W9-ACB-137

LION FEUCHTWANGER

THIS IS THE HOUR

TRANSLATED BY H. T. LOWE-PORTER
AND FRANCES FAWCETT

THE VIKING PRESS · NEW YORK · MCMLI

FIRST PUBLISHED IN MAY 1951

PUBLISHED ON THE SAME DAY IN THE DOMINION OF CANADA
BY THE MACMILLAN COMPANY OF CANADA LIMITED

PRINTED IN U.S.A. BY H. WOLFF, NEW YORK

1

Towards the end of the eighteenth century, almost everywhere in Western Europe, the Middle Ages had been rooted out. But on the Iberian peninsula, cut off on three sides by the sea and on the fourth by mountains, they persisted.

To drive the Arabs from the peninsula, Monarchy and Church had centuries before been forced to enter into an indissoluble alliance. Victory was possible only if kings and prelates succeeded in welding together by the strictest discipline the peoples of Spain. They had succeeded. They had united them in a mystically fervid belief in Throne and Altar. And this hardness, this unity, had endured.

At the end of the eighteenth century the Iberian tradition was frozen into a rigidity both tragic and absurd. Even two hundred years before, the country's greatest writer had drawn his material from this sinister and grotesque persistence. In the tale of the knight who could not abandon the ancient now meaningless customs of chivalry, he had created an eternally valid analogy, and his lovable hero, touching and ridiculous, had become famous all over the globe.

The Spaniards had laughed over Don Quixote, but had not given up their obsession with tradition. The chivalry of the Middle Ages had lasted longer in the peninsula than anywhere else in Europe. Prowess in arms, heroism carried to the point of madness, an exaggerated gallantry deriving from the veneration of the Virgin Mary—these characteristics remained the ideals of Spain. Chivalrous practices, long since obsolete, still persisted.

Bound up with this warlike habit was something of contempt for learning and reason; similarly, a monstrous pride, known and notorious throughout the world, general pride of country, individual pride of caste. Christianity itself lost in Spain its cheerful simplicity and assumed a fierce, gloomy, autocratic mien. The Church became arrogant, aggressive, masculine, and cruel.

Thus, at the turn of the century, the country was the most backward in Europe. Its towns, its dress, its gestures, yes, even the faces of the folk, struck the stranger as oddly rigid, relics of a time gone by.

Yet on the other side of the mountains to the north, cut off from Spain by these mountains alone, lay the most lucid, most rational country in the world: France. And over these mountains, in spite of all measures to shut them out, her rationality and suppleness found their way. Beneath the hard-baked surface the people of the peninsula, very slowly, were changing.

At that time foreign kings ruled over Spain, rulers of French origin, Bourbons. The Spaniards could well force the Bourbons to adapt themselves, as earlier they had forced the Hapsburgs. But the Spanish nobility learned the foreign customs from the French kings and their entourages, and many came to like them.

The people, however, while the aristocracy was slowly changing, stuck stubbornly to their old ways. Solemnly, zealously, they took over the rights and duties their masters were relinquishing. The noblest sport had always been the bullfight, preserve of the high aristocracy. Only the nobility could take part, only the nobility look on. Now, when the grandees no longer concerned themselves with bullfighting, the people practiced the savage custom with the greater passion. And as the grandees relaxed somewhat in their manners, the etiquette of the folk became correspondingly stricter. Shoemakers attached importance to being regarded as petty nobility, as *hidalgos*, and tailors addressed one another with cumbersome titles. Don Quixote had abdicated, Don Quixote had transformed himself into an elegant gentleman from Versailles; now the people took over his shield and his ramshackle war horse. Sancho Panza became Don Quixote, heroic and ridiculous.

Over on the other side of the Pyrénées the French beheaded their king and chased their nobility out of the country. Here in Spain the people deified their monarchs, French though they were in origin and highly unkingly. To the people, king was king, grandee grandee, and while these exalted ones, more and more committed to French customs, had even resigned themselves to the idea of a pact with a republican France, the Spanish people fought enthusiastically on against the godless French and let themselves be slain for their king, their nobles, and their priests.

True, in Spain existed Spaniards
Who perceived the contradiction
In themselves, and these would struggle
In their breasts to fight the fight out
'Twixt the old and modern usage,
'Twixt their feelings and their reason,
Oft with pain and oft with passion,
Winning sometimes, yet not always.

— 2 —

Doña Cayetana, thirteenth Duchess of Alba, was giving a theatrical evening for her friends in her palace in Madrid. A troop of royalist Parisian actors who had fled over the Pyrénées were putting on a piece by the dramatist Berthelin, *The Martyrdom of Marie Antoinette*, a drama which, in spite of its contemporary subject matter, was executed in the classical style.

The audience—not numerous, made up chiefly of ladies and gentlemen of the high nobility—was swallowed up by the large hall, which was only dimly lighted to show up more clearly the action on the stage. Noble and monotonous, the six-foot iambics rang out, their elegant French not always wholly understandable to Spanish ears. The hall was warm, and gradually a pensive, agreeable somnolence crept over the listeners in their comfortable armchairs.

The royal martyr on the stage was imparting noble precepts to her children, the fourteen-year-old Madame Royale and the nine-year-old King Louis the Seventeenth. Then, turning to her sister-in-law, Princess Elizabeth, she swore that whatever might come to pass, she would bear herself in a manner worthy of her murdered spouse, Louis the Sixteenth.

The Duchess of Alba herself had not yet put in an appearance, but in the first row sat her husband, the Marqués de Villabranca, who, following the usual custom, had added her title to the many others he already possessed. The quiet, elegant man, almost slight in build though full in the face, gazed thoughtfully with his fine dark eyes at the haggard actress up on the stage declaiming sentimental, pathetic verses and purporting to be the deceased Marie Antoinette. The Duke of Alba was fastidious about artistic performances not of the very highest class, and in this case had had his doubts from the first. But his dear Duchess had declared that life in Madrid had become mortally boring in consequence of the mourning ordained by the Court after the horrible death of Queen Marie Antoinette, and that she really must do something. A performance such as *The Martyrdom* would bring life into the house and at the same time express sympathy over the eclipse of the monarchy in France. The Duke could well understand that his wife, who was famous for her caprices in all the courts of Europe, might be bored in the spacious isolation of her Madrid palace; he had agreed without more ado and now, patient and sceptical, allowed the performance to wash over him.

His mother, widow of the tenth Marqués of Villabranca, sat next to him and listened indifferently. This Hapsburger on the stage, how loud and lachrymose she was! No, Marie Antoinette had not been like that. The Marquesa de Villabranca had seen and spoken to her in her time at Versailles. She had been a delightful woman, Marie Antoinette of Hapsburg and Bourbon, gay and lovable, a little showy perhaps, and loud. But when all was said and done she was only a Hapsburg and had nothing of the unobtrusive nobility of a Villabranca. The relationship of Marie Antoinette to her silent unassertive Louis, did it not somehow resemble that of Cayetana de Alba to her Don José? She stole a glance at her son; in his delicacy and weakness he was her favourite; what she saw and experienced was seen and experienced wholly in relationship to him. He loved his wife, as anyone could understand who had once seen her, but there was no question but that he stood in her shadow; to the world he was the husband of the Duchess of Alba. Ah, but few really knew her son José! They saw and commended his aristocratic poise, but of his inner musicality, the wonderfully balanced rhythm of his being, few were aware; even his wife knew too little of it.

Up on the stage the President of the Revolutionary Tribunal, a brutal man, now appeared to inform the Queen of the verdict. First of all he accused her once more of all her atrocities and read aloud a list of crimes as senseless as it was shocking.

Lost in his great armchair sat Monsieur de Havré, meagre and fragile in his splendid diplomatic dress. He represented the heir to the French throne, who was governing France from Verona in place of the little king held prisoner by the republicans. It was not easy to govern a country of which one possessed not a single square metre, and even harder to be the ambassador of such a regent. Monsieur de Havré was an old diplomat. For decades he had represented the brilliance of Versailles and was adapting himself only with difficulty to his wretched new role. The missions he had to convey at the behest of his master, the Regent, to the Court in Madrid, sometimes very grandiose ones, came oddly from the mouth of a man whose diplomatic dress was growing threadbare and who could not have paid for his meals without the help of the Spanish Court. There sat Monsieur de Havré, holding his hat so as to hide the shabbiest places on his coat, and beside him his slim, pale, pretty sixteen-year-old daughter Geneviève. She too could have done with some new clothes to the advantage of France and herself as well. Ah, how one had come down in the world! One had to be grateful when the Duchess of Alba invited one to her house.

Up on the stage the man from the Tribunal had conveyed the death sentence to the Queen and she had replied that she longed to be reunited with her husband. But dying was not going to be made as easy for her as all that; the godless scoundrels had conceived a final degradation for her. Marie Antoinette, thus declaimed the horrible man on the stage, all the time in verse, had with her unbridled licentiousness brought France low in the eyes of the world; therefore it was the will of the people that she, this time herself brought low, should go to the place of execution stripped to the navel.

The audience had read many reports of the horrible event, but this was something new. They pricked up their ears, shuddering and titillated; they shook off their drowsiness, and the play drew to a close amid general interest.

The curtain fell. There was polite applause. The guests stood up, glad to stretch their limbs. They began to move about through the hall.

More candles were lighted. It was possible to see who was there.

One man stood out among these polished men and women, a man who in spite of his meticulous, even costly dress was distinguished by a certain clumsiness. He was not tall, his eyes were deep-set beneath heavy lids, his underlip was full and forcibly thrust out, his nose, thick and fleshy, grew straight out of his forehead, his head had something of a leonine quality. As he strolled through the hall almost everyone recognized him and returned his greeting with respect. "A pleasure to see you, Don Francisco," he heard again and again.

Don Francisco de Goya was pleased that the Duchess of Alba had invited him to this select company; he was pleased by the respect shown him. It was a long way from the peasant village of Fuendetodos to this palace of Alba. The road had not been an easy one, but here he was, little Francho, a Court Painter now, *Pintor de cámara*, and when he painted the portraits of these great ladies and gentlemen it was a question who was doing whom the greater honour.

He bowed low before the old Marquesa de Villabranca. "How did the play and its performance strike you, Don Francisco?" she asked. "I can't think," he answered, "that Marie Antoinette really spoke like that, and if she had, then I should regret her death the less." The Marquesa smiled. "Nevertheless it is a pity," she said, "that Their Majesties weren't here." There was a trace of mischief in her tone. She looked at him with her beautiful, untroubled eyes, her wide, thin-lipped mouth just slightly awry. And he smiled too and shared the Marquesa's unspoken thought, that the Spanish Bourbons would have felt disagreeable titillation had they had to listen all evening to what had happened to the necks of their French relations.

"When are you finally going to paint me, Don Francisco?" the Marquesa went on. "I know—I am an old woman and you have something better to do." He denied it, passionately and with conviction. For the Marquesa at fifty-five was still beautiful and had about her the aura of a rich life not long since past. Goya looked at the wise, benignant face, the simple, dark, costly gown, the delicate white scarf from which a rose peeped out. She was exactly what in his youthful dreams he had imagined a great lady to be, and he looked forward to painting her.

The major-domo invited the company into the great reception hall, where the Duchess was awaiting them. Goya escorted the Marquesa. They went slowly through the picture galleries which led from the theatre into the reception hall. Choice paintings by old Spanish, Flemish, and Italian masters hung there. It was difficult not to stop in front of this one or that, so vividly, in the flickering candlelight, did the life shine forth from them.

"I can't help it," said the Marquesa to Goya. "I do love my Raphael. Of all the pictures here, 'The Holy Family' is my favourite." Goya, in opposition to the general opinion, was no admirer of Raphael—he was about to make some pleasant noncommittal reply.

But now they had reached the turn of the gallery, and through the double doors of the great reception room they saw Cayetana de Alba. She was sitting, following the old custom, on a low dais spread with rugs and shut off from the rest of the room by a small grille with a wide opening. And she was not wearing a modern gown like the other ladies, but a Spanish one of old-fashioned cut. The Marquesa smiled. That was Doña Cayetana for you. From France she took what good France had to offer, but she did not wish to conceal that she was a Spaniard. It was her evening, the invitations had gone out in her name alone, not those of herself and her husband together, and no one could take it amiss if she chose to conclude in Spanish an evening she had begun in French. But to show herself in her own house in the middle of an evening party in Spanish costume, almost as if she were a *maja*, such an effect was a bit conspicuous. "She is always having new ideas, our Doña Cayetana," the Marquesa told the painter. "*Elle est chatoyante*," she went on in French.

Goya did not answer. He stood there without a word and stared foolishly at the Duchess. Over a silver-grey gown she was wearing black lace; the warm pallor of her unpainted oval face gleamed white with a tone of brown; it was luxuriantly framed in wavy black hair crowned by a tall comb. Tiny, dainty in their pointed shoes, her feet peeped out under the voluminous skirt. An absurdly small, woolly white dog sat in her lap, and she was stroking it with her gloved left hand. But the right one, ungloved, narrow, childishly plump, lay half on the arm of the chair, and with the tapering fingers slightly spread held her fan, almost closed and pointing downwards.

The Marquesa, as Goya did not speak, thought he had not understood the French words and translated. "She is changeable as a tabby cat." But Don Francisco went on staring. He had met the Duchess often, had painted a portrait of her, with complete indifference; nor had it amounted to much. He had even playfully made use of the face of this great lady, about whom Madrid loved so well to prattle, in the showy stylized cartoons he had made for the tapestries in the royal castles. But now he did not recognize her, had never seen her before, and was this really the Duchess of Alba?

His knees shook. Every hair, every pore of her skin, the thick arched eyebrows, the breasts half exposed under the black lace, aroused in him unbounded desire.

The Marquesa's words echoed in his ears but he had not fully taken in their meaning; mechanically he answered, "Yes, she is refreshingly independent, Doña Cayetana, utterly Spanish." He was still standing in the doorway, his eyes on the woman. But now she raised her head and looked towards him. Did she see him? Did she look unseeingly past him? She went on talking, went on petting the little dog with her left hand. Meanwhile the right hand raised the fan and opened it wide so that the picture on it was visible—a singer sending his song up to a balcony—shut it up and spread it out again.

Joyful surprise took Francisco's breath away. There was a fan language by which the *majas*, the girls from the people, made themselves understood to strangers in church, at public festivals, and in the taverns; and the signal which came from the dais was a definite encouragement.

Perhaps the old Marquesa had spoken meanwhile; possible even that he had replied, he did not know. At any rate he now left her brusquely, rudely, and crossed the hall to the dais.

The murmur of voices was everywhere, and laughter, and the ringing of glasses and china. But through the decorous hubbub a voice came from the dais, rather hard, yet in no way shrill, a very young voice, her voice. "Was she not a little stupid, after all, Marie Antoinette?" asked the Duchess, and then as she obviously noticed how her downright words offended, she explained with good-natured mockery, "Naturally I mean the Antoinette in Monsieur Berthelin's play."

Now he was on the platform. "How did you like our play, Señor de Goya?" she asked. He did not answer. He stood there and looked at her, heedless of all else. He was no longer young, he was forty-five, and he was not handsome. The round face with its broad fleshy nose, the deep-set eyes and the full, protruding underlip were oddly framed by thick, fashionably powdered hair; his body, tightly encased in its elegant coat, inclined to stoutness. The whole man with his leonine face made by his very attention to appearances an impression of roughness, as of a peasant in a too fashionable Court dress.

He did not know if he finally answered her, did not know if others spoke, but now the startling voice issued again out of the proud capricious face with its brownish pallor. "Do you like my laces?" she asked. "Field Marshal Alba looted them three hundred years ago in Flanders, or in Portugal, I forget now which." Goya made no reply. "What else are you discovering about me?" she went on. "You have painted me, you ought to know me." "The portrait was a failure," he burst out; his voice, usually clear and gentle, was hoarse and uncontrolled. "And the faces on the tapestries were not serious at all. I should like to try again, Doña Cayetana."

She said neither yes nor no. She looked at him with her softly glowing face unchanged but the large metallic eyes full and urgently upon him. Three seconds long she looked at him thus, and in the eternity of these three seconds they were alone in the room full of people.

Abruptly, then, she broke the enchanted communion, casually remarking that for a time she would unfortunately be too busy to sit for him; she was occupied with the building and furnishing of a country residence in Moncloa. There was much talk of this project in Madrid. The Duchess, in emulation of the dead Queen of France, wished to build herself her own Trianon, a little castle where she might as occasion arose spend a few days alone, not with friends of the family but with her own.

Immediately she resumed her former tone. "Will you paint me something else in the meanwhile, Don Francisco?" she asked. "A fan, perhaps. Would you paint me *El Fraile y la Maja?*" She meant *El Fraile y la Maja, The Monk and the Maiden,* an entr'acte by Ramón de la Cruz, a daring little play which had been forbidden for public performance and had therefore been put on in private by amateurs.

The Duchess of Alba commissioned the Court Painter, Francisco de Goya, to paint her a fan. There was nothing unusual in that; ladies often had fans painted. And yet it seemed to the bystanders that they had witnessed a daring, forbidden spectacle.

"Poor Don Francisco," thought the old Marquesa down in the hall, and in her mind's eye she saw a picture by Rubens that she had just observed in the gallery, of Hercules being made to spin by Omphale. The old lady set store by good manners, but she did not hold it against the painter, who was, moreover, the only commoner in this assemblage of grandees, that he had so impolitely left her standing. She barely even held it against her son's wife that she had behaved herself in so shameless a way. She understood Doña Cayetana; she was herself a woman of great experience and love of life. Her son was weak and delicate, the thin stream of his life needed to be fed by powerful tributaries, it was good for him to have this woman at his side; one had much to thank her for. The great houses of Spain were in decline, their men were becoming finer and feebler, and what strength remained to them was in the women, in this one, for instance, the wife of her dear son, who had coquetted with such insolent grace up there on the dais with the painter, one of the few real men in the country.

The Duke of Alba himself followed with his large thoughtful eyes the game his wife was playing with the painter. There he sat, Don José Alvarez de Toledo, thirteenth Duke of Berwick and Alba, eleventh Marqués of Villabranca, and holder of many other titles. Among the hundred and nineteen grandees of the kingdom, two only were his equals in rank, and he was blessed with every conceivable worldly good. There he sat, slender, highly bred, very elegant, and he felt no desire to intervene in the destinies of this world to which his own descent and his acquired title gave him the right—the proud and sinister title of Alba, dreaded in Flanders even today. Rather was this Alba weary of his exalted station, weary of so much thinking about the complicated affairs of life. He took no pleasure in ordering one to do this and another to do that. He really felt happy only when he was listening to music or making music himself. When it was a matter of music, then he felt there was virtue in him, and he had dared to oppose the King when the latter refused further to subsidize the opera in the Coliseo del Príncipe. He had defiantly taken on the support of the opera himself, until the King forbade him. So now he looked at his beautiful Duchess throwing out the bait to the painter. He knew how slight was his own strength, knew that Cayetana felt attracted to Don Francisco, who was both a painter and a man. She was devoted to him, his Duchess, but he was well aware that this devotion was not free from pity. She had never given him a look such as the one with which she had gazed at Don Francisco. When he was alone he would take up his violin and with Haydn or Boccherini cleanse his soul of *The Martyrdom of Marie Antoinette* and all that had followed it. He became aware of his mother's delicately solicitous glance; with an almost imperceptible smile he turned his head towards her. They understood each other without words, and she knew that he did not grudge the woman on the dais her game.

Goya, on the dais, realized that the woman no longer had her mind on him, knew that she would not look at him again that evening. He left, too early for good manners.

Outside, inhospitable weather greeted him, one of Madrid's unpleasant January evenings, full of mud and showers of mingled snow and rain. His carriage was waiting, with servants in livery, as was proper for a Court Painter when bidden to the Duchess of Alba's. But to their amazement he sent it away. He preferred to go home on foot, disregarding the fact, careful man though he was, that his tall silk hat and his shoes might come to harm.

Mad and alluring, challenging and alarming, lay the future before him. Only two days ago he had written to his friend Martín Zapater in Saragossa that his affairs were at last in order; and it had been the truth. He had ceased bickering with his wife Josefa, he took pleasure in his children—true, of the many children she had borne him only three were still living, but they were nice, healthy children. Then, his wife's brother, the insufferable Bayeu, the King's First Painter, had stopped laying down the law to him about painting and life in general; there had been a reconciliation, and, moreover, Bayeu had a stomach ailment and could not last much longer. Goya's affairs with women no longer made such demands on him as once they had, either; Pepa Tudo, to whom he had stuck for the last eight months, was a reasonable girl. He had got over the severe illness which had fallen upon him a year before, and he was now hard of hearing only when it suited him to be so. Nor were his finances in such a bad way. Their Majesties showed him at every opportunity how much they prized him, as did Don Manuel, Duke of Alcudia, the Queen's favourite, and all that there was of wealth and title in Madrid was clamouring to be painted by him. "Come soon, my heart's dear Martín," he had concluded the letter, "and see for yourself how prosperous and contented is your eternal friend, forever your little Francho, Francisco de Goya y Lucientes, member of the Academy and Court Painter." And he had marked the letter top and bottom with a cross for good luck and in a postscript had commanded his friend to burn two fat candles to the Virgen del Pilar so that she would continue to favour him.

But crosses and candles had not availed, and what had been true two days ago was true no longer. The woman on the dais had upset everything. It had been bliss to feel her large metallic eyes resting on him; new life had flooded over him. But he knew that anything worth having must be paid for, the more desirable the thing, the higher the price. He knew he would have to fight and suffer over the woman, for one was forever beset with evil spirits, and if one did not take care, if one incautiously gave oneself up to dreams and desires, then the monsters were upon one.

He had not seen her aright. He had made a capricious doll of the woman. Which she was, among other things, but he had not seen the other things, the things that lay behind. Yet even then he had been no mean painter, better at any rate than all the others, even those two who stood higher than himself at Court, Bayeu and Maella. They might have learned more from their Mengs and their Winckelmann, but he had the better eye, and had taken Velázquez and nature for his teachers. And still he had been a bungler. He had seen only what was clear and well defined, he had not seen the complexity and confusion that is in all of us, and the danger. He had really started to paint only in the last few years, in the last few months even, since his illness. He had had to pass the age of forty before he even began to understand what painting really was. But now he understood, now he was learning, was working many hours each day. And then this woman had to come along and disturb him. She was a magnificent woman, it would be a magnificent experience, and she would give him much to think about, would rob him of time and the spirit for his work, so he cursed himself and her and fate that she should cost him so dear.

He heard a gentle tinkling sound coming through the snow and saw that a priest and an acolyte were struggling through the storm with the Holy of Holies, obviously on the way to a deathbed. Cursing softly, he drew out his handkerchief, spread it in the slush, and knelt down, as custom, the Inquisition, and his own feelings dictated.

It was a bad omen that he should meet the Host on the way to a dying man; things would not go well with him and the woman. "Better to meet a nine-year-old steer in a blind alley than a woman when you are ruttish." He was of the people and full of old folk sayings.

He snorted crossly as he trudged on through the snow, keeping along the walls of the houses, for the middle of the road was ankle-deep in slush. One had nothing but vexation. At once he thought of Monsieur de Havré, the French ambassador. He had painted his portrait, and the Frenchman had not paid him. And after he sent the bill in a third time, they had let it be known at Court that it would not be well received if the French gentleman was troubled further. Francisco had as many commissions as he could wish, but when it came to payment there were often difficulties. At the same time his expenses were multiplying. The carriage and horses were costly, the servants shameless in demanding more and more money; they stole too, but what could one do?—a Court Painter cannot be stingy. If his sainted father only knew that he, little Francho, spent more in two days than the whole Goya family in Fuendetodos in a year, he would turn over in his grave. But was it not glorious that he, Francisco, *could* spend so much? A grin passed over his face.

He reached his house and the *sereno*, the watchman, opened the gate to him. Goya went upstairs, threw off his wet clothes, lay down in bed. But he could not sleep. In his nightshirt he went to his studio. It was cold. On noiseless feet he slipped down the corridor. Light shone under the door of the servant Andreo. Goya knocked. If the lad had to have his fifteen reals, at least he could be asked to light a fire. Unwillingly the half-clothed creature did as he was bid.

Goya sat down and gazed into the fire. Shadows climbed up and down the wall, grotesque, intriguing, frightening. A tapestry hung on one wall, representing a procession, and the darting tongues of light picked out a part here and there, the huge saint borne on a platform, the faces of the wildly excited crowd. A bearded cardinal by Velázquez looking down with a gloomy, rather bored expression from the other wall became almost ghostlike in the fitful light, and even the ancient, blackened wooden effigy of the Virgin, the angularly charming Lady of Atocha, Francisco's patron saint, seemed to mock and threaten.

Goya stood up and stretched, shook off his fancies with a powerful shrug of the shoulders. He walked up and down. He took a handful of sand and strewed it over the table.

In the sand he started drawing.
And there grew a naked figure—
Woman-figure, squatting, idle
On the ground, cross-legged, squatting.
Back into the sand he blurred her,
Goya did and made another,
This one naked too, and dancing.
Back into the sand her also
Goya wiped and made another,
Made a third, erect and proudly
Treading, on her head a vessel
Bore she, yet she too must vanish
Back into the sand, and then he
Took his tool and drew a fourth one.
This one on her head upstanding
Wore a comb and from it falling,
Flowing, her black lace mantilla
Fell upon her naked whiteness.
Sighing, angry, baffled, snorting
Through his nose, Francisco Goya
Saw his sketch and so destroyed it.

— 3 —

He was working. From the canvas a lady looked down: very pretty, the rather long face like a mocking mask, the eyes far apart under arched eyebrows, the mouth wide, the thin upper lip and heavy lower one meeting firmly. She had already sat for him three times. Also, he had made several sketches of her. Now he was working on the completion of the picture. He was sure of himself and a rapid worker. But he had been tinkering at this picture for four weeks and it just would not come off.

Yet everything was right. This was the lady as he wished to present her. He knew her well and had known her a long time: she was the wife of his friend Miguel Bermúdez. He had got it all in, the mystery, the mockery, the fundamental artfulness hiding behind the fine-lady mask. But some little thing was lacking, and this little thing made all the difference. He had met her at a reception given by Don Manuel, the Duke of Alcudia, the all-powerful favourite whose confidential secretary Miguel Bermúdez was. She was wearing a pale yellow gown with white lace over it, and he had suddenly seen her as a whole, seen the fluttering, flickering, dissolving presentment which was her nature. There had been a certain silveriness about her appearance, and he had realized from one look at this Doña Lucía Bermúdez in her yellow dress with the white lace exactly what he wanted to do, must do. Now he tormented himself: there it all was, her face and flesh, her carriage and her dress, the pale grey background which was so entirely right. And yet nothing at all was there, the accent was missing on which everything depended; a mere trifle, and what was missing was everything.

In his heart of hearts he knew why the picture did not come off. More than two weeks had passed since the evening at the Palacio Alba, and he had heard nothing from the woman on the dais. He felt bitter. If the woman did not come, why at least did she not summon him and ask for the fan? Of course she was busy with her impudent, ridiculous castle in Moncloa. Of course he could have gone to her unbidden and brought her the fan. But his pride would not let him. She must summon *him*. She would summon him. That passage on the dais could not simply be brushed away like the pictures he habitually traced in the sand.

Francisco was not alone in the studio. As almost always, his pupil and helper, Agustín Esteve was there. The room was big enough so that they did not disturb each other.

Today Don Agustín was at work on an equestrian portrait of General Ricardos. Goya had painted the old General's cold, morose face; he entrusted to the conscientious Agustín the horse and the innumerable meticulous details of uniform and medals upon which the General set so much store.

Agustín Esteve was a tall, lean man in his early thirties, with a head full of bumps, hair swept back above a high, domed brow, hollow cheeks, thin lips; the whole face, long and rather pointed, bespoke reserve; whereas Francisco, confiding by nature, liked to chat even when he was working. But today he too was silent. Contrary to his usual habit, he had not mentioned the evening at the Albas even to his intimates.

Agustín, quietly as was his way, stepped up behind Goya and inspected the silver-grey canvas with the silver-grey woman on it. He had lived with Goya for seven years; they were together almost all day. Don Agustín was no great painter, and painfully aware of the fact. But he understood a great deal about painting, and no one else knew so exactly Francisco's strength and weakness. Goya had need of him, of his ungracious praise, his ungracious blame, his unspoken reproaches. Goya needed criticism, though he defied it; he mocked and scolded his critic, threw mud at him; but he needed him, his assent and dissent. He needed his laconic, always ungracious Agustín, his profoundly versed and understanding expert Agustín, who went round like the seven thin cows. He scolded him outrageously, cursed him, loved him. He could not get on without him; as little as could Agustín himself do without his big, childish, much admired, impossible friend.

Agustín gazed long at the picture. He too knew the lady who looked out so mockingly from the canvas at him; he knew her well, he was in love with her. He had no luck with women and realized how unattractive he was. Doña Lucía Bermúdez was known as one of the few women in Madrid who had no *cortejo* beside her own husband, no acknowledged lover. Francisco, to whom every woman succumbed if he gave his mind to it, could certainly have become her lover. That he obviously did not want to was a satisfaction to Agustín, yet at the same time an offence. Nonetheless he was enough of an expert to be able to judge the picture purely on its artistic merits. He perceived that it was good; also, that precisely what Francisco strove for had eluded him. He felt smug, felt pleased, went back to his big canvas and worked in silence on the hindquarters of the General's horse.

Goya was used to having Agustín stand behind him and look at his canvas. The portrait of Doña Lucía was not a success, but nevertheless what he was doing was new and off the beaten track and he awaited Agustín's judgment in some suspense. Now that the latter was once more standing silent in front of his equestrian General, anger mounted high in Goya. How impertinent he was, this nonentity! How far would the poor wretch have got if he, Francisco, had not taken him up? This eunuch, who languished after all the women yet ventured nothing and got nothing for his pains. And such a man had the cheek to turn away from one of his, Goya's, pictures without a word. But he controlled himself, behaved as if he had not noticed that the other had looked at his picture, went on with his work.

He held out for three minutes and then spoke, grimly, with dangerous mildness, over his shoulder. "What were you pleased to say? You know my ear is bad again today. You could have troubled to open your mouth a little wider." "I did not say anything," was Don Agustín's reply, very loud and very dry. "When one does want to get something out of you," Francisco scolded, "you are like the pillar of salt, and when one doesn't, you run on like a waterfall." Agustín made no reply. But Goya, still angry, went on, "I promised General Ricardos to bring him home the bacon this week. When will you be finished with that horse of yours?" "Today," Agustín replied, "but then you will find you still have a lot of work to do on the General's soul." "It will be your fault," Goya raged, "if I can't deliver it in time. I should have thought you had at least learned your job well enough not to have to spend a whole week on a horse's arse."

Agustín did not take his friend's coarseness amiss. What Francisco said did not count. Only what he could paint counted.

Goya applied himself once more to his portrait, and once more both worked a while in silence. Then there was a knock on the door, and in came an unexpected guest, the Abbé Don Diego.

It did not disturb Goya to be watched while he worked; he was a disciplined artist, despising painters like that incompetent Antonio Carnicero, who talked so much about moods. Francisco's friends were free to come into his studio at any time while he was painting. So he was not put off when the priest came; today, on the contrary, Don Diego was almost a welcome guest. Goya realized that today he would not grasp this nuance that was eluding him; it was one of those few things which were not to be mastered by effort, for which one had to wait.

He looked idly on while the Abbé walked about the studio. The heavy man was never still; he moved through the room with remarkably light tread; he had a free and easy way, wherever he was, of examining everything, picking things up, putting them down again—books, manuscripts, objects of all kinds. Goya, who as a rule quickly saw through people, had known the Abbé for a long time but had no clear picture of his personality: it seemed to him that this highly intelligent man permanently wore a very skilful mask. Beneath Don Diego's fine high brow, shrewd humorous eyes looked out; below them a broad, straight nose; his mouth stretched wide, full and sensual. The whole face, pale, jovial, and knowing, crowned most incongruously the black priestly habit. The priest was, if anything, a rather ungainly figure, yet everything about him was well groomed; he even contrived to make his priestly dress seem elegant.

Wandering about in the big studio, the Abbé retailed all kinds of gossip, amiably ironical, sometimes caustic, never boring. He was well informed, being as much at home with the gentlemen of the Inquisition as in the circles of the free-thinkers.

Francisco paid him little attention. Yet when he heard the Abbé say, "When I was at Doña Cayetana's levee today," he started in sudden excitement. But what was the matter? He saw the priest's lips moving but heard not a word. He was seized by a monstrous fear. Had that illness which he thought overcome forever come back? Was he deaf? He cast a look of pain and helplessness at the old wooden statue of the Virgin of Atocha. "May the Virgin and all the saints forbid," he thought and thought over and over; it was all he was able to think.

When he could hear again, the Abbé was speaking of Doctor Joaquín Peral who had, it seemed, also been at Doña Cayetana's levee. Doctor Peral had returned from abroad only a short while before and had overnight become the miracle doctor of Madrid society. It was said that he had raised Count Espaja from the dead. Moreover, recounted the Abbé, he was learned in all the arts and sciences, and excellent company; people were fighting for his favour. But he was spoiled and made himself dear. Of course he waited daily on the Duchess of Alba—she too valued him exceedingly.

Francisco strove to breathe calmly. He hoped Agustín and Don Diego had not noticed his seizure. The Abbé stood at Goya's back and looked at the portrait on which the latter was at work. Agustín observed him narrowly. The priest belonged to the Bermúdez' circle of friends, and Agustín had reason to believe that the attentions he paid to the fair Lucía in word and deed meant more than the customary gallantries of a worldly priest.

So now Don Diego stood there in front of Doña Lucía's portrait and Agustín waited in suspense to hear what he had to say. But the usually so eloquent gentleman gave no opinion.

On the contrary, he went on talking about Doña Cayetana's levee. Carnicero had also attended. "He too?" Goya could not prevent himself from saying. He bade himself keep silent, not to bring on himself another wave of rage and deafness. He succeeded, though only with an effort. He saw them all, saw them with his painter's eye, the priest, the barber, and Carnicero, that dauber and dabbler who had managed to get himself the title of Court Painter; three sickening people sitting there while the woman was gowned and coiffed. He saw them chatting, saw the sweeping gestures, how they feasted their eyes, saw the woman smiling at them, her glance haughty yet provocative.

He could quite simply have gone himself to the woman's levee. She would surely have had a more significant, more friendly smile for him than for the others. But she would have to catch another dog with that bone. He would not have gone there even in the certainty of going to bed with her; not for anything would he have gone there.

Meanwhile the priest was saying that as soon as the Court mourning was over—that was to say in a few weeks—the Duchess was thinking of giving a house-warming party at her little castle in Moncloa, the Palacio Buenavista. Of course, it was difficult to make plans now, after yesterday's military reports.

"What military reports?" asked Agustín more quickly than usual. "What sort of world are you living in, my dear friends?" cried the priest. "Am I really the first to bring you the bad news?" "What news?" insisted Agustín. And the priest replied, "You really did not know that the French have retaken Toulon? At the levee there was talk of nothing else." "Toulon has fallen?" Agustín asked hoarsely. "Apparently the news came some days ago," replied the Abbé. "They must have kept it back. A quite young officer recaptured the fort right under the noses of our fleet and that of the English. A simple artillery captain, Buonafide or Buonaparte or something like that, his name was."

Goya said, and there was no telling whether there was disappointment or cynicism in his voice, "Well, then, we shall soon have peace." Agustín gave him a dark look. "Few in Spain," he muttered, "will wish for peace under such conditions." "Some will certainly not wish it," agreed the Abbé.

He spoke lightly and noncommittally, and the others looked up. There had always been much obscurity surrounding the Abbé. For years he had officially been Secretary of the Inquisition. Even the new, ultrafanatical Grand Inquisitor had allowed him to keep the title. Some folk said straight out that Don Diego spied for the Inquisition. On the other hand, he was on intimate terms with certain progressive statesmen, and some declared him to be in secret a supporter of the French Republic. Nobody could quite make out this mockingly tolerant man, but one thing was certain: the cynical hedonism he displayed was only a mask.

When the priest had gone Agustín said, "Now your friend Don Manuel will surely allow himself to be persuaded to take over the government, and then you will sit even more comfortably." For it was whispered that Don Manuel Godoy had from the beginning opposed the war and for this reason had declined to head the government.

Goya had painted Don Manuel several times, to the complete satisfaction of the latter, and had boasted to Agustín that he thought he carried some weight with the most powerful man in Spain. So Agustín's gibe was doubly pointed. For the latter took a knowing interest in public affairs, discussed them with zeal and knowledge, and held it against his friend that he shrugged off any concern in that direction. What Agustín had just said cut Goya very near the bone. Actually his first thought had been that there would soon be peace and that his patron, Don Manuel, would take over the government. But was it not natural that this should please him? He was no politician; political matters were too involved for him. War or peace, that was the King's business and that of the King's counsellors and grandees. It was not his, Francisco's, affair, he was a painter.

He did not answer. He stood before the picture, the portrait of Doña Lucía. "You haven't said a word about this," he complained. "You know without my telling you what is the matter," replied Agustín and stepped in front of the painting in his turn. "Nothing is wrong and yet everything," he declared in a cross, authoritative tone. "A pleasanter companion for my dark hours I could not have found," said Goya bitterly. And then, as Agustín remained standing in front of the picture, contemplating it, he went on, "But there she is, your Lucía. Can one see her, or can't one?" Then, remembering how he could wound him, he added spitefully, "Go on, look at her, you can't do anything else with her, after all, can you, Platonic lover that you are?" Agustín pressed his lips together. He himself never spoke of his love for Doña Lucía, yet Goya taunted him with it every time he was in a bad mood. "I know I'm not attractive," he replied, and his voice sounded even rougher than usual. "But even if I were you, with all your gifts and titles, I would not try to seduce the wife of our friend Don Miguel Bermúdez."

"Noble words, forsooth!" there mocked him
Don Francisco. "Lofty precepts!
From the soles up to the narrow
Brow the prig complete! A pity,
Though, that she thy virtue never
Puts to proof, thy long-desired,
Thy long-languished-for beloved."
Never answer gave Esteve,
Stroked his chin, in dismal dumbness,
Gazing at his loved one's portrait.

Goya raged on, "Not to any,
Even the very best of painters,
Can come any rhythm or colour,
Light or shadow in the bitter
Breath thou givest out about thee."
And he took his hat and mantle
Angrily, and left the workshop.

When, as today, Goya had nothing particular to do, he loved to spend the evening with his family. He was fond of his wife and doted on his children. But he feared that in his present mood the harmless chatter around the family table would be hard to bear. He preferred to go to his mistress, Pepa Tudo.

Pepa was agreeably surprised. She was never carelessly dressed like other Madrileñas; today she was wearing a pretty blue negligee against which her white skin stood out radiantly. She leaned back on the sofa, languid, luxurious, playing with her fan, and conducted with him a slow conversation.

Her dueña, Conchita, came in and asked what Don Francisco would like for dinner. The withered Conchita had looked after Pepa from her birth and had stuck to her through all the vicissitudes of her young and eventful life. They conferred about the composition of the meal; then the old woman withdrew to buy what was necessary, above all the rather vulgar manzanilla, which was Francisco's favourite wine.

He was untalkative even after Conchita had gone. It was very warm in Pepa's pretty living room, the grate was heaped high, they both felt lazy and comfortable, although they both knew there were things to discuss. Pepa had an almost impudent way of turning her face towards one quite suddenly, for no reason at all: a very white face, with a broad low forehead under fine red-blond hair, and far-apart green eyes.

"How have you spent the last few days?" Francisco asked at last. She had sung. She had learned three pretty songs as sung by Mario Pulpilla in the new zarzuela, then she had played cards with her dueña: it was remarkable, Conchita was as honest as the day, but at cards she cheated, she certainly did—she had cheated Pepa out of three reals. Further, Pepa had gone to the dressmaker, Mademoiselle Lisette on the Puerta Serrada. Her friend Lucía had assured her that Mademoiselle Lisette would make a special price for her. But even with a special price the coat she needed would have come much too dear. So she would have to go on having the work done by Buceta. "Apart from that I went to see Lucía," she recounted, "and once Lucía was here."

Goya waited to learn what Lucía had said about the portrait. But Pepa let him wait; he had to ask. Yes, they had spoken of the portrait, more than once. "You're painting her in the yellow dress, aren't you? She got it from Mademoiselle Lisette. Eight hundred reals she had to pay for it. So you can see what her prices are like." Goya restrained himself. "And what does Doña Lucía think of the portrait?" he asked. "She is surprised," said Pepa, "that it isn't done. She thought you'd done all you could to it long ago and can't understand why you are so against showing it to her husband. I am surprised myself, I must confess," Pepa chattered on. "I admit Don Miguel is difficult and has some fault to find with everything. But you don't usually give yourself so much trouble. And, after all, what will Don Miguel pay you? Probably absolutely nothing, because he is your friend. Certainly not the three thousand reals you're asking."

Goya stood up and walked to and fro. Perhaps it would have been better to eat with his family. "Tell me, Francisco," Pepa persisted, "why are you taking so much trouble? You didn't work three days on my portrait for the Admiral and he paid you four thousand. Is Lucía so much more difficult than I? Or what is it? Do you want to sleep with her? Or have you slept with her already? She is very pretty, it's true." Pepa spoke casually, without emotion.

Goya's heavy face was black. Was Pepa trying to get a rise out of him? Probably not. She was often uncannily matter-or-fact, like that. If he seriously wished it he could certainly have Doña Lucía, for all her camouflage of gentility. But—there were many "buts." Pepa was sometimes hard to bear. And fundamentally she wasn't even his type. She was plump, a *jamona*, a pretty, charming, smooth-skinned little pig.

Pepa fetched her guitar and sang. She sang softly, with abandon. She was lovely as she sat there and warbled the old popular romances, accompanying herself on the guitar. Goya knew that in the old poetic stanzas she was reliving her own experiences.

The twenty-three-year-old girl had seen a deal of life. She had grown up in the colonies, in America, the daughter of a well-to-do planter. When she had been ten years old her father had lost his ships and his fortune. He had gone back to Europe with his family, and Pepa had exchanged a spacious, luxurious life for a narrow, needy one. A happy disposition had prevented her from suffering too much over the reversal. Then the young naval officer Felipe Tudo had come into her life. He was handsome and easy to manage —it had been a pleasant marriage, but he was poor and had run into debt for her sake. Probably in the long run they would have had little joy of each other. But he had perished, on an expedition of his squadron in Mexican waters, and was surely in Paradise; he had been a good man. Then, when Pepa had submitted her petition for an increase of pension to Admiral Mazarredo, the stout, elderly man had fallen head over heels in love with her. A *viudita*, a delicious little widow, he called her, and set her up in the pretty little dwelling in the Calle Mayor. Pepa understood his not introducing her to his friends in the high nobility; it meant much that he had had her painted by the celebrated Court Painter. Now, during the war, the Admiral was cruising with his armada in distant seas, and it had been a good thing she had met her painter, who had shown himself ardently anxious to console her lonely state.

Pepa was of a placid disposition, grateful for what she had; but she often recalled the spacious life in the colonies, the vast estates, the innumerable slaves. From all this superfluity nothing was left but her faithful old Conchita, who was as honest as the daylight and never cheated except at cards. Francisco, Francho, was a wonderful friend, a proper man in whom a *viudita* might well rejoice, and a great painter. But he had much to do: his art made demands on him, the Court made demands on him, his many friends and mistresses made demands on him, and even when he was with her his thoughts were sometimes elsewhere.

Of all this Pepa Tudo mused as she trilled her ballads. She dreamed, probably, that she herself was the heroine of such a ballad, a lovely young woman, for example, set upon by the Moors or sold to them by her lover. It must have its advantages, to be the idolized white beloved of a gallant brown prince. She probably also dreamed that fortune might smile on her here in Madrid, and she saw herself as one of those ladies who three or four times a year travelled from their palaces in the city to their castles in the country and back again to Court, always surrounded by chamberlains, ladies' maids, and hairdressers, decked out in the smartest Parisian gowns, with jewels which might have been looted hundreds of years before by the marshals of Catholic Isabella or Charles the Fifth.

The dueña asked Pepa to help her set the table. They ate. The meal was good and plentiful; they enjoyed it.

The picture of Admiral Federico de Mazarredo looked down upon them. The Admiral had had himself done for his sister and then ordered a copy for Pepa, which Agustín had executed conscientiously.

It was no great passion which had driven Goya to Pepa, but

the naturalness and warmth with which she had given herself to him pleased him and gave him satisfaction. His realistic peasant good sense reasoned that she was making sacrifices for her love. He knew all about her circumstances. After the death of her sailor husband she had taken lessons from the great actress La Tirana, thus consuming the little money she had left. Now, since the beginning of the war, she had been allotted five hundred reals a month. It was not quite clear how much of it was government pension and how much the personal gift of the Admiral. Five hundred reals were at once a good deal and very little. Gowns from Mademoiselle Lisette one certainly could not buy with them. Goya was not stingy, and he often bought his fair and agreeable mistress presents, sometimes small, sometimes of considerable value. But every now and then his calculating Aragonese peasant blood got the upper hand, and often, after hearing the price of some intended gift, he decided not to buy it.

The table was cleared. It was very warm. Doña Pepa reclined on her sofa, beautiful, compliant, languid, voluptuous, fanning herself idly. Obviously she was still thinking of Doña Lucía and the portrait. Pointing with her fan to the picture of the Admiral, she said, "You didn't take much trouble over that one either. Whenever I look at it, I think the right arm is much too short."

Goya was suddenly flooded by a feeling of the many knocks fortune had dealt him from all quarters in the last few days: the nervous waiting for the Duchess, his dissatisfaction with the portrait of Doña Lucía, the amazing political situation, and the carping of Agustín. And now, on top of everything else, these pert inanities from Pepa. Did a man who had, in the presence of the grandees of Spain, looked at the Duchess of Alba as though she were lying in bed with him have to listen to such trash, and from such a *jamona?* He took up his grey silk hat and pulled it down over her head. "You can see just as much of the Admiral's picture as you could before," he declared grimly.

She worked her way out of the hat. She looked funny and pretty with her high coiffure all in disarray.

"Conchita!" she called furiously, and, when the old woman appeared, "Open the house door for Don Francisco." But Francisco only laughed. "Nonsense, Conchita," he said, "go back to your kitchen." And when the old woman was gone he apologized. "I am a little hard to please today. I've had a lot of annoyances. Besides, what you said about the picture really wasn't very clever. Look at it carefully and the arm won't seem too short to you." She sulked and insisted, "Yes, it is too short." "You're blind, but you're pretty, with your hair all messed up," he said good-naturedly. "And I'll pay for you to have it done again," he consoled her further, and kissed her.

Later, in bed, she said, "Did you know that Don Federico is coming back very soon? Captain Morales gave me a message from him, and his greetings." This faced Don Francisco with yet another situation. "What will you do when the Admiral really comes back?" he asked. "Tell him how things stand," she answered. "Tell him, 'Between us—all is over,'" she quoted from one of her ballads. "That will be unpleasant for him," Goya reflected aloud. "First he loses Toulon and then you." "Actually it was not he who lost Toulon," Pepa defended her Admiral in her literal way. "It was the English. But they lay the blame on him; it is always like that."

After a while Francisco put into words a thought that had been occupying him the whole time. "And how will this affect your pension?" he asked. "I don't know," she replied unconcernedly. "I expect something will be left."

It was not Goya's business to keep a woman; a great painter has no need to do such a thing. Also, he reflected that he could very easily get along without Pepa. On the other hand, he found it natural that a pretty woman should want to live in comfortable circumstances, and it would have offended him if she, only because he did not give her enough money, were to fall into the clutches of somebody else or even go back to the Admiral.

"Don't"—he said—"let this distress you.
Surely I'll arrange the business
So that you can go on living
As you are." His tone was heavy.
"Thanks a lot," said Pepa idly.
"And the Admiral, we'll take him
Down from off the wall then, shall we?"
He proposed with animation.
"Why, whatever for?" she countered.
"Just because his arm is shortened?

No, for short it really isn't,
And I said it was because you
Take such trouble with Lucía."

— 5 —

He stood alone in front of the portrait and looked at it, scrutinizing it with the utmost sharpness for any mistake. That was Doña Lucía, no question.

Thus she was, living, in the flesh, as he saw her. Everything was there, the mask effect, the slight artificiality, the hint of something behind it all. For something there certainly was; indeed many people thought they had seen her before, this woman of perhaps thirty years; seen her without her fine-lady mask.

Did he want to sleep with this woman? Pepa had asked. Silly question. Any healthy man with red blood in his veins wanted to sleep with every halfway pretty woman, and Doña Lucía Bermúdez was excitingly pretty, fine-lady pretty, pretty in a rather unusual way.

Her husband, Don Miguel, was his friend. But Goya openly admitted to himself that it was not that which kept him from spending time and effort on the conquest of Doña Lucía. On the contrary, what hindered him was just that unknown something. It excited the painter in him, not the man. What she was, and what she was not, they ran into each other, could not be separated; it was uncanny. Once he had seen it, that time in Don Manuel's ballroom. It had been the silver tone in the yellow frock—the shimmer, the light that cursed and blessed. That was the truth of her, that was the picture he wanted to create.

And all at once he saw it afresh. At one stroke he saw how he could reproduce that glistening, silvery, flowing grey sheen that he had seen then. It wasn't the background that did it, or the lacy white web over the yellow gown. This line must be softened here, and this one here, the flesh tones must do their part, the light from the hand, from the face. It was a trifle, it was everything. He shut his eyes and saw. He knew what he had to do.

He worked. He made changes. Took a little away, added a little. It all came of itself, without effort. In an incredibly short time there it was.

He inspected his work. It was good. He had pulled it off. There was something new there, something great. It was the woman as she really was with all her shimmer. He had seized that thing which had floated and hovered before him. It was his light, his air, the world of his inner eye.

His face relaxed, became almost silly with satisfaction. He crouched in a chair, lax, with a feeling of exhaustion.

Agustín came in, greeted him grumpily. Took a few steps, passed the portrait without a glance. But something must have struck him; he turned abruptly and his gaze narrowed.

He looked long. He cleared his throat. "That's it, Don Francisco," he said at last hoarsely. "Now you've got it—you've got the air and the light. Now you've got your grey right, Francisco." Goya beamed like a boy. "Are you serious, Agustín?" he asked and laid his arm across the other's shoulders. "I seldom joke," said Agustín.

He was deeply moved, almost more than Francisco. He had not learned to lay about him with quotations from Aristotle or Winckelmann like Don Miguel Bermúdez or the Abbé. He couldn't do anything, he was a wretched painter, but he understood more about painting than anybody else and he knew that this Francisco Goya, his Francho, had achieved something of which as yet the whole century had no conception: he had broken away from line. The others had wanted only to develop ever greater purity of line; their painting was after all nothing more than coloured drawing. This Francisco was teaching the world to see anew, to see more fully. And for all his conceit he probably didn't even know that he had done this great new thing.

Goya, now, with marked deliberation, took his brushes and very carefully washed them. Then he stepped up to the General's huge equestrian painting on which Agustín was still working. "Good, that horse's arse," he acknowledged, and gave his brushes another, quite superfluous washing.

Meanwhile Agustín was feeling
Joy profoundest, at the knowledge

He was this man's friend and comrade.
Yes, he even in his clumsy
Way had helped him and had made him
Seek and find the way to follow.
And he looked with eyes of friendship,
Looked on Don Francisco Goya,
On his Francho, as a father
Looks upon a very gifted,
Admirable child, forever
Playing new, fantastic, silly
Tricks. And to himself Esteve
Vowed that he would bear forever
With this friend and dearest comrade,
Dear and yet so hard to suffer.

— 6 —

The next day, on learning that the painting was finished, Don Miguel and Doña Lucía Bermúdez betook themselves to Francisco's studio.

Francisco Goya and Miguel Bermúdez, though the one might have this or that to object to in the other, were intimate friends. Don Miguel, principal secretary to the all-powerful Don Manuel, Duke of Alcudia, did, while standing in the background, actually direct the destinies of Spain. A progressive, at bottom a Francophile, he had to use considerable skill to maintain his position against the intrigues of the Inquisition, and Francisco admired the modesty with which his friend concealed rather than displayed his power. As a scholar, on the other hand, particularly as an art historian, Miguel was not so retiring, and the big art lexicon published by him definitely laid down the law. Señor Bermúdez countenanced nothing but the imitation of the classical masters. Goya's brother-in-law Bayeu was for him the greatest contemporary Spanish painter, and he pedantically reproached his friend Francisco, though with courteously expressed regret, because the latter had more and more often of late departed from classical theory.

Francisco looked forward with malicious joy to showing his friend—and in a painting of the man's own wife—just what could be achieved by breaking the rules. He was convinced that Miguel, in spite of his strict orthodoxy, was susceptible to genuine art. He meant to get his conventional friend—who for all his assumed casualness was certainly very anxious about the new picture—to give once again an explicit exposition of his previous principles, before surprising him with the shimmering Doña Lucía. So he had turned with her face to the wall the woman with all her air and light and beauty, so that only the rough, bald grey-brown back of the picture was visible.

It turned out just as he thought. Don Miguel sat there, one leg thrown over the other, a little smile on his square, pale, lightly powdered face with the clear-shining brow above it. He pointed to a large portfolio he had brought with him. "I have succeeded," he declared, "in spite of the war, in getting hold of these Parisian engravings. They will make you sit up, Francisco, and you, Don Agustín. The engravings are reproductions of the best work that Jacques-Louis David has done in the last few years." Jacques-Louis David was the most famous painter in France and head of that classical school which Señor Bermúdez prized so highly.

Apart from scenes of classical antiquity, the engravings represented men and events of recent history, themselves conceived in the classical style. There were portraits of Danton and Desmoulins. There was Marat, murdered in his bath.

The work of the French painter was in direct opposition not only to Francisco's work but even to Francisco's whole nature. Nevertheless no one could realize better than Goya with how much art these pictures had been painted. The dead Marat, for example: his head hung limply to one side; limply his right arm hung out of the tub, while the left still held the petition which the cunning murderess had brought with her. It was done with a cool mastery, a calm superiority, and yet—how exciting it was! With all its realism, what grandeur and beauty leaped out from the ugly face of the dead man! How dearly the painter must have loved this "friend of the people"! So powerfully did the content of the picture in all its horrible reality strike Goya as he looked at it that for a time he was no longer the artist critically examining another artist's work. Instead, uneasiness seized him, fear of the fate that hangs over everyone, threatening to leap out from ambush unexpectedly, while one is at work in front of the easel; in bed while making love; as one relaxes in the bath.

"One shivers when one looks at his pictures," he said at last. "A great man, and a repulsive one." They all recalled how David, painter and revolutionary, had voted in the National Assembly for the death of his patron, the sixteenth Louis. "I wouldn't change my life for his, even for a month, not for the fame of Velázquez," concluded Goya.

But Señor Bermúdez was explaining how the pictures by the Frenchman proved once more that all true art was based on study of the antique. Nothing mattered but line. Colour was a necessary evil and had only one function—to obey.

Francisco grinned good-humouredly. But now Don Agustín put in his oar. He opened his wide, thin-lipped, ill-tempered mouth and said, making his rumbling voice sound unusually polite, "These pictures by David, Don Miguel, do really seem to reach a peak. Nonetheless I can imagine that even with colour, which you so roundly condemned, one might also achieve new and surprising effects." And he stalked over to the wall and with one powerful gesture held aloft the grey-brown canvas which had been leaning there.

"I can guess," Don Miguel said with a smile, "what you mean, Don Agustín. We are both, Doña Lucía and I, in suspense about the portrait that has so long—" He did not finish the sentence. For now, looking down from the easel, was the painted, shimmering Lucía.

Don Miguel stood motionless and silent. The connoisseur, accustomed to assessing pictures by his carefully constructed theories, forgot his principles. The woman on the canvas was the Lucía he knew and at the same time a bewilderingly different one. Again, against his principles, he looked over at the Lucía of flesh and blood, hiding his confusion only with difficulty.

Years ago, when he married her, Lucía had been a *maja*, a girl of the people, impulsive, incalculable, and to marry her was a decision that had been as sudden as it was bold and dangerous. But instinct, experience, and the study of the classics had taught him that he who does not grasp quickly often goes away empty-handed, and that the gods vouchsafe to mortals the great opportunity once only. And he had never regretted his rash act. He loved and desired his wife as much today as on the first day; moreover, she had transformed herself from the girl of the streets, of doubtful repute, into a presentable Señora Bermúdez, on whose account he was envied. It was as a lady of society, desirable and presentable, that she also looked down at him from the canvas; yet there was something intangible, silvery, changeable about her. Suddenly Don Miguel saw that this Lucía whom in all these years he had thought to have plumbed to her depths was today as exciting and unknown to him, as dangerously incalculable, as at the beginning, still a *maja* even today.

Goya was highly gratified to see the bewildered look on the face of his usually collected friend. Yes, my dear Miguel. Your David's methods are good. Pure line is a good thing in itself, and pure things allow themselves to be represented by it. But the world and the men in it are not pure. The bad, the dangerous, the supernatural, that which lurks behind, everything that does not let itself be expressed by your means, that's something you can't find in your respected classical masters. Your Winckelmann and your Mengs and your David can't help us there.

Goya, too, looked from the painted woman to the real one. She stood there, utterly silent, gazing. Her narrow, slanting eyes beneath the high, politely surprised eyebrows looked at the dancing light which played about her in the picture; her wilful face had laid aside the mask a little, she had slightly opened her wide mouth, a smile hovered round it, not fastidious and disdainful as usual, but deeper, more dangerous, more vulgar probably—perhaps even more vicious. And suddenly Goya recalled an episode which he had forgotten and had long sought to remember. Once he had been walking with a woman in the Prado—it had been many years ago—and an *avellanera*, a filbert- and almond-seller, half grown, she might perhaps have been fourteen or fifteen, had accosted him. He had wanted to buy almonds for his companion. The child had overcharged him; he had offered a lower price, and the young nutseller, a proper *maja*, had overwhelmed him with a flood of invective and abuse. "Two reals? I'll ask my master. You wait here, my fine gentleman, in half a year I'll be back with the answer." Her screams had brought the rest of her crew to the spot. "Come here, my dears. Here is a man who throws his money round. He has holes in his pockets—he wants to spend two reals for his lady." In angry chagrin he had flung the five reals to the impertinent urchin. It was a triumph for him to have painted into his picture of Lucía something of that forgotten scene, to have pictured her vulgar and mischievous side, her sly ways and fondness for rude answers and coarse jokes. It was another triumph that his picture had driven her to raise her mask a trifle.

Don Agustín, for his part, now that Doña Lucía was standing in front of the portrait, saw how the beauty of the woman in the flesh enhanced the beauty of the picture, the glory of the picture the glory of the woman. And his heart contracted with desire and pleasure.

They were all silent. Then at last Doña Lucía spoke. "I really had no idea," she said to Francisco in her rather halting tones, "that I was wicked as well." But this time her playful tone and her smile betrayed more than they hid. She was challenging Francisco, there was no doubt of it; she was setting out, in the presence of her husband, his friend, to play a dubious game with him. He, however, contented himself with answering politely, "I am glad that you like my portrait, Doña Lucía."

This exchange recalled Don Agustín from his rapture and reminded him of his purpose, the humiliation of Don Miguel. "I am anxious," he said in his brittle voice, "to know whether your good husband is as satisfied with the picture as you are."

Don Miguel had striven, after the first shock, to stifle his all-too-personal reactions; but even so the connoisseur stood in front of the picture in no less confusion than Doña Lucía's husband. He could not deny it: this iconoclastic creation moved him, spoke to him; it was beautiful. "It is all quite wrong," he said at last, "but I admit, it is magnificent." "You are a convert," said Agustín and grinned all over his bony face.

But Agustín's provocations did not succeed in angering Don Miguel, and the uneasiness and doubt which the portrait had at first caused ceased to plague him. He was a fanatical collector of great art, and his heart was warm with pleasure that for little, or in fact for nothing, this admittedly unorthodox but exciting and historically significant painting should fall to his lot.

Don Manuel's most important business was entrusted to him. His time was limited. Yet he lingered in his friend's studio. One leg over the other, toying mechanically with David's engravings, he said, "I am anxious to see, Francisco, if you will use your new methods when you come to paint my Duke." And as Goya looked up he went on, "Because, of course, now that Don Manuel has taken over the government we will have to ask you to paint at least two more portraits of him, and we shall need a lot of copies for the ministries and public institutions." Goya was happy. His friend Miguel would not accept gifts; he was paying nothing for Lucía's portrait, but he had procured for him this honourable and remunerative commission. The fall of Toulon was in very truth making itself felt in his life; it had thrust on him the provision for Pepa, yet it brought him this fat job as well.

Don Miguel meanwhile went on in the same light, casual tone. "If it's all right with you, I will arrange a good long sitting in the next few days, beginning with the levee." "That's extremely kind of you," said Francisco.

But Señor Bermúdez was not yet finished. "There will be some changes," he went on chattily, "now that Don Manuel has taken over the conduct of affairs in person. The country will have to get used to regarding the French Republic as a fact which will not let itself be ignored."

Agustín looked up. "Do I understand you aright?" he asked eagerly. "Will Don Manuel put the domestic policy of the country back on the old footing? Does he intend to rescind certain measures taken against the liberals?" "Just that," replied Bermúdez, and, still playing with the engravings, he turned towards Francisco without looking at him directly. "By the way, you could help us, Francisco. You know how Don Manuel likes to have you about him. Perhaps, during your sittings, you could suggest to him a certain political measure." And, more lightly still, in a conversational tone, swinging his leg, he concluded, "I think it is about time Don Gaspar was recalled."

The impassive Agustín rose to his feet in excitement. Goya breathed hard through his flat nose, uneasiness in every line of his face.

For this was Don Gaspar Melchor de Jovellanos, the most respected liberal statesman and writer in the country, commonly called "the Spanish Voltaire." As minister to the last king he had put through many beneficial reforms. But to Charles the Fourth and Don Manuel this upright man had soon become a nuisance with his constant demands; he was forever involving the Crown in fresh complications with the Inquisition and the reactionary high nobility, and the outbreak of the French Revolution had provided a welcome excuse to set aside this liberal leader and subverter. He had been banished to his far-off native hills and forbidden to publish any further works. It was no pleasant task to ask Don Manuel for this man's pardon.

Francisco was silent. Agustín stumped rudely up and down in his excitement. Doña Lucía, playing with her fan, peered under her lids at Goya's unwilling face. "Why should you want *me* to make such an approach, Miguel?" Francisco finally asked. "Why don't you intercede for Jovellanos yourself?" Don Miguel answered easily, "From the very hour that my Duke took over the government I was determined to ask for the rehabilitation of my liberal teachers and mentors. But of course Don Manuel, as well as everyone else, knows how much I am indebted to Don Gaspar, that I owe my whole career to him and even my whole outlook on life. You, Francisco, are above suspicion. You are regarded as politically neutral and in no way a partisan of Don Gaspar, although if I remember rightly he has done you one or two good turns. It would certainly be useful if the first approach came from you. Then I will apply pressure, and once we have got Jovellanos here again I shall be able to bring about the rehabilitation of Count Cabarrús and others."

Francisco pulled his thick hair over his ears with an angry gesture. The reference to the good turns Jovellanos had done him only annoyed him. It was true, when he had come to Madrid, unknown and poor as a beggar, Jovellanos had given him a large portrait commission and useful introductions. But at bottom the remorselessly severe man had remained a stranger; Goya felt for him the same chill admiration as for the painter David; he could understand why a light-hearted man like Don Manuel could not bear the grim, dour Jovellanos. Now the virtuous Miguel was challenging Francisco to show magnanimity and gratitude. "Good deeds," Goya thought, quoting the saying to himself, "are usually paid for in heaven, and bad ones on earth."

Don Miguel continued his persuasions. "Especially now, when Don Manuel is steering towards peace with France, the prospects for such an attempt are good."

Presumably that was correct. But it did not alter the fact that Don Miguel's request was a presumption, and Goya's ingenuous countenance plainly showed his reluctance. His rise had been slow; he had had to struggle for it with effort, tenacity, caution, and craft. Now he was being asked to endanger what he had won by involving himself in affairs of state. "After all, you're the politician," he said sulkily. "I am a painter." "But don't you see, Francisco," Señor Bermúdez patiently explained again, "in this case you are the better advocate precisely *because* you have no political ambitions."

Doña Lucía was still looking steadily at Francisco. She held her fan almost shut, pointing to her bosom. In the language of the *majas* this meant mocking rejection; the smile had deepened on her wide mouth. Agustín too stared at Goya, with almost scornful suspense, and the latter knew that his faithful friend disapproved of his hesitation. It was contemptible of Miguel to have made the disagreeable proposal in front of Doña Lucía and Agustín.

"Very well then," he conceded
Sulkily, without conviction.
"Good, I'll do it, and Our Lady
Of Atocha, may she keep me
Safe from any harm to follow."
So he spoke, with pious crossing
Of his heart.

But now Lucía,
Smiling, added to her husband,
"Well I know your friend Francisco
Has a noble nature, ready
Ever to be helpful, selfless,
Full of courage, a *hidalgo*
From his crown into his boot-soles."
Grimly Don Francisco listened.

When the two of them had left him,
Carrying Lucía's portrait,
Then he fiercely turned his anger
On to Agustín, beginning:
"There you sit and laugh, and hug your
Virtue, that's so easy to you,

Starveling, who loseth nothing."
And he muttered the old saying:
" 'Everywhere one turns there's trouble,
Everywhere the same old story,
Debts and duties, weeds and children.' "

— 7 —

On the next day but one, when Goya appeared at Don Manuel's levee to begin the commissioned portrait, he found the antechamber crammed with people. Through the open door he could see into the luxurious bedchamber where the Duke was being dressed and coiffed.

There were tradespeople of all kinds, lace dealers, jewellers, a sea captain just returned from America, bringing the Duke a present of rare birds. There was Señor Pavan, the editor of a recently founded geographical magazine, subsidized by Don Manuel, called *The World-Traveller;* and there was Don Roberto Ortega, the famous botanist, come to present his latest work. Don Manuel considered it his duty to further botanical science. The majority of the visitors, however, were pretty young women who wished to present petitions to the Minister.

As soon as Goya was announced, Don Manuel came into the antechamber, half dressed, his dressing gown thrown carelessly around him, followed by secretaries and government officials. The lackeys wore red stockings, a distinction properly reserved for the royal household; Charles the Fourth, however, had empowered the Duke to dress his staff in the distinctive stockings.

Don Manuel greeted Goya cordially. "I've been expecting you," he said and bade him enter the inner room, while he himself moved about in the antechamber. He addressed this person and that, in a casual yet not unfriendly way; had a few pleasant words for the captain who had run the enemy blockade; amiably thanked the botanist; sized up the women with jovial unconcern and had their petitions collected by his secretary. Then he dismissed the whole gathering and went back into his dressing room, to Goya.

While the Duke's toilette was being finished, Señor Bermúdez, with many oral explanations, laid all manner of papers before him for signing. Francisco set to work. The Minister's pretty face—plump, lazy, with a small, sensuous red mouth—had a curious fixed look about it. As he worked, Goya laughed to himself at the thought of the many bungling pictures that others had made of this face. They had come to grief because they had tried to make a hero of him. It was not easy to see Don Manuel as he really was; he was so greatly hated. Public affairs were going badly, and royalist Spaniards did not attribute the blame to the Monarch, but rather to the Queen, that alien, that Italian, and, above all, to her lover, her *cortejo*, Don Manuel. He had risen from below on nothing but his own shameless good luck, and he ought to behave himself like one of them, not like a nobleman or the King.

Goya thought otherwise. It was precisely Manuel's luck, that fairy-tale rise, that made the young man congenial to him.

Born in Badajoz, in the cattle country of Estremadura, of people in humble circumstances, Manuel had come to Court as a young lieutenant in the Guards, and his upstanding, well-built body and agreeable voice had come to the attention of the wife of the heir to the throne, the Princess of Asturias. This lady, with her lust for life, had never relaxed her hold on him, neither as Crown Princess nor as Queen. Today, at the age of twenty-seven, the impressive youth was known as Manuel de Godoy y Alvarez de Faria, Duke of Alcudia; he was Commander-in-Chief of the Walloon bodyguard, Private Secretary to the Queen, President of the Crown Council, Knight of the Golden Fleece, in possession of all the riches he could desire, and father of the two youngest royal children, the Infanta Isabella and the Infante Francisco de Paula, as well as numerous bastards.

Goya knew it was hard to support so much good fortune without becoming evil at heart. Don Manuel remained good-natured, he had respect for art and science, was susceptible to beauty, and became mean or cruel only when anyone did not do what he wanted. It would not be easy to paint any life into the broad face of the young Duke, who was fond of posing and to this purpose assumed a proud and blasé mask. Francisco, because of the sympathy he felt for him, would succeed in making visible the love of life and laughter which concealed itself behind the slightly bored manner.

Don Manuel had signed the documents which had been put before him. "And now," said Señor Bermúdez, "I have a few matters to impart to Your Excellency which are not suitable for the public ear," and he glanced smilingly at Goya. "Don Francisco is not the public," said the Duke amiably, and Don Miguel began to hold forth.

Monsieur de Havré, the ambassador of the Regent of France, had demanded in arrogant tones that Spain prosecute with greater intensity the war against the godless French Republic. Don Manuel was more amused than upset. "Our fat Prince Louis can afford to be warlike in his hotel room in Verona," he said, and he explained to the painter, "He is living in the Albergo Tre Gobbi, and if we don't send him money he'll have to give up one of his two rooms." He turned once more to Bermúdez. "Does he make precise demands?" "Havré declared," the latter replied, "that ten million francs and twenty thousand more men was the least his princely master expected from the Spanish crown." "Havré has a pretty daughter," Don Manuel meditated. "Thin, I admit, as thin as a rail. I have nothing against thin ones, but too lean just won't do. What do you think, Don Francisco?" And without waiting for an answer he instructed Miguel, "Inform Monsieur de Havré that we have done our utmost. And give him in God's name another five thousand francs. By the way"—he turned once more to Goya—"has he ever paid you for the portrait?" And as Goya said no, he observed, "There we have it. Five years ago this Monsieur de Havré was still one of the most brilliant gentlemen at the Court of Versailles. Now he doesn't even pay his painter."

"Monsieur de Havré," Bermúdez reported further, "is unfortunately not the only one to demand that reinforcements should be sent to the front. General Garcini does so with even greater urgency. The news from the theatre of war is bad," he continued and turned over his papers. "Figueras has fallen," he concluded.

The Duke had till now maintained the pose. Now he tilted up his head, unpleasantly surprised, and turned to Bermúdez. But at once he turned again and resumed the pose. "Excuse me, Don Francisco," he said.

"Garcini is afraid," declared Don Miguel, "that now our allies are defeated, the French will withdraw troops from the other fronts and send them into the Pyrénées. Garcini is afraid that if he doesn't receive reinforcements the French could reach the Ebro in three weeks."

Goya assumed that Don Manuel would now send him away. But he kept the pose. "I don't think," he mused aloud, in a gentle voice, "I don't think that I'll send reinforcements to Garcini," and when Bermúdez made as if to reply, he went on, "I know, the Church will be difficult. But I must put up with that. We have done more than the allies. Must the country bleed to death? The Court is cutting down more and more. Doña María Luisa has dismissed two equerries and ten lackeys. I can't impose any further privations on the Queen." He had raised his voice slightly, but his head stayed in the position that Goya had indicated to him. "So what shall I tell General Garcini?" Bermúdez asked dryly. "The French Republic," answered Don Manuel, "is in the habit of beheading generals who fail; we confine ourselves to not sending them reinforcements. That is what you should please tell the General, but in a polite form."

"Obviously," Don Miguel went on with his report, "our allies have given up all hope of defeating France. The Prussian ambassador has set down the views of his government on the war situation in a memorandum—in a long memorandum." "Please make it short," Don Manuel told him. "Herr von Rohde," replied Bermúdez, "indicates the intention of his government to make peace if they can get halfway tolerable terms. He counsels us to do the same." "What does he consider halfway tolerable terms?" asked Don Manuel. "If," replied Bermúdez, "the French Republic hands over to us the children of their deceased Majesties, then, in the opinion of Prussia, that would be an honourable peace." "The French royal children," opined Don Manuel, "if no territory comes with them, are going to be rather expensive at the rate of fifty million reals and twelve thousand Spaniards. Don't you think so, Don Francisco?" Goya smiled politely; he felt flattered that Don Manuel drew him into the conversation. He went on painting, but he listened with all his ears.

"If little King Louis and Madame Royale are saved and in our protection," Bermúdez explained further, "then the concept of the French monarchy will live on on our soil. That is no dishonourable peace." "I hope, Don Miguel," replied the Duke, "that you will at least be able to get hold of the Kingdom of Navarre." Bermúdez replied amiably, "I will do my best. But I am afraid that if we aren't sending reinforcements to Garcini we shall have to be satisfied with the children." He shuffled his papers together, made his adieux, and left.

In the course of this political conversation Goya had forgotten the purpose for which Don Miguel had arranged his meeting with the Duke. Now the matter of Jovellanos began to be heavy on his chest. He asked himself how he should introduce the subject. But before he could speak Don Manuel forestalled him. "Many people," he said consideringly, "will demand the recall of Garcini. Many people are calling for the recall of Admiral Mazarredo, because he did not prevent the fall of Toulon. But war is a matter of luck, and I am not vindictive. By the way, haven't you done a couple of portraits for the Admiral?" He went on with more animation, "It seems to me I saw a picture by you in his house. Yes, of course," he went on, "it was at the Admiral's that I saw that unusually good portrait of a woman."

Goya listened in surprise. What was Don Manuel getting at? The woman whom he had painted for the Admiral was Pepa Tudo. They had got to know each other during the sittings. He was on his guard. "Yes," he said noncommittally, "I painted a lady of his acquaintance for the Admiral." "The picture was a great success," opined Don Manuel. "What's more, the lady must be very pretty in the flesh. A *viudita* I think the Admiral told me she was. Her husband seems to have been killed in Mexico or somewhere, and the Minister of Marine has awarded her a pension. Or am I wrong about that? An exceptionally pretty woman."

By now, with his realistic peasant intelligence, Goya had grasped what Don Manuel was after, and he was confused, pulled this way and that. He saw himself suddenly entangled in a complex intrigue. He understood why Miguel did not want to speak for Jovellanos himself but sent him, Goya, instead; Miguel had no Pepa to offer in exchange for the old liberal. Francisco felt rather foolish. Perhaps it was Doña Lucía who was behind the whole deal. Perhaps that was why she had given him that look, so bold and questioning, when he hadn't said "yes" at once. For all his anger he could not but be amused at the strange ways taken by the irreproachable Miguel Bermúdez in order to recall from banishment a man even more irreproachable than himself. Quite likely Miguel conceived it his, Goya's, duty to give up his mistress if thereby something as important as the recall of Jovellanos could be achieved. Likely, too, that Miguel considered the sacrifice as not excessive, and in that he was right. After all, he could imagine life without Pepa. But the part they were forcing upon him was offensive, it hurt his pride. He did not care so enormously for Pepa, but he wasn't going to sell her. He wouldn't pass her on to this conceited lout of a Manuel simply because Manuel itched for her.

On the other hand, he owed a debt of gratitude to Jovellanos, and it wasn't right that Don Gaspar should go on sitting there in the mountains, condemned to idleness at a time when Spain was in trouble, simply because he, Francisco, hung on to a woman who didn't mean much to him, a *jamona.*

For the time being, at any rate, he would take the offensive himself and introduce the matter of Jovellanos. Don Manuel would make a face, but he who offers sour wine must not be surprised when he is given sour wine to drink, as the old saying went. It would be hard, the way matters stood, for Don Manuel to say no, and then he, Francisco, would see.

So without referring to the subject of Pepa Tudo, painting away, he said after a while, "The country will be grateful to you if you restore peace to it. Madrid will look as it did before, and one's heart will rejoice to get a glimpse of the faces one has missed so long." Don Manuel, as Francisco had expected, was astonished. "Missed?" he asked. "Do you seriously believe, Don Francisco, that Madrid has missed the few all too zealous progressives to whom we had to recommend a sojourn in the country?" "Something is missing when certain people aren't here," Goya replied. "You see, Your Excellency, my pictures would lose half their life if they lost certain tiny points of light. In the same way, something is lacking in Madrid when, for example, let us say, Count Cabarrús or Señor Jovellanos is not here." Don Manuel sat up angrily, but Goya, undaunted, bade him keep his head still.

Don Manuel obeyed. "If our friend Miguel were to say such things I would think nothing of it. Coming from you, they are surprising."

Goya painted away. "They were thoughts which came to me when you did me the honour of letting me be witness to your conversation with Don Miguel. I ask your forgiveness, Don Manuel, if

I was too forward. I had the feeling that I could allow myself to be open with you."

The Duke meanwhile had perceived how the bargain was going. "I'm always glad to hear a frank opinion," he said amiably, with a certain condescension. "I will give your suggestion my benevolent consideration." And then without transition and with much more animation he continued, "To come back to that lady about whose successful portrait we were speaking just now—do you happen to know if she is still in Madrid? Have you met her lately?"

Goya was amused at the clumsy circumlocutions the Duke seemed to find necessary. The police records of what every person did and did not do were as carefully kept as were the registers of the Holy Office of the Inquisition; and Don Manuel naturally knew all there was to know about Pepa Tudo and her relations with him, Francisco. Probably he had also spoken to Miguel about it. Don Francisco kept his counsel. "Certainly, Don Manuel," he replied rather coldly. "I see the lady from time to time."

There was nothing else for it, the Duke had to speak out. He held his head obediently in the prescribed position and said casually, "It would be kind of you, Don Francisco, if you could arrange an introduction to this lady for me. Perhaps you could also tell her that I am not so indiscriminately greedy as hostile rumours present me; rather that I have a warm and abiding feeling for genuine beauty. The Señora's picture shows her to be an intelligent woman. Without doubt one can converse with her. Most women can do nothing but lie down, and when one has been with them three times one doesn't know what to do with them. Am I not right?" To himself Goya was thinking something rather obscene. Aloud he said, "Yes, Your Excellency, philosophizing is possible only with the few." Now Don Manuel became quite open. "How would it be," he suggested, "if we were sometime to spend a pleasant and profitable evening together, you, the charming *viudita*, and a few other friends in whose company it is worth while to eat and drink and chat and sing. If I'm not mistaken, our Doña Lucía knows the *viudita*. But a condition of the whole thing, my dear Don Francisco, is that you should attend any such *tertulia*."

The transaction couldn't have been put more clearly. Don Manuel was ready to talk about Jovellanos if Goya was ready to talk about the widow. With his mind's eye Goya saw Pepa sitting there, languid, voluptuous, complacent, looking at him with her wide, green-eyed gaze. The picture of her that he had painted for Admiral Mazarredo hadn't been bad at all; at that time he had really been in love with Pepa and had painted the fact into his picture. It was certainly a joke that he himself had aroused Don Manuel's appetite with his good painting. He saw Pepa quite clearly now, as she was, as he ought to have painted her, and as he perhaps still might paint her. And although he had the intention of sleeping with her once or twice more, yet in this moment Francisco Goya bade farewell to his friend Pepa Tudo. "It will surely," he said formally, "be both an honour and a pleasure for Señora Josefa Tudo to meet Your Excellency."

Very soon thereafter one of the red-stockinged lackeys appeared and announced, "The lady has been waiting for ten minutes, Excellency." The man's immobile, respectful face betrayed the lady's identity: it was the Queen. "A pity," sighed Don Manuel. "I suppose we shall have to stop."

Goya went home in two minds. He had treated women badly, had given women up for the sake of his career. But no one had ever dared to make such a proposition to him, and he could not imagine accepting it had it not been a matter of Jovellanos.

In his studio he found Agustín. The man's sour, provocative face had played its part in goading him on to this uncomfortable bargain. Francisco took out the sketches he had made of Don Manuel. He went on working on them. Good nature and wit disappeared from the Duke's fleshy face; it grew more and more satyr-like, more and more swinish. Goya tore up the sketches, strewed sand over the table and drew in it. A lickerish, profoundly artful Lucía, with the face of a spiteful cat; a shy, angular, fox-faced Miguel. With an impatient sigh, he wiped the faces away.

Out of sorts, ill-humoured, Goya
Spent that night and still another
Just as bad. But by the third one
Came a message to him, from the
Alban house; a liveried lackey
Bore and handed in a ticket
Whereon Don Francisco Goya
Was invited to the fiesta
Made to celebrate the opening

By the Duchess of the palace
Buenavista, her new dwelling.
Further, on the card was written:
"And my fan, when do I get it,
Don Francisco?" Smiling, drawing
A deep breath, the painter read the
Small, ornate, beflourished writing.
Here was confirmation, here was
His reward, come down from Heaven
For the sacrifice he'd offered,
Sacrifice of pride and person
Made for Spain and Jovellanos.

— 8 —

The Prussian envoy, Herr von Rohde, reported to Potsdam on the subject of Don Manuel Godoy, Duke of Alcudia:

"He gets up early and gives his equerries and other officials precise instructions for the day and the immediate future. At eight o'clock he goes to the riding school at his country house; every morning at nine the Queen visits him there to keep him company during his ride. He is a capital horseman. This goes on till about eleven. When the King comes back from hunting he joins them. Meanwhile innumerable people are already waiting on the Duke, with all kinds of business they want to discuss with him. These are all dealt with inside a quarter of an hour. Then his official levee takes place; generally a half-dozen ladies of rank are present, and the best musicians give a concert. At one o'clock Don Manuel betakes himself to the Royal Palace. There he has his own large apartment, living room, workroom, bedroom. In his capacity as chamberlain he is present at the King's official dinner. After that he goes to his private apartments, which are immediately beneath those of the Queen, who comes down to him by a secret staircase; the King is already off hunting again. At these encounters

Doña María Luisa and Don Manuel are in the habit of concerting the measures they will propose to the King.

"At about seven o'clock Don Manuel goes to the King to give him advice. At eight he returns to his private quarters, where usually thirty to forty women of all ranks and classes have gathered with their petitions. Dealing with these petitions takes more than two hours. He usually summons his ministers for ten o'clock, and with them he embarks on his real work. Generally he only has these two hours of the night for this purpose. But he makes a point of dealing swiftly and punctually with current business. Letters which do not demand lengthier consideration he almost always answers on the same day. His understanding is quick and precise, and while he tends soon to tire of affairs he makes up by the accuracy of his judgment for any harm that might arise from his short hours of work.

"All in all, in spite of his youth he fills his difficult office not badly, and Europe would be well off if every state had such officials in responsible positions."

9

The party for Don Manuel and the *viudita* Josefa Tudo took place at Doña Lucía Bermúdez'.

Señor Bermúdez' house was large and spacious and full of objets d'art. High and low, the walls were hung with paintings, new and old, large and small, in bewildering profusion, like a tapestry.

Here Doña Lucía received her guests, sitting on her dais under a high canopy, in the old Spanish style. She was all in black, and her face looked out like the head of a lizard, delicate and mask-like, beneath the high combs. So she sat, slender and composed, yet looking forward to what was to happen with mischievous relish.

Don Manuel appeared early. He was carefully dressed, elegant but not exaggeratedly so. He was without a wig and had not even powdered his red-blond hair. Of all his many orders he wore only the Golden Fleece. On his broad face there showed nothing of his usual ennui. He put himself out to make conversation with the lady of the house, but he wasn't really concentrating, he was waiting.

The Abbé was standing in front of Goya's portrait of Lucía. At first Miguel had wanted to give the picture a place apart, but he found that its originality stood out even more when surrounded by other treasures. So there it hung among the many other pictures in the room. Don Diego realized that he could not stand there dumb in front of it any longer. Wordily, embellishing his speech with Latin and French quotations, he praised the novelty and excellence of the work, and it sounded like a declaration of love for Lucía. With mixed feelings Don Miguel listened to the panegyric of the living and the painted Lucía.

Pepa arrived. She wore a green dress with a mantle of light-coloured lace; as her single jewel, a crucifix set with precious stones, a gift from the Admiral. Just so had Goya seen her when Don Manuel had made his shameless proposal, thus had he wished to paint her with his newly discovered technique. She apologized casually for coming so late: her dueña had had trouble in finding a chair. Goya admired her airy manner. There had passed between them only the most indirect reference to what was to happen this evening. He had expected, he had hoped, that she would pour out complaints and reproaches. Nothing of the sort had happened, nothing but gently mocking, ambiguous phrases. Her present demeanour, of course, was studied and deliberate. She had come late on purpose, on purpose had disclosed the poorness of her circumstances. Her intentiton was to put him to shame in front of the Duke by showing that he behaved in a miserly way. Actually she had needed only to have opened her mouth and he would have ordered more servants for her—grumbling, to be sure. It was contemptible.

Don Manuel had very likely scarcely heard what she said. He had stared at her, certainly too long, but with a reverence of which the others would never have thought him capable. When Doña Lucía finally introduced him he bowed lower than he had ever bowed before the Queen or the Infantas. He spoke to her without restraint of how much the picture had impressed him from the first moment and how far in this particular case the portrait even by so great a painter was inferior to the reality. His gaze was homage itself.

Pepa was used to extravagant attentions; in that respect all Spaniards were the same, *majos* from Madrid, *hidalgos* from the provinces, grandees of the Court. But she had an instinct for nuances and she quickly perceived that this great gentleman had fallen for her more deeply than had that Admiral Mazarredo whose return was imminent; perhaps even more deeply than her husband, who now lay in the bosom of God and the deep. If Francisco was going to betray her and sell her, then he should see that he was giving up something very valuable, and she resolved to put her price high. Her wide mouth with the large, brilliantly white teeth smiled amiably and noncommittally; her fan did not, it is true, reject, but neither did it invite; and she saw with pleasure that Francisco was looking across, following Don Manuel's wooing with reluctant interest.

The page announced that supper was ready. They went into the dining room. Here, too, the walls were covered from top to bottom with paintings, with still lifes and kitchen scenes by Flemish, French, and Spanish masters. There was one painted by Velázquez of men busy around a hearth; a "Marriage at Cana" by Van Dyck; poultry, game, fish, and fruit pieces looking so succulent that one's mouth watered to look at them. The table itself was choice but not too luxuriant. There were salads, fish, cakes and sweetmeats, malaga and sherry, punch and sweetened icewater. No servants were present, only the page; the men waited on the ladies.

Don Manuel occupied himself zealously with Pepa. She was, he assured her, full of that same joyous serenity that radiated from the portrait by Don Francisco. But he had no idea of the exciting quality hidden in this very repose. For all her languor, how exciting, moving, overpowering she was! Did she speak French? "*Un peu,*" she replied with a strong accent. He had expected as much, he said: that she should be more educated than other women of Madrid. To the others, to the Court ladies and all these *petimetras* and *majas*, one could talk only empty gallantries; with her one could talk of life and the things of the mind. She ate and drank and listened. Through the lace of her gloves the flesh of her arms shimmered delicate and white.

Later, by means of her fan, she gave him to understand that his attentions were not unwelcome. Thereupon Don Manuel had tempestuously declared that Goya must paint another picture of her; just as she was sitting there he must paint her, he must gather all his strength together and paint her for Manuel.

Goya himself had been drawn into conversation with Doña Lucía. She sat there, quiet and composed, and looked across at Don Manuel exerting himself over Pepa. From the way in which he looked at her, bent over her, no one could help seeing in what an infatuation he had involved himself, and Doña Lucía relished the spectacle.

Very casually, sipping at her iced drink, she said, "I am glad our Pepa is enjoying herself. The poor child! So young a widow, and no parents on top of that. She has taken the ups and downs of her fate with admirable calm, don't you think?" And, still looking across at Don Manuel, she went on, "How remarkable, Don Francisco, that at bottom it was your picture that aroused Don Manuel's interest in Pepa. You shape destinies, Don Francisco. With your pictures, I mean."

Goya had believed he knew more about women than any other man he knew. But here sat this Lucía, sweet, slim, tall, enigmatic, ladylike, and unscrupulous, and made her impudent fun of him. In his ears rang the shameless shrieking of that almond-seller of the Prado, the *avellanera,* that guttersnipe, when she had set her gang of confederates on him. He felt foolish. He did not even know how far Pepa was acquainted with the background of the whole affair, or even if Lucía and Pepa were not laughing at him together behind his back. A great resentment seized him, but he controlled himself, answered monosyllabically, played the innocent, and returned without a flicker her wide-eyed, enigmatic glances. "You're even pricklier than usual today, Don Francisco," she said pleasantly. "Aren't you at all pleased at Pepa's good fortune?"

He was glad when the Abbé came up to them and he could escape from the uncomfortable conversation.

But scarcely had he left Lucía when Pepa called him. She asked him to bring her a glass of punch. Don Manuel observed that she wished to be alone with Goya. He understood this and did not want to cross her. He joined the other guests.

"How do I look?" asked Pepa, languid and dainty in her chair.

Francisco felt unsure of himself. He had been ready all along to speak openly with her; it would be her fault if they parted now without a talk, and not as friendly as they should be. If anyone had reason to be annoyed it was he.

"I don't want to stay long," she went on. "Should I come to you or are you coming to me?" His face was stupid with astonishment. What was she up to? She was not, after all, so stupid as not to understand, when she had been invited to this party, what was at stake. Or had Lucía not enlightened her? Perhaps it was he who had done everything wrong.

In reality, Pepa had known for days what it was all about, but the decision had not come as easily to her as he imagined. For days she had wondered why he did not speak and whether she ought to precipitate the discussion herself. For all her easygoing nature, she felt embittered that he could give her up so easily, whether it was for the sake of his career or because he wished to be rid of her and did not want to stand in her way. In the midst of these reflections she realized how attached she was to him. In spite of her experiences she had remained simple in her emotions. She had ogled and flirted with men, but her Felipe Tudo had been the first with whom she had slept. Later, particularly while she was studying for the stage, when the men became grosser in their attentions to the *viudita,* she had repulsed rather than encouraged them. Then the Admiral had launched into her life with all sails set, and that had greatly increased her self-esteem. But as for desire, deep, genuine desire, it was Francisco Goya who had first made her feel that. It was sad that he did not love her more passionately.

When Lucía mentioned to her that the all-powerful Minister set great store by making her acquaintance, she had naturally realized that a broad, sunlit path was opening before her. Her romance-fed dreams of magnificent castles and obsequious servants might come true. She had lost herself in fantasies of how it would be if the Duke of Alcudia, the Queen's *cortejo,* should become her *cortejo,* and when she played cards with the dueña she had let her cheat even more than usual.

At the same time she had been determined to preserve her relationship with Francisco, if only he wished it, and such was still her resolve.

So now she had asked him a plain question: "Should I come to you, or will you come to me?" And there he sat, looking as stupid as only he knew how.

As he did not speak she went on amiably, "Have you found someone else, Francho?" And as he still kept silent: "Have I become a burden to you? Why are you throwing me to the Duke?" She spoke in a friendly tone, not loud, and the others must have thought she was making casual conversation.

There she sat, desirable, a pleasure to the eye of a man and a painter, and, irritatingly enough, she was right: he had found someone else; she had simply walked into his life, this other one, had seized him neck and crop, and so he was abandoning Pepa to the Duke. But still Pepa was only half right. She had no idea of the connection between herself and the sacrifice he was making for Jovellanos and Spain. He felt a sudden wild anger. Always one was misunderstood. He would gladly have struck her.

Agustín Esteve looked from Pepa to Lucía and from Lucía to Pepa. Instinctively he grasped the situation. Francisco was in difficulty, Francisco needed him, otherwise he would not have brought him along this evening, and that showed how strong were the ties between them. Nevertheless he was not enjoying the evening very much. He stood around feeling lost and envying Francisco his predicament.

Lucía had had champagne brought in. Agustín, against his usual habit, began to drink. Alternately he drank malaga, which he did not like, and champagne, which he did not like either, and he felt sad.

Don Manuel felt he had now fulfilled the demands of propriety and could once more devote himself to the *viudita*. She was not sorry to see him. She had quite plainly offered herself to Francisco, had humbled herself, and if Francisco was going to spurn her, very good, then she would take the path he was pointing out to her. But then it should be as in her ballads. There she would be, rejected perhaps, but admired and exalted above the others. It was not the case that a great man like the Duke could simply come along and pick her up. On the contrary, she was going to ask her price of this Manuel, a good price, in fact a thoroughly high price, as he seemed to be prepared to pay it.

Pepa Tudo was on friendly terms with Lucía Bermúdez, appeared often at her *tertulias*, but she did not frequent the formal receptions which Señor and Señora Bermúdez gave from time to time. She was reasonable and understood that the widow of a mere naval officer would not be admitted into society. But now that would be different. If she was to embark on a liaison with Don Manuel, she was not going to be one of those hidden-away little women but his official mistress, the Queen's rival.

Don Manuel had been drinking. He was hot, excited by champagne and the propinquity of the *viudita*. He wanted to show off before her. Did she ride? he asked. It was a particularly foolish question; only the wives of grandees and the very richest people rode horses. Casually she answered that she had occasionally sat a horse on her father's plantations, but here in Spain only on donkeys and mules. There was much leeway to make up, he replied. She must ride; she would look like a goddess on a horse. He himself was no bad horseman.

Pepa saw her opportunity. "The whole of Spain knows," she said, "how well you ride, Don Manuel." And then, "Can I see you ride some time?" she added. Now this innocent question was extremely daring, a presumption really, even in the mouth of the fairest widow in the land; for the Queen was in the habit of frequenting Don Manuel's riding practice, and often the King as well. Must not Señora Tudo also know what was the talk of Madrid? The Duke was for an instant startled; what was more, he became sober, he saw a great cage opening, into which a lovely mouth was bidding him enter. But then he saw the mouth itself, beautiful, wide, enticing; he saw Pepa's green eyes on him, quietly waiting, and he knew, if he said no, if he drew back now, that he would lose the woman, this glorious woman whose red hair and white skin, whose odor even, so agreeably bemused him. Of course he would be able to sleep with her even if he said no; but he wanted more, he wanted to have her always about him whenever he desired her, and always meant always: he wanted her entirely to himself. He swallowed, drank, swallowed again, said, "Certainly, Señora, of course, Doña Josefa. I shall be honoured to show off my paces. The Court is going to the Escorial in the next few days. But the morning will come when your devoted servant Manuel Godoy will come back to Madrid, will shake off for a few hours the cares and affairs of state, and will ride before you and for you, Doña Pepa." It was the first time he had used the diminutive form of her name.

Pepa Tudo, within her, triumphed whole-heartedly. She thought of her ballads: what Don Manuel had said sounded as poetic as they did. Many things in her life would now be different, perhaps a few things also in Don Manuel's. And something even in Francisco's. She would be in a position to offer or refuse him favours. Of course she would not refuse them. But—and a vindictive light came into her green eyes—she would let him feel that it was she who was furthering his career.

Señor Bermúdez saw how Don Manuel was exerting himself for Pepa, and anxiety stole upon him. Impetuous his Duke had often been, but never had he thrown himself into the business so completely as now. One must take care that he did not do anything foolish. Sometimes he was too sure of the Queen. Doña María Luisa had nothing against Don Manuel's kicking over the traces from time to time, but she was not the woman to put up with a serious entanglement, and the affair with the widow Tudo did not look as if it was going to last only over Sunday. When Doña María Luisa got into a rage, she knew no restraint; then she would be capable of working against Don Manuel's policies, against his, Miguel's, policies.

He did not want to be prematurely anxious; he turned away from Manuel and Pepa, looked across to Doña Lucía. How beautiful she was, how much the lady! Admittedly since Francisco's portrait had been hanging among his pictures her fine-lady beauty no longer seemed as unambiguous as before. In many years of endless study he had established his principles; he had read his Shaftesbury and knew what was beautiful and what not. But now the boundaries began to blur, and from both the Lucías, the painted and the living one, emanated a glitter which filled him with disquiet.

Pepa, once the understanding had been reached that she might visit Don Manuel at the riding ground, became more confiding. She told him about her childhood, about the sugar plantations and the slaves, and her close acquaintance, friendship even, with La Tirana, the great actress, and how she had taken lessons from her.

She must be wonderful on the stage, Don Manuel ardently declared at once; her gestures few but eloquent, her expressive face, her voice which went straight to the marrow of one's bones, had made him think from the first that she was meant for the stage. "And you sing too, I'm sure," he said. "A little," she replied. "May I hear you sing sometime?" he asked. "I sing only for myself," she replied, and as he made a disappointed face, she added in her full, slow voice, "If I sing for someone I feel I am letting him come very close to me," and she looked him full in the face. "When will you sing for me, Doña Pepa?" he implored softly, eagerly. She did not reply but closed her fan in token of refusal. "Have you sung for Don Francisco?" he asked her jealously, and now her face too was forbidding. He begged in a tempest of remorse, "Forgive me, Doña Pepa. I did not wish to offend you, you know that. But I love music. I could not love any woman who had no music in her. I myself sing a little. You must let me sing for you."

The story went in Madrid that it was Doña María Luisa's greatest pleasure to hear her darling sing, but Don Manuel had to be asked many times before he would yield to her request, and three times out of four he would refuse. So Pepa was inwardly very proud to have the Duke so submissive to her at their first encounter; but she showed only casual amiability.

"Just think, Lucía," she called, "the Duke wants to sing for us." Everyone was surprised.

The page brought the guitar. Don Manuel flung one leg over the other, tuned the guitar, and sang. First, accompanying himself, he sang the old sentimental ballad of the youth who, chosen by lot for military service, has to go away to war. "Away, away sails the armada, and my Rosita stays behind. Oh, my Rosita!" he sang. He sang well and with feeling; his voice was trained. "More, more," begged the flattered ladies, and Don Manuel sang a couplet, a *seguidilla bolera*, a mock-sentimental thing about a bullfighter who had disgraced himself in the ring and could no longer appear before the people, not to mention the bulls. Two hundred beautiful and elegant Madrileñas, *majas*, *petimetras*, two duchesses even, had once scratched one another's eyes out over him; now he must be grateful if a girl from his own village lets him lie in the straw with her. There was loud applause, and Don Manuel was gratified. He laid the guitar aside.

But the ladies begged, "More, more." The Minister, hesitating, tempted, declared that he was prepared to give a real *tonadilla*, but for that another was needed, and he looked over at Franscisco. Goya, who loved singing and was probably also excited by the wine, was ready to oblige. The Duke and he took whispered council together, experimented, decided. They sang, played, danced the *tonadilla* of the mule-driver. The driver scolds his passenger, but the latter only grows more and more exigent. He is a nuisance to animal and driver, won't dismount when the road is uphill, and finally is niggardly and won't add a cuarto to the agreed price. Amid the quarrelling and cursing is heard the braying of the mule, faithfully reproduced now by Manuel, now by Francisco.

They sang and danced with abandon, the Prime Minister and the Court Painter of Their Catholic Majesties. The two elegantly dressed gentlemen not only played the scolding driver and the stingy traveller, they turned into them. They *were* the parts they played, far more than they were Prime Minister and Court Painter.

The ladies looked on, but the Abbé and Señor Bermúdez conversed in whispers. Then, as Don Manuel and Goya threw themselves with more and more abandon into their parts, even they fell silent, surprised for all their sophistication, feeling for the pair a mild, amused contempt derived from the consciousness of their own spiritual and intellectual refinement. How they were exerting themselves, the barbarians, to please the ladies! How they were lowering themselves without even being aware of it!

At last Manuel and Francisco had had enough of singing and prancing and stopped for breath, exhausted and happy.

Then, quite surprisingly, someone else put himself forward: Don Agustín Esteve.

To Spaniards drunkenness is something contemptible; it deprives men of their dignity. Don Agustín could not recall ever having lost the clarity of his mind through wine. Today, however, he had drunk more than he should have, and he knew it. He was vexed with himself, but still more with the other guests. There were these two men, Manuel Godoy who called himself Duke of Alcudia and festooned his stomach with glittering gold, and Francisco Goya who poured himself and his art out as if they were dish water. Luck had lifted them both from their lowly estate to the topmost heights and showered them with things they could only have dreamed of—riches, power, esteem, desirable women. And instead of giving humble thanks to Heaven and the fates, they made themselves ridiculous, bellowing and dancing about like stuck pigs, in the face of the most wonderful woman in the world. And he, Agustín, had to stand and look on and drink the champagne of which he was thoroughly sick. At least he was now in the mood to give the Abbé a real piece of his mind, and Don Miguel too, that learned and leathery ass who did not realize what he possessed in Doña Lucía.

In a rumbling voice Agustín began to expatiate on the empty erudition of certain gentlemen. They talked the hind leg off a donkey about their Greek and their German, their Aristotle and their Winckelmann. That wasn't difficult, if one had enough money for education, and time as well, and if one had belonged to the *colegiales* with their stiff collars and buckled shoes, and if one had not, like a certain Agustín Esteve, had to work oneself to death as *manteísta* in order to earn or beg his thin soup of an evening. Yes, certain gentlemen had had the necessary twenty thousand reals for their banquet and their bullfight and their doctor's diploma. "And the likes of us, who have no degrees but more understanding of art in our little fingers than the four universities and the whole Academy with all their doctors, we have to sit here drinking more champagne than we are up to and paint pictures of horses under the arses of defeated generals." Agustín's wine glass had tipped over and now he himself slumped over the table, gasping for breath. The Abbé said indulgently, "So now our Don Agustín has sung his *tonadilla* too."

Don Manuel understood perfectly his personal painter's lanky assistant. "As drunk as a Swiss," he said benevolently; the soldiers of the Swiss Guard were celebrated for the way they passed their evening leave, marching through the streets in long lines, arm in arm, drunken, bawling, and molesting the passers-by. Don Manuel remarked with satisfaction the difference between Agustín's heavy, irascible drunkenness and his own light, good-hearted, agreeable warmth. He sat down by Goya, in order while still drinking to pour out his heart to the painter, his wiser, older, sympathetic friend.

Don Miguel addressed himself to Pepa. As she was clearly going to have influence with his Duke for some time to come, he regarded it as desirable in the interests of Spain and progress to make sure of her good will.

Don Diego sat himself down by Doña Lucía. He believed he understood human beings, he believed he understood Doña Lucía. She was very experienced, she must be blasé, she had arrived at her goal; a woman such as she would be difficult to win. But he was a scholar, philosopher, and theoretician, and he had worked out his system, his strategy. If Doña Lucía occasionally displayed a gentle mockery which was hard to interpret, then it was probably because she was aware of her origin and proud of it. She belonged to the lower classes, to the *majas;* she never forgot it, and therein lay her strength. She deferred to no one; the *majas* and *majos* of Madrid felt themselves to be as purely Spanish as the grandees, perhaps more so. The Abbé took this great lady, Doña Lucía Bermúdez, for a secret revolutionary who might have played her part in Paris; and he laid his plans accordingly.

He did not know if Don Miguel discussed affairs of state with her or even if she was interested in them. Yet he behaved as if it was she who, from her dais or her salon, guided the destinies of Spain. The first tentative steps on the road to peace had not led very far; Paris was suspicious. Was it not conceivable that a priest who was certainly in the good books of the gentlemen of the Inquisition and an elegant lady who had one of the first salons in Europe might conduct the affairs of Spain with more freedom, and for that reason with more effect, than the politicians of the Court? Don Diego intimated that he had a certain influence in Paris, access to men who were scarcely accessible to others. Cautiously, larding his words with gallantries, he asked her for her advice, challenged her to make a pact with him.

The astute Lucía was well aware that his objective went beyond the political. Nevertheless the confidence of this cultivated intriguer and the subtle, difficult role he offered her flattered the spoiled woman. For the first time her slanting, enigmatic eyes looked at him with serious interest.

But then she showed signs of fatigue. It was late, and she set store by abundant sleep. She withdrew, taking Pepa with her, as the latter wanted to refresh her toilette.

Don Manuel and Goya stayed on. They noticed nothing of what went on around them; they drank and were absorbed in each other. "I am your friend, Francho," the Duke assured the painter, "your friend and your protector. We Spanish grandees have always been patrons of the arts, and I have a feeling for art. You've heard what a singer I am. We belong together, you and I, the painter and the statesman. You come of peasants, don't you, from Aragón? One can hear it in your speech. My mother is of gentle birth, but between you and me, I come of peasants too. I've made something big of myself and I'll make something big out of you, you can rely on that, my Francho. We're men, you and I, and there aren't many men in these parts. 'Spain breeds great men but she uses them up fast,' as the saying goes, and so she does. It is because of all these wars that so few remain. But you and I are left over, and that's why the women quarrel over us. There are a hundred and nineteen grandees at Court and only two men. My father always called me 'Manuel, my little bull,' and right he was. But the toreador for this bull hasn't appeared yet, he's still to be born. I'll tell you something, Francisco, my Francho: one must have luck. One must have it, it doesn't come to one. Luck is something you have, like your nose, your leg, your behind, and everything else; one either has it or one hasn't. You are a kindred soul, Francho. I am a grateful man and I owe you a debt of gratitude. I've got quite a good eye by nature, but it was you who first taught me to see properly. Who knows whether without your picture I should have come across the *viudita?* And who knows if without your picture I would have recognized the goddess in this woman? Where is she? She seems not to be here. Never mind, she'll come back again. My luck never fails me. I tell you she's right, this Señora Josefa Tudo. She is the right one for me. But of course you know, I don't have to tell you. She's clever, intelligent, she speaks French. And not only that, she's an artist, a friend of La Tirana. She doesn't butter one, she is reserved, one of the few real ladies. How much music she has in her only he can tell who comes really near her. But the day will come, or the night, rather, when I shall be able to tell. It's already here, that night, or don't you think so?"

Goya listened with mixed feelings, not without contempt and yet with understanding of the drunken man. What Don Manuel uttered was his inmost truth, and in the midst of his drunkenness felt sure of him, Francisco Goya, regarded him as his friend, was his friend. Remarkable how things link up. He had wanted to have Jovellanos called back, to conquer himself and give Pepa up to this end, and now Don Manuel, the most powerful man in the whole of Spain, had become his friend. Now he no longer needed that arrogant, pedantic Bayeu, his wife's brother. On the contrary, he was now certain, through his connection with the Duke, of becoming First Court Painter against no matter what opposition. Of course one mustn't tempt Providence; what Don Manuel had said about luck being a thing you just had, that was presumptuous. He, Francisco, was not presumptuous. He was aware of the dark forces that were always about one. Inwardly he crossed himself and thought of the old saying, "Good luck has long legs, bad luck has wings." A lot could still happen before he became First Painter to the King. But in one thing Don Manuel was certainly right: they belonged together, they were both men. And so, in defiance of all the dark forces, he was confident of success. For today happiness took only one form for him: not a diploma with a royal seal, but an oval face with a hint of brown in its pallor, narrow, childishly plump hands; it rippled and shimmered, it was *chatoyant*. And if she'd kept him waiting to the point of despair, she had at last invited him to Moncloa to the Palacio Buenavista, writing with her own hand.

Don Manuel had gone on prattling. But now he broke off. Pepa was suddenly among them again, freshly rouged and powdered.

The candles had burned down, the smell of stale wine was in the room, the page sat, dead tired, half asleep on his chair. Agustín crouched over the table, his big nobby head on his arms, his eyes shut, snoring. Don Miguel himself seemed tired. But Pepa sat there, languid as ever, yet physically fresh and resilient.

Señor Bermúdez set about lighting fresh candles. But Don Manuel, now perfectly sober, stopped him. "No, Don Miguel," he called out. "Don't trouble yourself. Even the best party must have an end."

He stepped up to Pepa with surprising alertness and bowed low before her. "Allow me the honour, Doña Josefa," he said in a cajoling voice, "of taking you home." Pepa gave him a calm, friendly look out of her green eyes and played with her fan. "Thank you very much, Don Manuel," she said and inclined her head.

Past Francisco as he sat there
Tiptoed Manuel and Pepa.
By the door outside there squatted
Sleeping the dueña. Pepa
Smiling waked her, and the porter

Sprang up too. With trampling horses
Came Don Manuel's stately carriage
And the lackey in red stockings
Held the door until they mounted.
Swiftly Manuel and Pepa
Thundered through the sleeping city
Homeward.

-- 10 --

A few days later as Goya was working without much enthusiasm on the portrait of Don Manuel, an unexpected visitor appeared: Don Gaspar Jovellanos. The Minister had been as good as his word.

Agustín's hatchet face was suffused with embarrassment, pleasure, and reverence when he saw the famous statesman walk into the studio. Goya himself was confused; proud and ashamed at once that the great man should come to him immediately on his arrival, to thank him.

"I think I can say," declared Don Gaspar, "that during my exile I have never doubted that in the end my opponents would have to call me back. The forces of progress are stronger than the tyrannical will of perverted individuals. But without your intervention, Don Francisco, it would probably have taken much longer. It is reassuring and consoling to see one's friends risking a bold word or two for the good of the country. It is doubly gratifying when those words are said by a man from whom, frankly, one would not have expected them. Accept my thanks, Don Francisco." He spoke with dignity; his austere, heavily lined, bony face remained sombre. When he had finished, he bowed.

Goya knew that in liberal circles big words were customary, but he did not care for pathos himself. The punctilious phrases of his visitor embarrassed him. He made some vague reply. Then, with more animation, he remarked that Don Gaspar looked gratifyingly well and strong. "Yes," replied Jovellanos grimly, "if some people thought I would eat my heart out during my exile they made a mistake. I love my mountains; I climbed about, I hunted, I pursued my studies in peace, and, as you rightly remark, it didn't suit me at all badly."

"They say," Agustín said respectfully, "that in this time of quiet you have produced several important books." "I had leisure," replied Jovellanos, "and I did put some of my ideas on paper. They are essays in philosophy and political economy. Close friends thought enough of my manuscripts to smuggle them into Holland. But I suppose little or nothing has reached Madrid." "I think you are mistaken, Don Gaspar," said Agustín, smiling and hoarse with enthusiasm. "For instance, there is a manuscript, not very comprehensive but still important. 'Bread and Bullfights' is the title. The author signs himself Don Cándido Nocedal, but anyone who has read a work by Jovellanos knows who this Nocedal is. There's only one man in Spain who writes like that." Jovellanos's thin, furrowed face had grown red, but Agustín in his enthusiasm went on, "The Inquisition has been on the track of the work, and anyone caught reading it has fared ill. But our Madrileños haven't let themselves be scared off; they have copied the work over and over again; many know it by heart." And he began to quote: " 'Madrid has more churches and chapels than dwelling houses, more priests and monks than laity. On every street corner faked relics are offered for sale, accounts of faked miracles. Religion consists in absurd externals, and too many brotherhoods have been the death of brotherly love. In every corner of rotten, degenerate, ignorant, superstitious Spain hangs a dingy picture of the Virgin. We go to confession once a month but we persist in our wickedness all the days of our life till we die. No heathen is as barbarian and criminal as we Spanish Christians. What we fear are the dungeons of the Inquisition, not the Last Judgment.' "

"Don Cándido Nocedal is right," chuckled Jovellanos.

But Francisco had listened to the ringing phrases with fear and indignation and he was angry with Agustín for uttering them under his roof. Goya had no great love for the Church and her governors, but such bold and slanderous talk was dangerous; it could bring down the Inquisition on their heads. And it tempted Providence. He looked at the Virgin of Atocha and crossed himself.

But the painter in him could not help noticing the change that had taken place in Jovellanos. His hard face had softened; he was enjoying the humour of having quoted to him the fine sentences he had had smuggled from his banishment into Madrid under a false name. Goya saw what was going on beneath Jovellanos's crusty exterior, and now he knew how he would paint him: as a great man in spite of the exaggerated harshness that masked his virtue.

Unfortunately Jovellanos soon dropped his genial mood and worked himself up to wilder and wilder accusations against the present regime. "In our time," he declared passionately, "we improved the living conditions of the lower classes by lowering taxes. We brought it about that at least every eighth child could go to school, and when our ships came back from America with gold we even managed to lay a little by. But the present regime has squandered it all. They have not grasped the fact that Marie Antoinette's extravagance was one of the chief causes of the Revolution. They are more wildly extravagant still. They keep favourites, and English and Arabian horses, instead of strengthening the army. We furthered education and welfare: those people sow ignorance and misery, and now they are reaping devastation and defeat. Under our regime the Spanish colours were yellow and red; under these they are blood and gold."

To Francisco, Jovellanos's words appeared distorted and exaggerated. In details he might be right, but hatred falsified the whole picture for him, and if Goya had had to paint him now he would have made a gloomy, narrow-minded fanatic and nothing else. At the same time this Jovellanos was undoubtedly one of the cleverest and most upright men in the country. Anyone who went in for politics was bound to exaggerate, on one side or the other. Goya was glad that he himself had nothing to do with politics.

The whole time Jovellanos had been darkly scrutinizing Don Manuel's portrait. Now he raised his finger and pointed accusingly at the Duke who, half finished and disdainful, looked out at him from the canvas. "If this gentleman and his lady," he raged, "were not so wildly extravagant, there would be more money for schools. But that's just what they don't want. They foster ignorance, so that the people shan't know where the cause of their sufferings lies. How does it happen that impoverished France is victorious over the whole world? It is because the French people adhere to reason and virtue, because they are civilized. And what have we got? A brainless King, a Queen who is governed solely by the lusts of her flesh, and a Prime Minister who has only one single qualification, a strapping pair of legs."

Francisco was outraged. The fourth Charles was not overbright, one had to admit, and Doña María Luisa was temperamental and concupiscent; but the King was well-meaning and dignified in his way, and the Queen diabolically clever, and she had presented the country with a whole troop of healthy Infantes and Infantas. As for Don Manuel, he was quite easy to get on with if one did not irritate him. At any rate he, Francisco, was happy to have these personages honour him with their friendship. He was convinced that the King's power was his by Divine Grace, and if Jovellanos really believed all that he said, then he was no Spaniard and ought to take himself off to France, that land of godless mutineers.

But Goya controlled himself and said only, "Aren't you a little unjust to the Duke, Don Gaspar?" "A little?" returned Jovellanos. "Very, I hope, very. I don't wish to be just to the scoundrel. That he was unjust to me is what I hold least against him. One can't be just, in politics. Virtue and Justice are not identical. Virtue demands that one should be unjust on occasion."

Still gently, savouring to the full the ironic ambiguity of his position, Francisco observed, "When all is said and done, Don Manuel seems to be concerned to make good what he did to you. Otherwise why should he have recalled you?"

Jovellanos, with an angry glance at the half-finished portrait, replied, "It keeps me awake at night, the thought that I am indebted to this creature."

With one of those sudden changes which caused many people to forget all that was hard, angular, and repellent in him, he went on, "But don't let us speak of that. Let us talk about art, your art. I owe you a debt of gratitude, Don Francisco, and when I think of your art I am glad I do. They tell me you now belong among the greatest portrait painters in the country." Don Gaspar's face, when he said things like that, beamed and was charmingly friendly. Goya's heart rejoiced at his words.

But not for long. For almost immediately Don Gaspar made himself unbearable again by remarking, "They tell me some of your things actually come up to Bayeu and Maella." Even Agustín started.

Jovellanos walked about in the studio, inspecting Goya's pictures and sketches seriously, expertly, at length, and in silence. "I am indebted to you, Don Francisco," he said at last, "and so I owe it to you to be frank. You have great ability, perhaps really as much as Bayeu and Maella, perhaps even more. But you experiment too much with established truths. You play with colour, you dissolve line. And in that way you waste your talents. Take Jacques-Louis David as your model. We could do with a painter like him in Madrid. A Jacques-Louis David would be fired with indignation at the Court and its corruption. He wouldn't paint elegant ladies but a thundering Jove." "The old fool," thought Francisco, recalling the saying "When a man with anger shakes, all his reason him forsakes." Aloud, and without concealing his scorn, he replied, "Shall I paint a portrait of you, Don Gaspar?"

For an instant it seemed as if Jovellanos would explode. But he controlled himself and only said, "It's a pity you don't take my criticism seriously, because I take it seriously myself. Next to politics nothing is nearer to my heart than art. Artistic gift united to political fervour might produce the highest things of which man is capable. A Jacques-Louis David would not be of less use to this country than a Mirabeau."

At first, after Jovellanos had gone, Francisco shrugged his shoulders; but then he felt his temper rising. There he was, having to listen in silence to that prig's schoolmasterish rubbish. "They ought to have left him sitting in the mountain fastness he so richly deserved," he raged, and he turned to Agustín. "It's your fault, you looked at me with your stupid, fanatical, reproachful eyes, and I was fool enough to say yes. And now I shall have this leathery old pedant hanging about me for who knows how long. My very palette dries up when he looks at it."

This time Agustín did not keep silence. "Don't talk like that," he retorted defiantly. "What Don Gaspar says about you and David is mistaken, of course. But he is right in wanting to make art political today in Spain. You should take notice of that." He expected that Goya would burst out violently. But he did not. In a voice subdued but full of the most venomous contempt he answered, "And I'm being preached at in this way by a man who when he is at the top of his form manages to paint a horse's arse. Are arses political? The Spanish David! What impudent rubbish!

The Spanish David, that's what you can be, Don Agustín Esteve, it's about what your talents run to."

But Agustín, his big, bony head thrust forward, went on with grim persistence, "Let me tell you something, Don Francisco, let me tell you something, Francho, let me tell you something, Señor Court Painter and member of the Academy. He is right a thousand times over, no matter how much you twist and turn or how much spite you spit out. Your pictures are tripe, Don Francisco Goya, for all your gifts, and there is more political sense in my horse's arse than in the lascivious faces of your grand ladies. And so long as you remain a cowardly neutral, so long as you either have no opinion or express none, so long will all your painting be nothing but filthy tripe." He pointed to the picture of Don Manuel. "Have you got the nerve to look at it? A disgrace, that's what it is, a disgrace. *Qué vergüenza!* You've been smearing away at it for a week and it all comes to nothing and you know it. You make a wonderful uniform and wonderful decorations in wonderful colours, and the face is empty and the whole thing is empty. It's shit, not painting. And why? Because you want to please your Don Manuel. Your Manuel is the same sort that you are, stuck up and vain and anxiously taken up with his paltry reputation. That's why you don't dare paint him as he is. You're afraid of the truth, of his truth and your truth. A piddler, that's what you are!"

But this was too much. Lowering over Agustín with his round, peasant, leonine face, Goya let fly; stood directly before him, powerful fists clenched. "Shut your mouth, you pathetic buffoon," he ordered in a voice that was ominously low.

"I shouldn't think of it," replied Agustín. "You daub and smear away ten hours a day and pride yourself on your industry and your hundreds of pictures. I tell you you're lazy, frivolous, and criminally careless. You dodge the issue, you're yellow, you don't deserve your talent. You did your Doña Lucía, you found your new light and your new atmosphere. And what are you doing with it? Instead of concentrating, instead of experimenting with this new thing till you've made sure of it, you fall back on your sleight of hand and daub away as you always have, without an idea in your head."

"Will you shut your mouth now, you swine?" Goya said, so

threateningly that anyone else would have drawn back. Not so Agustín. He saw that Goya was breathing hard, he knew his friend-enemy would be reduced to deafness by his rage; he raised his voice. "Your Manuel," he screamed, "may possibly be satisfied with your trash. But trash it is. Effective trash and therefore twice as trashy. And you know it. And why are you such a wretched failure? Because you're stinking lazy. Because you won't concentrate. Because you're too gross to concentrate. A disgrace. *Qué vergüenza!* Because you're waiting on a woman who won't say 'yes' to you at once, and who probably isn't worth waiting for."

The last words Goya heard were "*Qué vergüenza.*" A crimson cloud of rage had enveloped him, mounting to ears and brain so that he could no longer hear. "Get out!" he bellowed. "Go to your Jovellanos. Paint him, paint him the way your David painted Marat, killed in his bath. Get out, I say, get out and stay out!"

What Agustín answered Francisco did not hear; he only saw his lips moving. He wanted to rush at him. But this time Agustín actually went. With ungainly speed he stumped out.

So alone Francisco Goya
Stood there with his half-baked Manuel
Feeling foolish. "*Qué vergüenza!*"
He repeated. "*Qué vergüenza!*"
Ever and again he muttered.
On a sudden then he dashed off,
Calling, shouting, shrieking loudly,
Since he could by no means measure
How he sounded, since his illness
Stopped his ears. "But wait a minute,
Wait, you ass! Just let me finish!
Yes, I know you're always like that:
You can say the worst things to me,
But when I make any answer,
Then you are as peeved and angry
As an old Infanta-aunty."

11

Francisco Goya had painted the portraits of almost half of the one hundred and nineteen grandees of Spain. He knew their weaknesses and their little human foibles, and moved among them as one of themselves. Nevertheless, on his way to Moncloa, to the Duchess of Alba's, he felt as shy as he had felt when as a small boy he had had to appear before the Count of Fuendetodos, his father's all-powerful landlord.

He laughed at himself. What was he afraid of and what was he hoping for? He was going to a woman who had made quite open advances to him. There was no denying that. But then why had she been silent so long?

She had been very busy in those weeks, that was true. He had heard a great deal about her—the whole city talked of what the Duchess of Alba did or did not do. Wherever he was he had to expect to hear her name, and he had both dreaded and longed for the sound.

He knew that her name had the same effect in the taverns of the *majos* and *majas* as in the salons of the grandees. People gossiped and slandered; they told the ugliest stories about her and at the same time they were enchanted with the thought that the great-grandchild of the bloodthirstiest man in Spain, Field Marshal Alba, was so radiantly beautiful, so childlike, so arrogant, wilful, and spoiled. She would fall into conversation with street urchins about the coming bullfights; on the other hand, she would sometimes disdainfully ignore every salutation. Now she would challenge society with her penchant for French fashions; now she would show herself utterly Spanish, a real *maja*. But all the time she tried to make trouble with the Queen, the Italian, the foreigner.

All in all, Cayetana de Alba did not live less proudly and extravagantly than the Queen. She had just as many costly whims, and it could scarcely be said that she was virtuous. Yet when the toreador Costillares dedicated his bull to the Queen, there was silence; when he dedicated it to the Duchess the whole arena cheered.

It was an effrontery that she should build this new castle when the war was demanding the highest sacrifices from the people. Was not the extravagance with which Marie Antoinette built her Trianon one of the causes that had brought her to the guillotine? And yet with her smiling, insolent, unlimited Alba pride, Cayetana de Alba carried on the frivolities of Marie Antoinette from the point where the latter had had to give them up. And not many people, not even Francisco, would have been able to say whether they admired her or hated her for it. The people of Madrid always felt like that about the Duchess. They got angry with her. Joked about her. Loved her.

The palace was small; only Cayetana's most intimate friends were invited, and the most exalted grandees. That she counted him among them made him proud and happy. But she was as incalculable as next year's weather; perhaps she no longer realized she had invited him. How would she receive him? Would she carry his fan? What would the fan say? And would she call him Goya or Don Francisco or simply Francisco?

The carriage had reached the barred gateway of Buenavista; it drove up the ramp. Restrained, in the *estilo desornamentado* of Herrera, dispensing with all nonessentials, the façade rose up proudly before them. The double doors opened, the staircase curved nobly upwards, and from above, at the head of the stairs, the life-size portrait of an early ancestor of the Duchess gazed haughtily away past the heads of all beholders. Goya could not overcome a sense of oppression at the name of Alba, the first name in Spain, older, more famous, more exalted than that of the Bourbons. So, outwardly a courtier, inwardly a peasant, he ascended the grand staircase, escorted by the chamberlain, between two rows of servants; in advance of him, low-voiced, important, flew his name, whispered from mouth to mouth, till at the top an usher loudly announced, "Señor de Goya, the King's Painter."

This stair-climbing Señor de Goya, for all his awe and dignity, took note with surprise that the interior of the little castle was in bold and mocking contrast to its classically severe façade. Here all was of the gayest and most luxurious, the sort of thing created by the French Court of a generation past, the Court of Louis the Fifteenth and the du Barry. Did the owner of this castle wish to show that she was at once the bearer of the proudest and most fearsome name in Spain and an enthusiast of the gallant *savoir vivre* of the fallen French aristocracy?

On the walls of her palace, however, the Duchess had hung pictures quite other than those which adorned the similar chateaux of noblemen in France. Nothing by Boucher or Watteau and nothing corresponding to the tapestries of Goya or his brother-in-law Bayeu. On the contrary, there hung only paintings by the great old Spanish masters, a dark, cruel, grandee portrait from the hand of Velázquez, a gloomy saint by Ribera, a darkly fanatical monk by Zurbarán.

Beneath these paintings sat the not very numerous guests. Of the twelve topmost men who had the privilege of wearing their hats in the presence of the King, five were present with their ladies. Then there was Goya's perpetual debtor, Monsieur de Havré, the ambassador of the boy King of France and of his Regent; representative, shabby and defiant, he sat there with his thin, pretty sixteen-year-old daughter Geneviève at his side. There, too, was the Abbé Don Diego. Further, there was a blond, portly gentleman with strong features and a composed mien. Even before they were introduced Goya knew: this was Doctor Peral, the detested doctor, the barber.

But who was this stern, dignified, upright figure, a living negation of all the dainty, frivolous atmosphere of the palace? Yes, it was he, Don Gaspar Jovellanos, the opponent of Church and Throne, who, reluctantly recalled, had not yet been granted by the King the opportunity to kiss his hand in gratitude for this new favour. It was an incomparable piece of audacity that Doña Cayetana had invited him today, when Their Catholic Majesties were expected. The assembled guests did not know how to behave towards Don Gaspar. They greeted him politely and coldly and avoided conversation with him. He did not seem to mind. It was a triumph for his cause that the first noblewoman of the kingdom should invite him on such an occasion; besides, he set no store by mixing with these aristocratic celebrities. Solitary and defiant, he sat on his little gilt chair, and Goya had the feeling that the delicate piece of furniture must collapse beneath the weight of so much dignity.

The Duke of Alba and his mother, the Marquesa of Villabranca, greeted the guests. The Duke was more animated than usual. "You're going to have a little surprise, my friend," he told Goya. The Abbé explained to Goya that the Duchess intended to celebrate the opening of the theatre at Buenavista with chamber music and that the Duke himself would take part. Goya was not greatly interested. He was nervous, he missed his hostess, it was strange that she was not there to receive her guests. The Abbé had an explanation for that too. For better or worse, one would have to wait to view the house until Their Majesties had put in an appearance. But Doña Cayetana did not want to sit and wait, not even for the royal pair, so she had arranged to be notified, and would enter the hall at the same time as, and immediately ahead of, Their Majesties.

There she was. Many times Francisco had enjoined upon himself to remain calm at the sight of her, but it affected him just as it had when he had seen her on the dais. Everything else, the guests, the all-pervading glitter, the pictures, the mirrors, the chandeliers, everything sank away, and she was there alone. She was of extreme, challenging simplicity. Her dress was white and without ornament, such as the ladies of the Republic might be wearing now in Paris; from her slender waist, spanned by a wide scarf, the skirt with a pale golden hem spread down to the floor. Around her wrist she wore a band of smooth gold; otherwise she was without jewels. Her hair fell in thick, black masses and unruly ringlets over her bare shoulders.

Goya stared. Without regard for the others, who had the right to precede him in greeting her, he tried to press towards her. But just then, according to plan, the call came, swelling in volume from the staircase, "Their Catholic Majesties!" Those present formed two lines, and Cayetana went to meet the arrivals.

The major-domo, raising his staff, announced for the last time, "Their Catholic Majesties and His Highness, the Duke of Alcudia." And they came. The King, Charles the Fourth, stately, rotund, bulky, was wearing—a man of forty-six—a red frock coat embroidered in silver, over which was an impressive row of decorations and the Order of the Golden Fleece. Under his arm he had his three-cornered hat, in his left hand a cane; and his plump, red, good-natured face with the big fleshy nose, the sensual mouth, and the slightly receding brow culminating in a small patch of baldness, did its best to look imposing. Next to him, half a pace behind, taking up the whole double door with her hoop skirt, as sewn with jewels as a saint's image, holding her great fan in her hand, Doña María Luisa of Parma, the Queen, appeared; almost sweeping the archway of the door swayed the enormous plumes of her hat. Behind them Don Manuel was to be seen, the usual slightly bored smile on his handsome, rather heavy face.

Making a Court curtsy, Cayetana kissed the hand first of the King, then of Doña María Luisa. The latter, concealing her astonishment with an effort, scrutinized with her sharp little black eyes the defiantly simple dress in which the proud Duchess of Alba presumed to receive Their Catholic Majesties.

They held Court. There stood Gaspar Jovellanos, the rebel, as if he belonged there. The King, who was rather slow-witted, did not recognize him at once. Then, clearing his throat, he said, "We haven't seen each other for a long time. How have you been keeping? You look splendid." Doña María Luisa, on the other hand, for a moment could not hide her pained surprise; then she told herself that now that they had recalled the man they might at least make use of his financial abilities. So she graciously suffered the rebel to kiss her hand. "In these hard times, Señor," she said, "our poor country needs the services of every man, whoever he may be. So we have decided, the King and I, to give even you the opportunity to prove yourself." She spoke loudly in her not unpleasing voice, so that all could admire the amiable ambiguities by means of which she extricated herself from a difficult situation. "I thank you, Your Majesty," replied Jovellanos, and he too made use of his trained orator's voice so that it was audible throughout the whole hall. "I only hope that my abilities have not rusted during the long time I have been forced to be idle." You shall pay me for this, thought María Luisa, meaning the Duchess.

The guests were shown over the house. "Very pretty, very comfortable," praised Don Carlos. The Queen, however, inspected with envy and an expert eye the costly details of the delicately gay décor. She pointed to the old Spanish masterpieces looking down with incongruous austerity and grandeur on the agreeable trifles all around. "Strange things you've chosen to hang on your walls, my dear," she observed. "If I had to live with such pictures it would make me shiver."

In the theatre even the cold, reserved grandees indulged in cries of rapture. Spendid but nonetheless discreet, the blue and golden room shimmered in the light of countless candles. Loges and chairs fashioned of the finest materials were at once formal and inviting. The finials of the pillars supporting the balcony were in the form of antique heraldic animals, indicating that the members of the audience were guests of a lady whose titles represented seven grandees of Spain.

And now came the moment to which the Duke of Alba had been looking forward for weeks. The major-domo bade the ladies and gentlemen be seated. On the stage appeared the Duke, his sister-in-law Doña María Tomasa, and little Geneviève, Monsieur de Havré's daughter. The Duke's sister-in-law, a black-haired, well-built woman, appeared robust beside Geneviève and the Duke, but she played the smallest of the three instruments on the stage, the viola. Geneviève, on the other hand, thin, appealing, a little exiguous in physique and dress, sat behind her big cello. The Duke himself played an instrument which nowadays one saw more and more seldom, a barytone, a *viola di bordone,* a sort of knee-fiddle with many strings, not very large, with an affectingly hard and soft deep tone.

The three tuned their instruments, nodded to each other, and began a divertimento by Haydn. Doña María Tomasa played her viola with repose and certainty. Geneviève laboured at her powerful cello, big-eyed, eager, and shy. But the Duke, usually so cool and remote, came to life as he played; his fingers became creatures with a life of their own as they pressed or plucked the strings, the fine, melancholy eyes shone, the whole body, usually so controlled, let itself go, swayed backwards and forwards as he extracted from his instrument its hidden life. The old Marquesa of Villabranca, moved and enraptured, watched her son. "Isn't he an artist, my José?" she asked of Goya who sat next to her. He, however, looked only with half an eye and listened with only half an ear. He had not yet spoken a word to Cayetana; he did not even know if she had noticed him.

The guests enjoyed the music and greeted the exhausted, smiling Duke of Alba with genuine applause. Even King Carlos forgot that Don José over and over again and on the most transparent pretexts had defiantly refused the King's request to play in his quartet. He even exerted himself to say something gracious to him. The stout and ungainly monarch stood in front of his first grandee. "You are a real artist, Don José," he declared. "It's not really suitable for a gentleman in your position, but what's true must be said, and I can't come up to your barytone with my modest violin."

The Duchess declared that the stage was dedicated to the amateurs, and did not one of the guests wish to perform? The Queen, casually but so that everyone could hear, asked, "What about it, Don Manuel? Wouldn't you like to treat us to one of your ballads or a *seguidilla bolera?*" Don Manuel hesitated a brief instant. Then, obsequiously, he replied that he was afraid, in such refined surroundings and after so priceless a performance, his poor offering would be out of place. But Doña María Luisa insisted. "Don't be coy, Don Manuel," she coaxed, and it was no longer the Queen who was asking but a woman desirous of showing off to her friends the manifold talents of her lover. But Don Manuel—perhaps he was thinking of Pepa—was not in the mood to let himself be put on display. "Please believe me, Madame," he replied, "I am not in good voice, and I will not sing."

This was brusque. It was no way for a grandee to answer his Queen, or a *cortejo* his lady, least of all in the presence of others. There was an embarrassed silence. But the Duchess of Alba had the tact not to savour the Queen's defeat for more than a few seconds. Then, very amiably, she called her guests to table.

Goya sat at the table of the lower nobility with Jovellanos and the Abbé. Any other arrangement would scarcely have been possible. Nevertheless he was out of temper, said little, and ate much. He had still not spoken to the Duchess. After the meal—the Duke had immediately withdrawn—he sat alone in a corner. He was angry no longer, but overcome by a feeling of torpid disillusionment.

"You're positively avoiding me, Don Francisco," he heard a voice saying; rather a hard voice, yet it affected him more deeply than the music of the Austrian master had done. "First of all, you aren't seen for weeks," the Duchess went on, "and then you simply keep out of my way." He looked at her as before, without restraint, and she looked at him pleasantly, not at all as before. She played with her fan—it was not his fan, but at least the fan was saying something pleasant.

"Sit down by me," she ordered. "I haven't had much time in the last few weeks," she told him. "The building of this house has made great demands on me. Even in the near future I shan't have much time; I have to go to the Escorial with the Court. But as soon as I come back you must really make a portrait of me in your new manner. The whole world is raving about your new portraits." Goya listened, bowed, was silent.

"You haven't said a word to me about my house," the Duchess continued. "You're not polite. And what do you think of my little theatre? Not much, of course. You like a stage only for coarse masculine things, for women with big breasts and loud voices. I like that sort of thing too occasionally, but in my theatre I want things to be different; it will be very daring too, of course, but at the same time delicate and elegant. What do you think, for example, of Calderón's *There's No Trifling with Love?* Or would you like *The Girl of Gómez Arias* better?"

Francisco's hearing failed him, things swam before his eyes. *The Girl of Gómez Arias* was a colourful, sweetish, racy comedy of a man who falls wildly in love with a girl, seduces her, tires of her at once, and sells her to the Moors. Francisco's heart missed a beat. The Duchess knew all about his transactions with Don Manuel and Pepa. She despised him. He stammered something, rose, bowed clumsily, and left her.

He raged. He went over what she had said. Thought it over, weighed it. Don Gómez was a scoundrel, admitted, but a scoundrel of stature, run after by all the women. What the Duchess had said to him really only confirmed that his prospects with her were good. But he wouldn't be treated like that. He was no small boy to be played with.

Don Manuel sat down by him, addressed him, embarked on a confidential man-to-man talk. Enlarged on the game he had pulled off with the Queen, and in the Duchess's house into the bargain. "I won't let myself be talked into anything," he explained, "not by anyone. I sing when I want to. I sing for people who understand me, not for these grandees. I'm one myself, but what sort of company are they? You and I are both inflammable, Francisco; but are there many of the women here that you'd like to go to bed with? As far as I'm concerned, not even five. This little Geneviève is quite sweet, but no more than a child, and I'm not yet quite old enough to get fun out of children. And, by the way, I can get along without our amiable hostess too. She's too complicated for me, too capricious, too exigent. She expects one to court her for weeks and months. That sort of thing's not for Don Manuel. I don't like lengthy preliminaries; I like it when the curtain goes up at once."

Goya listened in sombre agreement. Don Manuel was right, the woman was nothing but a spoiled, arrogant doll. He'd had enough of her, he would pluck her out of his heart. As long as Their Majesties remained he would have to stay, but as soon as they left he would go too, and the Duchess of Alba and her castle Buenavista which was as crazy as she was would fade out of his life forever.

Meanwhile he joined a group around the two ladies who had played in the trio. The conversation was of music, and Peral, the doctor, in his composed, not loud, yet carrying voice held forth expertly on the subject of the barytone, an instrument that unfortunately was going more and more out of fashion; and of Señor José Haydn, the Austrian composer, who had written so much music for it. "Tell me, Doctor," came the voice of Doña Cayetana, "is there any single subject about which you know nothing?"

The Duchess's rather hard voice was slightly mocking but in it Goya thought he heard a tenderness, an intimacy with the doctor, which made him wild. He broke in, carefully schooling himself to calmness, and related an anecdote of a young man of his acquaintance who by a quite simple recipe had acquired a reputation for the highest erudition. This young man possessed, in all, three learned statements of fact, but understood well how to apply them. He would quote a phrase from a work of Saint Jerome. Then, as opportunity offered, he would relate that Virgil had made his hero Aeneas lachrymose and superstitious only in order to flatter Augustus Cæsar, who had the same propensities. Then he would speak of the unusual composition of dromedary blood. By skilful deployment of these three pieces of information the young man had established a reputation for great learning.

There was a short, astonished silence. Doctor Peral then asked the Abbé in casual undertone, "Who is the stout gentleman?" Then, with an amused little sigh, he observed, "The Court

Painter is right. Human knowledge is fragmentary. In my profession, for example, even the most learned know very little with certainty. There are scarcely four or five hundred facts that are established beyond doubt. What an honest doctor doesn't know, and isn't likely to know for a long time, would fill whole libraries." The doctor had spoken without pretension, with the good-natured superiority of the expert who effortlessly dispatches a raw ignoramus.

The violence with which the painter attacked her friends amused the Duchess. She wanted to show him what power she had over men. Without transition, she turned amiably to the Duke of Alcudia. "I could understand, Don Manuel," she said, "that you refused to sing just now in my little theatre. But this is no pretentious stage; here we are together without restraint. Sing us a song now, Don Manuel, give us the pleasure. We've all heard so much about your voice." Don Carlos, while the others looked at Don Manuel in slightly embarrassed suspense, observed, "An excellent idea, now we're getting quite cosy." Don Manuel hesitated for a moment; it would be unwise to provoke the Queen further. But he was no henpecked husband. He smiled graciously, feeling flattered, bowed to the Duchess, and took up position. Cleared his throat. Sang.

Doña María's little black eyes looked angry, but she bore with dignity this second humiliation in the house of her rival. She sat there in her flowing, jewel-studded gown, holding herself proudly, her sharp chin well up, slowly moving her enormous fan. Her lips smiled amiably.

Goya, who had often painted María Luisa, knew her with precision, knew every little wrinkle of her face, ravaged as it was by appetite, excess, and unsatisfied desire. She had never been beautiful, but as long as her youth lasted, so much wild and untamed life had emanated from her as certainly made her attractive to men. And she was well built; now, of course, her body had grown flabby from much child-bearing, and only the beauty of her arms remained. With bitter amusement and a little pity Goya saw how pathetically, for all her pride, decked in every magnificence, the Queen sat there, confronting the Duchess in her costly simplicity. The ageing María had the sharper wit and unlimited power, but the other was heart-breakingly lovely. Wicked they were, both of them, as witches, and it was a question which one was the more dangerous, the beautiful or the ugly. How unnecessary, how stupidly cruel, of the Alba to humiliate her rival for the second time! It was not good for him to look at the woman any longer. Grimly determined, he commanded himself for the tenth time to go as soon as the King left.

But he knew he would stay. He knew that this bad, beautiful woman was the ultimate temptation of his life and its greatest danger, something encountered only once in a lifetime, a source of supreme pleasure and supreme pain. But he was Francisco Goya and he would not run away from this unique experience.

This time Don Manuel sang only three songs. Scarcely had he finished the third when the Queen said, "You wanted to go hunting first thing in the morning, Carlos. I think we should go."

But the King unbuttoned his splendid waistcoat, and beneath it another simple one became visible, with several watch chains. He pulled out two watches, looked at them, listened to them, compared them. He loved clocks and accuracy. "It's only twelve minutes past ten," he stated. He put the watches away again, buttoned himself up, sat there, filling up his chair, lazy, massive, digesting his dinner, comfortable. "We can stay just a little half hour more," he said. "It's such a cosy evening."

The King's remark was a welcome signal to the Abbé Don Diego. Whole-heartedly an opponent of the war, he knew that Don Manuel and the Queen wanted to make peace but had hitherto hesitated to utter their opinions in public. Now the astute Abbé calculated that the temperamental Doña María Luisa, provoked by her defeat as a woman, would be glad of a chance to show statesmanship and shine in a sphere in which her rival could not follow her. He seized the opportunity and spoke. "Your Majesties have been pleased to extol the cheerful atmosphere which is so noticeable today, the 'cosiness' as Your Majesty was pleased to call it. You will perceive, Sire, this relaxation of tension everywhere where Spaniards come together, whether they are of high or low degree, for everyone feels that thanks to the wisdom of your government this cruel war is nearing its end."

Don Carlos looked with surprise at the heavy, ungainly man who wore his black priestly habit with such an air. What sort of queer bird was this, a courtier or a priest? And the King was quite at a loss to know what to make of the strange phrases which issued from his mouth. But the Queen, just as the Abbé had intended, snapped at the bait and seized the opportunity to shine, if not as a woman, then as a queen. She showed herself as the benevolent mother of her country, preferring a moderate peace to the continuation of the war, more glorious but more costly in blood and gold. "What you say, Abbé," she declared in her resonant voice, "fills us with satisfaction. We have, the King and I, defended the sacred principle of monarchy against the revolutionary French longer and more fiercely than anyone else. We have implored and threatened our allies, in order to hold them to their duty of restoring to power in France her divinely ordained ruler. But, alas, the princes and people who are in league with us are not so ready for sacrifice as we and our Spaniards are. They are ready to recognize the French Republic either with or without us. But if we endure alone we must expect that a certain other greedy nation, envious of our sea power, will fall upon us while we are involved on our frontiers in a life-and-death struggle. So we have come to the conclusion, the King and I, that we have satisfied our honour and the honour of our country, and that we are justified before God and the world in restoring peace to our people. It will be peace with honour."

Thus spoke María Luisa of Parma and Bourbon. She had not risen, she sat enthroned in her hoop skirt, her jewels and feathers, like an image. She had copied from their portraits the regal bearing of her ancestors; she had a good, practised voice, and the slight Italian accent with which she spoke heightened the ceremonial distance between her and her audience.

At her words despair overcame poor Monsieur de Havré. He had looked forward to this evening; it had been a satisfaction to him that the Duchess had invited him, and that his poor, beautiful, and so gifted daughter had been allowed to play in the trio. But the brief appearance of Geneviève on the stage had been the one ray of light in the darkness of the evening. First he had had to endure the sight of that crafty Abbé, the fat snake that spewed his poison against his royal masters; then the hated countenance of Jovellanos, the arch rebel, whose head should have been presented to Their Catholic Majesties by the hangman instead of by the Duchess of Alba. Not to speak of the sight of that impudent painter who was always vulgarly dunning him for money, instead of being glad of the honour of committing to canvas the envoy of the pathetic little Majesty of France. And now the most fearful blow of all had fallen. With his own ears he had had to hear the Queen of this country, in the presence of her grandees, in shameless, naked words betray the principle of monarchy, whose highest representative she was. And he had to sit there erect and calm, he must not bow his head on his arms and weep. Oh, had he only stayed in revolutionary Paris with his King and died under the knife of the guillotine!

All the greater was the rejoicing of the Abbé and Jovellanos. The Abbé felt proud of the psychological insight with which he had seized on the favourable moment. He was really the only statesman this side of the Pyrénées. His sense of victory was only slightly qualified by the fact that history would presumably not record his service to the cause of freedom. Jovellanos for his part well knew that it was not consideration for the welfare of the country which had made María Luisa, this Messalina, this crowned whore, declare her decision in favour of peace; but merely concern that with the mounting costs of the war she and her bedfellow would not have enough money to indulge their boundless lust for squandering. But whatever the reason, she had in the hearing of them all declared her readiness to end the war. Peace would come, and with it the time when a man filled with zeal for good would be able to put through beneficial reforms for the benefit of the people.

To most of the guests Doña María Luisa's announcement was not utterly unexpected and yet they were conscious of a certain surprise. They found the decision of the Crown inglorious but reasonable. They were content that the war should end; its continuance would mean forced economies for every one of them. One also had to allow that she had communicated her rather ignominious decision with skill and dignity.

So the Queen had pleased her grandees; but not Cayetana de Alba. The latter could not bear to have this woman, her rival, utter so proud and weighty a last word, and that here in her new house. She answered, she contradicted. "Certainly," she said, "many Spaniards will admire the wisdom of the royal decision. But I personally, and presumably one or two other Spaniards, will be deeply sorrowful that there should be a thought of peace while enemy troops are still on our soil. I remember how the poorest gave up their last penny for arms; I can remember how the people went to war, singing, dancing, stamping, with enthusiasm. No doubt I am a very foolish young woman, but I can't help it; after all that enthusiasm this finish seems to me to be—how shall I express it?—rather flat."

She had risen to her feet. White and slender, in the utmost simplicity, she stood before the sweeping magnificence of the Queen.

Poor Monsieur de Havré's heart leaped up. There were still voices raised in Spain for what was high and sacred, still people in this country who would protect the monarchy against revolt and godlessness. He looked reverently at this Iberian Maid of Orléans and gently stroked his Geneviève's hand.

Even the others were not unaffected by Cayetana's words. Of course the Queen was right and what the Duchess had uttered was romanticism, sheer heroic nonsense. But how lovely she was, and how daring! Was there another soul in Spain, man or woman, who would have dared open his mouth like that in front of Their Catholic Majesties? The hearts of the whole assemblage were hers.

No one spoke when she finished. Only Don Carlos shook his head and said soothingly, "Now, now, my dear."

With painful clarity Doña María Luisa realized that even this victory was going to turn into defeat. She could have reproved her impertinent antagonist, she had the power, but she could not afford to let herself go, could not admit that the other's words had struck home, dared not be vehement. "Your new house, my dear young friend," she said pleasantly, "has certainly a façade in the best old Spanish style, but inside you have adapted it to the demands of modern times. Perhaps you should make the same arrangement for yourself." A better riposte could scarcely have been found; the Queen had put her first noblewoman to rights in a dignified way. But Doña María Luisa knew that it was no use. She herself would always be the ugly old woman and the other would be right, however wrong.

Obviously the Duchess knew it too. She curtsied to the Queen and said with provocative humility, "I deeply regret having incurred Your Majesty's displeasure. I was orphaned in early youth and badly brought up. And so it happens from time to time that I offend against the wise and strict conventions of the Spanish Court." But as she spoke she cast a little sidelong glance up at the portrait of her ancestor, the blood-stained Field Marshal Duke of Alba, who, when the King demanded an accounting, sent in the following statement: "4 kingdoms won for the Spanish Crown by force of arms, 9 decisive victories, 217 successful sieges, and 60 years' service."

Goya had listened with mixed feelings to the battle of words between the two noble ladies. He believed in the divine origin of monarchy; the subject's duty of obedience was as sacred to him as the veneration of the Virgin, and the Duchess's words seemed to him outrageously arrogant; he had crossed himself inwardly as he listened; so much insolence must surely call down calamity on the head of the speaker. Nonetheless his heart contracted with rapture at the pride and beauty of the Duchess.

Their Majesties took leave soon after, with dignity and without much warmth. Goya stayed. So did most of the others.

And now Don Gaspar Jovellanos felt called upon to instruct the Duchess. He had wished to do so immediately after her speech; but the proud and lovely lady had appeared to him, in her burning love of country as well as in her reckless folly, as the embodiment of everything Spanish; and he had not had the heart to set her right in the presence of her rival. Now, however, he opened his mouth of weighty purpose. "Señora," he said, "Doña Cayetana, I understand your pain over the news that the war will end without being won. Believe me, my heart is no less Spanish than yours. But my mind works according to the laws of logic. On this occasion the counsellors of the Crown are right. It could only do harm to go on with the war, and there is no greater crime than an unnecessary war. It is not easy for me to ask a lady to envisage the horrors of war. But let me quote a few sentences from a writer, the greatest of the century." And he quoted: "'Candide clambered over a pile of dying and dead and reached a village, which was being turned to rubble and ashes. The enemy had set fire to it according to all the regulations of the laws of nations. Men, bent under the blows they received, looked on as their wives were strangled to death clutching their children to their bleeding breasts. Girls, with their bellies slit open, perished after having satisfied the natural desires of numerous heroes; others, half burned to death, begged for the *coup de grâce*. The ground was covered with spattered brains and hacked-off arms and legs.' Forgive me, ladies and gentlemen, the unpleasant description. But I can tell you from my own experience: the man is right. And, furthermore, I can assure you that such things as he describes are happening now, this very night, in our northern provinces."

It was tactless but not lacking in piquancy that Señor de Jovellanos, without fear of the Inquisition, should quote the most forbidden author in the world, Monsieur de Voltaire, and that in the palace of the Duchess of Alba to boot. It was proving an exciting evening, and they did not break up at once.

Goya, however, took the words of Jovellanos as a warning against the Duchess. What this woman did, what she said, was evil. He wanted no further part of her. He pulled himself together to go at last.

And then Cayetana turned to him. She touched his sleeve with her hand, gently; the other hand played invitingly with her fan.

"Listen to me, Don Francisco,
I have made a blunder, asking
You to wait and paint me later,
After the Escorial visit."
Dazedly he looked and listened,
Some new devilry expecting.
Till, confidingly and urgent,
Moving closer, she continued,
"That was wrong, it was an error.
I regret it, and I beg you
For forgiveness, since I cannot
Any longer wait, Francisco.
I will get an invitation
And you come to Court, or else I
Quickly will return; for straightway
You must paint me, Don Francisco,
Do you hear, and we together
Shall achieve a thing to make our
Friends stare open-mouthed in wonder."

12

When Goya ate his main meal in the family circle, as on most days he did, he was from head to foot the family man, rejoicing in his wife Josefa, in his children, in the eating and drinking and table talk. But today the meal passed gloomily, and everyone at table—

Goya, Josefa, the three children, and the skinny Agustín—was monosyllabic. News had come that Francisco Bayeu, Josefa's brother, who had been ailing a long time, had at most two or three days to live.

Goya regarded his wife sideways. She sat upright, as always; her long face showed nothing of her feelings. The clear, lively eyes looked straight ahead; the narrow-lipped mouth under the large nose was firmly shut. She sucked a little at her upper lip, and her chin was perhaps more pointed than usual. She had done her red-gold hair in heavy braids on her lofty brow; her hair sloped away to the back of her head like an old-fashioned priest's cap. In Saragossa, once, when their marriage was still young, he had painted her as the Blessed Virgin with two of their children as the boy Jesus and little John. Since then he had lived twenty years with her, through hopes and disappointments, through bad times and good, and she had borne him children both alive and dead. But even now he sometimes saw her as he had seen her then; in spite of her many pregnancies, there was about the forty-three-year-old woman a maidenly delicacy, a childlikeness, an austere charm.

He knew exactly what Josefa was feeling today and pitied her. She was losing much in her brother. When she had fallen in love with him, Goya, it had been with him as a man, his strength, his obstinacy, his richness of character; but she had never had much opinion of Goya the painter. All the more intense was her belief in the genius of her brother; he, Francisco Bayeu, First Painter to the King, President of the Academy, the most famous artist in the country, remained for her the head of the family; from him derived the reputation even of the house of Goya, and that Goya should rebel against him and his theories was a constant grief to Josefa.

She had an unmistakable resemblance to her brother. But to Goya what was unbearable in the brother pleased him in the sister. He found his brother-in-law irritatingly conceited and stiff-necked. The fact that she was proud of her respected family, that she was obstinate and taciturn, heightened her charm for him. He loved her for being as she was, loved her for being a Bayeu from Saragossa. He had often taken on unwelcome commissions only because he wanted to show her that he could earn the means necessary to provide her with the spacious life befitting a Bayeu.

Josefa never reproached him with his shortcomings as an artist or with his many affairs with women. He took her austere devotion for granted. The woman who had married Francisco Goya must understand quite clearly that he was no dutiful husband but a man.

Which was all the more reason for Bayeu to have tried to interfere in Goya's life. But the latter had told his brother-in-law, the King's First Painter, that exemplary schoolmaster of a man, exactly where he got off. What did his brother-in-law want? Didn't he, Goya, sleep with his wife as often as she wished, in fact even oftener? Didn't he share his board with her? Didn't he keep her even better than her position warranted? She was economical, one could almost say stingy; no cause for surprise in the sister of such a prig. Hadn't he positively had to force her to breakfast in bed? With chocolate in the aristocratic manner? The best chocolate, Moho chocolate from Bolivia, powdered by the dealer before Josefa's very eyes? Bayeu had replied haughtily, had drawn attention to Goya's village origins, used a contemptuous phrase about a woman with whom Goya had had relations, and Goya had been moved to seize his brother-in-law by the throat and shake him, in the course of which the latter's silver-embroidered frock coat had been torn.

Now Doña Josefa was about to lose her brother, and with him a light would go out of her life. But she sat there with an immobile face, bearing herself well, and Goya loved and admired her for it.

Gradually the silence and gloom around the board began to oppress him. Abruptly he declared that they must finish the meal without him, he wanted to go to Bayeu. Doña Josefa looked up. Then she thought she understood. She felt gratified. Obviously Francisco wished, in a conversation without witnesses, to beg the dying man's forgiveness for all he had done to him.

Goya found his brother-in-law lying on a low couch, propped up by many pillows. The thin, grey, sallow face was even more furrowed than usual, sick, weary, severe, suffering.

Goya observed that the familiar picture on the wall representing St. Francis hung head downwards; an old superstition had it that only by such an act of insolence could the saint be spurred to effective help.

His cultivated, austerely rational brother-in-law could scarcely expect much of such things; he had consulted the very best doctors too, but he obviously did not shrink from the most out-of-the-way measures in order to prolong his life for the sake of family, country, and art.

Goya enjoined himself to be sorry for the dying man. This was his wife's brother. He had meant well and had sometimes really been helpful. But Goya could not squeeze out a drop of pity; the sufferer had embittered Goya's life to the extent of his powers. This Bayeu had admonished him as one would a stupid, rebellious schoolboy, again and again, and in front of the whole cathedral chapter, that time when they were painting the frescoes in the cathedral of Saragossa. Even now the shame burned him, the *sarna*, the sting, the scalding irritation of that experience. And on top of all that the dying man had wanted to estrange Josefa from him, had tried to show her how despised her husband was and how highly respected her brother. Had succeeded in having the chapter throw his, Goya's, wages at his feet and ignominiously chase him away; at the same time the clerical gentlemen had presented his wife with a gold medal "as the sister of our great painter Bayeu."

Goya looked down at the suffering, dying man and grimly repeated the good old proverb to himself: "A brother-in-law and a plow are only good when they are in the ground."

He felt a strong desire to paint a portrait of Bayeu. He would have subtracted nothing from the man's dignity, his purposeful industry, his intelligence; but he would have put in also his rigidity, his cold-sober narrow-mindedness.

Bayeu meanwhile began to talk, laboriously but in well-rounded sentences, as always. "I am dying," he said. "I am clearing the way for you. You'll become President of the Academy. I've spoken to the Minister about it and to Maella and Ramón. Maella should really be president before you, and so should my brother Ramón. I owe it to you to be frank. You're certainly more talented, but you have no discipline and too much insolent self-confidence. On the other hand, I think I can answer before God for having favoured the worse man for love of my sister." He paused. It was an effort for him to talk; he panted. The fool, thought Goya, I could have had the Academy without him. Don Manuel would have got it for me.

"I know your unruly heart, Francisco Goya," Bayeu continued, "and perhaps it's a good thing for you that there is no portrait of you by my hand in existence. But the time will come when you will regret not having taken my irksome advice. I exhort you for the last time: stick to the classical tradition. Every day read a few pages of Mengs' theory. I am leaving you my copy with his dedication and many notes by me. You know how far he and I have gone. Tame yourself. Perhaps you may go as far yourself."

Goya felt contemptuous pity. Here this poor creature was exerting his last morsel of strength in an effort to convince him and others that he was a great painter. Without respite he had striven after "real art" and was always reading up in books to see if he was doing it right. He had a good eye and a skilled hand but his theory had ruined everything he did. You and your Mengs, thought Goya, you put me back years. One sideways glance, one twist of the mouth from my Agustín, is more valuable to me than all your rules and principles. You made things difficult for yourself, Señor First Painter, for yourself and others; the earth will be lighter for us when you're underneath it.

It was as if Bayeu had been waiting only to read his brother-in-law a last lecture. Immediately thereafter the death agony began.

With sombre faces Bayeu's nearest relatives and friends, Josefa, Ramón, the painter Maella, stood round the low couch. Francisco Goya regarded the gasping man with an unfriendly eye. The nose was insensitive, the deep lines running down to the mouth bespoke unblessed exertions; these lips were capable of uttering only schoolmasterish strictures. Even the hand of death could not make the haggard face significant.

King Carlos had valued his First Painter very highly. He gave instructions that he should receive the burial of a grandee of the Kingdom; the dead Francisco Bayeu was buried in the crypt of the Church of San Juan Bautista at the side of the greatest painter the peninsula had produced, Don Diego Velázquez.

The relatives of the dead man held an inspection of his studio, to decide what should be done with the works he had left behind. There were many pictures, finished and unfinished. The onlookers were most of all attracted by a painting in which Bayeu had depicted himself at his easel. Although some details, the palette, the brushes, his waistcoat, had been rendered with especial care, the picture was obviously unfinished; the conscientious man had not finished his own face. Half complete, out of dead eyes, as if he had perished before birth, the head stared down at them. "What a pity," said Ramón after a while, "that our brother was not permitted to finish this picture." "I will finish it," said Goya. The others looked up, surprised, not without scruples. But Goya had already taken possession of the canvas.

He painted for a long time on the picture of Bayeu, under Agustín's eye. He showed respect, he did not alter much of what was already there. The brows became only a trifle deeper, the furrows from nose to mouth wearier, the chin a little more obstinate, the corners of the mouth drooped a little more morosely. Love and hate worked together on the picture, but they did not cloud the cold, sharp, uncompromising eye of the painter. What finally emerged was the portrait of a sad, sickly, ageing man, who had driven himself his whole life long and who was now weary of dignity and everlasting effort but too conscientious to give up and rest.

Agustín Esteve stood next to Goya and inspected the finished work. From the canvas looked out a man who asked more of the world than he deserved and from himself more than he had it in him to give. But the whole thing was saturated in a silvery brightness deriving from Francisco's newly discovered, clear, shimmering grey, and Agustín maliciously noted that this sovereign silvery light served only to emphasize the hardness of the face and the priggish barrenness of the hand holding the brush. The picture was as attractive as the man it portrayed was the opposite. "You've done that magnificently, Francho," Agustín burst out, delighted, admiring.

And Josefa without speaking
Stood for long before the picture
Of her brother. Goya asked her,
"Have I to the dead done justice?"
"What will happen to the picture?"
Drawing in her upper lip she
Asked him. "It is yours," he told her.
And Josefa answered, "Thank you."

She considered where the painting
Was to hang, but nothing suited.
Finally she sent it to her
Brother Manuel Bayeu in
Saragossa.

— 13 —

Goya waited anxiously for word from the Escorial but Cayetana was silent, and the tedium of the weeks of mourning increased his nervous tension.

Then there appeared an unhoped for visitor from home, Martín Zapater.

When Goya caught sight of his heart's dear Martín he embraced him tempestuously, called all the saints to witness his delight, kissed him, pushed him into a chair, pulled him out again, dragged him by the arm through the studio.

For all his pride Goya was by nature confiding. Often and voluntarily he would talk his heart out to Josefa, Agustín, and Miguel. But his ultimate privacy, his most secret vanity and most hidden discontents, he could discuss only with his friend, his nearest and dearest friend, Martín. He asked a hundred questions of the worthy, portly, comfortable, good-natured man, and he himself gave a wildly confused recital while the envious Agustín listened jealously.

Since the six-year-old Francisco had left his village of Fuendetodos to go to Saragossa, he and Martín Zapater had been friends. Together they had learned to read and write in Fray Joaquín's school, but they belonged to two rival bands, Goya to the band of the Virgen del Pilar, Zapater to that of San Luis. After young Goya had once administered a frightful beating to young Zapater, the latter, full of admiration, had changed over to the other's band, and since that time they had been bosom friends. Francisco afforded Martín the exciting stimulus of his strong, unaccountable personality; the sensible Martín gave practical advice and performed material services. Francisco came of a poor family, Martín from the well-to-do, respectable middle class. From his earliest youth Martín had believed in Goya's artistic vocation; on the elder Zapater's recommendation, Count Pignatelli, the Saragossan Mæcenas, had arranged for little Francisco to receive lessons in drawing and painting.

"You're the same as ever, little one," Goya said to Zapater, who topped him by a head. "Only your great nose, *el narigón*, has grown even bigger. You look imposing, dignified; one can see all the great houses of Saragossa behind you, the Salvadores, Grasas, and Aznarez." "I hope," Martín succeeded in interposing, "you see the Castel and the Lonja and the Puente too." "Everything," Francisco replied heartily. In truth he did see quite clearly the city of his youth, Saragossa, with her tired magnificence, her dirt and dust, her Moorish towers, the ancient bridge over the sluggish grey-green Ebro, the flat-coloured, dusty plain with the distant mountains behind.

Both, now that they were together, became as boys. Again life lay before them, beckoning with adventure, and around every corner lurked something new that one had to discover, grapple with, conquer. They both felt how much they needed each other. Francisco needed his friend's down-to-earth good sense, his constant readiness to serve; for Martín the dull world took on colour when Goya afforded him glimpses into the revelations of his eye and heart.

In the days that followed Goya painted his friend; they were happy days. It was fun, a great pleasure to see Martín taking shape on the canvas just as he was, shrewd, dignified, lovable, warm-hearted, somewhat philistine. Wisely, with a kind of comfortable serenity, the sharp eyes looked out over the plump cheeks and powerful nose. "So that's what I'm like," said Martín and clicked with his tongue.

Francisco did not know which was better, the painting or the long pauses during which he chatted with his friend. He liked to send Agustín away on some pretext or other, and then let go. He could call up old memories in indiscriminate confusion—girls, money troubles, dealings with the police, exciting escapes from the Inquisition, wild challenges and dangerous brawls with knives and sabres, discord with the proud family of Bayeu. He held forth, naïvely boasting about the difference between his needy youth and his present flourishing state. Here he sat in his solid Madrid house with its expensive furniture and objets d'art, its liveried servants; elegant friends came to call, whom he did not even always receive, and he had the magnificent carriage, the gilded *berlina* in English style, of which there were only three in Madrid. Yes, this carriage, this *carozza*, was Goya's pride. Its upkeep, especially that of the horses, was high in Madrid, but Goya did not shrink from the expense; it was worth a sacrifice. And though it was hardly seemly during a period of mourning, he took his friend for a drive in the Prado.

Sometimes Francisco and Martín sang and made music, played *seguidillas, tiranas, boleros*. Both were passionately fond of folk music. They were always quarrelling over the merits of individual pieces; generally Francisco succeeded in convincing Martín and made fun of him for his backward taste. Or he would chaff Martín because he was a follower of the bullfighter Costillares, while he, Goya, swore by Ramiro. He strewed sand on the table and drew the two bullfighters, a small, powerful Ramiro and a big, stout Costillares with a monstrous nose, and they both roared with laughter.

But suddenly, in the midst of his laughter, Francisco stopped and his face clouded over. "Here I am, laughing and boasting to you how far I've got, marvellously far. I am a *Pintor de cámara*, and in a few days I'll be President of the Academy. I have the best eye in Spain, the most masterly hand, everyone envies me, and I tell you, Martín, that's all façade, and underneath it nothing, just dung."

Martín knew his friend's sudden changes of mood and uncontrolled outbursts. "Francho, Francho," he tried to soothe him. "Don't talk so wildly and sinfully." Francisco glanced swiftly across to Our Lady of Atocha and crossed himself. But then he went on, "It is true, Chico. All my good fortune has its bad side; behind everything the evil spirits are lurking, grinning at me. It is a piece of good luck that my brother-in-law, that sour-faced schoolmaster, is at last under the ground; but now I have Josefa sitting around day and night, pale and grieving. It's good luck to have Don Manuel become very friendly to me; he is the most powerful man in Spain and a fine young man; but he's a scoundrel too, and a fairly dangerous one. On top of that I'm irked by the circumstances under which we became friends. I can't get over what was expected of me for Don Gaspar's sake, and all the time I can't bear the sight of him, the prig. And I get no thanks either. Pepa looks at me sarcastically out of her green eyes and puts on airs as if she had got where she is by herself. Everyone wants something of me, and not a single one of them bothers to understand me." And he expressed himself forcibly on the way Miguel and Agustín every other week came and tried to persuade him to mix into the affairs of King and State. He was a Court Painter, he belonged to the Court, and that was good, that was how he wanted it, he was proud of it. By his painting he could render his country better service than all these smug, speechifying political reformers. "A painter's job is to paint," he said with angry decision, gloom spreading over his whole massive face, "a painter has to paint, and that's that.

"And I've also got to discuss my money affairs with someone who understands something about the subject," he went on. It was a surprising and welcome transition. Still, Martín had rather expected that Francisco would seek his advice; he had a bank in Saragossa and Francisco regarded him as an expert. "I'm always glad if I can advise you," he said heartily, and added cautiously, "As far as I can see the state of your finances is in no way disquieting."

But Goya would not have it so. "I don't look for trouble, and I don't like to complain. I don't care much for money, but I have to have it. Here in Madrid it's really, as the proverb says, 'For him who has no money there are only three places to go: prison, hospital, or the graveyard.' I have to spend a sinful amount of money for my clothes and the *carozza* and on my dishonest servants. I must keep up appearances. If I don't, my grandees try to beat me down. And anyhow I slave like a donkey and I want to have something to show for it. In this life there's no fun without money. Not that women actually demand money from me, but from time to time I sleep with great ladies and they have a right to expect that their lover look like a gentleman."

Don Martín knew that Francisco attached importance to having magnificence about him and throwing money about, and then again he would have qualms of conscience and attacks of peasant stinginess. He needed encouragement, his friend Francho, and so he encouraged him. Francisco Goya, a Court Painter, earned more in a few hours than an Aragonese shepherd in a whole year. Didn't he earn four thousand reals for a portrait that he could toss off in a few hours? Such a money-breeder need have no fears for his future. "Your studio is a better financial security than my bank in Saragossa," he assured Goya.

Goya wanted to hear more such reassurances. "All very well, Big-nose," he said, "but don't forget the endless demands that are made on me from Saragossa, especially by my brothers. You know all about it. 'Maggots are glad of a fat cheese,' " he bitterly quoted the old saying. "My mother shall, of course, lack for nothing, first because I love her and then because the mother of a *Pintor de cámara* must live in comfort. But my brother Tomás is as bold as a rat. Didn't I set him up in the gilding shop in the Calle de Morería? Get work for him? Give him his thousand reals on marriage and three hundred at the birth of each child? And with Camilo things are even worse. I'd rather bite off my tongue than ask for anything for myself, and for him I humbled myself and asked for the living in Chinchón. But he's never satisfied. Today he wants money for the church, tomorrow it will be for the rectory. When I go hunting with him a hare costs as much as a horse."

Martín had heard all this many times. "Don't talk nonsense, Francho," he said good-naturedly. "Haven't you got revenues like an archbishop's? Let's just go over your accounts," he suggested. "You'll see," prophesied Goya, "I haven't as much as thirty thousand reals." Martín smiled; his friend had the habit of expanding or contracting the figures according to his mood.

It turned out that, apart from his house and its furnishings, he possessed about eighty thousand reals. "Even that is miserable," he said. "All the same," Martín consoled him, "it will do to fill a hollow tooth or so." He thought a little. "Perhaps the Bank of Spain would sell you some preference shares. If Count Cabarrús has been able to take over the Bank again, it has only been by the intervention of Señor Jovellanos, in whose recall you have not been entirely unconcerned." Goya wanted to raise objections, but Martín assured him, "You can rely on me, Francho. I'll manage it with dignity and delicacy."

It was a relief to Francisco that Martín listened so well and gave such sympathetic advice. He prepared himself to tell him his great and final secret, his dreams about Cayetana. But he could not do it; he could not find the words. Just as he had not known what colour was before he discovered his grey, so he had not known what passion was before he caught sight of the Duchess of Alba on her dais. Passion was a stupid word; it expressed nothing whatever of all that he was full of. The truth was that you couldn't put it into words, and there was no one, not even his Martín, who would understand his babblings.

To Goya's joy his appointment to the presidency of the Academy came about while Martín was still in Madrid. There appeared in his house the Court Painter, Don Pedro Maella, and two other members of the Academy to hand over the document to him. How often these men had looked at him askance because he was not classical enough for them! And now they stood there and read out from the parchment with the stately seals formal expressions of recognition and repute. He listened to them eagerly.

But when the deputation had withdrawn, Goya did not let his wife Josefa or his friends Agustín and Martín see what he was feeling. He merely remarked with some contempt, "The thing carries with it twenty-five doubloons a year. I get as much for a single picture. And for that I have to put on Court dress as least once a week, spend hours of boredom sitting round with dull incompetents, listening to pompous nonsense, and emitting pompous nonsense myself. 'Much honour, small advantage,' " he quoted the old saying.

But later he was alone with Martín. "Good luck and blessings," said Martín heartily. "Good luck and blessings on you, Señor Don Francisco de Goya y Lucientes, Painter to the King and President of the Academy of San Fernando. And may Our Lady of the Pillar protect you." "And Our Lady of Atocha," Goya added hastily, and looked over at his Virgin and crossed himself. Then they both began to laugh and made a lot of joyful noise and clapped each other on the back. And then they sang the *seguidilla* of the peasant who had had an unexpected legacy, the *seguidilla* with the refrain: "And now dance, dance, dance, Now we will dance the fandango, Yes, he who has money may dance, Yes, he may dance the fandango, Whether he can, or no." And they danced their fandango.

The next few days brought many visits of congratulation.

The ladies Lucía Bermúdez and Pepa Tudo came too, escorted by the Abbé Don Diego. Goya was surprised, felt uncomfortable, contrary to his custom spoke but little. Zapater chatted, respectfully and with enjoyment. Agustín, agitated by a mixture of feelings, stared gloomily at the lovely ladies.

Pepa found an opportunity to speak to Francisco alone. With her dragging voice, a little ironically, she gave an accounting. She was living now in the little palace on the Calle de Antorcha. Don Manuel had procured it for her from the estate of the deceased Condesa Bondad Real. Don Manuel had come several times to Madrid from the Escorial in order to visit her; he had also invited her to the riding ground of his villa so that he could display his equestrian prowess. Goya had already heard of the ascent of the

Señora Tudo; he had tried to avoid hearing of it, but now he was forced to take cognizance of the event.

By the way, Pepa further reported, Don Manuel had told her that Goya was going to be invited to the Escorial in the near future. "I strongly supported the proposal," she said casually, and observed with pleasure the effort it cost Goya not to attack her with his fists.

"I," she told him, in her pleasant
Lazy accents, "have already
Been myself in the Escorial."
Pale and angry, he was silent.
She continued, "We are making,
Both of us, careers, Francisco."

"*Hombre!*" when the ladies left them
Said Don Martín, and again he,
Clucking with his tongue, said, "*Hombre!*"

Came next day a red-bestockinged
Runner, with a message, saying
Presidente Don Francisco
Goya was invited to the
Court and palace, the Escorial.

-- 14 --

Thirty miles northwest of Madrid, visible far and wide against the dark background of the Sierra Guadarrama, rises the castle El Escorial. There it stands, a vast, impressive mass of stone, coldly magnificent, grim, forbidding.

Next to the Vatican and the Palace of Versailles, the Escorial was the most famous building in Europe. Spaniards regarded it as the eighth wonder of the world.

Philip the Second had built it in the second half of the sixteenth century, that grim, fanatical, sensual, mistrustful, art-minded, bureaucratic ruler. With a threefold purpose. When his soldiers defeated the French army at St. Quentin, they had unintentionally shot to pieces a monastery of St. Laurence. Laurence had been a Spaniard by birth. The cruel manner of his martyrdom—he had been roasted alive—particularly endeared him to Spaniards, and King Philip wished to atone by building him a sanctuary such as the world had never seen. Further, he desired to fulfill a command of his father, the Emperor Charles, who had ordained in his testament that a fitting mausoleum should be built for the mortal remains of himself and his Empress. And, finally, Philip wanted to spend his latter years in solitude, in his own company and God's, surrounded by monks and prayers.

Nothing was too costly to make this retreat worthy of him, the world-conqueror. He ordered the finest woods from his West Indian islands, from his forests of Cuenca the best trees. In the mountains of Granada and Aracena he had brown-, green-, and red-mottled marbles quarried, white in the mountains of Filabres, jasper from the quarries of Burgo de Osmar. Not only in Spain did the best painters and sculptors work for him, but in Flanders, Florence, Milan as well. The transports for his castle rolled over distant highways, swam over the seven seas. With hand and eye the King tested every detail; if he was in the field he had to have a daily report sent to him. The revenues of entire overseas provinces went into the building.

The ground plan of the Escorial was such that the whole represented the instrument which God had chosen for the martyrdom of St. Laurence, the gridiron on which he was burned. The mighty four-cornered building itself, with its many courtyards, was a projection in reverse of the gridiron: the four towers at the corner were the feet, the projecting Palacio de los Infantes the handle.

So the building rose in severe and godly magnificence, a challenge, conceived and constructed for the most distant future; like the Pyramids, only of more durable stuff: the grey-white granite of Peralejos. The Escorial had 16 patios, 2673 windows, 1940 doors, 1860 apartments, 86 staircases, 89 fountains, 51 bells.

The Escorial possessed a magnificent library, 130,000 volumes and over 4000 manuscripts. The particularly precious Arabic manuscripts had been found on board captured vessels in which the treasures of Zidian, Sultan of Morocco, were being carried overseas. The Moorish King had offered two million reals for the return of the manuscripts; but the Spaniards had demanded on top of that the release of all his Christian prisoners. As the Sultan would not agree to this, the manuscripts were now in the Escorial.

There were 204 statues in the palace, and 1563 paintings, among them masterpieces by Leonardo, Veronese and Raphael, Rubens and Van Dyck, El Greco and Velázquez.

More than of all these works of art, however, the Spaniards were proud of the treasures that were hoarded in the *relicario*, the relics. More than 1500 containers were there, of gold, silver, gilded bronze, and the rarest woods, many of them studded with gems. Preserved in them were the complete skeletons of 10 saints and martyrs, 144 skulls, 366 arms and legs, 1427 fingers and toes. There was one of St. Antony's arms, a leg of St. Teresa, the tiny skeleton of one of the sucklings murdered by Herod. There was, further, a part of the cord with which Jesus Christ had been bound, two thorns from His crown, a portion of the vinegar-soaked sponge which the soldier had stretched up to Him, and a little piece of wood from the Cross on which He had suffered. Also, there was the earthenware vessel whose water Jesus had turned to wine, the inkwell of Saint Augustine, and finally a stone from the bladder of the Holy Father Pius V. A wicked rumour had it that once a monk whose senses had been confused by the Devil had emptied the magnificent caskets of their contents and thrown them together in such a hopeless heap that they had no longer been able to distinguish which arm was Isidro's and which Veronica's.

The proudest relic of the Escorial was kept in a special chapel; it was the Santa Forma, a Host in which the Godhead had manifested Himself in an amazing and sublime manner. Heretics, *Zuinglianos*, had got possession of the Host, thrown it on the ground, and trodden it with their feet. But the Host had begun to bleed, streaks of blood had become plainly visible. The Godhead had demonstrated that He dwelt in the Host. This had happened in Holland; from a Dutch monastery the Host was taken to Vienna and later to Prague for Kaiser Rudolf the Second. The world-conquering Philip had obtained it from the latter, paying a high price—three cities in his Low Countries and important trading concessions. So now the Santa Forma reposed in the Escorial and no heretic might set eyes upon it.

Court etiquette, as stern and stately as the Escorial itself, prescribed that the reigning King of Spain should spend time, and precisely how much time, in each of his castles. In the Escorial the King and his Court had to spend sixty-three days. The dates were laid down precisely. Charles the Third, the father of the present ruler, had died of this regulation: against the advice of his doctors he had moved to the Escorial on the prescribed date in spite of an incipient congestion of the lungs.

The gloomy magnificence of the castle depressed the easygoing Charles the Fourth. Therefore he had arranged his own apartments, for the nine weeks which he had to spend there, according to his own cheerful taste, and while on the floor below the rooms in which Philip the Second had spent his last years were severely and monastically bare, Charles the Fourth lived above them in comfortable apartments, among gay tapestries and pictures of children at play, dallying shepherdesses, plump, gossiping washerwomen.

But once a week, as usage dictated, even this monarch went to the church of the Escorial to visit his deceased ancestors. He went through the Patio de los Reyes, where the Kings of Judah stood in granite: David with harp and sword, Solomon with books, Hezekiah with a battering ram, Manasseh with sacred vessels, Jehosaphat with an axe. These were the tools with which these kings had built the temple of Jerusalem, and now the Escorial continued the tradition and was to the Christian world what the temple of Solomon had been to the peoples of the Old Testament.

Past these kings, then, went the fourth Charles. The main door of the church opened before him; it was opened only for persons of royal blood, living and dead. Uncomfortable, with severe and sombre face, the massive monarch strode through the bold and haughty harmony of the noble building, and, imposing as he was himself, he seemed a dwarf in the immense space beneath the giant dome.

He descended between walls and through arches of choice marbles, first to the Panteón de los Infantes, the burial place of princes, princesses, and those royal ladies whose children had not attained to the throne. Then, further down, still on steps carved out of granite, into the Panteón de los Reyes. He stood there in the octagonal room, the proudest, most splendid mausoleum in Europe, surrounded by walls inlaid with jasper and black marble. The graves had been placed directly beneath the High Altar of the

Capilla Mayor, so that the priest who elevated the Host stood directly over the dead kings, who thus were able to partake of Grace as well.

Here now stood Charles the Fourth, among the bronze sarcophagi which contained the remains of his forebears.

On the fine and simple lettering
Dwelt his eyes; upon the names of
Those there lying, and the other
Coffins standing empty, waiting.
Two there were, and on the first one
Stood the words: "Don Carlos, of his
Name the Fourth"; but on the other
Simply "Queen María Luisa."

There he stood, for full five minutes,
Satisfying thus the custom.
Counted to three hundred. Then he
Left the vault, the staircase mounted;
Fast he went and ever faster,
Echoed through the church his footsteps,
Through the courtyard, past the statues
Of the Kings of Judah, hasting,
Never heeding. So he reached his
Light, bright rooms. And there among the
Pleasant pictures all about him
Off he slipped his mourning garments,
Heavy, sombre, and arrayed him
For the hunt.

— 15 —

Goya was not lodged in the Escorial itself but in the *posada* of San Lorenzo. It was no more than was to be expected; the Escorial, in spite of its size, was not big enough to take all the guests. All the same he was put out.

Don Miguel came. Goya asked after Doña Lucía. Yes, she was here, she was well; Miguel was rather reserved. He grew more animated when the talk turned to politics. The peace negotiations, he related, which were being carried on with the French in Basle, were not going very well. The French were refusing to surrender the little son and daughter of the deceased Louis the Sixteenth. Spain, however, had staked her honour on liberating the royal children, and Don Manuel did not wish to yield on this point.

Later Goya met the Abbé Don Diego and Doña Lucía. The Abbé reported further on the political situation. Militarily speaking, the war was lost. But the Queen alone was being reasonable and showing a willingness to forego the royal children so that there might be peace at last. Charles was hesitating, abetted by Don Manuel. For the latter was playing with the idea of marrying the little French princess, in order to acquire the title of a sovereign prince.

"And our Pepa is backing him up in his schemes," Lucía related; the gaze of her wide-apart, shadowy eyes seemed to Goya to be twice as mocking and calculating as usual. "Is Pepa still here?" he asked, disagreeably surprised. The Abbé explained. "Since the dismissal of Admiral Mazarredo, Señora Tudo has been having difficulties with her pension. She is here at Court, petitioning."

"The Queen is surprised," added Lucía, "that Señora Tudo does not await the decision in Madrid. But you know our Pepa. Here she is and here she means to stay. She's got it into her head that her Manuel must marry the daughter of the King of France. Every other day she sings him the ballad of the youth Ramiro, the hero who abducted the Infanta." "So much is certain," remarked the Abbé, "the presence of Señora Tudo in the Escorial does not make the task of our peace delegation any easier."

It displeased Goya that his onetime Pepa should interfere in the affairs of princes. It wasn't seemly, it offended against the divine order of things. "You ought to visit her, Don Francisco," said Lucía with amiable guile. "She is living in the lower *posada.*" Francisco resolved to keep out of Pepa's way.

The following morning he betook himself to the Escorial as custom prescribed, to attend the levee of the Queen. He did not know if Doña Cayetana would be on duty, or whether he wished to see her or feared to.

The antechamber was full of dressed-up ladies and gentlemen.

The Abbé was there, and Monsieur de Havré. And also—Francisco's face darkened—Carnicero, his professional colleague, that botcher who understood nothing but getting effects and exorbitant prices.

The double doors of the bedroom opened. At her toilette table sat the Queen of Spain. Ceremoniously, with exactly prescribed movements, the ladies of the high nobility performed their duties: this Duchess handed over the skirt, this Countess the jacket, this Marquesa the ribbons. Their gestures calculated, their faces made up like masks, they went to and fro, glittering dolls, with frozen, rather melancholy smiles, and Goya looked on and could not make up his mind: this centuries-old formality, so full of colour, was it splendid, or was it ridiculous?

There was the Duchess of Alba, and his heart beat fast. She moved her limbs as the others did; she too was made up like a doll; but whereas the others, here in the Escorial, going through the outgrown motions above the tombs of dead world rulers were playing a part and were ridiculous, she, Doña Cayetana, belonged here; for her, what she was doing was inbred and innate.

Don Manuel sent for Goya. Told him he had been looking forward to sitting for another portrait. Unfortunately, however, he hadn't the time, for the moment. The peace negotiations, difficult enough already, were further complicated by private problems. "Our mutual friend, Señora Tudo," he explained, "wants to make a hero of me. That is charming and patriotic. But after all I can't let the country bleed to death simply to play the hero in front of our friend Pepa. I'm a statesman. I must obey the dictates of reason and political necessity, not those of feeling."

Goya listened uneasily. Clearly there was something behind all this, some further imposition, something humiliating.

"Moreover," the Minister went on, "the Queen is nervous, weighed down by the gravity of the decisions she has to make, and she takes exception to innocent trifles. For example, to the presence of Señora Tudo. The Señora is yielding, of course, to the royal behest, but she justifiably feels herself slighted. So before she goes back to Madrid I want to do a little something to please her. How would it be if we repeated that unconstrained evening which, thanks to you, inaugurated my friendship with the Señora?"

"Is this Pepa's idea?" asked Goya, concealing his reluctance with difficulty. "Half hers, half mine," Don Manuel admitted. "Pepa's conception of it is that we should arrange the party in my apartments in the Escorial. She promises herself particular enjoyment from that."

Now Goya was really put out. What had come over Pepa? Why was she arranging to have her dubious *tertulia* take place in the grandest setting in Spain? " 'A cathedral is no place for hens,' " he grimly repeated to himself the old adage. And why must she have him there? Did she want to show off to him how far she had come? But he could see no possibility of declining the Minister's invitation.

So on the following evening once again, up the formal staircase, through the long, solemn corridors, he went to Don Manuel.

In the antechamber sat Pepa's dueña, the skinny Conchita. She greeted Francisco obsequiously, but on her gaunt face there was an impudent and knowing smile.

The company was the same as on the former occasion at Doña Lucía's; only Agustín was missing, and the cautious Don Miguel. Pepa, in a simple green dress, was very lovely, as Goya had half-reluctantly to admit. He understood her feelings exactly, her chagrin and her triumph. She had only had to leave him, and everything had fallen into her lap that a woman could desire. There she stood, Pepa Tudo, insolent, proud, in the proudest palace in the kingdom, above the vault of the royal dead, and gave her *tertulia*, and she had required his presence and he could not refuse. "*Trágala, perro!* Swallow it, you dog!"

Pepa greeted him without embarrassment, with distant friendliness. "Lovely to see you again at last, Don Francisco. I hear you're here to paint Their Majesties' portraits. I'm sorry they're keeping you waiting. I'm here on business too, but I've almost achieved what I came for and can go back to Madrid tomorrow."

Goya would gladly have taken her by the shoulders, given her a good shaking, and hurled one or two strong and unseemly words into her insolent face; but in Don Manuel's presence he had to control himself.

The latter was behaving as though it were the most natural thing in the world for him to place his ceremonial apartments at Pepa Tudo's disposal for her *tertulia*. He was jovial, talkative, noisy. His easy manner was not genuine. It was true that Doña María Luisa had winked at a good deal, but this time hadn't he gone a bit far?

The Abbé's pleasure in the evening was unqualified. He delighted in the presence of Lucía. Slowly, by many devious routes, he was getting closer to her; she now saw political affairs through his eyes; like him, she took a mischievous pleasure in the cynical irreverence of this *tertulia*. Philip the Second in his wildest dreams could never have imagined that the first minister of the kingdom would one day divert himself with a mistress over his very grave.

On this evening Pepa sang one of her romances, a second, then a third. She sang the romance of King Alfonso who falls in love in Toledo with a Jewess, Raquel la Fermosa, Rachel, the fair, and lives with her for seven years, abandoning his Queen, the English Leonora. Then the grandees revolted and beat the Jewess to death. The King mourns her extravagantly. " 'Torn from him,' " sang Pepa, " 'Torn from him his lovely Jewess, Stood Alfonso sad and yearning, Grief and longing for his Raquel, In his heart revengeful burning.' " But then an angel comes and reproaches him for his sin. He repents, and as a penance puts to death a thousand Moors.

Thus Pepa sang. The others listened pensively. "Our Pepa," Don Manuel remarked with apparent irrelevance, "has set her heart on making me a real old-fashioned Spanish hero." And Pepa, with equal irrelevance, replied, "I haven't a single drop of Jewish or Moorish blood. I am the purest old Castilian," and she crossed herself. "I know," Don Manuel hastened to answer, "we all know it."

"You sing even better than you did, Pepa," said Goya, when he found an opportunity of speaking to her alone. She looked him full in the face with her green eyes, in her shameless way. "My romances are better than reality," she said. He said, "I hear you're taking an interest in politics these days." She replied amiably, "I'm not interested in politics, Don Francisco, I'm interested in Spain. And in Don Manuel. When my sainted Felipe was still alive and also during my time with the Admiral, I was interested in the Navy. During my friendship with you it was painting. Don't you remember how I drew your attention to the fact that, in your portrait of Señor Mazarredo, his arm had turned out too short? Now I'm interested in Don Manuel. He's the greatest statesman in Spain. Why shouldn't he be the greatest in the world? But don't think I forget old friends. At my instigation Don Manuel suggested to the King that he might appoint a new First Painter; unfortunately at the moment Don Carlos is being obstinate, and this is just the one salary he's determined to save."

Goya remained calm. "If I were you, Pepa, I'd leave it to the

King of Spain and the National Convention of France to decide what should become of the children of Louis the Sixteenth." She did not avert her gaze from him for an instant. "You're clever, Don Francisco," she replied. "You're not like the men in my romances. You've always understood how to use your work to the best advantage. Probably the advice you're giving me is good too. By the way, I'd followed it, even before you gave it to me."

Goya thought to himself, " 'Help a woman out of the water and she'll maintain that it was you that fell in.' " At the same time, although he could scarcely have put it into words, his good masculine peasant instinct told him exactly what she was feeling. Precisely the fact that she was doing her best to hurt him was proof of how much she cared for him. He needed only to give her a sign, and for all her apparent indifference she would jump into bed with him. Let her jeer at him, let her think herself superior; even so he pitied her.

He was interested to see how Manuel and Pepa would conclude the evening. Would they dare to spend the night together in the Escorial, under the same roof as the Queen, above the graves of Emperor Charles the Fifth and Philip the Second?

Lucía and the Abbé took their leave. Pepa made no move to go. Goya too felt he must get home. "Good night, Don Francisco," said Pepa in her indolent, attractive voice. "Good night, Francho," she said, and looked him full in the face.

Through the lobby strode Francisco,
Where the old woman, the dueña,
Squatted, drowsing. But she nodded,
Grinned, stood up, and made a curtsy.
Goya crossed himself. The presence
Of this withered crone beneath the
Roof of the Escorial palace
Seemed to him more sacrilegious
Than the rendezvous nocturnal
Of Don Manuel and his Pepa.

16

A letter from the Escorial was delivered at the *posada* for the Court Painter Don Francisco de Goya y Lucientes. It ran: "I am not on duty tomorrow with the Queen. Why do I never see you at my levee? Your friend, Cayetana de Alba."

He had waited for this message with a bitter heart. Now all the bad feelings were swept away. "Your friend, Cayetana de Alba." "*Elle est chatoyante*," he thought, almost with tenderness.

Next day, he had scarcely arrived when she beckoned to him. "How nice that you have come at last, Don Francisco," she greeted him. "We have so much to talk about. Do stay after the others go." Her rather light, rather hard voice was unconcernedly loud, so that the others heard her words, and full of undisguised cordiality.

There were unfortunately many others there, and some whom Goya was not pleased to see. The tall, blond Doctor Peral, of course; and his own colleague, the bungler Carnicero; there was the pretty, foppish Marqués de San Adrián, in whose amiable manner Goya thought to perceive a trace of condescension; there was the bullfighter Costillares, to whom the Escorial, God knows, should have remained closed.

And the woman had gracious looks for all of them. While he waited, Francisco's joy evaporated. He dealt monosyllabically with anyone who spoke to him.

He turned his back on the company, inspected the many-coloured gobelins which hung on the walls.

The Albas occupied one of the few apartments which the King had had decorated in the sprightly taste of the last decade. Among the gobelins was one executed after a design which he, Goya, had made at a time when he was blithely painting away for the sheer pleasure of it. It was a lively folk scene. Four girls were diverting themselves by making a puppet, a *pelele*, jump about by tossing him on a sheet. The grouping was not bad, the movements natural.

Nevertheless he did not like this earlier work of his. These *majas*, girls from the people, who were tossing the doll in the air, were unreal. They weren't *majas*, they were Court ladies playing at being *majas*, and their gaiety was of that painted frozen sort which he had observed at the Queen's levee. The absurd, jerky movements of the puppet were more realistic than those of the girls.

At the time he had greatly liked this sort of gay masquerade and had eagerly lent himself to it. Everybody had done the same. His French fellow-painters had painted the ladies and gentlemen of Versailles as shepherds and shepherdesses just as stiff and artificial as his *majas* and *majos*. A few of these gallant shepherds and pretty shepherdesses had meanwhile had their doll-like heads cut off. Even he, although he was actually better off now than then, had learned better, and now the gaiety of his scene struck him as stupid, stiff, annoying.

The laughing, empty faces on the gobelins were not exactly portraits, and yet they were. He could plausibly deny that the third of the doll-faced ladies was the Duchess of Alba, yet she it was. In this technique of suggesting a face and yet leaving it anonymous he was ahead of everyone else. She was tossing her puppet with real enjoyment, was the Duchess.

"Ladies and gentlemen, I am ready," the Duchess announced, unexpectedly soon, and pleasantly but decisively she dismissed her visitors. "You're staying, of course, Don Francisco," she repeated.

"We're going for a walk, Eufemia." She indicated her dueña, after the others had left, and made introductions. "This is Doña Luisa María Beata Eufemia de Ferrer y Estala." Francisco bowed low and said, "It is an honour and a pleasure to make your acquaintance, Doña Eufemia." In a love affair with a great lady the dueña was an important person who could cause it to rain or shine as she chose.

Ladies' maids rolled up a new toilette table with jars of cream and bottles of toilette water; the projected walk demanded protective measures against the sun. Goya saw Cayetana's brownish-pale oval face heavily whitened; even so, with the amazing arched eyebrows, it remained the unique face of the Duchess of Alba. Where had his eyes been when he painted the third girl on the puppet tapestry?

"And which dress does my lamb desire for her walk?" The dueña turned to Cayetana. "The green one from Paris, or the Andalusian, or the white muslin from Madrid?" "The white, of course," commanded the Duchess, "and the red sash."

She did not speak to him now; being dressed demanded her full attention. The ladies of Madrid were accustomed to having men about them as they made their toilettes, and they freely displayed arms, shoulders, backs, breasts; but they adhered to the old rule—that the legs must not be seen. Doña Cayetana did not conceal her legs. "If the foot does not decline, all the maid will soon be thine"—the refrain of the old *tonadilla* went through Goya's head.

With a practised eye, for all his passion and desire, he took in the whole complicated ceremony of the attiring. It was superintended by the dueña. Doña Eufemia was tall and thin; her broad head with its sloping forehead, flat nose, and puffy lips was perched on a skinny neck. The Duchess treated the black-garbed, dignified old lady at times imperiously, like a slave; at times with playful, almost shameless familiarity.

The white muslin gown was shorter than was actually permissible; it had no train; it was just the right dress for a walk. The red sash was tied in place and the luxuriant black hair confined in a thin black net.

The companions Doña Cayetana was in the habit of taking with her on her walks now appeared: Julio, the page, a whey-faced, sharp-nosed youth with saucy eyes, and the little five-year-old Negro girl, María Luz. The dueña took the parasol; the page the receptacle for powder and perfume; the Negro child held the tiny woolly white dog, Don Juanito, in her arms.

The little procession with Cayetana and Goya at its head walked through the solemn corridors, down the grand staircase, out into the garden. Down winding gravelled paths they went, between flower beds and hedges of box and yew, behind them the massive solemnity of the castle. Then Doña Cayetana left the realm of the gardens and took a path which quickly narrowed and led upwards to the Silla del Rey, the King's Seat, a rocky projection which afforded the famous view of the Escorial.

The air was agreeably fresh; a pale sun stood in a clear sky. A light breeze blew. The Duchess walked along in her delicate shoes, firmly and with enjoyment, her toes pointing outwards as the mode was; she held her fan closed in her left hand, swinging it slightly. Small, graceful, and decided, she went along the narrow stony paths which led upwards through the greyish brown wasteland into the foothills of the Guadarrama.

Diagonally behind her walked Goya. Court dress was *de rigeur* for everyone who entered the Escorial as a guest; he walked stiffly in clothes that were somewhat too tight for him, and discommoded by his hat, sword, and wig. In front of him he saw the slender body of the Duchess, the red sash tightly swathed about her delicately rounded hips. Thus she preceded him, tiny, slender, swift. She neither strode, walked, nor minced. It was hard to find the right word to describe the way in which she moved.

The path, climbing up the sunny, grey-brown and whitish expanse of stones, seemed long to Goya. The black-clothed dueña moved her old limbs with dignity and without complaint. The page looked bored as he carried the perfumes and powder boxes. The Negro child ran now before and now behind. The little dog barked with insistent ill-temper and had to be put down every moment to piss. Goya was aware of the funny side of the little procession as it marched along, through the primeval desert, elegant, affected, artificial.

The Duchess spoke to him over her shoulder. "Does Señora Tudo live in the same *posada* as you?" she inquired. "Señora Tudo has gone away, as far as I know," he replied, making an effort to appear disinterested. "I hear you gave a lovely party for Señora Tudo, or was it Don Manuel? Tell me something, don't be so prim and discreet. Don Manuel is persistent, but the Italian woman isn't exactly yielding either. Which do you think will bring down the bull?" "I am too little informed, Your Grace," he answered dryly. "At least don't say 'Your Grace' to me," she begged.

Here was the rocky spur, the Silla del Rey, King Philip's favourite spot, from which he had seen his castle grow, stone upon stone. The Duchess sat down; her fan lay closed in her lap. The dueña and the two children settled themselves near her. Goya remained standing. "Do sit down," she commanded over her shoulder. He squatted awkwardly on the ground, hampered by his sword and by the sharp little stones. "*Cubríos*, cover your head," she commanded further, and he did not know whether it was intentionally or not, seriously or with irony, that she had used the formal mode of address with which the King distinguished his twelve first grandees.

There she sat, a wilful, delicate little figure on her stone seat, and looked across the shimmering desert at the castle. So might her ancestor have sat, he whom the fanatical King Philip had often summoned hither; here might he, that earlier Alba, have pondered over the instructions the King had given him in his soft, polite manner, orders to fall upon some insubordinate kingdom or to wipe out some heretical province.

The Duchess sat perfectly still. The others, too, sat without moving. They seemed hypnotized by the shimmering of the great waste out of which the castle rose stiff and dead as the waste itself.

Goya stared out over the stony expanse with the others. Suddenly he saw something moving, across and out of the desert, a creature unsubstantial yet very distinct, whitish-greyish-brown like the wasteland, a giant toad, or was it a turtle? A something with a human head from which enormous eyes protruded. Slowly but relentlessly the creature crept nearer; squat, good-natured, devilishly grinning, sure of itself and of its prey, it came upon him. They ought to go. Why did they remain sitting there? There were ghosts who worked only at night and others who had power during the day. These were rare but more dangerous. Goya knew the spectre which was creeping up on them in broad daylight. He had heard of it even as a small child; it was called by harmless, even agreeable names, like *El Yantar*, the midday meal, or even more familiarly, *La Siesta*. But it was a malignant ghost for all its grinning and shimmering and good-natured air. It showed itself only in sunlight, and they ought to pull themselves together to get up and go away.

Then the Duchess began to speak, and straightway the spectral toad vanished, the desert was empty. "Did you know," the Alba said, "that this time during my stay in the Escorial something unusual is going to happen to me?" "What makes you think that?" asked Goya. "My Eufemia told me," replied Cayetana, "and you can rely on her. She knows a great deal about the future. She has dealings with witches. One of these days when she annoys me I'm going to report her to the Inquisition." "Don't talk so wickedly, little white lamb of my soul," begged the dueña. "Don Francisco is a clever man and can take a joke. But if you let yourself go, you might one day talk like this in front of others."

"By the way," the Duchess turned and spoke to Francisco over her shoulder, "I knew someone else who prophesied for me, a tire-woman of my grandmother's. This maid, her name was Brígida, was burned as a witch. Many people said she was innocent, but when the executioner asked her for the kiss of forgiveness she would not kiss him, a sure sign that she was a witch. She appears to me sometimes and tells me what is going to happen. She is very good at telling the future." "What did she foretell for you?" he asked. She replied dryly, "That I would not grow old, and that I must make the most of my time if I want to get anything out of life."

Then her face she turned full on him,
With her great, metallic-shining
Eyes she looked straight at him, and she
Asked, "Do you believe in witches?"
"Yes, of course," he brusquely answered,
Using now the homely dialect
Native and familiar to him.
"Certainly, I do believe in
Witches."

17

Days passed. Francisco saw and heard nothing of her. In his room in the *posada* he sat and waited. He drew the midday spectre he had seen, drew it a second and then a third time. "*Elle est chatoyante*," he thought.

Unexpectedly he was ordered to move into the Escorial. In the flush of his joyful surprise he assumed that she had procured this favour for him. However, it was not she but the King himself who wanted him in the castle. The awkward political tension was over, the tiff between Doña María Luisa and Manuel settled; the King had the time and inclination to be painted by Goya.

Carlos valued his Goya. For all his phlegmatic constitution, the King had a sense of his position. Nor did he find the traditional duty of the Spanish ruler to further the arts, especially painting, to be a burden to him. It was an agreeable concept to him that he should live on in the portraits of good painters.

Assiduously he debated with Goya how he should be painted this time. He wanted to have three representative portraits calculated to bring at once to the memory of every subject the signature of the King: "*Yo el rey*"—"I, the King."

Goya had always admired the way Velázquez contrived that the majesty of the royal robes should find their reflection in the face of the wearer. He had learned from Velázquez to create a unity out of men and apparel. He had painted Carlos in a red coat, in a blue, and a brown, with gold embroidery and with silver, with ribbons and stars, in purple and in ermine, in the uniform of the Gardes du Corps, on foot and on horseback. More than once he had succeeded in creating out of the good-natured, almost crude, purposefully dignified countenance of his King Carlos and his majestic garb, out of the double chin pressed against the chest, the plump belly and the brilliant constellation of orders, something new and organic, something which conveyed to the beholder an impression of royalty, without at the same time misrepresenting Carlos's comfortable corporality. He looked forward to discovering new and effective variations on the familiar theme.

Carlos was aware that it was his duty to assist his painter, and he stuck to the often fatiguing poses. Nor did he himself make interruptions, though he was grateful for them when they came. Then he chatted amiably with Goya, as one Spaniard with another. He would take off his heavy, regal robes, sit massively down in a wide armchair, or stump about in doublet and hose. His watch chains would thus become visible, and the King would often talk about his watches. In one thing, he would say, half in jest, half in earnest, he was superior to his great predecessor, the Emperor Charles: that he had reached the point where his watches all kept the same time to the second. And proudly he would pull them out, compare them, listen to them, show them to Goya, even make him listen too.

The great thing, he expounded to Goya, was that watches must always be worn. In order to attain its maximum efficiency a watch needed the direct contact of the human body. A watch was itself something human. He set great store by having his favourite watches worn continually; those which he did not wear himself he got his valet to carry.

Goya would actually have needed only three or four sittings for the commissioned portraits; with the help of the sketches he had made and the robes and uniforms which might have been sent to him in his studio, he might have worked even better and more rapidly. But Carlos was bored in the Escorial. He enjoyed the sittings; he sat to his painter five days long, eight days long, morning after morning for two or three hours. The conversations with Goya obviously afforded him pleasure. He questioned him exhaustively about his children, and told him about his own. Or he talked about hunting. Or he discussed his favourite dishes, never omitting to praise the splendid quality of the ham which came from Estremadura, the birthplace of his beloved Manuel.

Finally the Queen declared that Carlos had had Goya working for him long enough. Now it was her turn.

Doña María Luisa was in a good humour. She had taken the news of Pepa's "orgy" with less indignation than everybody had expected. For her the most important thing was that the female was no longer there, so that she could once more enjoy Don Manuel's society without sacrificing any of her own dignity. He for his part was relieved that Doña María Luisa had not made the dreaded scene, and it was also welcome to him that for a time he did not have to listen to Pepa's exhortations to heroism. Moreover, the astute María Luisa was treating him with the greatest magnanimity. She was behaving as if he had been working all along for a reconciliation with the French Republic. She extolled him in front of the grandees and ministers as the man who would bring peace to Spain. The friendship between the Queen and her First Minister was closer than ever.

So Goya found a cheerful and very gracious María Luisa. He had first painted her almost ten years ago while she was still Crown Princess. At that time, although she was sharp and ugly, she had still been able to attract a man. Now she was older and uglier, but still anxious for recognition not only as a queen but as a woman. She ordered gowns and lingerie from all the capitals of Europe, and the costliest salves, oils, and perfumes; at night she wore masks of dough and precious fats. She exercised with the dancing master and walked up and down before her mirror with chains on her ankles to improve her carriage. With sovereign lack of reticence she talked with Goya of the effort it cost her to assert herself as a woman. He was impressed by her fierce energy and wanted to paint her as she was: ugly and interesting.

He missed the resources of his studio, and even more he missed Agustín, the advice, the surly criticisms, the many services his helper rendered. But with accommodation at the Escorial limited as it was, he could scarcely expect them to let Agustín come too.

Now, however, it happened that as a token of their reconciliation Don Manuel had given the Queen as a present the stallion Marcial, the pride of his stables, and it was her wish that she should be painted for him on this horse. To paint so ambitious a picture without assistance in the allotted time was as good as impossible. Goya could therefore quite plausibly ask to call in his friend and pupil, Don Agustín Esteve.

Agustín came. Grinning broadly, he greeted his friend; he had missed him sorely, and it was a satisfaction that Francisco had procured an invitation to the Escorial for him.

However, he could not help noticing, almost at once, how, for all his industry, Goya would suddenly lapse into a brown study, in what torment he was waiting for something that did not come. Soon, from remarks dropped by Lucía, Miguel, the Abbé, he pieced together the situation, recognized how deeply and irretrievably Francisco had this time involved himself.

He began to pick holes in his friend's work. The portraits of the King had turned out not nearly so good as they might have been. Goya had certainly employed considerable manual dexterity but little inner concentration. They were purely representative pictures, and that was not enough, from the Goya of today. "And I know why you are failing too," he declared. "You're taken up with side issues, your heart is not in your work." "You envious old busybody, you plucked student!" Goya retorted, though with comparative calm. "You know perfectly well that these pictures are just as good as all the others I've done of Don Carlos."

"Exactly," replied Agustín, "and that's why they're bad. Because you can do better now than you could. I'll tell you again: you're too lazy." He thought of Lucía and lashed himself into a rage. "You're too old to be running after women," he said malevolently. "You've got a lot still to learn and your time's getting short. If you go on like this, everything you've done will be piecework and you yourself like nothing but a worked-out mine."

"Go on, go on," Goya replied with quiet venom. "My hearing's good today; today for once I can really hear exactly what you think." "You have unusual and undeserved good luck," replied Don Agustín, nothing loath. "The King sits to you and sits over and over; shows himself to you in his doublet and lets you hear his watches tick. And what do you make of this unique opportunity to look right inside the man? Have you painted into your Carlos's face what we patriots see in it? Blinded by your vacuous sensuality, you don't even see what any layman can. *Qué vergüenza!* Because Carlos has talked nicely to you about Estremadura ham, you consider him a great king and you paint him a dignified face on top of his frock coat and Golden Fleece." "All right," said Goya, still strikingly calm, "now you've said your say. And now I'm sending you home, on the oldest mule I can scare up in San Lorenzo."

He expected a rude answer. He expected Agustín to walk out, banging the door behind him so that the whole Escorial would shake. Nothing of the kind happened. Agustín had taken up a sheet of paper which Francisco had inadvertently stuck among the sketches for the King's pictures when he took them out of a drawer; it was that drawing of *El Yantar*, the midday spectre. Agustín stood there and looked and stared.

And Goya, almost embarrassed, though it was quite unlike him, said, "Oh, that's nothing. I just scribbled it down. A mood, a caprice."

From that moment Agustín said no more about Francisco's affairs with women and his neglect of his art. On the contrary, even when they were discussing only technicalities, he chose his words with care and tact. Francisco could not tell whether he was pleased or displeased to have Agustín look so deeply into his entanglement.

The Queen paraded in front of Goya on the stallion Marcial as the commander of the regiment of the Gardes du Corps. She sat astride her horse like a man; she was a good horsewoman. Her head rose bold and proud above the martial uniform.

It would have been enough if she had posed on the wooden horse for the rest of the sittings, but Goya derived a keen satisfaction from asking her a second and even a third time to display her horsemanship for him, and—what was more—in the presence of Agustín. He ordered the Queen to turn the horse this way or that, to hold her head thus or so. And he pushed Agustín into the foreground, emphasized his participation in the work in hand, asked, "What do you think, Agustín, should we leave it like this or would it be better so?"

Once, when years ago he painted
The first time a great *hidalgo*,
In the background he had put a
Figure of himself, a tiny
Shadowy form, that to the grandee
Offered the commissioned portrait.
So when to his pupil-helper
He today would give a pleasure,
Goya made the Queen of Spain go
Through her paces on her war steed
While his friend looked on, before he
Deigned to fall to on the painting.
What a pity, that his father,
The old Goya, lived no longer
To behold that sight. How widely
Would his aged eyes have opened!

-- 18 --

He went along the corridor leading from the Queen's apartments to his own room. He had come from the Queen; a red-stockinged lackey carried his painting things. Towards him, a small figure with firm, delicate tread, came the Duchess of Alba, accompanied by Doña Eufemia.

His knees trembled, the floor beneath him heaved. She stopped. "What a good thing that I met you, Don Francisco," she said. And in slow distinct French she went on. "I can't stand it here in the Escorial any more. I'm going to Madrid for a few days, starting on Wednesday. Will you be there too?"

An overwhelming thrill of joy shot through Goya. Here it was, the consummation. Promised for a definite time, for Wednesday, for Wednesday night. But at once, in the same moment, his good, calculating peasant sense reminded him that precisely that time did not belong to him. The Queen was expecting to sit for him on Thursday, early in the morning. If he did not appear his whole future would crumble to nothing. He would never again be permitted to paint a member of the Court, never become First Court Painter. He would fall back into nothingness. But if he did not utter a blissful "yes" to this woman with her arrogant, mocking, wonderful face while her last words yet hung in the air, she would go on down the corridor and out of his life forever.

She was already making an almost imperceptible move to walk on, and the mocking look about her mouth had deepened a trifle. He knew that this uncanny woman perceived exactly what he was thinking. Fear seized him lest he had misplayed his hand. Hoarsely he stammered in rapid, jerky Spanish, "Did I understand you aright? May I pay you my respects Wednesday evening in Madrid?" And she, still in French, replied, "You understood aright, sir."

He did not know how he reached his room. Heavily, vacantly, he sat a long while. All he felt was, "The die is cast, the die is cast."

But then he began to scheme with peasant cunning. He thought it only just that fate should ask a high price for a night with the Duchess of Alba; but did the price have to be his whole career? He would have to find a pressing and convincing reason for calling off the sitting with the Queen. If someone was ill, for example, mortally ill, someone of his immediate family. He would have to show a dispatch containing some such intelligence to the Queen's chamberlain.

"When are you going to Madrid, to Ezquerra?" he asked Agustín an hour later, with rather forced gruffness. "How much longer are you going to keep me waiting for the paints?" Agustín looked at him in surprise. "We can get along with what we've got for at least three more days," he said. "Besides, the daily courier can order them. If I give him clear instructions Ezquerra will know what we want." But Goya grimly insisted, "You're going to Madrid today." "Are you mad?" asked Agustín. "You promised faithfully to have the picture ready for Don Manuel's anniversary. You yourself asked for the four sittings from the Queen. And now you want to send me away?"

"You're going to Madrid," Goya commanded. Hoarsely and with even more brusqueness and decision he added, "And there you will learn that my little Elena is seriously ill and that Josefa is pressing for my immediate return." Agustín, in increasing amazement, said, "I don't understand a word." "You don't have to understand," responded Goya impatiently. "You're to bring me the intelligence that my Elenita is ill. That's all."

Agustín strode up and down, disconcerted, thinking hard. "So, you're going to put the Queen off," he said at last, drawing the correct conclusion. "You want to go to Madrid." Goya, tormented, almost beseechingly, said, "I *must* go to Madrid. My life depends on it." "And you can't find any other excuse?" Agustín asked hesitantly. Goya himself began to feel uneasy at having chosen this one, but he could think of no other. "Don't leave me in the lurch," he implored. "You know how I can work if we have a time limit. The picture will be finished, and it will be good. Don't let me down this time."

Ever since Agustín had seen the drawing of the noonday ghost he had known that Goya was on the point of committing one of his colossal acts of folly, and that no one and nobody could restrain him. "I'll go to Madrid," he said unhappily. "You'll get your letter." "Thank you," said Goya, and, "Try to understand," he begged.

Goya, when Agustín was gone, made an effort to work. He was a disciplined worker; but now he could not collect his thoughts. They circled around the night in Madrid and what course it would take. Transports of love overwhelmed him; then again in words and images he would call up the vilest obscenities he had ever seen or heard in the local taverns.

He was with Lucía and the Abbé. He felt Lucía's knowing, lightly mocking glance upon him. Of course he had evolved his own technique of dealing with women, from whores to duchesses, but on Wednesday night he feared he might make a fool of himself. He envied the Abbé his adroitness, the elegance which he himself had so often derided. He was afraid of the Duchess's laugh, still more of her smile.

Long after midnight Goya lay in restless sleep. Agustín came. Covered with dust, still in his travelling clothes, he stood in the doorway, a servant with a torch behind him. "Here's your letter," he said; the letter seemed to lie heavy in his hand. Francisco had half sat up. He took the letter, held it without opening it, he too as if he were weighing something heavy. "The letter is as you wanted it," said Agustín. "Thank you, Agustín," said Goya.

Next morning Goya announced to the Queen's chamberlain, the Marqués de la Vega Inclán, that to his bitter regret he would have to forego the sitting Doña María Luisa had so graciously granted him. He explained the circumstances and handed over the letter. The Marqués took the letter, put it down on the table unread, and said, "Her Majesty would have had to cancel the sitting in any case. The Infante Francisco de Paula is seriously ill."

Goya, staring at the Marqués,
Went all pale. Some words he stammered,
Then he staggered from the chamber,
In unseemly haste he left the
Chamberlain, who, in annoyance,
Muttered, looking after Goya's
Back, "What manners have these artists!
Such as him I must put up with
Here in the Escorial. Rabble,"
Was his thought. "*Canaille, chusma.*"

19

"We're going to the theatre, to the Cruz," declared the Duchess when he arrived at her house. "They're playing *The Hostile Brothers*. It's a silly piece from what I hear, but Coronado is playing the fool and Gizmana the soubrette, and the *tonadillas* are sure to be good." Goya was irritated by the casual tone in which she said it. Was this the overture to their night of love?

A crowd of youths were waiting at the entrance to the theatre to see the women descending from their carriages and sedans. It was the only occasion on which feminine legs were to be seen. The Duchess got out of her chair.

"That's a luscious little pair of legs," someone called to her, "plump, tender, good enough to eat." Goya stood there grimly. He would gladly have hit out but he feared to make a scandal.

To reach the interior one had to pass through a long, dark passage. There was noise and a press of people, pedlars offered water for sale, sweetmeats, the texts of the songs. It smelled and was dirty. Everybody pushed and shoved; great care was needed to keep shoes and clothing free from mud. There were not many boxes—only women with male escorts were admitted to them—and they were already full. It cost Goya lengthy negotiations and a shamelessly large bribe before he got one.

They were scarcely in their seats when there was an uproar in the patio and the parterre. The people there, the *mosqueteros*, had recognized the Duchess of Alba at once. They called and clapped. More ardently interested still, though less noisy, were the women; they sat in the part of the theatre reserved for them, in the *gallinero*, the hen-coop, all of them in the same prescribed black clothes and white headkerchief, and all now turned towards the box, cackling and laughing.

Goya kept his heavy, sullen face rigidly unmoved. Cayetana behaved as if the noise were directed at someone else and chatted with him amiably, unconcernedly.

The Hostile Brothers was indeed a stupid play, a watered-down version of a piece by Lope. The scoundrelly younger son supplants the noble elder one in the love of his father and in the heart of his girl. Even in the first act a duel took place in a graveyard, various ghosts appeared, the wicked brother drove the other one into the woods and locked his father up in a donjon to starve. The peasants were enraged against their wicked new master; so was the audience, and as the man who was taking the part of the police captain, Alguacil, stepped up from the auditorium to stand by the wicked brother, the audience spat at him and wanted to drub him. He had to protest that after all he was only the actor Garro.

"Are you a *Chorizo* or a *Polaco?*" the Duchess asked the painter. The Madrid public, passionately interested in their theatre, had for half a century been split into two factions; the members of one called themselves, after a long since dead comic actor, sausages, *Chorizos*, of the other *Polacos*, after an abbé who had published a polemic for the rival party. Goya admitted to being a *Chorizo*. "I thought so," said the Duchess crossly. "We Albas are *Polacos*. My grandfather was one."

The *tonadilla* sung after the first act was lively and united both groups in rowdy enjoyment. Then the second act began, in the tower, with the clanking of chains and the rustle of straw. A masculine angel, contemporaneously clothed in knee breeches but with wings at his shoulders, consoles the imprisoned old man. The girl, mistrusting the calumniations of the wicked brother, meets the Count in the savage forest. The audience, intent, gripped, had fallen silent. The Duchess said she thought they could leave.

They breathed the fresh evening air. "We'll go to one of your taverns," commanded the Duchess. Goya, deliberately misunderstanding, suggested an elegant restaurant. "To Ceferino?" he asked. "To one of *your* taverns," said the Duchess. "We can't go to the Manolería in evening dress," Goya said uneasily. The Manolería was the district on the outskirts of the city where the *majos* and *majas* lived. "You don't have to tell me that," said the Duchess in her small quick voice. "I will go home, change my dress, and await you."

He went home in a bad temper. Was it for this that he had gone through so much torment, contrived the risky dispatch about little Elena, jeopardized his whole career? "*Qué vergüenza!*" he seemed to hear within him in Agustín's rough voice.

Before he changed his clothes he went on tiptoe into the children's room and looked at little Elena. She was sleeping peacefully.

He put on his old *majo* costume. His ill-humour evaporated; pleasurable anticipation took its place. The various garments were well worn, it was true, and the trousers, the bright green waistcoat, the short red coat were all rather a tight fit. But he had had many experiences in these clothes; good experiences they had been. As he wound the broad scarf around his waist and stuck the knife, the *navaja*, in it, he felt a different man, young, ready for anything. "Put on the cowl and you can talk Latin," went the old saying. Then he wrapped himself in the *capa*, the vast cloak, which was actually forbidden, and put on the broad-brimmed hat, the *chambergo*, which threw a deep shadow over the face.

Thus, enveloped to the point of being unrecognizable, he went on his way. He chuckled when the Duchess's doorkeeper did not want to let him in. He showed his face and the man grinned. The Duchess smiled too at the sight of him—appreciatively, he thought. She herself wore an ample, gaily-coloured skirt and low-cut bodice embroidered in colours. She had her hair in a net. The whole became her very well, and one might have taken her for a *maja*.

"Where are we going?" she asked. "To Rosalía's wine tavern in the Barquillo," he replied. "But you'll have trouble if you wear your mantilla," he warned, for Eufemia had put the mantilla round her, and *tapadas,* women in veils, were not welcome in the Manolería. Cayetana, without replying, pulled the mantilla further over her face. "Let me come too," begged the dueña. "I shall die of worry as long as I know you're in the Manolería." "Nonsense, Eufemia," said Cayetana firmly, "Don Francisco is man enough to protect me."

The wine shop was full. People sat, drank, and smoked, monosyllabic, concerned to preserve a Castilian gravity. Most of the men wore their broad-brimmed hats. The women were sturdy, many of them pretty, all of them unveiled. Thick smoke lay over the room. Someone was playing the guitar.

The new arrivals were regarded with a restrained curiosity not exactly friendly. Someone offered Goya smuggled tobacco. "How much?" asked Goya. "Twenty-two reals," the man said. "Do you take me for a *gabacho?*" asked Goya. This was the contemptuous word used to signify a foreigner, especially a Frenchman. "I'll pay sixteen reals like everyone else."

One of the girls put her oar in. "Aren't you at least going to buy your girl a cigar?" she asked. "I don't smoke," said the Duchess beneath her veil. "Oh, but you should," said the girl. The youth next to her declared, "Smoking cleans the brain, stimulates the appetite, and keeps the teeth healthy." "Of course, the lady ought to take off her mantilla," taunted the girl. "Be quiet, Zanca, Spindleshanks," said the boy, "and don't make a stink." But Zanca persisted, "Tell your lady, Señor, that she ought to take off her mantilla. One isn't admitted veiled into the parks, and here it's even less called for." And a young fellow at another table suggested, "Perhaps the lady is a *gabacha.*"

Francisco had predicted to Cayetana that her mantilla would cause ill-feeling. He knew his *majos;* he was one of them himself. They were not ones to stomach prying looks; they regarded themselves as the best, the most Spanish of Spaniards, and were not disposed to put up with the condescending curiosity of foreigners. Whoever visited them in their own taverns had to comply with their customs and show their faces.

The man with the guitar had stopped playing. Everybody looked at Goya. Under no circumstances would he back down now. "Who said that about being a *gabacha?*" he asked. He did not raise his voice; he spoke evenly between two pulls at his cigar. There was a little silence. The hostess, the buxom Rosalía, said to the man with the guitar, "Don't be lazy now, play us a fandango." But Francisco repeated, "Who said that about a *gabacha?*" "I said it," said the *majo*. "Will you beg the lady's pardon?" asked Goya. "He doesn't have to," said another. "She hasn't taken off her mantilla." It was true, but Goya could not yield. "Who asked for your opinion?" he said instead, and, "Shut up, or I'll show you that I can dance a fandango over the dead bodies of the whole lot of you." This was just the sort of expression to go down well in the Manolería and it delighted the hearts of those present. But the young man who had called the Duchess a *gabacha* said, "I'll count up to ten, and if by then you haven't managed to make your girl take off her stuck-up veil, I'll give you such a kick that you'll fly all the way to Aranjuez."

Goya saw that action was now demanded of him. He stood up, the *capa* slipped off his shoulders, and he felt for his *navaja*, his knife.

But now arose a great cry of astonishment. The Duchess had lifted her mantilla. "The Duchess of Alba!" they cried. "Our Duchess!" And the young man said, "Forgive me, Señora. God knows you're no *gabacha*, Señora. You're one of us."

Goya found the bowing and scraping more odious than the altercation which preceded it. For what the boy had said was not true; the Duchess was not one of them. At best she was a lady of the Court playing at being a *maja*. He felt ashamed in front of the real *majas* because he had brought her here. Simultaneously he reflected that the girls he had painted in his tapestry designs had been no *majas* but dressed-up duchesses and countesses, and he was angrier than ever.

She talked with the others, after their own fashion; the words flowed from her mouth with unaffected friendliness, and, apart from him, no one seemed to notice that her manner was false, that condescension lay behind it, mere affability.

"Let us go," he said suddenly. It sounded more peremptory than he meant.

For an instant the Duchess looked up, surprised. But then she said quickly to the others, graciously, with a trace of mockery, "Yes, Señores, we must, alas, break up our party. Our Court Painter here is expecting a great man who wants to have his portrait painted." People laughed. The absurdity of this excuse amused them all. He felt a helpless anger.

Someone fetched a sedan. "Come again soon," they called after her, heartily, gratefully.

"Where are we going?" he asked bitterly. "To your studio, of course," she returned, "where you're expecting your model."

The promise her words implied took his breath away. But she was so inconstant; perhaps she would change her mind before they got there.

Excited, full of impotent rage at what had gone before, at her moods and his own helplessness, tossed hither and thither by anger, anticipation, desire, he walked by her sedan through the night. Now to crown everything he could hear a bell ringing, a priest coming with the Viaticum. The bearers put down the chair, the Duchess got out; he spread out his handkerchief for her and they all knelt down, till the priest and his acolyte had passed.

At last they reached his house. The *sereno*, the night watchman, opened the door. They went up to the studio. Goya, rather clumsily, lighted candles. The Duchess sat down languidly in an armchair. "It's dark in here," she pronounced, "and cold." He waked his servant Andreo. The latter brought two silver candelabra with many candles, and made a fire, with a great deal of fuss and grumbling. The Duchess looked on, unveiled. She and Goya kept silent as long as Andreo was in the room.

At last the lad departed. The room lay in warm, not very brilliant light. The gobelin of the procession with the huge saint and the excited crowd remained indistinct, indistinct as well the gloomy, bearded Cardinal by Velázquez. The Duchess stepped closer to the picture. "Who had this picture before you?" she asked, half to herself, half to him. "It was a gift from the Duchess of Osuna," he replied. "Yes," she said, "I remember seeing it in the Alameda. Did you sleep with her?" she asked abruptly in her rather hard, childlike voice but still amiably.

Goya did not answer. She was still standing in front of the picture. "I've learned a great deal from Velázquez," he said after a while, "more than from anyone else." She said, "I have a Velázquez in my country house in Montefrio, a remarkable little picture, as good as unknown. If you're ever in Andalucía, Don Francisco, please look at it. I believe it would go well in here."

She examined some sketches lying on the table, designs for the portrait of the Queen. "It seems you mean to paint the Italian woman almost as ugly as she really is. Does she permit that?" "As Doña María Luisa is an intelligent woman," Goya replied, "she doesn't want to be prettified." "Yes," observed the Duchess, "when a woman looks like that the least she can do is to be intelligent."

She sat down on the sofa. She leaned back comfortably, her pale brown face only lightly powdered. "I think I'll paint you as a *maja*," he said, "or, then again, perhaps not. I don't want to risk painting you again in a mask. I must find out what the real Cayetana is like."

"You never will," she assured him. "Anyhow, I don't know myself. I really think I'm more *maja* than anything else. I don't care at all what others think, and that's how *majas* are, isn't it?"

"Does it disturb you if I look at you like this?" he asked. She said, "I don't take it amiss, because you're a painter. Tell me, by the way, are you only a painter, never anything else but a painter? You might be a little more forthcoming." He remained silent. She reverted to her former topic. "I was brought up to be a *maja*. My grandfather had me brought up according to the principles of Rousseau. Do you know who Rousseau was, Don Francisco?" Goya was more amused than offended. "My friends occasionally allow me to read the *Encyclopædia*," he replied. She looked up for an instant. The *Encyclopædia* was anathema to the Inquisition; to obtain the work, to read it, was hard and hazardous. However, she did not take him up but went on with her own story. "My father died when I was very young, and my grandfather permitted me every freedom. Apart from that my grandmother's deceased chambermaid visits me from time to time and tells me what I should do and what I shouldn't. Seriously, Don Francisco, you ought to paint me as a *maja*."

Goya poked the fire. "I don't believe a word of it. You don't really think you're a *maja* any more than you really have nocturnal conversations with a dead servant maid." He turned round and looked her challengingly in the face. "I say what I think, when I feel like it. I *am* a *majo*, even though I do sometimes read the *Encyclopædia*." "Is it true," the Duchess asked with equable friendliness, "that you've killed four or five men in affrays or out of jealousy? And did you really have to flee to Italy because the police were after you? And did you get your living for a whole year as a bullfighter? Did you really carry off a nun in Rome so that only our ambassador's intervention could get you out of it? Or have you only put all these stories in circulation so as to make yourself interesting and get more commissions?"

Goya told himself the woman would scarcely have come to his studio at this hour of night simply with the purpose of offending him. She wanted to make him feel small so that, later, she should not feel small herself. He controlled himself and answered quietly, amiably, playfully. "A *majo* loves big words and bragging. You must be aware of that, Your Grace." "If you say 'Your Grace' to me once more, I'll go," replied the Duchess. "I don't think you'll go, Your Grace," said Goya. "I think you're bent on"—he searched for a word—"bent on ruining me." "And why should I want to ruin you, Francho?" the Duchess asked softly. "I don't know," said Goya. "How should I know what you want to do?" "That smacks of philosophy and heresy," said the Duchess. "I'm afraid you're a heretic, Francho, I'm afraid you believe more in the devil than in God." "If the Inquisition wants to concern itself with either of us it ought to be you," replied Goya. "The Inquisition does not concern itself with the Duchess of Alba," she answered so naturally that it did not even sound arrogant. "What's more," she said, "you mustn't take me too seriously if I sometimes say wicked things to you. Several times I've prayed to the Virgen del Pilar to send you peace and happiness, Francho, because the Devil seems to torment you so bitterly. But," and she looked over to the wooden effigy of Our Lady of Atocha, "you don't entrust yourself any more to the Virgen del Pilar. And yet before you surely did so more than other people because you're from Saragossa. So you're faithless as well."

She stood up and walked over to the ageless dark-brown figure, looking it up and down. "But I don't wish to speak irreverently in front of the Virgin of Atocha," she said, "and certainly not in front of this one who is your patron saint. She has great power, I'm sure, and one must under no circumstances offend her."

> And with tender care she wrapped the
> Great black veil, her large mantilla,
> All about the blackened wooden
> Image of Our Blessed Lady
> Of Atocha, that she might not
> Have before her eyes the sight of
> What now happened. From her black hair

Next she drew the lofty comb, and
Slipped her feet out of the high-heeled
Shoes, and smaller looked than ever.
Shameless in the flickering firelight,
Gravely and intent she dropped the
Heavy skirt and gaily coloured
Bodice.

-- PART II --

— 1 —

In the year 1478 the Catholic rulers Ferdinand and Isabella set up a special tribunal for the persecution of all offences against religion. This had happened after the defeat of the Arabs, when it was important to cement the hard-won unity of the kingdom with unity of faith. One flock, one shepherd, one faith, one king, one sword, the poet Hernando Acuña had sung at the time.

This spiritual court, the Inquisition, the Holy Office, had done its duty. Jew and Arab had been spied out, hounded, exterminated. The same fate had befallen all those who had tried to conceal their subversive views beneath the mask of their Catholic beliefs; the secret Moors and Jews, Moriscos, Judaizers, Marranos.

But after the Inquisition had fulfilled its purpose, it became an independent power within the State. Nominally, it is true, it confined its activities to the discovering and punishment of heresy. But what did the term heresy not comprise? Primarily, heresy was any opinion that conflicted with a dogma of the Catholic Church; and, accordingly, to the Inquisition fell the task of censoring everything written, printed, spoken, sung, and danced. Heresy was, further, any activity of importance to the general public if it was carried on by the descendant of a heretic. Thus the Holy Office had the duty of investigating the antecedents of all applicants for public office. Every candidate had to prove his *limpieza*, his descent from Christian parents and grandparents; there must have been no Moor or Jew among his ancestors. And the Inquisition alone could furnish certificates to this effect. It could prolong the investigations at its pleasure, it could demand as high fees as it liked, the final decision whether or not a Spaniard could be employed by the State lay in its hands. But heresy was also swearing, the representation of the nude, bigamy, unnatural instincts. Usury was heresy, because it was forbidden in the Bible. Even horse-trading with any but Spaniards was heresy because such trading might benefit the unbelievers on the other side of the Pyrénées.

By such interpretations of its sphere of jurisdiction the Inquisition appropriated to itself more and more of the rights of the Crown and undermined the authority of the State.

Every year the Holy Office proclaimed a public holiday on which to pronounce the so-called Edict of Faith. In this edict, all those who felt themselves guilty of heretical tendencies were admonished to denounce themselves to the Holy Tribunal within a period of thirty days. Furthermore, all the faithful were exhorted to report any case of heresy which came to their notice. A long list of suspicious acts was compiled. Evidence of clandestine heresy included all Jewish practices, the lighting of candles on Friday evening, changing one's linen on the Sabbath, abstaining from pork, washing the hands before meals. The reading of foreign books was an indication of heresy, as was the frequent reading of any profane works at all. Children had to inform on their parents, men and wives upon each other, on pain of excommunication, whenever they noticed anything suspicious.

The secrecy with which the Tribunal proceeded was oppressive. The charge had to be preferred secretly, and anyone who gave the accused notice of the indictment laid himself open to heavy penalties. The slenderest evidence was enough for the court to order arrest, and nobody dared to inquire after those who disappeared into the dungeons of the Inquisition. Informers, witnesses, accused were sworn on oath to silence; an infringement of the oath was punished as heavily as heresy itself.

Should the accused deny his guilt or persist in his error, torture was applied. In order to avoid having to pay torturers, the Inquisition would sometimes call upon high civil officials to exercise a function pleasing in the sight of God. Like other phases of the procedure, the torture was carried out with scrupulous exactness according to regulations and in the presence of a doctor and a secretary who set down a record of every detail. Through the centuries the spiritual judges had emphasized that they used the distasteful method of torture out of compassion; that is, in order to liberate the impenitent one from his heresy and lead him into the way of true knowledge.

Should the accused confess and repent, he would thereby have "made his peace with the Church." This reconciliation involved a penance; the penitent would perhaps be scourged or made to walk through the streets ignominiously clothed, in the garment of shame, or he might be handed over to the secular arm to serve a three- to eight-year or even lifelong sentence in the galleys. The penitent's worldly goods would be confiscated, sometimes his house would even be destroyed; he and his descendants to the fifth generation were disqualified from holding office or following any honourable profession.

The Holy Tribunal adhered firmly to the principle of clemency, even if the heretic did not confess or made only a partial acknowledgment of guilt. The Church did not put the sinner to death; instead she would thrust the obstinate or relapsing offender out of her communion and hand him over to the secular authorities. To the latter, also, she recommended avoidance of the sword, but exhorted them to take to heart the verse in Holy Writ: "If a man abide not in me, he is cast forth as a branch, and is withered; and men gather them and cast them into the fire and they are burned." In consequence of which the civil authorities did indeed burn the branches which had been cast away, those expelled from the Communion, and they burned them alive. If the case was one of a heretic already deceased, then the corpse would be dug up and burned. If the heretic confessed after sentence had been passed he was strangled and only his cadaver burned. If the heretic had escaped he was burned in effigy. In every case his property was confiscated; one part of the forfeited goods went to the State, the other to the Inquisition.

The Inquisition was very wealthy, acquittals were rare. From the institution of the Holy Tribunal in Spain until the coronation of Charles the Fourth, the total of those burned by the Inquisition or burdened with the severest penalties was 348,907.

The sentences of the Inquisition were proclaimed and carried out with a pomp and publicity exactly proportioned to the secrecy of its deliberations. Promulgation and execution of the sentence were called an Act of Faith, Proclamation of Faith, Manifesto of Faith, Auto-da-fé. To participate therein was regarded as an activity pleasing in the eyes of God. Magnificent processions took place, the banners of the Inquisition were ceremoniously broken out, the dignitaries temporal and spiritual sat on huge platforms. Every single criminal was announced by name and called up before the judges, attired in the sanbenito, the penitential shift, and tall pointed hat of the heretic. His sentence was pronounced in resounding tones. With a great show of military, the condemned were taken to the *quemadero*, the place of burning. The crowd witnessed the burning of heretics with an eagerness that exceeded the ecstasies of the bullfight, and if too many sinners repented after sentence, so that they got off with being strangled and didn't have to burn, the onlookers grumbled.

Such Acts of Faith were frequently held to celebrate happy events, the accession or marriage of a king or the birth of an heir to the throne; on these occasions the pyre was set alight by a member of the royal family.

Reports were published of every auto-da-fé, compiled by skilled ecclesiastical writers. These reports were very popular. Padre Garau might, for example, describe an auto-da-fé on the island of Mallorca: how three impenitent sinners met their death in the fire and how, when the flames reached them, they tried desperately to free themselves from the stake. The heretic Benito Terongi did indeed pull himself free on one side, only to fall into the flames on the other. His sister Catalina, who had boasted beforehand that she would leap into the flames of her own accord, shrieked and begged to be unbound. The heretic Rafael Valls at first stood as still as a statue in the smoke, but when the flames reached him he twisted and writhed. He was as fat and rosy as a sucking pig, and when one could no longer see the flames on the outside of his body, he went on burning inside, his belly burst open, his entrails fell out like Judas's. Padre Garau's little volume, *La Fée Triunfante*, had a particular success; it ran to fourteen printings, the last one appearing in the time of Francisco Goya.

Some of the Inquisitors were actuated by pure zeal for the Faith, others used their authority to satisfy their lust for power and possession, their carnal appetites. The accounts of such victims as managed to escape might be exaggerated, yet the Manual of the Inquisition, its rules of procedure, betrays how easy it was made for the judges to act according to their own inclinations, and the records show how arbitrarily they in fact proceeded.

The Inquisition claimed that by uniting all Hispanic peoples in the Catholic Faith they had preserved the peninsula from the religious wars which had befallen the rest of Europe. But this result was dearly bought. The Inquisition had implanted in Spaniards the conviction that more important than a moral way of life was an unshakable belief in dogma. Foreigners who travelled in Spain reported almost unanimously that precisely in the land of the Inquisition religion had little to do with morality and the passionate zeal for dogma was often coupled with immoral conduct. The Holy Tribunal often dealt leniently with offences which were viewed with revulsion by the whole world; such as, for example, the seduction of children in the confessional. But small technical transgressions against dogma were in all cases harshly treated. In Córdoba, for example, one hundred and seven men, women, and children were condemned to the stake at a single hearing because they had listened to the sermon of a certain Membreque who had been pronounced a heretic.

At about the time of Francisco Goya's birth a number of Judaizantes, among them an eighteen-year-old girl, were burned in a particularly splendid auto-da-fé for practising certain Jewish customs. Montesquieu, the greatest French writer of the time, puts into the mouth of one of them a speech in his defence composed by himself: "You accuse the Mohammedans," it runs, "of having propagated their religion by the sword; why then do you propagate yours by fire? To prove the divine origin of your religion, you make great play with the blood of your martyrs; but at present you play the role of Diocletian and make us assume the role of martyr. You would have us become Christians and you will not be so yourselves. But if you will not be Christians, at least treat us as you would if having only the weak sense of justice which Nature has seen fit to bestow upon every creature, however base, that wears a human face. So much is certain: your activities will serve future historians as proof that the Europe of our time was inhabited by barbarians and savages."

In Spain itself during the second half of the eighteenth century works were circulated which laid upon the Inquisition the chief blame for the decline of the country, its depopulation, its spiritual poverty, its emasculation. Even the rulers of the time, Bourbons of French origin, recognized that the country would go to ruin without certain modern, "heretical" reforms. So, pious and full of respect for tradition as they were, they left the Holy Office all the formal appearance of authority while depriving it of its most important functions and privileges.

Among the people, however, the influence of the Inquisition remained undiminished, and the darkness and secrecy which shrouded its power only increased its attraction. The day on which an Edict of Faith was pronounced was splendid and alluring just because of the grim menace of the edict itself. Even more was this true of the autos-da-fé, with their mixture of horror, cruelty, and lust.

Everywhere the Inquisition
Darkly peered and spied and threatened
Everybody with its menace.
Men must hide their thoughts and feelings
With pretence and whisper only
To their nearest what lay closest
To their hearts. Yet this perpetual
Threat gave life its charm: the Spanish
Could not spare their Inquisition,
For it gave unto the folks its
God, who was indeed the god of
Every other folk as well, yet
Eminently of the Spanish.
So the Spaniard, stiffly, stoutly,
Stuck up for his Inquisition.

— 2 —

The peace negotiations which the Madrid Court was conducting with the French in Basle were protracting themselves. The Spaniards, though privately resigned to giving up their demand for the surrender of the royal children of France, felt themselves in honour bound to press this very condition until the last moment. In Paris, meanwhile, no one had any intention of providing, by the surrender of the heirs of the Capets, a focus for royalist resistance, and they stuck by a chilly "No." Nonetheless and against all reason the royalist ambassador of France, Monsieur de Havré, hoped that the intensive pressure applied by the Spaniards would finally carry the day. In his dreams he saw the little King rescued and in Madrid, and himself as his tutor and guardian, the secret regent of glorious, sacred, beloved France.

Then fearful tidings came: the royal boy Louis the Seventeenth was dead. Monsieur de Havré doubted the truth of the news. Probably royalists had abducted the boy and were keeping him in hiding, but Doña María Luisa and Don Manuel were more than ready to accept the death of the little Louis as a fact; indeed the Court of Madrid received the evil news with a private sigh of relief. The troublesome issue was now disposed of without loss of honour.

But even after that the peace negotiations did not progress. The Republic, presuming upon the success of its arms, was demanding the cession of the province of Guipúzcoa with the important city of San Sebastián, and a war indemnity of four hundred millions. "I count on the peace to allow us a somewhat more spacious life," said Doña María Luisa to her First Minister, and Don Manuel realized that he could not pay the four hundred millions. Pepa, for her part, said, "I hope, Don Manuel, that you will enable a greater Spain to emerge from the war." And Don Manuel saw that he could not give up the Basque province. "I am a Spaniard," he declared grandly and darkly to his Don Miguel. "I will neither yield San Sebastián nor pay this monstrous tribute."

But the cunning Miguel had already, without compromising his master, put out feelers in Paris and was soon in a position to make interesting communications; the Paris Directory, over and above the peace, was anxious for an alliance with Spain; if they were certain of such an alliance they would considerably mitigate the terms of peace. "From what I hear," Don Miguel concluded cautiously, "Paris would be satisfied if you were to promise personally that the desired alliance would come to pass."

Don Manuel looked up. "I personally?" he asked, agreeably surprised. "Yes, Señor," Don Miguel affirmed. "In the event of your addressing a letter in your own hand containing such an assurance, in confidence of course, to one of the Directors, let us say to the Abbé Sieyès, then the Republic would no longer insist on the two troublesome clauses."

The importance which people in Paris attached to his person flattered Don Manuel. He believed himself able, he said to the Queen, to achieve a tolerable, even an honourable peace if he were empowered to embark on an unofficial personal exchange of opinions with the gentlemen in Paris. María Luisa was sceptical. "I think you overestimate yourself, Pico, my little one," she replied. Don Manuel was ruffled. "All right, Doña María Luisa," he said, "then I'll leave the deliverance of the kingdom to you." And in spite of Don Miguel's insistence, he did not send off the letter to the Abbé Sieyès.

The French, tired of the prolonged haggling, gave their General Pérignon orders to advance. In a swift train of victories, the republican army took Bilboa, Miranda, Vittoria, and pushed on to the borders of Castile. There was panic in Madrid. Rumours flew about that the Court was girding itself for flight to Andalucía. "I will save you, Madame," declared Don Manuel. "You and Spain." And he wrote the letter.

One week later the provisional peace treaty was signed. France contented itself with the Spanish half of San Domingo in the Antilles and withdrew its claim to the Basque province. The Republic also agreed to the Spanish suggestion that the war indemnity should be spread over ten years and paid in kind. Further, the Republic pledged itself to surrender the Princess Marie Thérèse, the daughter of Louis the Sixteenth, though only to Austria.

There was immense astonishment in the country, and great rejoicing that they had emerged from a lost war with as good as no loss of territory. This Manuel Godoy! "What a chap you are," said Don Carlos and clapped him heartily on the shoulder. "Shall I tell you how I worked it?" Manuel asked the Queen. "No, no," she said; she had sized up the situation and did not want to know anything about it.

As the favourable peace was thanks entirely to Don Manuel, honours were heaped upon him such as had not fallen to the lot of anyone for a long time. A crown demesne in Granada was made over to him as a present, he was made Príncipe de la Paz, Prince of the Peace, and Generalissimo.

Wearing the uniform of Generalissimo, he paid his visit of thanks to the sovereign pair. The tight-fitting white breeches spanned his thighs, proudly the coat embraced his chest, exuberantly the plume swayed from the hat which he carried under his arm. "You look magnificent," said Don Carlos, and added quickly, "Cover yourself." Only the first twelve grandees of the kingdom were entitled to put on their hats before replying. The grandees of second rank could put on their hats only after they had replied, those of the third rank only when they had been invited to sit down.

Doña María Luisa guessed that it was not Don Manuel who was

responsible for this peace but his advisers, the suspicious, enlightened rebellious *Afrancesados*, the Francophiles, and that the apparently so glorious event would bring in its train new wars and unforeseeable consequences, in all probability bad ones. However, for the time being it was a brilliant and honourable peace. And Manuel had signed for it. She had put the young man into this uniform herself, but she could not help it, he impressed her in his new and manly splendour, her heart warmed towards him.

There were still twelve grandees of the first rank, descendants of such families as had ruled in the peninsula since the time of Sancho the Great, that is, for nine hundred years and more. They addressed each other with the brotherly "thou." Now that the King's favour had added him, the most noble Príncipe de la Paz, to their number, Manuel overcame his instinctive awe and said "thou" to the Dukes of Arcos, Béjar, Medina-Sidonia, Infantado, and all the rest of them. They betrayed a faint astonishment and then returned his "thou"; he was overjoyed.

And he said to the Duke of Alba, "I'm happy, Don José, to see thee looking so fresh today." The frail, elegant man's calm, full face, remained unmoved; unmoved also his fine dark pensive eyes, and he said pleasantly, "I'm grateful to you for your interest, *Excelentísimo Señor*." Yes, he said "*Excelentísimo Señor*" and did not return the "thou."

And Manuel said to Don Luis María de Borbón, Conde de Chinchón, Archbishop of Seville, "It's a long time since I've seen thee, Don Luis." The very young, very solemn young man looked at him as if he were air and passed on. And yet this Don Luis María de Borbón was only half a Bourbon. Though the son of an Infante of Castile and a blood cousin of the King's, his mother had been a simple Doña María Teresa de Vallabriga, of the petty Aragonese nobility, and hitherto the King had not conceded him the title Infante. So that though Don Luis María was of the blood royal, he, Don Manuel, actually had the higher title and pretensions. He was certainly not a vain man, but he would not forget this bastard half-Bourbon's arrogance.

María Luisa, in order to make good any slights upon her favourite, devised new honours for him. A royal decree was issued that at official functions a head of Janus should be borne by a herald in front of the Príncipe de la Paz as a sign that he had rightly summed up both past and future.

Don Manuel displayed this new distinction for the first time at the opening of the Academy of Sciences.

Yet he drove not by the straightest
Route but rather in his carriage
With four horses made a detour,
And of all his friends 'twas Pepa
Tudo was the first to see his
New and double-headed grandeur.
For she stood there in her window
As he passed, and he saluted,
Bowing low in homage to her.
So she stood there and her bosom
Filled with pride at having made of
Him a man just like the heroes
Her romantic ballads pictured,
Saviour too of Spain, the kingdom's
Foremost man. And in this glory
She resolved that Don Francisco
Was to make a portrait of him
Just for her.

— 3 —

Spurred on by his enlightened friends and advisers, Don Manuel used his surprising popularity to introduce new progressive measures. He had set great store by appearing as a protector of the arts and sciences from the start; over and above this, by such liberal policies he was showing those in power in Paris his good intentions in the matter of the promised alliance.

But his measures remained ineffective since the Church fought them with all her influence. His friends advised him to limit the jurisdiction of the Holy Office still further and to claim a far larger part of the revenues of the Inquisition for the State; he might indeed, now that he was secure in the love and admiration of the people, revoke the tax immunities of the Church, and, at the same time, realizing an old dream, cleanse the finances of the State and break forever the Church's opposition to the modernization of the country.

Such open warfare, however, went against Don Manuel's nature. And Pepa did her best to keep him from decisive measures. As a child she had witnessed an auto-da-fé, and the fierce, sinister ceremonial, the banners and the priests, the condemned criminals and the flames in which they burned, were among her profoundest memories. Her confessor did his best to inspire her soul with the dark mystique of the Holy Tribunal. Gentlemen of the Inquisition visited her constantly; even the Archbishop Despuig of Granada, who stood close to the Grand Inquisitor, had received her during his last stay in Madrid.

In the sixties and seventies the influence of the Inquisition had shrunk. But it took on fresh strength as revolt and godlessness got the upper hand across the Pyrénées. The liberal Grand Inquisitor Sierra had been deposed and replaced by the fanatical Cardinal Archbishop of Toledo, the sinister Francisco de Lorenzana. With the approval of the government, the Holy Office had persecuted as godlessness, as "philosophism," any intellectual tendency which betrayed sympathy with French theories, and had instituted proceedings against a number of *Afrancesados*. But now a peace had been made with the Republic, plans for an alliance were contemplated; the free-thinkers were getting the upper hand again, the new-won power of the Inquisition was endangered.

Lorenzana, a shrewd politician and intriguer, took precautions. Almost all the ministers and higher counsellors were suspected of "philosophism" and "naturalism"; that is, the equating of God and nature. Lorenzana collected material against these gentlemen, denunciations piled up in the archives of his tribunals. Assistants, voluntary and paid, spied on the life of the Príncipe de la Paz, the friendship of certain prelates with Pepa Tudo did the rest, and the First Minister's every day and night were carefully recorded in the registers of the Holy Office. With exactitude the Grand Inquisitor examined and calculated the degree to which the favourite's relations with the Queen blew hotter or colder according to the temperature of his love for Pepa Tudo. He came to the conclusion that Don Manuel's position was not so strong and that of the Holy Office by no means so weak as was commonly assumed.

He took the offensive against the godless Prime Minister, hit back against the heretics. In several provincial capitals the Inquisition initiated proceedings, on the charge of philosophism, against men of great reputation, professors, high State officials. They arrested and sentenced the former ambassador to France, Conde de Azora, the philologist Yereguí, who had been tutor to the royal Infantes under Charles the Third, the famous mathematician of the University of Salamanca, Luis de Samaniego.

The Grand Inquisitor waited to see if the First Minister would intervene, whether he would try to wrest from his clutches these his companions in free-thinking. Don Manuel did not dare. He made half-hearted representations to the Holy Office that they should be lenient in their punishment of these men who had rendered good service to the Crown.

Lorenzana got set for the decisive blow: the destruction of a leader among free-thinkers who was known all over Europe, the writer and statesman Olavide.

Don Pablo Olavide was born in Lima in Peru. He had been regarded as an infant prodigy and was made a judge while still very young. When a terrible earthquake destroyed the city of Lima, he was entrusted with the administration of goods and moneys the right to which had become a matter of controversy after the death of their owners. The money to which claims could not be substantiated, the very young man used to build a church and a theatre. This annoyed the clergy. With the support of powerful Peruvian clerics, the heirs whose claims had been rejected addressed themselves and their complaints to Madrid. Olavide was summoned to the capital, brought into court, deprived of his office, in many cases declared liable for compensation, sentenced to prison. He was soon released on grounds of health and was hailed as a martyr by the progressives of the country. A very rich widow married him. He procured the remission of the sentence he had not yet served. He travelled. He was frequently in Paris. Acquired a palace in the Spanish capital, another in the French. Struck up a friendship with Voltaire, with Rousseau, exchanged letters with them. Maintained a theatre in Paris where he put on modern French pieces in his own translation. Aranda, Charles the Third's liberal Prime Minister, called him in to advise on important matters. In Pablo Olavide, Europe saw one of her leading progressive spirits.

Now there were on the southern slopes of the Sierra Morena wide stretches of country, earlier under cultivation, which had become waste land when the Moors and Moriscos had been driven out. The Mesta, an association of cattle-breeders, had contrived that these lands be given over to them free as grazing grounds for their large, roving herds of sheep. Now, on the initiative of Olavide, the government withdrew this privilege from the Mesta and empowered Olavide to establish settlements on the waste land, Nuevas Poblaciones. With the help of the Bavarian Colonel Thürriegl, he settled some ten thousand peasants there, mostly Germans, also silkworm breeders and silk-spinners from Lyon. He himself was appointed governor of the district, with wide powers. He was allowed to give his colony a liberal constitution. He received the concession that the new settlers could bring their own clergy with them from their former homes. Even Protestants were admitted. In a few years Olavide had made the wilderness into a blossoming countryside, with hamlets, villages, small towns, inns, workshops, factories.

Now settlers from the Palatinate had brought a Capuchin monk with them for the cure of their souls, Brother Romuald of Freiburg. This man did not get on well with the liberal Olavide. As their differences increased, Romuald notified him to the Holy Office as an atheist and materialist. In secret, and according to procedure, without Olavide knowing anything about it, the Inquisition interrogated witnesses and collected material. But it did not dare to bring formal charges against the highly esteemed man. The Mesta, however, had a powerful protector in Archbishop Despuig of Granada. He and the King's confessor, the Bishop of Osma, managed to extract from Carlos a vague declaration to the effect that he would not stand in the Inquisition's way if it arrested Olavide, in order to prevent the issues being obscured.

All this had happened before Don Manuel came to power. A severe Grand Inquisitor was replaced by a liberal one, and he by the even more liberal Sierra, and all this time Olavide had remained shut up in the dungeons of the Inquisition. There had been unwillingness to discredit the Holy Office by his release, but at the same time he had not been sentenced.

The forty-third Grand Inquisitor, the above-mentioned Don Francisco Lorenzana, was a man of a different kidney from his predecessor. He resolved that sentence should be passed on the heretic Olavide. It would be a warning to blasphemers even in the highest office that the Inquisition was still alive and powerful.

Lorenzana had realized Don Manuel's lack of resolution. Nonetheless he wished to reinforce his position by the support of the Vatican; he was sure of a sympathetic hearing from the indefatigable Pius the Sixth. He felt it his duty, he wrote the Pope, to see that the sins of Olavide should be expiated in an auto-da-fé. On the other hand, in the present godless state of the world, the public condemnation of a heretic so prized and protected by the philosophasters would surely provoke attacks against the Spanish Inquisition and probably against the Church throughout the whole inhabited world. He begged the Holy Father for instructions.

The Abbé Don Diego, one of the secretaries of the Holy Office, learned of the plans of the Grand Inquisitor. He and Don Miguel importuned the Príncipe de la Paz to take steps and to make a timely declaration to Lorenzana that the government would not tolerate such an auto-da-fé.

For a moment Don Manuel was startled. But even now he preferred to avoid open conflict with Lorenzana. Pablo Olavide, he declared, had been arrested under the progressive First Minister Aranda, and the King had acquiesced in the proceedings of the Inquisition. Under these circumstances it was not his business to obstruct the sentence. Moreover, it was his belief that Lorenzana wanted only to intimidate the government, and that if he passed sentence at all it would be behind closed doors and not in an auto-da-fé. He thought of Pepa, remained deaf to Miguel's entreaties, lapsed into complacency and indifference.

Now Don Miguel and Don Gaspar
And the Abbé Don Diego
Sat together taking counsel
Full of anxious apprehension,
And their fears made them determine
To seek out their friend the painter
Don Francisco, who was painting
In these weeks a portrait of the
Príncipe of Peace for Pepa
Tudo.

— 4 —

Goya was absorbed in his affair with Cayetana. He had both hoped and feared that his passion, flaring up with such incredible swiftness, would dissipate as quickly. More than once it had happened that he had believed himself fathoms deep in love with a woman, only to wonder after two or three weeks what he could have seen in her. But Cayetana was something new to him every time; he did not get to the bottom of her. With his painter's eye he had spied out every detail of her external appearance, so that he could draw her from memory, and yet she seemed different every time he met her; she remained incalculable.

Whatever he did, when he thought, painted, conversed, Cayetana was always somewhere in his head. The link with her was very different from the quiet, secure bond between him and Josefa, very different from the pleasurable or tormenting fancies he had had in the past for this or that woman.

Her changes of mood came about suddenly, and whatever she was she was with her whole self. She had many faces, he saw them all; the ultimate reality behind them he did not see. It was there, he sensed it, he knew it; but he could not discover the irreducible unity behind the baffling variety of masks. He played his old game, drawing this one of her faces in the sand, then that one; her true face escaped him, elusive like the sand itself.

He painted her. Posed her in the open air and painted in the landscape delicately, carefully—yet in such a way that it disappeared and nothing was left but Cayetana. White, proud, dainty, she stood there, with incredibly high eyebrows below the black tide of her hair, the scarf girt high about her, a red ribbon across her breast, and in front of her, unspeakably small and silly, her woolly white dog with a red ribbon round his hind leg, in ridiculous imitation of the one she wore. She was pointing, with a gesture that was stiff, haughty, affected, down in front of her feet, where in fine, thin lettering were the words: "To the Duchess of Alba from Francisco de Goya"; and the letters were turned in homage toward the eyes of the Duchess.

He was not satisfied. That which had overpowered him that time on the dais, which had thrown him into confusion on their walk, the thing which unceasingly angered and lured him on was not in the picture.

For all that he was happy. She showed herself with him without shame, and he was proud that he, a stout man, no longer young, who had risen from the people, was her *cortejo*. He dressed in the latest fashion even when he was painting—particularly when he was painting. He had done so when he had first come to Madrid; but Josefa had insisted that he should not soil his fine clothes and should avail himself of the customary working smock; gradually by her persuasions and his own parsimony the smock had been forced on him. Now it vanished again. And yet he knew that he cut a foolish figure in the tight-fitting, fashionable clothing.

Cayetana might be childish, he would be more so. If she came unexpectedly he would stand on his head and greet her by waving his feet in the air. With delight he used his art to make her laugh. Drew his own face making a crazy grimace; drew with magnificent distortion the heads of her dueña Eufemia, the foppish Marqués de San Adrián, the good-natured, clumsy, well-meaning King. They went frequently to the theatre, and he laughed happily at the simple jokes in the *tonadillas* and *sainetes*. Often they went to the Manolería, welcome guests in the taverns of the *majos*.

On the threshold of age he felt a new youth. Before, everything had seemed to pall, the good with the bad, always the same, familiar as the taste of food. Now the world had become rich and new for him. It was a second youth, more versed in desire and its enjoyment.

And yet he was aware that all the time the evil spirits lay in wait and that this great happiness must produce some great calamity. Had he not seen the noonday ghost? But to have Cayetana in his life was a joy without measure, and he was ready to pay for it.

His happiness communicated itself to his work; he painted a great deal and with enjoyment. His hand was light, his eye quick, keen, exact.

He received a letter from Don Gaspar Jovellanos with a politely pressing invitation "to tea." For the liberals preferred tea to the aristocratic, reactionary chocolate; had not this preference for tea and opposition to an arbitrary increase in its price brought revolution and then freedom to England's American colonies?

Goya was not fond of the insipid drink nor of the doctrinaire, fiery Jovellanos. But it would scarcely do to say no when a man like Jovellanos issued so civil and so stern an invitation.

It was only a small company which had gathered at Jovellanos's. Don Miguel Bermúdez was there, and Count Cabarrús, the great financier, and of course the Abbé Don Diego. The only guest whom Goya did not know was the lawyer and writer José Quintana. But Quintana's verses were familiar to him, as they were to everyone; the poet was said to have written them at the age of sixteen. Even today he seemed very young, scarcely more than twenty or twenty-one. Goya, who himself had come late to maturity, mistrusted success so early achieved; but the modest and at the same time lively José Quintana attracted him.

The talk, as Goya had expected, turned to politics. The position of the Príncipe de la Paz was strongly criticized. Granted, the Minister *was* supremely self-confident: Goya happened to have a chance to observe him closely, because just at this time Don Manuel was posing for him. He could see with what complacent nonchalance of mien and gesture Don Manuel was displaying his new importance. But was this vanity injurious to the country? Was not Don Manuel in fact showing a willingness to further the cause of progress? Was he not using his popularity to make useful reforms?

The measures taken by the Príncipe de la Paz were half-hearted, said Jovellanos. The important thing was, and would remain, the struggle against the Inquisition, against the Church, and the Minister gave way before the clergy with the same superstitious fear that the common people showed for the Holy Office. Any serious effort towards reform, he railed, in his blustering, fanatical voice, must have as its very first aim to break the power of the clergy. For the root of all evil was the ignorance of the masses, fostered and preserved by the Church. How could anyone put through measures of hygiene in a country where even a Duchess of Medina-Coeli had administered to her sick son the powdered finger of Saint Ignatius, half of it in a soup and half in an enema? But the Inquisition proceeded against anyone daring to question the miraculous efficacy of such measures.

All of a sudden, however, he interrupted himself and said, smiling, "Forgive me, I am a bad host. I set the bitter draught of my discontent before you instead of wine and something to eat." And he had them bring *hipocrás*, *pajarete*, fruits, pastries, and sweetmeats.

The talk was now of books and pictures. The Abbé called on the young Quintana to read a few of his poems aloud. The latter did not need to be pressed but preferred to read a prose passage written in a rather daring new manner. It was a short biography, he explained to his listeners, corresponding to the small portraits, the so-called "miniatures," which had once been found at the beginning of books and which were coming back into fashion.

And as all were agreeable he read a sketch of the Dominican Bartolomé Carranza, Archbishop of Toledo, the Inquisition's most illustrious martyr.

Even now, three hundred years since
He had died, it was forbidden
Ever in his praise to speak, yet
Everywhere among the common
Folk they spoke of him, remembering
In his praise his holy words and
Holy deeds. Of course they spoke in
Whispers.

— 5 —

Don Bartolomé Carranza had distinguished himself even in his early years as professor of theology, and soon ranked as the best theologian in Spain. Charles the Fifth sent him as his representative to the Council of Trent, where he rendered his country and his Church exceptional services. Charles' successor, Philip the Second, who benefited by his spiritual and political counsel in England and Flanders, made him Archbishop of Toledo and thereby Primate of the Kingdom. Carranza's strict conception of the duties of the priesthood and his unusual benevolence acquired for him all over

Europe the reputation of being the worthiest churchman of his time.

But he was no politician; his lofty state, his fame, the uncompromising severity of his judgments when the duties of the higher clergy were in question, aroused envy and hostility.

His bitterest opponent was Don Fernando Valdés, Archbishop of Seville. Carranza compelled him, indirectly of course, as the result of ecclesiastical arbitration, to pay fifty thousand ducats in war tax to King Philip out of the revenues of his Archbishopric, and Don Fernando Valdés was a man covetous of money. Later on Carranza even snatched away from under his very nose the richest benefice in the kingdom, the Archbishopric of Toledo, with its yearly revenue of from eight to ten million. Don Fernando Valdés waited for an opportunity to bring Carranza low.

This opportunity came when Valdés was appointed Grand Inquisitor. Archbishop Carranza had written a commentary on the Catechism which was much talked of but at the same time often attacked. The learned Dominican Melchor Cano, whom Carranza had offended by some differences of opinion in theological matters, declared that nine passages in the book were open to suspicion of heresy. Further testimony to the same effect came to hand; also information as to suspicious utterances of Carranza. The Grand Inquisitor read the evidence, studied it, found the material sufficient to justify an indictment.

Carranza, warned that an investigation of his book was pending, caused certain eminent theologians to furnish certificates testifying in no uncertain terms to the exemplary piety and orthodoxy of his work, and turned for protection to his pupil King Philip, who was at the time in Flanders. Grand Inquisitor Valdés knew that after the return of the King he would no longer be able to touch Carranza. He decided to strike.

Carranza was on an official journey in Torrelaguna. The Inquisition gave orders that for two days no inhabitant of the place was to leave his house, then it surrounded with a strong armed force the small palace in which the Archbishop lived. The call resounded, "Open to the Holy Office." With tears in his eyes the Inquisitor de Castro knelt by the bed of the Archbishop and showed him the warrant for his arrest, begging his forgiveness. Carranza made the sign of the cross and gave himself up.

And disappeared from the eyes of men as if he had vanished from the earth.

The Grand Inquisitor made a hasty journey to Flanders to make his report to King Philip. Prelates from the rank of bishop upwards did not come under the jurisdiction of the Inquisition, but only that of the Pope. Valdés however had caused the Holy Father to give him plenary powers in particularly dangerous cases to undertake the investigations without first procuring permission from Rome. Such a case, he explained to the King, they now had before them. He submitted the evidence, emphasized that he had already sequestrated the revenues of the Archbishopric of Toledo and that the Inquisition intended, after the costs of the trial had been met, to turn the income over to the Crown. Thereupon Philip agreed that his old counsellor and spiritual teacher Carranza smelled strongly of heresy and sanctioned the proceedings of the Grand Inquisitor.

Carranza was brought to Valladolid. There, in the suburb of San Pedro, he was locked up, with a single attendant, in two lightless, airless rooms.

A lengthy investigation began. Ninety-three witnesses were called, the whole vast archive of the Archbishopric of Toledo was ransacked. Drafts for sermons which the student Carranza had made forty years before were discovered; extracts from heretical books which as an expert at the Council of Trent he had written out in order to refute them; innumerable such suspicious documents.

The plenary powers which the Holy Father had bestowed upon the Inquisition merely authorized Valdés to secure the person of the accused and the evidence. Now Pope Paul demanded that the prisoner and the documents be delivered to him in Rome. The Grand Inquisitor made excuses, the King enjoyed the revenues of the Archbishopric of Toledo. Pope Paul died and was succeeded by Pius IV. The authority which Rome had given had been limited to two years. Pope Pius demanded the delivery of the prisoner and the evidence in the case. The Grand Inquisitor made excuses, the King paid the Pope's nephew a pension out of the revenues of the Archbishopric. Pope Pius extended the plenary powers for two years, then for another year.

Meanwhile the Carranza case had become a European scandal. The Council of Trent saw in the great injustice which was being done Archbishop Carranza an insult to the Church and an attack by the Spanish Inquisition on the immunity of prelates. The Council not only did not put Carranza's commentary on the Index, the very book which the Spanish Inquisition regarded as the chief evidence of his heresy, but found that the work was good Catholic doctrine, worthy of reading and being taken to heart by godly people all over the world.

Furthermore, Pope Pius gave the Council and all the world to know that the Holy See had been humiliated by the obstinacy of the Catholic King. The Inquisition's authority to try the Carranza case would expire once and for all on January first of the following year, and the arrested Archbishop and all the documents were to be handed over to the authorities in Rome. But King Philip protected the Inquisition. He did not want to relinquish the revenues of the Archbishopric and regarded it as a weakening of his prestige if he were now to give in to the Pope. Carranza remained in strict confinement in Valladolid.

The Pope solemnly declared: should the handing over of the Archbishop be postponed further, all those responsible would *ipso facto* come under the "anathema," be divested of their dignities and functions, be regarded as criminals and incapable ever again of being reinstated in office. Carranza was to be delivered without delay to the Papal Nuncio. King Philip did not reply; Carranza remained in his prison in Valladolid.

Finally it was agreed that a papal mission should, together with the Spanish Inquisition, examine the case of Archbishop Carranza on Spanish soil. Rome sent four legates, more exalted than any the Holy See had hitherto sent to any ruler. The first was later Pope Gregory XIII, the second later Pope Urban VII, the third was Cardinal Aldobrandini, brother of the future Pope Clement VIII, the fourth later became Pope Sixtus V. The Grand Inquisitor received the gentlemen with the reverence that was their due, but insisted that the trial should take place within the framework of the Suprema, the highest court of the Inquisition, that is to say, with fifteen Spaniards, which meant that they would be only four among nineteen.

While they were bargaining Pope Pius IV died. On his deathbed he declared that, to appease the insatiable Catholic King, he had in the case of Archbishop Carranza offended against canon law and the will of the Councils and the Cardinals; that nothing weighed on his conscience more than his failure in the Carranza case.

The dead Pope's successor was Pius V, a most difficult man. Very soon Spanish Ambassador Zúñiga complained to his King that unfortunately the Holy Father, having no experience in matters of State and no private interests of any kind, did only what he considered right and nothing else. Indeed, the new Pope declared that the authority of the Grand Inquisitor and his men had expired as from that moment. Grand Inquisitor Valdés was to set the imprisoned Archbishop free without delay so that he could betake himself to Rome to be judged in person by the Pope. The documents in the case were to be transported to Rome inside of three months. All this on penalty of the divine wrath, the displeasure of the Apostles Peter and Paul, and of excommunication.

The old money-mad and revenge-seeking Valdés was ready to take up the fight with the new Pope too, but the Catholic King, involved in difficult affairs of foreign and domestic policy, was afraid of the interdict. Carranza was handed over to the papal legates and travelled to Italy.

Eight years had the Archbishop spent imprisoned in Spain; now he was lodged in Castel Sant' Angelo, in comfort but still in prison. For Pius V, a thorough man, had ordained that the investigation should begin again from the beginning. The whole enormous collection of documents was translated into Italian and Latin. A special court, seventeen prelates of which four were Spaniards, sat every day under the presidency of the Pope. The Catholic King followed the proceedings with the greatest interest and sent fresh material all the time.

The case dragged on. Eight years of Spanish imprisonment were followed by five in Italy. But at last the Holy Father had weighed every pro and con. He and his court found Archbishop Carranza not guilty of heresy. The judgment was drafted with great care and the submission of many arguments, under the supervision of the Pope. The Holy Father did not promulgate the verdict but out of courtesy communicated it first to King Philip.

But hard on the heels of the draft of the judgment which announced and justified the acquittal, the news reached Spain that Pope Pius V was dead. The verdict was never delivered. It disappeared.

Pius V's successor, Gregory XIII, naturally knew of the acquittal, but as one of the four legates whom the Holy See had sent to Spain in connection with the Carranza affair he had become acquainted with the tenacity of the Catholic King. He declared that he would examine the whole matter afresh in person from the beginning.

King Philip sent more material. Then, quite soon, he wrote to the Pope that he was convinced with mind and heart of Carranza's heresy and demanded a speedy sentence. Three weeks later he wrote to the Pope a second time, in his own hand, forcibly, eloquently, demanded that the heretic should be sent to the stake. Any milder punishment would permit Carranza, even after a lapse of time, to be reinstated in his bishopric; and it was intolerable for the King of Spain to know that a heretic was in possession of the highest ecclesiastical honour in the kingdom.

However, before this letter reached the Pope, he had passed judgment on the Archbishop, a diplomatic judgment. Carranza was found guilty of fifteen instances of mild heresy. He was publicly to recant and to be suspended from his archbishopric for five years. During this time he was to live in a monastery in Orvieto with a monthly stipend of a thousand gold crowns. Further, a mild spiritual penance was imposed.

Pope Gregory informed King Philip of the verdict in a personal letter. "We regret," he wrote, "that we have had to condemn this man, pre-eminent as he is in conduct, in scholarship and good works, and that we could not, as we had hoped, acquit him entirely."

Seventeen years Don Bartolomé Carranza, Archbishop of Toledo, whom thousands regarded as the holiest man ever to tread the soil of the Iberian peninsula, had spent in Spanish and Italian prisons. Popes Paul V, Pius IV, and Pius V had died before sentence was passed on him.

After the Archbishop had abjured his errors in the Vatican, he submitted himself to the spiritual penance the Holy Father had laid upon him. It consisted in his having to visit seven Roman churches. As a sign of his respect and sympathy, Pope Gregory placed his own litter at Carranza's disposal for these visits, and horses for escort. But Carranza declined. He went on foot. Tens of thousands of people gathered, many had come from a distance to see him as he passed to pay him homage. His penance became a triumph such as had seldom fallen to the lot even of a Pope.

When Carranza returned from his penitential journey he felt

severe pains and had to take to his bed. After a few days it was recognized that he was beyond help. The Pope sent him general absolution from all his sins and the Apostolic blessing. Carranza bade seven high dignitaries of the Church come to him. In their presence, after he had received absolution and immediately before receiving the Viaticum, he declared solemnly, "I swear by the reckoning which in a short time I shall have to make to the Almighty, and by the King of Kings who comes to us in the Sacrament that I am on the point of receiving, that during the time I was studying theology, and in the years following when I was writing, preaching, disputing, and officiating in Spain, Germany, Italy, and England, it was always my purpose to insure the triumph of the religion of Jesus Christ and to oppose heretics. And I have even, by the Grace of God, converted many to the Catholic Faith. King Philip, long my confessant, was witness to this. I loved him, love him still with all my heart, no son could be more honestly devoted to him. I further protest that I have never fallen into the errors of which I have been declared suspect; my words have been distorted and false meanings have been assigned to them. Nevertheless, as it has been spoken by the Vicar of Christ, I recognize as just the judgment with which my trial ended. In the hour of my death I forgive all those who came forward against me in these trials. I have never borne them ill-will, and I will, if I go thither where through the mercy of the Lord I hope to go, pray for their souls."

An autopsy was ordered on his corpse. The doctors declared that the seventy-three-year-old man had died of a cancerous affection. Nobody believed it. Everyone assumed that this death, which occurred so conveniently for the Catholic King, was to be laid to his door. The proud man, as he himself had written, would never have borne to have Carranza reinstated in his Archbishopric. King and Archbishop could not live together under the same sky, and the King regarded it as his divine right to rid himself of his opponent by whatever means he could.

As he wrote the Pope, the judgment
Seemed to many Spanish clerics
Of experience and wisdom
All too mild. Yet he sincerely
Recognized the Holy Father's
Earnest pains to reach a judgment

Just and pious. And the more so
Since in truth God's hand already
Had applied the just solution
And the evil thus avoided
Which upon the Pope's mild sentence
Might have followed.

It was the story of the Archbishop, saint, and heretic Don Bartolomé Carranza which young Quintana read aloud to Jovellanos and his guests in the form of one of his "miniatures."

They all knew the story, but it seemed new and unfamiliar as Quintana read it. He did not shrink from representing as fact events about which little was known, about which one could at best conjecture. But how strange it was: as he told the story it was so and could not have been otherwise.

Goya, like the others, listened spellbound. The events, as this young man set them forth, had happened not two or three centuries ago, they were contemporary, exciting, outrageous. But precisely on that account, was not what was going on here seditious, and utterly dangerous? And was it not senseless, just now, when life was offering him fulfilment and promise, to be sitting round with these rebels and fanatics? And yet the rash young man attracted him as he recited his story. Goya, with barely controlled indignation, would have gone on listening even though he could well have made himself scarce without giving offence.

When young Quintana ended, an oppressive silence reigned. Finally Jovellanos cleared his throat and said, "Your offences against pure Castilian, my dear Don José, are without number. But there is power in your sentences, and of course you're still very young. Plenty of corners will be rubbed off in time."

The Abbé had risen to his feet. Perhaps of them all he had been the most affected by Quintana's recital. "We're clever, we men of the Inquisition," he said. He had the right to say "We men of the Inquisition," for although his patron the Grand Inquisitor Sierra had fallen into disfavour and was being impeached on a charge of dubious theology, he himself still held the title Secretary to the Holy Office. So now he walked up and down in Don Gaspar's spacious room, picking up an object here and there to examine it, making his little speech as he did so. "We of the Inquisition," he said, "have always been clever. We did not imprison Archbishop Carranza and put him to death: it was the Pope and King Philip. And now, if Grand Inquisitor Lorenzana should finally come to a decision in the case of Olavide, who can say it was he who had the great man arrested? Is it not his simple duty to make an end of a case which has been pending for so long?"

Goya pricked up his ears. He had known Don Pablo Olavide slightly; it had been a shock to him when, years ago, this brave, brilliantly clever man had been arrested and his great establishment on the Sierra Morena endangered. Goya too had heard in recent weeks that at last the Inquisition intended to destroy Olavide himself, but he had shut his ears, not wishing to have his happiness disturbed by rumours. Now, under the spell of Quintana's recital he could not help asking "Will they really. . . ?"

"Certainly they will," replied the Abbé, and his shrewd, merry eyes were no longer in the least merry. "Lorenzana has from the beginning had the ambition to become just as renowned in the fight for doctrinal purity as was Grand Inquisitor Valdés before him. He has already obtained the blessing of the Holy Father on the ruin of Olavide. If Don Manuel persists any longer in his lethargy, if the King doesn't put a spoke in the Grand Inquisitor's wheel, then the capital will witness an auto-da-fé the like of which hasn't been seen for centuries."

Goya distinctly felt that the Abbé's evil prophecies, perhaps even young Quintana's narration, had been directed at him alone, and now Jovellanos turned to him and said, without beating about the bush, "You're working now on a portrait of the Príncipe de la Paz, Don Francisco. At such sittings Don Manuel ought to be very approachable. How would it be if you were to discuss the Olavide case with him?" Although Jovellanos made an effort to speak casually, every word came out with emphasis. There was silence. Everyone waited for Goya's reply.

Uneasily he said, "I doubt if Don Manuel takes me seriously in matters outside of painting. Frankly," he went on with feeble humour, "I don't care much whether I'm taken seriously or not when it's not a matter of my work." The others kept a disapproving silence. But even at the risk of cutting a miserable figure in the eyes of these gentlemen, Goya would not a second time be beguiled into mixing himself in political affairs. "I regret that I must nonetheless say 'no' to you, Don Gaspar," he declared with increasing energy. "The proceedings against Don Pablo Olavide shock me as much as they do you; but I am *not* going to speak to Don Manuel about it. Our friend Don Miguel has surely discussed the miserable business with him, and surely you too, Don Diego"—he turned to the Abbé—"have importuned him with all the arts of skilled persuasion. If you have both failed, you two experienced politicians, what could I hope to achieve, a simple painter from Aragón?"

Don Miguel took up the challenge. "If many great men are glad to see you among them, Francisco, it is not solely for the sake of your portraits. They have specialists around them all day long, economists, scientists, politicians like me. But the artist is more than a specialist, he influences all, knows their inmost being, speaks for them all, speaks for the people as a whole. Don Manuel knows this, and that's why he listens to you. And that's why you ought to speak with him about this infamous and desperate trial of Don Pablo Olavide."

Modestly, yet glowing with zeal, young Quintana put in, "What you've just said, Don Miguel, is something I have often felt myself. Not we poor writers, but you, Don Francisco, speak the language that all understand, the universal idiom. Your pictures reveal more of the nature of man than the faces of men themselves, or the words of writers."

"You do my art great honour, young man," replied Goya. "But, unfortunately, what is being asked of me is that I should *talk* with Don Manuel, wherein I am deprived of my universal idiom. I am a painter, gentlemen," he said, his voice almost impolitely loud. "Can't you understand, I am a painter, and nothing but a painter?"

When he was alone he tried to shake off the painful memory of Jovellanos and his companions. He recapitulated the reasons for his refusal, and good reasons they were. "*Oir, ver y callar:* hear, see, and keep your mouth shut." Of the many good old sayings that was one of the best. But his discomfort persisted.

He had to explain himself to a confidant, justify himself. He told Agustín how Jovellanos and the others had once again expected him to intervene in the King's affairs and how he, of course, had refused. "A man," he concluded with rather forced joviality, "takes two years to learn to talk and sixty to learn to hold his tongue."

Agustín was troubled. He seemed already to have heard of the affair. "*Quien calla, otorga,*" he answered in his rumbling voice. "Silence gives consent." Goya did not reply. Agustín controlled himself, he did not scream, he made an effort to speak quietly. "I'm afraid," he said, "that if you curtain your windows against what goes on outside you'll soon be unable to see what's inside." "Don't talk nonsense," Francisco remonstrated. "Do I paint worse now than I used to?" But he too forced himself to keep calm. "Sometimes your priggish Jovellanos does impress me," he conceded reasonably, "with his obstinacy and his big words. But more often I find him ridiculous.

"When a man lives in a world that
Ought to be, instead of in the
One that is, the man is just a
Simpleton. The only way is
To adjust yourself," he shouted
In his anger. "Well, you do it,
Don Francisco," answered mildly
Agustín. But then Francisco
Spoke, not shouting, "Still there must be
In between those worlds a way that
Shall be found, and I will find it.
Agustín, my friend, have only
Patience."

— 7 —

Goya was working on a light-hearted picture of the pilgrimage to San Isidro. He painted with abandon, with joy. He was alone. Suddenly Francisco had a feeling that someone was in the studio.

Yes, there was someone there, someone who had entered without knocking, a man in the garb of a nuncio, a messenger of the Holy Office. "Jesus Christ be praised," said the man. "Forever and ever, amen," replied Francisco. "Be so kind as to confirm, Don Francisco," the nuncio said very politely, "that I have delivered to you a letter from the Holy Office." He handed him the receipt. Goya signed. The man gave him the letter. Goya took it and crossed himself. "Blessed be the Holy Virgin," said the nuncio. "Thrice blessed," replied Don Francisco, and the nuncio retired.

Goya sat down, the sealed letter unopened in his hand. Recently there had been much talk to the effect that the Inquisition was intending to announce the verdict on Don Pablo Olavide not publicly but in an *auto particular*, in a promulgation intended only for invited guests. To be invited to this was both an honour and a danger. It amounted almost to a warning. Goya was certain that the letter in his hand contained such an invitation. Only now did he feel the full shock which the sudden and noiseless appearance of the messenger had administered to him. He sat stooped in his chair, exhausted, weak at the knees. It was a long time before he opened the letter.

Josefa, when Francisco told her of the invitation, was greatly shocked. So her brother's prophecy was being fulfilled: Francisco's immoral ways had brought him under suspicion of heresy. Probably it was the shameless flaunting of his association with the Duchess rather than his intercourse with the ungodly which had prompted the Inquisition to send this dangerous invitation. The bad thing was that her Francisco really was a heretic. And worst of all, she clung to him as only one human being can cling to another. Even if the Inquisition tortured her she would never say one word against Francho. She was at pains to keep her face still, her proud, reserved Bayeu face. She only pressed her lips a little more tightly together. Then she said, "May the Virgin bless you, Francho."

Even the Duchess, when he told her about the invitation, made a gesture of pained surprise. But at once she regained command of herself. "Now you see, Don Francisco," she said, "what an important man you are."

For Grand Inquisitor Lorenzana had invited the most distinguished men in the kingdom to witness the triumph of the Inquisition: not only Don Miguel, Cabarrús, Jovellanos, but even Don Manuel. Rome had recommended that he not hold an *auto publico* in the case of Olavide lest it provoke the King, but at the same time to give the sentencing of the heretic much publicity. So he had ordered an *auto particular* "with open doors," so that in spite of the public being excluded the whole population of Madrid could participate in the humiliation of the heretic.

One week before the ceremony mounted servants and notaries of the Inquisition rode through the city of Madrid with drums, horns, and trumpets, and a herald gave all people to understand that to the greater glory of God and the Catholic Faith the Holy Office intended to hold an *auto particular* "with open doors" in the Church of San Domingo el Real. All believers were exhorted to attend the sacred spectacle as it was a Divine Service.

On the day before the *auto* the great green cross and the standard of the Holy Office were brought into the church. The Prior of the Dominicans carried the green cross, surrounded by monks with torches, singing the "Miserere." On the richly embroidered standard of purple damask were the arms of the King and those of the Holy Office, cross, sword, and rod. The standard was followed by the coffins of disinterred dead heretics on whom sentence was to be passed, as well as pictures of fugitives. A huge crowd lined the streets and knelt before the standard and the green cross.

Next morning very early the invited guests assembled in the Church of San Domingo el Real: ministers, generals, the Rector of the University, leading writers, all those men of rank who were suspected of being progressive. Failure to act on an invitation to such a ceremony would, even in the case of illness, have amounted to a confession of heresy.

Also invited, in order to gloat over their victory, were the men who had brought Olavide down: Archbishop Despuig of Granada, the Bishop of Osma, Brother Romuald of Freiburg, the men of the Mesta who had lost their free grazing rights because of Olavide's settlements.

All of them, friend and foe, sat together on a large platform; opposite them another platform awaited the gentlemen of the Inquisition. Above their heads hung the famous picture of San Domingo; he lay on the ground, exhausted by mortification of the flesh, and the Holy Virgin in her mercy allowed milk to flow from her breast into his mouth.

In the middle of the church a platform had been set up on which stood the coffins of the dead and the pictures, hung from black-draped crosses, of the fugitive heretics. A second platform awaited the heretics in the flesh.

Meanwhile, outside, the procession of judges and accused drew near. The cavalry regiment of Murcia was in the van, African cavalry brought up the rear of the train, the rest of the Madrid garrison lined the streets. In two long rows marched the officials of the Inquisition, between them the sinners.

At the entrance to the church the clergy of San Domingo received the Grand Inquisitor and his retinue. Immediately behind Lorenzana walked the President of the Holy Office in the capital, Doctor Don José de Quevedo, and the three honorary secretaries, all three grandees of the first rank, then the six officiating secretaries, the Abbé Don Diego among them. As the procession entered the church the guests knelt down.

When they looked up again the platform for the living heretics was also occupied. They, the living heretics, sat facing the platform with the coffins of the dead ones, on a low bench with a black-draped cross at their feet.

There were four of them and they were dressed in the sanbenito, the *zamarra*, the penitent's shift. The sacklike garment, rough and yellow, with the black cross of Saint Andrew on it, hung about them, the rope of broom dangled round their necks, the tall pointed hat, the *coroza*, perched on their heads; their naked feet were thrust into shoes of some rough yellow material; in their hands they carried snuffed-out green candles.

Deeply moved, Goya stared at the penitents in their sanbenitos. Such penitential shifts hung in all the churches, and the memory came to him of that sanbenito in front of which, as a small boy, he had first been told what such a garment of shame signified. It had been an ancient sanbenito, painted with frightening devils casting sinners into Hell; above it was written the name and the crime of the heretic who had worn it a hundred years or more ago. Vividly Francisco remembered the shuddering rapture occasioned in him by the realization that even today the descendants of that heretic had been excluded from the communion of the pure.

Avidly, with the intensity of a man possessed, he searched for the face of Pablo Olavide, for in their sanbenitos and beneath their pointed hats the four heretics looked almost exactly alike; they sat bent forward, with grey, lifeless faces. There seemed to be a woman among them. One could scarcely distinguish her from the men. Francisco had an exact memory for faces. Clearly he saw before him the Pablo Olavide whom he had met years before; he had been a slight, elegant, lively man, with an alert, friendly face. Now it took Francisco a long time to decide which of the four was Olavide; for he no longer had a face; it had been obliterated, its flame of life extinguished.

A secretary stepped into the pulpit and read the oath by which those present committed themselves to strict obedience to the Holy Office and unremitting persecution of all heresy. Everybody replied, "Amen."

Then the Prior of the Dominicans preached a sermon. His text was, "Stand up, O Lord, and give judgment," and he preached briefly and with violence. "The Holy Tribunal" he announced, "and this platform with the sinners, who are destined to suffer, are an impressive picture of what we shall one day all experience, with shudders, at the Last Judgment. But, ask the doubters, have you not other enemies, O Lord, besides Jews, Mohammedans, and heretics? Do not countless others offend daily against your Holiness by other sins and transgressions? Certainly, God replies, but these are venial offences, which I forgive. Irreconcilable abhorrence I have only for the Jews, Mohammedans, and heretics, for they befoul my name and my honour. That is what David meant when he cried to the Lord: 'Wake up out of the mildness in which over-great mercy lulls Thee. Stand up, O Lord, and give judgment in Thy affairs. Strike down with the fury of Thy anger the heathen and the unbelievers!' And the Holy Office is acting according to these words today."

Then the sentences were pronounced on the four heretics. It appeared that Pablo Olavide had been lumped together with persons lacking great name or rank, presumably in order to show that before the tribunal of the Inquisition the high and the lowly were the same.

First to be called up was José Ortiz, a cook, formerly in the Seminary of Palencia. He had expressed doubts as to the miraculous powers of the image of Our Lady of the Pillar. Further, he had declared that the worst that could happen to him after his death was that he might be eaten by dogs. The remark about the dogs was to be regarded as negligible heresy, since the corpses of martyrs too had been preyed upon by dogs, birds of prey, even by swine.

The other utterance was pronounced to be a monstrous disavowal of the true dogma. The man was sentenced to be led through the streets in public procession and to receive two hundred strokes of the lash; then he was to be handed over to the secular arm to serve a term of five years at the galleys.

After him was called up the book-seller Constancia Rodríguez. Seventeen books which were on the Index, three in false bindings with innocuous titles, had been found in her stock. The woman was condemned, apart from the usual "subsidiary" punishments such as exile, confiscation of property, and so on, to the punishment known as the *vergüenza*, that is, she was to be led through the streets naked to the waist while a herald proclaimed her crime and its punishment.

The licentiate Manuel Sánchez Velazco had, in the precincts of the Church of San Cayetano made blasphemous remarks such as that the saint could not help him, and similar utterances. He escaped with a mild sentence. He was banished from Madrid for life and deprived of the right to hold positions of honour or to follow reputable professions.

The judgments were read slowly, with pedantic enumeration of proofs and principles. The guests listened, at once bored and tense, waiting for Olavide to be sentenced. But they could not escape an uncomfortable sympathy for the wretched figures in their grotesque sanbenitos, whose lives had been ruined forever at one blow by a careless word; nor could they help being afraid of this tribunal, which with a million ears listened for every rash utterance and had the power to destroy anyone it pitched on.

At last Pablo Olavide was summoned; and, moreover, with all his titles—former auditor of the vice-regency of Peru, former Governor of Seville, former Governor General of the Nuevas Poblaciones, former Commander of the Order of Santiago, former Knight of the Cross of Saint Andrew.

It was very still in the crowded church as the little man, grotesquely heightened by his heretic's cap, was led forward. He attempted to walk, but the priest on his right and the warden on his left had to support him and pull him. One could hear his feet in the absurd yellow cloth shoes shuffling along the stone floor.

As he obviously could not hold himself upright, he was told to sit down. There he crouched. His body hung limp over the low rail which fenced off the platform of the accused, the high pointed cap thrust grotesquely forward, and round about sat the First Minister and the Rector of the University and many men of rank and scholars and writers, who were his friends, and also the miserable wretches his enemies, and all were witness to his disgrace.

The judgment was explicit, carefully weighed, buttressed with a good deal of theology. The accused had admitted to having made careless remarks but had nonetheless insisted that he had never abandoned the true Catholic Faith and had never committed the sin of heresy. But the Holy Office had examined the books and writings of the accused, they had heard seventy-two witnesses, and the guilt of Pablo Olavide had been proved. He had declared he did not believe in miracles. Had disputed the doctrine that non-Catholics were doomed to Hell. Had expressed the opinion that more than one of the Cæsars of heathen Rome had been preferable to some of the Christian princes. Had accused certain scholars and Fathers of the Church of hindering the progress of the human spirit. Had expressed doubts as to whether prayers would avert a bad harvest. These were more than careless talk, they amounted to heresy. Furthermore, Olavide had been in possession of many forbidden books; yes, he had even searched out Voltaire, the herald of Antichrist in Switzerland, shown him respect and friendship; and among his papers had been found letters which this arch heretic had written to him. Further, the accused had declared in front of witnesses that the ringing of bells in a thunderstorm was useless. Had ordered, during a plague, that the corpses should not be buried in the churches but far away from the villages in insufficiently hallowed ground. In short, Pablo Olavide stood clearly convicted of heresy in a hundred and sixty-six instances.

The enumeration of these hundred and sixty-six instances lasted more than two hours. At the end of the second hour Olavide fell over to one side, and everyone realized that he had fainted. He was sprinkled with water, and when, after a few moments, he regained consciousness the recital went on.

At last it came to an end. "For these reasons," ran the judgment, "we declare him to be a convicted heretic, an unsound member of the Christian communion, and we sentence him to forswear his heresy and to make his peace with the Church." As penalty he was to spend eight years in the Capuchin monastery of Gerona. Added to this were the usual incidental punishments. His property would be confiscated. He was to keep away from Madrid and all other royal residences, from the Kingdoms of Peru and Andalucía, as well as from the settlements on the Sierra Morena. He could neither bear title nor hold office. Forbidden to him were the professions of doctor, apothecary, teacher, advocate, tax-collector. He could ride no horse, wear no jewellery, no clothes of fine silk or wool but only those of course wool or other rough material. On his leaving the monastery of Gerona, his sanbenito was to be hung in the Church of the Nuevas Poblaciones, with a list of his heresies, so that all the world might know them. His descendants were to be subject to these subsidiary penalties to the fifth generation.

There were many candles burning, the air in the church was bad, cold and stuffy at the same time. The priests in their old-fashioned stoles, cowls, and robes, the great men in their gala uniforms, sat still, tired and strained, most of them breathing heavily, and listened.

The Abbé, as one of the secretaries of the Holy Tribunal in Madrid, sat among the Inquisitional judges. He was a friend of Grand Inquisitor Sierra, whom Lorenzana had deposed and impeached, and Lorenzana naturally knew that the fallen Grand Inquisitor had entrusted him with the drawing up of a memorandum on the methods by which the procedures of the Inquisition might be adapted to the spirit of the times. So the Abbé was well aware that he himself might easily have been sitting there in a shift on the bench with Olavide. If Lorenzana had for the moment not dared to touch him, it could be only because he was Don Manuel's official librarian and intimate friend. But he certainly was on the list of those who had been picked out to share the fate of the man down there, and after this auto-da-fé he could expect to be arrested any day. He should have got away long ago, should long ago have put the Pyrénées between himself and the Inquisition. The reason for his not doing so had a name: Doña Lucía. He could not leave Spain before he had completed her political education; he could not forgo the sight of her.

Don Manuel sat in the first row of dignitaries. He had an urgent desire to get up and leave the church with resounding tread. His friends were right; he should never have permitted this ignominious spectacle. But he had underestimated Lorenzana's impudence, and once the latter had announced the auto-da-fé it had been too late. To have forbidden an auto-da-fé that had been announced, such an outrage would have caused a disturbance which would have brought about his certain downfall. But it was a scandal all the same that this Lorenzana, who was enthroned opposite him in all the splendour of his God-given judicial dignity, was allowed to trample in this way on a man like Olavide, whose little finger was worth more than the whole of Lorenzana's swelled head. On the other hand, of course, Pepa was right; what was sitting opposite in ostentatious triumph was not Señor Francisco Lorenzana: it was Rome and the Altar, it was the Church itself. From the moment that he rightfully assumed the robe of the Grand Inquisitor, from that moment even as detestable a man as Lorenzana became the embodiment of divine justice and it was not safe to proceed against him. Nevertheless, Don Manuel assured himself, his friends should not feel he had let them down. He would not permit Lorenzana to go beyond this miserable performance; he would not suffer him to persecute Olavide further, unto death.

Francisco Goya looked at the criminal with fervid interest. What had happened down there could happen to all of us. It was the evil spirits who lay in wait everywhere who had forced the shift and the heretic's hat on the unfortunate Pablo Olavide and who were mocking him in the shape of the Grand Inquisitor and his associates. "*Trágala, perro!* Swallow it, dog!" And Goya sat and looked and took in every smallest detail of what was happening in the Church of San Domingo el Real. At the same time he lived anew events of his early youth. He had in those days in his native Saragossa witnessed an auto-da-fé more solemn, dreadful, and grotesque than this. It had been held inside and in front of the Cathedral of the Virgen del Pilar, and then they had burned the heretics at the Puerta del Portillo. Almost more clearly now than when it had happened, Goya saw those judges and criminals and witnesses of Saragossa, he smelled the burning flesh, the heretics of that time and the prisoners of today became one and the same.

On his knees now, facing the black-draped cross, one hand on the open Bible, Olavide retracted. The priest pronounced the words, and Olavide repeated after him that he forswore all heresy, particularly heresies of the kind he himself had perpetrated, in thought, word, and deed. The priest intoned, and he repeated, that he swore in the name of God and the Blessed Virgin to accept with patience and humility all the punishments imposed upon him and to submit to them to the best of his powers. Should he fail to do so, or commit a further offence, he would brand himself as an impenitent and persistent heretic who would without further trial be doomed to the severities of canon law and to the stake.

Faintly through the church's open
Door there came the voices of the
Mighty crowds outside; within it,
Though so full of human beings,
There was stillness, such a stillness
That one started when a halberd
Thudded though but lightly on the
Floor. And yet despite the stillness
Only what the priest said could be
Heard; of his, of Olavide's,
Voice there came not even a single
Sound; one only saw and noted
In the grey and light-quenched face the
Lips move painfully and close and
Open. And therewith the sacred
Ceremony ended. Clear and
Loud without the order sounded
And the tread of marching soldiers.
So as they had come, they went, in
Long procession, first the judges,
Then the sinners, left the sacred
Church of San Domingo.

Goya felt urged to communicate what he had experienced in the Church of San Domingo. Agustín did not ask about it, but he was obviously waiting for Francisco to tell.

Yet Goya was silent. He could not find the right words. The experience had been too complex. He had seen more than the misery of Olavide and the fanatic brutality of his judges. He had seen the demons who flew, crept, and cowered about judges, heretics, guests, those evil spirits who always surround one; he had seen their ghoulish glee. He himself, and that was something his good tea-drinking Agustín would never understand, he himself, for all the pity, hatred, and disgust which the grotesquely dreadful spectacle had inspired in him, had shared the exultation of the demons. More than that, the childishly greedy, shuddering pleasure had reawakened in him what he had felt as a boy at the sight of the condemned and burning heretics. But this confusion, this tangle of past and present sights and emotions, could not be uttered in words.

It could be painted.

He painted. Thrust all else from him and painted. Put off the sittings which the Príncipe de la Paz had granted him. Kept away from Cayetana. Admitted no one to the studio. Even asked Agustín not to take as much as a glance at his painting; when it was ready, he should be the first to see it.

He put on his most expensive clothes to work in; sometimes even, despite the discomfort, his *majo* costume.

He painted quickly yet with all the nervous energy he had. Painted even at night, when he wore a low, cylinder-shaped hat with a metal shield in front, to which were fastened candles to give him ample light at any time.

He felt that he had achieved new mastery of eye and colour. He was joyfully excited. Exultantly, modestly, he wrote to his dear friend Martín that he was working at the moment on some little pictures, entirely for his own enjoyment; he was following his own heart, his own eye and notions, in a way impossible with commissioned pictures; he was giving free rein to his imagination and painting the world as he saw it. "It's going to be magnificent," he wrote, "and I will exhibit the pictures here first for my friends, then in the Academy, and I wish only, Martín of my soul, that you may come quickly to see them." He made a big cross on the letter, lest the evil spirits should intervene at the last minute to set everything at nought because of his presumptuous self-confidence.

And then the day came when he said to Agustín with almost grim satisfaction, "There, they're finished. Now you can look at them, and if you want to, you can even say what you think about them."

There the pictures were.

One represents a shabby country bullfight. There is the bullring with bullfighter, horses, onlookers, and a few inconsiderable houses behind. The bull itself is bleeding and sweating, a poor, cowardly bull pressing itself against the side of the ring; it makes water, it does not want to fight any more, only to die. And the audience is furious at the cowardice of the bull which is not affording them the spectacle they have a right to expect, which will not go out into the arena and into the sun again but wants abjectly to stand in the shade and perish. The bull does not take up much room; it is not the bull that Francisco was interested to depict, but its fate; and the others, the fighter, audience, and horses, were just as much involved in it as the bull itself.

The second picture shows a crowd of lunatics in their asylum. It is a big room like a cellar, all of stone with a vaulted ceiling. The light falls through the arches and the barred window. Here a great many insane are shut up together, each one hopelessly alone. And each one is acting according to his mania. In the middle a powerful, naked young man is haranguing with wild, threatening gestures a nonexistent opponent, pressing him hard. Others are there, also half-naked, decked with crowns, bull's horns, bright-coloured feathers worn as Indians wear them round the head. They squat, stand, lie, in tangled heaps, under the eternal stone vault. But there is plenty of clear light around them.

The third picture is of a Good Friday procession. Though not an enormous crowd is visible, one gets a strong visual sense of the whole surging mass of flags, crosses, participants, onlookers, penitents. A heavy platform sways along in front of houses draped in black, borne by powerful, sweating men, and on it is a huge image of the Virgin with a halo. Behind it, in the distance, a similar platform with Saint Joseph: farther back still, a third, and on it a gigantic Christ Crucified. Flags and crosses are in the van of the procession. But clearly depicted are the penitents, the *disciplinantes*, some white and half-naked, with the peaked white penitential hat, others in black garb, with black devil-masks, all of them leaping fanatically, swinging their many-tailed whips.

In the auto-da-fé in which Francisco had participated as a nine-year-old child, in Saragossa, he had seen and heard a priest, Padre Arévalo, condemned for having whipped his confessants in the nude, and been whipped by them in turn, on the parts of their bodies which had offended. The sentence passed on the Padre had been lenient but lengthy, with extensive argument, and a description of what the Padre had imposed on himself and his confessants, going into every detail of the forbidden penance, had been read aloud. For decades Goya had not thought of it. But in the Church of San Domingo he had once more clearly felt the furtive, compelling, greedy interest with which he had listened to the reading of that judgment. There had risen in him too the memory of all the flagellants he had seen since then in the procession of those strange penitents who inflict pain upon themselves to ward off pain in the future. They chastise themselves passionately. Their whips sport the colours of their loved one, and if a penitent sees his mistress in the crowd he tries to sprinkle her with his blood. This is homage and a labour of love not only for the Blessed Virgin but for the beloved as well. So now he had painted them, the penitents. They march in the forefront of his picture, they dance naked, with bent, muscular backs, wearing white loin cloths and pointed white caps. The light beats harshly down on them. But from the Blessed Virgin it streams forth mild and gentle.

A quite different sort of procession is depicted in the fourth picture, "The Burial of the Sardine," the wild rite which brings the carnival to an end, the last festival before the long, hard period of fasting. The crowd is packed thick, on pleasure bent; there is a great banner with a diabolical moon on it, a couple of youths are carrying fierce, naïvely horrifying masks, two girls, looking like men dressed up, dance a lumbering dance with a third masked man. It is a strained, demoniac gaiety which emanates from the picture, a fanatical abandon. One feels that hard upon it is coming the time of sackcloth and ashes.

The fifth and last picture represents an auto-da-fé. It takes place not in San Domingo but in a well-lighted church with high airy vaults and arches. In front, on his elevated platform, sits the heretic in his shift, his pointed hat awry and sticking up grotesquely into the air. The man is quite collapsed, a bundle of misery and shame; his elevation makes his wretchedness doubly wretched. Separated from him and much lower down sit three other accused; like him, they have their hands bound; like him, they wear the penitential shift and the pointed hat; one of them has collapsed, the others still manage to hold themselves upright. In the background, before the enthroned tribunal, a secretary reads the verdict. Dignitaries sit round about, spiritual and temporal, in wigs and skullcaps. There they sit, rather detached, portly, pious, respectable, inscrutable, and in their midst the man they have caught, the heretic whose sentence they are pronouncing.

In front of these pictures Agustín now stood. Stood and looked; drank the pictures in; was startled, confounded.

It was a joyful shock. This was a kind of painting different from what one had seen till now. It was another Francisco who had painted them, and yet the same. The subjects of these pictures were complex events involving many people, yet nothing was superfluous. It was a carefully measured abundance. Whatever did not subordinate itself to the whole was omitted. The individual man, the individual object, was nothing but a contributory part of the whole. And even stranger: all five pictures, Agustín fully realized, all five pictures, diverse though their contents were, belonged together. The dying bull, the crazy carnival procession, the flagellants, the madhouse, the Inquisition—these were a unity, were Spain. The whole ferocity of it was there, the horror; and the dullness and darkness that are present even in Spanish happiness. And yet, despite all that—and only one man could paint it, only his friend Francisco—a lightness lay over it all, something rhythmic; the frightening impact of the action was mitigated by the tender clarity of the sky, the floating, delicately shaded light. And everything that Francisco had been unable to put in words for Agustín the latter now perceived from the pictures; particularly that to this extraordinary Francho even the wicked demons were welcome. For over the sombreness of what Francisco had painted shone his lust to live, to see, to paint, his immense joy of life, whatever it might be like.

Were these paintings, then, seditious?
Were they hostile to the ruling
Powers? Did they rise against the
Throne and Altar? Not so far as
Eye could see or lips express in
Words. And yet these little pictures
Were disturbing. They disturbed one
More than words howe'er disloyal.
There, that bull that watered in his
Dying, and that wild, forbidding
Carnival, did they not cause the
Heart to throb more hotly and the

Bitter gall to rise? Just so the
Judgment on the heretics.

"Well,
What have you to say?" asked Goya.
"Nothing," answered Agustín, "for
There is nothing, nothing one can
Say at all." Across his features,
Bony, haggard, gloomy, spread a
Grin, and his whole face was beaming.

9

Josefa came and looked at the pictures, and she shrank into a corner. The man she loved was uncanny to her.

Jovellanos came with the young poet Quintana. Jovellanos said, "You are one of us, Don Francisco. I had all but done you an injustice." Young Quintana exulted. "The universal idiom. Everyone understands your pictures, from the muleteer down to the First Minister."

Don Miguel, Lucía, Don Diego came to look at the pictures. It was absurd to try to measure such painting by the standards of Mengs and Bayeu. "I'm afraid we must rearrange our ideas, Don Miguel," said the Abbé.

But next morning Don Miguel came to Goya again. Francisco's pictures had not allowed him to sleep. They disquieted Bermúdez the connoisseur. And, moreover, would others not smell out the disguised indignation in the pictures, the enemies, Grand Inquisitor Lorenzana, for example? They wouldn't trouble about the artistic value of the pictures. They would merely feel that these manifestations were disturbing, seditious, heretical.

This was what Miguel now wished to make clear to his friend. With these pictures, he explained, Francisco had adequately proved his political courage and good will in the right direction. To do more, to exhibit the pictures, would be an act of madness. For a man who had been invited by the Inquisition to witness the auto-da-fé in the Church of San Domingo to exhibit pictures like these would constitute a challenge the Holy Office would not tolerate.

Goya, in chuckling surprise, regarded the pictures. "I can't see anything in them," he said, "which might prompt the Holy Office to proceed against me. My worthy brother-in-law finally impressed on me the rules of the Pacheco. I've never painted the nude. I've never painted the feet of Our Lady. There's nothing in any of my paintings that goes against the interdicts of the Inquisition." He let his eye stray once more over the pictures. "I can't find anything objectionable in them," he repeated and shook his head emphatically.

Miguel sighed over Francisco's naïve, peasantlike cunning. "One can't actually put one's finger on anything seditious," he explained patiently, "but the smell of it in your pictures is unmistakable." Francisco simply didn't understand what Miguel wanted. Obviously nothing was ever right as far as he was concerned. First he was too much just the artist, now too much the politician. What in the world had these pictures to do with politics? Hadn't plenty of others before him painted tribunals of the Inquisition? "But not now!" cried Miguel. "Not like this!"

Goya shrugged his shoulders. "I can't imagine," he declared, "that these pictures could get me into trouble. I *had* to paint them. They're what's in me to do, and I don't want to hide them, I want to show them. I'm going to exhibit them." As he perceived the anxiety and distress on his friend's usually severe features he added warmly, "You have so often exposed yourself to danger. It really is very good of you to want to keep me from doing something rash. But," he concluded firmly, "don't go talking your tongue sore. I'm going to exhibit them." Miguel gave up. "I'll see to it," he said in worried tones, "that at least Don Manuel comes here and declares himself for the pictures. Perhaps the Grand Inquisitor may take that as a warning to keep off."

Don Manuel soon came. He was accompanied by Pepa. It appeared that Pepa had been alarmed for Francisco when he was invited to the auto-da-fé. "I always told you, Don Francisco," she declared, "your views smell of heresy. If Don Manuel sometimes isn't quite so Catholic as I'd like him to be, at least he has an excuse; he is a statesman; he must protect certain rights of the Crown. But you, Francho, are only a painter." "Don't let her frighten you,

Don Francisco," Manuel consoled him gaily. "I'll look after you. I've let the Holy Office go through its big performance once, I'm not going to do it a second time. And now show us the pictures. Miguel has told me so much about them."

They looked at the pictures. "Magnificent!" said Manuel. "Actually you ought to be grateful to me, Don Francisco, for having allowed this auto-da-fé to take place. Otherwise you'd never have painted these pictures." Pepa examined the pictures a long time in silence. Then, rather haltingly, in her full, lazy voice, she said, "You've really done it marvellously, Francho—I must say I don't understand why the bull's so small and the *torero* so big, but you'll have your reasons for it. You're conceited, Francho. One shouldn't praise you too much, but I believe you really are a great painter." And she looked full at him, shamelessly, with her green eyes.

Don Manuel didn't much care for this. "We must go," he said. "Send me the pictures please, Don Francisco. I'll buy them."

Goya was agreeably surprised that the pictures he had painted purely for fun should actually bring him in money, and he could ask a steep price of Don Manuel. The only thing was that he had not painted the pictures for him, and certainly not for Pepa—he didn't like to think of them being in the hands of people with so little appreciation of them. It was rash and ill advised to annoy the Príncipe de la Paz, but nonetheless: "I'm very sorry, Don Manuel," he said, "I can't let you have the pictures. They're already promised to someone else." "Now, now," said Manuel ungraciously, "you'll be able to let us have at least two of them all the same, one for Señora Tudo, one for me." He spoke imperiously, so that a refusal was impossible.

All Goya's friends had now seen the pictures with the exception of Cayetana. He waited. His passion broke over him in a great wave, he was filled with a black rage.

At last she came, but she was not alone. She came escorted by Doctor Peral, the physician.

She said, "I've missed you, Francho." They looked at each other ardently, without shame, joyfully. It was as if they met again after an eternity.

Then she stood in front of the pictures. Her large metallic eyes beneath the proudly arched brows devoured his work. She looked with the observation, the absorption, of a child. He was bursting with desire and pride. Life had nothing more to offer him. Here he had between four walls, in the smallest possible space, the work that only he could do, and the one woman in the world, the only one for him.

"I'd like to be there myself," she said. He understood at once, was filled with profound joy. That was just what he had felt and tried to make others feel. He had wanted to take part in the bullfight, in the carnival, even in the tribunal of the Inquisition. More than that even; if anyone could look at the madhouse without being seized by a dark desire to be free of everything himself for once, clothes, standards, reason, then he had painted in vain. "I'd like to be there myself." She, Cayetana, had felt it.

They had forgotten Doctor Peral. Now he recalled himself to them by saying in his composed voice, "What you have just said, Duquesita, has more wisdom than all the art experts can produce in their fat volumes." That this fellow could call her *duquesita*, "little duchess," with such impertinent familiarity tore Francisco abruptly from his bliss. How did things stand between them? "What I most admire"—Peral now turned to Francisco—"is that in spite of its gloomy subject matter your painting is so imponderable, so supple, one might almost say gay. Doña Cayetana is perfectly right. As you paint it, Don Francisco, the horrible has something seductive about it." And abruptly he concluded, "Will you sell me one of the pictures, Don Francisco?"

Goya could not help laughing wryly to himself. This Peral appreciated his pictures, one had to admit. He was no blockhead like Pepa. Nevertheless he replied quite gruffly, "My prices are high, Doctor." Peral very politely answered, "I'm not exactly poor, Sir Court Painter." But the Duchess in her good-natured, decisive way commanded, "Let me have two of the pictures, Francisco."

Goya was furious. Smiling with particular graciousness, he said, "Permit me to make you a present of the two pictures, *amiguita de mi alma*." He had to pay off this "barber" for his "*duquesita*" with his own "little friend of my soul." "It's up to you, then, whether you give them away or not." "Thank you," said the Duchess with unruffled good humour.

The art-collector Peral, unmoved by Goya's incivility, delighted that he was to receive one or perhaps even two of the pictures, raved on. "These pictures," he declared with obvious conviction, "are the first creation of a new art, the first pictures of the next century. How one feels oneself drawn to this creature!" he observed in front of the heretic in the "Inquisition." "It is madness, but you're quite right, Doña Cayetana, one wants to be in his place."

He tore himself away, and, still excited, went on, "Your instinct, Don Francisco, is confirmed by the facts of history. There were Judaizantes, Marranos, who could perhaps have escaped, but they stayed within reach of the Inquisition, waiting for it to come and fetch them. They must have been tempted by the thought of sitting there in just such a sanbenito." "You're remarkably conversant with the feelings of Judaizantes," Goya said spitefully. "Take care the Inquisition doesn't mistake you for one yourself." "How can I tell," Doctor Peral asked quietly, "that I really have no Jewish blood in me? Which of us can maintain it with certainty? One thing is certain. The Jews and the Moors have produced the finest doctors. I've learned a great deal from their works. I'm glad I was able to study them abroad." Goya had to concede that it was plucky to utter such words after the fall of Olavide, and his chagrin increased.

Soon after this a consignment of antique silver from the treasures of the Albas was brought to Señora Doña Josefa de Goya y Bayeu, with greetings from the Duchess. Josefa stood bewildered at the profusion of valuables. She was shrewd in material things and the superabundant gift pleased her, yet it was also offensive. Goya explained, "I felt called upon to present the Duchess with two of my pictures. It's natural that she should return the gift. You see," he ended with satisfaction, "if I'd let myself be paid for the pictures I could scarcely have asked more than six thousand reals. What's lying there in front of us would fetch its thirty thousand. I'm always telling you: Generosity pays more than stinginess."

He exhibited the pictures in the Academy. Not without anxiety Goya's friends waited to see what the Inquisition's reaction would be.

He received a communication to the effect that experts from the Holy Office would inspect his pictures; he was told to be present.

At the head of the ecclesiastical gentlemen appeared Archbishop Despuig. Goya was aware that Pepa was on friendly terms with this prelate. He told himself, perhaps she had sent him. To help him, or to ruin him?

The Prince of the Church examined the pictures. "These are

good, pious works," he pronounced. "From this 'Inquisition' there emanates that salutary shock which the Holy Office strives to administer. You ought to give us the picture, my son. You should make a present of it to the Grand Inquisitor." Goya was bewildered and delighted.

Casually he informed Josefa that he had presented the "Trial of the Heretics" to the Holy Office.

She, transfixed by such bravado,
Said, "They'll throw your pictures on the
Bonfire, you yourself into their
Dungeons." Airily he answered
As before, "The Grand Inquisitor
Asked, himself, to have the painting."
And amazed Josefa stood there.
"How you manage it, my Francho,
That I cannot understand," she
Said. "It must be, Francho, that you
Cast some sort of spell upon the
People."

-- 10 --

Since the Abbé had seen Pablo Olavide sitting on the penitential bench he had an actual physical awareness of the danger creeping upon him, nearer hour by hour. He knew Lorenzana hated him as the friend of the deposed Sierra, as the enemy within the gates of the Inquisition. The time that remained to him for flight was running out, but he could not tear himself away from Madrid and Lucía.

Manuel made him large promises of protection, but the Abbé did not rely on them. There was only one way of putting a spoke in Lorenzana's wheel. Don Manuel would even now, precisely now, have to wrest Olavide from the clutches of the Inquisition.

The Abbé and Miguel urged Don Manuel to help Olavide escape. The Minister himself still smarted and burned over the *sarna*, the degradation of the spectacle in the Church of San Domingo, and he felt greatly tempted to snatch Olavide away from these overbearing churchmen. But he was aware of the danger of such an undertaking. He would not venture upon it without the express sanction of the Queen, and this, he thought, would be impossible to obtain. For María Luisa, angry at the continuation of his affair with Pepa, was just at this time making frequent scenes, doing her best to offend him, mocking him for the defeat he had sustained in the case of Olavide. She would be certain to tell him he had made his bed and must lie in it by himself.

He assured his liberal friends that he would not allow Olavide to rot in the monastery of Gerona, but that the abduction of a convicted heretic was a ticklish business and he would need time to win Carlos over to it.

For the time being he shifted his fight against the Inquisition to another ground.

The Spanish currency, more and more unstable since the war, was in need of support, and foreign men of business had declared themselves ready to negotiate a not inconsiderable loan. Unfortunately, however, these courageous financiers were Jews. For hundreds of years the Inquisition had insisted that no Jewish foot should defile the soil of Spain; but the Jewish gentlemen who were willing to sanify the finances of Spain set store by being able to study economic conditions in the country itself. Don Manuel made representations to the Queen, mentioned the size of the loan, two hundred million. María Luisa had no objection to her Minister asking the Grand Inquisitor, with polite emphasis, for the admission of the two gentlemen.

Lorenzana at once returned a decided "No." He was summoned by the King, and a discussion took place in Manuel's presence, during which Don Carlos was less accommodating than usual. All the Grand Inquisitor could achieve was that not more than two Jews would be admitted and that during their entire stay they should be under the surveillance, though unobtrusive, of the Inquisition.

The Jewish gentlemen, a Monsieur Boehmer from Antwerp and a Mynheer Pereira from Amsterdam, caused a sensation in Madrid. All the progressives vied with one another in showing them attentions.

Lorenzana, provoked to the uttermost that during his term of office Jewish breath should poison the air of the capital city, intensified his measures against the liberals. In recent years the Inquisition had winked at the fact that persons of influence were in possession of forbidden books. Now the house-to-house searches increased in number, and with them the records of the Inquisition.

On one occasion when the Abbé came home at an unusual time, he saw coming out of his door a certain López Gil whom he knew to be a spy for the Inquisition. He begged Don Manuel not to allow a second Olavide affair, implored him to warn Lorenzana, or, better still, procure Olavide's escape.

Don Diego's representations made an impression on the Minister. He half agreed. But he remained undecided.

Then the Grand Inquisitor himself came to his assistance. Recently clerical authors had published a whole series of papers exhorting the populace to burn the seditious works of Jovellanos, Cabarrús, Quintana, and thus show these authors conclusively that Spain was a Catholic country. Now a particularly poisonous pamphlet was even saying that it was not to be wondered at that foul and atheistical works were tolerated and admired, since the highest official in the kingdom was himself furnishing an example of unheard of licentiousness with the cooperation of the kingdom's first lady.

When the police submitted the pamphlet to him, Don Manuel was delighted. This time the fellow Lorenzana had gone too far. He brought the scurrilous work to the Queen. María Luisa read it. "Lorenzana ought to be rapped over the knuckles," she said with dangerous calm. "Madame is right, as usual," replied Manuel. She said, "Of course you're pleased that I'm going to put right what you've bungled and spoiled." "Do you mean the case of Olavide, Madame?" Manuel asked innocently; then, "Yes," he went on, "I certainly think Olavide ought to be got away from them." "I'll speak to Carlos," she answered.

María Luisa spoke to Carlos, then Manuel spoke to Miguel, then Miguel to the Abbé, then the Abbé spoke to the Grand Inquisitor.

This interview was conducted in the Latin tongue, and the second person singular used throughout. The Abbé began by saying that he spoke not as a humble servant of the Holy Office to its highest official but as a private individual; though, of course, Don Manuel and the Catholic King were themselves interested in the interview and its outcome. Lorenzana replied that he was glad to hear it. Perhaps Don Diego would inform Don Manuel, and His Majesty Don Carlos, unofficially too, of course, that unfortunately the grounds for suspicion against the former Grand Inquisitor Sierra had multiplied, and that his conviction was unavoidable. "You, O Brother," he said, "as you know the man well, will have anticipated something of the kind." "I know him, and I know you, O Father," replied the Abbé, "and so I foresaw it." The Grand Inquisitor asked, "Are you still working on the memorandum, O Brother, which that man requested of you?" Don Diego's reason told him to say "No," but his rebellious heart did not let him. "I was not ordered," he said in golden Latin, "to interrupt the work." And he went on, "The Almighty bids the moon to wax and wane. The Almighty imbues the Holy Office now with mercy, now with severity. For that reason I am of the humble opinion that one day perhaps my work will be of use after all." "I fear, O Brother," replied Lorenzana, "you are stronger in hope than in purity of doctrine. But deliver your message," he went on imperiously. The Abbé replied, "The Prince of Peace, O Father, wishes me to draw your attention to the fact that the condemned heretic Pablo Olavide has a very delicate constitution. Now should this constitution succumb while it is under the protection of the Inquisition, the Prince of Peace fears that all Europe will bitterly condemn this country and the Catholic King. Therefore the Prince of Peace requests you, *Reverendissime*, to be especially solicitous for the health of this heretic." "You know, my Brother," rejoined the Grand Inquisitor, "that the sum of days which a man may attain to is determined not by the Holy Office but by the Holy Trinity." "True, my Father," answered Don Diego. "But should the Holy Trinity allot so short a span that the heretic passes away while he is yet in the hands of the Holy Office, then, *Reverendissime*, the Catholic King would perceive therein a sign of the divine displeasure. His Majesty would find himself compelled to suggest to the Holy Father the necessity of a change in the conduct of the Holy Office." Lorenzana remained silent for a full half-minute. "What are Don Manuel's orders to the Holy Office?" he asked then, harshly. The Abbé, with careful politeness, answered, "Neither the Prince of Peace nor the Catholic King would dream of intervening in the affairs of the King of Kings, whose legal representative on Spanish soil you are. But these two temporal princes do beg you earnestly to consider that the body of the aforementioned heretic is feeble and in need of healing waters. Would you, my Father, therefore consider whether the heretic could conveniently be sent to a watering place? The Prince of Peace would be glad if you could let him know the result of your deliberations within three days at the most." Lorenzana said, "I thank you for this communication, and I will never forget the consideration which you and your master have shown." Throughout the interview the Abbé had been enjoying to the full the difference between his own polished Latin and the crudity of the Grand Inquisitor's.

Briefly and simply, the Grand Inquisitor informed the First Minister that the Holy Office would send the penitent heretic Pablo Olavide to Caldas de Montbuy, that he might make use of the warm baths there to restore his impaired health.

"Well, Señores?" said Don Manuel proudly to his friends Miguel and Diego. "Did I do it all right?" "What do you imagine comes next?" asked the Abbé. Don Manuel gave a sly smile. "I've thought of a part for you to play there, my dear friend," he replied. "For a long time I've been considering sending a special legate to Paris on a confidential mission connected with the alliance negotiations. I ask you to assume this task, Don Diego. I will give you plenipotentiary powers, which will place at your disposal the services of any of the King's subjects. It will scarcely take you out of your way to look up your friend Olavide at his spa. You oughtn't to find it hard to persuade him to take an extended walk. If he should lose his way and find himself in France, that's his affair."

The Abbé, otherwise never at a loss for a clever reply, went pale and was silent. Ardently he wished to accept Don Manuel's offer that with his own hands he snatch Olavide from Lorenzana and escort him across the Pyrénées to safety. But if he did so he would be forced to remain in France, not for a short time, but forever. For should he venture back into the country after so monstrous a transgression as the abduction of a condemned heretic, no one in Spain, not even the King, could protect him; then the Grand Inquisitor would lay hands on him—and he had seen the fierce hatred in his eyes—send him to the stake to the fanatical rejoicing of the whole country.

"I am very grateful to you, Don Manuel," he said. "May I beg one day in which to consider whether I am the right man for such an adventure?"

He spoke with Lucía, expounded to her that his inclinations and his convictions bade him take on the proposed mission but that he could not bring himself to banish himself forever from Spain and from her presence. Lucía was more thoughtful than usual. "Didn't Olavide, in his day," she encouraged him, "create a new Spain in Paris? You told me about it yourself. Why shouldn't you and Olavide do the same now?" As he was silent she went on, "I used to know Madame Tallien when she lived here and was still Teresa Cabarrús; I can claim to have been a friend of hers. I would dearly love to see her again. I hear she has influence in Paris. Don't you think, Don Diego, I could serve the cause of Spain in Paris?"

Don Diego, the politician, the smooth, witty cynic, blushed like a youth when a girl first says "yes" to him. "You could—? You would—?" was all he could answer. But she asked matter-of-factly, "How long will it be, do you think, before you reach the first stopping place inside France?" The Abbé considered briefly. "Two weeks," he replied. "Yes, in two weeks we should be in Cerbère." "If I should go travelling I shall need a little preparation." Lucía calculated. She looked at him. "Please, before you go on to Paris, put in a week's rest in Cerbère," she said.

The heavily built man forgot all his elegance and wit; he panted like a youth out of pure joy.

"Truly, if it were to happen,
Come to pass that in Cerbère
On the soil of France, in safety
I might be vouchsafed to see the
Pyrénées with you beside me,
At my side, Doña Lucía,
And Don Pablo Olavide
Rescued, safe, beside me also,
Seen with my own eyes, then truly
I might once again be able
To believe in God."

11

Some three weeks later Miguel sought out Goya. "We have reason to be pleased," he reported. "Pablo Olavide is in safety. Don Diego has got him across the frontier."

Wrapped up in himself and his happiness as Goya was, yet the rescue of Olavide moved him. And so almost equally did the flight of the Abbé. He realized that the latter would not soon, perhaps never, be able to return. He remembered how he himself had had to flee, as a young man, after they had found that dead body. As clearly as if it were today, he saw the white coast of Cádiz fading from sight, felt the sharp pang of realizing that he was leaving his Spain behind him—for who knew how long! And yet he had been young then, fleeing from the extremity of danger, the distance lay before him azure and enchanted. But Don Diego was no longer young. He was leaving an existence he loved, going into the unknown. Francisco could not imagine anything more terrible than to have to run away now. To leave Madrid, Saragossa, the Court, the bullring, Josefa and the children, his fame, the *majas*, his house, his carriage, and her, Cayetana—that was not to be thought of, he would never bring himself to do it.

Miguel sat in his favourite posture, one leg over the other, his pale, lightly powdered, clear-browed pleasant face very calm. Yet as Goya re-emerged from his memories and scrutinized his friend with his piercing eyes he thought to perceive a faint, hardly perceptible disquiet in his face.

Count Cabarrús, Don Miguel related further with forced casualness, had long been urging that Lucía should visit his daughter, her old friend Madame Tallien, and now that Olavide and the Abbé were also in Paris he had accepted the invitation. In combination with the other two, Lucía might have some political success with her influential friend.

Goya was put off. Then he saw the connection. He was sorry for his friend, who had raised Lucía up, a small, glittering piece of dirt, and fashioned her into one of the first ladies of Madrid. Poor Miguel! And how chivalrously he stepped in to cover up for her!

Moreover, Francisco would not have thought her capable of such a passion. It would have been understandable if she had run after some dandy, the Marqués de San Adrián or some other aristocratic fop. But the Abbé! A plump man, ageing, moneyless, without a title. And what a miserable figure he would cut in Paris, a wanderer, a fugitive official of the Inquisition. Women were incalculable. All of them.

That evening Señor Bermúdez sat alone in his study, sorting notes for his big lexicon of painters. He had hoped this occupation would distract him. But something drove him away from his beloved papers, drove him to stand before the picture of Lucía.

Francisco was right. The shimmering light of the picture, the sense of something deeply equivocal, of subtlety, behind the fine-lady mask, that was the reality. Line and clarity, what were they, when everything was disorder, confusion, within and without? And he, Miguel, had been a fool to think he could reform the untamable *maja*.

He had always overestimated himself. He, a belated, incorrigible humanist, a Don Quixote, had believed in the divine power of reason, in the mission of intellectuals to overcome the stupidity of the masses. What insane arrogance! Reason would always be ineffective, doomed to live out in the cold, lean and lonely.

He remembered an evening spent with Olavide. The latter had raved about how he would drive the wild beasts from the Sierra Morena and make the desert into cultivated land. For two or three years it had looked as if the experiment would succeed, but then he had had to pay with his own destruction, and now the land was as much a waste as before. It was just the same with him, Miguel. Never would wisdom succeed in exorcising what was rude, ugly, and violent in man. Reason would never be able to turn barbarism into civilization.

He had first been conscious of his miserable failure when he had seen Olavide sitting in his sanbenito in the Church of San Domingo. Success is only for a short moment. Then men relapse and once more become the animals they are. For two years in France reason had dragged the masses up into the light, and then unbridled savagery had triumphed and night had fallen deeper than before.

Brightness, clarity and hope there
Were in art alone—not even
There indeed; the Mengs and Bayeus
Were all thin and artificial
And their pictures were not right, their
Line not true, for human beings
Are not like that, all within them
Being dark, opaque and sightless,
Dull.

Don Miguel sat there lax and
Fear seized on him at the strangeness
Of his nearest, of Lucía,
Of his friend Francisco Goya:
So much of the unknown was in them,
Dark and heavy, blurred and hostile.
So he sat, still staring at the
Picture of Lucía as his
Friend had painted it for him and
Cold he felt, and lonely.

12

When Grand Inquisitor Lorenzana considered the brazen openness with which Manuel Godoy, that scum of the earth, had given orders to have the heretic put where he might the more conveniently be carried off abroad, especially when he recalled the Latin conversation he had been forced to have with that renegade, the Abbé, the ageing man was consumed with a white heat of anger. Not since its inception had the Holy Office suffered such provocation.

Lorenzana's closest friends and advisers, Archbishop Despuig of Granada and the Bishop of Osma, implored him to take stern measures. If Don Manuel's monstrous transgression were to go unpunished the power of the Inquisition would be destroyed forever.

The Grand Inquisitor, they urged, should have the insolent heretic arrested at once and brought before the Holy Tribunal. The whole of Spain would be grateful to him.

There was nothing Lorenzana would rather have done. But he was afraid Doña María Luisa would not permit her bedfellow to be taken from her. To arrest Don Manuel, he was well aware, would mean embarking on a struggle with the Crown such as the Holy Office had never had. Nonetheless he finally declared himself ready to proceed against the First Minister, but only if he were to receive the Holy Father's express approval.

Archbishop Despuig addressed himself to a friend in Rome, Cardinal Vincenti. The latter expounded to the Pope the dangerous decision which faced the Grand Inquisitor. The Pope, Pius VI, was himself under pressure. General Bonaparte had invaded his territories and was threatening to take him prisoner. But the Pope was a man whom threats only made more pugnacious, and it was in such a mood that he advised Lorenzana. He commissioned Cardinal Vincenti to answer the Cardinal-Archbishop Despuig's question point for point, so that the latter could convey the Pope's opinion to the Grand Inquisitor. The sin of the so-called Prince of Peace, so ran the document, which was couched in Latin, stank to Heaven, and it was a disgrace that the most Catholic King should have such a man as his chief adviser. Therefore the Holy Father emphatically approved the action contemplated by the Grand Inquisitor. If the Grand Inquisitor could put a stop to the crimes of Manuel Godoy, he would be ridding not only Spain but the Vicar of Christ of a wicked enemy.

But now it fell out that the courier who was to bring this letter from the Vatican to Seville was attacked by soldiers of General Napoleon Bonaparte in the neighbourhood of Genoa. Bonaparte read the letter. Though no great Latinist, he at once understood the snare the Grand Inquisitor had woven against the Príncipe de la Paz with the help of the Pope. The young French General felt an affinity with the young Spanish Minister who had had just such a fairy-tale rise to fame as himself. Moreover, he was anxious to further the not yet concluded Franco-Spanish alliance. He had a copy made of the Pope's letter, sent the copy to Manuel with cordial greetings, and informed him that he would send the letter itself to the addressee after a lapse of three weeks.

Manuel was delighted at the comradely service General Bonaparte had rendered him. He conferred with Miguel, who exulted inwardly. He had a hatred for the Grand Inquisitor which went beyond political antagonism. It was Lorenzana who had driven the Abbé out of the country, and with him Lucía. Lorenzana had ruined his life. And now the cunning foe had been delivered into his hands.

The documents, he expounded to Don Manuel, proved conclusively that Lorenzana and the two Bishops had misused their Holy Office to prescribe to the Catholic King a policy inimical to Spanish interests. Behind the King's back they had intrigued with a foreign power at war with the Republic friendly to the Spanish Crown. Don Manuel ought to have all three arrested and charged with high treason before the High Court of Castile.

But Don Manuel shrank from such extreme measures. He would have to think it well over, and in the first place he had three weeks' time.

Several days passed, a week. Don Manuel still vacillated. He felt sufficiently secure in the possession of the treasonable letter; he was obviously disinclined to take the offensive himself.

The usually composed Miguel could not curb his ill-humour. Bitterly he complained to his friend Goya. Here was a superb opportunity to get rid of this vicious animal Lorenzana, to make the Spanish Church independent of Rome, to deal a mortal blow to the Inquisition. And everything was foundering on Manuel's lack of decision. Clearly he would be acting against his own advantage if he now failed to rid himself of his arch enemy. But he was simply too sluggish to fight, and, encouraged therein by Pepa, mistook his lazy complacence for the traditional Spanish pride.

With melancholy ferocity Don Miguel poured out to Francisco all the rage and misery that was bottled up inside him. This amiable, good-natured Don Manuel was of a scarcely imaginable obstinacy, soft and tough at once, a smooth, sluggish mass which could not be budged. At the same time he was egregiously vain. Every proposal one made to him had to have a sugar-coating of flattery. His, Miguel's, life was a daily capitulation, an ignominious daily genuflection before conceit and caprice. "How sick I am," he burst out, "of the compromise, the endless detours I have to make in order to get an inch nearer my goal. I have grown old and tired before my time. And if it doesn't come off this time," he ended, "if Manuel doesn't send Lorenzana to the devil, then I give up. I shall give up politics and occupy myself solely with my poetry and pictures."

Never had Goya seen the even-tempered, steadfast Miguel so depressed and broken. He considered how he might help him. Had an idea.

He was working at this time on the last of the portraits which the Príncipe de la Paz had ordered. When Don Manuel posed he was always in a particularly expansive mood. It was likely that Manuel would tell him in his blasé, ironic way of the Grand Inquisitor's plot and how it had failed. Then Goya would make his proposal.

And Manuel did tell him about Lorenzana and the amusing, highly complimentary way in which the latter's proposed attack had come to his notice. He laughed, he behaved as if he took the base intrigue as a joke.

Goya joined in his hilarity. "A man like you," he said, "will know how to repay the Grand Inquisitor Cardinal's bad turn in some witty way."

Manuel stood stiffly in the pose, in gala uniform, resplendent with orders and ribbons, his right hand pointed to an as yet indefinite allegorical representation of his official activities. Throwing back his head, he said, "What do you mean by that, Francisco?" Quietly going on with his work, Goya answered slowly, "The Holy Father is in serious difficulties as a result of General Bonaparte's activities. Shouldn't the Spanish Court send him someone to comfort him? The Grand Inquisitor, for example, and the two Bishops?" For a moment Don Manuel considered, then he abandoned his pose and clapped the painter on the shoulder. "You are a humourist, Francho," he cried. "You have marvellous ideas." And with noisy frankness he burst out, "We're friends, you and I. I knew it from the first moment. We help each other. We belong together. The rest of them are nothing but grandees. At a pinch they can manage to sleep with a woman, but to take a woman and knead her into what one wants her to be, that's something only we can do. That's why we have so much luck. Luck is a female too."

Now Manuel was sure of himself. He went in high feather to Carlos and María Luisa and told them, with the letter to support his story, of the machinations of the cunning priests.

Carlos shook his head. "Lorenzana really shouldn't have done it," he said. "If he wanted to complain about you, Manuel, he ought to have applied to me, not to the Pope. And behind my back! You're quite right. It's improper, it's high treason. He really shouldn't have done it." But there was an evil gleam in Doña María Luisa's eyes and Manuel saw that she was glad of the chance to pay off the Grand Inquisitor for that libellous pamphlet.

"This is what I thought we'd do," said Manuel. "We'll send him and his two Bishops to the Holy Father, who in his extremity is much in need of comfort and advice." The King did not understand at once. But María Luisa smiled. "Excellent," she said, and then, "Did the idea come from you, Manuel," she said, turning to him, "or from your Señor Bermúdez?" "I swear by Our Lady," Manuel replied indignantly "that it did *not* come from Don Miguel."

It was disclosed to Lorenzana and the two Bishops that they were to go to the Holy Father on a mission from the King. As Bonaparte had in mind to declare the Papal States a republic, they were to offer him the Island of Mallorca as a refuge, and whatever he should decide, they should afford him comfort and companionship through the years.

When the Cardinal Lorenzana,
Grand Inquisitor, took leave of
Their most Catholic Majesties to
Journey to his Roman exile,
Said the Queen, María Luisa,
To him, with especial blandness,
"Pray convey unto the Holy
Father my most humble greeting.
And upon your journey thither
Ponder well upon the question
Whether such a man as you are,
Who his King's own wife has slandered
Wantonly, bears not his share of
Guilt for that unbridled spirit
Of revolt that all through Europe
Lifts its head. So God be with you,
Highly Reverend Sir, and favouring
Winds behind.

13

At first the liaison with Cayetana had given Francisco a feeling of contentment, of stability, which he had never had before. But then, and ever more frequently, in the midst of pleasure and fulfilment restlessness overcame him. Although he was convinced that she loved him, her incalculableness gave him no peace. Never could one foretell her reactions. Sometimes things seemed valuable to her which to him were insipid; sometimes she was politely indifferent to things and events which moved him.

He showed her his work. Sometimes, often even, she understood what he was painting more profoundly than anyone else; then sometimes she would turn away indifferently from a picture that he felt certain would move her. If she approved she said so at once, without reservations; if something left her cold, nothing could change it. Sometimes, contrary to his custom, he tried to explain to her why he did something in one way rather than another, but she did not really listen, she was bored; he gave it up.

He gave up painting her too. The whole world, including the Duchess herself, acclaimed his portraits of her, but he himself did not. They furnished, he felt, only a partial truth, and therefore none at all. She kept urging him to paint her as a *maja*, a real *maja*, not a dressed-up one. But he did not see her as one, did not paint her as one.

She was a real *maja* in so far as she was quite open in her liaison with him. She showed herself with him everywhere, at the play, at bullfights, walking in the Prado. In the beginning this had been a source of pride to him, but gradually it began to irk him that his love was made a spectacle for all the world to see; besides, he was afraid of unpleasantness. When he hinted as much to her, she raised her eyebrows higher than ever. She was the Duchess of Alba, no gossip could touch her.

He was invited to all the entertainments given in the palaces of the Duke and the old Marquesa de Villabranca. And not by the slightest gesture did they betray that they were aware of his relationship to Cayetana. To Goya the Duke was a stranger for whom he felt a kind of pitying contempt. And then he would observe how the man's face came to life when there was music. This touched and impressed him; most grandees had nothing to them but their pride.

For the old Marquesa, Goya felt respect and sympathy. She had great understanding of men and women; "*elle est chatoyante*," she had said of Cayetana, and since then he had found out how right she had been. He would gladly have discussed Cayetana further with her, but for all her naturalness and good nature, she was so much a *grande dame* that he did not dare.

Among those who constantly surrounded Cayetana, the one who disturbed him most was Doctor Joaquín Peral. He was annoyed at the beautiful carriage in which the doctor drove about, at the expert assurance with which the man discussed anything in the world, the Duke's music, his, Francisco's, pictures. What irked him above all else was that he who was usually so quick to see through human relationships could not decide what was the exact nature of Cayetana's relationship to her doctor. There was as little to be learned from the polite reserve of the doctor's expression as from the mocking familiarity of Cayetana's. Gradually the mere presence of the doctor became an annoyance to Francisco. Whenever he met Don Joaquín he firmly commanded himself to keep calm, only to make some childishly uncivil remark immediately afterwards, received by others with astonishment, by Peral himself with a placating smile.

As the doctor had been unable to find a worthy habitation for the pictures he had collected abroad, the Duchess had finally placed at his disposal two rooms in her vast Palacio Liria, and she invited their common friends to view Peral's collection.

It was quite a miscellaneous assortment: Flemish and German masters, early, little-known Italians; a Greco, a Mengs, a David, and the Goya which Cayetana had given to her doctor. Yet underlying the diversity a unifying factor was perceptible, the well-defined though arbitrary taste of a connoisseur.

"What I haven't been able to acquire," the doctor complained in the hearing of Cayetana and others, "is a Raphael. Posterity may find that we overestimate Raphael, but I can't help it, I'd willingly exchange any of the pictures hanging here for a Raphael. You seem to disapprove, Don Francisco"—he turned amiably to the latter—

"and I'm sure you're right. But tell us your reasons." "It would be a very complicated matter to expound my reasons to you, Don Joaquín," Francisco answered brusquely, "and it would probably be about as much use as if you were to explain your medical theories to me." Without altering the amiability of his countenance, Doctor Peral turned to the rest of the group and spoke of other matters.

Cayetana too continued to smile, but she had no intention of letting Francisco's churlishness go unpunished. When the customary ball began she had the musicians play a minuet, a dance that was going out of fashion, and she called on Goya to be her partner. The portly Goya was well aware that in his tight-fitting gala attire he would not cut a pretty figure in the dainty, formal minuet, and he had no wish to play the puppet for her amusement. He grumbled. But she gave him one look and he danced. Danced grimly. Went home in a temper.

In the middle of July it was the custom for the Court to go to the castle of San Ildefonso to spend the hot months in the fresh mountain air; as the Queen's first lady-in-waiting Cayetana had to go too, and Francisco dreaded the long, lonely summer in Madrid. But one day she declared, "Don José is too ailing this year to be at Court during the hot weather. I have asked for leave of absence. I want to keep Don José company during the summer at our country seat in Piedrehita. You, Don Francisco, are invited to come with us to Piedrehita. You can paint Don José and Doña María Antonia; perhaps you'll even condescend to paint me. We have time there; you can have sittings from all of us, as many as you like." Francisco beamed. He realized that Cayetana was making a sacrifice for his sake; for in spite of her antipathy to the Queen, she preferred life at Court to the long, tedious months in the country.

Next day, after the levee, Doña María Luisa detained the Duchess of Alba. She cordially hoped, she said, that the sojourn in Piedrehita might benefit Don José's condition. She also welcomed the fact that Doña Cayetana had decided to accompany her spouse. "In that way," she concluded amiably, "the Court and the townspeople will have less opportunity for circulating rumours about one of the first ladies of the kingdom."

The Duchess replied sweetly, "I think you are right, Madame. It is difficult to protect oneself against rumours at this Court. I never cease to be astonished at the number of men with whom gossip links me. There's Count de Teba, there's Don Agustín Lancaster, Count de Fuentes, the Duke of Trastamara, and I could name a dozen more." These were all men who were regarded as paramours of the Queen.

Doña María Luisa, as smoothly as ever, replied, "From time to time, Doña Cayetana, you and I have an urge to thrust ceremony aside and play the *maja*. You can afford to do so because you're young, and not ill-looking, I because by the grace of God I am the Queen. But it's more difficult for me because my youth is over and some men don't like my looks. I have to make good the deficiency by artistry and intelligence. As you know, I have had to replace some of my teeth with ones made of diamonds, to be able to seize and hold"—here she made a small pause and smiled—"when I want to hold."

The Duchess smiled too; but it was the stiff smile displayed by the dressed-up *majas* of the tapestries. What the Italian woman said sounded very much like a threat.

"In Piedrehita," the Duchess said, "we will have but little company. We've invited only the painter Goya to visit us. He never seems to be able to finish my portraits."

"I see," Doña María Luisa answered, "that you are a real art lover and are giving your painter opportunity to study you." Then she added lightly, "Well, see to it, Madame Duchess of Alba, that there's no more gossip about you."

"And is that a royal order
And a warning?" Cayetana
Asked her offhand, though she fixed her
With her eyes. The other mildly
Answered, "Take it for the present
As the advice of a maternal
Friend."

And Cayetana shuddered
Slightly. Then there came into her
Mind the thought of weeks that were to
Come, of weeks spent with Francisco,
And she shook them off like water,
Shook the low, sharp words her Queen had
Uttered.

14

When the Court had taken up its summer residence at San Ildefonso, Doña Josefa Tudo too found that the heat of Madrid was insalubrious. Don Manuel did not hesitate to invite her to San Ildefonso.

She stopped in the village, in the Posada de los Embajadores, and spent the hot months in tolerable boredom with her dueña Conchita. She played cards with her, or she studied French, or she strummed on her guitar. Don Manuel contrived that at certain times she should be admitted to the gardens of the castle. Then she would sit for hours by one of the celebrated fountains, the Font of Fama, Diana's Pool, or the Fountains of the Winds, listen to the splashing of the watery masterpieces, hum one of her romances to herself, and think with idle, comfortable melancholy of her young husband drowned in the ocean or perhaps of her painter Francisco.

In Don Manuel's company she made expeditions into the magnificent mountain forests which surrounded the castle. The paths were kept in good condition for the royal hunt. They rode in the Lozoya valley and the forests of Valsain. She had learned to ride in Madrid.

Sometimes Manuel spoke of Goya and his summer sojourn with the Albas, uttering jesting salacities about the union of the bull Francisco with the small, fragile Cayetana. Pepa listened with passive face, attentively, saying nothing. Don Manuel spoke often of Piedrehita. It was a source of satisfaction to him that the supercilious Duke, who had not been willing to return his "thou," was now to the general amusement so intimately associated with Francisco. And he welcomed the painter's infatuation in so far as it kept him from running after Pepa. On the other hand, he could not understand what a man who might have enjoyed the affections of a Pepa could see in a woman like Cayetana. She was repugnant to him, the fastidious, artificial, affected doll. Once, though he had never told Pepa this, when at the Queen's levee he had jokingly presumed to ask, "And what is our friend Francisco doing today?" she had ignored it as completely as the Duke had on another occasion ignored his "thou."

One day, on a horseback ride to the ruins of the old hunting box of Valsain, he began to make merry again over the fact that Francisco, still in Piedrehita, did not seem to tire of the Duchess. Pepa made no answer to this. But later she unexpectedly referred to the subject. They had dismounted, settled themselves on the ground; the groom had laid out a small collation for them. They were eating. "Actually," she remarked suddenly, "Francisco ought to paint me on a horse."

Don Manuel was in the act of lifting a small piece of game pâté to his mouth. He let his hand fall. Pepa was not exactly a skilled horsewoman, but she looked marvellous in the saddle, everyone would agree; it was more than understandable that she should wish to be painted in her habit. On the other hand, until recently riding had been a privilege of the grandees. Not that it was now precisely forbidden to people who did not belong to the nobility to be painted on horseback; simply that it had never happened, it was, to say the least, unusual. And what would the Queen, what would the whole world, say if the First Minister were to have the young widow Tudo painted sitting on a horse? "Don Francisco," he demurred, "is on holiday in Piedrehita with the Duchess of Alba." Pepa, somewhat surprised, replied, "Perhaps if you really wanted him to, Manuel, Don Francisco might condescend to take his country vacation in San Ildefonso instead." "*Vous avez toujours des idées surprenantes, ma chérie,*" said Don Manuel. But in laboured French she persisted, "*Alors, viendra-t-il?*" "*Naturellement,*" he answered, "*comme vous le désirez.*" "*Muchas gracias,*" said Pepa.

The more Manuel considered her request, the more he enjoyed the prospect of taking the painter away from that arrogant Alba clan. But from what he knew of Francho he was quite capable of evading the summons on some pretext; if he really wanted to have him here he would have to think of some very effective form of invitation.

He begged María Luisa to employ the leisure of San Ildefonso in having her portrait painted for him once again, and by Goya; and then he might have his own portrait done, for her. Doña María

Luisa was tempted by the thought of disturbing the impertinent Duchess's pastoral happiness. It wasn't a bad idea, she said. Manuel could let Goya know that he was to come; she could probably find time to sit for him.

To emphasize the importance of the errand, the Príncipe de la Paz sent his special messenger to Piedrehita.

There Francisco was passing weeks filled with tranquil happiness. Naturally the quiet, elegant presence of the Duke laid some restraint on him and Cayetana. But Don José and the old Marquesa clearly regarded Cayetana as a spoiled, attractive child whose whims they accepted indulgently even when they went very far, and they left the couple alone as much as the latter could wish.

Two or three times a week the Duke made music. The Marquesa listened with admiring attention but obviously only out of love for her son. And Francisco's and Cayetana's taste was only for folk songs and dances, for *tonadillas* and *seguidillas;* the Duke's harmonies were too choice for them. The only one to understand them was Doctor Peral.

Goya painted the old Marquesa, and as he painted he came to know her better. She was still the great lady he had perceived in her from the beginning, always equable, serene, and gracious, but now he saw the faint melancholy on her beautiful, still youthful face. She certainly understood and forgave the conduct of her son's wife, but to Doña María Antonia, widow of the tenth Marquis of Villabranca, dignity was something to be cherished, and sometimes Goya thought he detected in her words a faint trace of concern lest Cayetana's attachment prove deeper and more dangerous than was seemly; her words sounded like a warning to him, and her portrait did not emerge so readily beneath his brush as he had expected.

But finally there it was, and Goya felt that the animated face, fine-boned and vivid, the delicate blue ribbons and the rose which he had given the Marquesa, made all in all a happy picture of it. But she stood before it and said with a smile, "You've made me look old and fretful, Don Francisco. I had no idea I showed it all so plainly." Then she ended more cheerfully, "But it's a wonderful picture, and if you still have any time left for ladies of my age you must paint me again."

Cayetana herself was full of constant gaiety. Goya had been housed in the casino, or *palacete*, a small annex to the main building, which he had to himself. Cayetana visited him there every day. Usually she came just before dark, as it was getting cooler; she would be escorted by her dueña Eufemia, who was passing the summer in sable dignity; sometimes she brought the Negro girl María Luz with her and the page Julio, and almost always she was accompanied by two or three of her cats. She behaved naturally, almost childlishly. Might even bring a guitar with her and demand that Francisco sing the *seguidillas* and *sainetes* they had heard together.

Sometimes the old dueña was made to tell stories about witches. Cayetana was of the opinion that Francisco had a talent for witchcraft and challenged him to take lessons from a celebrated witch. But Doña Eufemia questioned his aptitude, on the ground that his ears were not set close enough to his head. People with exceptionally well-developed lobes to their ears should eschew attempts to practise magic; it had come to pass that pupils of this kind had got stuck in the middle of a transformation and had perished miserably.

On one occasion Cayetana had been visited by her dead maid Brígida. The dead woman had prophesied that her liaison with the Court Painter would last a long time and end only after many misunderstandings, much loving and suffering.

Once again, yielding to her importunity, he tried to paint her. He painted slowly. She grew impatient. "I'm not Hasty Luca," he said crossly. That had been the nickname of Luca Giordano, who had done a great deal of painting for Charles the Second; highly esteemed, highly paid, and a quick worker. But in spite of all his efforts, Francisco was unable to produce a picture of her this time either.

She declared, only half jokingly, "That's because you will not see that of all the ladies of Madrid I'm the only real *maja*."

His failure to paint a portrait of Cayetana was the only shadow over his stay in Piedrehita. All else was light-hearted and serene.

Into this atmosphere of calm and happiness broke the red-stockinged courier with the letter from the Príncipe de la Paz, inviting Goya to San Ildefonso.

Goya felt both proud and dismayed. No doubt the Spanish kings devoted their sojourn in the mountains of Segovia at their summer residence of San Ildefonso entirely to rest and recuperation; the business of government would be pursued less energetically, the intricate ceremonial would be relaxed, Their Majesties would see only grandees of the first rank and intimate friends; to be invited to share their leisure at the castle of San Ildefonso was a distinction indeed. Nevertheless, and for all his pleasure, Goya felt uneasy. These weeks in Piedrehita had been the loveliest of his life, nothing could outweigh them, and what would Cayetana say when she heard he wished to leave?

He showed her the letter. She had not done her enemy the honour of speaking to Goya of her malevolent threats. Nor did she now; she controlled herself. "You will have to justify your refusal with great skill and civility, Francho," she said quietly. "That Italian woman obviously thinks she's hit on a very elegant and clever way of spoiling our summer together. She'll be green with rage when she gets your letter of regret."

Goya looked at her almost stupidly. It had not occurred to him that perhaps the letter had not been written for his sake as a painter, but because Doña María Luisa wanted to play a trick on her enemy, Cayetana. Faintly now he began to suspect the truth, namely that Pepa was at the bottom of the invitation.

Meanwhile Cayetana was tearing up Don Manuel's letter, idly, childishly, with her delicate, tapering, yet plump little fingers. He watched, without being aware of what she did, yet so exactly that the picture of her gestures was imprinted on his mind forever. "I am a Court Painter, and the letter refers to the Queen," he said hesitatingly. "The letter does not come from the Queen, as far as I can see," replied the Duchess. And she concluded, not loudly, yet her childish voice was hard, "Must you come running when Manuel Godoy calls?"

Goya was filled with helpless rage. Did she not understand that he was still not First Painter to the King? That he was dependent on Doña María Luisa's favour? On the other hand, it was on his account alone that she was sitting here in the boredom of Piedrehita, and she would be bitterly offended if he went. "I can postpone my departure for two or three days perhaps," he said lamely, "perhaps for four or five. I can say I have a portrait I must finish." "That is kind of you, Don Francisco," said Cayetana with that icy graciousness which she alone could put into her voice. "Please tell the major-domo when you would like to have the carriage."

There came back to him now all the agony of that night when for her sake he had awaited word of the mortal sickness of his little Elena. "You must understand," he burst out, "I'm not a grandee.

I'm a painter, a quite ordinary painter, dependent on Doña María Luisa's commissions. And," he added grimly, looking her full in the face, "on Don Manuel's." She made no reply, but the faint, infinitely haughty contempt of her expression maddened him more than anything else could have done. "You care nothing for my success," he raged. "You care nothing for my art. All you care about is your own pleasure."

She left the room, without haste, with her small, firm, yet floating step.

He took his leave of the Marquesa, of Don José.

And he forced himself to go and
Take his leave of Cayetana
Also. But was dryly told by
The dueña that Her Highness
Was too busy. Don Francisco
Asked, "When might I hope to see her?"
"All today and all tomorrow
Is Her Highness occupied," said
Doña Eufemia, courteous
But detached.

-- 15 --

In the sixteenth century there had been two great representative types of Spaniard. The one was the knight, the grandee; the other was the *pícaro*, the underprivileged, the wretch who spent his life in a permanent subterranean struggle against all comers, a struggle waged with cunning, treachery, and constant wariness. The people and their poets sang the praises of the knight and hero, but the *pícaro* and the *pícara* they celebrated no less, and they loved them even more; the rabble, the lower classes, unfailingly shrewd, crafty, gay, vital, never at a loss. To the folk the *pícaro* was a Spanish manifestation just as valid as the grandee; they complemented each other, and great poets have immortalized the *pícaros* Guzmán and

Lazarillo, those rascals and ragamuffins, with their poverty, their full-bodied and unscrupulous materialism, their lively, cheerful, earthy good sense, in equal measure with those representatives of chivalry, the Cid and Don Quixote.

By the eighteenth century *pícaro* and *pícara* had become *majo* and *maja*.

Majismo, the customs and ways of life of these people, was as little to be dissociated from the Spain of that time as was the absolute monarchy or the Inquisition.

There were *majos* in all the big cities. But the headquarters of *majismo* would always be Madrid, a certain quarter of Madrid, the Manolería. The *majos* were farriers, locksmiths, weavers, small innkeepers, butchers, or they lived by smuggling, peddling, or gambling. *Majas* might keep winecellars, mend clothes and underlinen; or they were street vendors, fruit pedlars, sellers of flowers and provisions of all kinds. They and their cheapjack wares were a feature of every fair and every pilgrimage. Nor did they shame to extract money from rich men.

The followers of *majismo* clung to the outmoded Spanish costumes. The *majo* wore tight knee-breeches, buckled shoes, the short jacket and the wide scarf, the mighty broad-brimmed hat. Nor was the long mantle, the *capa* ever lacking, nor the *navaja*, the collapsible knife, nor the powerful black cigar. The *maja* wore flat-heeled shoes, a low-cut embroidered bodice, a many-coloured shawl crossed over the bosom; on feast days she decked herself out with lace mantillas and high combs. Frequently she carried a small dagger stuck in the left garter.

The authorities regarded the long mantle with disfavour, and the *majo's* hat with its great brim obscuring the face. The *majos* themselves loved their mantles because the stains and grime of trade could be concealed beneath them, and sometimes other things they might not wish to have seen; they loved the broad-brimmed hat too, for it cast shadows across a face perhaps unwilling to be recognized. "My Madrileños," Carlos the Third complained, "slink through the streets with their faces covered like conspirators, not like the peaceful subjects of a civilized monarch." His First Minister Squillace, whom he had brought with him from Naples, finally forbade the mantle and hat altogether. Then the *majos* rose in revolt and the alien Minister was hounded out of the country. A more astute successor decreed that the hangman should wear the undesirable hat while plying his trade; some people did give up the hat as a result.

Just as they had their own costumes, the *majos* and *majas* had their own customs, their own philosophy, their own language. The *majo* revered the old Spanish traditions and fanatically defended the absolute monarchy and priesthood, but he hated the changing laws and decrees and took no notice of them. He felt it was his privilege to smuggle; it was a point of honour for him to smoke only contraband tobacco. The *majos* considered dignity a virtue; they were taciturn. But when they did speak they used high-sounding, poetic words, and their bragging and colourful boasts were a source of poetry and famous beyond their own borders.

The *majo* was proud. Nobody could push him aside or even look at him askance. He dwelt in a constant state of feud with the backbone of the middle classes, the *petit-maître*, the *petimetre*. To ruin the exquisite suit of some small bourgeois boy, to tousle the careful coiffure of a *petimetra*, were among his chief amusements. The police kept out of their way. Others gave them a wide berth too, for they were quarrelsome, used strong language and even blows, and were quick to reach for their knives.

In the struggle against enlightenment and reason, against the spirit of France, against the Revolution and everything connected with it, the *majo* was the best of allies to monarchy and Church. The *majo* loved the splendour of the royal castles, the colourful parades of grandees, the magnificent processions of the Church; he loved bulls, banners, horses, and daggers, and in his furious national pride regarded with hatred and suspicion the intellectual, the liberal, the *Afrancesado*, who wanted to do away with all these things. In vain did progressive writers and statesmen promise him better dwellings and more plentiful bread and meat. He would gladly go without them, only so they left him his fiestas and his toreros.

For on such occasions the *majo* and the *maja* were the motley and fanatical public. They jostled one another in the patios of the theatres, they were the shock troops of the *Chorizos* and *Polacos*, they made a great disturbance when the *autos sacramentales* were forbidden, the popular religious plays wherein, for example, Christ might descend from the cross, exchange the loin cloth and the crown of thorns for a *majo* costume, and dance a *seguidilla* with the other actors in the passion play. The *majos* were enthusiastic supporters, *apasionados*, of the autos-da-fé, and just as enthusiastic followers, *aficionados*, of the bullfight, outraged whenever a *torero*, a bull, or a heretic made a bad end. They were sticklers for good form.

In the things of the heart the *majo* was fiery, open-handed, broad-minded. He gave his loved one gaily coloured presents, beat her if she did the slightest thing to annoy him, and demanded his presents back if he left her or she left him. The *maja* had no scruple in plundering an infatuated *petimetre* down to the last peso; and a married *maja* liked to keep a wealthy *cortejo*, or perhaps even two. Spanish men eulogized the *maja* as having those qualities they most prized in women: she was said to be proud and inaccessible in public, an angel in Church, a devil in bed. Even foreigners agreed that no other woman in the world could arouse so much desire, afford such satisfaction, as the real *maja*. Louis the Sixteenth's envoy Jean-François de Bourgoing in his famous book on Spain found many words with which to condemn the shameless licentiousness of the *maja* and even more to extol the fascination and allurement that emanated from her.

The *majo* regarded himself as the finest exponent of the spirit of Spain, of *españolismo;* he yielded to no grandee therein. Every true Spaniard must have something of the *majo* in him; *majo* and *maja* were the favourite characters in the *sainetes* and *tonadillas*, the favourite subjects of writers and painters.

> And the Señors and Señoras
> Of the Court, the rule ignoring
> Which forbade the wearing of the
> *Majo* costume and the *maja's*,
> Liked to slip into the dashing
> Garb and weave into their speech the
> Large words which both *majo* and *maja*
> Loved to use. And many grandees,
> Even many a wealthy burgher,
> Liked to play the *majo* and the
> *Maja*, yes, there were among them
> Some who truly were.

— 16 —

At San Ildefonso, Goya was received with the greatest courtesy. He was accommodated not in the *posada* but in the castle itself. Books, sweetmeats, wine stood ready, clearly selected with a knowledge of his tastes. One of the red-stockinged lackeys was detailed as permanent attendant. His apartments consisted of three rooms of which he was at liberty to turn one into a studio.

Manuel sent a request that he should come to the riding school at about six o'clock. It was a strange place for an evening rendezvous. Did Manuel or even once more Doña María Luisa herself wish to be painted on horseback?

At the riding school he found Manuel and Pepa. She greeted him with a beaming smile. "It was a capital idea of Don Manuel's to invite you here," she said. "We've had some wonderful weeks in this glorious mountain country. I hope you have been having a good time too, Francisco." Manuel stood by her, in riding clothes, looking virile, complacent, proprietary.

So Cayetana had been right. They had played a stupid, impudent trick on him. What they had done in destroying the greatest happiness of his life they probably did not know themselves. On the other hand, that might be just why they had done it. It was shocking, and ridiculous too, that a whim of Pepa's, the *pícara*, the discarded whore, could smash his wonderful summer to bits. "I intend, Francho," said the Príncipe de la Paz, "to make great demands on you. First of all, I would like to have you paint Señora Tudo for me. Mounted. Don't you think her habit becomes her wonderfully?" He bowed to Pepa. The groom was already running to fetch the horses.

Dearly would Goya have loved to give Pepa a tremendous box on the ear in proper *majo* style. But he was a *majo* no longer; he was corrupted by success and life at Court. He told himself that now he had come, there was no point in spoiling everything in a fit of rage. On the other hand, of course, he would not dream of painting her, this *jamona,* on horseback. "The eagle belongs in the sky, the sow on the midden." The cheek of it, this dolled-up creature climbing onto a horse and asking to be painted! As a grandee! And by him! "Unfortunately such a task is beyond my powers, Don Manuel," he said politely. "The fact is I'm not a painter of beauties. If I were to paint anything like Señora Tudo on horseback, I'm afraid my picture would fall far short of the reality as you see it, Don Manuel."

Pepa's composed white face wore a little grimace. "I might have known you would spoil my fun, Francho," she said. "You want to spoil all my fun for me." Her broad low forehead was furrowed in a frown. "Please, Don Manuel," she said, "give the commission to Maella or Carnicero."

Manuel appreciated that the proposition looked too risky for the painter. At bottom he was not ill-pleased himself to have escaped in this way from a dangerous situation. "Let us think it over, Señora," he said soothingly. "If a Goya doesn't trust himself to paint you on horseback, how could a Maella or Carnicero be expected to do you justice?"

The Pico de Peñalara looked down on them, a pleasant little breeze blew, but there was a feeling of discord in the beneficent fresh air. "I might as well withdraw," said Francisco. "Nonsense, Francho," replied Manuel. "I've kept myself free for this evening. Pepa will listen to reason, of course. You'll stay with us."

During the meal Pepa sat in silence, composed and lovely. Goya felt a desire to sleep with her; that would be a revenge on the Duchess, on Manuel, on Pepa herself. But he did not wish to show her that she could attract him even now. He too was monosyllabic.

Manuel, on the other hand, was spasmodically cheerful. "I know," he said as if suddenly inspired, "how you must paint Pepa for us: with her guitar." Goya felt that would not be so bad. "The eagle up in the sky, the sow on the midden," Pepa with her expression of rapt stupidity and her guitar.

He threw himself with enthusiasm into the work. Pepa was a docile model. She sat there languidly, evoking desire, and looked him shamelessly full in the face. He desired her extremely. He knew she would spurn him at first only to be more accommodating in the end. But he was engrossed by Cayetana. "Not now, of all times," he thought. But he painted all his desire into the picture. He worked swiftly; when he felt like it he could compete with

Hasty Luca. In three sittings "The Lady with the Guitar" was finished. "You *have* done it well, Francho," Pepa said. Manuel was delighted.

Francisco was summoned to Doña María Luisa. So she really had been in the plot too. He answered her summons with bitterness in his heart.

She greeted him warmly, and his common sense prevailed. He had no cause to be angry with the Queen. It was not he whose summer and whole happiness she had wished to spoil but exclusively that of her enemy, the Duchess of Alba; which was understandable after the way the latter had repeatedly provoked her. Deep down Francisco felt a certain satisfaction that the Queen and the Duchess should be fighting over him. He would have to write Martín in Saragossa all about it.

María Luisa was genuinely pleased to have Goya there. She valued his shrewd, independent, and yet modest judgment, and she appreciated his art. And of course it amused her that Goya was there and not in Piedrehita. Not that she grudged the Duchess her stout and ageing Francisco; for her part she required virile youths for her bed, not too intelligent; the kind that knew how to wear their uniforms with an air. But the lady had grown too insolent; now and then she needed to be slapped. That was why Goya was now painting her, María Luisa de Borbón y Borbón, and not Cayetana de Alba.

Her reflections about the Duchess gave her a good idea. She suggested to Goya that he should paint her as a *maja*.

He was disagreeably surprised. First he was to do an equestrian portrait of Pepa, and now the Queen as *maja*. He tacitly admitted that there was something of the *maja* in the way she disregarded ceremony and despised gossip, and above all in her unquenchable thirst for life. But the ladies of grandees were permitted to wear the *maja's* costume only at fancy-dress balls, and if Doña María Luisa had herself painted thus, it would be surprising to say the least. And it would certainly give rise to fresh unpleasantness with Cayetana.

Very tactfully he advised against it. She insisted. She made only one concession: that the costume should not be coloured but black. In other respects she was as always a good model, supporting rather than hindering him. Again and again she said to him, "Make me as I am. Don't idealize me. I wish to be as I am."

Nevertheless the work on the picture did not progress as it should. It was not only that she expected a great deal of him, and he the same of himself; she was nervous also, no doubt, out of jealous anger with Manuel, whose affair with that person was still going on, and she frequently cancelled the sittings.

When he was not working he idled about the castle and grounds, bored and irritable. He could not endure to be with the ladies and gentlemen of the Court, and the society of Manuel and Pepa annoyed him. But when he was alone, surrounded by the stiff, brilliant, contrived, and offensively French splendours of the palace and the gardens, then, however hard he tried to exclude them, he would be overwhelmed by thoughts of Cayetana. Against all reason he believed Cayetana would write to him, send for him. It was unthinkable that all should be over between them; she was bound up with him and he with her.

He longed to be away from San Ildefonso. He felt he would have more peace in his studio in Madrid. But the work on the portrait dragged on. María Luisa, as nervous as he, cancelled more and more and more of the agreed sittings.

And then something happened which postponed the completion of the work for several weeks more.

A small nephew of the Queen had just died in Parma, and as she was concerned to emphasize the dignity and eminence of the grand-ducal family from which she sprang, she went beyond what ceremonial prescribed and ordained Court mourning for the little prince. Which meant that the sittings suffered a fresh interruption. Goya petitioned to be allowed to return to Madrid; the portrait was as good as done, he could put the necessary finishing touches to it in Madrid. He received the meagre intelligence that Her Majesty wished the work to be concluded on the spot. A new sitting might be vouchsafed him in perhaps ten days.

At last he was summoned to another sitting. He worked one more week. Then the portrait was finished. He stepped back. "Queen Doña María Luisa as *maja* in black," he presented his Queen to the Queen in flesh and blood.

There she stands, in a natural and at the same time stately pose, *maja* and queen. The eyes above the predatory beak are shrewd and eager, the lips above the firm chin are pressed together, because of the diamond teeth. The whole painted and powdered face is eloquent of worldly wisdom, cupidity, and force. The mantilla falling from the wig is crossed over a bosom youthfully enticing in its deep décolletage, the arms are round and shapely, the beringed left hand hangs at her side, the right holds across the breast a tiny fan, closed in the gesture of invitation and expectancy.

Goya had been at pains to paint not too much and not too little. His Doña María Luisa was ugly, but he had made something vital of this ugliness, something almost attractive. In her hair he had put a bow, red with a good deal of blue in it, and the light from this ribbon gave a glow to the austere black of the lace. He gave her gold shoes, which stood out brilliantly from all the blackness, and he accented the whole with the subdued gleam of the flesh tones.

At last the Queen could find nothing to criticize. She declared her satisfaction in flattering terms and bade Goya stay and make two copies there in San Ildefonso.

Respectfully but decidedly he declined. After he had put so much serious effort into a work, he said, he could not reproduce it. But he would like to have his assistant, Don Agustín Esteve, with whose skill and reliability Doña María Luisa was familiar, execute the desired copies.

At last he could return to Madrid.

But he was no better off there than in San Ildefonso. A hundred times he told himself that the wisest thing would be to write to Cayetana, or simply to go back to Piedrehita. But he was unable to pocket his pride to that extent.

So he cursed himself for being
As he was. And why, precisely,
Over Cayetana had he
Had to sink himself in folly?
Time and time again this stupid
Passion had demanded of him
Sacrifices. He had had to
Pay for everything about her,
Dear. His wrath now turned against her,
Cayetana. And the demons,
All those evil spirits in corners,
Lurking, lowering, pouncing on him,
All of them became one with the
Alba.

17

In the late summer the Albas returned to Madrid. Cayetana remained invisible and sent no message. Many times Francisco encountered one of the carriages of the house of Alba. He would command himself not to look inside. And looked. Twice it was the Duke, twice a stranger, another time the old Marquesa.

A card was delivered, inviting the Court Painter de Goya y Lucientes and Señora Doña Josefa to one of the Duke's musical soirées; an opera by Don José Haydn was to be performed. For a whole hour Francisco was resolutely determined to decline, for the next hour as firmly decided to go. Josefa took it for granted that they would accept the invitation.

As on that other evening which had seen the origin of Goya's ill-starred entanglement with her, Cayetana was at first not visible. Goya had first to listen to the whole of Señor Haydn's opera. He sat there next to Josefa, consumed with impatience, dread, and hope, tortured by memories of the hours in Piedrehita where he had listened to similar musical offerings of the Duke's with Cayetana at his side.

At last the opera was at an end. The major-domo summoned them into the large salon.

As on that other occasion, Doña Cayetana received her guests in the old Spanish manner on her dais. This time the high baldachin under which she sat was embellished by a wooden statue of the Virgin, executed by Juan Martínez Montanés. With folded hands, her head humbly inclined, the Virgin stood there, very charming, wearing a faint smile entirely Spanish in its pride; her foot rested on a half-moon supported by delicately carved heads of angels. The sight of the Duchess, herself so lovely, sitting there beneath this lovely statue, had something blasphemous and seductive about it. She was painted and powdered this time; she wore a gown cut after the fashion of Versailles, the full skirt flowing from the tiniest possible waist. She looked deliberately doll-like and almost comically haughty. Her white face smiled stiffly; the metallic eyes beneath the lofty brows were disconcertingly alive; the face seemed doubly wicked in its confrontation with the countenance of the Virgin listening with a smile of chaste gratification to the Annunciation.

Francisco, shaken with rage and ravishment, had a wild desire to say something to her which concerned them alone, something extravagantly devoted or extravagantly indecent. But she gave him no opportunity to speak to her alone; on the contrary, she treated him with a remote, exaggerated politeness.

In other ways too the evening afforded him nothing but annoyance. Of course his colleague Carnicero was there, the bungler. He had designed the sets for the opera; Goya's eyes still hurt from looking at the sickly lemon-yellow daubs. The Duke and the old Marquesa irritated him by their very cordiality. Don José, although he thought Maestro Carnicero's scenes very pretty, expressed regret that it was not Goya who had designed the sets; but of course he had been quite inaccessible lately, so Cayetana had told him. The old Marquesa also found it sad that Goya had no time to present himself at Villabranca and paint the second portrait of her. Francisco detected a gentle irony in her words; certainly she must be aware of what had passed between him and Cayetana.

Doctor Peral was quite intolerable. With offensively expert knowledge of the subject, he expatiated upon the music of Don José Haydn. But what rasped Francisco even more than the learned windbag's clever chatter were the intimate, inaudible words he saw him exchanging with Cayetana, and Cayetana's laughter at some joke of the doctor's which obviously only he and she could understand. His way of speaking to Cayetana had something maddeningly proprietary about it.

For days Goya had been looking forward to this evening with torment and desire. Now it was a bitter satisfaction to him to be able to take his leave, to escape from the atmosphere that surrounded Cayetana. On the ride homewards Josefa observed that the evening had been exceptionally successful. Don José was really a great musician and the opera very pretty.

Another week passed without a word from Cayetana. Now Goya knew that he would not hear from her in three months, nor yet in a year. More fervently than he had ever regretted anything, he regretted that he had gone away from Piedrehita and from her.

Then the dueña Eufemia came to his studio and in the most natural way in the world asked if Don Francisco had time and inclination to go to the Cruz with Doña Cayetana the next evening; they were giving *The Betrayer Betrayed* by Comella, and Doña Cayetana was expecting great things of the *seguidillas.*

They went to the theatre, they behaved as if they had last seen each other yesterday, they asked no questions, spoke not a word of what had passed in Piedrehita.

In the weeks that followed they saw a great deal of each other, they lived with each other, they loved each other just as they had before their quarrel in Piedrehita.

Usually when Cayetana meant to come she would give notice of her intention, so that Goya could make sure to be alone. Once, when she came unannounced, Agustín was at work on a copy of "The Queen as *Maja* in Black."

Cayetana regarded the picture of her enemy, who stood there with such easy dignity. Francho had not minimized her ugliness, one had to admit, but he had been at pains to make the most of what little María Luisa had, the flesh of the arms and bosom. And he had given her stature. As she stood on the canvas she was in every way a *maja* and a great lady, and in no way ridiculous. Cayetana felt that slight shiver which had come over her when the Queen had warned her.

"Why did you paint her like this?" she asked crossly and directly, unconcerned at the presence of Agustín. "It's a good picture," Francisco answered her literally, in great surprise. "I don't understand you," said Cayetana. "This woman wrecked our summer, your happiness and mine, in a cheap, spiteful way. We both know from experience what she is, an Italian seamstress, and you paint her as a queen, Spanish from the crown of her head to the soles of her feet." "If I paint her like that, then that is how she is," replied Francisco calmly, but with a pride which fell in no way short of the Duchess of Alba's. Agustín was delighted with his friend.

Henceforth Cayetana laid herself out to provoke the Queen more bitterly even than before. She had somehow discovered that María Luisa had ordered a particularly daring gown from Paris. She managed to procure the model, and on the day after the reception at which María Luisa had worn the gown there appeared on the promenade of the Prado two carriages of the house of Alba full of Cayetana's maids attired exactly as the Queen had been the day before. Everyone laughed. María Luisa was angry, but scarcely to the extent Cayetana had hoped. The old Marquesa did not find the jest a happy one; even less so did Francisco.

> Yet whatever the reproach he
> Felt, it melted when he saw her,
> Saw her childlike ladylikeness,
> And as strong as ever in him
> Was his bliss, though always came the
> Threat which with it twined together,
> Deeply mingled.

-- 18 --

At this time an epidemic broke out in Madrid, an infection of the throat which principally attacked children. It began as a kind of inflammation of the tonsils. The glands in the children's necks would swell; soon they could swallow only with difficulty. Then pulse and heartbeat grew weak, a discoloured evil-smelling fluid was discharged from the nose. The little victims suffered from increasing shortness of breath, threatened to suffocate. Many of them died.

Of Goya's three children, first Mariano fell ill, then the youngest, little Elena.

Francisco, although he was only in the way, could not tear himself from the bed of the suffering, struggling Elena. With growing panic he recognized the extremity of the child's condition. From the very first he had known that that letter with which he had purchased his first night with the Duchess had defied the demons and must be avenged.

Doctor Gallardo, the family physician, ordered hot drinks and compresses; later, when the fever rose, cold baths. He quoted Hippocrates. Seemed confident and was clearly groping in the dark.

Goya sought refuge in religious remedies. Strips of paper dedicated to the Blessed Virgin of Recovery and bearing the invocation "*Salus infirmorum*, Saviour of the Ill," were rolled into little balls and given to the children to drink in a glass of water. It was a bad sign that they were unable to swallow them. For Elena, Francisco borrowed a blanket incorporating parts of the clothing of her patron saint, after depositing a large sum of money with the convent where it was preserved, and wrapped the sick child in it.

He recalled all that he had undertaken when Josefa had been pregnant with this child. How he had brought images of Saint Raymond Nonnatus and Saint Vincent Ferrer into the house and had urgently besought these helpers in time of trouble to make the mother's hours of labour as short and easy as possible. And how happily they had all gone in pilgrimage to San Isidro to thank him and the other saints because all had gone well. And all would have continued to do so had he himself not criminally sacrificed the child to the powers of darkness.

He went out to the suburb of Atocha, and accused himself before the Virgin of Atocha. For satisfaction of his own lust he had betrayed his child. He repented and besought her to accept his contrition and help him. He confessed to an unknown, rustic, and stupid-looking priest. He hoped the latter would not grasp what it was he had to confess, but apparently he did. He was merciful. He imposed days of fasting on him, many Our Fathers, and forbade further adultery with the woman. Goya solemnly promised to defile his eyes no more with the sight of the witch and whore Cayetana.

He knew all this was nonsense. He bade himself subject his wild emotions to the restraining power of reason. If one permitted reason to sleep, one was overtaken by dreams, evil dreams, bat-winged, cat-faced monstrosities of dreams. He must lock his madness up within himself, tame it, not spread it abroad. So he held his peace, held it with Agustín, Miguel, Josefa. But he wrote to his friend Martín Zapater. Wrote him how he had conceived the wicked, accursed excuse in order to satisfy his own lusts, and how the Devil had now made his lie come true, how he was to blame for the mortal illness of his beloved child, and how he knew that all this had no foundation in reason and no reality but was yet his truth. He equipped the letter with three crosses and begged his friend to spare nothing and light many fat candles to the Virgen del Pilar, that she might deliver him and his children from their sufferings.

The Duchess of Alba came to hear of the illness of Francisco's children. He had never told her of the excuse he had employed, but she divined the turmoil in his bosom. She dispatched her dueña to give notice of her intended visit. She was not surprised when he declined to see her. She sought out Josefa and promised to send her own physician, Doctor Peral.

Goya did not appear when Peral came. Josefa praised his calmness, skill, and expert knowledge. Goya said nothing. Two days later Mariano was obviously better, the doctors declared him out of danger. On the third day little Elena died.

Goya's despair, his revolt against fate, was unbounded. From the little one's deathbed he ran to his studio, cursed the saints for not helping, cursed himself, cursed her who was to blame for it all, the she-devil, the doxy and duchess who by her arrogance and lust had forced him to sacrifice his best-loved child. Back again at the deathbed, he recalled the child's dreadful attacks of choking, and how he had helplessly looked on. His big, leonine face became a mask of extreme suffering; no one had ever been through what he had suffered and was suffering. Then he rushed back to the studio and his pain turned to rage and a thirst for revenge, into a longing to hurl all his anger, contempt, and disillusion into the accursed one's haughty puppet face.

Agustín was almost always with him, but he effaced himself. Spoke only when it was unavoidable; it was as if he went on tiptoe. He attended without asking, on his own responsibility, to all business, of which there was at the time a great deal. The way in which his friend revealed his sympathy did Goya good. He was grateful to Agustín for understanding him and not bothering him with cheap, rationalizing condolences.

To Josefa's almost disapproving surprise he ordered a funeral for Elena such as might have been for an Infanta.

Then they sat in the darkened salon. Many people came to console with them. On the second day Goya could no longer stand the empty, factitious melancholy on the visitors' faces; he went to his studio.

There he sat or lay or prowled restlessly about. Took pencil and dashed his dreams off on paper, tore up the drawings before they were finished.

In came the Duchess of Alba.

He had awaited her coming, dreaded it, longed for it. She was beautiful. Her face was not a mask; it was the face of a woman in love, come to comfort her lover in his extremity. With his penetrating gaze Goya perceived this and said to himself that though she might have offended him, yet he had offended her more deeply. But reason was swept away by wild orgiastic rage at the sight of her. All that he had ever felt against her since the time he had seen her sitting on her dais, his anger at her moods of insolent cruelty, his vexation with his own enslavement, his panic fear of fate which was making use of this woman to torment him, all this boiled up in him.

He thrust out his thick underlip; his fleshy face, though he attempted to control it, quivered with ungovernable hatred. Involuntarily she recoiled.

"You! You dare to come here!" he said. "First you kill my child, and now you come to mock me."

Still she controlled herself. "Pull yourself together, Francho," she begged. "Don't let your grief drive you out of your mind."

Of course. She had no notion of what he was suffering. She was barren. She could bring nothing forth, nothing came to life within her, neither joy nor pain, nothing but empty lust. She was barren, a witch, evil itself, sent by the Devil into the world.

"You knew it all perfectly well," he allowed his rage and frenzy to burst forth. "This is how you meant it to be. You put into my head the idea which brought this illness down on my little Elena. Either I was to sacrifice my Elena to you, or my career, my art. That was the price I was to pay for being allowed to come to you. Then you tried it a second time in Piedrehita, when you didn't want me to go to Court, so that I should lose my reputation and my art. But that was one of your traps I didn't fall into. And then you want me to make something shameful out of María Luisa. You want to rob me of everything, my children, my career, my painting. To satisfy the lust of your accursed unfruitful womb"—he used an obscene word—"you would deprive me of everything I have."

Boundless fury seized her. She was transformed from the loving comforter into the Duchess of Alba, granddaughter of the late Marshal, the destroyer. It had been a great favour that she had allowed this creature to address as much as a word to her, that she had let him breathe the same air as she did. And now the clumsy peasant could find no better outlet for his stupid remorse over a stupid excuse than in berating her. "From the very beginning," she said softly with cutting politeness, "you've been no good for anything, Señor Goya from Fuendetodos, but a Court jester. You want to be a *majo*, do you? You've remained a peasant no matter how you've dressed yourself. Why do you think the others let you get anywhere near them, the Duchess of Osuna, of Medina-Coeli? They wanted to have their sport with the country lout and his ways. One doesn't have to be a witch to set you dancing, you *pelele*, you puppet." She still spoke softly but her childish voice had grown sharp and ugly.

He saw that her arched brows were drawn together in rage, and he was pleased that he had succeeded in so enraging her. But his satisfaction was submerged in frenzy because she had touched on a sore spot in him, mocked him with something that he had himself sometimes suspected in his secret heart. But it was not true, must not be true. It was not for fun and simply to pass the time that they had invited him into their beds, neither the Osuna nor the Medina-Coeli, nor she herself. He thought of how she had melted beneath him a hundred times, dissolved in desire, and he wanted to throw the coarsest, most indecent words he could think of in her accursed, lovely, insolent, arrogant, furious face. And then he would take hold of her, carry her to the door, and literally throw her outside.

She saw him advance upon her. He was going to strike her. She wished he would. Though that would be the end of everything. Perhaps she would kill him. "Come on then, peasant," she challenged him. "You can be proud because your arms are stronger than mine—"

But he did not reach her. He did not strike her, did not lay hands on her. He stopped in mid-stride. He had seen her mouth opening and shutting but he had heard no words. His infirmity was come upon him again; he was deaf.

Then he flung himself into his
Armchair and in desperation
Buried in his hands his face.

She
Started, then she understood, ran
To him, stroking him as though he
Were a child. He heard no single
Sound, he only saw the movement
Of her lips, yet comprehended
They were gentle words she uttered.
He relaxed, his eyes closed, from them
Tears fell.

—19—

Don Miguel's days were filled with political activity, but somehow it gave him less pleasure than formerly. In the evenings he tried by occupying himself with the arts to distract his mind from anxiety over Lucía and his rising anger at the humiliations involved in his services to Don Manuel.

Over and over he read the account by his great preceptor Niccolò Machiavelli, of his life, after his downfall, on his little estate San Caciano. He would rise with the sun, go into the woods and give instructions to his woodsmen. Then he would walk for about an hour, would rest by a spring or a fowling floor, and pull out his book, Dante, Petrarch, Tibullus, Ovid, or some such master, read of their loves, recall his own, and amuse himself a while with such memories. Then he would look in at the inn on the road, ask travellers for the news, and probe their reactions to it. Then back to his own bare dwelling to consume a meagre meal. To the inn again to play checkers or cards with the innkeeper, the butcher, the miller, and two tile-makers; there would be the usual quarrel over the tiny stakes, the noise of which would resound as far as the village of San Caciano. But in the evening Machiavelli would lay aside his shabby garments, dress himself with formality, and repair to his books, to the company of the great ones of old. He would converse with them and they would make friendly answer. In this way he would pass four carefree hours in his chamber, forgetful of his dreary daily round, careless of his poverty, no longer haunted by the fear of death. He lived with his classical authors, he asked and they answered, they asked and he answered, he read their books and worked at his own.

Miguel Bermúdez tried to follow his example. Surrounded by his pictures, books, manuscripts, he worked away at his lexicon of artists, and sometimes he was able for an hour or even two to sit at his work, without going over to stand in front of Lucía's picture.

Moreover, Lucía wrote him frequently and without embarrassment. She behaved as if she had really undertaken the trip to Paris at his behest, and wrote a great deal about politics. She was in touch with influential people and they were one and all surprised and angry that Spain still delayed concluding the alliance.

She reported also on the Parisian painters, above all on the development of the painter Jacques-Louis David. Since Robespierre's downfall he had twice been in prison, he had conducted himself with dignity and astuteness, had been able to adapt himself to the new regime, the Revision of Freedom and Equality, without surrendering his classic republican ideals. He had a seat once more among the Five Hundred, arranged the art collections of the Republic, and was the most esteemed and influential of all the French painters. He was working on a large painting, "The Sabine Women." It was intended to depict in classical style and with classical nudity the ravished women mediating between the enemies; by these means the artist wished to illustrate the necessity of the reconciliation of opposites. Monsieur David had conceived the design for the painting while he was still in prison; now he had been working on it for months; he was a slow, thorough worker. All Paris, so Lucía wrote, was taking a passionate interest in the progress of the work; bulletins were issued every two weeks.

Later on she rounded out her reports on the Parisian masters by sending Miguel some engravings, then even paintings which she claimed to have acquired cheaply, once actually a picture by David. Miguel regarded the priceless works with mixed feelings. As a zealous collector he delighted in their possession. But he told himself that political services were expected of him in return, above all that he should do his best to hasten the conclusion of the treaty of alliance. Such action would be in accord with his own convictions, but it was distasteful to him that his convictions were now open to misinterpretation.

Moreover, it was quite obvious that even without the written pledge of Don Manuel the alliance would have to be concluded. Admittedly the alliance would involve an ominous dependence of the Kingdom of Spain on the much stronger French Republic; but without French assistance Spain was no longer in a position to defend her colonies against the superior English fleet. So that the Príncipe de la Paz could have redeemed his promise at last without exposing himself to criticism.

But he hesitated as before, sought ever new excuses to put the French off. To the Queen and his own Don Miguel he indulged in patriotic protestations, such as that he feared to lay fetters on Spain from which she would not soon be able to free herself. María Luisa smiled broadly. Miguel kept his amusement to himself. Both were well aware of the extremely private nature of the motives which determined the First Minister's attitude.

Don Manuel had embarked upon an affair with little Geneviève, daughter of Monsieur de Havré, the royalist ambassador.

He had slipped into the liaison without enthusiasm, half against his will. One evening in the course of a tedious official reception he had felt a fleeting fancy for Geneviève; the girl's childlike thinness, which he usually found so displeasing, had attracted him, as well as the consideration that she belonged to the most ancient French nobility. Then too, without actually admitting as much to himself, he was slightly jealous of Goya; he had a vague impression that Pepa had never really shaken off her attachment to her painter; it would be seasonable to remind her that she could not be entirely sure of him, Manuel. He summoned Geneviève on some pretext and assaulted her without preamble. She fled in affright and, white in the face, informed her father of the brutal attack. Monsieur de Havré saw himself confronted with a thorny problem. The Republic was urging that Spain should withdraw her support from the French royalist *émigrés;* there was indeed a rumour that the Directory was demanding their extradition. It was possible that this was a condition of the pending alliance. His royal master Louis the Eighteenth was wandering about, a fugitive, in Germany, in miserable circumstances, dependent on such financial assistance as his wretched envoy could beg from the ministers of the Catholic King. Perhaps he ought to see the hand of Providence in the fact that this brutish Prince of Peace had fallen in love with his daughter. Was it not his patriotic duty to throw his sweet Geneviève to the Minotaur?

In this manner was Geneviève incorporated into the ranks of Don Manuel's conquests. As a matter of fact, he had soon lost any inclination for the little creature, especially as Pepa seemed more amused than offended at his new affair. But the girl though slight showed herself to be tough, and behind her stood, politely threatening, her father; the picture of a Monsieur de Havré who wandered about Europe making sinister accusations to the effect that Spain was taking advantage of the plight of the French monarchy to ravish the daughters of the French aristocracy was one which Manuel found unpleasing.

The trouble was that the Directory in Paris was not disposed to have its policies disarranged by the amours of Manuel Godoy. Ambassador General Pérignon was recalled for being too gentle with the Spaniards; he was replaced by Citizen Ferdinand Pierre Guillemardet.

Reports furnished by Spanish agents in Paris on the previous career of Citizen Guillemardet struck a painfully discordant note in the summer repose of the Court at San Ildefonso. Guillemardet, still quite a young man, had been the doctor in a village in the vicinity of Paris. The Department of Saône-et-Loire had sent the fanatical republican to the National Convention. During the trial of Louis the Sixteenth he had declared, "As judge I vote for the death sentence. As statesman I vote for the death sentence. So I register two votes for the death sentence." After his appointment as special commissar for three northern departments, he had decreed that the public buildings known by the names "Temple," "Church," or "Chapel" were no longer to be used in support of superstition but only for the purposes of the public weal. Such was the man, regicide and atheist, whom the Republic now sent to San Ildefonso to bring about the banishment of the royalists and the conclusion of the alliance.

Citizen Guillemardet arrived and presented himself to the Spanish cabinet. He proved to be a man of good appearance, correct, haughty, with a somewhat brusque formality of manner. Or so at least he appeared to the ministers of the Catholic King. He for his part reported back to Paris that the Spanish cabinet consisted of four idiots led by a turkey-cock.

When Citizen Guillemardet had entered government service he had according to the rule sworn the solemn oath, "I swear sincere devotion to the Republic and eternal hatred of kings." However, as ambassador at the Court of the Catholic King, he could not very well openly display his hatred of this monarch, and he had referred back to the Directory for instructions on this point. They had advised him to conform to Spanish Court ceremony in every respect, so that he would be able to press his political demands more forcefully. As a result of these instructions, the new Citizen Ambassador had to undergo a variety of humiliations.

First he had to present his credentials to the Catholic King in a solemn audience and be presented to the entire royal family. Besides the royal pair there were assembled in the throne room all the Infantes and Infantas, and the regicide had reverently to kiss the hands not only of that idiot Carlos and that Messalina María Luisa but of every single one of those rascally little girls and boys. What was more, the youngest, little Francisco de Paula, the turkey-cock's bastard, ran up to him merrily calling out, "Papa, Papa."

The unpleasantness to which Guillemardet had to submit for the good of the Republic was somewhat compensated for by the fact that the King arranged a banquet in his honour.

The new French ambassador had found favour in María Luisa's eyes. His features were proud, clear-cut, rather severe, and the many-coloured magnificence of the uniform which the Paris Directory had lately prescribed for its officials was becoming to him. He looked well, anyhow, considerably better than the thin, shabby, elderly Havré. She declared that it was important to keep Citizen Guillemardet in a good temper; so she wanted to give a banquet for him. This idea was unwelcome to the Príncipe de la Paz. He foresaw little Geneviève's reproaches; she would be mortally offended if he permitted the Court to distinguish the executioner of her King with such an unusual honour, and he did not care for it himself that the disgusting plebeian should receive such a mark of esteem. He explained to the Queen that to distinguish the *gabacho* in this way would be nothing less than capitulation to the demands of the Republic. María Luisa was aware of her Manuel's motives and was delighted at his embarrassment. "Talk yourself blue in the face, *chéri*," she said amiably, "it's no good. I've taken a fancy to Citizen Guillemardet." Don Manuel suggested that they could at least invite Monsieur de Havré too. María Luisa, foreseeing the fresh embarrassments that would inevitably accrue to Manuel, acquiesced with a smile.

For the occasion of the banquet San Ildefonso put forth all the splendour with which Versailles had been wont to celebrate such feasts a bare decade earlier. But now the regicide and commoner sat high up the table in bloated magnificence, while the representative of the banished king in a threadbare uniform sat far down the board next to his skinny daughter.

The colourful Citizen Guillemardet was shocked by the tactlessness of inviting the royalist traitor at the same time as himself. He quickly forgot the honour done him and as quickly his anger grew at the ignominy to which he had been subjected. He sat down and wrote a sharp note, harking back to previous demands, in which he demanded in menacing terms the immediate extradition of the French royalist fugitives.

María Luisa gently drew Don Manuel's attention to the fact that his having invited Havré was responsible for this sharpening of the old conflict. He could not think of much to say in reply. And for that very reason he would have felt it to be an ignominious defeat to accede to the plebeian's demand.

Anything rather than that.

He had himself driven to Guillemardet in his ceremonial carriage, with the head of Janus borne before him. At great length he explained that it would be contrary to the most elementary rules of Spanish courtesy to violate the rights of hospitality once they had been extended. "If the government of the Catholic King continues to tolerate the presence of royalist traitors on Spanish soil," Citizen Guillemardet answered coldly, "and even goes so far as to support them, the Republic will be forced to interpret it as a hostile attitude." Don Manuel blanched slightly, but he was prepared. Monsieur de Havré, he replied courteously, would be given to understand in the discreetest possible way that he would be relieving the Spanish Court of a great embarrassment if, say within the year, he were to join his master, who as far as one knew was staying in Germany. "The Republic," icily replied Guillemardet, more threateningly than before, "could not accept this fresh delay—" "Please let me finish, Excellency," the Príncipe de la Paz interrupted. "To avoid having to endanger its good name for hospitality the government of His Catholic Majesty would be willing to make sweeping concessions to the Republic in other fields." He stood up, his orders jingling, and solemnly announced, "I am authorized, Your Excellency, to make the following declaration to you in the name of my royal master. In the event of Your Excellency's accepting the fact that Monsieur de Havré will not leave the country till a year has elapsed, the Catholic King is prepared within two weeks to conclude the treaty of alliance in the form which the Republic suggested in its latest note."

In this way the conclusion of the long-prepared offensive and defensive alliance was agreed upon between the Catholic King and the one and indivisible French Republic, and the Spanish Crown had to accept as part of the bargain the inevitable conflict with Great Britain.

Readiness for war was ordered
For the fleet and all the ports. Then
In the castle Ildefonso
With due form and ceremony
There was signed and sealed the contract
'Twixt the King and the Republic,
Making them allies and partners.
The ambassador, however,
Of His British Majesty, the
Lord Saint Helens, now requested
His safe-conduct.

-- 20 --

For several days Goya had remained completely deaf, locked up with his fury. He was beyond bounds, angrily repulsed all approaches, did all he could to exaggerate his state of frenzy in the presence of others. Everyone now followed Agustín's example and proceeded with great caution when he was present; they knew he would not let himself be helped.

For days, for more than a week, Goya would have no one about him but Josefa and Agustín; and even to them he was full of ill-tempered complaints.

The indefatigably industrious Agustín, who had little to do at this time, spent his time perfecting his technical skill at etching. The engraver Jean-Baptiste Leprince had invented a method of reproducing ink and wash drawings by copper-plate printing. He had kept it a secret during his lifetime, but after his death it was published in the *Encyclopédie Méthodique*, and now the zealous Agustín Esteve was trying his skill at it. Goya looked on, for the most part absent-mindedly. In earlier years he himself had made etchings after Velázquez, without much success. Agustín suspected that his master would be tempted by the new technique, but he prudently refrained from saying anything to him. Francisco asked no questions either, but again and again went back to Agustín's work table to watch.

From time to time Don Miguel dropped in. The first few times he said little or nothing, later he spoke in low tones with Agustín. They could not tell whether Francisco was able to follow their conversation or not.

But on one occasion Goya did not trouble to conceal his interest. It was when Miguel told in detail how the painter Jacques-Louis David had gone over to the new regime. After he had finished his story Agustín commented on it scornfully. He had always had the impression that David's work, for all its formal perfection, had something empty, shallow about it; it did not surprise him that David had fallen away from Liberty, Equality, and Fraternity and had come down on the side of the ruling powers, the big businessmen. Goya smiled maliciously. So even Jacques-Louis David, the exemplary republican, idol of the *Afrancesados*, had adapted himself to the force of circumstance. And here were his friends asking him, Francisco, to become a revolutionary. "If gold rusts, what can you expect of iron?" "I find it understandable," he said at last, bitterly, "that he shouldn't want to go to the scaffold. But it would have been more classical, more in his line, if he had let himself be put to death."

Goya cheered up for the first time when Zapater came unexpectedly, his heart's own Martín. Josefa had written to him in Saragossa, but neither she nor Martín let Francisco know that his friend had come for his sake alone.

Here at last was someone to whom Francisco could speak without restraint of his suffering and anger. How the woman had forced him into telling that lie that his daughter was mortally ill: for none other than she, the she-villain Cayetana, had conjured the idea into his head. And now, when he had thrown her guilt in her face, she had assailed him with foul language like a whore dissatisfied with her wage. And how then his rage had overcome him, and his deafness.

Martín listened with silent attention, smoking. He made no reply; his shrewd, kindly eyes above the powerful nose were thoughtful, sympathetic. "I can see you think I'm out of my mind," Francisco raved. "Everyone thinks I am; they tiptoe softly around me as if I were a raving lunatic. I'm not a lunatic," he stormed. "It's an insult. And if I am mad it's because she's bewitched me; she suggested it to me. That time that she looked at the picture of the madhouse, she said, 'One would like to be there oneself.'

"I've got to tell you something," Francisco began again after a pause, and while before he had been talking rather loudly, now he came close to Martín and spoke softly, mysteriously. "I'm not mad *yet*," he said, "but it is not impossible that I should become so. Sometimes, often, I feel that I shall." Martín Zapater was cautious and did not say much in reply; but the mere fact of his quiet presence had a calming effect.

Shortly before Martín had to go back to Saragossa a message came from the old Marquesa. Doña María Antonia wished to know if Goya now had the time to do that second portrait of which they had spoken in Piedrehita.

To Martín, who urged him to accept the commission, Goya behaved as if it would cost him an effort of will. But at bottom he had already quite made up his mind to take it on. Perhaps Cayetana was behind the commission, and even if she wasn't, perhaps some chance might bring her to the Marquesa's house while he was working there. He burned to see her again, burned with anger and desire. What he would do he had no idea, but see her again he must. He accepted.

He very soon realized that Doña María Antonia de Villabranca had more idea of what had passed between him and Cayetana than was welcome to him. Sometimes when she calmly looked him straight in the face with her proud, gracious gaze, he felt as if he were standing there naked and exposed. He regretted having taken on the commission.

At the same time he spun out the work. Not only did he both hope and fear that Cayetana might come, but he began to perceive, through the presence of the Marquesa, the existence in Cayetana's life and nature of twilight depths which he had hitherto shrunk from acknowledging and considering. In his rage he had called her barren. Was she? If she were to bear a child by one of the men with whom she slept, would the Duke and the Marquesa agree to bestow the titles of Villabranca and Alba on the bastard? Perhaps in order to evade such problems she had had recourse to the skill of Doctor Peral, of Eufemia, or of both. Possibly that was the explanation of her intimacy with the doctor. As he painted away at the picture of the Marquesa the realization came to Goya that life in the house of Alba was not so simple as he had been pleased to believe.

And then the portrait of Doña María Antonia just would not come off. Almost never before had he made so many sketches for a picture, almost never before had he been so uncertain of what he really wanted to do. Moreover, his hearing remained as poor as ever. He could read words easily only from the lips of those in whose presence he felt sure of himself; he understood little of what the Marquesa said. And he had abandoned the hope of meeting Cayetana at her house.

Martín had gone back to Saragossa. But Don Miguel dropped in more and more often; perhaps, without Francisco saying much about it, he understood his friend's anxieties and bewilderment. He had a proposal to make him, which he disguised as a favour; the fact of the matter was, however, that this understanding friend wanted to do something to help his Francisco.

Relations between Don Manuel and the envoy of the French Republic remained as cool as ever. Political wisdom dictated that Citizen Guillemardet should be kept in a good humour; but the Príncipe de la Paz could not refrain from showing his dislike of this plebeian who had administered a personal defeat to him. Señor Bermúdez, for his part, did all he could to propitiate the important man and used every opportunity to be agreeable to him. Now Guillemardet was interested in the arts; it piqued him that the greatest painter in Spain should have painted the royalist ambassador Havré, and he had let Don Miguel know that he would be pleased if Señor de Goya were to paint him also. Should Francisco accept the commission he would be rendering a service to the cause of

Spanish liberalism; possibly the work might even prove a welcome distraction. But he must get to work without delay. The Frenchman was an impatient fellow, irritable because Don Manuel had so often been pleased to keep him waiting.

Francisco was delighted to have a pretext for interrupting the work on the Marquesa's portrait. She brushed his excuses amiably aside. Whenever he had the time and inclination, she encouraged him, he could resume work on it.

Despite her kindness he left the Palacio Villabranca in irritation. He felt mortified, in her eyes and his own, that he had not managed to complete the portrait; such a thing had almost never happened to him before, and as time went on he was often tormented by thoughts of the unfinished picture.

With all the greater zeal therefore, he threw himself into the new task. Guillemardet, flattered that Goya had accepted his invitation with such alacrity, was disposed to be friendly. He wanted to be painted in uniform, with all the attributes of his office. "Don't paint me, esteemed *maître*," he exhorted, "paint the Republic. The Republic," he enlarged, with a sweeping gesture, "has undergone changes in the course of the years. You have surely heard, Citizen Goya, of Aristotle's dynamis and entelechy, of the seed, the potentiality, which resides in all things from their inception and strives for fulfilment. In the same way the Republic has become ever more maturely republican and at the same time Ferdinand Pierre Guillemardet has become more and more Citizen Guillemardet."

Francisco understood little of the stilted French words. But the thought of the painter David crossed his mind and he knew how the regicide and iconoclast Citizen Guillemardet must have struggled and suffered as he saw the Republic slipping out of the hands of the people and being taken over by the profit-seeking bourgeoisie. He perceived that Guillemardet was seeking to conceal this transformation from himself. He felt the constant strain and effort in the ambassador's bearing; he saw the almost insane pride in his eyes and realized that the self-deception into which the man retreated must drive him into ever-deepening delusion.

To paint all this was a grateful task, and so, without having properly understood him, he painted what the man had wanted him to paint. He painted the victorious Republic, her grandeur and her theatricality, her flaunting, utterly crazy pretensions.

Francisco could not hear, but that only made his eye the sharper.

As he was deprived of the sound of voices he compensated with colour. He painted the colours of the Republic as they had never been painted before, an orgy of blue, white, and red.

There he sits, Ferdinand Guillemardet, the little country doctor, now ambassador of the one and indivisible Republic, who had twice condemned King Louis the Sixteenth to death and had forced the Spanish monarchy into a relationship of subjection to his own country; there he sits in his blue-black uniform, in a rather extravagant pose, the figure almost in profile but the head directly facing the beholder. What strikes the beholder first is the glittering hilt of his sabre, the brilliant blue, white, and red of his sash. He has thrown onto the table his magnificent cocked hat with its blue, white, and red feather and blue, white, and red cockade. One hand grips the arm of the chair, the other he rests powerfully, provocatively, effectively, on his thigh. The short black curls have been brushed forward onto his broad, well-formed forehead, the lips are curled, the nose juts out uncompromisingly. It is a long, well-modelled face, intelligent, full of the owner's self-importance. The properties—chair, table, and fringed tablecloth—have a dull golden-yellow finish with bluish shadows. The sharply defined dissonances of the colours play upon one another in an artistically ordered confusion.

Ferdinand Guillemardet
Stood in flesh and blood before the
Ferdinand Guillemardet,
Citizen, there painted, sitting.
And each looked the other in the
Eye; till bursting with his feelings
Of his own importance and his
Country's, the ambassador of
France gave vent and spoke, "Yes, that is
The Republic."

Though Francisco
Could not hear the words exactly,
Yet he saw the man's eyes, saw the
Lips move, and within him heard the
"Marseillaise."

21

The epidemic which had caused the deaths of so many children in Madrid had almost died down when María Luisa's youngest son fell ill, the Infante Francisco de Paula. María Luisa had borne eight children; of the six remaining to her this little prince was her favourite. He was reddish-blond, without question Don Manuel's little son. And now this her best-beloved son lay helpless in his bed, fighting for breath, fighting with death.

The old Court physician, Vicente Piquer, ordered ice water and cold compresses. María Luisa drew her brows together and called in Madrid's most celebrated and most hated doctor, Doctor Joaquín Peral. He listened to his elderly colleague with polite attention, and then prescribed measures of such a kind that the Court physician was unable to close his mouth for shocked astonishment.

The child recovered.

Doña María Luisa asked Doctor Peral if he would continue to care for the small Infante: him, herself, and her family.

The Queen's offer was a great temptation. It would mean that he would have influence wherever he wished it, in political and in personal matters, and it also meant that the wonderful art collections of the kings of Spain would be at his disposal. But if he accepted he would have little time left for research or for his own pictures, and he would have completely to renounce the bittersweet delights of his intimacy with Cayetana de Alba. He begged respectfully for time to think it over.

Usually so serene and confident, he was in a state of confusion. Should he refuse, not only would he be ignoring a chance which fortune would not offer again, but he would also make an enemy of the Queen. Yet he could not bear to lose his Duquesita.

No one, not she herself, knew Cayetana better than he did. With a matter-of-fact absence of shame she had exposed her body a hundred times for examination, had confided its infirmities to him, had requested his help and accepted it. But Doctor Peral was an educated man and knew that the ladies of ancient Rome had behaved no differently to the learned Greek slaves whom they purchased as medical advisers; they had suffered their beautiful bodies to be tended by them, yet the skilled hands of their attendants had been no more to them than the brushes and oil sponges they used. And even if the Duquesita did treat him as friend, adviser, and confidant, Don Joaquín often questioned whether he meant more to her than one of those Greek slave physicians.

Doctor Peral regarded himself as a free-thinker of the purest persuasion. His masters were La Mettrie, Holbach, Helvétius; he was firmly convinced that thought and feeling were as much products of the body as urine and sweat. Human anatomy was always the same, lusts remained the same, between the sensations of the steer mounting the cow and Dante's emotions towards Beatrice there was only a difference of degree, and to think of love as something fundamentally different from lust was superstitious idealization. Doctor Peral described himself as a materialist hedonist; he declared that the sole purpose of life was enjoyment; he liked to describe himself with Horace as a "little pig from the herd of Epicurus."

The trouble was that this philosophy failed him where Cayetana de Alba was concerned. He believed that had he seriously applied himself to it he could have "had" his Duquesita. But strangely enough, and contrary to his convictions, this was not enough. He wanted more from her. He observed how she chose her men and that there existed for her but one criterion: her own feeling. This feeling might last only for an hour or even less, but exist it must; she never wanted just any man, but one particular one. Unfortunately he never seemed to be the one.

As this was the case it would be madness if he were to refuse Doña María Luisa's offer. No love-offering, however great, would sway Cayetana's capricious affections to his advantage, and should he now decline he would only be throwing the chance of a lifetime to the winds. And yet he knew he would decline. His life would be meaningless could he no longer breathe the same air as Cayetana, no longer closely observe the incalculable humours of her supple body.

He told Cayetana of María Luisa's offer. He spoke lightly, casually. "For courtesy's sake I asked for time to consider the matter. Of course I shall refuse."

The past weeks had not been happy ones for Cayetana. She missed Francisco sorely; to lose Peral as well would be hard to bear. Her enemy, the Italian, had chosen well her time to strike. But she controlled herself. In a conversational tone which matched his she said, "You know I shall be glad if you stay with me, but I hope if you do refuse that it won't be on my account," and calm, coolly friendly, she looked full at him with her metallic eyes under the arched brows.

He knew exactly what was passing in her mind; she was expecting him in recompense to ask her to sleep with him. Possibly, probably, she would do it; but he would not really touch her, he would lose her forever.

> And she said, "There is no doubt you've
> Realized by now that I am
> Never grateful." "Yes, I know," he calmly
> Told her. "But if I refuse the
> Offer, it is true I do so
> On my own account, not yours." She
> Answered, "So, 'tis good, Don Joaquín."
> Reaching up then like a child she
> Gravely, softly, kissed him on the
> Brow as he bent down.

-- 22 --

She went on living just as she always had. She was the center of a whirlpool of activity. She had endless engagements, she was seen at the play, at the bullfights, she gave and attended receptions and associated cheerfully with Don José and the Marquesa.

But in the well-bred relationships of the trio there was now perceptible a faint irritation.

When the Marquesa had affianced her son to the last and only remaining bearer of the proud and fateful name of Alba—the couple had been scarcely more than children—she had not only wished to unite the wealth and titles of the two houses; she had felt drawn by Cayetana's strong, self-willed, and charming personality, and had hoped that Don José's thin and tentative hold on life would be nourished by the full richness of the girl's. To be sure, from earliest youth Cayetana had been *chatoyante*, somewhat eccentric—her grandfather had had her brought up according to the precepts of Rousseau; but Doña María Antonia had calculated that an Alba, however brought up, would have an infallible sense of tradition and propriety.

And indeed for all her moods and excesses Doña Cayetana had remained a lady. Often as she had been involved in love affairs she had never confronted the Marquesa and Don José with the problem of deciding whether or not to recognize a bastard as the bearer of Spain's greatest name. She had contrived, without bothering the Marquesa with embarrassing questions and requests for help, tactfully to find means of avoiding just such a situation.

And now, all of a sudden, Cayetana failed them. She, who had effortlessly extricated herself from so many difficult affairs without giving offence. No one thought ill of a great lady for having a *cortejo*. No one thought ill of the Duchess of Alba for having chosen the Court Painter Francisco de Goya as her *cortejo*. But the way she now openly displayed her passion was no longer quite seemly. And that she should so precipitately break off the relationship instead of gradually and quietly dissolving it was going too far. Now all Madrid saw that it was more than trifling; smiled, and felt sorry for the Duke. So the Marquesa, against her will, was forced to open her eyes and see how deep this passion went.

The Duke's reactions were similar to his mother's. Cayetana had never made any pretence of loving him but she had given him companionship and understanding and so he had accepted her caprices with composure. Now all at once one of her outbreaks had turned into a naked passion which offended his sense of proportion and good breeding. It disturbed him and made him irritable, for all his outward appearance of control.

It was this irritation which prompted him to a surprising and momentous decision. He had always loved music above all else, and suffered from the shrieking banalities which the King uttered on the subject, and the clumsy jokes with which he used to chaff him. Now he could stand it no longer. One day after he had had to listen to a quartet in which Don Carlos scraped away as first violin, he declared to his mother that the King's crass stupidity had stifled any real music in Spain. He could not any longer endure it at Court and in Madrid. He intended to travel in Italy and Germany, to wash his ears and his heart clean again.

He was afraid his mother would advise against the journey. And in fact María Antonia was disquieted by the thought of the effort which such an expedition would cost her son. Yet she hoped that the change and the music would refresh him; and above all, she said to herself, such a journey would in itself be a solution to the problem of Cayetana. So she gave Don José's plan her approval without hesitation.

They resolved to set out without any great delay. "I think," said Don José, "that we will travel in the smallest possible company, only you, Mama, Cayetana and I, and we will take few servants with us." "And Doctor Peral, of course," observed the Marquesa. "Preferably not the doctor," said Don José. The Marquesa looked up. "I think," Don José repeated, pleasantly but with unwonted firmness, "that we won't take Peral." The Marquesa understood. José wanted to have Cayetana to himself, without the accessory to so many of her secrets. "Very well," she said, "we'll leave Don Joaquín here."

When Don José informed Cayetana of his intentions, her whole being was in revolt. For her there was no life outside Spain. The very names of the German cities and German musicians which Don José mentioned seemed to her barbaric. And then, Francisco would place the worst interpretation on this journey, would assume that she was leaving Madrid only to torment him; he would give her no opportunity to explain herself to him, she would lose him forever. But if she did not go with her ailing husband on his journey she would have the Court and the whole country against her. She saw no possibility of denying Don José her company.

When the Duke was informing Doctor Peral that he was going to travel for several months abroad, Peral was confounded. Was Cayetana sending the Duke away? Did she want to stay behind alone? Cautiously he inquired if His Grace did not fear the fatigues of the journey. Don José answered lightly that the sight of new faces, the influence of new music, would revive him. Peral, still groping—for he did not know whether the Duquesita was going—asked if the Duke desired his company. The latter, with the same unaccustomed, almost frivolous gaiety, replied that he thanked Don Joaquín very much but he did not want to pamper himself, he would try to get along without his assistance.

Doctor Peral betook himself at once to the Duchess. She had not been aware that he was not to come with them, and she only just managed to hide her surprise and distress. They both stood helpless. He asked if her decision to go with the Duke was final. She did not reply; she made a small, resigned, almost forlorn gesture. He had for the first time the experience of seeing grief in her eyes, and a plea for help. Never, even when she had been far more in need of his help, had this woman, among all the grandees of Spain the proudest and most independent, permitted him to see her in such agitation. He felt a faint stirring of satisfaction that Cayetana de Alba confided her troubles to him alone.

For only two brief moments could he read the distress signals in her eyes, and in those moments it seemed to him that a deeper understanding existed between them than ever before.

The necessary provisions for the journey were made. When people of the rank of the Albas and Villabrancas decided to travel, even with the smallest retinue, many preparations were necessary.

So there ran and so there sweated
Couriers and major-domos,
Tailors, footmen, servants male and
Female; and the foreign envoys
From Bavaria, Austria, Parma,
Tuscany, and Modena had
All their work cut out for them, with
Writing and dispatching missives.
For the Duke with unaccustomed
Firmness drove them on to hasten,
Since he felt an urge within him
On this journey soon as might be
To set forward.

23

They never did set forward. During the preparations the Duke complained of a strange debility. The trip was first postponed, then abandoned.

Don José had always been ailing. But now his lassitude paralyzed him to such a degree that he could scarcely move. Reviving draughts were of no avail. The doctors were unable to explain the profound and unremitting fatigue.

Most of the time Don José sat in an armchair, huddled in a voluminous dressing gown, emaciated, his eyes shut, in a painful state of exhaustion. When his eyes opened, they looked larger than ever in his face, which was becoming more and more haggard. His features hardened, acquired a look of severity and suffering. Everyone could see that his vital powers were ebbing.

Towards Cayetana he showed a polite, haughty, unspoken aversion. The same courteous aloofness was shown her by the Marquesa. In her suffering the serenely cheerful Doña María Antonia had become more like her son. She never as much as hinted that she in any way blamed the recent events for her son's decline, but Cayetana recognized that she would never again have a friend in Doña María Antonia.

When it was clear that the end was approaching, Don José expressed a wish to be taken to the Palacio Villabranca. Up till now he had not suffered himself to be put to bed, but now he refused no longer. Attended by his mother, his brother Luis, his sister-in-law María Tomasa, he lay there, weary of pomp and circumstance, and Cayetana felt herself a stranger.

In the antechambers of the Palacio Liria and the Palacio Villabranca lay open books in which visitors who came to inquire after the condition of the illustrious invalid inscribed their names. People stood in whispering groups in the nearby streets. It was being said that Don José had always been delicate, had never expected to attain a great age, but that the suddenness of this end was surprising all the same. It was being said that interested parties had had a hand in producing his mysterious prostration; a creeping poison had been administered to him. It was also being said that Don José's existence was an inconvenience to his Duchess; were not her love affairs the talk of the country?

The end came at high noon. The priest spoke the prescribed Latin prayers, pronounced absolution, and offered the dying man a crucifix. Don José had no particular reputation for piety; moreover, he appeared to be preoccupied with other matters; possibly he could hear music; but though it cost him an obvious effort, he kissed the crucifix politely and reverently as was fitting. Then the priest took cotton wool impregnated with oil from a golden vessel and anointed the dying man's eyes, nose, lips, hands, and feet.

Immediately after Don José's death began the solemn, exactly prescribed business of mourning. His face was rouged, Franciscan monks dressed him in the habit of their Order. The room in which he died was hung with black damask, three altars were installed, on which rested very old and very valuable crucifixes from the treasuries of the Albas and Villabrancas; beside the bed and on the altars tall candles burned in golden candlesticks. Thus, austere and solemn, lay in state the dead Don José Alvarez de Toledo, thirteenth Duke of Berwick and Alba, eleventh Marqués of Villabranca.

The Patriarch of both the Indies came, the King sent the choir of his Chapel Royal to sing the Mass for the Dead. Present at this office were the family, representatives of the King and Queen, the highest grandees, and the closest friends. The singers and players put forth their best efforts; the dead man had been their brother-artist. The illustrious guests stood with stiff, dignified expressions as custom decreed. Doña María Antonia knelt, her face rigid. But two of the women wept aloud, which actually usage did not permit. One was Doña María Tomasa; she had been very close to her brother-in-law. When they had made music together she had known what it was to see his soul break through his dignity and reserve. The other was poor pathetic little Geneviève de Havré. In a few weeks she would be leaving this gloomy country. She had gone through terrible things here, had yielded to her father's wishes and for the sake of the lilies of France had sacrificed herself to the lusts of that brute Don Manuel. Her happy days on the peninsula had been few in number, and among them she counted those in which she had been allowed to make music with the kindly, well-bred man who lay there in his coffin.

Later the crowd was admitted to file past the body, and all night long Masses were said at the three altars.

Then the dead man was placed in a coffin covered with black velvet and furnished with golden nails and golden borders. This coffin was in its turn enclosed in another of bronze, beautifully chased. Thus the dead man was brought to Toledo to be buried, according to custom, in the family vault of the Dukes of Alba.

So their title bore alone now
Cayetana. But the ancient
Villabranca coat-of-arms was
Taken from the house of mourning
And with solemn ceremony
Brought unto the brother's dwelling.
Now was Don Luis María
Called the Marqués Villabranca,
Of this name the twelfth, till later
On the death of Cayetana
Came the time when he himself might
Take in turn the name and wear the
Title of the Duke of Alba.

-- 24 --

In the Palacio Villabranca members of the immediate family received the visits of condolence of their friends and acquaintances.

Goya was among them. It would have been a grave affront had he not come.

He had heard that the Albas were planning a journey abroad. He was convinced that they were doing so solely because Cayetana wished to show him how little she cared for him. Then he had heard of the Duke's mortal illness and of those rumours which hinted foul play. Of course that was foolish gossip, his reason dismissed it. But he could not help it; these rumours which would not die down aroused his fear and aversion, and a faint, sinister satisfaction.

He had not seen Cayetana again since that senseless quarrel. He entered the Palacio Villabranca more wrought up almost than he had ever been in his life.

The mirrors and pictures in the big salon had been shrouded. On low chairs, in deep black, sat the mourners. There were four of them: the Marquesa, Doña Cayetana, the dead man's brother, Don Luis María, and his wife.

Goya, as custom demanded, began by taking a seat without speaking. He sat there grave and silent, but inside he was a tumult of half-formulated thoughts and torrential emotions. Of course Cayetana was innocent of the Duke's death. The rumours were absurd. They were *not* absurd. There was always a kernel of truth in what people were saying, and Cayetana *had* had something to do with this sudden, mysterious, fatal illness. If it were true that Don José had had to die because of him it would be dreadful. It would be wonderful. "Bloody hands and clever brains go down from generation to generation," he said the old saying to himself, and, sitting there in the gloomy hall, he was overcome by that strange mixture of dread and fascination which the name of Alba had power to evoke.

He stood up, walked over to the old Marquesa, bowed, and, lowering his voice, uttered the usual, meaningless words of sympathy. Doña María Antonia listened with a controlled expression, but behind this mask of calm his searching artist eye detected a frozen violence of feeling which had never been in her face before. And suddenly he became aware of another shocking thing. The mourners' chairs were not far apart, about a yard perhaps, but it was as if this yard between the Marquesa's chair and Cayetana's was as wide as the whole world, such immense, wordless, well-bred hostility existed between the two women.

And now he stopped in front of Cayetana and bent over her very politely. She turned her full face to him, he looked at it from above; it was white with powder against the shrouding black, very small; the black veil was drawn down to her brows, the throat covered to the chin.

His lips uttered the proper words of condolence. To himself he thought, "You witch, you murderess, seductress, you aristocrat, you bring nothing but ill fortune to everyone. You killed my child, what had she done to you? You killed your husband, what had he done to you? Woe is me that I ever fell into your hands! But now I have seen through and through you and I am seeing you for the last time. I shall never see you again, never come to you again. I will not, I have made a vow and I shall keep it." And even as he thought thus he knew that he would be fettered to her forever. And together with his hatred and despair he felt a fierce and vulgar exultation that he knew her in a guise other than the one in which she now sat before him. He called up an image of her small naked body quivering in his embrace. He pictured to himself how he would crush this proud unapproachable creature again in his arms, how he would bite the arrogant lips till they melted beneath his, till the hatefully mocking eyes swam and closed. He would not stroke her, nor would she get any flattering words of admiration out of him; he would take her like the meanest whore.

Such were his thoughts and feelings as he spoke his measured sentences of sympathy and consolation. But his eyes bored imperiously into hers. These same eyes had seized, amassed, and stored up so much of human nature that often he could take another unawares with his observing, searching look and make him expose himself. He wanted to see, to fathom, what went on inside that small, insolent, fragile, proud, and violent head.

She looked at him steadily, with polite detachment, or so it must have seemed to the others in the room. But in reality she too had wild thoughts behind her made-up face, not clear even to herself, and such as he imagined there might be.

Till now she had scarcely listened when her Eufemia had told her what the people were saying about Don José's death. Now for the first time as she looked into Goya's painstakingly composed face and into his probing eyes it occurred to her that it was not only the rabble that believed the gossip. She despised Francisco and rejoiced that he credited her with the murder. She exulted that he could not break away from her though he might be shuddering with aversion. Agitated by these and similar thoughts, she returned a few meaningless words of thanks.

He withdrew in a helpless rage. He could believe all the evil in the world of her; told himself this was madness, knew he would suspect her again and again and would tell her so against his will.

A few days later Doña Eufemia came to his studio and informed him that Doña Cayetana would come to him that evening; would he see to it that no one else should be about?

He could barely reply for excitement. He made a firm resolve to say nothing of their last encounter or of Don José's death.

She came, heavily veiled. They did not speak, not even words of greeting. She unwrapped herself from her veil. The warm pallor of her face, unpainted, gleamed in a brownish white. He snatched her to him, dragged her down upon the bed.

Even afterwards they did not speak for a long time. He no longer knew what he had said to her when they were last together, could only vaguely remember what his thoughts had been in the hall of mourning in the Palacio Villabranca. But he knew this much: it had all happened quite differently from what he had expected, and fundamentally it was a defeat for him. But it was a joyful defeat, he felt exhausted and happy.

She—was it hours or minutes later?—said, "I knew beforehand that there would be trouble. Immediately after we had been to the theatre to see *The Betrayer Betrayed* Brígida came to me again —you remember, the dead maid—and told me that trouble was coming. She didn't tell me exactly what, she was vague. She can be quite plain when she wants to be, but sometimes, to tease me, she's vague. All the same, when the trouble came it didn't take me by surprise." She spoke quite objectively, in her small, hard voice.

"Trouble!" Their horrifying quarrels, the circumstances attending Don José's death, to her these were "troubles." She thrust all responsibility from her, put it all upon fate. "Troubles!" Suddenly the evil thoughts were with him again which he had woven about her in the hall of mourning at the house of Villabranca. Once more he saw the old Marquesa sitting drawn away from her, leaving her to herself in the faint odour of blood. Even as he thought thus he told himself it was nonsense, against all reason. But the talk of the common folk, the gossip from Rosalía's tavern was stronger than his reason. "Think the worst of everyone and you think the truth."

She went on, "And our troubles aren't over yet. We won't be able to see each other very often. I must be doubly careful now. Human beings are incalculable. They're either cheering at one, Heaven knows why, or they're loathing and execrating one, again Heaven knows why."

"Murder will out," he thought. "She has to talk about it whether she wants to or not. If she says she hasn't done it I won't believe her, and if she says she has I won't believe her either. For no other woman can lie as well as she can, and she herself never knows what is truth and what falsehood."

"You know it too, you've often spoken of it," she continued with the same quiet detachment. "The evil demons lie in wait for one everywhere, and if one of them manages to penetrate one's defences then they all attack one at once. If I weren't the Duchess of Alba, perhaps the Holy Office would really come and try me as a witch. Haven't you yourself warned me to beware of the Inquisition, Francho?"

"Don't speak," he commanded himself. "I am not going to be involved in any argument. I've sworn it to myself." Aloud he said, "The wisest thing naturally would be for you to dismiss your Peral. If people don't see the doctor with you any more the rumours will soon stop."

She drew away from him, raised herself up. Thus she sat, half reclining, propped on one elbow, naked in the black torrent of her hair, and looked at him. There they had lain, flesh against flesh, and of what was within her he knew nothing. Clearly he was demanding of her that she feel guilty. But she didn't feel the faintest sense of guilt. If Peral had really done something to prevent this journey, he had not done it to help her but only because Don José had wished by this foolish expedition to deprive the doctor of her company for a long time. He, Don Joaquín, had himself expressly declared, when he had rejected the appointment as Court Physician, that it was done for his own sake, not for hers. How much better Don Joaquín understood her than Francisco, how much more pride he had! She would be under an obligation to no one, could not bear dependence, and he understood this, had never given the faintest hint that a new link had been forged between them by these stupid rumours. He passed unscathed through all the insolent whispering that went on around him, through all the filthy, prying curiosity.

She felt chilled, alienated by Francho's ignorance of her. He was an artist, as such ought to be one of them, a grandee, and most of the time he felt as they did, with infinitely more subtlety and refinement than the common man. Then suddenly he would relapse and become as small-minded and plebeian as a mule-driver. What was he imputing to her? If Joaquín had done this thing, ought she to abandon him in his hour of danger? She felt worlds away from Francisco. But in the next minute she was laughing at herself. He was a *majo*. She loved that side of him. A *majo* ought to be jealous, and when he was jealous a *majo* turned nasty.

"It's a pity, Francho," she said, "that you hate Don Joaquín. I don't think he hates you, and he's the cleverest man I know. That's why the Inquisition puts it about that he has Jewish blood and thinks night and day of nothing but daggers and poison. He is really very clever. And courageous. It's a pity you hate him."

Goya was profoundly angry with himself. Once again he had done everything wrong. You couldn't persuade Cayetana of anything, he should have known that by now. She did as she liked, she spoke and slept with whom she wished. He couldn't have done anything more foolish than to try to turn her against Peral.

At least he gave up the argument for the time being, and they parted on good terms.

In the weeks that followed they saw each other frequently. They spoke neither of their great quarrel nor of Don José's death. Their relationship was made darker, fiercer, more dangerous by what remained unspoken.

He did a great deal of work at this time. Agustín reproached him with working only with hand and eye, not with the heart. Agustín had again grown more morose, quarrelsome, and Francisco responded with ill-natured gibes.

Privately he admitted that Agustín was right. More than once the memory of that unfinished portrait of the old Marquesa rose to torment him. He felt an urge to complete this picture.

He sent to Doña María Antonia to ask whether she was willing to vouchsafe him the two or three more sittings necessary for the completion of the portrait. The Marquesa instructed her secretary to inform him that she had no time for him for years to come; enclosed was a draft for the agreed price of the finished portrait.

The letter came like a blow in the face. The Marquesa would never have insulted him thus were she not convinced of Cayetana's guilt and of his own complicity.

Even Cayetana, always so composed, grew pale when he told her about it.

A few days later there was public announcement of the gifts and endowments which the Duchess of Alba was distributing on the occasion of her husband's death to public bodies and private individuals. Doctor Don Joaquín Peral received "The Holy Family" by Raphael, from the gallery of the Palacio Liria.

Of all the great masters there had ever been, Raphael Sanzio was the one which Spaniards prized most highly, and this *tondo* of the Holy Family was as a work of art the proudest possession of the Iberian peninsula. One of the Dukes of Alba had made off with the valuable canvas from Nocera, when he was Viceroy of Naples, and since then the Dukes of Alba had regarded it as the finest work of art they owned, and this Virgin of Raphael's was the patron saint of the ladies of the house. If Doña Cayetana now made the suspected doctor such a truly royal present, it could mean only that she was wholly identifying herself with him. If he was guilty, then so was she.

"Keep calm," Goya told himself when Miguel and Agustín told him of this fresh outrage which Cayetana had perpetrated. He felt the dreaded black and red wave sweeping over him, to strike him deaf. He exerted all the will-power he possessed. The wave broke before it reached him; he could hear what the others were saying.

He looked over to the Virgin of Atocha and crossed himself. In so impudently giving away her patron saint the woman was challenging the very heavens. She was challenging the Marquesa, the Queen, the Inquisition, the whole country. Of all the things she had done, this was the most foolhardy, the most arrogant, the stupidest, the most magnificent.

He was weighed down by anxiety for her and for himself. He was no coward, he had a reputation for courage, but he knew what fear was. Danger lurked in every cranny, around every corner. When a cat eats it looks around all the time to see if an enemy is coming, and one could profit from its example. If one did not look ahead one was lost. Fear was essential if one wanted to survive, to stay on top.

She, meanwhile, she, Cayetana,
Had been born upon the heights where
One was free with crazy, splendid
Freedom from that fear which hampered
And tormented all the others
Not like her at home upon the
Heights. He felt an envious wonder

At her all because she was just
What she was, so crazy and so
Fearless. And it seemed to him that
Cramped and petty was his own heart
Looking at this woman's wildness
And her freedom.

Hated more than
Ever Don Joaquín Peral,
Knowing deeper still than ever
From this woman he would ne'er be
Free.

-- 25 --

Till now the people of Madrid had regarded the Duchess of Alba as a spoiled yet lovable child, and wherever she appeared, on the street, at the theatre, at the bullfights, they had acclaimed her because, great lady as she was, she bore herself like a *maja* and identified herself with the people. But now that she had made a present of Raphael's Virgin, that precious, sacred masterpiece, to the man who was her husband's murderer, popular feeling swung round. Now they put her in the same class as the foreigner, the Italian woman; she became for them the aristocrat who, protected by her privileges, stops at nothing however shameless. They no longer had any doubt that her Doctor Peral, with his black arts, had done away with the poor young Duke, and they looked to the Inquisition to shed its fiery light on the affair.

"Who would have thought it of Cayetana, *chérie*," said Don Manuel as he sat playing cards with Pepa. "The way she has compromised herself for our friend Francisco is unheard of. *Ce n'est pas une bagatelle, ça.*" Pepa herself felt a certain admiration for the Alba. She was impressed by the open defiance with which the woman admitted her love. Pepa inspected the cards, deliberated a while, played a trump. "But," she observed, "the lady achieves real grandeur only if she can also accept the consequences of her actions with dignity; for I suppose one can take it for granted that you will institute proceedings against the Duchess and her doctor."

Don Manuel had no intention of instituting such proceedings. It would be unwise, for presumably the other grandees would protect the Duchess. It was for Doña María Luisa to decide whether or not she wished to take steps against her enemy. He didn't want to get mixed up in it. He played his cards, let Pepa win, made no reply.

But he could not rid himself of thoughts of the Duchess. This insolent gesture with the Raphael was fresh proof of how unspeakably proud they were, these Albas. And just at the moment they really had no cause to be so. Fate had dealt them some ugly knocks. The man who had not returned his "thou" lay beneath the sod, and Cayetana's position was not an agreeable one either. There was too much odour of blood about her.

Presently he received even better satisfaction.

Immediately after Don José's suspicious death Doña María Luisa had begun to consider whether she ought to punish the Duchess and with her the doctor who had so insolently turned down her generous offer. Political considerations had given her pause. The war with England was going badly. More and more war contributions had to be demanded of the grumbling grandees; under such circumstances the nobility would have taken it as a provocation if the Queen had publicly displayed her displeasure with a lady of the rank of the Duchess of Alba. But now that the gift of the Raphael had provoked even the grandees to outraged protest, she could call the insolent one to heel without fear of opposition.

Doña María Luisa commanded the widowed Duchess of Alba to appear in Aranjuez, where the Court was then in residence.

She received her in her study, a light, cheerful room. White damask covered the walls, the chairs were upholstered in the same material. The writing desk was a present from the so shockingly deceased Louis the Sixteenth; the famous Pluvinet had built it of the finest mahogany, Dupin had embellished it with the choicest carving; the dead King himself had fashioned the ingenious lock. At this desk then, magnificent, in summery attire, sat the Queen; opposite her, in deep black, sat Cayetana; both ladies were drinking iced lemonade.

"Once already I have had to recommend to you, my dear friend," said María Luisa, "to take care that there should be an end to the scandal about you. Unfortunately you have thrown my motherly counsel to the winds and have given no thought to the wild rumours which your ill-considered generosity towards your doctor could not but occasion." Cayetana looked straight at her with an expression of innocent astonishment.

"Of course the simplest thing would be," María Luisa continued, "to have the affair of Doctor Peral thoroughly investigated. If I have asked the King to refrain from instituting such an investigation I did it only for your sake, Doña Cayetana. That is to say—I will be frank with you—I am not so much concerned with you but with those who will bear the name of Alba after you." "I don't understand a word, Madame," replied Cayetana, "but I do understand that I have incurred Your Majesty's displeasure." The Queen continued, as if the other had not spoken, "You, my dear, are obviously unwilling or unable to protect this noble name as it should be your duty to do. Therefore I must help you." "I do not ask for your help, Your Majesty," said the Duchess. "I do not wish it."

"You are always ready with an answer, Doña Cayetana," replied the Queen, "but you see, I have the last word." She had put her lemonade glass aside and was playing with the quill that could turn her words into a command which there was no gainsaying. "So, whether you like it or not, I am going to protect you from further rumours. I suggest that for a time you absent yourself from Madrid. For the duration of your mourning," she elucidated.

For the duration of the mourning! From the moment that she had been commanded to Aranjuez, Cayetana had anticipated that she would be banished. But that the exile should last three years—for such was the term of mourning prescribed for the widow of a grandee of the first rank—was something she hadn't reckoned with. Three years without Madrid! Three years without Francho!

Doña María Luisa watched her, still playing with the fateful quill. She had parted her lips slightly, a flash of her diamond teeth was visible. For one moment Cayetana had changed colour, but she was in command of herself at once; the other could scarcely have noticed her consternation.

"You have three weeks, my dear, to make your preparations," the Queen now said, relishing her triumph so profoundly that her voice sounded almost kind. The Duchess, apparently wholly indifferent, stood up, made a deep curtsy and spoke the usual formula, "I thank Your Majesty for your concern," and, as etiquette prescribed, kissed her hand. It was a well-kept, fleshy, almost childish hand, heavily ringed.

Cayetana told Francisco what had happened. "You see, I was right," she concluded with rather forced gaiety. "The Italian woman isn't quite as generous as your portrait made her out to be."

Goya was dismayed. Cayetana banished! Cayetana away from Madrid! The event would change his whole life. She would surely expect him to accompany her into exile. It was a tempting prospect, to be with Cayetana on one of her estates, without the bustle of the Court, the bustle of Madrid, without prying eyes round about them. But he was the King's Painter, he was President of the Academy; if he could leave Madrid at all it would be for only the shortest possible time. He was bewildered. In the midst of all his indecisions, expectations, calculations, there was a secret pride that in the end it had been he who had intervened in the destiny of this haughty noblewoman.

Before he could marshal his thoughts she went on, "I think it has its advantages, to live quite detached, to know that the gossip of Madrid has been forgotten there before it reaches me."

He had to say something. "Where will you go?" he asked stupidly. "For the time being I shall stay here," she replied, and as he looked at her in amazement she explained, "I'm going to force her to use her pen. Let her send me a royal command. I shall go when I receive the *Carta Orden*, and not before."

Meanwhile he had reached a decision. "May I accompany you, Cayetana?" he asked clumsily, proud of his courage. At the same time he had already calculated with peasant cunning that his ear trouble would afford a good pretext for taking leave of absence. "Of course you'll come too!" she cried, delighted. And he said exultantly, "This is something Doña María Luisa certainly hadn't thought of, that she might be doing us a favour."

But María Luisa had thought of it. To Goya's petition for leave of absence the Lord Chamberlain replied that the President of the Academy should postpone his departure, for the King had it in mind to give him an important commission. He was bidden to Aranjuez where Their Majesties would discuss further details with him.

Cayetana, when she heard it,
Went quite pale. "The underhanded
Bitch!" she burst out, but her reason
Soon returned. "A month," she said then,
"Or at most two she can keep you.
So you will be coming later.
And we luckily have lots of
Time, alas! Come soon, and work well.
Make her look just like herself, she
Finished with a smile of malice.
Yes, do make her look exactly
Like herself, precisely as she
Does look, your black *maja!*"

-- 26 --

When Goya reached Aranjuez he was conducted immediately to the King.

The monarch took a walk in the gardens with his painter. The portly man plodded along with Francisco half a pace behind him. The alleys stretched farther than the eye could see, the branches of the lofty trees formed a broad, arched canopy of leaves through which a little sunlight filtered. "Now listen, my friend," the King expounded, "to what I have in mind for you. It happens that during this merry month of May I have got all my loved ones about me here in Aranjuez. And so I had an inspiration. You must paint us, Don Francisco, all together in one picture."

Goya's hearing was good that day, and His Majesty had a loud voice. Nevertheless he supposed he must have heard wrong. For the prospect which arose before him at the King's words was one of unique, fairy-tale good fortune, and he feared that if he snatched at it too eagerly it might vanish into air.

Seldom could a King have the inclination to sit with his whole family for a painter. Persons of blood had little patience, and if the one had time to spare, another would be busy. Only highly prized masters had been permitted to execute such group pictures, and none since Miguel van Loo.

"This is how I've pictured it to myself," Don Carlos went on. "You will do something pretty, intimate, and yet dignified. I could, for example, be comparing my watches or playing the fiddle. The Queen could be reading, the little ones playing tag. Everybody pleasantly occupied and at the same time there is a certain dignity about it. You know what I mean, Don Francisco."

Don Francisco knew. But it was not his idea of the thing at all. A genre painting? Never! But he was cautious, he did not wish to spoil his wonderful opportunity. He thanked the King for his confidence in him, he answered respectfully, and for the exceptional honour. He asked for a day or two's time, after which he would put suggestions to His Majesty. "Granted, my friend," replied Carlos. "I'm never in a hurry, least of all in Aranjuez. If something occurs to you, let Doña María Luisa and me know."

On that day and the one following the usually gregarious Goya avoided company. Immersed in himself, almost bemused by his good fortune, not hearing or not wishing to hear when people called to him, he walked through the light, cheerfully formal castle of Aranjuez, strolled about in the wonderful gardens, beneath the leafy arcades in the Calle del Alhambra and the Calle de los Embajadores, past bridges large and small, grottoes and fountains.

Something "intimate." Well, His Majesty would just have to get on without that. Van Loo's "Family of Philip the Fifth" with its artificially natural grouping was stupid theatre, bungling insipidity; he himself could not descend to such depths. And then, Velázquez' "Court Ladies," the "*Meninas*"; to be sure, Spanish painting had produced nothing finer, and he admired the picture. But it was alien to him, with its frozen gaiety. As always, he did not wish to compete with anybody, as little with the great Velázquez as with the insignificant Van Loo. He wanted to compete only with himself, his picture must be by Francisco Goya, no one else.

On the second day he saw faintly, as from a distance, what he wanted. But he did not dare approach it too closely lest it vanish. Seeing vaguely and from afar, pondering and dreaming, he went to bed, slept.

Next morning when he awoke he knew quite clearly what he was going to do.

He had himself announced to the King and Queen. Expounded his idea, speaking more to Doña María Luisa than to Don Carlos. He would best succeed, he observed modestly, in his representation of the Catholic King if he were allowed to emphasize the grandeur, the unique dignity which radiated from their supreme persons. He was afraid of a certain artificial informality which could have the effect of seeming to portray merely noble or even bourgeois persons. Therefore he would respectfully urge Their Majesties to bid him strike the representative note in the projected family portrait. The members of the royal family should stand there as what God had made them, kings and infantes. They should stand there quite simply in their full glory.

Don Carlos was disappointed. He gave up only with reluctance the idea of seeing himself on the canvas with a watch in his hand and his fiddle on the table. On the other hand, his Court Painter's proposal recalled to him more forcibly than before an idea which had occupied his thoughts more than once in the last weeks. Confidential reports had come from Paris that a royalist conspiracy was in the making, and Manuel had hinted that if one were adroit in one's support of this movement the French people might offer him, Don Carlos, the head of the House of Bourbon, the Crown of France as well. "*Yo el rey de las Españas y de Francia,*" he thought to himself. If he stood there surrounded by his own in the pride of his uniform, with brilliant ribbons and glittering orders, with his imposing figure and dignified head, and if he kept zealously repeating to himself, "*Yo el rey,*" then surely this Court Painter should be able to convey a reflection of the same onto his canvas. "Your idea isn't half bad," he announced. Goya breathed again.

The significance of the Court Painter's words had at once been obvious to the Queen. She was majestic. Goya had often painted her thus, and in the midst of her own family she would appear doubly so. But wasn't Goya making it a little too simple for himself? "How do you conceive it, Don Francisco?" she asked, not ungraciously but still in doubt. "All of us in a row? Isn't that rather monotonous?" "If you will grant me the favour, Señora," Goya replied, "of letting me try, then I think I will be able to give you satisfaction."

It was agreed that the King and his family should assemble the next morning in the Green Gallery, all in gala dress, and then they would finally determine exactly how Don Francisco would paint "The Family of Carlos the Fourth."

Accordingly the Spanish Bourbons turned up the following day in the Green Gallery, all of them, young and old; yes, a lady-in-waiting was even holding with awkward carefulness a baby princeling who apparently was also to be in the picture. The ladies and gentlemen stood or sat in the sunlight which streamed through the large windows. The two youngest Infantes, the twelve-year-old Isabel and the six-year-old Francisco de Paula, romped about. All were in gala dress, which had a strange effect in the broad daylight. A crowd of attendants effaced themselves along the walls. There was considerable noise and at the same time constraint. A performance of this kind was not provided for by the Court rules.

Doña María Luisa took the situation in hand. "Here you have us, Don Francisco," she said; "now make something good of us."

Goya set to work. In the middle, between her two youngest, the twelve-year-old and the six-year-old, he placed the Queen; on her left, very much in the foreground, he planted the massive Don Carlos. This group simply made itself. The second group was simple to make too; there was the unobtrusively pretty Infanta María Luisa with her baby, whom the lady-in-waiting had handed over with a deep curtsy, and on her right her husband, the hereditary Prince of Parma, a tall man who did full justice to the space allotted him. The link between this group and the one in the centre was supplied by the placid old Infante Don Antonio Pasqual, the King's brother, who looked absurdly like him; the left side of the picture as seen by the beholder was adequately filled in by the three remaining Bourbons: Don Fernando, heir to the throne, a sixteen-year-old youth with an insignificant, passably handsome face, his younger brother Don Carlos, and their aunt, the King's eldest sister, the unspeakably ugly Doña María Josefa. It was a composition of childlike simplicity, and Goya anticipated that it would be disparaged for its lack of imagination; yet for his purpose it was exactly the thing.

However, "Stop! Stop!" the King ordered suddenly. "There are two Infantas missing," and he explained to the astonished Goya, "My eldest daughter, the reigning Princess of Portugal, and the Neapolitan Princess, my Crown Prince's future wife." "Does Your

Majesty wish," Goya asked, "that I should paint Their Royal Highnesses from pictures or from descriptions?" "Do it as you see fit," said the King. "The main thing is that they must be in the picture."

But now Don Fernando, Prince of Asturias, the Crown Prince, spoke up. "I don't know," he declared crossly in his harsh, breaking voice, "that it's fitting for me to stand here in the corner. After all, I am the Prince of Asturias. Why should the little one"—and he pointed to his six-year-old brother—"stand in the middle and I in the corner?" Goya, excusing himself and addressing the King rather than the Prince, replied tolerantly, "I felt it was artistically more desirable that there should not be a grown-up Infante between Your Majesty and Her Majesty but a small one, so that the figure of the King might appear to the better advantage." "I still don't see," grumbled Don Fernando, "why my dignity shouldn't be preserved." The King declared, "Because you're too tall," and María Luisa commanded, "You're to be quiet, Don Fernando."

Goya stepped back a little and surveyed the Bourbons standing there in a ragged line. "Might I ask Their Majesties and Royal Highnesses to move to another room?" he said after a while. "I need light from the left," he explained, "plenty of light from above falling to the right." María Luisa understood at once. "Let us go to the Ariadne Room," she suggested. "There I think you'll find what you need, Don Francisco."

With a great clatter and commotion the brilliant company set out on its march through the castle, the burly King and bedizened Queen in the van, the ugly old Infantes and the nice young ones behind, the rear brought up by the ladies and gentlemen in attendance. Thus they marched through rooms and along corridors to the Ariadne Room. Here the light was immediately congenial, falling from up high on the left just as Goya wanted it, and the vast paintings of mythological subjects on the walls were swallowed up in shadow.

There stood the King, the Queen, and the Princes, and in front of them stood Goya. He contemplated them and his eyes apprehended them, seized them, sucked them in with unbridled avidity. He observed them critically, clearly, with precision, stared long at them. There was silence in the room, and the attendants felt that what was happening, that is, that a subject of the King's should stare at him and his family like this, was unseemly, impertinent, disrespectful, and should not be allowed. Moreover, on this occasion Goya was wearing his working overalls though it was against the custom and his own habit; nor would he have been able to explain why he did so.

And now he actually said, "I have two more requests. If His Royal Highness the little Infante could wear bright red, then Your Majesties as well as His Royal Highness himself would appear to greater advantage. And then, it would be better for the picture as a whole if His Royal Highness, the Crown Prince, were not to wear red, but a pale blue." "This red is the same as in my General's uniform," angrily protested Don Fernando, "and it's my favourite color." "You'll wear blue," said the Queen dryly. Don Carlos said placatingly, "If Don Francisco has no objection you can wear more orders and ribbons to make up for it, the Golden Fleece as well." "His Royal Highness the Crown Prince," Goya said soothingly, "will be standing full in the light. Orders and ribbons will be particularly resplendent on him."

Working rapidly, he dashed off the sketches on his drawing board. Then he explained that he would have to ask the individual ladies and gentlemen for one or two more sittings, either alone or in small groups. He would need them together only once more for a last, large colour sketch. "Granted," said the King.

Goya did not sleep well that night either. No, he wasn't going to paint any meaningless episodes like Van Loo, and no one should say that what was all right for Velázquez was not all right for Goya. "Velázquez is great, and dead," he thought, almost exultantly, "and times have changed, and I'm not exactly small, and I am alive." And in the darkness, with inward exultation, he saw exactly what he wanted to paint, the conflicting colours that he would force to harmonize with each other, the whole shimmering glittering unison, and, in the midst of all this sparkling extravaganza, nakedly clear, the faces.

Before he could start work on the individual sketches he was summoned to the King's Chamberlain, the Marqués de Ariza. The latter received him in the presence of the King's Treasurer, Don Rodrigo Soler. "I have one or two announcements to make to the Señor Court Painter," declared the Marqués; he spoke politely but stared ahead into space without looking at Francisco. "Although it is quite proper to regard Her Royal Highness Doña María Antonia, Crown Princess of Naples, as the betrothed of His Royal

Highness the Crown Prince Don Fernando, still the negotiations between the high contracting parties are not wholly concluded, so that changes are still within the realm of possibility. It is therefore to be recommended that the Señor Court Painter give the betrothed Highness a certain indistinctness, almost an anonymity of feature, so that in case other dispositions are made the figure created by the Señor Court Painter could be used to represent another noble lady. Does the Señor Court Painter take my meaning?" "Yes, Excellency," Goya replied. "Further, it has been pointed out," went on the Marqués de Ariza, "that the number of princely personages to be depicted, if the future hereditary Prince of Parma, I refer of course to the baby, and the two absent Infantas are included, come to thirteen. Now it goes without saying that the noble personages to be depicted are above such and every superstition, but not so all possible beholders. In consequence it has been suggested that the Señor Court Painter should, as has been done before in such paintings, include himself in the picture, in an unobtrusive way, of course. Does the Señor Court Painter take my meaning?" Goya dryly replied, "Yes, I think so, Excellency. I am requested to put myself in the picture, at work in the shadows." "I thank the Señor Court Painter," returned the Marqués. "The Señor Court Painter has understood."

Goya was thinking furiously. He recalled how Velázquez had portrayed himself in his picture "The Royal Family," large, assured yet unassuming, in no wise in the shadow, and how King Philip had with his own hand painted the Santiago Cross on the breast of the painted Velázquez. He, Francisco, would paint himself in the shadow, but he would for all that remain entirely visible, and his King would reward him, probably with less grace than Don Felipe had rewarded Velázquez, but he would surely make him First Painter, at last; after he had imposed this momentously heavy task upon him there could be no doubt of that.

"There remains only the question of the fee to be settled," the Treasurer Don Rodrigo Soler spoke courteously, and at one stroke Francisco became the calculating peasant and resolved to hear very well indeed. For sometimes in such cases they might offer a very meagre fee, assuming that the painter would consider himself recompensed by the honour of the commission. "I thought at first," Francisco cautiously explained, "that the preparatory work could be limited to the execution of rough sketches of the individual figures; but it has turned out that I shall have to execute even the individual portraits down to the smallest detail. It will amount to four small group pictures and ten single portraits."

The Marqués de Ariza stood in silence, exuding haughty distaste. "It has been decided," said Treasurer Soler, "not to take the time spent as a basis for reckoning your fee. Rather will the value of your painting be assessed according to the number of exalted personages to be depicted. We will pay you for the heads of Their Majesties and Their Majesties' children two thousand reals each, for the heads of the remaining members of the royal family, one thousand reals each." Goya wondered whether he was to be paid for the heads of the absent Infantas, the babe-in-arms, and his own; but he did not ask.

He smiled to himself. The payment wasn't at all bad. He was in the habit of raising his price when the client wished to have his hands painted too. This time hands had not been mentioned, and it had been his intention from the beginning to paint very few hands, at most four to six. No, the payment was quite decent, even if they should pay for only ten heads.

The same day, in the makeshift studio which had been set up in the Ariadne Room, he began to work.

Here he could place each single model in exactly the light in which he or she would stand in the family picture, and he executed the sketches to the last detail. He painted Don Luis, the Prince of Parma, young, dignified, passably good-looking, a trifle stupid. He painted the old Infanta María Josefa. Although he had determined that not more than her face should peer out between the full-length figures of the Crown Prince and his anonymous noble bride, he spent two whole mornings on the sketches: the old Infanta's repellent ugliness fascinated him.

The King himself was a thoroughly cooperative model. He held himself very upright and threw out his chest and stomach. Thereon shimmered the pale blue ribbon of the Order of Carlos, shone the red ribbon of the Order of Christ of Portugal, glittered the Golden Fleece. The grey facings on his chestnut-brown velvet coat caught the light, the hilt of his sword flashed. The wearer of all this splendour stood there, erect, steadfast, impressive, proud of being able to stand for so long in spite of his gout.

If it was a pleasure to the King to stand there and pose, the rests between afforded him no less enjoyment. Then he would lay aside his sword, sometimes also perhaps his heavy velvet coat with all the ribbons and orders on it, would stretch out in a chair, lovingly compare his watches, and converse about hunting, farming, children, and other everyday topics. "You're going to be in the picture too, Don Francisco," he observed one day, benevolently. He surveyed his painter appraisingly. "You'll make quite an imposing figure," he declared. Then, "How about a little wrestling?" he suggested unexpectedly, with animation. "Of course, I'm much taller than you and probably more heavily built, but then, there's my age and my gout. Let me feel your biceps," he commanded, and Goya had to bare his arm. "Not bad," he pronounced, "but now feel mine." Goya did so. "Remarkable, Your Majesty," he acknowledged. Suddenly the King attacked him. Goya, taken by surprise, defended himself with some force. He had tried many a fall with *majos* in the Manolería, in play or in earnest. Carlos, breathing heavily, had recourse to unorthodox grips. Goya, angered by these, forgot that he hoped to become First Painter and, using a real *majo* grip, squeezed the inside of the King's thigh in a most painful way. "Ouch!" exclaimed Don Carlos with some vehemence. Francisco, controlling himself and for his part also breathing heavily, said, "I most humbly beg pardon." All the same it was quite a time before he allowed Don Carlos to put his knee on his chest. "You're a caution," said Carlos.

He showed Francisco favour in every possible way. He always felt particularly well in Aranjuez and wanted to communicate his good-humour to Francisco, thereby disturbing the progress of the work. More than once he took him hunting. On another occasion he summoned him to the great music room and there, a solid figure amid the delicate Chinese appointments, he played the violin for him. "Don't you think I've made progress?" he asked. "There are certainly better fiddlers in my orchestra, but among my grandees, now that our good friend Alba has been called home so early, I imagine I'm the best musician."

Of all Goya's sitters there was only one who was refractory, the Crown Prince Don Fernando. Goya treated the sixteen-year-old youth with special deference and did his best to win him over. But the violent, conceited Fernando continued stubborn. He knew that Goya was a friend of the Príncipe de la Paz, whom he hated. Early initiated into the pleasures of sex by servant maids, governesses, and ladies-in-waiting, the little Prince had soon discovered that Don Manuel was his mother's lover, and he had regarded him with a mixture of curiosity and jealousy. And now he had to pose for this Don Manuel's friend, in a coat whose colour he disliked, and to crown all the painter had the impudence to wear his working smock in front of him, the heir to the throne.

On the other hand, Doña María Luisa was a particularly willing model. She posed now by herself, now with the two children, according to Goya's wishes, or would permit each of the children to pose by itself.

At last the time came when he respectfully asked the ladies and gentlemen to assemble once more and in gala dress in the Ariadne Room to pose for the large colour sketch.

They stood there, a delight to Goya's eye; the harmonizing of clashing colours was there, as he had dreamed of it, rich, new, significant. The detail was subordinated to the whole, and the whole was in each detail. The conflicting colours were an effulgence, red and gold on the right, on the left blue and silver; in every gleam of light there was a shadow, each one differently shaded, and in each shadow a light, and in all the dazzlement the faces stood out naked, hard, the commonplace in the midst of the uncommon. He did not think of it in that way, he would have been unable to put it into words; he felt it.

He looked, he stared, penetratingly, irreverently, and this time the retinue were really shocked. The fellow stands there, this paltry underling in his shabby smock, and in front of him the Kings and Princes in all their glory, and he looks at them like a general inspecting his troops. This was rebellion, no less; such a thing would have been impossible before the French Revolution, and why did the Bourbons put up with it?

Francisco began to paint, rapidly and at length. The old Infanta María Josefa complained that she couldn't stand any longer, and Carlos put her in her place by telling her that a little endurance was the least one could expect of an Infanta. But Goya did not hear, genuinely did not hear; he was abandoned to his work.

At last he broke off, and everybody stretched themselves and wanted to be off. "Another twenty minutes," he asked, and when he saw the reluctant faces he begged and besought them. "Only twenty minutes more, then I won't need to trouble you, not so much as once more." They capitulated. He painted. There was silence, one could hear a big fly buzzing against the window. At last

Goya said, "Thank you, Your Majesty. Thank you, Your Majesty. Thank you, Your Royal Highnesses."

When he was left alone he sat for a long time, blissfully exhausted. His vision had taken shape, it could no longer elude him.

Suddenly, abruptly, a violent longing for Cayetana seized him. From the violence of it he realized the effort it had cost him to suppress all thought of her for so long.

It would have been more sensible, would have been the only sensible thing, for him to have stayed in Aranjuez and gone on with his work. But he asked himself, "Is she still in Madrid? And for how long or how short a time?" And he

Sent a message to Madrid, to
The Duquesa, he would be there
On the following day. His brains he
Cudgelled searching for the reason
Why his painting really needed
And required his presence briefly
In Madrid. All this was very
Stupid and he knew it, yet he
Did it nonetheless.

He rolled the
Sketches, the great colour one and
Also all the single studies
Carefully together; took them
With him in great pride, much hope and
Most almighty haste, and with them
Drove off to Madrid.

-- 27 --

On the first night after his return she came to him. The summer nights were short, and for Cayetana there was the risk that she might be surprised on her way from his house to hers in the morning. Nevertheless she stayed till dawn.

The next evening she came very early. He told her about his work, showed her the colour sketches, tried to explain to her the novelty and importance of what he was going to do. But she scarcely listened to his fumbling words; she looked at the sketches, at the assemblage of self-satisfied, puffed-up heads above the magnificent apparel; her mouth twitched, she laughed. Laughed aloud with delight. He was offended. Was this to be its effect on people? He regretted having shown it to her.

But his annoyance was of short duration. He was happy to see her, to touch her, to possess her. Everything about her made him happy. "*Ven ventura, ven y dura*, come fortune, come and stay," he thought, humming it to himself over and over again.

This, the second night, she also spent with him. Perhaps they were her last hours in Madrid; on the morrow the three weeks were up which María Luisa had permitted her. But she did not believe that they would really dare to banish her by edict, and he could not believe it either.

The following afternoon he received a hasty note from her: "Come at once." And he knew she had been exiled. He rushed to her.

In the great Palacio Liria all was confusion. Servants ran up and down everywhere, orders were given, revoked; even the dignified Doña Eufemia did not hide her excitement. Yes, Cayetana had received the *Carta Orden*, a command written by the King's own hand.

She received Francisco in her bedchamber. He found her on the point of being dressed for the journey; in her petticoat, without shoes, giving orders to her maids all the while, she told her story. She was to leave the city that very day, and to stay on one of her Andalusian properties till further notice. She was expressly forbidden to leave the kingdom of Andalucía without special permission. "I shall travel by roundabout ways," she said. "I shall travel in such a way as to pass the night only on soil that belongs to me." She laughed at the hubbub around her. The little woolly white dog barked.

His heart yearned to go with her, to be with her now, just when she was so open-hearted and of such good courage. And he must forgo this, forgo just those weeks when she would wholly and solely be his. He would not forgo it. Rather would he renounce the picture which he already carried with him in imagination, rather renounce career and fame. He must be with her now, he glowed with the desire to do as she did, to defy all the world as she had defied it with her rash, proud, foolish, admirable present to that wretched doctor. But in the next moment he glowed just as hotly with longing for his picture. The picture summons him imperiously, the picture is within him, the whole sparkling, glittering, shining flashing deluge of colour, and the naked faces emerging therefrom—"The Royal Family" by Goya, not emulating "The Royal Family" by Velázquez but in its own right a picture that is worth looking at. He said a little hoarsely, "May I escort you, Doña Cayetana?" and then at once, rather half-heartedly he added, "At least for the first day?"

She had been looking at him with her discerning eyes as all this went through his mind, and he had the uncomfortable feeling that she had read his thoughts. And now that he had made his rather lukewarm offer she was laughing, if not unkindly. All the same he was offended. Did it mean nothing when the King's Painter abandoned in midstream the work which was to make him First Painter, and declared his readiness to accompany a lady who was in disfavour on her journey into exile? "I am fully able to appreciate what you have offered me, Don Francisco," she said. "But you are a prudent man, and this time I am going to be prudent too. If you were to ride for a day beside my carriage and swallow the dust it raises only to give up all hope of ever being First Painter in return, three days later you would regret it and would regret it for the rest of life. Isn't it so? And I'd rather not think of all the lovely names you would silently hurl at my head all those years, perhaps not even so silently. And so—thank you, Francho," and she rose on her toes and kissed him.

Then she added casually, "And anyhow, Don Joaquín is accompanying me, of course, so I shall in every respect be in good hands."

He had already assumed that Doctor Peral would go with her, it went without saying. But still it was a blow to him.

Servants called her to the carriage.
"Follow after soon, Francisco,"
Said she and the simple words rang
Full of longing. "Paint your picture,
Paint it to the very end, like
Lightning Luca, and then travel

Off to Andalucía swift as
Though the Holy Office on your
Heels came riding."

— 28 —

Till now Goya had given Agustín no opportunity for a real talk with him. But scarcely had Cayetana left when he said, "Now, you sour-faced old Agustín, I'm going to show you what I've been doing." And he unrolled the sketches and fastened them on boards with little nails.

Agustín stood in front of them, stepped back, went up again, thrust his big bullet head close to first one sketch, then another, swallowed, smacked his long thin lips. "Let me explain," Goya began, but with a "Don't say anything. I know already," Agustín waved him away. "You don't know a thing," said Goya, but he said no more and let the other go on looking.

"*Carajo*," Agustín broke out at last. It was a huge, mouth-filling obscenity, a real mule-driver's oath, and from the way in which Agustín brought it out Francisco realized that he had grasped the significance of the picture. Even so he could not restrain himself, he had at least to put into words what he was trying to do, had to explain it. "I don't want anything contrived," he said. "I'm not going to imitate Velázquez with some ridiculous tableau, you understand. I simply put these people down on the canvas, quite artless and childlike." He felt that words, above all his own words, were clumsy and inadequate for the delicate complexities he was trying to analyse, but something forced him to continue. "The details must be quite clear, and at the same time one mustn't notice them at all. The faces alone must look out at one, hard, real, exact just as they are. And behind all this it's dark, one no more than senses the huge daubs in the Ariadne Room. Do you see what I'm trying to do? Understand?"

"I'm not a complete idiot," answered Agustín. And with quiet exultation he added, "*Hombre!* This is going to be something really great. And something really new. Francho, Francho, what a painter you are!" "So you've noticed it at last," Francisco returned with satisfaction. "Day after tomorrow we go to Aranjuez," he went on. "Of course I'm taking you with me. We don't take long to finish it. All I have to do is to transfer the portraits to the main canvas. Here we've already got everything that matters. It will be magnificent." "Yes," said Agustín with conviction. He had waited anxiously to see if Francisco was going to invite him to come too; now he was childishly pleased. And he struck a practical note at once. "So, day after tomorrow it's Aranjuez," he said. "There's a great deal to see to first. I must go to Dacher about the frame and the canvas, to Ezquerra about the paints, and I must mention the varnishing to him too."

He thought for a while and then observed hesitatingly, "You haven't seen your friends all this long time—Jovellanos, Bermúdez, Quintana. And now you're going to Aranjuez for several weeks more. Don't you think you ought to meet them?"

Goya's brows had darkened, and Agustín was afraid he was going to fly into a passion. But he controlled himself. He could hardly understand how he could have got on for so long without Augustín, he couldn't imagine doing any further work in Aranjuez without this most understanding of all friends, so he really must give him this pleasure. Besides, Agustín was right, it would be taken amiss if he did not see his friends.

He met Miguel and Quintana at the house of Jovellanos. "We haven't met for ages. I was completely tied up in my work," he excused himself. "Of all the good things in the world," Don Miguel observed bitterly, "work is the only one that doesn't leave a bad taste in the mouth."

And then, of course, they spoke of politics. Things were going badly for Spain, worse than Goya, who had held affairs in general at arm's length in Aranjuez, had been willing to admit to himself. The fleet, forced into war by the allied French Republic, had never recovered from the heavy defeat off Cape Saint Vincent. The English had taken Trinidad, had cut the supply line from India, were ever threatening the coast of the Spanish motherland. The heavy cost of the war was bringing misery and famine in its train. But the Paris Directory intended to let Spain suffer for having delayed so long over the conclusion of the alliance. The Republic basked in the victories which its armies had won in Italy and left Spain everywhere in the lurch. General Bonaparte had gone so far as to dethrone the Italian relations of the royal house of Spain and confiscate their territories. Of course the alliance with France was sound politics and remained the only possible course. But instead of insisting that the Republic should in turn fulfil her commitments under the treaty of alliance, Spain was giving in all along the line. The reason for this was that the Queen and Don Manuel had quite openly sold offices or given them away to their favourites. Evil men were occupying the important posts, men who instead of cherishing the interests of Spain took bribes from the Republic. Even María Luisa herself was not unsusceptible. If she screwed herself up to the point of making strong demands, then costly presents would arrive from Paris and the sharply worded protests would become tame complaints.

Goya listened in silence, defensively. He belonged to the Court. Fundamentally these people here, inasmuch as they were inveighing against the Court, were his enemies. It was strange that Spain's curse should be his own blessing. Likely enough that the cheerful good-natured Carlos was a bad king, that the domination of Doña María Luisa was her country's misfortune; yet if these two had not been as they were, there would be no commissions for him. Even the fact that General Bonaparte had taken the Grand Duchy of Parma away from María Luisa's brother struck Goya as an advantage. For if the Prince of Parma and his Infanta had not thereby been compelled to spend the summer in Aranjuez, who knows if Don Carlos would have hit on the splendid idea of having "us all painted together."

These considerations did not prevent Goya from sharing in the indignation over Spain's evil and self-seeking government. "These gentlemen must have had to try very hard to bring so blessed a land as ours so low." The words, and the way Jovellanos said them, rang in Goya's ears.

But he shook his big head, he had other things to think of. He was preparing for his return to Aranjuez.

He had barely had time for Josefa in these few days; now it lay on his conscience. After all, since he had shown his work to Cayetana and Agustín, he didn't want to keep it a secret from her. With a faint, slightly embarrassed smile he led her up to the mounted sketches.

Tried to explain his intentions to her. She knew enough about painting to make sense of his explanations and the sketches. She pictured the finished painting to herself and could not tell if she liked it. That wonderful glittering confusion of which he spoke would surely emerge from the canvas, and the faces of the Kings and Princes would sharply stand out. But the sketches seemed to look evilly at her, and the idea of the finished picture made her shiver. She was afraid it would contain an evil spirit, something dangerous, heretical, seditious. Their Majesties were, to be sure, not exactly beautiful in real life, but in the portraits by Raphael Mengs, by Maella, by her brother, and even in earlier portraits by Francisco, for all that they were good likenesses they had not been *quite* so ugly. Would they tolerate it? Surely the picture could bring only misfortune.

"Well, what do you think?" asked Goya.
"Are the King and Queen," she queried
Back, "and even more the aunt, the
Old Infanta not"—she hunted
For a word— "Too like?" he helped her.
"Yes." Attracted yet repelled, she
Stood and looked at them and answered
Finally, "Well, after all it
Is a masterly achievement,
Only so surprising."

-- 29 --

In Aranjuez, in the Ariadne Room, Agustín's expert and admiring eye saw his friend's inward vision now made visible to all by the skill of his hand.

There was something else which Agustín now realized with deep satisfaction: namely, that "The Family of Carlos the Fourth" was a political picture. But he was careful not to give utterance to the thought. For of course Francisco would never think of painting politically. He believed in the absolute monarchy, he felt drawn towards this good-natured king, so full of the sense of his own importance, and towards Doña María Luisa who with her insatiable appetite cut herself such a vast slice of the world's cake. But the ugly events which were besetting Spain, the shattered ships, the ransacked treasury, the Queen's weaknesses and arrogance, the misery of the people—all this was in Goya's head as he painted, whether he wished it or not. And it was precisely because he painted without hatred that amid the glittering pride of uniforms, orders, and jewels, amid the sparkle of all these attributes of monarchy by divine right, the pitiable humanity of every single one of those representatives of royalty leaped to the eye with stark, factual brutality.

Goya worked with the utmost perseverance, industry, and a sovereign contempt for the irrelevant. He had been directed to render anonymous the features of the Crown Prince's noble bride since no certain choice had been made; he simply made the magnificently adorned unknown Infanta turn her head away. He had actually gone so far as to forget till the last moment the King's eldest daughter, the absent Princess Regent of Portugal. Agustín reminded him. Francisco waved him away. "All right, all right, I can do her in two minutes," and he went on painting away at the big head of the Infante Don Antonio Pasqual with its expression of sour dignity. A meal was announced; he went on working. The head was finished, and again he was summoned. "You just sit down," he told Agustín. "I'm coming directly. I'm just quickly going to paint the Princess Regent." And in fact the soup was not yet cold before the completed face of the Infanta, indifferently, exaggeratedly inexpressive, peered out between the Infante Antonio and the tall Prince Luis.

To paint himself into the picture took him less than an hour. Then the living Goya nodded with mischievous pleasure at the painted Goya looking out of the darkness, somewhat shadowy as desired but easily recognizable and by no means subservient.

Altogether Goya was in a consistently good temper the whole time, contrary to Agustín's expectations. As on former occasions, the King and Queen did all they could to facilitate his work. They sent him the gala costumes and orders which he needed, and Goya must have laughed as he hung the ribbon and cross of the Golden Fleece around Agustín's neck or, to Agustín's own grim amusement, stuck some stout lackey into Don Carlos's royal robes and told him to stand there and be stately, like the King.

There came a day when he put in the last highlights. And then, addressing both himself and his friend, he asked, "Is it finished?"

Agustín looked at it. There were the thirteen Bourbons. There was the stark, cruel reality of their deplorable faces, the magical, staggering profusion of colour which was their royal inheritance. "Yes, it's finished," said Agustín. "Has it anything in common with Van Loo's 'Family of Philip?' " Goya asked and grinned. "No," said Agustín, grinning broadly. "Nor with Velázquez' 'Court Ladies,' " he said, and his deep rumbling laugh mingled with Goya's clear and happy one.

"Perhaps we ought to show it to Don Miguel," suggested Agustín. Senor Bermúdez was in Aranjuez with Don Manuel and Agustín looked forward to seeing the great connoisseur's astonished face.

Don Miguel came, looked, and made up his mind at once. The picture disturbed him inwardly, repelled him, he found it barbaric for all its artistry. All the same, he hesitated before he spoke. Hadn't he been quite sure of himself in the case of Lucía, and hadn't Francisco turned out to be right with this picture too, not from genuine æsthetic knowledge but from the uncanny depths of his intuition?

"An unusual picture," Miguel said at last. "Very different, very original. But—" He stopped. For meanwhile his self-confidence had returned. It was impossible that his theoretic principles, evolved after decades of labour and effort, could be so utterly mistaken. He owed it to the æsthetic wisdom of the great ones of the ancient world, the mantle of whose humanism after a course of two thousand years had fallen upon his, Don Miguel Bermúdez', shoulders, that he now took up the cudgels against this piece of barbarity. "I admire your colour effects, Francisco," he said. "They are against the rules, but I must allow that this whirlpool of lights, this controlled turmoil of colour is high art. But why do you confront the beautiful with so much that is repellent? I delight in any genuine realism, but your Bourbons are not portraits, they are caricatures. And why the oversimplified, primitive composition? I can't think of any work, either by an old master or a contemporary, which you could cite as a precedent. Don't hold it against me, Francisco, I look up to you, you are my friend, but

I can't go along with you in this." He finished by saying in a tone of authority, "This picture is not a success."

Agustín was sorry they had ever shown the picture to this erudite ass, whose sufferings over Lucía had not made him any wiser. Angrily he thrust his knobbly head forward, made ready to reply. But Goya gave him a warning sign. "I don't hold it against you, my friend," he said lightly to Miguel.

Meanwhile the latter returned to the charge. "Have the King and Queen seen the picture?" he asked anxiously. "I made sketches of the individual figures," Goya replied, "and those they must have seen. I haven't allowed them to see the picture itself while I was at work on it." "Forgive me, Francisco," said Don Miguel, "advice is seldom welcome, I know, but I owe it to you to be frank, and I can't withhold my advice. Don't show the picture as it now stands. I beg you not to." And, fearless of the displeasure which he saw mounting in Goya's countenance, he went on, "Can't you at least treat your Carlos and your María Luisa with a little more"— he groped for a word—"kindliness? After all, among the lot of us you are the one who sees them with the most charitable eye." "I have been neither charitable nor uncharitable with them," Goya replied. "I have made them as they are. That's how they are and that's how they will remain, forever."

The painting got dry, was varnished. Señor Julio Dacher, the famous French frame maker, stretched it into its frame. A day was fixed on which the royal family was to inspect the picture.

Then for the last time Goya was in the Ariadne Room, walked back and forth in front of his completed work, waited.

The doors opened, Their Majesties and Royal Highnesses entered. They had been strolling in the gardens, they were simply dressed, wearing only a few orders, and with them, himself modestly turned out, was the Príncipe de la Paz. A considerable retinue, including Miguel, came with them. Don Carlos, as he entered, fumbled under his coat and waistcoat, produced two watches, compared them and pronounced, "10:22, 14th of June, 10:22. You have delivered the picture on time, Don Francisco."

There they stood, the Bourbons, not grouped as they were in the picture but haphazardly, and the Bourbons in the flesh inspected their painted counterparts, each one his own and all the others. Behind them, in the shadow, both in reality and in the painting, stood the painter who had so arranged and painted them.

The canvas glittered and sparkled most royally, and they stood there on the canvas large as life, larger than life, true to life, truer than life, unmistakable for anyone who had ever, however fleetingly, beheld them.

They gazed and were silent, somewhat bewildered; it was such a large picture, they had never been painted on quite such an expanse of canvas before or surrounded by quite so many other Highnesses.

Don Carlos stood massively in the middle both of the picture and of the room. He was pleased with the whole, he was pleased with himself. How wonderfully his chestnut-brown coat was executed, one could see that it was velvet; and how accurate was the hilt of the sword, was every star and every ribbon; and he himself was most effective, he stood solidly there, unshakable, one could tell how much strength and marrow there still was in his bones, despite his years, despite his gout. "Like a rock," he thought. "*Yo el rey de las Españas y de Francia*," he thought. "A very impressive picture." He was about to make a good-natured jest to Francisco but decided to wait for some utterance from his María Luisa.

She, the ageing, ugly, unadorned María Luisa, stood between her husband, her lover, and her children, and her sharp, darting eyes scrutinized the ageing, ugly, bedizened María Luisa of the picture. There was much that might displease many people in this painted woman, but it pleased her, she liked this woman. The woman had a face ugly but unique, it constrained one to look at her, it lodged in the memory. Yes, that was she, María Luisa of Borbón, Princess of Parma, Queen of the whole Spanish Empire, Queen of the two Indies, daughter of a Grand Duke, consort of a King, mother of future Kings and Queens, willing and able to wrest from life all that life had to offer, without fear or regrets, till the time should come for them to carry her out to the Escorial and down into the Panteón de los Reyes. If she were to die today she could truly say she had made of her life what she had wanted to make of it. And around her stood her children; she looked with satisfaction at the sweet little Infante whom the painted Queen holds by the hand, and at the pretty little Infanta around whose shoulders she lays her arm. She had had the children she had wished for, living, healthy children, not only from the fat stupid man whom she had to use to ensure to herself and her children forever the position which was theirs by right, but also from the man whom she had desired more than any other, and unless the whole world were to perish, these children would one day also sit upon the thrones of Europe. Yes, they were fine, healthy, intelligent children, her lover had bequeathed his looks to them, she her intellect. It was a good honest picture, not sentimental or flattering but realistic and proud. The only pity was that her Manuel was not also in it.

The silence lasted a long time. Goya began to be uneasy. He looked grimly across at Don Miguel. Had he brought bad luck with his peevish, pessimistic prognostications? Josefa had also had her doubts. Was it possible that Their Majesties might really think he had painted them too unkindly? When all the time, far from harbouring any irreverent thoughts about them, he had actually felt something like respect for this well-meaning King and a certain sympathy with the lust for life of this woman who was at the same time both Queen and *maja*. He had painted the truth, as he always had, and till now his truth had always found favour in the eyes of grandees and *majos* alike, yes, even of the Inquisition. He had actually counted on becoming First Court Painter on the strength of this picture, and was even that going to go wrong? Were they never going to open their mouths, the idiot and the whore?

At this point María Luisa spoke. "You have done well, Don Francisco," she said. "It is a sincere, faithful portrait, well calculated to show posterity what we Bourbons are like." And immediately Don Carlos loudly chimed in, "An excellent picture, a family picture, exactly as we wanted. And by the way, what is its size, how high, and how wide?" Goya was ready with the information: "2.80 metres high and 3.36 metres wide." "A great picture in every respect," Don Carlos declared with satisfaction, and he added archly, "*Cubríos*, put on your hat, Goya," as if Don Francisco were one of his twelve first grandees.

Everyone now congratulated Francisco extravagantly. Don Miguel warmly pressed his hand, his countenance unusually moved. He had waited apprehensively for what the King would say. He was whole-heartedly pleased that the doubtful affair had turned out so well for his friend, and, moreover, found therein confirmation of his own views. It was really not to be wondered at that a barbaric work should appeal to the barbarian King.

Meanwhile the Príncipe de la Paz was whispering in the King's ear. The latter replied, aloud, "Yes, a gentle hint is certainly permissible." And, turning to Goya, he announced in ringing tones, with a broad smile, "Yes, my friend, in a few days I think you will have an agreeable surprise." And Manuel underlined it: "Yes, Francho, we've made it this time."

Ever since Bayeu's death Francisco had hankered after the appointment as First Painter, it would be the explicit and formal recognition of what he knew himself to be already. Yet two minutes ago he had doubted that it would come to pass. And now the fulfilment was at hand. There was nothing left to wish for. He was sensible of his own power, of his growth and consummation, his efforts had been crowned with success. Agustín recognized it, the experts recognized it, these bone-headed rulers recognized it. And so would the French and even the Germans. And so would those to come after. *Idioma universal.* Young Quintana had hit the nail on the head. And today he had this palpable, tangible success, and tomorrow his glorious beloved.

He travelled back to Madrid, made ready for his journey to Andalucía.

As long as he had been working on the "Family of Don Carlos" he had scarcely spared a thought for Cayetana, but now he burned with desire, was stung by impatience. He was unable to work, the smell of the paints, the very sight of a canvas, was repugnant to him. But he did not dare to leave Madrid till he held documentary evidence of his appointment in his hands. He could not believe in it as long as it was not signed, sealed, and delivered. There was many a slip between a promise and its fulfilment, and he feared his demons who always lay in wait. For that reason, in order not to call down the demons upon himself, he breathed no word of the King's promise, neither to Agustín nor to Josefa. He consumed himself with waiting and dared not leave Madrid.

The Treasurer of the Crown, Don Rodrigo Soler, paid him a visit. "In the matter of your fee, Don Francisco," he explained, "I imagine we are agreed that there are in question six exalted heads at two thousand reals each, and five exalted heads at one thousand reals each. You will perceive that I have included the head of His Highness the baby Prince in the reckoning. On the other hand, I am sure you will accept the fact that heads twelve and thirteen, those of their absent Highnesses, are not to be paid for. In the same way, head fourteen, your own, need not be considered." Goya found the payment not generous, but not niggardly either.

Another day passed, another, then a third. An appointment took effect only when it had gone through all the ministries concerned, with the result that slack or ill-disposed officials could delay the matter as long as they wished. Therefore it was natural that Goya had to wait. But his impatience became morbid, his hearing deteriorated. He was more and more often assailed by the idea of journeying at once to Andalucía, to Cayetana, let come what might.

Then, on the fourth day after the Treasurer's visit, Don Manuel appeared, accompanied by Pepa. One of his red-stockinged servants, carrying a great portfolio, stood modestly in the background.

"I've heard all about your picture, Don Francisco," prattled Pepa, "and, with Don Manuel's permission, I even went to Aranjuez, rather behind Their Majesties' backs, and had a look at it. It's not like me to do such a thing, but you know how interested I am in your work. It certainly is a good picture, a real tableau, I must say. Not only the largest, but the best you've produced. Of course you've taken it rather easy in parts. The Prince of Parma, for example, is certainly too tall. But, taking it all round, it's an excellent picture. And so colourful."

Don Manuel said, "I come in an official capacity. I have an agreeable communication to make to you." He gave a sign to the red-stockinged one, who handed him a document with a large official seal. "I intervened in person," he declared, "otherwise it would have taken another three weeks. As it is, I am in a position to hand the document over to you today. Shall I read it out to you?" he asked ponderously.

Goya naturally knew what this was all about, and Don Manuel had a right to look for thanks; nevertheless he had difficulty in mastering his irritation at so clumsily patronizing an approach. "My hearing isn't very good today," he replied. "May I be allowed to read the document myself?" "As you like," said the Minister, somewhat offended.

Goya read: "The King our master desires to reward you for your outstanding services and to give you a mark of his exalted favour such as may act as an encouragement to the other professors of the Academy and afford them proof of how highly His Majesty values pre-eminence in the noble art of painting. For this reason the King our master has been pleased to appoint you to be First Court Painter, with an annual emolument of 50,000 reals, payable as from today. Further, the Treasury is instructed to pay you yearly 500 ducats to defray the expenses of your carriage. The Treasury will also negotiate with you over the payment of an adequate subsidy towards a representative residence. May God preserve you for us for many years to come. The First Minister Don Manuel Príncipe de la Paz."

Goya, now genuinely moved, said hoarsely, "Thank you, Don Manuel." "Not at all, my friend," said Don Manuel, his faint displeasure dissipated by the painter's visibly profound gratification. Pepa, however, looked full at him with her beautiful, bold green eyes and said, "I wanted to be the first to congratulate you, Francho."

When Goya was alone he read the document over and over again. He was delighted with the subsidy on his residence and even more by the five hundred ducats for the carriage. His conscience had never ceased to prick him because of this carriage, and now his purchase of it was to be vindicated. He had sometimes thought the King was being stingy in trying for so long to save himself the expense of a First Painter's salary. But he had done him an injustice. Don Carlos was generous and knew the value of the arts. And in future he wouldn't listen to a word his friends might say against him.

When he told Josefa of the appointment she heaved a sigh of relief. Her brother, now asleep in the Lord, had ever and again declared that a painter must combine the true with the beautiful. Francho had transgressed these principles, and to the last she had been afraid that Their Majesties might not approve his representation of their sacred persons. Now for the first time she was convinced that her Francho owed his rise not to her brother or to his connection with the great name of Bayeu, but to his own achievements, and that he was a painter in his own right.

To his friend Martín Zapater, Goya wrote: "I have not written for a long time, but I have been overloaded with work. With satisfying work. Even today I have no time for a long letter, I must make all haste to the south, to a certain great lady. I think you can guess her name. Also I have been appointed First Court Painter, and will need to seek your advice in the matter of new investments. I have commissioned my Agustín to send you a copy of my diploma. Show it to my mother and my brother and indeed to everyone in Saragossa. I am about to step into my carriage, for which, by the way, the King will in future pay me five hundred ducats a year. The Virgin be praised. I am absolutely exhausted by the work accomplished and by my good fortune. Buy two fat candles for the Virgin of the Pillar. Martín of my heart! The King and Queen vie with each other over your friend Francho."

He travelled to Aranjuez to render thanks to Their Majesties. He ordered post horses for the south. Immediately after the audience he changed his clothes, sent his Court dress back to Madrid, and embarked at once on the journey to Andalucía.

"Hurry, hurry!" But upon the
Second day the experienced driver
Thought they'd better make a detour,
Told the painter that the highroad
Was no good, being full of potholes
And of bandits. Goya, however,
Would hear nothing of a detour.
A whole golden ducat piece he
Gave the astonished driver, saying,
"Have no fear, old man, for in your
Wagon here there rides a child of
Fortune."

-- 30 --

Goya sat half-dressed in an easy chair and watched Cayetana drinking her chocolate in bed. The curtains of the alcove in which the wide bed stood were parted. On either side of the bed stood an antique figure of a goddess, carefully wrought out of the finest wood; the breasts of both goddesses supported candlesticks, and although it must have been high noon the candles were lit. They gave but little illumination, the room lay in a beneficent twilight, one could only imperfectly distinguish the frescoes which ran along the walls, an absurd garden panorama. The walls of the alcove itself were painted to represent tall windows, the shutters had amusing peepholes painted in them through which could stream in an imaginary sun, and it was pleasant to sit in the cool room and picture to oneself how warm it must be outside.

Cayetana toyed and nibbled, dipping sweet pastries into the thick chocolate. The dueña looked on anxiously lest any of it should run down. Goya looked on too, lazy and contented. No one spoke.

Cayetana finished her breakfast, the dueña relieved her of the cup. Cayetana stretched languidly.

Francisco's happiness was complete. When he had arrived the day before, late in the afternoon, she had run out to greet him, had shown her joy in a most unladylike way and embraced him in the presence of the major-domo. And then while he was bathing and changing she had talked to him through the open door. They had dined alone, and it had been a gay meal; they had chatted and made childish jokes and also some less childish ones, no barbed words were spoken, and throughout the long, voluptuous night no evil thought had come to trouble him; they had been wonderful hours.

She threw back the bedclothes, sat on the side of the bed. "You need not attend my levee, Don Francisco," she said. "Sleep a little longer or inspect the castle, or go for a walk in the garden. I will meet you at the belvedere half an hour before we eat, for a little walk."

He came early to the belvedere. It afforded a fine view of the house and the surrounding landscape. Like most houses here in the neighborhood of Cádiz, the extensive building was in the Arabian style, the walls, broken by only a few windows, were very white, a slender lookout tower thrust up into the sky from the flat roof. The gardens sloped away in terraces. Broad and sluggish the Guadalquivir flowed on its way to the sea. The town of San Lúcar and its *vega* lay, like an oasis, entirely surrounded by sand; the flat landscape stretched for miles on each side of the vineyards and olive groves, yellowish-white. Scanty growths of pine and cork oak struggled for existence amid the sand. The dunes undulated. The salt mines shimmered white.

Goya regarded the landscape without much interest. Whether

it was the mountains of Piedrehita which furnished the background or the dunes of San Lúcar, what mattered to him was that he was alone with Cayetana, far from the Court, far from the city of Madrid.

Doctor Peral joined him. They made desultory conversation. Peral told him something of the history of the house which lay before them. Count Olivares had built it, he whom Velázquez had so often painted, the all-powerful Minister of Philip the Fourth; here Olivares had spent the last bitter years of his exile. Then Don Gaspar de Haro, his nephew and heir, had built onto the house, and he it was after whom the castle came to be named Casa de Haro.

After that, on his own initiative, Peral rehearsed the events of the past weeks. Cayetana had naturally not been able to give any large evening receptions as she was in mourning, but there had been many guests nonetheless, from Cádiz, from Jerez, even from Seville. "Where there's a good bone the dogs gather," Goya called the old proverb to mind. From time to time they had themselves gone to Cádiz, to the Duchess's palace there, also called Casa de Haro. Once, veiled, Doña Cayetana had attended a *corrida* in Cádiz; and the bullfighter Costillares had been a guest for two days in the castle here. Goya had not expected Cayetana to stand the whole time on her lookout tower, watching for his coming, as did the ladies in Pepa's romances, but he felt rather put out nonetheless.

Cayetana appeared; in her train were the dueña, the page Julio, the little Negro girl María Luz, the small dog Don Juanito, and several cats. She had dressed herself with especial care, obviously for Goya's sake. He was delighted. "It's a good thing," she observed, "that we no longer do as our grandmothers did, when a widow had to wear black till she died or remarried." He was taken aback at the lack of constraint with which she spoke of her widowhood.

Peral asked leave to withdraw. The others walked through the gardens, a small procession: on either side of it, their tails held high, went the cats. "Your index finger points downwards perhaps a little more imperiously than before, Cayetana," he said, "but otherwise I can't see much change in you." "And your underlip sticks a little further out, Francisco," she returned.

There were a number of sundials in the garden, one with the

pointer painted on. "Count Olivares," Cayetana explained, "became a little strange here in his banishment, it seems. Obviously he dreamed of being able to make time stand still till his stars became more favourable."

They had a light meal. Around the walls of the dining room ran the washed-out fresco of a garden, with many columns, garlands, Egyptian motifs. Here too the painted finger of the sundial pointed always to the same hour.

After the meal Cayetana withdrew. He went to his room; it was warm, he lay down naked on the bed for a long siesta. He felt lazy, without initiative, for him a very unusual state of affairs. He was always busied with schemes, he could never lie in bed without thinking of the coming day, of the weeks to come, of fresh undertakings. Not so today. Today he wasted no regrets on the sleep which overcame him as so much time lost. He savoured with pleasure the enveloping mists into which his body sank away. He slept deeply and awoke in joyous mood.

The days that followed were like the first, relaxed and happy. Much of the time he and Cayetana were alone. With Eufemia, Cayetana had absolutely no reserve or sense of shame.

Once they were sitting, Cayetana and Francisco, half-naked in the darkened room. It was warm and Cayetana was fanning herself. Eufemia entered, bringing iced lemonade. She noticed the fan, stopped dead, let fall the glass of lemonade, ran to Cayetana and snatched the fan from her. "Not with that one, not when you're sitting there like that!" she cried. It was a fan on which was painted the Virgin of the Pillar.

Such an occurrence was, relatively speaking, an important event in San Lúcar. They had both been through much, Francisco and Cayetana. Seldom in all their lives had they experienced so calm and contented a time, and they rejoiced in it.

He did little work. He did not touch canvas, brushes, palette. These were the first weeks since his apprenticeship in which he had not painted. On the other hand, he drew a great deal, but only for his own pleasure. He simply committed to paper what pleased him in Cayetana's daily round. Once she asked him if he did not wish to paint her, as *maja* perhaps. "Let us be lazy," he begged. "Painting is my way of thinking. Don't let us even think."

"How many names have you actually got," he asked her on another occasion when confronted by a document in which her titles took up row upon row. *Hidalgos* could have up to six Christian names, grandees up to twelve, but grandees of the first rank were under no restriction as to the number of their baptismal names. It was a good thing to have many names; one enjoyed the protection of as many saints. Cayetana had thirty-one names, and she recited them: "María del Pilar Teresa Cayetana Felicia Luisa Catalina Antonia Isabel" and the rest. He remarked that for all his good memory he didn't think he could remember so many names, but one thing he did know, that she had as many faces as she had names. "Recite me your names once more," he demanded, "name for name, and for each one I'll draw you your face." She repeated the names, he drew; both women, Cayetana and the dueña, looked on. He drew fast, boldly, with zeal and wit, and the faces, though all were faces of Cayetana, were quite noticeably different; there were many amiable ones among them, but also some uncanny, evil.

Cayetana laughed. "How do you like me, Eufemia?" she asked, turning to the dueña. "What the Señor First Painter has drawn is splendid," replied Doña Eufemia, "but it would be better were he to go no further. It's sinful, putting everything down on paper." "The next name, please," said Goya. "Susana," said Cayetana, and Goya went on drawing. As he drew, and without looking at the dueña, he asked, "Do you think I'm a sorcerer, Doña Eufemia?" The dueña replied, choosing her words with care, "Excellency, I believe that the artistic gift, as it is from God, should preferably be used for the presentation of what is holy." Goya went on with his drawing and remarked casually, "I have painted plenty of saints. In many a church you will find holy pictures by me, Doña Eufemia. I've painted San Francisco de Borja alone nine times for the Osunas." "Yes," said Cayetana, "they're very proud of their family saint, are the Osunas. We Albas have no saint."

Goya had finished his sketch. Neatly he appended name and number: "24, Susana." Cayetana looked out from the paper, charming, mocking, enigmatic. Eufemia turned to her mistress in extreme disapproval. "It would be well, my lamb," she said beseechingly yet with emphasis, "if one or two of these sheets did not exist. Please ask the Señor First Painter to tear up this 'Susana' and some of the others. These pictures will bring down the demons on you, believe me. May I?" Already she had her hand on the "Susana." "Kindly leave that alone!" shouted Cayetana and rushed at her, half laughing, half in earnest. The dueña held out towards her the golden cross which hung about her neck, in order to ward off the evil demon which had clearly taken possession of her ewe-lamb.

Several times, morning or afternoon, while Cayetana slept, Francisco rode on a mule to the town of San Lúcar. There in the Venta de las Cuatro Naciones he drank the jerez which grew in the neighbourhood and chatted with the other guests in the tavern, men in big round white hats and, even in summer, their violet-coloured coats. The age-old town of San Lúcar—thought by many to derive its name from Lucifer—was known and notorious as the cradle of a breed of daredevils who knew how to lie and steal their way out of any difficulty. The *pícaros* in the old romances came from here, and a *majo* who could claim San Lúcar as his birthplace could feel proud. The place had grown rich by smuggling, and now that a powerful English fleet was blockading Cádiz it hummed with life and affairs. In the tavern de las Cuatro Naciones too, one always met mule-drivers in the gaily coloured costume of their trade, and they could tell stories from all over the country such as one never heard from anyone else. With these muleteers then, and with the other guests, Goya made idle conversation full of insinuation and innuendo. He understood their language and their ways and they his.

Sometimes too he would ride to some little place in the neighbourhood, to Bonanza or Chipiona. The path led through thin plantations of ilex, over glaring yellow sand dunes, and everywhere the shimmering white of salt mines. Once as he was riding across the sand he saw *El Yantar* again, the midday ghost. Slowly it crawled along, half-man, half-tortoise, hypnotizing rather than frightening the beholder, as its other name, *La Siesta*, implied. The ghost crawled slowly and inevitably on its way, but not in the direction or across the path of Francisco. He reined in his mule and watched it a long time. From far away on the shore came the sounds of children at play, hidden from sight by the dunes.

When he came back he found a letter from Cádiz. Señor Sebastián Martínez wished to present three pictures to the Santa Cueva and inquired whether the Señor First Painter felt inclined to take on the commission. Señor Martínez was known everywhere as the owner of Spain's largest merchant fleet; he commanded a respectable share of the trade with America and was regarded as a generous patron of the arts. The proposal came opportunely for Goya. He could ask a stiff price of Señor Martínez, and the work for the Santa Cueva afforded him the desired pretext for his prolonged absence from Court. To himself he also argued that the execution of religious works of this kind might do something to expiate what was sinful in his infatuation and the happiness it brought him. He decided to discuss the matter with Señor Martínez in person; Cádiz could be reached in a few hours.

Cayetana, when he told her of his intention, replied that it was a happy coincidence, that she had herself in any case been on the point of proposing that he go with her for a few days or even weeks to Cádiz. The war had brought a good deal of life into the place. And the theatre was good too. They decided to go at the end of the week.

That night Goya was unable to sleep. He went to the window. The moon was almost at the full; Goya looked out over the garden and the shining, distant sea.

Cayetana in the garden
Walked to taste the evening coolness,
Walked alone. He asked himself if
He should not go down to join her.
She did not look up, however,
At him, nor did he go down. Some
Of the cats were with her. Strangely
Soundless she was moving up and
Down and to and fro across the
Terraces, where fell the soft and
Blurred uncertain light. But Goya
Stood for long there at the window,
Watching her, as through the lightness
Of the night she passed, and with her
Went the cats, their tails like banners,
High and solemn and amusing
As they went.

31

The Duchess was showing Goya around her palace in Cádiz, the Casa de Haro. Count Olivares and Gaspar de Haro, the builders of the house, had spared no expense. While most of the houses in this city, which was unable to expand at the head of an extremely narrow promontory, were tall and narrow, they had constructed spacious salons around a large, quiet patio, a wonderful paved courtyard which itself looked like a magnificent room. Around this court, on the inner side of the three stories, there were galleries. From the flat roof a lookout tower aspired into the sky.

A musty coolness pervaded the whole spacious house. As in San Lúcar, here also there was a sundial with the hand painted to make the time stand still. There was a wealth of marble, there were paintings, sculpture, chandeliers. The *señores antepasados*, the noble ancestors, had not counted the cost. And yet the house now had a somewhat neglected air, the frescoes on the walls were fading and flaking off, some of the many steps were caved in.

They walked, Goya and the Duchess, on worn-down marble staircases large and small. Pedro, the old caretaker, himself somewhat gone to seed, preceded them, walking ceremoniously on stiff legs, gently chinking his bunch of keys. Finally, also on yellowed and worn-down marble steps, they ascended the *mirador*, the lookout tower. The spiral staircase led past a closed door, and then they were standing on the flat roof of the tower and looking down over the low parapet at the city which lay like an island shining white in the middle of the very blue sea, joined to the mainland only by the extremely narrow neck of land.

The Casa de Haro stood on high ground, at almost the highest point of the city. Francisco and Cayetana looked northwest and saw the harbour and its many guardian forts. They saw the strong squadron of Spanish warships and they saw the plains of Andalucía, bounded by the mountains of Granada. They looked westward and saw the wide ocean, and on the horizon the English fleet which was blockading the harbour. They looked south and saw the coast of Africa. And at their feet lay the houses of Cádiz with their flat roofs like gardens, adorned with plants of all kinds. " 'The hanging gardens of Babylon,' as His Excellency Your Grace's deceased grandfather was wont to say," observed the old caretaker.

Cayetana and Francisco were as good as alone in the great house. They had come in advance, with only the dueña; the others, Doctor Peral, the major-domo, the secretary, the whole household, were to follow after a few days. They ate their meals alone, waited on by Pedro and his wife, they were almost always by themselves, they knew that this could not last, and they made the most of their isolation.

Goya had made an appointment for the second day with Señor Martínez, his client. He had plenty of time, so he strolled through the city which, built as it was on a limited area, was very populous. He walked through the narrow streets between tall white houses with flat roofs to the Puerta de la Mar, where he revelled in the noise and bustle. The Mohammedan poultry vendors who had brought their ducks and chickens across from nearby Africa, the fishermen whose fish and mussels, vivid of smell and colour, lay spread out before them, the fruit-sellers standing by their mounds of many-coloured fruits, the pedlars selling sacred pictures, amulets, and sailors' caps, all this teemed and stank, assailing eyes, ears, and noses, beneath the brilliant sky, framed by the blue sea with the Spanish and English squadrons. More than once black-clothed women accosted Francisco and offered him girls, describing them in juicy terms. They reminded Francisco that the *solano* was coming, that sultry African wind which kindles desire; he might well regret having repulsed their offers. "Such a pretty round belly," they extolled, sketching it with their hands.

It was time for him to go to Señor Martínez.

Goya had heard a good deal about Sebastián Martínez. He had the reputation of being an enlightened man and had played his part in the modernization of industry and agriculture in Spain's overseas empire. He was not satisfied, as were many of the rich merchants of Cádiz, to amass profits, but had often, and under the most unpleasant circumstances, led his fleet in person to America and had acquitted himself well when his privateers had been involved in clashes with the enemy. After all this, Francisco was astonished to find in Señor Martínez a spare man dressed with exaggerated plainness, more resembling a pedantic scholar than a great merchant, pirate, and politician.

It was soon apparent that his famous art collection was less a matter of prestige than of love and understanding. He revealed his treasures lovingly to Goya, he emphasized that he himself had catalogued his galleries. He was almost prouder of his collection of reproductions of works which might be of significance in the history of art than he was of the paintings and sculpture he possessed. It was virtually complete, he boasted, the only one of its kind in Spain.

In three of the salons antiquities from Cádiz were on display. As he showed them to his visitor Señor Martínez said, "I don't pride myself in the least on my having contributed to the welfare of some of our possessions beyond the seas or on the fact that my fleets have more than once proved a match for the English, but I am proud of belonging to the oldest family of commoners in the oldest city in Spain. Even the historian Horozco speaks of a forebear of mine, a Martínez." "There's no fool like a learned fool," Goya thought, recalling the old saying.

Then Señor Martínez pointed out the oldest example of his city's coat of arms, which had adorned a long since vanished gateway. The relief showed the pillars which Hercules had erected when he came to this most westerly country of the inhabited world. "*Non plus ultra*, so far and no farther," Hercules had said, and there it was on the coat of arms. Of course he had not said it in Latin but in Greek, οὐκέτι πρόσω, and Señor Martínez quoted in Greek the lovely verses of Pindar from which the words were taken. Emperor Karl the Fifth had appropriated the proud motto, but had dropped the "*non*." "*Plus ultra*, ever onwards," he had created the device, and the forebears of Sebastián Martínez, those doughty burghers, had followed its precept and had thrust with their daring ships ever farther westward.

Goya observed with a smile the way in which the man's arid countenance was rejuvenated as with spirit and not without charm he recounted the antiquarian history of his city.

"But I'm keeping you with my stories, Don Francisco," Señor Martínez interrupted himself, "and I asked you here on business. I want to ask you, Excellency," he said, all of a sudden very dry, "to execute some paintings for the Santa Cueva. Let us make a deal, Señor First Painter. To be quite frank, I would rather have asked you to paint a portrait of me, but you might have turned that down, whereas one can scarcely reject a commission from the Santa Cueva. Am I not right?" And he tittered.

"Frankness for frankness," replied Francisco. "What do you propose to pay?" "Allow me to give you some confidential information," Señor Martínez answered. "I have the intention of running the English blockade with some of my ships and of taking the ships to America and back myself. For certain reasons my little fleet must not put to sea before three weeks from today, but not after that time either. Now I want to hand over the pictures to the chapter of Santa Cueva in person, so I must ask you to work fast, Don Francisco. On the other hand, should the pictures be delivered inside of three weeks, I am prepared to pay not the three thousand reals you usually ask, but six thousand per picture. You see, Excellency, even at the hands of a commoner one doesn't fare badly," he concluded, and tittered.

Goya often felt annoyance
At the supercilious manners
Of his grandees. This white city,
Cádiz, rich, luxurious city,
Richest and most pleasure-loving
In the world, than blazoned London
Even richer, had by burghers,
Sailors, merchants, been created.
But he did not like her either.
He could understand a burgher's
Pride, and yet this man Martínez
With his money, and his knowing
Zeal for art, did not attract him.
Neither did the subjects please him,
Miracle and allegory,
Supper, feeding of the thousands;
Still, a painter could not always
Choose for whom and what he painted;
After all, six thousand is a
Lot of money. Thin and dry he
Saw his patron's hand extend and
In it laid his own strong, plump one,
Saying, "Check."

-- 32 --

Cayetana invited Francisco to go up the *mirador*, the lookout tower, with her. But this time she did not go past the closed door halfway up the stairs, but opened it and bade Francisco enter.

The chamber was small; musty air hit them in the face. The interior was dim. She opened the shutters and abruptly light streamed full into the room. It was virtually empty; a single picture hung on the wall, a wide picture of medium height in a magnificent frame. In front of it stood two worn, comfortable armchairs. "Sit down, Don Francisco," Cayetana invited with a faint and as it seemed to him mischievous smile.

He inspected the painting. It depicted a mythological scene, with muscular men and fleshy women; it seemed to have originated in the workshop of Peter Paul Rubens, and evidently it had not been his most gifted pupils who had worked on it. "You have better pictures than this," Francisco observed after a while.

Cayetana pressed a button in the wall. The mythology shifted sideways, apparently by means of a spring, and revealed another picture.

Francisco stiffened, rose to his feet, went and stood behind his chair. His face became tense, almost dark with concentration, his lower lip thrust forward. He was all observation and attention.

In the picture was to be seen a reclining woman who, supporting herself on her right arm, looks at herself in a mirror and turns her back on the beholder. The woman was naked. In the mirror, which a little kneeling, winged boy is holding up to her, her countenance is faintly visible. But it was no foreigner who had painted this naked woman. She had not originated in Antwerp, nor yet in Venice; no, the picture before which Francisco now stood was from a Spanish hand, could have been painted by only one person, by Diego Velázquez. It was, there could be no doubt, the daring, famous, forbidden "*Doña Desnuda,*" the "Naked Woman" of Velázquez, a Psyche or a Venus or whatever one liked to call her, and in any case a very real naked woman.

Goya forgot that the picture was a good hundred and fifty years old, that he was in Cádiz, that Cayetana was at his side. He looked at his colleague's painting as if it had just been finished, at his colleague's, Velázquez', most daring and dangerous picture, the "*Doña Desnuda.*"

Every man selects some other man, alive or dead, for emulation. If Francisco had been allowed to ask some favour of fate, he would have asked for the fame and genius of Velázquez; he acknowledged no other Spaniard as a great master, apart from Diego Velázquez. Nature and this Don Diego had been his masters, and all his life he had struggled wholly to comprehend his painting. And now, here was this great new, mysterious, and extremely celebrated picture. Goya, quick in feeling and perception, quick to love and hate, to honour and despise, reacted before even half a minute had passed: he admired the picture, and he rejected it.

He admired the way the extremely graceful woman was posed; he admired the artifice whereby his colleague had left the woman's countenance to the undefining obscurity of the mirror while focusing all the beholder's attention upon the wonderful lines of the body; but above all he was full of admiration that Don Diego had undertaken to paint the picture at all. The interdict of the Inquisition upon the pictorial presentation of nakedness was unequivocal and strict, and no other Spanish painter had attempted to paint this most enticing of all subjects, naked female flesh. Don Diego might to some extent have been protected by the favour of his sovereign, or some other powerful client, but one could be sure the priests and bigots of the Court of Philip the Fourth had not lacked influence either, and the whims of the great are unpredictable. Velázquez had painted this woman because he had felt the urge to prove that nakedness could be presented otherwise than as by Titian and Rubens. He had put himself in danger because he was a great artist and full of Spanish pride, and because he had wished to prove that we Spaniards could also bring it off.

He had proved it.

Wonderful how the colours melted into each other! The mother-of-pearl of the flesh, the whitish draperies, the greenish grey of the looking glass, the dark brown of the hair, the reddish purple ribbons on the naked boy, the faint rainbow hues of his wings. The nude woman was painted with an airy delicacy, a severe elegance, there was nothing cheap about her, nothing of the crude, shrill sensuality which emanated from the female flesh of the Dutch and Italians. On the contrary, there was something almost sombre about the picture, and the sobriety of the whole colour scheme forbade any sense of intimacy. Don Diego was a Spaniard. For him love and beauty were no airy frivolities; they were something savage and profound, often the occasion of tragedy and suffering.

Francisco gazed and admired. As Don Diego had no doubt intended one should. But when one painted a woman in all the splendour of the flesh which nature has given her, and painted her in such a way as to leave the beholder cold, was that right? All right then, Don Diego had achieved it, that mastery beyond love and hate, that pure objectivity of art. But if the Devil were to offer him, Francisco, this mastery as a gift, he wouldn't want it, he would say, "*Muchas gracias*, no!" And he was happy because he was the painter Francisco Goya and not the painter Velázquez.

Suddenly a shrill, croaking voice was heard in the room. "The lady is a lazy lady," said the voice. "Ever since I've known her she's been lying here on the divan looking at herself in the glass and taking it easy."

Goya had swung around. There stood a monstrosity, a crippled, shrivelled old man, dressed in very loud colours and plastered with medals and the highest orders. "You shouldn't always give people such a fright, Padilla," Cayetana reproved him, but without asperity. She explained to Goya that he was the court jester of her dead grandfather, that he was called Padilla, that he lived here in the protection of the old caretaker and his wife, was very shy and seldom appeared in public.

"It's sensible of her to live in Cádiz, the *Doña Desnuda*," Padilla croaked on. "She wouldn't be allowed to live anywhere else. And at that she's really such a fine lady, actually a grandee of the first rank. She hasn't lifted a finger for a hundred and fifty years." To a grandee work of any kind was considered a disgrace.

"You must go away now, Padilla," Cayetana said still gently. "You mustn't disturb the Señor First Painter any longer." Padilla bowed, his orders jangled, he went.

Cayetana sat in the armchair. She looked up at Goya and asked with an expectant smile, "Do you think Padilla is right? Do you really think she *was* a grandee? Great ladies sat in the nude for Titian and Rubens, that has been proven." And in her rather hard, childish voice she repeated, "Do you believe she was a grandee?"

Till that moment Francisco had thought only of the painter and the painting without even the most passing thought for the model. But now that Cayetana asked he knew the answer at once, his excellent visual memory gave him certainty. "No," he said, "she was no grandee, she was a *maja*." "Perhaps she was a *maja and* a grandee," said Cayetana. "No." Francisco waved her away with the same certainty as before. "She is the same woman as in the picture 'The Spinners,' " he declared. "There's no doubt of it, the one who is unwinding wool from a reel. Think of the back, the neck, the arm; think of the shoulder, the hair, the whole carriage.

"Yes, she was a *maja*, not a
Grandee," he decided firmly,
Yet with calmness.

Cayetana
Could not call to mind "The Spinners"
But she thought Francisco surely
Must be right. She was a little
Disappointed. She had fancied
That it would be nicer, standing
Thus with him before this picture.
Once again she pressed the button
And the naked goddess, naked
Spinner, hid herself away then,
Hid in myth.

— 33 —

As they sat at dinner that evening Cayetana, prompted no doubt by the appearance of the court jester Padilla, gave Goya some reminiscences of her past life.

As a child she had been several times in Cádiz, with her grandfather, the twelfth Duke of Alba. He had counted as the proudest man in Spain, had regarded no one as his equal save the King, the coarse-fibred Carlos the Third, whom he could not endure. For a time he had been ambassador in France and had been the wonder of the Courts of Louis the Fifteenth and Sixteenth, for his luxury and pomp. After his return to Spain he had flouted the Inquisition; for his standing was so high that in spite of his respect for tradition he could afford to play the philosopher, free-thinker, which was forbidden to everyone else. From the dungeons of the Inquisition he had extracted a young man crippled by the tortures to which he had been subjected and had made him his court fool, the very same dwarf they had seen today; he had incited him to make bold and seditious remarks, named him Padilla after the hero of the early great insurrection, had allowed him to wear his own orders and decorations. No one was worthy to consort with the Duke of Alba except this fool. Because her grandfather plumed himself much on his free-thinking he came of choice and often to Cádiz; this city, which through its commerce had many links with abroad and was always full of foreign merchants, was the most enlightened in Spain. "My grandfather," Cayetana recalled, smiling, "brought me up on the principles of Rousseau. I was to learn in three ways: from nature, by my own intuition, and by luck."

Goya ate and drank and listened. Real grandees were quite different from what he had imagined them to be, proud in a very much more subtle way. One had clocks and time stand still when his luck was bad. Another kept an embittered court fool because no one else was worthy of having speech with him. And then there was Cayetana. Seventeen empty castles waited for her coming, and a court jester whom all through the years she had forgotten.

He ate with her, he slept with her, he was closer to her than he had ever been to anyone, and further apart.

Next day Cayetana's household arrived in Cádiz, and from that time Francisco was seldom alone with her. Since the beginning of the war Cádiz had become more and more the capital city, gentlemen from Court, high officials of the Crown, members of the council of the Indies, came there, and all were anxious to wait on the Duchess of Alba.

Francisco also met many friends and acquaintances from Madrid. He was pleased though not surprised when one day, representing Don Manuel, Señor Miguel Bermúdez turned up.

Miguel naturally talked politics. Don Manuel had veered round again and as it was easiest for the moment he was treating with the reactionaries in the Church and aristocracy and holding up the very same liberal measures which he himself had introduced. In foreign politics he was uncertain. The new French ambassador, Truguet, was a clever, quiet man. Don Manuel was still less a match for him than for the departed Guillemardet; he was first too aggressive and then too servile.

"What actually happened to Guillemardet?" Goya asked. Scarcely had the ambassador returned to Paris, Miguel informed him, when he had to be put away in a madhouse. Goya was strangely moved: had not his painting of the man foretold this fate? What had deprived Guillemardet of his reason, Miguel went on, was presumably his inability to follow and adapt himself to rapid changes in the public events in France. He had probably at a pinch been able to justify to himself the swift change from revolutionary radicalism to a moderate bourgeois democracy; but to accept the much more extreme swing over to a definite plutocracy was apparently beyond his powers.

Then, in his capacity as one of the agents of the Bank of Spain, young Quintana also appeared in Cádiz. Accompanied by Miguel, he visited Francisco in the Casa de Haro. The Duchess and Doctor Peral were also present.

Quintana lighted up at once when he saw Francisco and began to rave over "The Family of Carlos." "You, Don Francisco," he cried, "are Spain's saviour in her spiritual crisis!" "How so?" the Duchess asked with curiosity. She sat there, dazzlingly beautiful in her black dress; she was not offended that Quintana was clearly more interested in Goya than in herself; she examined without embarrassment the young man who was capable of so much honest enthusiasm; she herself gave encouragement to the arts, because it was proper for a grandee to do so, but her interest was not very deep. "This Spain of ours," Quintana explained, "drags her history and tradition with her like a chain. For someone to come along and expose what these originally great institutions have become today is what I call a feat. You see, Doña Cayetana," he told her eagerly, "a king of today, the Catholic King for example, is certainly furnished with all the outward symbols of power, but his functions have been whittled away. The Crown has become nothing but an obsolete head-covering, for a government of today a constitution is more necessary than a sceptre. And this is made visible in 'The Family of Carlos.'" "You don't say, young man," observed Goya.

Doctor Peral asked Quintana to tell him more about the picture. "You are not familiar with it?" the young poet queried, astonished; "nor you either, Duchess?" "You must understand, Don José," the Duchess answered kindly, "that I'm not here exactly of my own free will. I have been banished from Madrid." "Where are my brains, Duchess?" Quintana excused himself with a slight, agreeable laugh. "Of course you haven't seen the picture. But one can't describe it in words, no one could," and at once he began to describe it, raving about the flood of colours, the realism of the heads emerging from it, naked, hard, and ugly. He spoke as if Goya were not there. "It's a particular device of the painter's," he declared, "that in a picture so rich in figures so few hands are visible. Thereby the naked faces are permitted to stand out doubly sharply from the blaze of uniforms and gala apparel."

"If they'd paid me more," Goya said dryly, "I would have painted more hands. I ask a high price for hands." But the young man went on, "We all thought Spain was senile. And then Francisco Goya came and showed us how young she still is. He *is* the painter of youth, Francisco Goya." "Well, well," said Goya; he sat in his chair, stout, his shoulders drooping a little, fiftyish, hard of hearing and in other ways the worse for wear, and it seemed a little odd for Quintana to be calling him the painter of youth. But no one laughed. And Quintana continued, "Don Francisco's most recent pictures have proved it; this country has had the honour of producing three undying masters, Velázquez, Murillo, Goya.

"Moreover, Velázquez had a much easier time of it," mused Quintana aloud. "He revered the Crown and the nobility with his whole soul, and in those days that was the natural accepted thing. He must and could be inwardly in harmony with the King and his Court. To glorify the concept of monarchy was to him the noblest duty of the Spanish painter, and he had himself to be an aristocrat, had to feel he belonged, in order to achieve his artistic purpose. Our Goya on the other hand is unaristocratic through and through, and that is what is right for today. He looks at his King with eyes just as sharp as Velázquez', but there is a bit of the *majo* in him, he is a Velázquez of the people, and his painting has something refreshingly brutal about it." "I hope you won't take it amiss, Don José," Goya replied easily, "if I brutally and unaristocratically remind you of the old saying, 'I've let you pull out three hairs, at a fourth I will get unpleasant.' " Quintana laughed, and the talk turned to other things.

Cayetana, later, told him,
Told Francisco though his friends were
Surely clever, yet for her part
She could not imagine either
Of them as *cortejo*, even
Not the young one. "Curious," she
Mused naïvely, quite forgetting
That she might wound Goya's feelings,
"Curious, that very clever
Men, for instance your Don Miguel,
Or Quintana, or my Peral,
Never have a proper charm for
Me."

-- 34 --

The presence of the Duchess of Alba, Spain's most celebrated woman, excited the Caditani, and they vied with each other for her company. The Duchess was in mourning, which afforded a convenient excuse for receiving or not as she felt inclined.

Francisco maliciously observed how uncertain the proud citizens of Cádiz were in Doña Cayetana's presence, and the intrepid, learned, self-possessed Señor Sebastián Martínez, Francisco saw with grim enjoyment, was more deeply affected than anyone else.

On the pretext of wishing to discuss with him the pictures for the Santa Cueva, Martínez had more than once sought him out in the Casa de Haro. Francisco could not avoid introducing him to the Duchess. Señor Martínez had been received at Court, great men put themselves out for his favour, his immeasurable wealth and the fame of his exploits rendered the thin, almost ugly man attractive to many women; there were stories of occasional wild excesses on his part. But Doña Cayetana obviously aroused in him from the first moment a boyish romantic passion, and when he spoke to her this sophisticated and usually reserved gentleman was unable to master himself; his gaze flickered, his dry visage reddened. Cayetana enjoyed the sight, she treated him with that amiable, almost imperceptible hauteur which only she possessed. The experienced Señor Martínez must have realized that he was no more to her than a toy, a *pelele*. Yet in spite of his burgher's pride it was clearly just this inborn arrogance which he found so attractive.

At the end of the second week Goya was able to inform Señor Martínez that the pictures were ready for delivery. Señor Martínez inspected the product of his eighteen thousand reals. His comments were highly flattering and not wholly undiscerning. Perhaps now, he concluded, the Señor First Painter might have the time and inclination to execute a portrait of him, Sebastián Martínez, merchant of Cádiz; as Don Francisco was already aware, his fleet was not going to put to sea till the following week.

"I don't know," Francisco answered indifferently, "that I shall feel like working for the next few days. I have come here for a rest." "What remuneration could tempt you to interrupt your holiday for two or three days?" asked Señor Martínez. "Twenty-five thousand reals," Francisco replied without hesitation, astounded at his own effrontery. "Agreed," said Señor Martínez, also without hesitation.

But then, and rather tentatively, he asked if he might be allowed to invite the Duchess and Francisco to a small celebration at his house. The occasion offered; the pictures for the Santa Cueva were finished. Goya answered dryly that he was not in a position to accept invitations for the Duchess. Furthermore, he knew that Her Grace had already made plans for the next two weeks, after which Señor Martínez would be safely at sea, leading his ships to America.

Señor Martínez was silent for a while, his dry visage working. Then he said that if he could have the honour and pleasure of being allowed to welcome Doña Cayetana and Don Francisco under his bourgeois roof he would let his squadron put to sea without going with it himself. Goya was taken aback. He shrugged his shoulders. "Speak to the Duchess," he advised.

In the circle of intimate friends, and in Doña Cayetana's presence, the talk was of how Señor Martínez had given up his intention of accompanying his fleet for the sake of giving a party for the Duchess. "It must be disagreeable for a woman to arouse desire wherever she goes," Quintana commented with obvious disapproval. "You are extremely young, Señor," said the Duchess.

In deference to Doña Cayetana's mourning, Señor Martínez had invited only a small company. The usually self-assured Don Sebastián was at pains, even on this occasion, to display bourgeois moderation. As was only fitting, he devoted himself to the Duchess scarcely more than to his other guests, but he could not prevent his admiring, entreating gaze from turning to her again and again.

The custom was to sit down at the gaming tables after dinner. But Señor Martínez had made other plans. "Allow me to invite you into the theatre, Doña Cayetana," he said to the Duchess. "Serafina is to dance for you." "Serafina?" she asked, genuinely surprised.

Serafina was Spain's most famous dancer, popular to the point of idolatry. For she had won a great victory for the Spanish people. The Cardinal-Primate in Toledo had received numerous complaints, chiefly from foreign dignitaries of the Church, that such vulgar and indecent dances as the fandango and the bolero should be tolerated in a devout country like Spain. The Cardinal-Primate had finally summoned a consistory council to decide whether there should be an eventual interdict on these dances. The Archbishop of Seville, fearing the dissatisfaction which such a decree would arouse, particularly in Andalucía, had suggested that the venerable priestly tribunal should first of all see the dances for themselves. Serafina and her partner Pablo had danced before the consistory council. The prelates had had difficulty in keeping their seats, and the fandango had not been forbidden.

But almost immediately afterwards Serafina had disappeared; it was said that she had married. Whatever the truth was, she had not danced in public for two or three years. So the Duchess spoke her name with pleased surprise. "Serafina?" she asked. "Did you say Serafina?" "She is living in Jerez now," Señor Martínez informed her. "She is the wife of Vargas, my manager there. It is not exactly easy to persuade Señora Vargas to dance for any but her most intimate friends. For you, Duchess, she is going to dance."

The company betook itself to the theatre hall. The room had been cleverly arranged to give the impression of being one of those places where dancers from the people are accustomed to give their performances. The theatre, which was certainly an elegant one in its normal state, had been transformed into the dirty, wretched remnants of what had once been the drawing room of a noble Moorish house. There were darned and threadbare, once costly, carpets, the walls were hung with soiled white linen, the ceiling cunningly decorated with red and golden arabesques. There were a few shabby wooden chairs, a few candles afforded meagre light.

The guests sat down, and from the stage, behind the closed curtains, could be heard the sharp and stirring clatter of the castanets. The curtain parted, the scene revealed a primitively painted Andalusian landscape, a solitary musician sat abandoned in a corner with his guitar. The castanets sounded louder; from the wings there emerged on the left a *majo*, on the right a *maja*. They advanced upon each other, lovers, long parted and finding each other again. Their vivid costumes were of the cheapest material, bestrewn with gold and silver spangles, the boy's trousers and the girl's skirt fitted tightly over the hips, the skirt was of some thin stuff, not long, but wide at the hem. They took no notice of the audience, looked only at each other. With arms raised they danced towards each other.

Still nothing was to be heard but the low, exciting clatter of the castanets. Now the dancers were quite close to each other. Suddenly she drew back, danced backwards, still with her arms outstretched; he followed her, slower, faster, both had their lips slightly parted. It was now more a pantomime than a dance. They looked at each other, looked at the floor. She still evaded him, more slowly now, she lured him on, flirted with him; he followed her, still timidly, but with mounting eagerness. And now she turned towards him. The castanets grew louder, the guitar came in, as did the small invisible orchestra; the dancers had reached each other, already their clothes were touching, their faces close. Then, suddenly, in the middle of a beat the music stopped, the castanets stopped, the dancers stood rigid, rooted to the spot. The pause lasted a few seconds and seemed endless.

Now the guitar struck up again, a quiver passed through the girl's body, slowly her rigidity melted, she swayed back, then forwards. Now he was in motion again too. More passionately he danced towards her. More slowly, more lovingly, she swayed towards him. The movements of both of them became more vehement, their glances more challenging, every muscle quivered with passion. With eyes closed they advanced towards one another. Yet again, at the last moment, she darted back. And again one of those fierce, exciting, voluptuous pauses.

But then they both drew back, disappeared into the wings, and the audience knew that now would begin that variation which Andalucía had appended to the fandango, the solo, deriving probably from the gipsies and the Orient of long ago, which Serafina and many another dancer before her had made famous throughout the kingdom.

Here she comes from the wings, alone this time and without her castanets. But offstage can be heard a rhythmic, monotonous stamping and clapping, and a single deep voice sings a banal, yet eternally poignant song:

Therefore let us
Plunge into the
Deepest lap of
Love; because we
Live but such a
Short time here on
This our earth and
We are such a
Long time dead.

Soon even the words are lost and unrecognizable, the lonely voice no longer sings anything but a rhythmic, monotonous, almost plaintive "Aaah" and "Aaii," slowly but with a savage vehemence. And the girl's dance is slow, savage, and vehement too, always the same and always different, a stilly raging dance, a dance involving the whole body; obviously the girl is showing herself off to her lover, letting him see all the lust, sweetness, and savagery her body has to offer.

The audience sits silent. They feel the wild monotonous stamping in their own limbs but they do not stir, they are frozen as they watch. Nothing indecent is happening on the stage, there is no nakedness, but in complete innocence and in every detail is being shown the most natural of all appetites, fleshly desire, dissolved into rhythm.

The audience has seen this dance many a time, but never so perfectly performed. The erudite Miguel and the bookish Martínez watch Serafina's deliberate artistry with admiration and the eyes of experts. It must have been women like this whom the Romans carried away from sinful Gades to their own city, so that bankers and senators who had tasted all the pleasures of the flesh could revel in their dancing. It must have been women like this whom the early fathers of the Church, full of pious wrath, had likened to the dancing daughter of Herodias, and surely the tradition was right which maintained that the dancer Telethusa from Gades had served as model to the sculptor who created the "Venus Kallipygos."

Serafina danced on, abandoned, her face without expression, full of artistry, full of raging voluptuousness, natural and assumed. The monotonous stamping and singing grew wilder. And now the audience joined in. These grandees and rich gentlemen clapped their hands, stamped their feet, shouted "*¡Ole!*" And Serafina danced. Scarcely moving from the spot, she turned towards the audience first her back, then her side, then her face. Shudders passed ever more rapidly over her body, pulling up her arms, which twitched in the air; then suddenly there was one of those pauses which froze her and everybody else, then there was another very short dance passage almost unbearable in its sultriness, another quivering spasm of longing.

The solo was finished, and now they danced with breathless speed in a pantomime of love: longing, dark determination, fresh misgiving, mounting desire, yielding, consummation, release, torpid languor of satiety.

There was nothing light or frivolous about this dance; it was savagely and convincingly in earnest. And that was how the audience took it, and gave themselves to it. This song with its eternally true banalities, the music which was not music but noise, stupefying, spell-binding noise, no other art form could so well express what this Spanish man and woman were feeling. In the face of this dance, rational thought and ponderous logic dissolved into nothing. One had only to look and listen, had no choice but to abandon oneself to the swell of sound and the palpitation of these movements.

The Duchess of Alba felt as the others did. Unconsciously her little high-heeled shoes were beating time on the floor, her shrill childish voice was shouting "*¡Ole!*" She shut her eyes, unable any longer to bear the rising tide of desire.

Francisco's rugged face was melancholy, solemn, almost as empty as those of the dancers. Much was going on inside him which was not conscious or put into words. His eyes followed this Andalusian bolero or whatever the dance might be called; but inside himself he was dancing his native Aragonese jota, a positively warlike dance in which man and woman threaten each other, a dance without grace or restraint, full of suppressed passion; he had danced it often, holding himself very upright as the dance demanded, as if one were going into battle. And, like the rest, he clapped his big hands in time with the rhythm and shouted "*¡Ole!*" in a high key.

Then the dance was at an end, and the dancers, without once having touched each other, had experienced all the phases of earthly love, carrying the audience along with them. United now as the curtain fell, they vanished into the wings. The music broke off. Nobody clapped. The onlookers sat dumb, themselves emptied and exhausted.

Señor Martínez said to Goya, "I am delighted to have been able to give you this pleasure." There was a nuance to his words which angered Goya; he was angry that his feelings had been so plainly written on his face, that he had so obviously betrayed how much Serafina had aroused him. Cayetana too with her sharp eyes must have perceived what his feelings were. Indeed she now said to him, "A man like you ought to find Serafina attractive. You're very famous in Cádiz, Don Francisco. If Señor Martínez could persuade Serafina to dance for me he could certainly induce her to to do *you* a favour." And Señor Martínez broke in at once. "A portrait of Serafina would surely be more interesting to you, Excellency, than that of an old businessman. Señora Vargas will consider it an honour to sit for you, especially if you dispose of the portrait to me. I told you, did I not, that Señor Vargas is my agent in Jerez?"

Serafina joined them. They showered her with compliments and gallantries. She thanked them calmly, agreeably, without smiling. She was used to adulation.

Goya said nothing, only stared at her. Finally she turned to him. "How long will you be staying in Madrid, Señor First Painter?" she asked. "I don't really know," he answered, "probably another week or two. And then I shall spend a little time nearby, at San Lúcar." She said, "I live quite near here too, in Jerez. I had meant to hold my gala-bed in the late fall, but now I've decided to have it earlier, and I hope you will visit me." It was the custom in this region of Spain for women of some standing to be "ill" for one or two weeks during the year, to take to their beds where they were pampered and spoiled and given presents by their friends and acquaintances; a magnificent bed, for use only on these occasions, belonged in the trousseau of all self-respecting girls.

Goya looked at her, looked long and
Heedless of the others round them;
And she gave him back his look and
In them both there beat the wailing,
Stamping and monotonous rhythm
Of that song, of ancient wisdom:
"Therefore let us plunge into the
Deepest lap of love; because we
Live but a short time here." Then
He unclosed his lips, as though he
Broke a spell, and as a *majo*
Spoke he to the *maja,* saying,
"As to gala-bed, forget it;
For such matters, Serafina,
Must not be between us. I will
Paint you also. And we two shall
See each other without pretext,
Serafina."

-- 35 --

Two days later, in the evening, he was alone with Cayetana. The *solano* was blowing, that sultry African wind; between gusts one could hear the evening signals of the opposing squadrons, the nearby Spanish and the distant English.

Francisco was nervous and irritable. He wanted to go back to San Lúcar and have Cayetana to himself again. Suddenly he had had enough of life in Cádiz and all the people one had to be with. Was it for the sake of consorting with Señor Martínez and his friends that he was overstaying his leave and jeopardizing his favour at Court? Cayetana for her part obviously enjoyed the attentions of these people. She did not consider him at all. She ought to have the kindness and decency to notice that he didn't want to stay here any longer.

Scarcely had he finished saying these things to himself when she opened her mouth. "You don't even need to say it, Francisco." "Say what?" he returned with feigned innocence. "What don't I need to say?" And she, smiling, said, "If you would like it, we can go back to San Lúcar tomorrow."

All his ill-humour dispersed as soon as he was alone with her once more at San Lúcar; he was as radiantly happy as in the weeks before the visit. His memories of Cádiz became rosier. The men had made much of him, the women had fallen in love with him; he had been paid prices unheard of by almost any other painter; obviously his fame had spread throughout the whole kingdom. What was more, he had only just begun to show what he could do, his art was still developing. And now he was here, alone with his wonderful beloved, who bent herself to all his moods. He was young, he had proved himself, he possessed everything he wanted. "Sitting at the golden tables of life and art," came to him, a line of poetry which Don Miguel had probably quoted.

Once, in bed, stretching herself idly, Cayetana demanded, "Will you still not paint me as a *maja?*" "Of course I will," he said at once, and painted a gay, delicate picture in which he was going for a walk with her. She was in *maja* costume, she wore a black mantilla; he was a little behind her and she was turning round to him, supplely and coquettishly bending her wasp waist; one hand held a fan invitingly open, the other pointed challengingly at the fan with an imperious forefinger. He himself was addressing her with courtly gallantry, he was most elegantly dressed, quite foppish in fact; he was wearing a brownish frock coat, costly laces, and high boots; he had become unrecognizably young and was obviously as enamoured as a cockchafer.

She realized clearly enough that he still would not see her as a *maja*, that again he had painted her only as a great lady dressed up. But she was pleased with the picture all the same. His teasing was high-spirited but harmless, and after all he had made fun of himself like an urchin.

Next day she told him that she had had another visit from her dead maid Brígida. She had again told her she would die young, but not before she had been painted as a *maja*. Goya was stretched out lazily in an armchair. "I'm afraid in that case your end has come," he replied. "Don't be silly," she said, "you know exactly what she meant." "I think it's a very happy prophecy," Goya returned. "All you have to do is not to be painted as a *maja* and you'll live to be a hundred and fifty." "As I have made up my mind to it," she said, "I shall be painted as a *maja*. Brígida knows that as well as you and I do." "By the way, what was she wearing, this Brígida of yours?" Francisco asked. Cayetana, surprised, answered, "She was dressed like any other maid." But then she exclaimed, "What was she wearing! You question one like the Inquisition." Goya replied pacifically, "I'm a painter; if I can't see a thing it doesn't exist for me, it isn't a real ghost."

If Doctor Peral had kept himself in the background in Cádiz, here he extinguished himself completely whenever he felt he was not wanted. For the rest he showed himself a clever and amusing companion and was at great pains to show Goya how instructed his admiration for him was. Goya could not understand how a man who had played so dark a role in the Duke's death could now be so unwaveringly cheerful and contented. If he was implicated in the Duke's death, and of course he was, then he had done what he did coolly and without scruple, and it had never occurred to him that devils could lurk in corners and spy on one.

Peral was talkative and gave an appearance of frankness, though there always remained something hidden, undecipherable; Goya was deeply intrigued by the man, even became fond of him, however much he might be repelled by an occasional glance, an occasional gesture. A strange, friend-enemy relationship sprang up between the two men; they felt the existence of a link between them, wanted to get to the bottom of each other; they enjoyed exchanging penetrating truths.

As Goya never spoke of Cayetana, Peral did not mention her name either. But of love in general they often talked. Once the doctor asked the painter if he had ever heard of the distinction which the ancient philosophers drew between a hedonist and an erotic. "I'm an ignorant painting master, Doctor," said Goya good-humouredly, "and you are a *tertuliante*, a trebly wise Tullius Cicero. Instruct me, please." "A hedonist, then," Peral explained, "is a man who wishes to afford enjoyment to himself alone; an erotic is one who wishes to give pleasure when he experiences it himself." "Very interesting," said Goya rather uneasily; he could not tell whether Peral had the Duchess in mind. "The philosopher Cleanthes," Peral continued, "exhorts us, 'Woe to him who falls into the lap of a hedonist,' and he advises those whom this fate does befall to seek refuge in some great general undertaking, the fight for freedom and fatherland. It sounds well, but as a doctor I have my doubts of its efficacy."

Naturally Peral talked a great deal about art. He especially admired Francisco's technique for painting such expressive eyes. "I've found out what your trick is," he said. "You make the white smaller than nature and the iris larger." And when Goya looked up in surprise he declared, "The usual measurement of the iris is about eleven millimetres, but your subjects have irises of thirteen millimetres. I've measured." Goya did not know whether to laugh or not.

From Jerez came a letter, unhandily written, Serafina recalling herself to mind. "I may go to Jerez for a few days perhaps," Goya said to Cayetana, "to paint Serafina." "Wouldn't it be more convenient," she replied, "if you were to have her come here?" She spoke calmly, casually, but behind her words there was a mischievous, good-natured comprehension which provoked him. "It was just an idea which came into my head," he said. "Probably I'll neither go there nor will she come here. All the same," he added spitefully, "she'd make an ideal *maja*. If I ever paint a *maja* again she'll be the one."

Soon afterwards, when he went to Cayetana at the usual hour, he found her lying on the sofa in a costume such as had been worn many times in the past winter at fancy-dress balls. It was a garment of fine costly white material, a costume more *torero* than *maja*, half shirt, half trousers; with its many folds clinging to the body it revealed more than it hid. Over it Cayetana wore a bolero jacket, bright yellow, decorated with shimmering black metal paillettes forming a butterfly pattern; a wide pink belt held the garment together. There she lay, her hands behind her head.

"If you wanted to paint Serafina as *maja*, would this pose and this costume be the right ones?" she asked. "H'm, well," he made answer—it was neither yes nor no. The woman lying on the sofa was an attractive woman daringly dressed as a *maja;* but in a tavern in the Manolería not a single soul would have taken her for a *maja*, and Francisco could well imagine himself painting Cayetana, but never Serafina, like that. "If you were painting such a *maja*," she pursued, "would you do her life-size?" Rather surprised, he answered, "It's the first time I've known you to be interested in technicalities." She answered a little impatiently, "Well, today I am." He smiled. "I think I'd do it three-quarters life-size," he informed her.

A few days later she led him into one of the little-used rooms in the house, a magnificent, somewhat neglected bedchamber which some former mistress of the Casa de Haro may well have used for her official levees. On one wall hung an indifferent painting, representing a hunting scene. Cayetana, by means of the same device employed in the Casa de Haro in Cádiz, shifted the picture to one side. Behind it the naked wall was visible, space for another picture. He stood there stupidly. "Don't you understand?" she asked. "I want you finally to paint me as *maja*, as a real *maja*." He stared at her. Had he understood her aright? Velázquez' naked woman, he had told her, was neither goddess nor grandee, she was a *maja*. "I want to commission two portraits from you, Don Francisco," she said, "one as a *maja* in costume, the other as a real *maja*."

If that was what she wanted she should have it. He painted her in her costly, garish fancy dress, and even then he was really painting her nakedness beneath the transparent material. There she lay on a couch designed for pleasure, on dull green pillows, her hands linked behind her head, the left leg drawn up, the right thigh lying softly over the other, and he emphasized the pubic triangle. He had her put on make-up and paint her face, but it was not her face; rather was it an anonymous, ambiguous face such as he alone could paint, someone's face, anyone's face.

Cayetana delighted in the proud rivalry upon which she had embarked. She had got her way: Francisco was painting *her* as *maja;* Serafina, the *maja majada*, the prototype of the *maja*, had bidden him to her gala-bed in vain.

He worked in the room for which the paintings were intended. The light, which came from the left, was just right for the *maja* clothed. The naked one, however, he painted on the flat roof of the observation tower, the *mirador*, for here the parapet caused the light to fall in the right direction. The dueña, thoroughly disapproving, kept watch; they were protected. All the same, they were doing something extremely risky, for undertakings of this kind did not remain hidden forever.

Goya painted in a sour temper. He felt that she was forbidding him Serafina, that she wished to be more to him than Serafina, even to be more *maja* than Serafina was. But that was one thing she couldn't have. Ill-humour boiled up in him. As she lay there before him it was no longer he who was her *pelele;* for once it was she who was his. The thing that was emerging on his canvas was no *maja.* And though birth and riches had given her all that Spain could give, she was still cut off forever from the people, she remained nothing but a pitiable grandee. She'd never be a *maja* no matter what tricks she played. And least of all was she one when stripped of the final covering.

His thoughts turned aside from the woman in the flesh and fastened on his work. He could not tell if what he was doing was art. What would Luján, his teacher in Saragossa, have said to this? Luján had permitted him to copy adequately clothed plaster casts, having been a censor for the Inquisition. Certainly what he was doing was miles apart from that indifferent, uninteresting art about which Mengs and Miguel raved. But *carajo!* He wasn't going to compete with the dead Velázquez. And this was his "*Doña Desnuda.*" In this clothed and this unclothed nude he painted all the women he had ever lain with in bed and in corners. Painted a body calculated to arouse all the passions. And two faces to go with them; one full of appetite and expectancy, vacant almost with lasciviousness, the expression hard, alluring, and dangerous; the other a little drowsy, slowly awakening from satisfied desire, already thirsty for new fulfilment. What he was trying to paint was neither the Duchess of Alba nor any *maja.* It was lust itself, lust the insatiable, with its torpid blisses and all its perils.

The pictures were ready. Cayetana looked uncertainly from one to the other. The woman in the *torero* costume had a different face from the naked one. Both were her face and yet not her face. Why hadn't Francho painted her face as it really was?

"You've done something unique, Don Francisco," she said at

length. "Something disquieting." She tore herself away. "But I'm not quite as fat as all that," she said with artificial playfulness.

Then with help of the dueña
On the wall they hung them both and
Covering the naked *maja*
Lay the other. Cayetana
Said her guests would surely make big
Eyes at this one. Like a child she
Worked the mechanism, pushed the
Button, and the naked *maja*
Sprang to sight. In holy horror
Black and stiff, lips pressed together,
The dueña stood; and smiling
Cayetana hid the naked
Painting with the gay-hued other
Maja. Smiling still with outstretched
Pointing finger and her lovely
Large head held erect above the
Little body, with a light and
Gracious tread and beckoning to her
Goya that he follow her, the
Duchess of the house of Alba
Left the room.

— 36 —

A guest arrived at San Lúcar. Don Juan Antonio, Marqués de San Adrián.

Goya was put out. He had known the Marqués a long time. He had painted him, and it had turned out to be one of his best portraits. He had placed him in an open landscape; the young man stood there, very affected, leaning against a stone pillar—actually he wasn't so very young, in the early forties perhaps, but he looked no more than five-and-twenty, with his proud, pretty, mischievous face. He was in riding clothes, white waistcoat, narrow yellow trousers, and blue coat, a sort of Werther get-up. The hand holding the riding crop was placed elegantly on his hip, the other, painted with great care, was holding a book, neither model nor painter could have told why; he had placed his tall hat on top of the column. Goya had in no way modified the arrogance of the pretty, utterly spoiled young man who, one of the first grandees at Court, had in his early years been made president of the influential Council of the Indies. Goya had also encountered the Marqués many times in Cayetana's set; it was assumed that he had been one of her lovers. What was certain was that he was counted among the Queen's favourites; probably the Duchess had let him be her *cortejo* for a while to annoy Doña María Luisa. The Marqués of San Adrián was intelligent and exceptionally cultured; he had lived a long time in France, had the reputation of being progressive and probably was, but when he gave vent to one of his affectedly cynical and amusing remarks in his high, somewhat drawling boy's voice, it irritated Goya and he had difficulty in refraining from saying something coarse and abrupt in reply.

The Marqués was at pains not to intrude. He was of a naturally amiable disposition, and his presence at mealtimes and at Cayetana's levee was stimulating rather than annoying. Cayetana treated him with a kind of gentle sarcasm, as one might a precocious schoolboy; her liaison with him was clearly at an end. At all events Francisco was able as before to be alone with Cayetana to his heart's content.

One evening at table he became involved in a conversation with Peral on art; the other two did not take part. Then, while he was in the middle of a sentence, he intercepted a look from Cayetana to San Adrián. It was a slanting look such as a *maja* would have given; she ogled across at Don Juan, challenging, expectant, desirous. The look held less than two seconds. Perhaps he had imagined it. Of course he had imagined it. He commanded himself to forget the look. But it was only with difficulty that he completed his sentence.

That night he told himself it was all nonsense, that for a moment he had taken Cayetana for his "*Doña Desnuda*"; such things happened to him occasionally. Then again he told himself it was as good as certain that Cayetana had once slept with San Adrián, and why else should he have come if not to resuscitate the old friendship? And surely he hadn't come without her approval. It was all quite clear and he was the fool, the *pelele.* He imagined her lying with San Adrián, that fop, that stuck-up coxcomb, lying with him at that very moment while he was writhing in sleepless torment. And then she would show him the "*Doña Desnuda*" and San Adrián in that revolting voice of his would point out how many beauties Francisco had failed to see in her.

It was all madness. He was simply a jealous fool. He had reason for his fears. He was old and stout and hard of hearing and beginning to stoop, which was a disgrace, particularly for an Aragonese; also he had ungovernable moods and was inclined to sulk. Cayetana was *chatoyante,* the old Marquesa was right. Even if he had been young and dazzlingly handsome she might perhaps suddenly have lost interest in him and taken a fancy to someone else. But as he looked now, it was obvious that she must prefer to sleep with this young, slender, amusing, and always good-tempered dandy. *Trágala, perro!*

These were chimeras. Had she not teased the Marqués mercilessly on the subject of María Luisa? Had she not shown him quite plainly that he, Francisco, was her *cortejo?* But that sidelong look —that he hadn't imagined. It came not from the "*Doña Desnuda*" but from the hard metallic eyes of the living Cayetana. She had looked quite indifferent in the next moment, but she was as changeable as a cat's eye, nothing about her was straightforward and tangible. The fault did not lie with him that he was unable to paint Cayetana. Velázquez would not have been able to paint her either; nobody could paint her. One couldn't even paint her nakedness, even her nakedness was equivocal. And her heart was as made-up as her complexion. She was evil through and through. A line came to him from one of the old romances Pepa liked to sing: "In a lovely bosom an ugly heart."

Next morning he began a new painting. For at last he had caught a glimpse of the real Cayetana. He had her flying through the air; with her, beneath her, like the clouds which supported them, hovered three male figures. But this time there was nothing anonymous about the woman's features. This pure, proud face could belong to only one woman in the world, Cayetana de Alba, and the men's faces were clearly recognizable also; one was the bullfighter Costillares, the second was the President of the Council of the Indies, San Adrián, the third Don Manuel, Príncipe de la Paz. From the ground a freak looked up, grinning at the flight, the court jester Padilla. It was an ascension which Francisco had painted, but it was a most unholy one and its destination was assuredly not Heaven. The woman above the men's heads was holding her legs apart inside the wide-flowing garments which were bellying out in the flight through the air. One could easily credit this hovering figure with all the seven deadly sins. The owner of that face, how easily one could believe it, might well, without so much as a movement of the lips, have ordered the death of her innocent husband simply because he was rather in the way. Yes, at last he had seen it, at last he had got it, and this was once and for all her last face, her true face, pure and proud, Cayetana's face with its depth of deceit, vice and innocence, lust, allurement: a living lie.

On the following day Cayetana did not appear. The dueña made her excuses to the gentlemen. Her little white dog Don Juanito was ailing. She was grieving and could see no one. Goya went on painting on the "Ascensión," on the "Lie."

Next day the dog was well again and Cayetana was in radiant mood. Goya was monosyllabic but she was not put out by it, she tried many times to draw him into the conversation. But gradually, as he made no response, she turned to San Adrián, who spoke to her in his affable, childishly flattering way. He made a French quotation, she replied in the same tongue, they slipped entirely into French. Peral, snatched hither and thither first by malicious satisfaction, then by pity, attempted to steer the conversation back into Spanish, but they went on speaking French, a rapid French which Goya was unable to follow. Finally Cayetana turned to Francisco and said something to him in French, using some out of the way expression which he did not understand. Obviously she wished to expose him in front of San Adrián.

After dinner she declared that she was feeling gay and didn't want to go to bed yet, that she wanted to do something. She wanted to have her servants come to dance the fandango. Her maid Fruela was an excellent dancer, the groom Vicente wasn't at all bad either. It often happened that grandees would dissipate the boredom of their parties by having their servants dance for them.

Five couples appeared, willing and able to dance the fandango; about twenty others came too, to look on, servants and peasants from the estate. The report had spread that there was to be a fandango and they knew they might all come without the formality of asking. The people danced neither well nor badly, but a fandango was a spectacle calculated even without much art to carry everyone away. At first the audience sat serious and attentive, but then they began to tap their feet on the floor, to stamp, to clap in time to the music, to shout "*¡Ole!*" Only one couple danced at a time, but a fresh couple was always ready to come forward to relieve them.

Cayetana said, "Wouldn't you like to dance, Francisco?" For a moment he was tempted. But then he remembered how she had made him dance the minuet in front of the Duke and Peral; he saw before him San Adrián's charmingly pert face and asked himself whether he was going to let her make a fool of him again. He hesitated. She turned at once to San Adrián. "What about you, Don Juan?" The Marqués answered immediately, in his somewhat affected way, "Nothing I would like better, Duchess. But in this costume?" "The trousers will do," said Cayetana judicially, "and someone can lend you a jacket. Be making yourself ready while I change."

She came back, and she was wearing the costume in which Goya had painted her, that garment half shift, half trousers, of thin white stuff, which revealed more of the body than it concealed, over it the gay yellow bolero with the glittering black paillettes and the wide pink sash. Thus attired, she danced with San Adrián. It wasn't the proper costume, nor was his, nor was it a proper fandango they danced; even the maid Fruela and Vicente the groom did it better, not to mention anyone in Seville or Cádiz, and Serafina could not have been spoken of in the same breath. All the same it was a fandango, that naked, unambiguous spectacle, and there was something unseemly, even indecent, in the fact that the Duchess of Alba and the President of the Council of the Indies were performing in front of the maids, peasants, coachmen of San Lúcar, this pantomime of lust and longing, of hesitancy and repletion. They might just as well, Goya felt, have taken all these people into the robing room, pressed the button, and showed them the "*Doña Desnuda.*" But what angered him most of all was that the couple who were dancing were only playing at being *majo* and *maja*, without being it. It was a stupid, frivolous, impertinent game, and one they had no right to play. It was an outrage against all true *españolismo*. A heavy distaste possessed Francisco, rage against

Cayetana and Don Juan, against all the grandees and their ladies among whom he lived, these popinjays and puppets. True, he had played their false, stupid game enthusiastically himself when he had made the gobelins. But since then he had looked deeper into men and affairs, had lived and felt more deeply, and he had believed Cayetana to be something more than just one of these. He had believed that there existed between them not a game but the truth—passion, desire, love, the real fandango. But she had lied, all the time she had been lying, and he had let himself be misused, a *pelele,* a doll on strings, by this *grande dame.*

The lackeys and maids, the peasants, footmen, kitchenmaids and stable boys had a wonderful evening of it. They sensed the effort which Cayetana was making to be one of them, and they appreciated it, but they sensed also its failure and were embarrassed. They stamped on the floor, clapped and shouted "*¡Ole!*" and without putting their thoughts clearly into words felt themselves to be better than the people up there; and that when the maid Fruela went to bed tonight with Vicente the groom it would be better, more natural, more Spanish, more in the order of things, than when the fine lady slept with that dandy or with her painter.

The dueña could not bear the sight. She loved her Cayetana, Cayetana was her whole life, but now her lamb had let the painter put a spell on her. With angry grief she looked on as the first lady of the kingdom, descendant of the great Field Marshal, degraded herself in front of the *canaille*, the *chusma*, the common people.

Peral sat and watched. He did not clap, nor did he shout "*¡Ole!*" He had experienced many such outbreaks on Cayetana's part, not quite so crude as this perhaps, but not so very different. He looked at Goya, read his feelings in his face, felt satisfaction and regret.

Cayetana and San Adrián grew heated. The music became more fiery, the acclamations louder, they danced as hard as they could. "Dance as hard as you can," thought Goya, "you'll never be a *maja.* And you've no conception of a fandango either. All you want is to add a little spice to the night before you go to bed with this pathetic buffoon, this coxcomb and dandy." He left before the dance ended.

That night also he slept badly. Next morning she probably expected him to fetch her for a walk before luncheon, as he had done till now. He did not go to her. He sent a message that he had a headache and would not appear at luncheon. He got out his picture, the "Ascensión," the "Lie." It was ready, it did not need another stroke. Nor was he in any mood for work; the *solano* plagued him, he had the feeling that his hearing had got worse. He put the canvas away, sat down at the writing table, began to draft a letter. He thought to himself, "The old man kept a court jester. She keeps her court painter, but I'm not going to play any more." He roughed out a letter to the Court Chamberlain, a second to the Academy, announcing his return to Madrid. He abandoned the drafts without copying them out.

In the afternoon she came to him, her absurd dog was with her. She behaved as if nothing had happened, was agreeable, almost gay. Regretted that he did not feel well. Why hadn't he called in Doctor Peral? "It's not a thing in which Peral could help me," he replied darkly. "Send your San Adrián away!" he demanded. She said, "Be reasonable. You know I'm not going to offend him just because you're in a bad temper." "Send him away!" he insisted. "Why are you trying to dictate to me?" she said. "You know I won't stand for it. I've never told you what to do, I've never said to you, 'Do this' or 'Don't do that.' " The monstrous effrontery of it embittered him. She had demanded of him all that a human being could ask of another, the most cruel sacrifices, and she could stand there and say innocently, "Have I ever demanded anything of you?"

He said, "I'm going to Jerez, to paint Serafina." She sat there quite quietly with the little dog in her lap. "It's perfectly convenient," she said, "that you want to go away just now. Actually I'm going away myself for a few days. I'm going to visit some of my estates, to see what my tenants are up to. Don Juan is coming with me and will give me the benefit of his advice." His underlip was thrust violently forward, his deep-set brown eyes grew darker. "It's not for a few days that I'm going away. You needn't make the trip on my account. Just you stay here with that popinjay of yours. I shan't be in your way any more. From Jerez I shall go back to Madrid." She stood up. The dog barked. She wanted to say something violent in reply. She looked at his rugged face in which the eyes burned quite black; the whites were scarcely visible. She controlled herself. "It would be very foolish of you, Francisco," she said, "not to come back to San Lúcar, and I should be very sorry." As he remained silent she begged, "Be reasonable. You know me. Don't ask me to change. I'm not capable of it. Let me have four or five days, take as long as that yourself. And then come back, and I shall be here alone, and everything will be as it was before."

Still he stared at her, filled with hatred. At last he said, "Yes, I do know you," and pulled out the picture, the "Ascensión," the "Lie," and placed it on the easel.

Cayetana saw herself in flight, graceful, light, with that oh! so innocent face, and it *was* her face. She didn't flatter herself that she knew much about painting, but this much she could see, that no one had ever insulted her so rudely, not even María Luisa, no one. And the worst of it was she couldn't even see how this effect was achieved. Yes, she could though. It was the three men he had given her, these three of all others, and why Don Manuel? He knew perfectly well how repellent Don Manuel was to her, and he had deliberately chosen Manuel as her companion on this witches' Sabbath. "I went into exile on his account," she raged inwardly. "I've let him paint me as no grandee has ever before been painted by a wretched artist. And this is how he treats me."

A scraping knife lay on his work table. She picked it up, not even quickly, and with a powerful movement slit the canvas diagonally from top to bottom. He rushed at her, seized her with one hand, the picture with the other. The little dog ran between their feet, barking. Easel and picture crashed absurdly to the ground.

Panting violently they stood there.
Quietly then, but with hauteur, she
Spoke, as only she, the Alba,
Could. "I much regret the picture
Has been spoiled. Pray put your price, Sir,
On it; they will—" But she spoke no
Further. For that wave, the seizure
Always feared, came over him, and
Nerveless, lamed, collapsed, he sank down
In a chair and crouched, his features
Like a mask of ruin.

37

For hours Francisco sat fixed in a torpor of despair. Again and again the same bald phrases ran through his head. "This is what comes of it—I was mad—I'm going mad—this time she's really got me into trouble, the wretch—this is what comes of it—I'm really done for this time!" Then he spoke the same words, very loud. He thought he heard them, knew he could not hear them. He walked up to the mirror, saw himself opening and shutting his mouth, without hearing what he said. In his earlier attacks the high tones had become inaudible first and last of all the lowest. He spoke in a very deep voice, very loud. Heard nothing. In past attacks, if a noise had been very loud he had been able to catch a faint echo. He hurled a vase onto the stone floor, saw it smash to pieces, heard nothing.

"That's what comes of it," he said. "Trapped, swindled, betrayed. My child killed, my career ruined, my hearing stolen." Mad rage seized him, he poured out a stream of curses. Smashed the mirror which had once held her image. Looked in consternation at his cut and bleeding hand. Then he relapsed into grim resignation. "*Trágala, perro!* Swallow it, you dog!" he said to himself, and sat on in a kind of dull despair.

Peral came to him. Took pains to speak very plainly, so that Francisco could read the words from his lips. But he sat, a picture of obdurate hopelessness. Peral wrote, "I will give you a sedative. Please lie down." "I don't want to!" Goya shouted. "Be reasonable," wrote Peral. "After a long sleep everything will be better." He came back with the draught. Goya knocked it out of his hand. "I'm not going to let anyone do me in," he said, quietly this time but with sinister emphasis, and was not sure he had said it. Peral looked at him consideringly, not without pity, and left him without replying. An hour later he came back. "Shall I give you the medicine now?" he asked. Goya made no answer, sat there with his underlip thrust out. Peral mixed the draught and Goya took it.

Slowly, waking from an endless sleep, he rose to the surface of reality. He saw that his hand was bandaged. He saw that he had a new mirror, one that had not been sullied by Cayetana's lying image. He stood up, walked about the room, tested his hearing. Put a chair down hard on the stone floor. Yes, there was a faint thud. He tested with desperate anxiety. Yes, he was quite sure, the noises were far from clear but they did not come only from within himself. He *could* hear. There was hope.

Peral came again. He did not try to persuade him, but informed him that he had sent for a doctor from Cádiz, a specialist with a good reputation. Goya shrugged his shoulders, exaggerated his deafness. But he clung with all his soul to his hopes.

Late in the morning, at the time when he was in the habit of going to her, Cayetana appeared. He felt a shock of bitter joy. He had expected her to go away with her dandy as she had said she would; she was not the woman to give up a project simply because he was ill. But there she was. She spoke to him, took pains to form her words clearly. He was too agitated to understand, nor did he wish to understand. He was silent. She sat with him for a long time. Then tenderly she stroked his forehead. He jerked his head away. She sat for a while longer, then left him.

The doctor from Cádiz came. Wrote Goya encouraging messages, said the same words to him, moving his lips with careful distinctness. Spoke rapidly and at length with Peral. Wrote down for Goya that he would probably be unable to hear the high tones for a long time to come but would hear the lower ones. It was confirmation. Goya's hopes rose.

But the next night all the spectres came to him that he had ever known in a life rich in spectres. They had dogs' heads and cats' heads, they goggled with huge owl-eyes, snatched with monstrous claws, flapped gigantic bats' wings. It was night and utterly dark; he kept his eyes tightly closed, and still he saw them, with horrible faces—and pleasant ones, which were even worse. He could feel them sitting around in a circle, breathing on him with their horrible breath, and in the dead and deafening silence which now hemmed him in they were more menacing than ever before.

Towards morning, as the first light began to show, the realization of his deafness overcame him in its full horror. It was as if a huge bell-glass were being put over him, to shut him in forever. It was unbearable that he, who always must communicate his joys and sorrows to others, should be shut away from men from this time forth. No more would he hear the voices of women, no more the voices of his children, no more Martín's friendly voice, Agustín's scornful comments, Josefa's loving and solicitous reproaches, no more the praises of connoisseurs and potentates. He would no longer hear the hubbub of the Puerta del Sol, the sounds of the bullfight, no more music, no more *seguidillas* and *tonadillas*, no more gossip with *majos* and *majas* in the taverns. He would be shunned by other men, for who wants to talk with anyone who cannot hear? It was to be his lot to make a fool of himself constantly, to answer the wrong thing. From now on he would always have to strain to hear what it was impossible for him to hear. He knew all about the world's chill indifference. It was bad enough for one who was healthy and in a condition to protect himself, but quite dreadful for anyone who was as he was today. He would have to live on his memories, and yet he knew how the demons could distort them. He listened, within himself, trying to hear the familiar voices of friends and foes, and already he was uncertain whether he was hearing aright. Then he cried aloud. Raved.

He went up to the mirror. It was a fine big mirror in an expensively carved gilded frame. But the thing that looked back at him was worse than the monsters that had stared at him during the night. Could this be he? His hair was wild about his head; a tangled beard curled with weird and at the same time absurd effect down his hollow cheeks and around his chin; huge, almost entirely black, his eyes glowered in their deep sockets; his thick eyebrows zigzagged across his forehead, grotesquely cleft; deep furrows ran from nose to mouth, one side of his mouth was slack and unlike the other half. The whole face was sinister, full of impotent fury, resigned as a trapped animal is resigned, a face such as he himself might have painted among those in his own picture "The Madhouse."

He sat down in a chair facing away from the mirror and closed his eyes. There he sat, inert, for a long hour.

Towards midday a terrible suspense seized him as to whether Cayetana would come or not. He told himself she had surely gone away but he could not believe it. It drove him out of his chair; he paced up and down. The hour came at which it was their custom to meet. She did not come. Five minutes passed, ten. A monstrous anger filled him. If her dog was constipated she worried as if the world were coming to an end, but while he sat here, smitten like Job, she could run off with the first fop that came to hand. A crazy desire for revenge flared up in him. He wanted to strangle her, kick her, beat her, drag her to the ground, destroy her.

He saw her coming. All at once he grew quite calm. All urgency fell away from him; it was even as if the bell-glass which had been placed over him had lifted slightly. Perhaps the worst was over, perhaps he could hear again. But he dared not put it to the test. He did not wish to let her witness the struggle and suffering of his pitiful attempts, all he wanted was to enjoy her presence, nothing more. He did not even want to look at her, wanted only to be sure she was there, feel her near him. He threw himself in a chair, closed his eyes, breathed audibly, regularly.

She approached. She saw him sitting there in the chair, apparently asleep, the man, the only man who had ever defied her, again and again, who had enraged her as no one else had, to whom she was bound as to no other. All the women there had been in his life and might still be in his life meant nothing, the men who had been in her own life and those who still would be, they meant nothing either; even that she was going away that day with San Adrián meant nothing. She loved this man only, had loved only him and no other, and it would always be so. But even if it should bring ruin on him, and herself as well, she was not going to change herself for his sake, would give up nothing to which she had made up her mind.

There he sat, asleep now from exhaustion and despair, a most unhappy man, unhappy because of her just as he had been happy because of her, and as, because of her, he would continue to be both happy and unhappy.

And she comes up to him and she
Speaks to him, for this once only
Must she tell him, since he hears it
Not, he sleeps, and if he did not
Would not hear it either. But he
Hears it, hears her voice, that hard and
Childish voice. "You stupid Francho,"
Says the voice, "you know just nothing,
Nothing at all. For you, you only

Have I loved, O silly Francho,
Old fat man and *majo*, and you
Think that I am flying into
Hell with all these others. O, you
Hateful only one, how stupid,
For I care for you, you only,
Rude, insulting painter, always,
Only you!" He sleeps, he does not
Stir, and she can hear his breathing,
Plainly audible, until she
Leaves the room.

— 38 —

He was pleased with his own cunning in having deceived her, and slept well that night.

When he awoke next day he discovered with a shock that his hearing was again entirely gone, that he was shut up once and for all in the dark dome of deafness. With mingled pain and pleasure he reflected that the last sounds he would ever hear had been Cayetana's words, and that it had been his own work, his own cunning, which had extracted them from her.

The hour struck when she was in the habit of coming. He ran to the window and peered out, opened the door and peered along the corridor, for he was unable to hear her coming. Half an hour passed. Obviously she was not coming. Was it conceivable, after all that she had said to him, that she had gone away with that coxcomb?

Peral came to him, begged him to keep him company at luncheon.

Francisco, as casually as he could, asked, "Has Doña Cayetana gone away?" "Did she not say good-bye to you?" Peral asked in surprise. "She went to say good-bye to you, I know."

After luncheon they had a long talk. Goya became impatient because Peral would insist on trying to make himself understood by clear articulation, before resorting to writing his words down.

He was ashamed of his infirmity. He scanned Peral's face, which he knew so well, for any sign of malicious satisfaction. He found none, but mistrusted him as before. In future he would mistrust everyone, he would be regarded as a lugubrious fellow, a misanthrope, which he wasn't at all. He enjoyed good noisy conviviality, he liked to share his joys and pains, but if his ears were closed then his mouth would be closed too.

Peral drew a diagram of the inner ear and tried to explain to him the nature of his malady. There was not much hope of recovery, and he would do well to begin learning the sign language. A Frenchman, Doctor de l'Epée, had invented an excellent method, several people in Cádiz had mastered it, and it would be a good thing for Goya to begin on the exercises. "Yes," replied Goya fiercely, "cripples are to be my only companions from now on, deaf mutes, nothing but cripples. I'm no longer wanted in the company of normal people."

The doctor's lame words of comfort, his inadequate palliatives, showed him, more vividly than anything else could have done, how horrible his suffering would be amidst the world's cruel silence. Would he ever be able to sleep with a woman again? Till now he had always been the one who gave; from now on would he not be paralysed by the feeling that it would be as a favour that a woman would condescend to him, a cripple? Oh, they had devised a harsh punishment for him, the demons, because he had sacrificed his child to his wicked infatuation and very nearly his art as well. "Tell me," he said abruptly to Peral, "what is actually the cause of my illness?"

Peral had expected this question, had dreaded its coming, yet hoped it would come. He had for some time had a definite opinion of Goya's illness, and since the latter's last dreadful attack had considered whether he ought not to tell him the truth. He hesitated. He admired Goya's work, liked his rich, overflowing nature, but he also envied him his gift of attracting people, his faith in his own luck, his sure self-confidence; and the fact that catastrophe had at last befallen this man too had gratified him. He asked himself whether, in telling him the merciless truth, he was really doing it in fulfilment of his duty as fellow-man, as friend and physician, or whether it was not rather in order to savour his revenge on this fortune's favourite.

But when Francisco asked him the direct question he thrust his scruples aside and addressed himself to making the painful incision. He chose his words carefully and simply and took pains to articulate them clearly. "The seat of your illness," he said, "is in the brain. The slow destruction of your powers of hearing has been accomplished inside your brain. The affliction can ensue from some venereal disease which you may have had or inherited from one of your forebears. You can count yourself fortunate, Don Francisco, that the consequences have taken this form. In other cases, in most other cases, the brain is affected in a more dreadful manner."

Goya gazed into the other's face, at the thin expressive lips as they shaped the deadly words. There was turmoil within him. He thought, "He wants to poison you, the murderer, in some malignant, hidden, undiscoverable way, just as he poisoned the Duke." He thought, "He's right, I'm going mad, I'm mad already. All he's saying, in those learned words of his, is that it's sin, demonic possession, witchcraft at work in my brain." To himself he said this. But aloud he said, "You mean I am insane." First he spoke the words in a low, grim tone, then screamed them. "Insane! I am insane, you say! Did you say I am insane?" Peral very calmly and clearly replied, "It's lucky for you that you are *not* insane, but merely hard of hearing. Do try to understand this, Don Francisco." "Why do you lie?" Francisco screamed back. "If I'm not mad, yet I shall go mad in the end, and you know it. Didn't you say 'hard of hearing?' " he asked. "I told you you were lying," he went on, exultant at having got the best of the other. "You know perfectly well that I'm not hard of hearing but deaf, stone deaf, and permanently so. Deaf *and* insane." Peral answered patiently, "The fact that you are hard of hearing gives good grounds for hope, almost certainty in fact, that the original infection has burned itself out, once and for all." "Why do you torture me?" Goya railed. "Why don't you just say honestly, 'You are insane'?" "Because I don't wish to lie," Peral replied.

But later several remarkably frank conversations took place between the two men. Don Joaquín would console his patient and provoke him by turns, and Goya apparently wished it to be so; he would thank him for his solicitude and next moment do his best to insult him. "Even in your affliction," Doctor Peral would write, "you are luckier than others. They have to lock up their dangerous emotions inside themselves till sometimes the barriers of their reason do indeed break down. But you, Don Francisco, can paint them. You can paint your troubles clear out of your body and your soul." "Would you care to change places with me, Doctor?" Francisco inquired with a mocking smile. "Would you care to be hard of hearing and in exchange capable of painting certain troubles out of your soul?" Such were the jests they made with each other. But once, overcome by his suffering, Goya seized the other by the arm and laid his massive head on his enemy's breast; he was shaken, he felt he must cling to someone who understood him, and though they had never spoken of Cayetana he knew: his enemy understood him.

When he was alone, then sometimes he was as though stunned by the realization of what his life would be in future. Sometimes, when he was in company, he would shout, at other times whisper, would never be able to gauge the loudness of his own voice when he spoke, would often utter aloud without knowing he had done so what he had only meant to think; people would look at him in surprise, he would never have anything but uncertainty and suspicion. It was unbearable to the proud man that he should be to other men an object of pity and sometimes of derision. Of course Peral was right. He would lapse inevitably into insanity.

He would have liked to say straight out that his deafness was a punishment. But if he confessed he would be unable to hear the priest's reply, and if he told it to Peral the latter would merely regard it as fresh proof of his aberration.

Peral was an extremely clever physician. He must surely have seen through him long ago, surely for years have known of his insanity. For he was insane, had been for many long years. How many attacks of rage and raving had overtaken him throughout the years! How many ghosts and demons he had seen, quite palpable ones, but only he had seen them, no one but him! And this had all happened while the world still had voices: how would it be now, with nothing but this intolerable silence all around him?

Would he ever again be able
To distinguish what was real for
Everybody else, and what for
Him alone? Which Cayetana
Was the true one? Her he had painted
As Duquesa? Her as naked
Lust he had painted too? Or as a

Witch, as innocently swaying
Through the air away?

Oh, there they
Were again, there were the demons!
Broad daylight it is, and he has
Always known it: known the monsters
Who by day present themselves are
Worst of all, more fearsome than the
Ones by night. He dreams, but yet is
Frightfully awake. He writhes and
Flings himself across the table
Desperately, not to see them,
But he sees them, notwithstanding,
They are in him, are his very
Self, at once inside and outside
Him.

-- 39 --

Peral informed him that Doña Cayetana would return in about ten days.

Goya thrust out his underlip, his face grew dark. He said, "I'm leaving in three days." "Doña Cayetana will be extremely sorry, I know," answered Peral. "She's counting on finding you here. And as a doctor I ought to warn you against undertaking so long and arduous a journey so soon. You should first adapt yourself to your new condition." "I leave in three days," Goya returned. "Shall I come with you?" Peral offered after a short silence. "It's very kind of you, Don Joaquín," Goya answered glumly, "but my future will be bitter indeed if I can travel only with nurses and attendants." "Then I'll have the large travelling coach made ready for you," said Peral. "Thank you, Doctor," Goya replied, "but I won't need the large coach. I won't need post horses, or even the ordinary stagecoach. I'm going to take a mule-driver. I shall get Gil to come, the muleteer from the Venta de las Cuatro Naciones. He is a good man. If I give him a *gratificacioncita*, a small gratuity, he'll look after me and have consideration for my infirmity." Then, as Peral could not hide his astonishment, Goya concluded irritably, "Don't look at me like that, Don Joaquín. I'm not crazy. I have my reasons."

He could not bear the sight of the woman who had abandoned him in his misery. He must leave San Lúcar immediately, he knew. He also knew he must not make the journey in state, as might befit the First Painter to the King. Peral was right in saying he must adapt himself to his new condition. Must become entirely familiar with it. Must drain the bitter cup of his infirmity to the dregs. Not till then, fully conscious of his new state, could he let himself be seen by his family, the Court, his colleagues. That was why he was going to journey across his Spain as an ordinary man, and get used to exhibiting his ailment and excusing himself. "Your Excellency will excuse me," he would say, ten times a day. "I can't hear very well, I'm more or less stone deaf."

He would not take the direct route back to Madrid either. He would go much farther to the north. Avoiding Madrid, he would go to Aragón, to Saragossa, to confide all his troubles to his friend, his heart's dear Martín. Not till he had received Martín's comfort and advice would he be ready to see Josefa, his children, and his friends.

The mule-driver Gil, with whom Francisco had already had many lively conversations in the *venta* at San Lúcar, was a real *arriero*, a mule-driver after the old Spanish pattern, who could howl out his "*Arré, arré*," so that the mountains echoed far and wide. When he was told that Francisco wished to employ his services he appeared at the Casa de Haro in the costume of his trade. Around his head he wore a coloured silk kerchief with the Alhambra painted on it. The corners hung down behind like pigtails; over it he wore the pointed wide-brimmed hat. His jacket of black sheepskin was lavishly embroidered and furnished with large silver filigree buttons. Around his body he wore a wide silk scarf, the *faja*, in which he kept his knife. His breeches of blue velvet were striped vertically in many colours and also had silver buttons; his yellow boots were of untanned calfskin. He stood in front of Francisco in all his glory. When the latter revealed that he wished him to accompany him to Saragossa, skirting Madrid, he took it to be the crazy whim of some great gentleman. He whistled through his teeth, gesticulated expressively, and observed, "*Hombre!* That's a long journey!" And though he knew Goya to be familiar with the customs of the country, he asked the enormous sum of eight hundred reals, five times the yearly wage of a shepherd.

Goya took a good look at this *arriero* Gil with whom he intended to share four weeks of his life. He was no longer First Painter to the King but a man of the people, and so they confronted each other, one peasant's son to another, one much-travelled man to another of the same kidney. And as Goya was so long silent and only looked at him Gil finally said, "For such a damned long journey we'll need two mules. And of course I must let you have the *garañón*, the *Valeroso*, the most remarkable mule in Spain. One of his ancestors was the ass Constante who in his day threw the heretic Tomás Trebino as he was carrying him to the pyre, such a God-fearing ass he was." At this point Goya opened his mouth and said amiably, "I must surely have misunderstood you. My hearing's bad as a matter of fact, as you probably noticed in the *venta*, and now I'm as deaf as a post, as you might say. Did you really mention eight hundred reals?" Gil, gesticulating even more wildly, replied, "I wish Your Excellency well, but the fact that your hearing is weak won't make the journey any easier either for me or my animals. Eight hundred reals."

Goya began to swear horribly. He gave the mule-driver *carajos*, curses and maledictions, garlic and onions, *ajos y cebollas*, in such profusion as the other had never had hurled at his head before, and he shouted very loudly in the process. The mule-driver cursed back. Goya did not hear him but he saw how Gil was exerting himself and in the midst of his imprecations he broke off and suddenly burst into roars of laughter. "Save yourself the trouble," he said. "I win every time; for you hear me and I can't hear you." Gil saw the sense of that, and he also saw that he would not be able to put anything over on this man. "You're a great man, Don Francisco," he said. "You're one of us. So let's say seven hundred and eighty reals." They finally settled for six hundred and fifty. They also reached full agreement on itinerary, lodging expenses, provisions, and fodder for the animals, and Gil's respect for his traveller greatly increased. "*Por vida del demonio*, as true as there's a Devil in Hell," he said, "Your Excellency knows more about it than we do ourselves," and they shook hands on it.

Goya equipped himself for the journey as simply as possible; he procured a jacket of black lambskin, wide plain scarf, and a pointed hat with a black velvet brim. Nor did he forget the wineskin, the *bota*. But in the saddlebags, the *alforjas*, he stuffed only the barest necessities.

They set forth. Goya took no care of his appearance, never shaved, and soon a tangle of beard had grown about his face. No one would have taken him for a great gentleman.

It was a long journey and they did only a small stretch each day. First they took the road to Córdoba. It was on this road that he had come before to Cayetana, with post horses, six of them, in haste, full of expectation, fortune's favourite. He savoured it to the full that he was now retreating along the same road, humbly, with difficulty, slowly, through a silent world, often misunderstood and derided, an ageing peasant.

In the *venta* of La Carlota they were told that the famous bandit José de Roxas, called El Puñal, the Dagger, was to be executed in Córdoba in three days' time. The execution of a robber, particularly of a robber as famous as El Puñal, was a tremendous popular spectacle, more exciting than the finest *corrida*, and if Divine Providence should bring one into the neighbourhood at the time of such an execution it would be madness, sinful even, to let slip the opportunity of seeing the spectacle. The muleteer therefore immediately put it to Francisco that as they were in no hurry they should spend a day in Córdoba and take part in the great affair.

The idea of observing other men in their misfortunes had always had a fascination for Francisco; now that he had himself fallen on evil days it was doubly attractive. He decided to attend the execution.

The mule-driver Gil, in common with other members of his profession, had an appetite for the latest news, for anecdotes of all kinds, and he had already entertained Goya on the journey with numerous stories. Everything he related grew in the telling and became more vivid, *en luengas vías luengas mentiras*, long journeys call for tall stories. He had even been able to give a good deal of information about the bandit El Puñal. Now that the whole neighbourhood was full of stories about the bandit he thought up fresh embellishments. The robber El Puñal was an outstanding devout and God-fearing robber; he wore always two amulets, a rosary, and a holy image of the "Mother of Sorrows" of Córdoba, and he conscientiously gave half of his gains to the almsbox, which had been set up in front of the Cristo del Buen Ladrón, or the Christ of the Good Robber, in order that in this way bandits could atone for at least part of their sins. The Virgin herself had taken the Puñal under her protection, and he would never have been caught by the soldiers if a rascal from his own band, who had sold himself to the police, had not secretly abstracted his "Sorrowful Mother of Córdoba" while he slept. And although the population breathed a sigh of relief at being at last safe from the bandit, nevertheless their sympathies were with him and they disapproved of the way the authorities had proceeded. For they had promised to show clemency to the Puñal and his men should he deliver his band into the hands of the soldiery. He had succeeded in persuading his band to surrender, but the authorities had declared that the men had submitted not to the Puñal but to the escort of soldiers and had condemned him to the garrotte, to being throttled.

As soon as Goya and Gil reached Córdoba they went to the prison to see the bandit; for on the day before the execution anybody who liked could visit the condemned man and give expression to such sympathy or disapproval as he might feel. In the corridor outside the condemned cell Franciscan friars were collecting money so that Masses could be said for the criminal's soul. They sat with their tins and plates, smoking their cigars, and from time to time, by way of encouragement, called out the figures which their collection had so far attained.

The condemned cell, the *capilla,* was rather dark. There was a table, and on it a crucifix, a statue of the Virgin, two wax candles. In one corner, on a wooden pallet, lay the Puñal. He had pulled the striped blanket up to his mouth, only the upper half of his face was visible, with dishevelled locks and sharp black eyes which rolled unceasingly in their sockets.

The guards ordered Francisco and the driver to move on as others also wanted to see something. But Francisco was waiting for the Puñal to sit up. He gave a large tip and they were allowed to stay.

After a while the Puñal actually did sit up. He was almost naked, but around his neck hung the rosary and the amulet of the "Mother of Sorrows." A boy, so the guards said, had handed it in, he had been given it by some unknown person, and when this unknown was run to earth he said he had obtained it from a second unknown. Clearly whoever had stolen the Puñal's "Sorrowful Mother" did not want him to die without it.

There sat the bandit then, after so much fame and such dishonour, almost as naked as he had come into the world. On his bare body he wore the rosary which had been hung about his neck immediately after his birth, the image of the "Sorrowful Mother" which he had worn, lost, and found again on the next to the last day of his life; also the chains and shackles which men had hung on him before his end. Those in the cell abused him or commiserated with him. He made no response. From time to time, however, he raised his head and said, "It is not men who are responsible for my death but my own sins." He said this over and over again, mechanically. Obviously the monks had taught him to do so. But Goya saw that his look was crazed, hopeless, despairing; he looked like the man who had looked back at Goya from the mirror.

Next morning, very early, two hours before the appointed time, Francisco and his driver repaired to the Corredera, the big rectangular square in Córdoba where the execution was to take place. A dense throng was already on the spot; windows, roofs, and balconies were crowded with spectators. An area immediately in front of the scaffold was barred off by soldiers; only the privileged were allowed into it, officials, ladies, and gentlemen of society. "Will Your Excellency not make yourself known?" urged the driver. But though it was a strain to stand among the crowd, buffeted and hemmed in, and although the view of the execution platform was not precisely uninterrupted, yet Goya preferred to experience what was to come to pass up there in the company of the common people. For the first time since the blow had struck him he forgot his misfortunes and waited in the same suspense as everyone else.

Vendors of sweetmeats and sausages pushed their way through the crowd, romances telling of El Puñal's exploits were hawked about, stools were for hire on which to stand in order to get a better view. There were women with their infants; they complained as they were squeezed and jostled, but no one took any notice. The impatience of the crowd grew. There was still an hour to wait, still half an hour; how slowly the time passed. "It's going faster for him," a man said, grinning. Goya could not understand what was being said but he could guess it, he was at home with the mob, felt with it. He waited with the same dark sadism, the same pity and enjoyment, as the others.

At last ten struck from the cathedral, and now everyone pushed harder and craned his neck. But the Puñal still did not appear. For Spain was a devout country and the hour of execution had been fixed for ten minutes later. Ten extra minutes were given to the criminal, for absolution perhaps, and above all for repentance.

But now even the ten minutes were up, and there he was. Clothed in the yellow shift of the criminal, surrounded by Franciscan monks, supported by them, he made his last short, endless journey. A monk held the crucifix up to him, and again and again he halted to kiss it and thus prolong his life. All those present sympathized with the delay, nor did they grudge it him, and at the same time they would have liked to push him on his way.

Now he was on the steps of the scaffold. He knelt down, closely surrounded by monks, so that he could make his last confession unseen by the crowd. Then, accompanied by a single monk, a paunchy, good-natured-looking one, he ascended the steps.

From the top he addressed the populace in disjointed sentences, his breath often failing him. Goya could not understand what he said but he could see his face, and behind the pretended composure his boundless terror. He waited in suspense for the phrase with which the criminal, as the custom was, granted the executioner his forgiveness. For the Spaniard had a deep contempt for the executioner, and the words of forgiveness which religion dictated must have made the Puñal's last moments more bitter than they already were. Narrowing his eyes, Goya looked fixedly at his mouth and thus was able to understand the words. El Puñal said, "My transgressions kill me, not this creature." "This creature," he said, "*ese hombre*," a particularly derogatory usage, and Goya felt gratified that El Puñal had met his religious obligations and at the same time shown his executioner the contempt he deserved.

Now the bandit spoke the final words. "*Viva la fe*," he shouted, "*viva el rey, viva el nombre de Jesús*, long live the Faith, long live the King, long live the name of Jesus." The mob listened unconcernedly, without joining in. Not till El Puñal shouted, "*Viva la Virgen Santísima*," did they break out in a tremendous shout, "*Viva la Santísima*," and even Francisco joined in.

Meanwhile the executioner had made his preparations. He was a young man, officiating that day for the first time, and all were waiting eagerly to see how he would acquit himself.

A strong post had been driven through the scaffold into the earth. In front of it stood a rough wooden stool, upon which the executioner now pushed El Puñal. Then he bound his naked arms and legs so tightly that they became purple and swollen. Such precaution was indicated; shortly before this a criminal had murdered his executioner in the fulfilment of his duties. Fastened to the post was an iron collar. This, the garrotte, the executioner now put round the Puñal's neck. The paunchy monk thrust a small crucifix into his manacled hands.

Now all was ready. The man about to die sat there, bound hand and foot, his head pulled backwards against the post by the iron collar; he was grinding his teeth; his face, upturned towards the blue sky, was crazed with terror. The monk at his side had stepped back a little and was shading his eyes with one hand against the blinding sun. The executioner seized the handle of the screw, the judge gave the signal, the executioner threw a black cloth over El Puñal's face, and then with both hands turned the screw so that the iron ring throttled El Puñal. Holding their breaths, the mob watched as the suffocating man's hands flapped and his chest swelled monstrously. Then the executioner peered cautiously beneath the cloth, gave the screw a final turn, removed the cloth, folded it up, put it in his pocket, gave a sigh of satisfaction, and left the scaffold to light himself a cigar.

Clearly visible now to one and all in the crude sunlight was the dead man's face, distorted, blue and suffused in its frame of disordered beard, the eyes rolled upwards, the mouth open with the tongue hanging out. Goya was certain he would be able at any time to recall this face.

A large candle was now set up on the platform, and in front of the platform appeared a black bier and a table with two large plates on it, into which the people were supposed to throw coins so that Masses could be said for the dead man. The spectators eagerly discussed what had taken place. You could tell quite easily that the executioner had only just finished his apprenticeship, and, taking it all round, El Puñal hadn't made quite as brave an end as one might have expected of so great and celebrated a bandit.

The body remained on display till the afternoon. Most of the spectators, Goya and Gil included, stayed where they were. At last the carrion cart appeared. Everyone knew that the corpse would now be taken outside the city, into the wild hills, to a small plateau called the Mesa del rey, there to be hacked into pieces and thrown over a precipice. Slowly the mob dispersed. "The legs of the robber are thrown in the hole, the wolves get his bones, the devil his soul," they sang and hummed on their way home.

Goya and Gil left Córdoba and went on northwards.

As was customary when one travelled by mule, they often avoided the main roads and took paths which made short cuts over mountains and through valleys. On the main roads there were *fondas* and *posadas*, hostelries and inns, but on these bypaths there were only *ventas*, mean lodging houses with little to eat, a pair of straw pallets, and many fleas. Gil never ceased to wonder that the First Painter to the King should prefer such miserable accommodation, but Goya said, " 'No softer pillow than a tired back,' " and he slept well and dreamlessly.

It was an experience which never lost its novelty when they emerged from these desolate side paths once more onto the main road. There could be seen travelling in the carriages of the Royal Post, in the *galeras*, *tartañas*, and *caroches*, merchants, priests, and lawyers, while by mule and on foot travelled students, monks, small traders, ladies of doubtful virtue, hawkers seeking their luck at the next fair. Merchants from Cádiz drove by in elegant travelling coaches, and grandees in old-fashioned *coches de colleras* with a good deal of gilding, heraldry, and numerous extra horses and coachmen in livery.

These roads were familiar to Francisco, and perhaps he saw their motley traffic the more sharply now that the noise of them was silenced. But he knew what the sounds were, knew the *chirrio*, the wild rattling of wheels which were seldom greased so that their violent clatter might announce one's coming from afar and scare off wild animals. He knew the gay voices of the travellers, the full-throated bellow of coachmen and drivers. He could still see the wheels turning, the mouths of travellers and coachmen opening and shutting, but the sounds he had to supply out of his own memory. It was an exacting game, sometimes funny, for the most part sad.

The remarkable thing was that since he had witnessed the animal suffering of the bandit El Puñal his own burden had become lighter.

Once he stood with his Gil outside an inn, with many others, and looked on while the eight beasts were harnessed to the big post coach. Now all was ready, the *mayoral*, or head coachman, took the reins of the many bridles in his hand, the *zagal*, his assistant, swung himself up next to him, drivers and stable boys from the inn removed chocks and stones, and next moment the huge coach would begin to move. Goya saw them all shouting to urge the horses on, and he could not restrain himself, his mouth seemed to open of its own accord, and shrilly he joined in the shrill cry of coachmen and drivers: "*Qué perro-o-o! Macho—macho—macho —macho-o-o!*"

Then Goya and Gil turned aside once more from the main roads and took to the side paths. Here, more frequently than on the roads, did they come across little piles of stones, with crosses and coloured pictures on them, erected to the memory of persons who had died on that spot. It was amazing how many people did die on the road; there must have been quite an army of them. The pictures showed them falling over precipices, ravaged by roving animals, swept away by torrents, hacked to pieces by bandits, or quite simply polished off by a stroke. In addition, there was always a rhymed exhortation to the devout traveller to stay his steps and say a prayer for the soul of the unfortunate one. Gil noticed with surprise that Don Francisco would often do no more than take off his hat and cross himself.

On some stretches they would join up with other trains of muleteers; for on these remote paths it was better not to travel alone. Goya did not try to force himself on the others; nor did he avoid them; he did not mind telling them that he was deaf; Gil felt more and more liking and respect for this gentleman to whom he had hired himself. He cheated him only seldom and then for small sums. Sometimes, too, he was unable to resist telling the others, in defiance of Goya's prohibition, who his traveller was and what misfortune had befallen him.

Once they encountered some bandits. They were well-mannered bandits who knew their business and dispatched it quickly. While two of them searched Francisco, Gil whispered with the others; clearly he was telling them who Goya was. So then, this being the man who had so lovingly depicted scenes from the lives of robbers and smugglers on the royal tapestries, they relieved him of only half the six hundred reals which he had on him, and when they were finished they invited him to take a pull from their *bota*, flourished their hats respectfully, and called politely, "*Vaya usted con la Virgen!* May Your Excellency go with the Virgin."

So then Goya, poor and shabby,
In the prison of his deafness,
Sitting on his Valeroso
Moved through Spain, his Spain, so queerly
Soundless. Wretched, yet determined,
He would make his shoulders stronger,
Strong against the demons squatting
On them with intent to break them.
They had missed their guess, the demons.
He would walk the more erectly,
He, Francisco Goya, painter,
Man from Aragón. And all the
Stronger would he grow, and wrestle
With the ill-fate that befell him,
All the sharper see and all the
Sharper draw. His laugh resounded
Loud, until his Gil, mule-driver,
Looked at him, amazed and anxious.

Thus did Goya, lightly, grimly,
Leave the southern city where he
Had his highest joy experienced
And his deepest pain. He travelled
North, and towards the northern city
Saragossa, whence so many
Years ago he came.

-- PART III --

— 1 —

At that time, in the last five years of the century, the government of the French Republic had slipped from the hands of the people and been taken over by men of business. "There is no more dangerous creature alive than the businessman seeking his prey," Baron Holbach, the Encyclopædist, had recently proclaimed, and the leading men of the Revolution had seen it in the same light. Now, however, Gracchus Babeuf and his followers had been executed for having wanted to inaugurate a "community of equals" and to bring about equality of incomes, and the slogan of France's new masters was "Enrich yourselves."

In that other land also which had tried to realize the ideals of enlightenment by revolution, the United States of America, the leading men were flirting with the old ideas. They had denounced that France without whose help they could never have won their independence, they insulted the French ambassador and conducted a cold war with the Republic. They passed the Alien and Sedition Acts, which were contrary to the spirit of the Constitution, they watered down the principles of the Declaration of Independence. When the first President of the country, George Washington, laid down his office, a paper in Philadelphia exulted: "The man who is responsible for all the misery of our country descends today to the level of his fellow-citizens and no longer has the power to multiply the sufferings of these United States. Every heart which beats for freedom and the happiness of the people must today rejoice at the thought that the name of Washington now ceases to spread injustice and legalize corruption."

The impassioned efforts to create a new order of human existence in the shortest possible time had left the world exhausted. Society, exerting its powers to the utmost, had attempted to regulate affairs public and private in the light of reason. Now it had relaxed its effort, was fleeing from the dazzling light of reason back into the twilight of the emotions. All over the world the old conservative ideas were acclaimed. From the chill atmosphere of thought men ducked back into the warmth of faith, piety, and sensibility. They sought refuge in the quiet harbours of authority and discipline from the storms which freedom had brought with it. Romantic spirits dreamed of re-creating the Middle Ages, poets sang of their hatred of the clear sunlight, waxed lyrical over the moonlit enchantment of the night, extolled the peace and security to be had in the lap of the Catholic Church. "The enlightenment hasn't as much as scratched our skins," one Cardinal exulted.

That was a mistake. The sharp, clear, new ideas had taken possession of too many people to be eradicated. Privileges, till now unshakable, had been undermined. Absolutism, belief in the Grace of God, the segregation of castes and classes, the prerogatives of Church and nobility, all this had been called in question. France and America had provided the great example, and, in spite of the reinforced hostility of Church and nobility, the idea was gaining ground that human affairs should be conducted according to the principles of scientific knowledge and not according to laws laid down in old, professedly sacred books.

In that last five years of the century there were in France about 25,000,000 people, in England and Spain about 11,000,000 each; Paris had a population of 900,000; London 800,000. The United States of America were inhabited by about 3,000,000 whites and 700,000 coloured slaves. America's largest city was Philadelphia, with 42,000 inhabitants; New York had 30,000, and Boston, Baltimore, and Charleston 10,000 each. During these five years the English political economist Malthus published his essay on the principles of population and pronounced his conclusion that humanity was multiplying more rapidly than were the food supplies necessary for its maintenance, hence that propagation must be limited.

In these five years the human race turned a farther area of its planet to its own use. The United States of America exerted themselves to attract settlers and to this end set up companies and corporations which with ample long-term credit sold land at a dollar an acre. Also during these five years Alexander von Humboldt began his great voyages of discovery to Central and South America, the results of which were to make the world better understood and easier to live in.

In those five years, all over the world and above all in Europe, there took place many violent political changes. Old kingdoms collapsed and were constituted in new forms, chiefly as republics. Numerous ecclesiastical territories were secularized. The Pope was brought a prisoner to France, the Doge of Venice espoused the sea for the last time. The French Republic won many battles on land, England many at sea; and England won her decisive victory in India. Towards the end of the century England concluded a pact with almost the whole of Europe, with the purpose of preventing the farther spread of the French Republic and of progressive ideas. All in all, there was more conflict and violence in the world during these last five years than in all the rest of the century, and in the same five years the German philosopher Immanuel Kant wrote his "Design for Eternal Peace."

In their private lives the military leaders of this divided world showed little concern for the gossip of the mob and the newspapers. In these five years Napoleon Bonaparte married Josephine Beauharnais, and Admiral Horatio Nelson met Emma Hamilton and fell in love with her.

In those five years men and women emancipated themselves from the burdensome splendour of the clothing they had worn till now and at the same time blurred the distinction between the clothes of the privileged and those of the lower classes. In France, under the influence of the painter Jacques-Louis David, a simple, archaizing style became popular, *la merveilleuse*, and people began to wear long trousers or pantaloons, a costume which spread rapidly all over Europe.

In those five years Alessandro Volta constructed the first apparatus to produce electric current, Priestley discovered carbonic oxide, Stanhope invented the iron printing press. Yet everywhere humanity held fast to superseded theories and techniques; they believed those who discovered and made use of hitherto unknown laws of nature to be agents of the Devil, and they went on tilling the soil as they had tilled it thousands of years ago. In those five years Doctor Edward Jenner published the results of an investigation indicating that inoculation with cowpox was efficacious against smallpox and was laughed at for his pains. Yet no one laughed at those who bathed in miraculous springs and waters, thereby contracting infections, or at those who to recover their health made waxen images of their affected parts and offered them up to all manner of saints; on the contrary, the Inquisition punished anyone who dared question the healing powers of such procedures.

In those five years Shakespeare was everywhere hailed as the greatest poet in a thousand years. Many people translated him into many tongues; August Wilhelm von Schlegel produced a translation which transformed and beautified the German language for a hundred years to come. In those five years Goethe wrote his poem *Hermann und Dorothea,* Schiller his tragedy *Wallenstein.* Alfieri wrote his classicist tragedies *Saul, Antigone,* and *The Second Brutus,* and there died that great creator of colourful and imaginative fairy stories, Carlo Gozzi, leaving behind him three volumes of *Useless Memoirs.* Jane Austen wrote her delicately dispassionate novels *Pride and Prejudice* and *Sense and Sensibility.* Coleridge published his first poems, as did the Swedish poet Tegnér. In Russia, Ivan Ivanovitch Chemnitzer wrote the tragedy *Moscow Delivered,* and Vasili Vasilievich Kapnist, in his rhymed comedy *Yabeda,* which means "pettifoggery," scoffed bitterly at the venality of justice. Millions of those who had never before held a book in their hands began to read books and enjoy them. But the Church forbade most of the books the critics recommended; in Spain infringement of this interdict was punishable with the pillory and imprisonment, and in the Hapsburg Monarchy high officials were dismissed from their posts if it was proved they read forbidden books.

In those five years the bones of the foremost free-thinker of them all, the revered bones of the revered Voltaire, were laid to rest in the Panthéon with the enthusiastic approval of the populace, and in the same five years, in the same Paris, Madame Marie Anne Lenormand opened a fortune-telling salon which enjoyed a great run of customers. And at Madame Tussaud's waxworks, Saint Denis, carrying his head under his arm, and the heretic Voltaire stood peaceably side by side.

In those five years, in the Egyptian city of Rosetta, the Arabian Raschid, there was found a stone covered with inscriptions, which enabled the researcher Champollion to decipher hieroglyphics. Antoine-Nicolas de Condorcet founded the collectivist materialist philosophy of history, Pierre-Simon de Laplace explained the origin of the planets in terms of natural science. But whoever did not confess the belief that the world was created according to the Biblical account in the six days between the 28th of September and the 3rd of October 3988 B.C. was debarred from public office in the Spanish Empire and the Hapsburg Monarchy.

In those five years Goethe wrote in his *Venetian Epigrams* that of all things the four he hated most were "the smell of tobacco, bugs, garlic, and the Cross"; and Thomas Paine was at work on that textbook of rationalism, *The Age of Reason.* At the same time Schleiermacher wrote his book *On Religion, Words addressed to the Educated among its Detractors,* Novalis his *Theodycee,* and the French author Chateaubriand was converted to a romanticized Catholicism. The book *Decline and Fall of the Roman Empire,* in which Edward Gibbon with delicate wit and chilly irony represented the rise of Christianity as a relapse into barbarism, was everywhere acclaimed as the most important historical work of the age; at the same time the *Apologies* in which Bishop Richard Watson sought with elegance and moderation to confute Gibbon and Paine had no less success.

In those five years many important discoveries were made in physics, chemistry, biology; important sociological principles were propounded and proved, and their discoverers were attacked, pilloried, thrust into prison. New scientific methods of healing were tried out, and priests and medicine men drove out devils from the ailing and effected cures with prayers and amulets.

Philosophizing statesmen and greedy businessmen, retiring scholars and mountebank quacks, ambitious priests and enslaved peasants, artists sensitive to every stimulus and brutish murderous foot-soldiers, all lived together in restricted space, rubbed elbows, jostled one another; clever and stupid ones, those whose brains were scarcely more developed than those of earliest man and those whose minds conceived thoughts which the majority would not grasp for another ice-age, the poetical ones who were susceptible to beauty in all its forms and those who were unmoved by any manipulation of words, sounds, or stone, industrious and active or lazy and stupid, they breathed the same air, touched one another's skins, were in constant direct proximity. They loved and hated one another, waged war, concluded treaties, broke them, waged new wars, concluded new treaties, hacked one another to pieces, mated and bore children, and only seldom understood one another. The clever, gifted few thrust forward, the vast host of others held them back, attacked them, shackled them, killed them, sought in all manner of ways to be rid of them. And yet they came on, the gifted few, imperceptibly no doubt, with much suffering and sacrifice, and as they came they forced, they hoisted the mass of the others a little way forward with them.

The ambitious and those of limited vision made use of the lethargy and stupidity of the masses in attempts to preserve outworn institutions. But the French Revolution had blown fresh air into the world, and Napoleon, consummator of the Revolution, set himself to the task of sweeping away much that was useless, once and for all.

More now than mere sound and fury
Was the idea of the human
Rights of man. In many countries
It was real: weak, young, and narrow,
Yet reality, a charter,
Written into law. And thus at
End of century and of lustrum,
Spite of all, there now existed
In the sorry world a little
More of reason than a hundred
Years before had been.

-- 2 --

Don Manuel had left San Ildefonso half an hour since. Tired and despondent, he leaned back against the cushions of the carriage. Before him lay the long journey to Cádiz, where disagreeable tasks awaited him. Of course he meant first to permit himself a few days rest in Madrid, incognito with Pepa. But not even this prospect served to cheer him.

Caramba! In the last few weeks he had had nothing but vexation. For the French to force him to continue the unpopular war against England was bad enough, but now they were insisting, the *gabachos*, that he undertake unconsidered, irretrievable steps against Portugal.

For the English fleet was using the Portuguese harbours as bases, and the French, invoking the treaty of alliance, were demanding that Spain bring about the closure of these ports. Again and again, with unpleasant logic, the French ambassador, Citizen Truguet, insisted that if Portugal refused, Spain should compel the closing of the harbours by force of arms. Now, of course, it was certainly a tempting idea to fall upon the small, helpless neighbour and procure an easy victory. But the Prince-Regent of Portugal was the son-in-law of the Catholic King, and Carlos and María Luisa were unwilling to make war against their own daughter. Apart from this, Portugal had given him, Don Manuel, splendid gifts; and so, by a kind of tacit agreement, Don Manuel had almost allowed the war against England to drop.

The Portuguese question was not his only worry. Long-forgotten affairs, for instance that with the skinny Geneviève, daughter of Royalist Ambassador de Havré, were flaring up. For after his banishment from Spain the Marquis had taken refuge in Portugal with his daughter and was living there on a subvention from the private fortune of the Catholic King. That troublesome Frenchman, the vulgar tactless Citizen Truguet, had got wind of it and was now making the shameless request that not only should Manuel break off all relations with "the Royalist adventurer" at once, but on top of that should effect his immediate extradition.

So he leaned back in the carriage, the Príncipe de la Paz; the bad taste of affairs in San Ildefonso was still in his mouth, and in Cádiz disheartening negotiations awaited him. María Luisa had planted several of her favourites in important positions in the battle fleet there, men who brought to the job nothing but exalted titles and the Queen's favour, and the very able officers who were subordinated to these incompetents were threatening resignation. All around him was nothing but discomfort.

Not quite everywhere. The nearer Don Manuel came to the capital, the more his disagreeable thoughts dissipated themselves. He decided to stay a day longer in Madrid with Pepa. He would forget that fate had burdened him with guiding the destinies of the Kingdom of Spain; during the next few days he would be no statesman but simply Don Manuel, enjoying life.

It turned out otherwise.

Pepa had been passing weeks of boredom and irritation. Francisco was away; for weeks now, months, imperilling his career, he had been sharing the Duchess of Alba's exile. With bitterness in her heart she reflected on the passion of which he was capable, and the scant regret with which he had relinquished her to Manuel. And Manuel himself! He talked very big about his love for her, but most of the time he was in San Ildefonso or in Aranjuez or at the Escorial, leaving her alone, and when he did come he came clandestinely. So it was an irritable and sulky Pepa who received Manuel.

She invited him to take her to a bullfight, to the *corrida* of Pedro Romero. He replied with a sigh that by Sunday he would already be on his way to Cádiz. "Is it too much to ask," she said, "that you should spend two days longer with me?" "*Chérie*, I had great difficulty in making these three days free for you," he answered. "I have a war to fight, apart from other urgent business. Please don't add to my burdens." "I can tell you why you don't want to go to the *corrida* with me," Pepa replied. "You're ashamed of me. You don't want to be seen with me."

Manuel tried to make her listen to reason. "Do understand," he begged impatiently. "I really have a devilish lot on my shoulders. I'm supposed to make Portugal give up her dealings with England, and at the same time I'm to spare the feelings of Portugal's Prince-Regent. I'm to dismiss six imbecile grandees from the fleet, and I'm to post three more imbecile grandees to the armada. On top of that Truguet has already sent me two insolent notes to the effect that I should have Monsieur de Havré banished from Lisbon. As it is there'll be sour faces in Cádiz because I'm two days late, and here you expect me to stay with you over Sunday. Do try to understand my difficulties." "Your difficulties," Pepa returned pugnaciously, "all arise from one source: from your cheap, unbridled sensuality. Your differences with Spain and Portugal all derive from your feeling you had to sleep with poor, thin, miserable Geneviève." Manuel, angry now in his turn, answered, "You drove me to it. If you'd shown me the sort of love a man like me has a right to expect, I'd never have laid a finger on that beanpole." Pepa, goaded beyond endurance, said, "And I suppose it's my fault too that you still climb into bed with old María Luisa?"

This was too much. His real nature, that of a *majo* from the hog-raising province of Estremadura, broke through. He lifted a plump hand and slapped her hard across the face.

For a second she wanted nothing but to strike back, to scratch, to bite, to wring his neck. Then she mastered herself. Pulled the bell. Called, "Conchita!" and again, "Conchita!"

He saw the imprint of his hand flaming on her very pale face, saw her green wide-set eyes blaze with outrage. He stammered apologies, spoke of how irritable he was from overwork. But Conchita was already there, thin and severe, and Pepa, her voice under control, said, "Accompany the gentleman to the door, Conchita!" Overcome with remorse, full of desire and raging at the stupidity by which he had ruined the holiday, he redoubled his apologies, tried to grasp her hand, embrace her. But she cried, "Are you ever going to get rid of the fellow, Conchita!" and fled into the next room. There was nothing else to do but to go.

He told himself bitterly that fate vouchsafed him no respite in his exertions for the good of the kingdom, and he drove as fast as possible to Cádiz, angry and eager for action. He hoped to forget his discomfiture in the eddy of business and pleasure, and then, on his return to Madrid, to find Pepa restored to reasonableness.

And in fact he had not one unoccupied minute in Cádiz. He negotiated with shipbuilders, the heads of export and import firms, and with bankers. Promised the professional officers of the fleet to put a stop to the activities of the noble and dunderheaded admirals. In a secret meeting with gentlemen of the English blockading fleet he confirmed the unwritten agreement that the two fleets should of course threaten, but not attack, each other. And while his days were given to activities for his country, his nights were devoted to the celebrated pleasures of Cádiz.

But neither business nor amusement served to drive the thought of Pepa out of his head. Again and again he saw the mark of his hand on her cheek, and the memory filled him with remorse, longing, and lust.

His business scarcely concluded, he drove by the quickest route back to Madrid. Hastened, still in traveling clothes, to the Palacio Bondad Real. He found the house in disorder, the furniture pushed against the walls, carpets rolled up; he found crates and packed trunks. The major-domo was unwilling to admit him. Conchita stood by with a severe, shut-up expression. He slipped three golden ducats into her hand. They kept him waiting but finally showed him into Pepa's apartment.

"I am going south," Pepa announed to him in her rich, slow voice. "I'm going to Málaga to go on the stage there. Señor Rivero was here; his company is becoming well known, and he has given me a good contract. When your fleet is once more in a condition to keep the sea lanes clear, I shall go back to the land of my birth, to America. They say Lima still has the best theatre in the Spanish world."

Inwardly Manuel was furious. True, he had hit her, but he had abased himself before her and had come back to do so again. She had no need to threaten him with putting the ocean between herself and him. He felt an impulse to strike her again. But her skin was so dazzlingly white against the black negligee, her green eyes looked huge, solemn, seductive; he inhaled her odour. He was fresh from nights spent with women of Cádiz, fascinating women practised in all the vices, but he knew that he could not get on without this woman who alone could afford him the height of voluptuous enjoyment, true ravishment, Heaven and Hell together, overwhelming. He dared not allow himself to be carried away by his anger, he must employ both eloquence and cunning to keep her.

Once more he made a vehement, thoroughgoing apology. Just now he was being pulled this way and that, by Madrileño free-thinkers and hide-bound grandees or ultramontane fanatics, by France and by Spain. That vulgar Citizen Truguet and that cold, petty Talleyrand, sly as a fox, had no regard for his subtle, wholly statesmanlike solutions. He stood alone. The only one who understood him, General Bonaparte, was fighting somewhere in Egypt. No wonder that under such circumstances a person should momentarily take leave of his senses. "I deserve to be punished," he admitted. "But you need not punish me quite so severely, Señora. You mustn't punish me like this, Pepa," he finished and seized her hand.

She withdrew it quite calmly. Life in Madrid did not satisfy her, she said. For a long time, he, Manuel, had been her consolation. His strength, his impetuous good-nature, had seduced her. She had believed him to be a *majo* and grandee in one. But now even he had disappointed her. Madrid had nothing further to offer her.

Her romantic lament impressed him. He could not allow her to leave Madrid, he assured her ardently. If she went away he would lay down his office and go into retirement, devote himself to his grief and to philosophy. "For Spain's sake you must stay with me, Señora!" he cried. "You are the only light in my arduous existence. Without you my onerous life would be unthinkable."

She held her white face turned toward him and looked at him in her peculiar, insolent way. Then, deliberately, in her rich, slow voice which made his pulse quicken, she replied, "If that is so, Don Manuel, then do not only tell it to me but demonstrate it to the world. I've been content too long to be your mistress. You would never have insulted your wife in this way. I think I have a right to ask that you acknowledge me publicly."

He was startled. Marry! And marry Pepa! All the really unpleasant Spanish proverbs passed through his mind "*Antes de casar, ten casas en que morar*—have someplace to live in before you take a wife"; and, "He who marries for love dies of rage." But he felt he could not risk taking leave a second time without having settled matters.

All these months, he assured her, he had had the intention of asking for her hand. But such a marriage would mean difficulties with Doña María Luisa, would mean his dismissal, would mean disaster for Spain. For nobody but himself could bring the tight-rope walking game between France and Portugal to a happy conclusion. "If I follow the dictates of my heart and marry you, Señora," he concluded, "it will mean war either with Portugal or with France." Pepa, still looking him unwaveringly in the face, said dryly, "You're probably right. And so—good-bye."

He had to find some way out. "Give me time, Pepa," he begged urgently. "Give me just a little time."

"Three days," she said.

On the third day he announced he had found the solution. He would marry her, but for a time the marriage must remain a secret. As soon, however, as he had brought about a decision in the Portuguese question, he would risk incurring royal disfavour and announce his marriage to the kingdom and the world at large.

Pepa agreed.

A venerable priest was unearthed, a certain Father Celestinos from Badajoz, who had a weakness for petty political intrigue and who was more than ready to do his omnipotent fellow-countryman a service.

> In the Prince's city palace
> In the private chapel, after
> Nightfall, there took place the marriage.
> Lights were dim, it was romantic,
> Truly after Pepa's heart. The
> Witnesses were the dueña
> And Don Miguel. And the Padre
> Swore them all to strictest silence,
> By an oath, he bound them over
> Not to speak about this marriage
> To a soul, an 'twere forever
> They were mute.

— 3 —

When the Queen heard the rumour that the Príncipe de la Paz had married Señora Tudo she abandoned herself to unbridled fury. She had fished this good-for-nothing from the filthiest depths, made him the most important man in the kingdom, only for him to seal himself, lock, stock, and barrel, to this whore. On her, on this brainless lump of female flesh, this goose, this *jamona*, he was conferring the resplendent title with which she, María Luisa, had so graciously endowed him. She pictured him to herself, lying in bed with his Pepa and laughing at her, the old woman whom they had made a fool of. But he would find out his mistake, this scum! There were a hundred instances of treason and embezzlement in which proceedings could be taken against him. He had stolen without scruple from the Royal Treasury. Had taken bribes from foreign powers. Had betrayed the Holy Father, their best allies. Had intrigued against the Catholic King with the godless men of the French Republic. Had betrayed everyone, friend or foe, out of greed, out of vanity, for a whim. But she would have him brought to justice, would hail him before the Council of Castile, would have him ignominiously put to death, publicly, while everyone rejoiced, prelates, grandees, the whole Spanish people. And this creature, this whore, she would have driven through the city streets, naked to the waist, and then publicly flogged.

She knew she would do none of these things. She was clever. She knew the world and she knew men, and women, knew her Manuel and herself. Now and again she had, by skilful exhibition of her intelligence and power, inspired some degree of sympathy and emotion in him, had even perhaps occasionally succeeded in transforming this feeling into love and desire. But how artificial it was, how transitory! How long could an ugly, ageing woman hope to hold a strapping young lad such as he was? Suddenly the wretchedness, the whole misery, of her four-and-forty years swept over her. Her life had been one long struggle against thousands, tens of thousands, of pretty young Spanish women. She could always try some new remedy, clothes from Paris, make-up, creams, powder, the best dancing masters and hairdressers, but, pitted against the fresh skin of some silly Pasquita, Consuela, or Dolores, these things were merely laughable.

And yet it was better as it was. In not so many years the Duchess of Alba would be as old as she was now, and then what would she be like, the Duchess? Worn out, withered. But she, María Luisa, had by her very ugliness been compelled to develop her mind. She had become clever because she was ugly, and her cleverness would endure.

Finally, she still counted for something herself, by the Grace of God Queen of all the Kingdoms of Spain, the West and East Indies, the islands and *terrafirma* of the ocean sea, Archduchess of Austria, Duchess of Burgundy, Countess of Hapsburg, Flanders, and the Tyrol. This empire was no longer in its first youth, like her it was beginning to age, and Citizen Truguet had the impudence to dictate to the Catholic Kings. But in spite of this she was still the most powerful woman in the world. For the world knew that it was not the simple-minded Carlos but she who ruled Spain, the Indies, and the ocean.

And to such a woman this fool could prefer a Pepa Tudo!

She scrutinized herself in the mirror. But the mirror showed her only as she was then, in the fleeting moment of abandonment under the impact of the offensive news. It was not she, not her true self.

She set out to face her true self. Left her boudoir. The chief lady-in-waiting, the *Camarera Mayor*, who was waiting in the antechamber, made as if to accompany her, as Court etiquette dictated. The Queen waved her impatiently back. She traversed alone the wide galleries and corridors, past priests and lackeys, past officers of the watch who presented arms as she went by, past courtiers who bowed down to the ground. She stood alone in the magnificent reception room in front of "The Family of Carlos."

The María Luisa in this picture was her true self. This artist knew her, understood her as perhaps no other. As she stood in the circle of her family of reigning kings and kings and queens to be, dominating them all, there was the reality, ugly, proud, and impressive.

Such a woman would not let herself be floored by the fact that a booby with whom she happened to be in love had married his kept woman behind her back. She would not punish the man. He was not worth the trouble of fighting for, but she was the Queen, she owed it to herself to take what she had a mind for, to keep what she intended to keep. She did not yet know how, but she would keep this man.

She slept well the night that followed, and by next morning had hit upon an excellent plan.

She spoke to Carlos of the never-ending political crises. Enumerated the bickerings with the merchants of Cádiz who would not pay their taxes, the negotiations with the insolent Truguet, the trouble with the mutinous ships' officers. One man had the job of fighting all these matters out singlehanded, the First Minister. He must be helped, his authority must be reinforced. Carlos considered. "Gladly," he said, "but with the best will in the world I can't think how. What titles and dignities are there that we have not already given Manuel?" "We might perhaps kill two birds with one stone," observed María Luisa. "I mean that we might at the same time settle the unpleasantness over the children of the late lamented Uncle Luis." Uncle Luis, brother of Carlos the Third, was the Infante who had married a Vallabriga, a mere noblewoman; their children had only the rank of Count or Countess of Borbón and Chinchón, and the question of their precedence at Court was a constant source of trouble.

Carlos betrayed no sign of comprehension. "How would it be," María Luisa explained, "if we were to make them both Infantes of Castile and married our Manuel to Doña Teresa, the Infanta? Then he would be an Infante too, and one of the family." "A good idea," Carlos agreed. "But not, I am afraid, one which accords with the wishes of my late father. My late father made Don Luis and Doña Teresa Excellencies. He did not make them Royal Highnesses." "Times change," stated María Luisa with forbearing patience. "You yourself, my dear Carlos, have on several occasions given directions which have gone beyond the ordinances of your deceased father. Why should you not make a similar disposition in this case?" "You're right as usual," Carlos conceded.

The Queen set to work energetically. She was not well disposed towards the future Infanta Teresa. This daughter of a minor noblewoman had an air of aristocratic ease about her which annoyed María Luisa, and although the little hypocrite would not dare to utter a word, she obviously disapproved of her, the Queen's, way of life. It amused her to think of pushing the quiet, blond, nun-like Teresa into bed with that bull Don Manuel.

On the very same day on which she achieved the King's consent to the union between Doña Teresa and Manuel, she sent word to the latter that she wished to speak to him. He had fully expected the Queen to find out about his marriage in spite of all attempts at secrecy, and he was conscious of discomfort, of fear even, at the prospect of the storm that was gathering.

But María Luisa's face was all smiles. "Manuel," she said, "Manuelito, I have some wonderful good news for you. Don Carlos is going to make the Count and Countess of Borbón and Chinchón Infantes of Castile, and you shall marry Doña Teresa and have the benefit of the title. I am overjoyed that in this way the intimate relations between you and us shall be made apparent to all the world."

When, instead of the anticipated violent thunderstorm, this shower of graciousness and good fortune descended upon him,

Manuel was at first unable to grasp what was happening; he stood there, an expression of stupidity on his face. Then a flood of exultation swept over him. "*Por la vida del demonio!*" He really was fortune's favourite child. Whatever he put his hand to turned out to his advantage. And what a good joke it was this time! Now he could pay back Don Luis María who had had the impertinence to look through him. Now he, Manuel, would sleep with the arrogant fellow's sister, and it was he, Manuelito, the despised one, who was making a whole Bourbon out of half a one, was making the bastard Luis legitimate.

Such were Manuel's reactions. He was bursting with pride. His father had been right to call him his sturdy little bull. By his own efforts he had possessed himself of this Queen, and he looked upon his old María Luisa with proprietary pride, affection, and tenderness.

She observed him closely. She had expected her communication to embarrass him, had expected him to stand there in confusion, thinking of that person, of his Pepa Tudo and his reckless marriage. But there was not the faintest sign of embarrassment or confusion to be detected in him. On the contrary, he was standing there, splendid to look upon in his magnificent uniform; his face beamed with joy and gratitude, nothing else. For a moment or two María Luisa believed the rumours were lies, that the disgraceful marriage had never taken place.

The fact was that Manuel had completely forgotten Pepa and his secret marriage in the surging tide of his rejoicing. But after a few moments he did remember. "*Carajo!*" he thought, and "*Carajo!*" was written on his face. But the feeling of bliss in which he seemed to be floating swept his confusion away again immediately. The task of disposing of his marriage seemed easy to him. All he needed was a little time.

After he had thanked the Queen in extravagant terms, covering her plump, bejewelled hand with burning kisses, he begged leave to postpone for two or three weeks the public announcement of his happy union with Doña Teresa and the royal family. The Queen, with inner bitterness but preserving a gracious smile, casually asked the reason for the delay. He was mysterious, declared that he had certain political designs to bring to completion which might be prejudiced by his promotion.

Meanwhile the longer he thought of it the more difficult appeared the task of extricating himself from his secret marriage with Pepa. Of course he could quite simply deny the marriage. One hint to the Grand Inquisitor and Padre Celestinos would disappear within some distant monastery. But what steps would Pepa take? When she discovered that her marriage had not taken place she would become the heroine of one of her romances. Would kill herself in some grandiose manner or perpetrate some other vastly dramatic folly which would make his marriage to the Infanta impossible. Of course he would have the means of ridding himself of Pepa once and for all, but a life without Pepa was no longer conceivable for him.

He could see no way out and took Miguel into his confidence.

The latter listened to him, outwardly with a politely sympathetic face, inwardly disturbed. Manuel had become more arrogant with increasing prosperity and treated Miguel more and more like a servant. His shameless greed, indiscriminate lechery, and boundless vanity were increasingly repellent to Miguel. Now, when Manuel came to him in this new emergency, he felt tempted to let him lie in the bed he had made for himself. The purpose of the Queen's cunning was doubtless to separate Manuel from Pepa forever. But he would never break away from Pepa, while Doña María Luisa on her part would never tolerate this permanent liaison; the vindictive woman would depose Manuel if he, Miguel, did not help him. Should he help him? Wouldn't it be a stroke of luck, the best thing that could happen, if he were to be rid of the fellow and his empty arrogance? If he could devote all his time to his pictures? If he could finish his great work, his lexicon of artists?

But in his mind's eye he saw himself sitting there in immeasurable loneliness, surrounded by his pictures and papers, and knew that just as Manuel was a prisoner to his Pepa, so would his own thoughts never cease to revolve agonizingly round Lucía. Only the exciting game of politics had the power to divert him; he could no longer do without it, could not renounce his part in steering the kingdom out of the shadows. He *would* help Manuel out of his embarrassment.

He considered the situation, conceived a plan which he propounded to Manuel. The latter seized upon it eagerly, embraced Miguel, his happiness restored.

Don Manuel sought out the King. Declared mysteriously that

he had come to ask his advice and assistance in a personal matter, man to man, *caballero* to *caballero*. "What's wrong?" Carlos asked. "We've dealt with France, we should be able to deal with your love troubles." Thus encouraged, Manuel disclosed to him that he had a tender attachment to a wonderful woman, though not of the nobility, a certain Señora Josefa Tudo. The liaison had existed for years and he was racking his brains to think of a way of breaking news to her of his impending marriage. He could see only one way out. One would have to explain to Señora Tudo that the proposed marriage with the Infanta was for the good of the Crown, in that lustre would be added thereby to the person of the First Minister in his negotiations with France, England, and Portugal. "Well, and so?" asked Don Carlos. "Why don't you explain it to her?" "It should be done by the highest authority," replied Manuel. "Only if you yourself, Sire, make it clear to Señora Tudo that my marriage is taking place in the interest of the State, will she be able to withstand the terrible blow I am dealing her." The King considered. Then, with a smile and a twinkle in his eye, he said, "You mean I should put it to her that she should let you have what you want even if you do marry the Infanta?" "This is how I've pictured it," replied Manuel. "Once more I ask Your Majesty to do me the great honour of dining with me, informally, the dinner to take place in the Señora's house. Your Majesty's presence will overpower Señora Tudo. You then address to the Señora one or two of those affable phrases with which you know so well how to delight your subjects, make it clear to her that it is to the advantage of the whole country that Señora Tudo should not rupture her relationship with me, and you make me happy for the rest of my life." "All right," said Carlos after some reflection. "You can count on me." He promised to appear at the Palacio Bondad Real disguised as a mere general the following Wednesday at six forty-five.

Don Manuel asked Pepa if he could dine with her on Wednesday and bring a friend with him. "Who?" Pepa asked. "The King," replied Don Manuel. Pepa's placid face was transfixed with astonishment. "Yes," Don Manuel declared solemnly, "the King our Master is eager to make your acquaintance." "You've told him of our marriage?" Pepa inquired happily. Manuel evaded the question. "The King has something important to tell you," he answered. "Please tell me what it's about," Pepa demanded. "I don't wish to be unprepared when the King does me the honour of dining at my table." And Don Manuel, perceiving his opportunity, said bluntly and with finality, "The King wishes me for reasons of State to marry his cousin, Doña Teresa. That is what he wishes to tell you. He is going to make her an Infanta and thus make an Infante of me also. So our marriage must never have taken place."

When Pepa revived from her faint he was all concern for her, the doting lover. It had become clear, he told her persuasively, that he could carry through the diplomatic tasks which the Crown and the fatherland demanded of him only if he were clothed with the highest authority, that is to say, with that of a member of the royal family, of an Infante. He realized what a tremendous sacrifice was being expected of her. It was for that reason that the King was honouring her with his presence. And once the King got to know her, her position in Madrid society was assured. She could be confident of acquiring a great title. He was negotiating with Count Castillofiel, an elderly gentleman, a very old gentleman in fact, who, being overburdened with debts, spent all his time on his estate near Málaga. The Count was prepared to marry Pepa. Then he would continue until his imminent end to live in Málaga as before, while she, a *señora de título,* would maintain her residence in Madrid. "But you and I are married already," Pepa objected. "I know," replied Manuel. "But I don't know that we could prove it. The only reliable witness, Padre Celestinos," he declared with concern, "has disappeared. Disappeared without trace."

Pepa realized that fate was against her legitimate union with Manuel. For all her love of the poetic she had a healthy sense of reality, and the nocturnal wedding had never seemed quite natural to her. She decided to submit. "The tricks fate plays!" she said musingly. "So now you're to be an Infante after all, Infante of Castile!" "It is entirely in your hands," said Manuel gallantly. "And the King will sanction our illicit relationship by his presence?" Pepa asked. "He'll even ask you to sing," replied Manuel, "just wait and see." "And shall I really become Condesa Castillofiel?" Pepa asked, wishing to make sure. "*Oui, Madame,*" Manuel answered. "But you say the Count is heavily in debt?" Pepa asked rather anxiously. "Please, let that be my concern," Manuel returned grandly. "The Condesa Castillofiel will live as befits the fairest lady of the realm and the mistress of the Infante Manuel." "I am prepared to immolate myself for your sake," said Pepa.

On Wednesday, at six forty-five, Don Carlos appeared at the Palacio Bondad Real, accompanied by Manuel. He wore a simple general's uniform and was informal in his behaviour. He had a good look at Pepa and remarked appreciatively that his old Manuel was clever at other things besides matters of state.

And he patted the Señora
Tudo's shoulder and he praised her
For her appetizing *olla*,
And his heart leaped up within him
When she sang the old romances.
And he promised that next time he'd
Play upon his fiddle.

And at
Leave-taking he made a little
Speech. "The conduct of an empire
Such as this," he said, "costs pains and
Sweat. Our Manuel has many
Heavy cares and difficulties.
Go on being, as you are, a
Spanish lady, good and lovely,
And for him, my good friend Manuel,
Make the rare hours of his leisure
Blithe and happy."

The Condesa Doña Teresa de Chinchón y Borbón was summoned from the solitude of her country seat, Arenas de San Pedro, to Court at San Ildefonso. Doña María Luisa, in the presence of the King, informed her that Don Carlos had arranged a marriage for her, had set aside a dowry of five million reals. As spouse he had chosen for her the first and best of his advisers, his beloved Don Manuel, Príncipe de la Paz. Furthermore, he had decided to make this the occasion of conferring on her the title of Infanta of Castile, so that henceforward she would belong to the royal family in the eyes of all the world.

Doña Teresa scarcely heard these last words. A fragile twenty-year-old who looked much younger, she held herself upright with an effort, her deep-blue eyes looked fixedly out of her face, from which all the blood had receded; her mouth was slightly open. The idea of having to bear some man's kisses and embraces terrified her, and the thought of Don Manuel filled her with revulsion.

"Well," Don Carlos was saying meanwhile, complacently, "have I done right? Am I a good cousin?" And Doña Teresa kissed his hand, and the Queen's, and uttered the appropriate words of respectful thanks.

Don Manuel paid his respects to his future bride. She received him in the presence of her brother, the same Don Luis who had on one occasion so arrogantly overlooked the Príncipe de la Paz.

There he stood, Don Luis, in the garb of a prelate, young, slim, serious. In the course of a few weeks he had been amazingly advanced. Not only had the King made him an Infante, but he had also, in place of his Archbishopric of Seville, been given the Archbishopric of Toledo, the highest spiritual office of the realm, and the Cardinal's hat as well. Of course he knew the reason for it all, saw through the vile dirty game the Queen and Don Manuel were playing. It was utterly offensive to him that he should owe his advancement to this vulgar Manuel Godoy, and his heart was heavy at the thought of his shy, delicate sister, of whom he was extremely fond, sacrificed to this unimaginably horrible lover of María Luisa. But there was no possibility of disregarding the King's word. Moreover, the young Prince of the Church was extremely devout and passionately patriotic. He was entirely free of ambition but had a justifiably high opinion of his own ability. If Providence now saw fit to make him Primate of Spain and gave him the opportunity to intervene in politics while at the same time sacrificing his sister to the vulgar, base-born Manuel, then they must both submit with humility.

Don Manuel inspected his future wife. Blond, very thin and

fragile, she sat there, looking a little like that Geneviève de Havré who had later given him so much trouble. No, these skinny, aristocratic misses were not at all to his taste. Pepa would have nothing to fear from his bride-to-be. Would she even be able to bear him a child, an Infante? But he gave no sign of his thoughts and bore himself irreproachably, like a grandee. Assured the Infanta of his good fortune and his gratitude, treated that urchin Don Luis with the reverence his hat and staff deserved, although it was he himself who had procured them for him.

Then the marriage of Don Manuel to the Infanta Doña Teresa took place, in the church in the Escorial, over the graves of the dead conquerors and in the presence of the sovereigns and grandees of Spain. Don Manuel not only acquired the title of Infante of Castile, but the King conferred on him on the occasion of his marriage a dignity which had been enjoyed by no one else except Christopher Columbus. He made him Grand Admiral of Spain and the Indies.

At about the same time, in Málaga, Señora Tudo became the wife of Count Castillofiel. The new Countess remained for a few weeks with her husband in Andalucía, then, leaving him in Málaga, she herself returned to Madrid.

Don Manuel, true to his promise, made it possible for her to lead the life worthy of a lady of title. Of the dowry of five million which the Infanta had brought with her he made over a half-million to the Countess Castillofiel. "Half a million"—these words were poetry to her ear and heart. They reminded her of her romances; she sat alone in her boudoir, strummed at her guitar, and sang dreamily to herself, "Half a million."

She made use of her new wealth, kept house lavishly, and summoned her friends to share her splendour. She invited actors with whom she had studied, minor officers who were acquaintances from the epoch of Lieutenant Tudo, even ladies of mature years and doubtful reputation who were friends of the dueña Conchita. One could be sure of meeting Señor Rivero there, that theatrical producer who had once engaged her for his troupe in Málaga. He was a resourceful financier, had contacts with celebrated bandits and smugglers, and even indulged in a little privateering. The Countess Castillofiel entrusted him with the management of her finances, greatly to her advantage.

Amid the sweetness of her success there was one bitterness: she was not received at Court. For Doña María Luisa did not admit the new Countess Castillofiel to the kissing of hands. And a person of title achieved full enjoyment of her title and dignities only after being received at Court.

However, the Court and town were not at all deterred by the fact that Countess Castillofiel still did not really belong to the five hundred and thirty-five persons of title, and people flocked to her levee. She was believed to have influence, and it was good fun at the Palacio Bondad Real, in the weirdly mixed gathering of grandees and prelates, actors, actresses, and officers.

People waited eagerly to see whether the First Minister would turn up there one day. But he kept away from Pepa's set. Instead, he was living on the best of terms with his Infanta, gave a series of large receptions for her in his Palacio Alcudia, and showed himself to the world as a good, assiduous husband. If he did enter the Palacio Bondad Real it was by the back door.

But after two months had passed, in his opinion a sufficiently long concession to decency, he appeared one morning at Pepa's levee, though for a few minutes only. On the next occasion he stayed longer, and then began to appear more and more often. Finally an office was fitted up for him in the Palacio Bondad Real, and soon foreign envoys were writing home that most of the affairs of state were settled in the Palacio Bondad Real, that Señora Pepa Tudo had offices and dignities in her gift, and that even her dueña Conchita had more to say in public affairs than Don Manuel's ministerial colleagues.

The Queen, when she heard of this, was not surprised. She had been sure that Manuel would not break with this creature. She raged. Railed at herself for being unable in her turn to break with him. But nature was like that. Other great queens had been infatuated with men who were nothing to be proud of. The great Semiramis, daughter of the air, had had her Menon or Nino or whatever his name was, Elizabeth her Essex, Catherine the Great her Potemkin. So she would not even bother to try to wipe Manuel from her life. Nor, on the other hand, would she accept his effrontery without more ado.

She naturally wouldn't be so foolish as to make a scene about his "Countess," she wouldn't waste a word over the continuance of her lover's affair with his Pepa; she would dismiss her incompetent First Minister with ignominy. Reasons for such a disgrace existed in plenty, good, impersonal, political reasons. He had failed, failed again and again, had impaired the honour of the Crown by incompetence, laziness, by a greed which bordered on high treason.

But when he next stood before her in all his insolent masculinity she forgot her resolutions. "I hear," she let fly at him, "that the Catholic King's political decisions are now made in that female's bed." Manuel saw at once that he could not get by this time with denials and protestations. This would have to be fought out. "If Your Majesty's ungracious words are intended to refer to the Countess Castillofiel," he retaliated with cold politeness, "then it is certainly correct that I sometimes ask this lady's counsel. It is good counsel. She is a Spaniard through and through and exceptionally clever."

María Luisa could restrain herself no longer. "You wretch!" she burst out. "You vain, greedy, boastful, thieving, dissolute good-for-nothing! You lewd, empty, faithless, doltish brute! It was I who dragged you up out of the mire. It was I who stuck you lump of filth into a uniform and made an Infante out of you. What little you know of politics I drummed into you, and it was difficult enough, and you can stand there, you scum, and tell me to my face that you take advice from that hussy of yours!" And suddenly she struck him a sharp blow left and right in the face with her bejewelled hand, so that the blood came and spotted his dress uniform.

Don Manuel seized her by the wrist with one hand, wiping away the blood with the other. For a split second he was tempted to strike back and to tell her one or two things which would hit her even harder. But he remembered the evil consequences of the box on the ear which he had given Pepa and felt it to be only fair that he should receive a slap in the face himself. Calmly and courteously he said, "I cannot believe, Madame, that you meant that seriously. A Queen of Spain would scarcely appoint as her chief adviser a man possessed of the qualities you have just been pleased to describe. You were momentarily not yourself." He concluded respectfully, "After what has happened I can assume Your Majesty no longer requires my presence." He lowered himself onto one knee as ceremony required, kissed her hand, and withdrew backwards from the room.

When he reached home he saw that his jabot, his coat, even his white stockings were stained with blood. "The old harridan," he swore angrily to himself.

He took counsel with Miguel, assuming that Doña María Luisa would now be set on revenge. Señor Bermúdez did not regard Manuel's situation as threatening. The Queen could put difficulties in his path, he opined, she could deprive him of office, but over and above that she could do little. She could hardly banish the Infante Manuel from Court. Moreover, Don Miguel observed cunningly, it would not be the worst that could happen if another were to step into Don Manuel's shoes. Disagreeable concessions would have to be made to France, and it might be a good thing if a successor were to take the responsibility while Don Manuel, patriot and martyr, stood disapprovingly by.

Manuel took thought. Don Miguel's observations appealed to him. He became more cheerful. "Manuel Godoy has once again turned up trumps," he exulted. "And you really think, my friend, that I should wait and do nothing?"

"In your place," Miguel advised, "I would forestall Her Majesty. Why don't you simply go to Carlos and ask to be relieved of your duties?"

Don Miguel went to Carlos. There had recently been differences of opinion between the Queen and himself on important political questions, he told him, differences so acute that further collaboration was hardly possible. This being the case, he felt he was doing his fatherland a service in asking the King to deliberate the conduct of affairs in future with the Queen alone. And as Carlos obviously did not understand, he concluded explicitly, "Sire, I ask leave to put my office back into your hands."

Carlos was upset. "You really can't do this to me, Manuel," he pleaded. "I respect your Spanish pride. But María Luisa surely didn't mean anything by it. I'll fix it up. Come on, don't be like this, my dear Infante." As Manuel seemed obdurate he shook his big head and said, "It was all so convenient. In the evening when I came back from the hunt you would come, both together, or you alone, you would tell me what was going on and I would sign things and put in my flourishes. How am I going to have confidence if someone else takes your place? I simply can't imagine it." He sat there despondently. Manuel too was silent.

"But at least you can give me one piece of advice," he began after a while with more animation, "as to who should be your successor."

Manuel had anticipated this request and had concocted a plan so bold, shrewd, and unscrupulous that he had not even dared to discuss it with his Miguel; for the latter was frequently a prey to scruples of conscience. Manuel wished to suggest to the King that the two most important government posts be entrusted to men of opposing political views. His calculation was that whenever the one sought to put measures through, the other would seek to frustrate them; whereby the domestic affairs of the realm would be paralysed. Their Majesties would soon have to look round for someone to rescue them, and there could be only one rescuer.

Manuel therefore advised the King to appoint a liberal as First Secretary of State, and an ultramontane as Minister of Justice; in this way the King could be certain of giving offence to neither of the great political parties. "Not a bad idea," Don Carlos observed, "but would the Queen agree?" "She will," Don Manuel assured him, for he had naturally thought of that. And he named the two men whom he had in mind. Doña María Luisa had slept with both of them, to both she had given visible tokens of her favour.

The one was Don Mariano Luis de Urquijo. He had lived a long time in France, consorted with French philosophers, translated French books, quoted Voltaire in public. Although she was opposed to radical liberalism, María Luisa had taken a fancy to Urquijo's bold features and fine build, and when the Holy Office had wished to proceed against him she had stretched out a protecting hand.

The other was Don José Antonio de Caballero. He was an obscurantist, his political views belonged to the Middle Ages, he supported every denunciation from Rome of the progressive faction among the Spanish clergy. María Luisa had as little sympathy for radical ultramôntanism as for its opposite, but Señor de Caballero's physical attributes had also won the monarch's approval. She had given him one of her ladies-in-waiting in marriage and attended the marriage feast herself.

These were the two men whom Manuel mentioned to the King. He nodded sadly. "Is there really nothing to be done?" he asked once more. "Do you really want to go?" "It is my firm, unshakable resolve," answered Manuel. Don Carlos embraced him with tears in his eyes.

Then he sat down to write his Manuel a heart-felt letter of thanks.

"In the many offices," he
Wrote, "that were entrusted to you,
You have borne yourself as statesman
And as friend of peace, before all
Spain, the world, and history. Of
My profound and lifelong thanks pray
Rest assured." With care and pains he
Wrote, with his own hand, and under
All with pains and care he set his
Yo el rey, and then the flourish,
His unique one, own and only,
Like a treble clef to look at,
And he painted this his flourish,
This his *rúbrica*, with loving
Care, as only once before he
Had, and that was when he made it
For the Escorial, to have it
Chiselled under all the names of
Those who ever ruled as monarch
Over Spain.

5

In the summer Martín Zapater lived in his country house outside the town, the Quinta Zapater. He was quite overcome when Francisco unexpectedly arrived with Gil the driver and the mules, and more so when he caught sight of his friend's face under the broad-brimmed hat, bearded, aged, and hardened.

The driver Gil explained what had happened to Francisco while the latter stood darkly by. Then, before Zapater had time to speak, Francisco imperiously ordered him to give the driver his *gratificacioncita*, his little gratuity, so that he could at last betake himself to a *venta,* as they had a strenuous day's journey behind them. "Give him two hundred reals," he commanded. This was an unheard of "little gratuity." Francisco and Gil had one last pull from the wineskin, the *bota.* Looking deeply moved, the muleteer commended his extraordinary patron to the protection of the Virgin and all the saints, and then Goya watched the companion of his long journey disappearing into the night with his two beasts in the direction of Saragossa.

Though Francisco was burning to tell his friend of the horrors that had befallen him and in particular of the dreadful disclosure Peral had made to him of the possibility of madness, at first he held his peace. He was afraid of what Martín might write down. Francisco had at all times feared the magic of the written word. A clearly formulated thought would bring down the demons, more insidious still was the spoken word, and most of all what was written.

During the first few days they lived alone in the Quinta Zapater, tended by Martín's old tenant Tadeo and his wife Farruca. Tadeo was of melancholy temperament and extremely devout; for hours on end he would sit, silent, his eyes closed, absorbed in religious meditation. Farruca's enthusiastic piety was of a milder nature. She had declared herself an "*esclava de la Santísima Trinidad,*" a slave of the Holy Trinity, her confessor had confirmed her declaration in writing. Farruca was obliged to act as lady's maid to the waxen statue of the Virgin which was to be found in her room; she regularly renewed the flowers and lights which trimmed it; she said certain prayers before the waxen image at certain times, changed the statue's clothes according to the day or season; nor did she omit putting on its nightgown before going to bed herself. Moreover, every week she had to pay four reals to her confessor as the representative of the Holy Trinity.

Martín did not say much but he was always with Francisco. The latter noticed that Martín had frequent, severe attacks of coughing. Farruca had been urging him for a long time to go to the doctor. But Martín didn't want any fuss made of his cold, and for doctors, the "barbers," he had, like Francisco, a healthy Spanish contempt.

Francisco insisted that Martín should not always keep him company but should attend to his own affairs in the city. When he was thus alone Farruca would come to him. She was unable to write, and he did not make it easy for her to communicate with him, but she was as patient as she was garrulous and regarded it as her duty to console and advise the unfortunate deaf man. She told him, for instance, about Pedro Sastre. He was the grandchild of Braulio Sastre, the lamplighter in the cathedral, whose lost leg had grown again because he had rubbed the stump for a whole year with consecrated oil from the lamps of Our Lady of the Pillar. The Sastre grandson was also endowed with great power and had effected some amazing cures. He was hard to get at; but he might be accessible to a gentleman like Don Francisco. To encourage him she told him where the man lived. Francisco recalled how as a boy he had been afraid to pass the house of this Pedro Sastre; the man must be very old.

Next evening, alone and unobserved, wearing the simple Aragonese costume which he had borrowed from Martín, the round hat pulled well down over his forehead, Goya set out for the outskirts of Saragossa. He found Pedro Sastre's house without difficulty, pushed aside the woman who sought to hold him back, and confronted the miracle doctor.

He was a small shrivelled-up man, old as the hills, just as Goya had expected. He was full of mistrust towards this impatient intruder who was deaf or pretended to be deaf and gave himself an incomprehensible name. Pedro Sastre, who lived in constant fear of the Inquisition, looked with suspicion on this violent visitor. On the other hand, he was convinced of the efficacy of his remedies; they worked, as long as the patients believed in them. He listened to what the deaf man had to say, gave him an ointment prepared from the fat of the wild dog, a creature with unusually good hearing, and recommended him to dedicate to our Lady of the Pillar some candles whose wax had been mixed with wax from his own ear. Goya thought of the diagrams of the middle ear which Peral had drawn and the enlightening explanations he had given him; he gave Sastre a dark look and without a word of thanks thrust ten reals at him. That was an absurdly inadequate payment; Pedro Sastre expressed himself in strong terms to that effect, speaking clearly and articulately. But Goya did not understand and went away.

Meanwhile the faithful Martín had in an astonishingly short time mastered the elements of the sign language. He and Francisco practised; Francisco often joked during these exercises but more often he swore and scolded Martín. He noticed that since he now had to observe lips and hands more closely there were things to be discovered in these hands and lips which had hitherto escaped him.

A few days later, while Martín was pursuing his business in Saragossa, Goya set out to see how a deaf man fares while walking about alone on the streets of a city. In the same simple coat and round hat which he had worn on his visit to the miracle doctor Sastre, he slipped away to Saragossa. Avoiding the main street, the Coso, he walked about in the familiar town.

He leaned against the railing of the old bridge and looked across over Saragossa, and the famous city with its great river Ebro seemed to have become smaller and greyer. It had always in his mind and heart been a gay, colourful city. Now it seemed serious and faded. Yes, it was severe, sad, depressing. Could it have been his own gaiety with which young Francisco had endowed it?

There were the churches and the palaces, and his heart was as deaf to them as his ear. He went past the house where he had spent many years apprenticed to the painter Luján, that pious, honourable, industrious man. He had frittered away many a year with him, yet he felt neither anger nor contempt. He passed the Aljafería, where the Inquisition had held its terrifying secret sessions, without a tremor. And he went past the Palacio Sobradiel and the monastery of the Escolapios, whose walls he had painted with frescoes. A host of hopes, triumphs, and defeats had been associated with these works. He had no desire to look at them, he was disappointed even as he saw them again in his mind's eye.

And there were the ancient, most holy churches. There was the statue of Christ which had opened its mouth and spoken to Canon Funes. Here was the Chapel of Saint Michael, and here was where the severed head had rolled up to Archbishop Lope de Luna to confess and receive absolution from him at the Saint's behest; for not till this had been achieved would the head consent to be buried. This same head had rolled through many of the boy Francisco's nightmares, but now the sacred and dismal spot evoked in the ageing Francisco neither shudder nor smile.

Here was the Cathedral of the Virgen del Pilar, the shrine of his highest hopes, scene of his first great success and his deepest disgrace, the *sarna,* that stinging humiliation to which his brother-in-law Bayeu had subjected him. There was the little choir, there was his fresco. "Señor Goya, the commission is yours," Canon Don

Mateo had informed him; he had then been twenty-five years old; it had been the 19th of December, and the greatest event of his life. He had never been so happy since, not even in the best moments with Cayetana, nor yet when the Queen had told him his "Family of Carlos" was a masterpiece. He had been convinced that what he was going to paint on the ceiling of the little choir would be the talk of the century. So there it was, and it was trash, rubbish, that botcher Carnicero would do it better. Was that meant to be the Trinity, that insipid, nebulous, and jejune triangle with the Hebraic capitals? And what clumsy angels! What woolly clouds! What a stupid flabby mess the whole thing was!

He went over to the chapel of Our Lady of the Pillar, to the scene of the *sarna*. There were the little cupolas which he had painted, there were his "virtues," Faith, Works, Courage, and Patience, the paintings which Bayeu and the arch priest of the cathedral chapter, Gilberto Alué, had pronounced to be the work of a bungler. They weren't very well painted, the virtues, the gentlemen had probably been right, but what his brother-in-law had wanted and had executed himself wasn't of eternal significance either. Though his triumph over the pictures in the choir had evaporated, the *sarna* of the chapel burned today as it had then.

"*Carajo!*" he thought, and was shocked that the oath should come to mind in this thrice-hallowed place. For here was the pillar which had given the cathedral its name, the pillar on which the Virgin had appeared to the apostle Santiago, patron saint of Spain, to charge him with erecting the Sanctuary on the banks of the Ebro. Here was the shrine with the sacred pillar. And inside the shrine the opening through which, if they wished, the faithful might kiss the pillar.

Goya did not kiss it. Not that he felt rebellious or wanted to deny the Santísima her due in reverence, but he felt no desire to ask the Virgin for help. How often in trouble he had prayed to this Virgin of the Pillar, how much doubt and conflict he had been through before he had gone over from the Virgin of the Pillar to the Virgin of Atocha. Now he stood without piety in front of this Holy of Holies, which had absorbed his entire youth. Part of him had died, and he did not even regret it.

He left the cathedral and went back through the city. "There are no birds in last year's nest," he thought to himself. Nor had there been any the year before that. The picture of Saragossa which he had carried in his heart, that gaily animated picture, had been the years of his youth, not the town of Saragossa. Probably the town of Saragossa had been just as dreary and dusty then as he saw it now in the day of his deafness. The silent Saragossa was the reality.

He went home and sat by himself between the white walls of his bare room in the Quinta Zapater, desolation around him and within him.

And then, in broad daylight, the nightmare of despair came back. It squatted by him, flew about, spectral, cat-headed, owl-eyed, bat-winged.

With a fearful effort he pulled himself together, seized a pencil. Dashed them down on paper, the evil spirits. There they were.

He spent almost a whole week alone in his bare room with his ghosts. He did not shut his eyes against the demons, did not throw himself across the table to hide his head from them. He looked them in the face, held onto them till they had revealed themselves to him fully, then forced them and his fear and madness onto paper.

He looked at himself in the mirror, hollow-cheeked as he was, with unkempt hair and tangled beard. His face had certainly filled out, the furrows were not so deep, he was no longer the man of ultimate despair who had looked back at him from the mirror at San Lúcar, after his collapse. But it was still an easy task to recall that face, and that face he now drew, the face of his uttermost extremity.

He conjured up Cayetana's face too, again and again. Of course the picture which had so disturbed Cayetana was ruined forever, and he did not think of painting it again. But he drew Cayetana's flight to the witches' Sabbath, and as a drawing it was even sharper and clearer than before. And he drew many other faces and forms of the ever-changing Cayetana. Here she was a pretty, dreamy young girl, listening to a procuress; here again surrounded by a crowd of suitors, fending them off and luring them on. Here she was pursued by demons, fleeing from them and ogling them. And finally he drew the witches' Sabbath itself, the *aquelarre*, the pandemonium, the monstrous celebration. The Master, the huge he-goat, sits upright on his hind legs with towering, garlanded horns and vast, round, rolling eyes of fire. Witches dance around him, offering him sacrifices, deaths' heads, babies that have been skinned alive, while he, the goat, one foreleg raised, blesses his community, the company of witches. And the company's comely ringleader is Cayetana.

Day by day now Goya draws, flings
Out and off what passes through his
Mind. He gives his dreams their fullest
Play. He lets them creep and fly out
Of his head, the demons, spectres—
Rat-tailed, dog-faced, toad-mouthed—always
Cayetana is among them.
So he draws her, raging, lusting,
Holds her fast; both lust and torment
'Tis to him to draw her so; he
Feels it is a better madness,
Almost blithe, not quite so beastly
'Tis to draw her so, as when he
Sits and thinks, the other madness
Crushing head and breast and never
Finding end to thinking. No, so
Long as he can draw he may be
Foolish, for there is clear-sighted
Folly in it, he enjoys it,
And he draws.

Martín did not question him and he was glad of it. No, he was not glad of it. The drawings which he had made in the last few days had been a means of relief, a method of communication; but he had to talk, to speak plainly about what was oppressing him, of what Doctor Peral had disclosed, of his fear of insanity. He could bear it no longer alone, he must have someone to share his terrible secret.

He showed Martín the drawings. Not all of them, but certainly those of the protean Cayetana, lovely, lying she-devil that she was. Martín was profoundly affected. His emotion brought on a prolonged and heavy fit of coughing. He examined the sheets of paper one by one, laid them aside, picked them up again and examined them afresh. Struggled anxiously to fathom what his friend was trying to say.

"It can't be put into words," Francisco declared, "that's why I've expressed it like this." "I think I understand," Martín answered modestly, rather unsure of himself. "You must have courage," Francisco exhorted him, "and then you'll understand exactly. *Idioma universal*," he added impatiently, "no one could help understanding." "I do understand," Martín assured him. "I can see how it all came about."

"You don't see a thing!" said Goya angrily. "No one can understand what a living lie she is." He began to speak of Cayetana's inconstancy, of the abyss of evil within her, he told of their great quarrel, how she had slashed the picture. But, strangely enough, while he talked he could feel nothing of the angry scorn to which he laid claim; rather could he hear quite plainly Cayetana's last words ringing warmly in his ears, that deeply felt, sincere declaration of her love. He did not wish to dwell on it, forbade himself to think of it, revived the anger of his drawings and boasted to Martín that he had cast her out of his life forever, that it was better so.

Then he set about disclosing to his friend his dreadful secret, showed him the other pictures, the grotesque faces and apparitions, and again he asked, "Do you understand?" Martín looked at them in dismay. "I'm afraid to understand them," he said. "Go on, you must," commanded Goya and then showed the picture of himself, the bearded one with the eyes, from which all the despair of the world looked out. And while Martín, shocked and confused, was looking from the drawing to the living model and back to the drawing again, Francisco said, "I'll try to explain it to you," and he spoke so quietly that the other could scarcely hear him. "It's something of the utmost gravity, very secret and very dreadful; before you reply you must consider your answer well and carefully, and under no circumstances must you write it out for me." Then he related what Doctor Peral had disclosed to him of the close affinity between his deafness and insanity. Doctor Peral was perfectly right, of course, he concluded, for he had been half-crazy for a long time, the monsters he had drawn he had really seen with his own mad eyes, and the crazy Francisco whom he had drawn was the real Francisco.

Martín made an effort to hide his consternation. Goya said, "There you have it. Now think it over, and then speak slowly, and please be patient. Then I'll be able to read what you have to say from your lips." The humility with which he said this made Martín's heart sore.

After a long pause he gave his answer. A man who could see his own madness so clearly, he said, was more reasonable than the great majority, and anyone who could make so penetrating an exposition of his own madness was his own best doctor. He chose his words with care; they were simple but well-considered, and to Francisco they were words of comfort.

Up till now Francisco had not been to see his mother. He longed to speak to her, and she for her part might have heard of his visit to Saragossa and be hurt that he did not come to her. But he had not been able to bring himself to see her, he was ashamed of his condition. Now that he had confided in Martín he felt ready to do so.

But first he got himself better clothes. Then he went to the barber. Imperiously he gave orders for the removal of his beard and made brusque incomprehensible answers to the man's friendly chatter. It took the barber some time to discover that his customer was deaf. Moreover, Francisco's skin had grown sensitive and shaving hurt him.

The face that emerged, now that the uncouth beard was removed and the hair tidily combed, astonished the barber. He looked in awed surprise at the gentleman who had entered his shop in such a shocking state of neglect and was now leaving it in such high-flown elegance.

Francisco had not given his mother notice of his visit. He was nervous, yet full of anticipation, as he strode along the street. His face felt unusually cold and naked, and burned at the same time. By a roundabout route he reached the little house where his mother lived, stopped in front of it, walked up the street once more and back again; finally went up to the second floor and knocked at the door. The door opened, and Francisco in his deafness confronted his mother.

"Come in," said Doña Engracia. "Sit down," she said with exaggerated distinctness, "and drink a *rosolí*." He had always been given *rosolí* as a child, when illness or some other misfortune had befallen him. "I already know all about it," she said, articulating as before with great care, while she produced the bottle of *rosolí*. "You might have come a bit sooner," she scolded.

She put the bottle and glasses in front of him, set out a few cakes, and sat down opposite him. He sniffed appreciatively, with recognition, at the strong, sweet-smelling liqueur and poured some out for himself and her. He took a sip. Smacked his lips, dipped a piece of cake in the *rosolí*, and thrust it into his mouth. He looked attentively at her face. "You're so arrogant and swell-headed," he read from her lips. "You must have known yourself it couldn't go on like this, and I told you myself you'd have to pay for it. 'The worst deaf man is the one who won't listen,' " she quoted the old saying. "And you'd never listen. God in His mercy has sent you a light punishment. How would you have felt if He had made you poor instead of deaf?"

These were lines of thought which Francisco could appreciate. Doña Engracia was right, she had sounded a warning note from the beginning and had made light of his fame and success to the point of offending him. She was the daughter of a *hidalgo*, she had the right to call herself "Doña," but at his father's side she had lived the penurious life of a peasant, counting every penny, humbly clothed, adapting herself in every way to the straitened reality. After his father's death he had brought her to live with him in Madrid, but she had not stuck it out there for long and had begged to go back to Saragossa. She had always mistrusted his good fortune and had made no bones of the fact that she did not believe it would last. And now here he sat, deaf, a cripple, and allowed her to scold him and console him with her *rosolí*.

He nodded his big round head, and to gratify her even exaggerated his misfortunes somewhat. Even professionally, he told her, he might now encounter more difficulties. Great ladies and gentlemen were impatient, and if he was slow to understand their chatter he would receive fewer commissions. "Do you want to cut down on the three hundred reals for me?" she asked at once angrily. "I'd send you those," Francisco replied, "even if I had to shovel coal with one hand." "As boastful as ever," answered his mother. "But you'll learn, Paco. Now that you're deaf you'll see a thing or two. You've always bragged to me about your wonderful friends. You've been quick to believe in everyone's friendship. But no one enjoys the companionship of a man who can't hear. Now you'll discover who are your real friends." But behind her harsh words Francisco could sense her pride in him, her hope that he would be a match for his misfortune, her unwillingness to humiliate him by a show of pity.

When he left she invited him to eat with her whenever he wished. He came several times during the week. She could remember exactly what he had liked as a child and set before him simple, highly seasoned food, with plenty of garlic, onions, and oil; sometimes she made a sustaining *puchero*, a kind of simplified *olla podrida*. They both ate copiously, without wasting words but with enjoyment.

Once he asked her if she would like him to paint her. "You want to try it out with a well-behaved model before you risk your luck again with clients who pay," she teased. But she was flattered.

His suggestion was that he should paint her in her everyday clothes. But she wanted to be painted in her Sunday finery. He had to buy her a new mantilla, and even a lace bonnet to hide her baldness.

The sittings took place in silence. She sat there quietly. The sunken old eyes looked out beneath the high forehead, the wide lips under the expressive nose were compressed. In one hand she held a closed fan, in the other a rosary. Both of them enjoyed the sittings, both were patient. Finally there looked down from the canvas an old woman who had been through much, whom nature had made clever and fate had made wise, who had learned to resign herself but was ready to enjoy the years which still remained to her. Francisco had painted her two strong bony old hands with particular affection. Doña Engracia was satisfied with her portrait. She was glad, she said, that he had not minded expending so much effort and canvas on an old woman who couldn't pay.

Francisco now looked up his brother Tomás, the gilder. He was offended that Francisco was so tardy in seeking him out. In the course of their conversation he asked Francisco if he did not feel, after this portent from Heaven, that he should do more for his family, and urged Francisco to make it possible for him to move to Madrid. Francisco replied that yes, he was going hunting with Martín tomorrow.

Francisco's brother-in-law, the priest Manuel Bayeu, had expressed the opinion that since Goya had hesitated so long before seeking spiritual consolation from his own brother-in-law, it must be a sign that he still had not sufficiently understood the heavenly warning. When Goya visited the priest he noticed that the picture of the deceased Court Painter Bayeu, which he, Goya, had painted and which Josefa had sent to Saragossa, was hanging in a poorly lighted corner. Goya asked directly what his brother-in-law thought of the picture. He replied that the artistry the picture displayed was considerable but sprang from a hardened heart. His regret at Francisco's misfortune was sincere, but it was mingled with a slight, almost unconscious satisfaction that the proud and godless painter had had a fall.

The great families of Saragossa, the Salvadores, the Grasas, the Aznarez, vied with each other for Francisco's attentions. But he made polite excuses and declined their invitations. After Francisco had failed to accept his second invitation, Count Fuendetodos asked Martín to find out if he, the Count, might pay him a visit; conversation should not be difficult as he had learned the elements of sign language. This persistence, this almost humble pursuit, touched Goya. He recalled how his family had lived in fear and trembling of the Count, who had been master of their native village, Fuendetodos.

Even the archpriest of the cathedral chapter sought him out. It was the same Don Gilberto Alué who had been so ill-natured and overbearing to Francisco in the quarrel with Bayeu. There could be no more striking proof of Goya's extraordinary rise to fame than the visit of this highly respected and ancient priest. Don Gilberto was extremely polite; in tiny, spidery capitals he wrote out for Francisco that the Archbishop deeply regretted the misfortune which had befallen the Señor Court Painter, the greatest painter Saragossa had ever produced. And Goya's heart swelled with bitter satisfaction that the deceased Bayeu was no longer Aragón's greatest artist.

Then Don Gilberto wrote out that it would give the Archbishop especial pleasure if Don Francisco would undertake to execute certain works for the cathedral, works of small dimensions which would not demand much time. Delicately, with graceful flourishes, the archpriest appended the information that the cathedral chapter suggested a fee of twenty-five thousand reals.

For a moment Goya believed he had misread or that the arch-priest had made a slip of the pen. The cathedral chapter was thrifty, and twenty-five thousand reals was an enormous sum for something that would take two weeks. "Don't be too proud of yourself, my heart!" he told himself, and determined to devote himself humbly and lovingly to the work and to grudge no time spent on it.

But before the pious task could
Be begun, there came from Madrid
News. In simple words Don Miguel
Told Francisco of the death of
Mariano, Francho's son; and
Counselled him to come to Madrid,
To Josefa.

Goya travelled
Post this time, and comfortably.
He was even glad to have his
Martín by his side upon the
Journey, giving tendance.

— 7 —

He looked at Josefa, watched her lips moving, could not make out the words. She made a great effort to suppress her horror at the sight of her so greatly altered Francho.

Little Mariano had been buried several days before. They exchanged awkward words of comfort. There was no need of speech between them. They sat long together in silence, and their silence was more eloquent than if they had spoken.

He pulled himself together and with a somewhat convulsive smile showed her the sketch book that he always carried about him now so that people could write out what they had to tell him. "When you want to say something to me," he explained to her, "you must write it down. I understand very little, I have to guess everything. Actually I'm absolutely stone deaf." She only nodded. She could not bear to ask him what had happened in the interval.

She was even more reserved than before, she shut herself away entirely. Yet he saw her with greater depth and clarity. He had always taken Josefa for granted as something always there, which called for no deciphering or subtlety of interpretation. He had not given much thought to what she might think of the part of his life which he led apart from her. A man of his station permitted himself the women his fancy demanded, such was the custom. Josefa was there when he needed her; this was what he expected, what he wanted, and how it was. He for his part had not held it against her that she should consider her brother to be the better artist, that she understood nothing about his work, and that she was full of unspoken pride in her family which was so much more estimable than his own. It had taken her years even to begin to understand what an artist he was and what the world thought of him. But she had loved him before she knew this, from the very beginning; otherwise she, a Bayeu, would never have married a Goya. *He* had married her partly because he loved her, partly, if not chiefly, because she was a Bayeu. She had surely realized that long since. But she had continued to love him and put up with him. He had always felt he gave her a good deal to swallow, and he had often pitied her. He felt an inner warmth, a satisfaction, that now she had a reason to be sorry for him.

But his heart swelled at the sight of his son Javier. He was no longer a boy, he was a young man now, whom not many women could pass by without a glance. Javier told him he had been thinking a great deal in the past months, was now decided upon being an artist, and hoped his father would accept him as a pupil. Goya looked at his beloved Javier, full of pride and affection. It was a powerful consolation to have this son after the loss of Mariano. He did not want the lad's path to be as hard as his own had been. He would send his son abroad, to Italy, to France; he himself had gained artistic understanding in Italy, but he had had a struggle to scrounge enough rice, bread, and cheese for his next meal. Javier should have his living and learning made easy for him.

Agustín's grim features twitched convulsively when he saw Francisco again. Francisco wished to hear no word of sympathy. He said brusquely, "Has much gone wrong while I've been away?

Have you done a great deal of damage?" and told him to go over the books with Zapater.

But later he asked to be shown what Agustín had been doing all this time, and Agustín showed him his engravings executed according to the new method of Jean-Baptiste Leprince. Agustín Esteve had improved on the method. Goya was surprised at what could be achieved by it. "*Hombre!*" he said several times and, sparing with praise though he was, he congratulated his friend and helper in the strongest terms. "The process ought to be called the Esteve method now," he declared. The old deep bond was there once more between them.

And then Francisco showed him the drawings he himself had made in Saragossa. Agustín was shaken to the depths. His lips moved, but Goya could not tell if he spoke or not. When he was excited Agustín had a funny way of swallowing and smacking his lips. He gazed and gazed, he could not have enough of looking.

Next day Francisco reported back at Court, not without some uneasiness and anxiety. But he was treated with particular consideration; even the arrogant Marqués de Ariza was assiduously sympathetic.

Don Carlos himself tried to overcome by joviality the embarrassment he felt in the deaf man's presence. He walked close up to him and absolutely bellowed, "Painting's done with the eyes, not the ears, eh?" Goya, rather taken aback, failed to understand and respectfully handed him the pad and pencil. The King's face lighted up, he understood, was delighted that there was a means whereby he could converse with his First Painter. He wrote down the consoling sentence which he had screamed at him. "Painting's done with the eyes and hands, not the ears," and while he was at it he attached his customary signature, "*Yo el rey*," and the usual flourish. Goya read the message and bowed reverently. "What did you say, my dear fellow?" asked the King. Goya replied, unusually loudly, "Nothing, Your Majesty." The King pursued the conversation in his customary affable way. "How many portraits of me have you actually painted by now?" he asked. Goya did not know exactly, but to have admitted this would have been impolite. He replied, "Sixty-nine." "Did you ever!" Carlos wrote out, and then solemnly added, "May the blessed Virgin grant us years enough that the number may reach a hundred."

The Príncipe de la Paz summoned Goya to him. Manuel awaited

the encounter expectantly. He felt the bond between himself and the painter even more strongly than before. They must have been born under very much the same constellation, and after a fairy-tale success fate had simultaneously dealt them both a severe blow. Francisco had brought about his first meeting with Pepa, that connection which had had such a decisive influence on his life, and he, Manuel, had been powerfully instrumental in Goya's success. They were friends, they understood each other, they could speak openly, each to the other.

When Manuel saw how Goya had aged a tide of genuine compassion swept over him. But he was outwardly as gay as in their best times together. Again and again he assured Francisco that they belonged together. Had he not predicted that, each in his own sphere, they would both scale the highest peaks? And now Francisco was First Painter and he himself Infante of Castile. "At the moment there is a cloud or two in the sky, but I tell you, my Francho"—and here he brushed the clouds away with a sweep of the hand—"these discordancies will pass away and our stars will shine all the brighter. Anyone who has to fight, like us two, to achieve power and position," he continued, solemnly confidentially, "values it much more than he who is born to it, he never lets go. *Plus ultra!*" he cried, and as Goya did not understand he wrote down, "*Plus ultra.*" He had taken a fancy to the expression during his recent stay in Cádiz. He had had a gay time in Cádiz, he related. And Francisco was said to have had a pretty wild time of it too, he said, winking; there was talk about a certain naked Venus.

Francisco was taken aback. Had she shown the picture to a third person? Wasn't she afraid of the gossip? Wasn't she afraid of the Inquisition?

Manuel noticed Francisco's confusion, wagged a threatening finger. "They're only rumours, and I'm not asking you either for confirmation or for a chivalrous denial. Of course I'd like to order a Venus like that from you myself, and I have a couple of extremely appetizing models. But for the moment you can paint my Infanta. You've already painted her as a child, I hear."

He came quite close and confided with genuine affection. "By the way, I'm learning sign language. I want to be able to converse fully and openly with you, Francho, my friend. And I've given orders for a plan for erecting an up-to-date institution for the deaf and dumb, according to the principles of Doctor de l'Epée. And it shall bear your name because it was you that gave me the idea. Believe me, it's not just presumption on my part, giving commissions of this kind. My period of idleness won't last long. I shall climb higher still. We shall both climb higher still. You can count on it, Francho!" And though Goya could not hear him, his throaty tenor took on a metallic ring.

Next day Andreo announced a lady. Goya, who had given orders that no one should be admitted, was annoyed. Andreo declared the lady would not be turned away, that it was a very grand lady. Goya sent Agustín. He came back, rather confused, and said it was Countess Castillofiel, and as Goya did not understand he shouted at him, "Pepa! It's Pepa!" And sure enough, there she was.

Pepa was doing well. She appeared to have acquired even greater glamour through Manuel's temporary eclipse. No one believed he would be long out of favour, and those who for safety's sake avoided the Infante showed themselves the more frequently at the levee of Countess Castillofiel. Moreover, her wealth was growing astonishingly.

When she had first heard what fate had overtaken Francisco she had experienced a certain satisfaction. At last he had been punished for the disrespect he had shown her. But this gratification did not last long. She sensed that his malady was in some way connected with the ardency of his passion. She was chagrined that it had not been she who had aroused this ardour in him.

She had come to make him feel that retribution is in Heaven and on earth. But when she saw him, saw the new, different Francisco, she was shaken, and her old affection for him came to the fore. She contented herself with letting him know how wonderfully she had got on. "I'm pregnant," she confided proudly. "My son will be Count Castillofiel, born in lawful wedlock." He noticed the effort she was making to prove both to him and to herself that she was not only successful but happy. Yet she was not happy. She was sick for him as he was for the Duchess, and he began to feel the old, good-natured, easy, half-pitying affection for her.

They spoke like intimate friends who know much about each other that no one else knows. She looked at him with her bold green eyes; he could easily read the words from her lips. He had observed that the only people he had difficulty in understanding were the ones to whom he was indifferent. The people he was fond of, and, what was more, those he hated, he could understand without effort.

"Does Conchita still cheat at cards?" he asked, and then added, "If I may, I'll come and dine with you soon, and drink manzanilla." She could not help pluming herself. "But you must give notice first," she said, "otherwise you might possibly find Don Carlos with me." "What Don Carlos?" he asked. "Don Carlos, King of all the Kingdoms of Spain and both the Indies," she replied. "*Carajo!*" he said. "You mustn't swear," she corrected him, "least of all in the presence of a lady who is about to bring a little count into the world." And then she told him more about Don Carlos. "He comes as an ordinary general," she reported, "and doesn't expect what you've been thinking. He shows me his watches, lets me feel his biceps, we eat our *olla podrida*, he plays his violin to me, and I sing him a romance or two."

"And now you must sing a few romances for me," he begged. And as she looked bewildered and clearly didn't know what to make of his words, he said with grim humour, "You're quite right, I *am* stone deaf, but I can still hear better than most.

"Sing now," he commanded grimly,
"I will play." And so they sang and
Played—she sang, he played, it sounded
Just as in the ancient ballads,
Sad and mild and sweet, and sometimes
It would happen that his playing
And her singing came together.

Martín Zapater stayed in Madrid longer than he had originally foreseen; ostensibly he had business to attend to. But in reality he devoted his whole time to his friend. He took care that Francisco should never be on the street alone; for he feared the deaf man might meet with an accident. Francisco hated protection of any kind, but Martín contrived it so cunningly that, without noticing it, Goya was always under surveillance.

Francisco's commissions piled up as never before, and Martín was forever getting him new ones so that he should never receive the impression that his disability alienated people. Goya accepted but little work, consoled the other customers with promises for the future.

Martín tried to find out anything that could be of interest to Goya. He even unearthed some news of Cayetana. The Duchess of Alba, he was able to report to Francisco, had asked for permission to travel abroad, to relatives in Italy, and would probably not return to Spain till the ban on her coming to Court had been lifted. "Wherever she is," Francisco remarked, "she won't be troubling herself much about a cripple."

To stay in Madrid with its frequent and abrupt climatic changes was obviously a great strain on Martín. He did not look well, he coughed a great deal, and was glad Francisco could not hear how sinister his cough sounded.

Finally he announced he must go home. The friends took leave of each other noisily, as was their way. They were at pains not to show any emotion, slapped each other roughly on the shoulders, joked about their age and their illnesses, and then Martín went back to Saragossa.

He had hardly left before Goya set out, alone and unhindered, to discover how the deaf Goya and the city of Madrid could get on together. It was only a short stretch from his house to the Puerta del Sol, the main square of the city. There several large thoroughfares come together, the Calle Mayor, the Arenal, the Carmen, the Alcalá, and many others.

Goya now took his stand on the Puerta del Sol at the time when traffic there was at its height. At first he stood by the booths and tables of the dealers on the Red de San Luis, then he went to the Gradas, the large square in front of the Church of San Felipe el Real, then to the Mariblanca Fountain. The Puerta del Sol was supposed to be the noisiest square in the world. Goya looked at the noise and bustle. He was jostled and sworn at, he was in the way wherever he stood but he did not care; he looked and enjoyed the noise. Madrid seemed to him as alive as Saragossa had seemed dead.

"Fresh water!" screamed the *aguadores* around the Mariblanca Fountain. "Who would like a drink? Fresh from the spring."

"Oranges," shouted the *naranjeras*, "two for a quarter." "A little carriage, Señor," invited the cab drivers. "Look what a tidy little carriage I've got. Look what a good little animal I have. A ride into the Prado, or wherever you wish." "A little something," begged a cripple, "for the blessed Virgin's sake. A little something for a brave veteran who lost both legs in the war against the infidel." "How are you, dear heart?" a pleasing young woman accosted him. "Do you want to see my little room, little one? Do you want to see my little bed? A soft pretty white bed, there isn't another like it." "Repent!" thundered a preacher from his bench. "Repent and win indulgences!" "Paper, paper, *Diario*, *Gaceta*," shouted the news vendors, "last three copies!"

Goya stood and looked on. He heard yet heard not; he knew every cry and every word, knew it no longer and knew it better than ever before.

Then a blind ballad singer appeared, and the sight of her snatched him rudely back to consciousness of his deafness. She sang and accompanied herself on the guitar, and she had clearly composed a good ballad, for everyone listened sympathetically and with suitable reactions of fear, suspense, and joy; he for his part, though he looked intently at her mouth, could understand nothing. Meanwhile the singer's partner displayed illustrations of what she was singing, variegated daubs, and suddenly Goya had to laugh; it had suddenly struck him that he couldn't hear the words and she couldn't see the pictures.

Apparently, the ballad was about El Maragoto, that fierce bandit whom the brave monk Zaldivia had taken prisoner. El Maragoto was not one of the noble bandits, he was a greedy, bestial, insensitive, blood-thirsty desperado, and when the monk had offered him all he had, his sandals, he had wanted to strike him down with his firing-piece. "You're not worth the shot, you and your sandals," he had screamed. But the courageous monk had hurled himself at him, wrested the gun from him, shot the fugitive in the hindquarters, and tied him up. The whole country was proud of the brave Capuchin, and the crowd on the Puerta del Sol listened enthusiastically as the ballad singer recounted the events, obviously with a wealth of colourful detail. Goya felt himself excluded. He purchased the text of the ballad, to read it at home in peace.

It was late afternoon, bells were ringing, the Angelus was being said, the dealers began to light up their shops, lanterns were lit in front of houses and statues of the Virgin. Goya set out on his way home.

People sat out on the balconies and enjoyed the cool of the evening. On the balcony of a dark, almost windowless, sinister-looking house sat two girls, fair and plump and pretty; they sat leaning over the balustrade, they had important things to tell each other but at the same time they ogled the men as they passed down below. Behind the girls, deep in the shadows, and so wrapped in their cloaks that their faces were invisible, two young men stood motionless. Goya saw them, slowed his steps, finally stopped altogether. He must have looked too long; the cloaked figures moved. It was only a small movement, but a threatening one, and Goya thought it prudent to move on. Yes, the girls on the balcony were real *majas* from the Manolería, *majas* with all their tinsel allure, and behind them, quite as it should be, was menace and shadow.

Next day Agustín asked if it wasn't about time for them to begin at last on the picture of the Marqués de Castrofuerte. But Goya only shook his head. He had something else to do. He painted his experience of yesterday. Painted in six small pictures the story of the robber El Maragoto threatening the Capuchin monk at the door of the monastery, and the monk bravely and with presence of mind shooting him and taking him prisoner. It was a fresh, simple presentation, the whole ballad was there, and all the deep simple pleasure the Puerta del Sol had taken in it.

Then he was assailed by the memory of that other bandit whose execution he had witnessed on the Corridera at Córdoba, the memory of El Puñal. So he painted the dead bandit strangled on the pillory, bearded, in his yellow shift, alone in the harsh light.

On the same day, for he felt he must begin this picture that very day, he started to paint the *majas*, the genuine *majas* on the balcony and their dangerous friends in the shadow; he painted the fascination which these women transmitted to a man, and the darkness and suspicion behind them, enhancing the fascination.

He showed Agustín the pictures. "Well, would I have done better to have painted the Marqués de Castrofuerte?" he asked, pleased and proud. Agustín swallowed and smacked his lips. "You have always something new up your sleeve," he said, and indeed this was a very different kind of painting from the style in which Francisco had painted such scenes before. For he had executed scenes with bandits and *majas* before, on the tapestries for the King, but they had been gay, harmless pictures, whereas these were by no means harmless, and to Agustín it seemed strange, disturbing, and gratifying that the First Court Painter should have begun to paint in such a manner. Meanwhile Francisco was gloating and patting himself on the back. "Can't you hear Maragoto threatening?" he asked. "Can't you hear the gun go off? Can't you hear the *majas* whispering? Could anyone tell they were painted by a deaf man?" And before Agustín could answer he said proudly, "You see! I've learned something new! *Plus ultra!*"

"What are you going to do with the pictures?" Agustín asked. "The Duchess of Osuna wanted a pair of small pictures. She'd certainly be glad to have the robber Maragoto." "I'm not selling these pictures," answered Goya. "I painted them for myself. But I can give them away. I'll give one to you, and the others are for Josefa."

Josefa was astonished, but she blushed with pleasure. Smiling, she wrote down for him in the deliberate capitals she had learned in the convent, "Thank you," and added a cross, as she did to everything she wrote.

He looked at her. She seemed recently to have grown thinner and more shut away than ever. They had never had much to say to each other, yet now he sometimes felt he would like to talk to her. So many of his friends and even strangers had learned sign language that it hurt and annoyed him that she had not made the effort to do so.

Suddenly he felt inspired to paint her. He saw her afresh, more clearly than before. Saw what had so often made him impatient before, her likeness to her brother, her lack of faith in his artistic powers. But he also saw what he had hitherto been unwilling to see, her grief and anxiety, arising out of her love, over his profoundly irreligious attitude, his unruliness, his lack of moderation.

She was a good, patient model. She sat erect in her chair as he had bidden her, with a rich, rather stiff shawl around her shoulders. He underlined her Aragonese stiffness and pride, made her dignified, gave her a kind of aloof charm. He saw her with eyes of affection; without flattering her, though he made her a little younger. There she sits holding her head high under the heavy braids of golden-red hair, her thin lips tightly compressed beneath the large nose. There is a faint sharpness in the features of the long face, her skin, still rosy pale, shows the first signs of withering, there is a slackness about the sloping shoulders. The large shining eyes have an expression of sadness and look past the beholder away into the distance. The hands, in grey gloves, are lying heavy in her lap, the fingers of the left oddly and stiffly splayed out over the right.

It was a good picture, full of affection, but not gay. Very different from the one he had painted of her in Saragossa with two of the children. But it was no carefree Goya who had painted this last picture.

This last picture. A few days after the completion of the portrait Josefa fell ill and took to her bed. She wasted away with great rapidity. The cause of her mortal exhaustion was clear. It was the treacherous climate of Madrid, the icy winters, the burning summers, the rough winds; and, further, her many pregnancies.

Now that her end was near this taciturn woman found much to say. He found that he had been offended without reason because she had not learned sign language. She had learned it, and if she did not use it, it was from obstinacy. Now she spoke to him with her weary fingers, but only for two or perhaps three days, and then her hands grew too heavy for her. He watched her as with a tremendous effort she moved her lips to utter a final message, and he read off the words, "Be careful, Francho! Don't waste either yourself or your money!" And so she died as she had lived, quietly, without fuss, admonishing him.

The dead woman's face beneath the mass of red-blond hair seemed less tired than in recent days. He thought of all he had been through with her, the stiffness of her fragile, slender, girl's body when he had taken her for the first time, of the uncomplaining effort with which she had borne his children, of the long, silent suffering he himself had caused her, of her incomprehension in face of his work, of her stubborn love. It was a malicious trick of fate that she should have to die just when they had come to know each other better.

But he felt none of the fierce agony of despair which so often assailed him. Instead, he was paralysed by a dull, flat desolation, a consciousness of inescapable loneliness.

For Josefa he had ordered
Simple funeral pomp, not splendid,
Like the one he once commanded

For his little Elena. Then
Coming from the churchyard, to his
Friends and fellow-mourners, grimly
Did he quote the ancient saying:
"To the grave the dead, the living
To the table."

With relief they
Saw that he this new misfortune
Without rage or raving bore. And
He himself believed that now of
That old foe within his bosom
He was free.

— 9 —

From Saragossa unexpectedly his mother came to comfort him. She had words of appreciation for the dead woman. When she had been in Madrid before she had not got on well with Josefa.

She had made the journey alone. Of course Tomás had wished to accompany her, and the priest Manuel Bayeu. But she had wanted to spare Francho that, for neither would have done anything but press him for more money, and that was unnecessary. She would have allowed Martín Zapater to come with her. But he was unfortunately ill again, his old cough; this time he had brought up a good deal of blood.

Goya was disturbed. His mother's sober words evoked a superstitious fear in him, he was afraid for Martín. Many of his friends whom he had painted had died in the flesh and lived on only in his pictures. Had not his Josefa just died? Just after he had done her portrait? It must be the case that when he put all he had into painting someone he deprived him of some part of life, for the subject would really exist in the picture and the greater part of his living and breathing self would thereby be taken away. He,

Francisco, brought bad luck, just like Cayetana; probably it was just that which bound him to her.

Doña Engracia's sensible presence helped to dispel his black thoughts. The old woman was hale and hearty; even though he had painted her she showed not the faintest indication of decay.

It was a pity that she simply could not bear her grandchild Javier. "I don't like the boy," she said in her outspoken way. "He has all the bad Bayeu points and all the Goya ones too. He's stuck-up, deceitful, and extravagant. You ought to give him a piece of your mind for once, Francho," and she quoted the old saying, " '*Al hijo y mulo para el culo*'—'the boy and the burro, the better you beat them, the better they are.' "

The polished and elegant Javier liked his homely grandmother from Saragossa as little as she liked him. On the other hand, Goya's friends, Agustín, Miguel, Quintana vied with each other in their attentions to the mother of their friend Francisco. Don Miguel suggested to Francisco that he bring Doña Engracia to Court and present her to Their Majesties so that the Señora might see with her own eyes how much the King and María Luisa valued her son. But the old lady resisted. "I don't belong at Court any more than you do, Francho," she said. "If you're born an onion you'll never be a rose."

She did not stay long and in spite of his pleas insisted on making the return journey alone. Hadn't he come to Saragossa by himself? "Even an old woman can get along better than a deaf man," she declared.

Just before she left she gave him some advice which recalled Josefa's warning. He should be careful, she said, be economical, should not give too much to those vultures, his brother and brother-in-law. "You can leave them something presentable in your will," she observed, "but in your lifetime I would not raise the allowance you make them. And, above all, act small rather than big, Paco! Don't get above yourself again. You can see what comes of it. 'The finer the clothes, the worse the dirt that falls on them.' "

She settled herself in the stagecoach. The *mayoral*, the head coachman, and his assistants urged the animals forward. "*Macho, macho!*" they bellowed, and as the leading beast did not begin to pull at once they swore at it, "*Qué perro!*" In the midst of the hubbub his mother looked out of the carriage and said, "May the Virgin protect you, Paco!" Francisco saw the curses and the blessing and they mingled within him. Then the great coach drove away, and he knew it was improbable that he would ever see the very old woman again.

He was concerned that Doña Engracia had not been able to get on with his son Javier. He continued to love and spoil Javier as before. He liked the things Javier said and the way he said them. Javier twined himself ever more closely about his heart. His mother was wrong, had to be wrong. The young man deserved to be spoiled, and it was precisely his affectations and youthful taste for elegance and luxury that pleased him.

On the other hand, he discovered that he no longer liked the house in which he lived, the magnificently furnished house in the Carrera San Jerónimo. Elena was dead, Mariano was dead, he was alone with Javier. The house and furniture belonged to a part of his life that was over forever.

He bought himself another house, just outside Madrid but entirely in the country, on the banks of the Manzanares near the Puenta Segovia. It was a roomy, old two-storied building, a real country house, a *quinta* with a good bit of open country round it. He had a wonderful view; on one side he looked out on the beloved Pradera de San Isidro which he had painted so often, and spread out above it was his own city of Madrid; on the other side he saw the hills of Guadarrama.

He furnished the *quinta* almost meagrely. With faint amusement he noticed that his son Javier had little liking for this new parsimony, so he encouraged the boy to trick out his own room with as much magnificence as he wished. He gave him the expensive chairs and sofas, the footstools covered in cloth of gold, from the house on the Carrera San Jerónimo. Most of the paintings too he handed over to him; but he kept for himself that portrait of Cayetana which he had painted not for her but for his own pleasure. And into his own large room he put only the essentials, and while the walls of his former studio had been decked with gobelins and costly paintings, he left the walls of the *quinta* quite bare.

He often sat and looked at these bare walls, and sometimes there was a subtle smile on his lips. He was toying with the idea of painting these walls; they should be pictures out of his world; his observation, his imagination, should guide his brush, he should follow no other rules but those he had made himself; and his inner world should be the real one.

But he still had a lot to learn before he could give expression to what was floating before his mind's eye. He had certainly achieved something in his art, but it was no more than a beginning. Just as when a climber attains the first mountain ridge and can see the whole cloudless sweeping range behind it, so had he, in this year of madness, suffering, deafness, loneliness, and dawning reason, caught a glimpse, high up and far off, of his true goal; and now he knew: the external eye must be complemented by the inner, the naked reality of the world by the fantasies of his own brain. Not till he could paint all this would he paint the walls of his *quinta*.

Meanly though he had furnished his house, he paid great attention to his dress. Moreover, he now dressed in the new fashion of the Paris bourgeoisie, appearing only in Court dress when it was prescribed. Otherwise he wore long trousers instead of *calzas*, or knee breeches, and substituted for the tricorne the tall stiff hat, the *prolifar* or *bolívar* as it was called. He combed his hair over his ears, which could no longer hear in any case. People often saw him walking in his big overgrown garden, powerful, dignified, leonine, looking quite awe-inspiring, with his tall hat and cane. They called him *El sordo en la huerta*, the deaf man in the garden, and they called his house *La quinta del sordo*, the deaf man's house.

He had paper and pencil always by him so that people could say what they wished to him. More and more often he would jot down small rapid sketches in this notebook, first drafts, snapshots of his inner and outer landscape. And he mastered Agustín's new technique, worked a great deal, and did not mind asking him for advice.

Here in the *quinta* as in his house on the San Jerónimo he shared his studio with Agustín. But now that he was beginning to paint his new discoveries and engrave them on the plates, he found even the presence of his faithful and understanding assistant disturbing. So he rented a room on the top floor of a tall house full of people and in the noisiest quarter of the city, on the corner of the Calle San Bernardino. He furnished this room very sparsely too; apart from the essential pieces of furniture he brought in only the utensils he needed for his engraving—copper plates, a press, and the rest of the technical equipment. It was a large room whose bareness was underlined by an abundance of light.

Here Goya would sit, his elegant clothes contrasting oddly with the poverty of his workshop, and he may have smiled to think that Josefa was no longer there to look askance because he did not put on his smock to do his dirty work in. Here then he sat, and from all sides, above, below, and from the bustle of the Calle San Bernardino, the noise rose; but he sat in his own vast silence and made his new, daring, powerful experiments, and his bare workshop became his favourite retreat, his *ermita*.

Agustín's new process made possible shadings which had never been known before, and that was as it should be. For the world which he carried in his head and wanted to etch onto his plates was rich and many-sided. For a long time he had believed the lowly past to have died, and that only Goya the courtier remained. But since the onset of his deafness, since his journey with the mule-driver Gil, he had noticed that his old self was still very much alive, and this pleased him.

In his youth he had been impatient and had pitted himself against the world. But he had had to learn that whoever seeks to get the better of the world gets knocked on the head by fate. Later on he had adapted himself, had joined gaily in the easy, extravagant life at Court. But he had learned that whoever betrays himself, adapts himself entirely, he also gets hit on the head by fate and loses himself and his art. He had learned that one may not seek to kick over the traces but must try to bend and mould both the world and oneself.

It seemed to him that all he had ever experienced had the single purpose of leading him to this bare room on the Calle San Bernardino; as if everything he had drawn and painted till now were only finger exercises for that which he had now to do. He sat there in his *ermita* and allowed the world to force itself upon him and at the same time forced it to conform to his vision of it.

The simplicity and economy which the matter of his new art forced upon him was as welcome to him as the baldness of his *quinta*. Light and colour were glories on which he had often intoxicated himself and would often do so again. But now sometimes in his solitude he would curse his earlier pictures; they were as loud-coloured as a monkey's rump! No, for his new, piercing, bitterly humorous insight there could be only one medium, graving tools and a respectable black and white.

He had informed the Academy that with a heavy heart he must ask to be relieved of his office, that his deafness compelled him to this step. The Academy made him Honorary President and on the occasion of his retirement from office organized a representative exhibition of his works.

The King loaned "The Family of Carlos" as his contribution to the exhibition.

There had been much talk about this daring picture. At the opening of the exhibition there appeared not only members of the Court who wished to display their patronage of the arts and their friendship for Goya, but everyone in Madrid who had a reputation for enlightenment.

There hung the picture about which there was so much talk and to-do and whispered amusement, and most of those seeing it for the first time found that it took their breath away.

Then, escorted by the President of the Academy Committee, the Marqués de Santa Cruz, Goya stepped into the midst of the excited, admiring throng in front of his work. A square-built man in clothes rather too tight for him, older than his years, with his narrowed eyes, he stood and inspected his Bourbons, his underlip thrust out, while behind him were courtiers, burghers, and artists of the city of Madrid. When they saw him in front of his picture a thunder of applause broke out. "Long live Spain!" they cried, and "Long live Francisco Goya!" and "*Viva!*" and "*Ole!*" and they clapped violently. But Goya noticed none of all this. So the Marqués de Santa Cruz plucked his sleeve and gently turned him round to face the others, and Francisco saw what was happening and bowed solemnly.

The Grand Inquisitor Don Ramón de Reynoso y Arce inspected the picture which had been described to him as a shameless defiance of the Grace of God.

And he found that what his people
Said was no exaggeration.
"If I were myself King Carlos,"
Quoth he in the Latin language,
"I would not have made this Goya
My First Painter; rather from the
Holy Office asked a verdict
Whether this were not a matter
For a charge to lie of *crimen*
Læsæ Majestatis."

— 10 —

It had been clever of Don Manuel to suggest to the King that he should make the liberal Urquijo First Secretary, and the reactionary ultramontane Caballero Minister of Justice. But he had left one thing out of account: namely that Don Mariano Luis de Urquijo was something more than a self-interested politician, and that the progressive ideas which he professed were more to him than a favourite topic of conversation in fashionable salons. The two Ministers did indeed oppose each other and attempted each to thwart the other's measures, as Don Manuel had anticipated. But Urquijo showed himself to be a zealous patriot and a statesman of considerable stature for whom the cunning, self-seeking, narrow-minded Caballero was by no means a match. In spite of Caballero's machinations Urquijo succeeded in weakening the influence of Rome on the Spanish Church and in forcing the Spanish ultramontanes to hand over to the Crown moneys which had hitherto gone to Rome; he even contrived to restrict the jurisdiction of the Inquisition. But Urquijo's greatest success was in his foreign policy. Not only did he avoid having to make the concessions to the French Republic which Don Manuel had held to be inevitable, but he was able, by a supple alternation between astute concessions in small matters and polite resistance in great ones, considerably to strengthen the position of the Spanish Crown in relation to its powerful, victorious, and troublesome ally.

Don Manuel was disappointed. Doña María Luisa, far from stretching out her hands imploringly to him, continued to look frostily over his head, and, instead of himself, loaded the new Minister-President with tokens of her favour and satisfaction.

On the surface Don Manuel was Urquijo's good friend, but privately wove a hundred intrigues against him in order to frustrate his policies. Came whenever it was possible to the assistance of the bigoted Caballero, encouraged the ultramontanes to raise the cry in press and pulpit against the godless Minister-President, caused representations to be made to the King over the laxity with which the censorship was administered under Urquijo.

Above all, Don Manuel sought to hamper Urquijo's foreign policies. The potentates in Paris found an unexpectedly clever and determined opponent in the new First Secretary of State and did what they could in Madrid to bring about his fall. Manuel recalled himself favourably to the minds of those in Paris by providing the Directory with the desired pretext for requesting Urquijo's dismissal.

King Carlos's brother, that is, Ferdinand of Naples, had to Carlos's secret delight joined the coalition against France and in a rapid campaign had been both defeated and deposed. Now Manuel advised the monarch to demand the Crown of Naples for his second son. It was an audacious request, since King Carlos as France's ally should have influenced his brother to remain neutral. Urquijo then expounded to the King that his demand was an offence against political expediency and could have only the most unfortunate consequences. But the King, acting on Manuel's advice, stood firm; Urquijo was compelled to demand the Crown of Naples for the Spanish prince. His apprehensions were realized. The Directory considered the request to be insolent and absurd, sent a sharp reply, and begged the King to dismiss the Minister who had addressed so unreasonable a demand to the Republic. Manuel persuaded the King that it was only Urquijo's awkward manner which had offended the French and provoked the unpleasant note. The King, partly to please the Queen and partly to preserve his own dignity, kept Urquijo in office but let him feel his displeasure, and he informed the government of the Republic of the reproof administered. " 'This fox is soon going to end up at the furdealers in Burgos,' " Manuel quoted the old saying exultantly.

And then there occurred one of those strokes of luck on which Don Manuel so firmly relied and with which his life had in fact been so well provided. Napoleon Bonaparte returned from Egypt and appointed himself First Consul. The statesman and general, exalted by his triumphs, had no intention of treating with the difficult Urquijo over the Spanish question and had no hesitation in saying that he would be glad to see his friend the Infante Don Manuel once more at the head of the Spanish government.

Napoleon was not the man to permit his wishes to remain wishes. He recalled Ambassador Truguet and replaced him with his own brother Lucien. The latter brought with him the draft for a new treaty between Spain and the Republic, an agreement shrewdly calculated with an eye to María Luisa's family pride, and Lucien had instructions not to deal with Urquijo over this new treaty but with Don Manuel.

Lucien therefore disclosed to the Infante Manuel in a secret conversation that the First Consul wanted to create a new kingdom out of the Grandduchy of Tuscany and some papal possessions, a Kingdom of Etruria, the crown of which he designed to bestow on the Prince of Parma, son-in-law of the Spanish royal pair, as compensation for the loss of the Duchy of Parma. In return for this concession the First Consul expected Spain to hand over her American colony of Louisiana to France.

Manuel perceived at once that, though scarcely advantageous to Spain, these suggestions would sound sweet in María Luisa's ears, and he promised the new envoy, Lucien Bonaparte, to lay them before the royal pair with a warm recommendation.

Since their great quarrel María Luisa had given Manuel no opportunity of speaking to her alone. Now he asked for a confidential interview to discuss a purely political matter. Put the situation before her, expressed his satisfaction that the unfortunate tension which Urquijo's clumsy behaviour had occasioned between France and Spain had been removed, as could be seen from the First Consul's generous offer. And one could scarcely take exception to the First Consul's being reluctant to negotiate with so maladroit a person as Urquijo over such delicate matters as the creation of a Kingdom of Etruria and the Spanish *quid pro quo*.

Doña María Luisa listened attentively; she preserved an air of disdain, yet she was affected. Now that Manuel stood alone opposite her for the first time after so long, she realized how much she had missed him; her whole body yearned for him. Of course Mariano Luis Urquijo was a statesman of a quite different calibre, but Manuel was probably right in saying that the First Consul wished to treat with Manuel rather than Urquijo.

"If I understand you aright, Infante," she said, "you are assuming that the treaty of which you speak could be concluded only by you." Manuel favoured her with a smile. "The fact that His Excellency the Ambassador Lucien Bonaparte has discussed his brother's secret plans with me," he answered, "is proof of trust such as is not given to many. But perhaps, Madame, you would rather ask

Ambassador Bonaparte direct," he went on boldly. "So you're ready to use any means to become First Minister again, Manuelito," said the Queen with a dreamy sweetness. "You're trying it in this roundabout way with General Bonaparte." "You're utterly and absolutely mistaken, Madame," Don Manuel declared amiably. "As things stand today it would be impossible for me to resume office as First Minister. Every time you called me in to advise I would be reminded of the humiliation dealt me by your hand." "I know how sensitive you are," said the Queen. "What are you trying to get out of me this time, Chico, my little one?" "You must appreciate, Your Majesty," declared Don Manuel, "that I cannot return to office without asking satisfaction." "Open your shameless mouth," answered María Luisa, "and tell me what demand you have to make in return for my daughter becoming Queen of Etruria." Manuel answered in his sonorous tenor, "I respectfully beg that Your Majesty include the Countess Castillofiel among the number of your ladies-in-waiting." "You are contemptible," said María Luisa. "I am ambitious," Infante Don Manuel corrected her, "both for myself and for those who are near and dear to me."

When Pepa received the written communication of the Marqués de Ariza, First Royal Chamberlain, summoning her in the name of Their Majesties to the Escorial for the *besamanos,* to kiss hands, on the King's birthday, her whole face lit up. As her pregnancy advanced so did her contentment. That she should now be presented at Court on one of the eight great gala occasions was a wonderful new stroke of luck. Manuel would be there, everyone would be there, the whole Court. Francho would be there too; the First Painter would not dare to miss the King's birthday. And she would confront the Queen, she would be compared, everyone would compare them, Manuel, Francho, the whole Court.

She made her preparations with joyful energy. She sent a special courier off to Málaga to drag that old dotard, her husband, to Madrid, for he must not be absent at her presentation. And she was indefatigable in her study of the *Handbook of Ceremonial.* The book comprised three hundred full-size pages; it was not on sale to the public, it was distributed by the seneschal's office only to such personages as were received at Court.

On the day of the reception she drove in splendour to the main entrance of the castle, her tottering Count at her side. This time she was not entering the Escorial by the back door but by invitation from the master of the house. She swept through galleries and corridors built over the graves of dead kings, past guards presenting arms and lackeys making deep obeisance; for on the eight great state occasions the King's whole household was mustered, the Walloon and Swiss Guards and the entire domestic staff high and low, one thousand eight hundred and seventy-four strong.

Pepa was received by the *Camarera Mayor*, the Marquesa de Monte Alegre, whose duty it was to prepare the ladies who were to be presented to Their Majesties. Today there were nineteen of them, most of them very young. They all seemed agitated by the task that lay before them; the only one among them who was entirely at ease was the Countess Castillofiel, who had had to master many more difficult roles while she was studying for the stage.

When the *Camarera Mayor* appeared in the throne room with her little flock, grandees, prelates, and ambassadors were already assembled. A mob of lesser nobility and high officials filled the sides of the room and the galleries. Pepa's entrance created a sensation. She looked about her unconcernedly for people she might know. Many of them gave her formal greeting, which she acknowledged easily with a gay nod of her head. In the gallery she detected Francisco and jauntily waved to him.

Small trumpets were sounded in the antechamber, commands rang out, the halberds of the watch clashed. Then the major-domo knocked three times with his staff and announced, "*Los reyes católicos.*" And now the royal Catholic pair made its entrance while all present made deep obeisance, and behind them members of the royal family, Manuel among them with his Infanta. Their Majesties sat down upon their thrones. The major-domo announced that the grandees of the kingdom had assembled on this propitious occasion to transmit to the King the good wishes of the nobility. "May the most Holy Virgin grant the King a long life for the welfare of Spain and of the world," he called out. Everyone repeated his cry, trumpets sounded all over the castle, the bells of the great church began to ring.

While the solemn sounds floated muffled into the vast, gloomily magnificent room, the twelve grandees of first rank and their wives approached the royal pair for the *besamanos*, the hand-kissing. Then came the presentation of the nineteen ladies, who were arranged according to rank, the Countess Castillofiel being the seventh. When the Marqués de Ariza called Pepa's name and the Marqués de la Vega Inclán repeated it, a tremor of anticipation and curiosity went through the room. The First Lord-in-Waiting conducted Pepa to the King; as she kissed his hand Carlos was unable to suppress a faint, slyly paternal smile.

The Countess Castillofiel stepped up to María Luisa. This was the moment for which all had been waiting. There was Don Manuel Godoy, Infante, Príncipe de la Paz, the man of whose influence on the Queen and the destinies of Spain all the chancelleries of Europe spoke with interest, hope, or concern, the man whose amours were discussed by the whole world with abhorrence, or with leers and nudges. And there, confronting each other, stood the companions of his couch, the Queen who could not break away from him, and the woman of the people from whom he could not break away, while Doña María Luisa's lawful husband, Don Manuel's lawful wife, and Pepa Tudo's lawful husband looked on.

María Luisa sat there arrayed in the royal robes of heavy damask studded with jewels, the diadem upon her brow, a veritable idol. Pepa Tudo stood before her, graceful in her amplitude, ripe and blooming with youth, her skin dazzlingly white against the red-blond hair, entirely at ease and confident of herself and her beauty. She curtsied, not quite so deeply as was prescribed, by reason of her pregnancy, kissed María Luisa's hand, came up again. The women looked each other in the eye. The Queen's small, piercing black eyes surveyed the lady presented to her with suitably polite indifference. But there was tumult within her. The creature was more beautiful than she had imagined and apparently cleverer too, the creature was invincible. But Pepa's eyes shone. She savoured to the full the pleasure of parading herself before this impotent potentate. For two seconds, the prescribed length of time, Countess Castillofiel looked the Queen in the face. Then she turned away towards the chair of the Prince of Asturias, the heir to the throne.

Goya was standing in the gallery and had a good view of the faces of both women. He smiled. "Hens don't belong in cathedrals," but now she did belong in the cathedral, Pepa, this *jamona* of his. She'd brought it off. She was a *señora de título*, had her accredited title; the child she carried within her would be born a count.

After they had eaten, Pepa took part in a game of cards with the Queen. María Luisa addressed now this guest, now that, with neutral amiability. Pepa waited to be addressed in her turn. She had long to wait. "Are you winning, Countess?" asked Doña María Luisa at last in her resonant, not unpleasing voice; she had decided to be friendly to the creature, it was the wisest course. "Not very much, Madame," answered Pepa. "What is your first name, Countess?" asked the Queen. "Josefa," Pepa replied, "María Josefa. The people of Madrid call me Countess Pepa, or just Pepa." "Yes," remarked the Queen, "the people of my capital are friendly and confiding." Pepa was astonished at the effrontery of this; María Luisa, "foreigner, Italian, whore, robber," was hated, to the extent that when she drove out in Madrid the police had to take extensive precautions to prevent demonstrations. "You have property in Andalucía, Doña Josefa?" the Queen went on. "Yes, Madame," answered Pepa. "But you prefer to stay in Madrid?" asked María Luisa. "Yes, Madame," Pepa replied. "As you yourself remarked, Madame, the people of your capital are trusting and friendly. To me." "And the Count, your husband," the Queen inquired further, "does he share your enjoyment of life in Madrid?" "Of course, Madame," Pepa returned, "but unfortunately the state of his health dictates that he should spend the larger part of the year in Andalucía." "I see," said the Queen, and added, "You are in a family way, Doña Josefa?" "Thanks to the most blessed Virgin, yes," answered Pepa.

"Tell me then, how old the Conde
Is, your husband?" asked the Queen with
Amiable consideration.
"Sixty-eight," said Pepa. "But I
Am in hope, I feel I have the
Inward certainty Our Lady
Of Atocha means to bless me
With delivery safe and happy
And a strong and healthy little
Son." And then she looked the Queen with
Innocent and beaming eyes full
In the face.

11

For the sake of her own dignity Doña María Luisa wished to avoid the appearance of being dictated to by Consul Bonaparte in the matter of appointments to office. For the time being she put off the dismissal of Urquijo.

Don Manuel was glad of it. He had recognized from the beginning, and Miguel had demonstrated to him with decisive logic, that the treaty which Lucien had suggested was entirely to Spain's disadvantage. If France were to invest Doña María Luisa's son-in-law with the Crown of Etruria, such an elevation would nourish María Luisa's vanity but Spain would foot the bill. It could be nothing but acceptable to Manuel that another should be in office when such a treaty was signed. Indeed, he could not imagine a more favourable arrangement: he, Manuel, would negotiate with Lucien Bonaparte and have all the credit in the Queen's eyes, Urquijo would lay before her all the arguments which spoke against the agreement, she, out of vanity, would refuse to listen to them, in the end Urquijo would have to sign the treaty and take the blame.

Don Manuel was certain he could depose Urquijo whenever he wanted to, and with this certainty at his back he made himself agreeable to the man. He stuck to this even after information had come to him that Urquijo spoke of him with malice and contempt. He smiled and said to himself, "Give me good enemies, Virgen del Pilar, and a lingering, sweet revenge."

Don Manuel was satisfied, happy and good-humoured, and in a mood to share his well-being with others. Good old María Luisa had been most reasonable, had taken it very decently, so he showed his gratitude, sang for her, endeavoured to make his relationship with Pepa less obvious. He explained to Pepa that he already had the tenderest feeling for the child she carried within her and wished to prevent even the shadow of a suspicion arising about this child. He had for this reason prevailed upon Count Castillofiel to stay in Madrid up to the time of her confinement; he himself, hard though it was for him, would for reasons of propriety see her less often in the last months of her pregnancy. Pepa made no objection; it was her own wish also that little Count Castillofiel should make his entry to the world in the most dignified circumstances possible.

Don Manuel even allowed his Infanta the benefit of his good humour and treated her with a sort of clumsy, pitying affection. The Queen of Spain had borne him children, but alas! they did not bear his name; the woman he loved would bear his child; yet it too, alas! would bear another's name. But surely this Infanta of the blood would bring a son into the world for him who would bear his name. He had actually not believed the skinny she-goat capable even of conceiving a child. Now he wished to show her that he appreciated her achievement, desired to pay her some attention. He knew how she longed to be away from Madrid. Of course there were definite reasons why her confinement would have to take place in Madrid. But for the time being there was nothing against Doña Teresa spending two or three weeks in the quiet of her country seat, Arenas de San Pedro, which she loved so much.

Furthermore—and this would please her too—it was quite time Francisco did a portrait of his Infanta.

Francisco was not loath to go to Arenas; the name of the place evoked pleasant memories.

At a time when he had been unknown and obscure, Doña Teresa's father, the old Infante Don Luis, had summoned Francisco to Arenas on the recommendation of Jovellanos to paint portraits of himself and his family. It had made a deep impression on Goya; his view of life had been turned upside down by the discovery that this prince of the blood, the King's brother, made no more of himself than any Pedro or Pablo in Madrid or Saragossa. Francisco had spent a whole month in Arenas, and Infante Luis and his family had treated him like one of themselves. During that happy time in Arenas he had become acquainted with Doña Teresa and had painted her; she had been a small child, and a shy one, but she had trusted him.

Goya now understood much better than he had then what a wise, warm-hearted man the Infante had been. According to the Bourbon laws of inheritance, Don Luis had a claim to the Crown, but he had renounced it in order to marry a woman of lowlier birth, the lady Vallabriga from Aragón. He had preferred to live on his Arenas estate with the woman he loved and the children she bore him, to devote himself to husbandry and hunting, to his books and his pictures. At bottom Goya had thought him slightly crazy. Now he understood him better, though had he been in his shoes he himself would still not have made the renunciation.

He had painted Doña Teresa a second time when she was seventeen and both her parents long since dead. She was a true daughter of those parents, contented with her quiet life far from the strident, absurd pomp of the Court. And now in her licentiousness María Luisa had thrown this harmless, lovable child to the vulgar, dissolute Manuel as the price for his continuing to creep into her bed from time to time. And Manuel had accepted Doña Teresa as a troublesome appendage to a desired title which, save through her, he would have been unable to acquire.

Since Francisco himself had been plunged so deeply into misfortune he had more understanding for the misfortunes of others. He observed her pathetic pregnancy. He observed how profoundly she suffered from the offensive foolishness of the situation into which she had been dragged and which outraged her whole being. He painted with the utmost care and tenderness. Painted all the sympathy he felt for the daughter of his patron into the portrait.

The result was a picture of great delicacy. There sits the little princess. The frail, childlike, pregnant body is veiled in a soft white dress fastened beneath the bosom, neck and breast emerge gracefully, above them, beneath a cloud of fair hair, the rather long face, not beautiful but yet attractive. All the pregnant child's troubled soul was visible in this countenance; huge, sad, dismayed eyes look out at a world the hideousness of which they cannot comprehend.

When Don Manuel saw the portrait he was startled. He had no idea his Infanta looked so touchingly fragile.

A feeling almost of reverence came over him, with it a faint sense of guilt, and he cried noisily, "*Por la vida del demonio!* The way you've painted my Infanta, Francisco, why, I may end up by falling in love with her after all."

Manuel had not come to inspect the portrait of Doña Teresa but to fetch her back to Madrid. His child must be born in Madrid. The Court must be present at the child's baptism. Both

Doña María Luisa and Don Manuel wanted to let all the world know that they were friends again.

On the 15th of October a special courier from Don Manuel reached the Escorial and informed the Queen that the Infanta was delivered of a fine healthy daughter. Doña María Luisa betook herself at once to Don Carlos and asked that the Court should interrupt its sojourn in the Escorial, so that the baptism of the little Princess might take place in the castle at Madrid, in the King's apartments. Don Carlos was doubtful. It was true that such a trip to Madrid would spare him a disagreeable visit to the crypt of his ancestors in the Escorial, but the duration of the sojourns in the individual castles was prescribed with the greatest exactitude, and his deceased father had risked his life to avoid infringing these regulations. María Luisa, however, declared that the Infante Manuel had rendered such exceptional services to King and State that they were bound to grant him this his fondest wish. She insisted, and the King gave way.

He summoned his First Lord-in-Waiting and communicated the proposal to him. The Marqués de Ariza, much disturbed, objected respectfully that the ruling in the *Handbook of Ceremonial* was quite unequivocal and had not been infringed for a quarter of a millennium. "Everything must have a beginning," said María Luisa coolly. The King wagged his big head and said to the Marqués, "There it is, my friend." The Marqués de Ariza, the Marqués de la Vega Inclán, and the Marquesa de Monte Alegre huddled together, shocked and perplexed. The Marqués de Ariza, who had never in his life been known to display excitement of any kind, was red in the face as he declared, "I would like to tear out page fifty-two of the *Handbook* with my own hands and then retire to my estates."

The breach of etiquette caused an immense sensation. All the envoys reported the occurrence to their governments as a sure sign that Don Manuel had once more taken the guidance of Spain's destinies absolutely into his own hands.

A mere thirty-six hours was to be the extent of the royal pair's stay in the capital. But every minister, every Court official, all those in waiting on the King and Queen down to the very humblest, the royal musicians, the entire households of the royal couple and the Infantes had to accompany Their Catholic Majesties.

The baptism took place amid celebrations such as were usually reserved for the baptism of an heir to the throne. The *Camarera Mayor*, with an escort of the Swiss Guard, repaired to the Palacio Alcudia to fetch Don Manuel's child to the royal castle. The nurse followed in a royal carriage. The baptism was performed in the Catholic King's apartments by the Grand Inquisitor Don Ramón de Reynoso y Arce. He baptized the child with the names Carlota Luisa. Then Don Carlos asked to have the child handed to him. Cautiously, lest his many orders should injure the baby, he rocked it to and fro, held his fingers up to its face and said, "Ta ta ta." "A pretty child," he pronounced, "a strong healthy Princess who will do the house of Bourbon credit." Then the *Camarera Mayor*, escorted this time by a detachment of Walloons, brought the little Infanta back to Don Manuel's palace.

An hour later Their Catholic Majesties themselves repaired to Don Manuel's. They drove for the first time in the State coach which the French Republic had presented to them a week before. It came from the stables of the guillotined Louis the Sixteenth but had undergone certain modifications.

At Don Manuel's a gala banquet took place. In addition to the royal couple almost all the dignitaries were there, as well as Ambassador Lucien Bonaparte. The presents which the little Princess had received were exhibited; they took up two rooms. Lucien Bonaparte had given a golden rattle in the name of the First Consul. María Luisa scrutinized the gifts, estimated their value at two or three millions. She for her part had invested the small Infanta with the order she herself had created "For nobility, virtue, merit, *nobilitati, virtuti, merito*."

Infante Don Manuel caused money to be thrown down to the mob, fifty thousand reals. And still they grumbled, the *populacho*, the *chusma*.

A few weeks later Pepa was brought to bed. The little Count Castillofiel was baptized by the Bishop of Cuenca with the names Luis María and a string of other names, among them Manuel and Francisco. The celebrations took place in the Palacio Bondad Real.

And Don Manuel too was present,
Representing the King, as one of
Carlos' chamberlains; and from the
King he bore a rare and precious
Gift, a tooth of San Isidro

Set within a golden setting.
Wonder-working was the jewel,
For whoever wore it had the
Power to make himself attractive,
Drawing all men to him and their
Friendship ever winning for his
Own.

-- 12 --

On the day before the Court travelled back to Madrid for the little Infanta's christening Lucien Bonaparte sought out First Secretary Urquijo in a political matter. When the gentlemen parted, the ambassador remarked casually that they would probably see each other next day in Madrid. Urquijo replied that he was not feeling well and would not be going to Madrid. Whereupon, somewhat surprised, Lucien Bonaparte answered with a hint of irony, "A most unfortunate circumstance, Excellency, that you should be indisposed just tomorrow."

And it was this indisposition of Urquijo's which was to bring about his fall. In recent weeks his contemptuous references to Don Manuel had been more and more frequent; his absenting himself from the Infanta's christening was a challenge. Don Manuel accepted it. He had waited long enough; with Dona María Luisa's approval he decided to ask Don Carlos for Urquijo's dismissal at the next opportunity.

Nor was the opportunity slow in coming. In a confidential message Pope Pius complained of certain philosophistic utterances made by the Spanish ambassador to the Holy See. The ambassador had also mentioned reforms which First Secretary Urquijo had in mind, reforms of such a nature as gravely to infringe upon ancient rights of the Holy See. The Pope begged the Catholic King to intermit these reforms, and not in his turn to ally himself with the persecutors of the hard-pressed Church, but to solace and defend her.

The Pope had commissioned the Nuncio to deliver this letter into the King's own hands. The Nuncio, aware of the hostility between Don Manuel and Urquijo, held a consultation with the former; Manuel contrived that the King received the Nuncio in his presence and the Queen's.

The prelate handed the King the letter and, in the name of the Holy Father, begged him to read it at once. Carlos read it and was thrown into confusion. The reforms of which the Pope complained were intended, as Urquijo had expressed it, to set the seal on his great undertaking, the liberation of Spain from Rome, and he, Carlos, had signed two weeks before the edict whereby these reforms became law. He had hesitated long, but on one occasion Urquijo had got him to himself, had demonstrated the advantages and asserted the legality of the edict with such insidious skill that Carlos had finally agreed. Further, when Urquijo had talked of the terrible wails and lamentations which the ultramontanes were sure to raise, Carlos had even expressly promised him protection against the attacks of the *frailucos,* the priests. A fine mess he'd got himself into!

In great embarrassment the King stammered apologies, assurances of the deepest respect for the Holy Father, of warmest sympathy. The Nuncio answered that he would convey these messages to the Holy Father, who would, however, or so he feared, scarcely be satisfied by them.

After the prelate had withdrawn, Manuel and María Luisa set to work to talk Carlos round. The fox Urquijo had betrayed him, had tricked the unsuspecting King with his devilish eloquence into signing the blasphemous edict. The King's regrets changed into rage against Urquijo. Manuel and María Luisa took advantage of his anger. Urquijo must be called to account immediately.

Urquijo was ill in bed. He was forced to get up and to appear, after making a hasty toilet, before the royal couple and Manuel, his bitterest enemy. "How dare you!" the King shouted at him. "You've betrayed me right and left! You've got me into difficulties with the Holy Father and called down the wrath of God on my head! You heretic!" "I laid the pros and cons before Your Majesty, as was my duty," the ailing Minister replied. "You listened to my arguments, Sire, and approved them before you were pleased to sign. More than that, Sire: you promised to protect me against the anticipated attacks of the ultramontanes." "What a barefaced lie!" bellowed Don Carlos. "I promised you protection from the priests, the *frailucos*, but not from the Nuncio and the Holy Father. It's your fault, your fault entirely, that I'm now as good as at war with Rome. And then you try to shove the blame off on me." Then, lest his fine rage should evaporate, he screamed, "To Pamplona with him! To the fortress!" and had to be restrained from assaulting Urquijo.

When the Minister had left, pale as death but still dignified, it occurred to María Luisa that it was after all rather a pity she had lost him. But Carlos remarked with a shake of his head, "Strange. This morning I rather liked him, and now he's a criminal and I have to have him locked up."

"Think no more about him, Sire," so
Said Don Manuel as he sought to
Soothe the King. "Be tranquil, Sire, and
Leave the rest of the affair to
The good offices of your zealous
Inquisition."

-- 13 --

On the advice of the Infante Manuel and with the purpose of showing his respect and good will for the First Consul, King Carlos had ordered a painting from the great Parisian painter, Jacques-Louis David. It was to be a glorification of General Bonaparte. As a subject for the picture David had suggested "The Crossing of the Saint Bernard." The painter was by no means cheap, he demanded a quarter of a million reals as well as the right to make three copies with slight variations. But it was important to maintain good relations with the First Consul; the Court granted the commission, David painted, the picture arrived and was hung at Aranjuez, where the gentlemen Francisco Goya, Miguel Bermúdez, and Agustín Esteve went to inspect it.

It was an imposing picture, more than two and a half metres high and nearly two and a half wide. In the middle of a wild mountain landscape Napoleon sat victorious astride a spiritedly rearing steed; small, shadowy shapes of soldiers and cannon eddied about his feet; faint inscriptions on slabs of rock recalled the two other martial heroes who had crossed the Alps, Hannibal and Charlemagne.

After a long silence Miguel was the first to pronounce judgment. "The apotheosis of genius—one can scarcely imagine anything more sublime. The vast world of the Alps is dwarfed by Bonaparte's greatness. And for all the classic grandeur of the work as a whole the painter has contrived to furnish a likeness of his hero." "One can afford to furnish something of likeness for a quarter of a million," said Goya objectively. "The horse isn't a good likeness," Agustín remarked dryly, "the horse is a prodigy of nature." "Yes," agreed Goya, "your horses' rumps are better."

Miguel admonished Agustín. "You can't forgive David for not having got himself guillotined on behalf of the Revolution," he chided. "I for my part am happy that so great a painter should have been spared. Nor can it be said that he has been untrue to his supreme example, ancient Rome. As a Roman, he would presumably—and since the Republic rotted from within, rightly—have taken the part of the Emperor Augustus. When they announced to him the formation of the Empire by the First Consul he said something wonderful. He said, 'We were not virtuous enough for a Republic.' "

Goya had not understood. "What did my colleague David say?" he asked. The room was vast. Miguel repeated in resounding tones, " 'We were not virtuous enough for a Republic.' "

Goya confined himself to saying, "I see," in reply. What he did see was that this David was the young general's barker, just as he had been barker for the Revolution. He called it "virtuous" and presumably he was at least sincere. He himself, Francisco, once in Parma when he was very young, had painted a crossing of the Alps for a competition, that of Hannibal. There had been a wealth of martial pomp in his picture, armed warriors, elephants, standards. David had been more sparing, and he had his mastery of technique, but the fifty-year-old David's insight was no deeper than had been that of the twenty-year-old Goya.

Agustín continued to sneer. "David is as supple in his politics as he is rigid in his painting," he observed. "A slow painter but a rapid politician." "You allow yourself to be swayed too much by your emotions, Don Agustín," Miguel lectured him. "Let him who pronounces in political matters do so without hatred. Whoever wishes to have anything to do with politics, either actively or as a spectator, must be endowed with impartiality. And in any case," he concluded, casually but articulating the words clearly, "we shall soon have some first-hand news of Monsieur David. Doña Lucía's mission in Paris has been completed. I am expecting Doña Lucía back in two weeks' time."

Goya saw Agustín's face change. So he had heard aright. He himself was not unmoved. Here she was coming back to Miguel as if nothing had happened, and he was receiving her as if nothing had happened. And what was to become of the Abbé? First she left the one and then the other. That's what they were like, the Cayetanas and Lucías.

And sure enough, two weeks later, Doña Lucía was in Madrid.

She invited her closest friends to a *tertulia*. The company was the same as on the evening when Manuel had seen Pepa for the first time; only the Abbé was missing.

Lucía was as unconcerned as if she had just returned from a short stay in the country. Goya observed her closely. His portrait of her was good. It was almost more true of the Lucía of today than of Lucía as she had been then. She sat there, rather enigmatic, strangely intriguing, disturbingly at ease. She was a lady without reproach, yet the atmosphere of adventure about her had become thicker than ever. There was something in common between him, Francisco, and this Lucía. Both of them belonged incontestably to those on top, but something lived on in them both of the depths from which they came.

Lucía told of Paris, but she did not mention what they were all so eager to hear, the fate of the Abbé. And her cool ladylike civility seemed to repel personal questions.

Later Lucía and Pepa sat together, close friends as before, with a mutual understanding which excluded others. One could see how they took a faint perverse pleasure in the men's inferiority. It was clear that if Lucía was going to tell anyone what had passed between her and the Abbé it would be Pepa.

Lucía spoke little to Francisco. She had not the habit of speaking very clearly, perhaps she found conversation with the deaf man too much of an effort. Perhaps, too, she felt he understood her better than the others did and was on her guard. He did not blame her.

He was agreeably surprised when after this she came frequently to see him in his *quinta*. She sat with him and Agustín in the studio. She continued to show little consideration for his deafness. She did not speak clearly, and when he did not understand something she did not trouble herself to write it down for him. But she obviously enjoyed his company and looked on while he worked.

Sometimes they both came, Lucía and Pepa. Then they would chat with each other or just sit there, silent and relaxed.

In spite of his love and admiration for Francisco, Agustín felt the old envious bitterness at the sight of these two beautiful women. Here this Francisco was, old and deaf, and the women still ran after him. They hadn't a glance to spare for *him*. Yet he knew more about painting than anyone else in Spain, and without him Goya would never have become Goya. At the same time Goya made it quite clear how little the two women meant to him. He was still thinking only of that high-born one who had plunged him into disaster. His portrait of the Duchess of Alba was the only one of his pictures he had kept. She looked down on the two other women and they accepted it.

When Agustín saw Lucía sitting thus beneath the picture of the Duchess he was unable to understand how anyone who could have a Lucía could be content with an Alba. No matter how much the latter disguised herself she would remain a ridiculous duchess; not even the artistry of a Goya had sufficed to turn her into a *maja*. Lucía, on the other hand, had genuinely become a great lady and had remained a *maja* at the same time. She was in very truth indifferent to the world's opinion of her. She went to Paris with her Abbé when she felt like it, and when the longing for Madrid came upon her, back she came with equal unconcern to her pedantic donkey of a husband.

Once when Lucía came to see them in the studio without Pepa she said unexpectedly, "I thought you were both friends of the Abbé. I think it rather unkind that you haven't once asked after him." She looked straight in front of her as she spoke, and it was not clear for whom the reproach was intended, Goya or Agustín. Goya went on painting, having clearly not been watching her lips. Agustín, dumbfounded, finally offered, "I will write down what you said for him, if you wish." "What are you two talking about?" Goya asked from his easel. "About the Abbé," Agustín replied very clearly. Goya stopped painting and looked attentively at Lucía.

"He's coming back soon," she told them composedly. Agustín sat down. Goya laid aside brushes and palette and began to walk up and down. "How have you managed it, Doña Lucía?" he asked. Lucía gave him a veiled, mocking look. "I wrote and told him he ought to come back," she said. "But the Inquisition!" shouted Agustín. "This will mean the stake for him!" And Goya too cried, "The Holy Office will never let this pass!" "Pepa and I have consulted Don Manuel," Lucía explained in her rather halting voice, "and he has spoken to the Grand Inquisitor. Of course the Abbé will have to put up with a certain amount of unpleasantness, but he is willing to do so. At least then he will be in Spain."

Doña Lucía spoke casually, without a trace of pride. Yet Francisco and Agustín were chilled by her words. They thought almost with abhorrence of the triumph which the woman must be feeling. For she had contrived the return of her lover by recourse to her husband's superior. And her lover was coming back ready to accept danger and sacrifice in order to breathe the same air as she did. Nor would the Grand Inquisitor Reynoso have exacted a modest price for denying himself the satisfaction of burning this arch heretic alive. The effects of the "conversations" which Don Manuel had had with Reynoso would no doubt be felt in many people's lives. Yet there the woman sat and spoke of it all, calmly, urbanely, casually, as if she were talking of a *tertulia* or a new hairdresser. Once again Francisco was forcibly reminded of the almond-seller in the Prado who long ago had cursed him up hill and down dale, giving him "*ajos y cebollas*," garlic and onions, reminded of that vulgar urchin Lucía with her fondness for impudent answers and rough jokes. Now she was having her joke with the First Minister, the Grand Inquisitor, the whole country.

Anyhow, or so it seemed, she
Had too early boasted of her
Triumph. Weeks and weeks went by, a
Month, and then another month and
Nothing all this time was heard of
The homecoming of Don Diego.

14

Goya was sitting at work in his studio on the Calle San Bernardino, in the *ermita.* He paused, pushed away his plate and graving tool, and looked down with a small absent smile at his dirty hands. He got up to go and wash them.

A man was standing in the room, might have been standing there for some time, a nuncio, one of the green-clad messengers of the Inquisition. The man bowed politely, said something which Goya did not understand, handed him a receipt, and indicated a sealed letter. Goya knew he must sign and did so mechanically but with great care; the man took the receipt, handed over the letter, bowed, said something to which Goya answered, "The blessed Virgin be praised," and withdrew.

Goya sat in his solitude which seemed to have grown deeper; he held the letter in his hand and stared unthinkingly at the seal, the cross, the sword, and the rod. The Inquisition had plenty of evidence against him, he knew. Cayetana, the witch, the destroyer, had permitted other eyes to look upon the picture he had painted, the picture of her nakedness; if Don Manuel knew about it, the Inquisition would also know. Many of his utterances could be construed as philosophisms by men of ill-will, and whispers had reached him which showed that the Grand Inquisitor looked with an unfavourable eye at him and his paintings. But he had supposed himself safe in the King's favour and his own reputation. And now he sat with the summons of the Holy Tribunal in his hand.

He breathed with difficulty, his chest constricted with panic. Now, just when he was re-emerging from the abyss of destruction, familiar with every eddy and whirlpool, he must not be sucked down again. Not till this past year had he learned what it was to live, to paint; had learned the meaning of art. It must not be that he should be snatched up by the terrible hands of the Inquisition.

He could not force himself to open the letter but continued to pursue his aimless reflections. They had waited so long, without daring to proceed against him; how was it that they had now struck, all of a sudden? He recalled how the two of them had sat together, Lucía and Pepa, as mischievous, dangerous, and seductive as the *majas* on the balcony. Perhaps he was included in the bargain which Lucía had struck over the Abbé's return. Since his experiences with Cayetana he was full of suspicion; one could believe anything of anyone.

He opened the letter.

The tribunal of the Inquisition in Tarragona invited him to attend an *auto particular* which was to pronounce judgment on the heretic Diego Perico, onetime abbé, onetime Secretary of the Holy Tribunal in Madrid.

For a moment Goya was relieved. Then anger overtook him that the Inquisition should have sent him this malicious summons. They were compelling him, a deaf man, who would not understand the sentence when it was read, to submit himself to the rigours of the long journey into farthest Aragón. It was arrantly presumptuous, and a sinister threat for that very reason.

Had he not been hampered by his infirmity Francisco would probably have confided his anxieties to Miguel or Agustín. As it was he was ashamed to do so. For so dangerous a matter could be referred to only in hints and vague allusions; he would not have understood the answers, and would feel foolish at having to ask to have them repeated. Should his friends, on the other hand, write down their answers for him, it would only bring the demons threateningly closer. More than once he asked himself whether he should confide in his son Javier. With him he would feel no shame. But Javier was too young.

So Goya carried his melancholy knowledge about with him unshared; tossed hither and thither by hopes and fears. For a time he felt sure the Grand Inquisitor would send the Abbé to the stake now that he had him in his power in spite of Don Manuel, and take him, Goya, into custody. Then again he told himself Manuel was astute enough, and Lucía as cunning as a snake, they must surely have obtained guarantees that the trial would be no more than a sombre farce and his own summons an empty threat.

Meanwhile the Inquisition itself, though traditionally committed to secrecy, spread rumours of the impending auto-da-fé, representing the Abbé's return as a glorious victory. God, they said, had awakened the heretic's conscience, so that he had returned to Spain of his own free will, to submit himself to the Holy Office.

When Agustín learned in this way of the impending auto-da-fé he was deeply moved. Although the Abbé's precious pedantry, his foppish, witty personality, were antipathetic to Agustín, and though he was wildly jealous that Lucía could have fallen in love with the fellow, he could not help admiring Don Diego for delivering himself into the jaws of the Inquisition for Lucía's sake. He was also honest and intelligent enough to acknowledge the Abbé's progressive opinions, so that the Inquisition's triumph over just this very man was galling to him.

Buffeted by the ambivalence of his feelings, he asked Goya, "Do you know that the Abbé has in fact come back? Have you heard anything about this auto-da-fé?" "Yes," grimly answered Goya, and showed the invitation from the Holy Tribunal.

It was a shock to Agustín, yet at the same time he felt proud. The spiritual judges were so afraid of this deaf, lonely man, considered his work so influential, that they found it necessary to send him this warning. But Agustín did not put these thoughts into words. Instead he took refuge, as Goya had done, in anger that so exacting a journey was expected of him. "It's monstrous," he railed, "that they should impose these hardships on you." Goya was glad that Agustín was taking the summons in this way. They both vented their rage not against the Inquisition, not against Lucía, but against the rigours of the journey.

"I will come with you, of course," Agustín said after a while. Goya had secretly been playing with the idea of asking Agustín to accompany him, but he would have found it hard to do so; for it took courage to escort a threatened man to the place where he was to receive his warning. But now that Agustín had offered of his own accord he murmured something of a refusal, then thanked him and accepted.

Since the government presumably had not agreed to an auto-da-fé in Madrid itself, the Grand Inquisitor had been deliberate in his choice of the city of Tarragona. The very name of the place called to every Spaniard's mind one of the Inquisition's greatest triumphs.

This had been in the year 1494. At that time plague was raging in Barcelona, and the Inquisitor of Barcelona, de Contreras, fled with his officials to Tarragona. The authorities appeared at the gates of the city and put it to the Inquisitor that if they permitted *him* to stay in the city, then officials of the *King* would ask to be exempted from the quarantine too. The Inquisitor replied that he might consider the matter for as long as it would take to say three "Misereres." If the gates were not then opened the city would be subjected to interdict and excommunication. He said three "Misereres" and then ordered the notary of the Holy Tribunal to knock three times at the gates. As they did not open he withdrew to the nearby Dominican monastery, wrote out the order of excommunication, and caused it to be nailed to the gates of the city of Tarragona. A week later Tarragona informed the Inquisitor that the city was now open to him. But now the offended prelate demanded that all officials and leading citizens must do solemn penance. The city was forced to comply. In the presence of the Viceroy of Catalonia, the civil authorities and most distinguished citizens had to appear in the Cathedral before the Inquisitor in penitential garb, candles in their hands, thus sustaining an irredeemable disgrace to themselves and their posterity.

It was to recall these events to the memories of all sinners that the Inquisition had selected the city of Tarragona for the Abbé's auto-da-fé.

After a long and troublesome journey Goya and Agustín reached Tarragona in good time. They put up at a simple *posada*, and Francisco called at the archiepiscopal palace, the Palacio del Patriarca. But he was received by a mere *vicarius*, who told him that the auto-da-fé would take place on the day after next in the council chamber of the archiepiscopal palace, adding dryly that it would surely be of use to the Señor First Painter to be present at the spectacle.

Francisco had never been in Tarragona. He and Agustín inspected the city; those huge ramparts, the Cyclopean walls, erected long before the time of the Romans, the innumerable Roman antiquities, and the cathedral, glorious, ages old, with its towers and cloisters, its Roman columns and the pagan sculptures which had artlessly been chiselled over into Christian ones. Goya enjoyed the little jokes which here and there some long-since perished sculptor had allowed himself. He stood for a long time chuckling at the story carved in stone of the cat who had shammed dead and let itself be borne to its grave by mice, only in order to fall upon them when a sufficient number had assembled. Probably at the time when the old artist had chiselled it into the stone the story had had some by no means harmless significance. Goya took out his notebook and drew his own version of the story of the cat.

He went with Agustín to the harbour, into the warehouses. Tarragona was famous far and wide for its wines, its nuts, its marzipan. Girls were sorting nuts in an enormous room, separating the good from the bad; they threw the bad under the table, the good into baskets on their laps. They worked with a rapid, mechanical dexterity, talking all the time, laughing, singing, even smoking. There must have been close on two hundred of them, the place buzzed with life; Goya forgot the auto-da-fé and drew.

Then on the day following he made his appearance in the council chamber of the Palacio del Patriarca. The room was large, up to date, and sober. Most of those invited appeared to be from Tarragona or the nearby capital of Catalonia, Barcelona. It seemed rather sinister that Francisco had been summoned thither from far-off Madrid; people looked at him with nervous curiosity, but no one addressed him.

The tribunal made its entry. The standards, the green cross, the dark robes of the spiritual judges, the wholly gloomy pomp contrasted strangely with the modern furnishings of the room and the soberly contemporary attire of the guests.

The Abbé was brought in. Goya had expected him to wear the yellow penitential shift, the sanbenito, but—and this must have been one of the concessions exacted by the government—Don Diego was wearing an ordinary suit of clothes, cut after the Parisian fashion, and he was obviously taking pains to give the appearance of being a calm, elegant gentleman. But when he was led up onto the defendant's platform and shut up inside the low wooden railing, his face began to twitch, it slacked, so that within the confines of his wooden fence and before the dread magnificence of the Holy Tribunal, the cynical man of the world in his everyday suit made an impression as wretched as though he had been stuck into a sanbenito.

The prior of the Dominicans began his address. Goya did not understand, made no effort to follow it: he looked. And although this tribunal involved a much lesser display of pomp and power than that other trial of Olavide in the Church of San Domingo el Real, it was no less sinister and oppressive. For no matter what bargain Lucía and Manuel had struck with the Grand Inquisitor, and whether Don Diego received a mild sentence or a severe one, here too—the Abbé's face made it all too plain—an individual was being destroyed. No one could recover from as terrible a humiliation as this man was now suffering, let him surround his heart with no matter how thick a crust of scepticism, courage, and reason. And even if he were set free after a lapse of years, he would bear the stain of being a condemned heretic and Spaniards would turn from him with loathing.

Meanwhile the reading of the sentence had begun. This time too it lasted long. With horrified fascination Goya looked on as the Abbé's features crumbled and collapsed, as the mask of worldly sophistication fell utterly away, revealing the degradation behind it, the animal despair and torment.

The Abbé had in his time watched the annihilation of Olavide in the Church of San Domingo and was now shut up in the pillory of the Palacio del Patriarca, while he, Goya, looked on: might not he too one day stand inside a wooden railing, face to face with just such a green cross and such candles, such a majestically menacing tribunal? Goya once again felt the demons creeping nearer, clawing at him. He could feel in his own flesh what was going on in the mind of the persecuted Abbé. There was no more thought of the beloved woman, no more thought of future happiness, of achievements past and to come, there was nothing but the boundless, eternal misery of the moment. In vain Goya told himself that what was taking place before his eyes was all a stupid make-believe, a grisly jest with a pre-arranged happy ending. He felt as he had felt when he was a boy and had doubted the reality of El Coco, the bogey-man, Black Peter, and had been oppressed with fear when he came.

And now the Abbé recanted. To see the man in his elegant modern clothes kneeling in front of the black-draped cross with his hand on the open Bible was more horrifying than had been the spectacle of the penitent Olavide in his sanbenito. The priest recited and the Abbé repeated the shocking, degrading formulas.

Before Goya was aware of it the religious transaction was at an end, the criminal was led away, the guests dispersed. Goya was left ominously alone. Staggering a little, unsure of himself in his deafness, and strangely benumbed, he left the twilight gloom of the chamber.

Agustín was sitting in the *posada;* contrary to his custom, there was a bottle of wine in front of him. He asked what sentence had been passed on the Abbé. Goya did not know, he had not understood. But the landlord was able to tell them that Don Diego had been condemned to three years' confinement in a monastery. It seemed the landlord was secretly a liberal, full of reverence for the Señor First Painter; he waited on them assiduously, but with a strange diffidence, almost with pity. He told them of a particularly excellent wine, thirteen years old, of which he had only seven bottles left, for himself and especially respected guests; he produced one of the bottles. Goya and Agustín drank in silence.

On the return journey they were still rather silent. Only once did Goya let himself go, unexpectedly, saying with a sort of grim satisfaction, "Now you can see where it gets you if you go in for politics. Had I done what you all wanted me to do, I would have rotted long since in the dungeons of the Holy Office."

Yet within his heart he thought and
Planned. For now, precisely now the
Holy Office will he paint, will
Draw it, in the quiet of the
Ermita, his study, draw it
As it truly is, the priesties,
The *frailucos*, fat and greedy,
Looking on, the while their sinner
In the snare tormented wriggles.
Also the garrotted man once
More he'll draw, more true than ever,
Likewise draw the Coco-spectre,
Nightmare, scarecrow, black man, creature,
Who does not exist at all—and
Yet he does.

15

When he reached Madrid his son Javier told him that the Duchess of Alba had been inquiring after him. She was once more living in her Palacete Buenavista in Moncloa; indeed, Goya's new house, the *quinta,* was very near this small country seat. Francisco did not know whether Javier was informed of his relationship to Cayetana, or to what extent. He controlled himself, swallowed, and said as lightly as he could, "Thank you, my boy."

He had believed that Cayetana's uncanny dominion over him was broken; only images remained, dreams good and bad, but always held in leash by reason. And this had indeed been so as long as she had been in Italy, with the sea to divide them. But now that a short walk could bring him to her, the leash which had held his dreams in check was broken.

He did not go to Cayetana. He sat helpless, wretched with longing, imprisoned in the glass dome of his silence.

Suddenly Doña Eufemia stood before him. She stood there, black and dignified, quite unchanged, full of polite hatred, age-old in spite of her ageless appearance. "May the Virgin protect Your Excellency," she said. "You don't exactly make it easy for anyone to bring you a message," and she looked round disapprovingly at the poorly furnished, untidy studio. He could not tell if he had understood her, he was too excited. "You will have to write down anything you have to say to me, Doña Eufemia," he replied hoarsely. "My hearing is much worse than it used to be. I am stone deaf, as you might say." Doña Eufemia wrote down her message, and while she wrote she remarked, "I always told you, Señor First Painter, that no good could come of painting such devilish things." He made no reply. He read the message attentively. He said that he would expect Doña Cayetana the following evening at half-past seven. "Here, in my studio in the Calle San Bernardino," he added very loudly.

He dressed himself for the evening with special care, and

despised himself as he did so. He looked absurd in his elegant clothes, in this studio which was as shabbily and wretchedly furnished as in the time of his poverty, a place only for working and experiments. Why had he chosen it for his meeting with Cayetana? It was a foolish, puerile gesture of defiance. He had known it as such himself, Doña Eufemia's expression had confirmed it, and yet he had persisted. Would she even come? Did she know, could she have realized, how much he was changed? Wouldn't the dueña let her know that he had turned into a morose, deaf old man living in a spider's web of owlish dreams?

It was half-past seven, and then ten minutes after. Cayetana did not come. He began to reflect what her life must have been like in the interval, always under silent pressure from the hopelessly enamoured Peral, or with Italian gallants who were even more frivolous than their Spanish counterparts. He ran to the door and looked out; perhaps she stood there and knocked, forgetting that he could not hear, wrapped up in herself as usual. He left the door a little open, so that light could escape. It was eight o'clock, she was not there, and now she certainly wasn't coming.

At five minutes past eight she came, late as always. She took off her veil in silence and stood before him utterly unchanged, the pure oval of her face wonderfully luminous above her small, slender, black-clothed form. They stood and looked at each other, and it was like the time that he had seen her on her estrade, and as if their great quarrel had never been.

In the days, weeks, months that followed everything was as it had been before. Perhaps they talked less, but then, had they not always communicated better by looks and actions? Words had never caused anything but trouble. Moreover, he could understand her more easily than anyone else, he could read everything from her lips, and it seemed to him that his memory had retained her hard, childish voice better than any other; he could at any time recall to his inward ear the exact sound of those last words she had spoken to him, not knowing that he could hear her.

They went to the theatre together although he no longer could do more than look at the music and dialogue; they visited the taverns of the Manolería and they were as welcome there as ever. *El Sordo*, the deaf man, that was his name everywhere. But he didn't pester one with dreary expatiations on his disability, he laughed with everyone else when he was responsible for some amusing misunderstanding, and anyhow he must be a splendid fellow or the Duchess of Alba wouldn't stick to him as she did.

His memories were not dead, he knew all about Cayetana's treacherous depths, but the dreams were once more safely on the leash. He enjoyed being in the light of day all the more for having recently been forced down into the suffocating abyss. His enjoyment of her had never been more rapturous, and she reciprocated his ecstasies.

He no longer felt any desire to paint her, nor did she ask him to. His big portraits of her were false, they gave only the surface, but he knew what lay beneath, he had seen it, and in his loneliness and misery he had painted and drawn it; that had been the truth, and it had been his medicine, his salvation. She had wronged him as bitterly as one human being can wrong another, full of artless cunning and vicious innocence, but she had thereby afforded him something that was more than a cure, something that had left him stronger than he had been before.

Goya painted a number of portraits at this time; with a light hand, not exactly scamping them but doing them as he had known how to do them years ago, and both he and Agustín were aware that by now he was capable of something better. He painted several lovely women, with a sort of gay sensuousness which enhanced their beauty. He painted gentlemen of the Court or the military or rich burghers, and made them appear more significant without suppressing their weaknesses. His portraits brought him fresh fame and fresh money, and the Court and city were convinced Europe had no greater painter than the deaf man, Francisco Goya.

He continued to spoil his son Javier. Took a passionate interest in everything the young man did. Sent him to Ramón Bayeu's school lest he acquire mannerisms from his father's tuition. He took Javier's art criticisms seriously; often when Cayetana visited him in his bare, spacious house, the *quinta,* he invited Javier to be present. These were great occasions for the boy. She treated him half as a boy, half as a young cavalier. Kindly, imperceptibly, she taught him what to do and what not to do. Subdued his tendency to exaggeration in dress. Brought him presents, trinkets, gloves, a ring, and trained him to replace the gaudily magnificent objects which he loved to wear and have about him with things of purer taste. He enjoyed to the full the advantages of being admitted to the circle of the first lady in the kingdom. And the Duchess of Alba's openly displayed relationship with his father he took as confirmation of the latter's supreme importance as an artist.

About this time the ship-owner Sebastián Martínez arrived in Madrid from Cádiz and paid Goya a visit. They conversed in writing; Goya observed with fascination the speed with which long, involved sentences grew under the great merchant's agile fingers, and he almost regretted not having given more care to his own rendering of these hands.

Finally Señor Martínez wrote out: "They say it wasn't only pictures for the Santa Cueva that you painted while you were in Cádiz, and San Lúcar. There's talk of a Venus. Would it be presumptuous of me to ask you to make me a copy of this Venus?" He tittered as he wrote, then he showed Goya what he had written. "You are presumptuous, Señor," Goya answered. Swiftly Señor Martínez wrote once more: "I'll give you fifty thousand for a copy." He underlined the word "copy" and held the paper up to Goya, but before the latter could answer he withdrew it and added deftly, "Am I still presumptuous?" "You are presumptuous, Señor," Goya repeated. "A hundred thousand," Martínez wrote, making the zeros very large, the one even bigger, and swiftly appended, "Still presumptuous?" "Yes," Goya said simply. Señor Martínez shrugged his shoulders sadly and remarked, not in writing this time, but speaking articulately, "You are hard to please, Excellency."

Señor Martínez waited upon the Duchess of Alba. She invited him to a party. The evening was a long one. They danced the *desmayo*, the dance of swoons and langours, in which first the man, then the woman, their eyes closed, fall upon their partner's bosom, limp with abandon. Later they also did the *marcha China*. In this Chinese march the men first crawl across the room on all fours while the women form a "Chinese wall." Standing in a row, the women bend forward till their hands touch the floor and the men crawl through the row of women's arms; then the women through the men's arms.

Cayetana took part in both dances; she danced the desmayo with the Marqués de San Adrián, the *marcha China* with Señor Martínez. Francisco watched the distasteful spectacle, and was reminded of his drawing of the *aquelarre*, the witches' Sabbath in which he had depicted an enormous goat squatting upright on his haunches and giving his blessing to the dancing troop of witches; the radiant leader of the troop is Cayetana.

Yet the melancholy distaste which filled Francisco was far from being the senseless rage which he had felt at Cayetana's fandango. Now, while he watched Cayetana, San Adrián, Martínez, and their other friends crawling around the floor in this absurd and vulgar way, he realized more deeply than by mere reason, he felt with his whole being, all the contradictory qualities which can exist at once in a single person and do exist in us all. This woman, he knew for he had experienced it, could surrender herself wholly, be tenderly, passionately selfless, as no other. She could say "I love only you" in a voice that melted one, which could penetrate his bell of silence, yet here she was crawling about on the floor, undignified, playfully bawdy, with a laugh the lascivious shrillness of which was so palpable that it pierced his deafness. But that was how she was. So was everyone. So he was himself. He ascended into the purest Heaven and plunged down into the abyss of filth. He could be utterly enraptured by a magical interplay of colour, then cast his brushes aside, go away without even washing them, and throw himself, hot with lust, on some woman. That is how human beings are made. They eat *olla podrida,* wax enthusiastic over Velázquez, pride themselves on their own work, wallow in dirty beds with some creature they buy for five reals, draw pictures of demons, and consider whether they can squeeze a thousand reals more out of so-and-so for the portrait.

He left the party and went back through the night to his *ermita.*

Here in the uncanny stillness he had it all out yet once more between himself and Cayetana de Alba, knowing she was the only woman he had ever loved or ever would love.

The uncertain light of the candles flung itself first at one part of the room, then another, and in these dancing shadows, as they spread and shrank, he saw the faces of the Duchess of Alba. All the evil faces of her he saw again anew, scornfully grinning, witchlike, corrupting; but he saw others too, surrendering to love, dissolving in passion. "Do not forget! Do not forget the others!" he commanded himself.

He strove to be fair to her. Mightn't she have her demons too? And even joy in these demons? Would he himself care to live without his demons? Life would be boring without them; one would become like Miguel. He, Francisco, had his demons on the leash, he could draw his own evil and debasement. But Cayetana had not got hers on a leash, she could not even describe her dead maid Brígida, let alone set her down on paper. So that what was evil and discordant in her found vent in words and deeds, in following her dead Brígida's whispered behests. That was why she had to dance the *desmayo* and the *marcha China*. She was now Cayetana, now Brígida.

He shut his eyes and saw her, Cayetana and Brígida in one person. Then he drew her, the ultimate truth about her, and about himself. He drew the dream, the lies, the inconstancy.

There she lay in her loveliness, and he gave her, this one woman, two faces. One is turned towards a man who is embracing her with complete self-oblivion, and the man unmistakably bears his, Francisco's, features.

Still, the other face, so lovely
This one too, yet domineering,
Looked with hard bold eyes aside and
Ogled other men. The two-faced
Woman had one hand surrendered
Gladly, wholly, to her lover;
Yet the other hand received the
Message of a likewise two-faced
Brígida, a second, fat one,
Who with a grimace and gesture
Laid her finger to her lips. And
Round about the lying figure
Crawled and coiled and wreathed and wound a
Leering breed of toads and vipers,
Even grinning wide a demon.
While remotely in the distance
Light and airy, inaccessible,
Gleamed high up a castle, builded
Of the dreams, at least it seemed so,
Dreamed by the besotted fool, the
Lover.

16

In the valley of the Manzanares, in the region of the Casa del Campo where the King was wont to hunt, in the Florida, there was a little church dedicated to Saint Anthony of Padua. It lay in the King's path when, returning from the hunt, he wished to perform his evening devotions. It had fallen into disrepair, and Don Carlos, who was fond of building, had entrusted the architect Ventura Rodríguez with the work of restoring it. Goya was to paint it.

He was pleased with the commission. The fact that the King, devout as he was, should entrust him with the decoration of his favourite church so soon after that ominous invitation to the auto-da-fé would serve as a useful shield against further attacks on the part of the Grand Inquisitor. On the other hand, he always felt rather uncomfortable when asked to paint religious subjects. "Of course," he told Cayetana, "a man who knows his job can paint everything. But I must admit I'm not very good at painting saints. I'm excellent at depicting the devil, I've seen him often enough, but I've seldom seen the saints."

He was to illustrate one of Saint Anthony's chief miracles. An innocent man was accused of murder and the Saint restored the murdered man to life so that he could bear witness to the accused man's innocence.

Francisco had just found his way back to happiness and gaiety after a period of sorrow and affliction, so that the portrayal of violence and the sublime did not attract him. But he hit upon a way out.

Fair and square in the vaulting of the cupola he painted the miracle. There stands Saint Anthony in his Franciscan habit, a haggard figure against the grey sky; he leans forward with urgent gestures, and the decaying corpse rises terrifyingly from its rigidity while the innocent man devoutly and joyously stretches out his arms. But this miracle was being performed in the presence of a considerable audience, and while the Saint, the corpse, and the innocent man were requisites, Goya put all he had into the crowd of onlookers. Into it he painted all his new-found mood of happiness, wisdom, and experienced youth.

The people he painted are no contemporaries of Saint Anthony but rather Madrileños of his own environment, genuine Madrileños, many probably from the Manolería. Nor does the miracle seem to have provoked feelings of piety in them; in fact they appear to be observing it more as if it were a glorious bullfight or an *auto sacramental* of the first order. They are leaning, these spectators, comfortably against a balcony which is splendidly draped with a *mantón;* one or two urchins are actually climbing about on and bestriding the railing. They are talking among themselves, these Madrileños, drawing one another's attention to what is happening. Some of them are excited and are looking on professionally to see if the putrefying corpse is really going to come to life, others seem relatively uninterested, they make eyes, tell each other stories not necessarily connected with the miracle. Nobody cares anything about the innocent man.

In the arches over the door and leading into the dome and in the tympana he painted angels and cherubs. The angels are noticeably pretty and feminine, with voluptuous expressions; they are very much clothed, in conformity with the laws of the Inquisition, but at pains not to hide their physical charms under a bushel. Goya painted these angels with the utmost gusto. Apart from their wings there is nothing angelic about them; he gave them those anonymous yet entirely identifiable faces which only he knew how to paint, faces of women well known to him and others.

While he was painting the Ermita de San Antonio, Goya changed back into the carefree, irrepressible Goya of his first years at Court, when he had thrown himself whole-heartedly into the life of frivolity around him. His deafness was no more than a minor annoyance, he was once again the *majo* disguised as courtier, boisterous, colourful, full of swaggering vitality. A last gleam from his happy, heedless past shone upon him. The frescoes in the Ermita turned out to be new gobelins, but painted by one who knew far more than before about colour, light, and rhythm.

The little church was near Goya's *quinta*, and near the Palacete Buenavista. Cayetana often came over from her country seat to watch him at work. Javier also came often, Agustín was there almost all the time, and other friends of Goya came too, grandees as well as men and women from the taverns of the Manolería. Goya worked with great facility. They were all delighted to see the youthful agility with which he clambered about on the scaffolding and even lay on his back to paint. It was amazing to watch this animated, variegated throng growing out of nothing, these sprightly buxom cherubs and seductive angels.

Two days after Goya had announced that the work was finished the King inspected his new church on the way back from the hunt with his retinue.

The ladies and gentlemen in their hunting attire stood there in the little church, which was not particularly well lit but was lent light and gaiety by the typically Goyesque bustling gaiety of these winged and wingless Madrileños. The grandees and their ladies were somewhat surprised at the highly secular treatment which the sacred theme had received. But had not other masters, admittedly foreigners, sometimes given a very vivid and cheerful interpretation to sublime events? They themselves, these elegant onlookers, had had many anxieties in recent months; they were pleased that this deaf, ageing man should profess his love of life with such *élan*. It was pleasant to take a leap back to the years when they had been able to conduct themselves like these angels and this happy crowd.

Such were their thoughts, and they would gladly have expressed their approval. But they awaited their monarch's judgment in silence. They had a long time to wait, and no sound was heard, save, through the open door of the church, the murmur of an assembling crowd and the neighing and stamping of the horses.

Carlos was taking his time. He wasn't quite sure what to make of these paintings. He was no spoil-sport, he loved a joke as well as the next man; nor did he wish to make his prayers and piety too dismal; in principle he had nothing against bright, happy faces and raiment in the illustration of sacred events; had he not himself directed that his church should be cheerful? But weren't the pictures his First Painter had painted a little bit too profane and frivolous? The angels were so very unangelic. "That one there with the folded wings, surely I know her," he said suddenly. "Why, it's Pepa, to be sure! And that one there is Rafaela, the girl who had an affair with Arcos and then was kept by the younger Colomero and now appears so often in police reports. My dear Don Francisco, I don't approve of angels like these. Of course I know, art ennobles. But it seems to me you haven't ennobled Rafaela quite as much as was necessary." The King's loud voice filled the little church, sounding to them all like thunder, all except Francisco, for he had not heard. He handed his notebook to the King. "I humbly ask your pardon, Sire," he said, "but would you be pleased to write down your exalted words of appreciation for me?"

Doña María Luisa intervened. Of course it was true the angel with the folded wings was that creature Pepa; the other one with spread wings did call to mind the notorious Rafaela, and Goya might very well have taken other models. But after all they weren't portraits, they were only resemblances, and one could discern as many resemblances as one wished among the terrestrial and celestial creatures of the frescoes, that was Goya's way, and actually it was a pity he hadn't included her, María Luisa. At least he had put Pepa next to that whore Rafaela. Furthermore, the paintings on the ceiling reminded María Luisa of a similar painting by Correggio in Parma, and she was always glad to be reminded of her beloved Parma. "Another of your masterpieces, Don Francisco," she said very distinctly. "Of course, your angels and some of your men and women are conducting themselves rather too boisterously, there I can only agree with the King, but I daresay the angels and the crowd are carried away by the sight of the miracle."

Since María Luisa approved the work Don Carlos was mollified at once. He patted Goya kindly on the shoulder. "It must have been a strain," he observed, "climbing about up there all the time and painting. But then we all know you have marrow in your bones." And now everybody, grandees and priests, fell to praising Francisco's work.

Meanwhile people from the Manzanares valley had gathered outside to watch the departure of the King and his retinue. They greeted the King and cheered him. Goya was among the last to leave the church; many people recognized him, and his appearance caused a renewed outburst of loud cheering. Goya saw that they were acclaiming him; he knew himself to be a popular figure in his own Madrid, he realized that these last cheers were directed at him. He was in gala dress, carrying his three-cornered hat under his arm. He put it on his head and took it off again, to acknowledge their greetings in the customary way, and observed that the crowds redoubled their shouts.

His carriage drove up and he asked his servant Andreo what it was that the people were saying. Andreo, who had become less sulky and more attentive since the onset of Goya's deafness, did his best to articulate the words with particular clarity. They were calling out, "Long live Saint Anthony! Long live the blessed Virgin and all Her heavenly Court. Long live Francisco Goya, Court Painter to the Saint."

In the days that followed all Madrid drove out to the Florida to inspect Goya's frescoes. A shower of praise descended on him. Men wrote and spoke ecstatically of Goya's new creation. "There are two miracles to be seen in the Florida," wrote the art critic Yriarte, "the one by Saint Anthony, the other by Francisco Goya."

But Grand Inquisitor Reynoso highly disapproved of Goya's work. They had summoned the heretic to Tarragona, and here he was, more barefaced than ever. "When he paints the saints," grumbled the Cardinal Inquisitor, "he paints the seven deadly sins as well and makes them more attractive than the virtues." He would really have liked to arrest the malefactor and close the church. But this Goya was a cunning fellow. There was no nakedness to be seen, no indecency that one could put one's finger on, and unfortunately the King was as blind as the crowd to subtleties of vice and impiety.

Yes, the people of Madrid delighted in the frescoes. The *majos* from the taverns, Goya's friends, the peasants and washerwomen of the Manzanares valley, had been among the first to see them, they had spread the report of them far and wide, and now the people of Madrid flocked to look at the miracle of their best-loved saint. They could identify themselves with the figures on the balcony; just so would they themselves have behaved had they been witnesses to the miracle. That was how they liked their religion, vital, exciting, spectacular; when they saw the great processions and autos-da-fé, they felt just as the figures on the balcony were feeling. They were completely at one with the merry, colourful throng with which the painter had filled the church. He had painted *them,* and they were grateful for it.

A few days later, about noon, when the Florida was empty of visitors by reason of the heat, Goya went to inspect the completed frescoes undisturbed. He posted himself in a dark corner; from here he had the best view of the part of the painting he wished to contemplate.

An old woman came into the church without noticing him. She inspected the frescoes, tipping her head right back to see the miracle in the dome, nodded approvingly, shuffled about full of joyful devotion, looked here, looked there. Finally she came back into the center and bowed deeply on all sides. The Saint was over her head, so that it cannot have been he, but rather the jolly angels and the common folk in the audience, to whom she was paying her respects.

Goya was amazed. He asked her,
"What is it you're doing, Mother,
And why do you do it?" But of
Course he could not estimate the
Volume of his voice, it boomed like
Thunder through the church and deeply
Startled the old soul, and looking
Round she saw the stranger. Goya,
Smiling, asked her once more, "What is
That you're doing, Mother, and why
Should you curtsy to that painted
Crew up there?" She answered gravely,
And he read her answer from her
Lips: "When you see something lovely,
Then of course you have to make a
Bow to it."

-- 17 --

As long as the Directory had been at the helm in Paris the Spanish government had always been able to put off a settlement of the tiresome Portuguese question. But now Napoleon Bonaparte was First Consul and he was not the man to accept excuses and fair words. He tersely requested that the Infante Manuel should force Portugal, by means of a stated ultimatum, to break off relations with Great Britain; should Portugal refuse, then an army of the allies, Spanish and French troops, was to take Lisbon. To reinforce his demand Napoleon had a detachment of French under the command of General Leclerc march up to the Spanish border, and gave Leclerc orders to place himself and his troops, within ten days, *and on Spanish soil*, at King Carlos's disposal, for his support in the Portuguese undertaking, whatever might or might not have been decided in the meantime at Aranjuez.

To a disgruntled, complaining Manuel there appeared Ambassador Lucien Bonaparte. He could well understand, he explained, that it might not come easy to Their Catholic Majesties to proceed against their relatives of the royal house of Portugal. But he had a plan to lay before the First Minister, admittedly for the moment a mere figment of his own imagination, of which, however, his brother Napoleon was informed and which might make easier for the Queen the harsh decision to take military action against her daughter in Lisbon. The fact was that the First Consul could not look for an heir from his consort, Josephine, and intended shortly to have a divorce in order to contract a new marriage. He, Lucien, had been enraptured by the charms of the Infanta Isabel, who though, of course, scarcely more than a child, would nonetheless soon be ripe for betrothal; he had given his brother the First Consul a hint to this effect, and Napoleon had received it with great interest.

Doña María Luisa's youngest daughter was one of his, Manuel's, children, as the resemblance plainly showed, and for a moment he was overcome with joy that such an elevation was considered for a daughter of his. But immediately he told himself that Lucien was probably talking the purest humbug. As always, he was glad to be able to save his face. Under the circumstances, he answered formally, he felt able before God and his own conscience to take the responsibility of the desired ultimatum to Portugal; and he would recommend to the Catholic King the course of action proposed by the First Consul.

In veiled terms the two gentlemen then struck a bargain on how they should divide between themselves the personal commission on the indemnity to be demanded of Portugal.

General Bonaparte's proposals made an impression on Doña María Luisa. Of course it went rather against the grain to hurt the feelings of her good-natured, tractable daughter Carlota, now on the throne of Portugal, by making war on her. But on a former occasion Napoleon had been as good as his word; he had made her daughter María Luisa Queen of Etruria. It was entirely possible that he was ready to ally himself by marriage to the house of Bourbon, carry her daughter Isabel off to Versailles, and reign with her there. Then there would once more be Bourbons on all the thrones of Europe.

She urged Don Carlos to submit to the inevitable. With a heavy heart he summoned Lucien Bonaparte and told him he would send the ultimatum to Portugal. "Now you can see, my dear Ambassador," he said with tears in his eyes, "the heartbreak that can go with the wearing of a crown. If I know my dear son-in-law at all he will refuse to yield, and then I will have to send an army against my own daughter who hasn't done me any harm and indeed has no idea what all this is about."

The Prince-Regent of Portugal did in fact reject the ultimatum, and a Spanish army marched into Portugal with Don Manuel at its head. This took place on the 16th of May.

On the 30th, defenseless Portugal was already suing for peace. The negotiations were conducted at Badajoz on the Portuguese frontier, Manuel's birthplace. Agreement was reached with surprising speed. Manuel, who had received rich gifts from Portugal, granted the defeated enemy generous terms. Lucien Bonaparte, also in receipt of a commission and sumptuous presents, appended his signature to the treaty in the name of France.

Once again the Príncipe de la Paz had distinguished himself and in spite of glorious military successes had allowed his conquered foe a magnanimous peace. The "Peace of Badajoz" was celebrated in both countries. A decree of the King approved a triumphal entry into Madrid for the victorious Infante Manuel.

But Napoleon, who had just decisively defeated the Austrians at Marengo, declared in a sharp note that Ambassador Lucien had exceeded his powers; he, the First Consul, had no intention of recognizing this absurd Peace of Badajoz and regarded himself as still at war with Portugal. To avoid further misunderstanding he sent a second detachment of French "auxiliaries" into Spain.

Manuel's vision was obscured by the clouds of incense his country was showering on him. In a note no less firm than Napoleon's, he requested that the French government immediately withdraw its troops from Spain as they were now superfluous; till then he would not even discuss a revision of the "Peace of Badajoz." Napoleon replied he could only interpret Manuel's arrogant words to mean that Their Catholic Majesties were weary of the troublesome business of sitting on thrones and were longing to share the fate of the other Bourbons.

Manuel had concealed from the people of Spain, and even from the royal pair, the fact that the First Consul had raised objections to the Peace of Badajoz, and Court and people continued to hail him with salvo and fanfare. And he, more and more dazzled by their acclamations, proceeded to return Napoleon's effrontery in kind. He drafted a dignified reply which the Spanish envoy in Paris, Azara, was to hand to General Bonaparte in Manuel's name in a personal interview. In this reply Don Manuel drew the upstart's attention to the fact that Almighty God, and no First Consul, determined the destiny of states, and suggested that a young ruler just in the saddle might more easily lose command than an anointed majesty whose forebears had worn crowns for a thousand years before him.

When Miguel scanned the draft of this reply he felt uneasy. To send such a note to Napoleon, victorious as he was on every front, bordered on madness. The secretary put it to Manuel that the First Consul would answer a communication of this nature with military measures against Madrid. The Minister gave Miguel a dark look, but the mists had been dispersed; he knew Napoleon was not a man to stand upon trifles. Sulkily he said, "Then I have concocted the whole speech for nothing?" Miguel proposed that Don Manuel's fine, dignified reply be sent to Paris but with instructions that Ambassador Azara should hand it over only in the last resort. Manuel reluctantly assented.

Meanwhile, however, Napoleon's final terms for the conclusion of peace with Portugal had arrived in Madrid. And hard terms they were. Portugal was to surrender her colony of Guiana, to sign a trade agreement most advantageous to France, to pay an indemnity of a hundred million, and, it went without saying, to break off relations with England. To ensure that these conditions were adhered to, a French army was to remain on Spanish soil till the conclusion of a peace with England. The one concession the First Consul made to his Spanish allies was that this treaty too should be concluded in Badajoz.

Don Manuel in reply was peevish and refractory. Whereupon Napoleon instructed his brother Lucien not to waste time on further dealings with Manuel and sent a note which he was to convey to Doña María Luisa without notifying Manuel. The First Consul's command was couched in such unequivocally severe terms that Lucien had to submit. Napoleon Bonaparte's personal message to the Queen ran: "In recent months Your Majesty's First Minister has addressed a series of offensive notes to my government and has spoken insolently against me over and above that. I have had enough of this foolish and unseemly behaviour. I beg Your Majesty to bear in mind that if I receive one more such note I will cause the lightning to strike."

Aghast, María Luisa at once summoned Manuel to her. "There's your friend Bonaparte for you!" she said and threw the letter at him. She watched him as he read it. Usually so sure of himself, his plump face was disturbed, his stout body slackened. "Your advice, if you please, Sir Minister!" she said contemptuously. "I am afraid," he answered dejectedly, "that if Bonaparte is to ratify the Peace of Badajoz your Carlota will have to give up Guiana." "And the hundred million," María Luisa added angrily.

So there was a second treaty
Of the Peace of Badajoz and
This time signed by the First Consul.
But this Peace had naught in common
With that famous earlier Peace of
Badajoz except the name.

But
Little was communicated
To the Spanish of the terms, and
So they went on feasting Manuel.
And the soldiers of the Frenchman
Still remained upon the soil of
Spain—and still remained at Spanish
Cost.

18

Goya, in Aranjuez, was at work on a portrait of Don Manuel.

For all the loud acclaim, many had perceived the rottenness of the Peace of Badajoz, the astute Francisco certainly among them, and Manuel, who felt there was a bond between them, was anxious to win him to his side. He loaded him with delicate small attentions, took his meals with him, drove out with him.

Sometimes he employed sign language, more often he simply talked away, frequently so rapidly and indistinctly that Goya could understand but little. Francisco would ask himself if Manuel really wanted to be understood. Obviously he was under pressure to unburden himself, but felt it wiser to do so to a listener whose receptive capacity was impaired. For Manuel uttered a number of dangerous things. Spoke his mind bitterly and extravagantly on the subject of the First Consul and was not sparing of ironical references to Doña María Luisa and the King, our lord.

Don Manuel had ordered Goya to make an important portrait of him, with the insignia of the Generalissimo; he had in mind something like David's painting of General Bonaparte's crossing of the Alps. Goya had therefore reproduced Don Manuel on the battlefield in glittering uniform, resting on a grassy bank after a successful engagement, a dispatch in his hand.

During the sittings a comfortable sofa did duty for the grassy bank. Upon it lolled the Infante, talking away. Goya no longer felt indulgent towards his powerful patron; he recognized that not only his face and figure, but also his soul, had run to fat. He thought of the callous indifference with which Manuel had wrecked the life of the Infanta Doña Teresa, thought of the underhanded revenge he had taken on his opponent Urquijo because the latter had shown himself the better man. For the former First Minister was being held in a damp, dark cell in the fortress of Pamplona, receiving insufficient food and denied the use of pen and paper. Thinking of all this, Goya indeed painted all the brilliance of the Generalissimo, but his indolence also, his fatty degeneration, his blasé, peevish arrogance. " 'The higher the monkey climbs the more he shows his rump,' " he told himself in the words of the old saying.

Sometimes Pepa was present at the sittings. She felt at home in Aranjuez, she was one of the Queen's ladies-in-waiting, her relations with her were good, better still with Carlos. There was scarcely a peak left for her to climb; all around her was blue sky. For Goya to have painted her as an angel in the Florida seemed to her to be confirmation of the place she still occupied in his heart.

When the picture was finished she and Manuel came to inspect it.

There sat Don Manuel, leaning back against his little hillock, in full military fig; he glittered with gold, the Order of Christ flashed from his sword belt. To his left a captured Portuguese flag fluttered limply; horses and soldiery moved like shadows in the background. A small figure behind Manuel, stood his adjutant, the Conde Tepa. Thus under a sombre leaden sky sat the commander-in-chief, obviously weary of his victories, reading his dispatch with a faint expression of boredom; very much to the fore were the fleshy, well-groomed hands.

"The pose is so unnatural," Pepa pronounced. "However, it's very like him otherwise. You really have got a little fat, Infante." Manuel did not take her up. The painting was the picture of a man and his triumph. Only a man who had power could sit like that, dress like that, look like that. "An excellent picture," he applauded, "a real Goya. What a pity I haven't got time to sit for a second picture, my friend and painter. But alas!" he sighed, "government business takes up my whole day."

And in fact he did have a great deal to do. Since he was prevented by General Bonaparte from demonstrating his power to Europe, he wanted to let the Spaniards feel it. Wanted to show them that a man different from Urquijo was now at the helm, a man who wouldn't have the godless French interfering in his policies. The result was that Don Manuel governed in opposition to the liberals and drew ever closer to the reactionary nobility and the ultramontane clergy.

In his unobtrusive way Miguel Bermúdez did his best to mitigate these tendencies, warned him with blandishments and mild, subtle arguments. But Manuel would not listen; actually gave him to understand that his advice was uncalled for. Manuel's relationship to Miguel had undergone a change. He had been forced to seek Miguel's help in embarrassing circumstances and did not wish to be reminded of it. The fact that his secretary had conducted himself in such an unmanly way in the affair of Lucía gave the Infante an excuse to forget all he owed him.

For all his equanimity it was a blow to Miguel that Manuel was slipping away from him. He already had enough anxiety and disquiet in his life without that. Instead of affording him the tranquillity he had expected, Lucía's return had brought nothing but fresh confusion. Now she was even weaving intrigues with Manuel from which he was excluded and of which she must know he would disapprove. The lenient sentence on the Abbé was unquestionably to be attributed to dubious bargaining between Manuel and the Grand Inquisitor; unquestionably Lucía and Pepa were behind the whole affair.

Miguel saw himself further and further dislodged from his intimacy with Don Manuel. Against his advice Manuel proceeded more and more oppressively against the liberals and he was now drawing off to deal his heaviest blow.

The fact was that Grand Inquisitor Reynoso had demanded only one thing in return for the merciful treatment of the Abbé Diego Perico: the expulsion of the arch heretic and rebel, Gaspar Jovellanos. Manuel had been reluctant to proceed against a man for whose pardon and promotion he himself was responsible. But in his heart of hearts he was glad to be rid of the sour moralist the very sight of whom was a reproach. So after a certain amount of havering and haggling he had agreed to the Grand Inquisitor's terms. And now the time seemed to have come for him to carry out his part of the bargain.

A convenient pretext soon offered itself. Jovellanos had published a daring new book, and the Holy Office had demanded in a stern communication that the government should ban the godless and seditious work immediately and call the author to account. "He'll never learn, this Don Gaspar of yours," Don Manuel said to Miguel with a sigh. "This time I'm afraid I shall have to take action against him." "You're surely not going to allow the book to be banned?" asked Miguel. "Let me draft a reply to Reynoso," he begged, "something soothing and reassuring." "I'm afraid we won't get away with that this time," Manuel said and looked full at Miguel, bright-eyed but obviously with some mischief up his sleeve. "You're really thinking of reprimanding Jovellanos, are you?" asked Miguel, now seriously alarmed. He was unable to maintain the composure which his clear-browed, square white face usually wore. "I'm afraid," Manuel replied, "that this time even that won't be enough." He raised his fleshy hand in an elegantly weary gesture of rejection. "Don Gaspar is forever getting me involved with the Grand Inquisitor and with Rome, and he simply will not understand." Throwing aside the mask, spitefully now and flaring out like a sulky child, he concluded, "I'm sick of these endless troubles. I shall send him back to his Asturias. I shall ask the King to serve a *Carta Orden* on him."

"You won't!" cried Miguel. He had risen to his feet. Bitterly he recalled the long struggle it had cost to get Jovellanos back from exile. Francisco's and Pepa's fate, his own and Manuel's, had been altered by that struggle: was all the effort and sacrifice to have been in vain? "I beg you to forgive me, Don Manuel," he said, "but if you now yield so unconditionally to the Grand Inquisitor he'll only be more audacious in the future." "Kindly remember, Don Miguel," Manuel returned quietly but with a sneer, "that when it comes to the point I can stand up very well against the Pope and the Grand Inquisitor. Has it ever been heard of before for someone who has smuggled a condemned heretic over the border to return to Spain and remain alive? Well, my friend, I pulled it off. Our Abbé *is* in Spain, he's not having too bad a time, and he'll have a better one. You must admit, Don Miguel, we dealt the Holy Office a heavy blow, and now it's only fair that we should do them a small favour." "A small favour!" cried Don Miguel, scarcely in command of his voice. "Jovellanos, the greatest man in the kingdom, banned! We shall never recover from such a defeat! Think twice, Don Manuel," he besought him, "before you take this step!" "Your advice has seemed to me rather importunate of late, *mi amigo*," Manuel replied with conspicuous calm. "Believe me, I can think perfectly well for myself. You liberals are getting too big for your boots, I've been spoiling you." Large, fleshy, imposing, he confronted the slender Miguel. "It's all settled," he said. "Your friend Don Gaspar will receive his *Carta Orden!*" His tenor voice vibrated, it rang with vicious triumph.

"I must ask to be relieved of my duties," said Don Miguel.

"You ungrateful dog!" cried Don Manuel. "You stupid, blind, ignorant, thankless dog! Have you still not grasped how it all fits together? Haven't you been able to figure it out for yourself, that this is the price for your Abbé's return? Hasn't your Lucía got it across to you? Why, I settled it all with her and Pepa. And this is the blockhead who wants to advise me!"

Don Miguel did not let Manuel
See that his whole body trembled.
In his inmost soul already
He had known it all, but yet he
Would not know it, had not known it,
Had ignored it. Now dry-lipped he
Answered, "For the explanation
Thank you." It was hard for him to
Speak. "Then that is all, of course," he
Said to him, and bowing stiffly,
Went away.

19

Influenced by his quarrel with Miguel, Don Manuel refrained from sending Jovellanos into exile by royal decree. Instead he put it to him in a personal interview that his presence in Madrid constituted a standing challenge to the Grand Inquisitor and those of the clergy who were friendly to Rome, thus endangering the policies of our lord the King. He therefore recommended that Don Gaspar withdraw to his native Asturias; in fact the Crown expected him to have embarked on the journey to Gijón within two weeks.

Don Miguel, oppressed by the knowledge that Lucía was largely to blame for Don Gaspar's unhappy fate, tried to persuade him to go to France instead of the Asturias. Feeling that it was scarcely advisable to stay in Spain himself after his dispute with Manuel, he too would have preferred to seek refuge in Paris. But he could not bring himself to appear before Lucía in so cowardly a light. He employed all his powers of eloquence, urging that at least his revered friend should take the journey over the border.

But Jovellanos growled at him. "What do you take me for? Even on top of the Pyrénées I would feel my opponents' laughter like an ill wind at my back. That scoundrel Manuel shall not gloat over me and say, 'There's your hero for you, he's made himself scarce, he's off.' No, Don Miguel, I stay in Spain."

On the day before he was to embark for the second time on an exile of indefinite duration, Don Gaspar gathered all his friends about him. Miguel and Quintana were there, Goya, Agustín, and, oddly enough, Doctor Peral.

In his misfortune the old man showed the dignified composure which one expected of him. It was understandable, he observed, that Don Manuel should seek to conceal his failures in foreign policy behind a display of power on the domestic scene. But peace with England could not be put off much longer, and then the miserable, inconstant time-server would certainly try to make friends again with the bourgeoisie and the free-thinkers. His own exile would not last long.

The others listened to Don Gaspar's confident statements with embarrassed faces. Everyone felt his hopes were groundless; the cruelty which Manuel had shown in his treatment of Urquijo boded ill for Jovellanos.

It was Doctor Peral who finally spoke after a strained silence. In his quiet, reasonable way he argued that now Manuel had taken the first step he would be unlikely to shrink from others. For that reason they would all prefer to see their revered host in Paris rather than in Gijón. The others hastened to agree with the doctor. Young Quintana was the most animated. "You owe it not only to yourself but to Spain, Don Gaspar," he declared enthusiastically, "to put yourself beyond the reach of this vindictive scoundrel. You are indispensable in the struggle for freedom and civilization."

The unanimous advice of his friends, above all the persuasiveness of Quintana, whose zeal and uprightness he prized highly, seemed to make some impression on the inflexible Don Gaspar. He looked thoughtfully from one to the other. But then, almost with a smile, he replied, "I think you are worrying yourselves unnecessarily about me, my friends. Even were I to perish in Asturias it would still be a better thing for the cause of progress than if I were to sit in Paris, an idle, prating refugee. No one who has died in the struggle for the spirit has died in vain. Juan Padilla was defeated, but he lives and fights today."

Francisco had understood, if not every single word, at least the sense of Don Gaspar's declaration, and had difficulty in hiding a melancholy smile. Assuredly Padilla was alive today, but in the shape of Cayetana's forgotten jester, the stunted, crippled Padilla of the Casa de Haro in Cádiz.

Doctor Peral spoke of Napoleon Bonaparte. Unquestionably the latter was honestly anxious to promote the cause of enlightenment all over Europe. But unfortunately Don Manuel's machinations forced him for the moment to look for military guarantees in Spain. This caused bad blood, and the First Consul could scarcely wish to aggravate the dissatisfaction of the Spanish people by underwriting progressive measures in the Iberian peninsula. The way matters stood today, Napoleon would certainly do nothing to obstruct the First Minister in his conflict with the free-thinkers. "For that reason," Peral reverted with characteristic tenacity to what he had said before, "if I were in your place I would not stay in Spain."

The others, and Miguel in particular, expected Jovellanos to administer a thunderous rebuke to his pertinacious counsellor. But Don Gaspar controlled himself. "I look back without bitterness on my last period of exile," he said. "The enforced idleness was not unwelcome. I could hunt, could read what I wanted, I studied, and I wrote a thing or two, some of it perhaps not without merit. If Providence is sending me back to my mountains, no doubt she has her reasons." The others preserved a polite but sceptical silence. As paper and ink were being withheld from Urquijo in his prison, it was unlikely that Don Gaspar would be permitted to write in Asturias another book like *Bread and Bulls*.

"My friends," Jovellanos consoled them, "you must not lose sight, in the defeat we have suffered, of all that the brave and noble Urquijo achieved. After all, the independence of the Spanish Church is an established fact. After all, huge sums which used to go as tribute to Rome now remain in the country. In the face of these successes, of what significance is the trifling inconvenience which I must accept as part of the bargain?" But now Agustín opened his mouth and said darkly, "If they have the nerve to send you away from Madrid, Don Gaspar, they won't hesitate to revoke the edict too." "That they would not dare!" cried Jovellanos. "They couldn't allow Rome to fall upon us again and drain us of the last drop of blood. I tell you, my friends, they wouldn't dare. They won't revoke the edict."

The others welcomed his comforting words but in their heart of hearts they were depressed at Jovellanos's naïveté. Even Francisco who did not take much interest in politics could clearly see how childish it was of Jovellanos to think so little evil of the world after so many evil experiences.

But for all the banal emotionalism of his personality Jovellanos was more touching than ridiculous. He was really going to remain within reach of the powerful enemy instead of making all haste to put the Pyrénées between them. He had still not learned that if one wants to fight for something the first necessity is to stay alive. And yet Jovellanos's folly was no contemptible folly; yes, Goya almost admired the obstinacy with which Don Gaspar lived up to his ideals.

Suddenly he became aware that Jovellanos was speaking to him. "It now lies with you, Don Francisco," he said, "to take my place here in Madrid. Our rulers of today are singularly blind where your pictures are concerned and fail to notice how effective they are in the struggle against the obscurantists and exploiters. You must turn the blind good-will of the King and his grandees to the best advantage. There must be no shirking, Goya. You must hold a mirror up to our dissolute times. You have only to will it and you can be the Juvenal of this Court and this city."

Nothing was further from Goya's intentions. He felt like repudiating Don Gaspar's bombastic phrases, his impertinent suggestion, in strong terms. But then he reminded himself that the old man was facing an uncertain fate and that one who asked so much of himself had the right to make demands on others. "I'm afraid, Don Gaspar," he answered civilly, "you overestimate the effects of my work. The government knows how slight the influence of my pictures is, and that is why they don't intervene. If the King and the grandees permit me to paint them as they are, they do it from pride. They think themselves so great that no truth can belittle them, whether told them by a Court fool or painted for them by a Court Painter."

"You do yourself an injustice, Don Francisco," Quintana cried impetuously. "All we writers can offer is polished Castilian, which rings agreeably in the ears of the educated few. But your 'Family of Carlos,' your frescoes in the Florida, find their way to every heart. *Idioma universal.*" Goya gave Quintana a kindly smile, but he made no reply.

He looked at Jovellanos. He would have liked to do a new portrait of him.

> Now and only now did Goya
> See this man. To him the victory
> Did not matter, but the struggle.
> He was the eternal warrior.
> And a piece of Don Quixote
> Was in him—as in what Spaniard
> Was there not? In this Don Gaspar
> Burned the zeal for justice's sake to
> Battle, where he saw the wrong he
> Must fall to, to right it. Never
> Could he understand that justice
> Is an empty goal, ideal, and
> Unattainable as ever
> Don Quixote's was. Ah, no, he
> Had to, knightly Don Quixote
> Had to ride abroad.

-- 20 --

The engravings which Francisco had done in recent months were adapted from the sketches he had made during that happy time in San Lúcar. But the gay, harmless drawings of those days had with their new form taken on a new meaning, fuller, sharper, more caustic. Cayetana was no longer just Cayetana. The dead maid Brígida peered out from behind the dueña Eufemia. The maid Fruela and the dancer Serafina appeared as Madrilenian *majas* in many forms. And he himself, Francisco, also appeared in many forms: now he was a foolish gallant, now a dangerous *majo*, but almost always infatuated, betrayed, the *pelele*, the fool.

In this way there came into being a wild, chaotic book of pictures in which was recorded everything that could happen to a woman in the city of Madrid—much bad and a little good. They marry rich men of horrible appearance, they lead astray innocent swains, they exploit those who let themselves be exploited, and are themselves exploited in their turn by usurers, lawyers, and judges; they flirt and make love, they preen themselves in seductive clothing, and even when they are very old and have faces like death's-heads they sit in front of mirrors and have themselves painted and powdered. They walk or drive in splendour or squat miserably in penitential clothes before the Grand Inquisitor, lie despairing in prison, stand in the pillory, are led ignominiously half-naked to the place of execution. And always they are surrounded by a swarm of elegant libertines, brutal policemen, truculent *majos*, sly dueñas, and procuresses.

There are demons around them too, not only the dead Brígida, but a whole army of ghosts, some of them benign, others to make one shudder, most of them grotesque, bizarre. And nothing is unambiguous, everything is fluid, shifting under the eyes of the beholder. The bride walking in the marriage procession has a second, animal face, the old woman behind her turns into a horrible ape, knowing onlookers leer out of the shadows. And the men, the covetous, the swains, flap about like birds with recognizable-unrecognizable faces, fall to earth, literally get plucked, and once plucked are swept out of doors. The bridegroom is shown the unblemished record of his affianced's lofty ancestors and does not notice, not yet, the living bride's simian countenance. She herself does not see it. Everyone wears a mask and appears even to himself as what he would like to be, not as he is. No one recognizes anyone, not even himself.

Such were the drawings Francisco had made in the last few weeks, with abandon, with grim energy. But since Jovellanos's departure his enthusiasm had evaporated. He sat idly in his *ermita*, unable to get the conversation at Don Gaspar's out of his head, conducting imaginary arguments with the others. What was it they wanted him to do? Was he to go to the Puerta del Sol and show the people seditious pictures? Couldn't they understand, the Jovellanoses and Quintanas, that martyrs are no use at all? For three hundred years they have let themselves be flayed and tortured and put to death for the same purpose, and where had it got them? Let the old man sit and wait in his Asturian mountains till the green messengers of the Inquisition came to fetch him; he, Francisco, wasn't going to let false courage becloud *his* reason. *A tuyo tú!* Each man for himself!

But he could not get away from what had been discussed at Jovellanos's. He thought of Don Manuel lolling indolently, overfed and arrogant, on the sofa which represented the battlefield, and he thought of how the Infanta had gazed big-eyed at the incomprehensibly horrible world, delicate and fragile.

Suddenly he sat down again at his table, his underlip thrust right out, and began to draw. No women this time, no great ladies, no *petimetras*, *majas*, or procuresses, nothing shadowy or ambiguous either, but simple drawings which anyone must understand.

In one, a large, elderly donkey is teaching a younger, smaller donkey the ABC with admirable zeal; or again, a monkey plays the guitar to an enraptured old she-ass, while her retinue applauds enthusiastically; or an elegant donkey studies his family tree and the donkeys on it go back a thousand years; a clever, industrious little monkey is painting a proud, magnificent donkey and a face looks out from the canvas, not without some likeness to the sitter, yet somehow more lion than ass.

Goya inspected what he had drawn. It was too easy, too simple, too much merely what his friends had said. So he drew two large, heavy donkeys sitting on the breaking backs of two men who were almost bent double. He smiled wickedly. Yes, that was better. One could see clergy and nobility astride the backs of the patient Spaniards.

To expect such scribblings to be politically effective was nonsense, of course. But it did him good to put the things on paper, it amused him.

In the days that followed he was often in the *ermita,* drawing with quiet ardour. Hitherto he had given no name to his drawings and etchings, but now he called them *Sátiras*, "Satires."

He drew women again, with more malice this time and less pity. A couple are making love and at their feet are two tiny, fashionable lap-dogs, as busy as the lovers. In front of a huge boulder a lover stands in despair at the sight of his dead beloved. But is she really dead? Isn't she peeping, to enjoy his despair?

The demons penetrated ever more deeply into the life he was drawing. The human, the divine, the diabolic, mingled bewilderingly together; in the midst of the bizarre miscellany Francisco, Cayetana, Lucía went dancing, and everything became a dashing, daring game.

He painted the delights of the game. Drew a satyr reclining on a sphere, probably the terrestrial sphere, and his goat-footed companion, a large, jovial demon, is passing the time doing a few acrobatics. With a dreamy, childlike expression of enjoyment on his face, he holds aloft a man in a splendid uniform with many orders, and the man is wearing an enormous wig which is smoking and flaming, and in his hands he carries smoking, flaming torches. From one side of the globe a figure is falling, some creature with whom the satyr has obviously tired of playing, and the falling man's posterior and splayed legs thrust grotesquely out into space. On the other side also a man is falling head-down into emptiness, arms and legs spread-eagled, another of the satyr's discarded toys.

Francisco enjoyed the ambiguity of what he had drawn. He smiled at the sight of the smoking wig and the smoking torches: for the word *humear*, to smoke, also meant to brag, to show off; he delighted in the gay, swaggering harlequin, the *pelele*, with whom the goat-footed one is playing, unaware as yet of how quickly he is going to fall after the other two discarded toys. And he asked himself whether Don Manuel was the childishly playing satyr or the complacent toy, the harlequin. So much was certain: even the simplest person could see from this drawing that luck was no pretty, capricious female but a big, jovial, comfortable, and, in his stupidity, positively dangerous satyr. Goya thought too of himself, of his own *subir y bajar*, his own ups and downs. But he would never be caught again like the smoking harlequin. He could be swept away, but he'd never let himself be taken by surprise by a satyr or any other demon. He couldn't be made a fool of any more. He was prepared for anything.

As it soon turned out, his confidence was no more than foolish boasting. The satyr could fool him, like the rest.

News came from Saragossa: Martín Zapater was dead.

Francisco spoke to no one of his misfortune; he rushed to the *ermita*. He sat there a long time, benumbed. Another fragment of life torn away, lost, finished. And there was no one left with whom he could talk of what had been, with whom he could laugh over silly things, to whom he would not mind showing himself mad with rage over annoying trifles, no one with whom he could "puff" and brag to his heart's content. Martín dead! Big-nose Martín, his heart's dear Martín!

"How could you do this to me, you blackguard!" He believed

he had said it to himself, but he had uttered it aloud. And suddenly, alone in his studio, he began to dance. He trod amidst the confusion of copper plates, presses, paper, brushes, graving tools, heating pans large and small, he danced wildly, yet at the same time stiffly. He was dancing the jota, that stately yet violent warlike dance which belonged to his and Martín's native land: it was his farewell, Martín's funeral rite.

Towards evening he remembered that he had an appointment with Cayetana. "The dead into the grave and the living to table," he told himself grimly. Contrary to his habit, he was untidily dressed, he had not ordered a carriage, and it was a long way up to Moncloa. He went on foot. Cayetana was astonished when he arrived all dusty and unkempt, but she asked no questions and he did not mention Martín's death to her. He stayed a long time with her that night, and took her with savage violence.

Next day in the *ermita* his old madness came over him in full force. *He* was to blame for Martín's death, his portraits were to blame. And this time he had not the courage to resist the ghosts, they clawed their way to him, he heard their silent laughter.

A long time he crouched there, oppressed with fear. Then suddenly inordinate anger seized him. First against himself. Then against Martín. Martín had made up to him, insinuated himself into his heart till he could no longer do without him, and, having made himself indispensable, had abandoned and betrayed him. Everyone was his enemy; those who pretended to be his intimates were the worst. Who was he anyway, this Martín? A shrewd ignoramus, a banker, a man who understood about as much about art as the little dog Juanito, a nobody. And how abysmally ugly he was! How dared anyone with a nose like that pry and ferret among his secrets? Angrily he drew him, sitting gulping down a plate of soup, and the nose grew bigger and bigger till suddenly the guzzling, gulping, snuffling fellow's face became something monstrously obscene. It was no longer a face, it was a man's privy parts.

Francisco was shaken with rage and remorse. He was sinning against the dead man. It was his own ugliness that he had drawn, his own abysmal vileness. Because Martín had been the best of friends to him, had done everything for him, he, out of envy for his goodness, was drawing into him all his own evil, swinish thoughts. Martín had been of a blessed simplicity, that was why the demons had never been able to get at him. Him, Francisco, they could reach, and he had been a fool to imagine he was their master.

They sat around him, horribly palpable, their croaking, growling, and shrieking penetrated his very deafness, he felt their dreadful breath.

He controlled himself with a colossal effort, sat up, clamped his lips together, pulled down his coat, brushed his hair over his ears. He, Francisco Goya, First Painter to the King, honorary President of the Academy, didn't shut his eyes and hide his face from the ghosts, he looked at them, even now, after they had killed his heart's dear Martín.

He will get the upper hand of the brood, force it down onto paper.

He drew. Drew himself, thrown across the table, hiding his head in his hands while around him they squatted, the hideous brood of the night, cat-creatures, bird-creatures, monsters, owls and bats, gigantically oppressing him. They crowd right in upon him—is not one of the monsters already on his back? But they can only come up to him, they can no longer get inside him. For into the claws of one of the bird-spectres he forced a tool, a graver. They must serve him, these ghosts, must hand him his tools, the weapons he needs to exorcise them, to consign them to paper where they no longer had power to harm.

From that moment he no longer feared the spectres. He felt compelled to wrestle with them, to get the upper hand of them. He called them, and behold! They were tamed, they came. They showed themselves to him everywhere.

From earliest youth he had been interested in the natural history of demons, and he knew more about them than most other artists and poets in Spain, more even than the demonologists, the professional experts of the Inquisition. Now, overcoming his reluctance, he forced himself to study those which till now had held aloof; and soon he knew them all. Knew the albs, mandrakes, and hobgoblins, the lemurs, changelings, and werewolfs, the elves, fairies, and gnomes, vampires and ghouls, ogres and basilisks. But there were also the *duendes* and *duendecitos*, droll little kobolds who willingly and gratefully performed the household tasks during the night for their unsuspecting hosts.

Many of the ghosts had human features, the characteristics of friend and foe bewilderingly mingled. One and the same witch would look to him now like Cayetana, now like Pepa, or Lucía. One and the same loutish spectre would be Don Manuel one minute and the next Don Carlos.

The ghosts came freely and often in clerical guise, as monks, as judges of the Holy Tribunal, as prelates. And they liked to imitate the rites of the Church and administer Communion, the Anointing, the Extreme Unction. A witch appeared to him, sitting on the shoulders of a satyr and making the vows of obedience; blissful ghosts in bishops' robes hover in the air, and hold the book up to her from which she is making her vows, and from the depths of a lake novices look up and sing.

He lost the last remnant of fear of the ghosts and felt a deep, angrily contemptuous pity for those who passed their whole lives in terror of spectres and chimeras. He showed them, the crowd, reverently worshipping Coco, tricked out by a tailor as a ghost. He showed the people, the exploited, the poor in spirit, blindly, with endless patience, feeding and tending their oppressors, the chinchillas, the giant rats, the grandees and priestlings, the brainless sluggards whose eyes are stuck together, whose ears are closed with enormous locks.

Ever bolder they became, the progeny of his imagination, ever more equivocal. And he no longer called them Satires, he called them Ideas, Whims, Caprices, *Caprichos*.

He spied on the ghosts in their most intimate occupations, getting drunk, making their toilette, cutting one another's coats and claws. He made them show themselves to him riding to the Sabbath, to the *aquelarre*. They had to initiate him into the ceremonial to be observed at the *besamano*, the hand-kissing of the enormous he-goat, had to reveal to him the incantations and specifics which they used to turn a human being into an animal, into a goat or a cat.

Often he brought his midday luncheon
With him to the *ermita*, bread and
Cheese, a little manzanilla
Wine. And he'd invite some of the
Spectres to partake, he gave them
Bread and cheese and sat at table
With them. Called the ghostly goat-foot
Mi amigo, friend; another
Towering, gigantic devil

Called he Chico, little one, and
Thus he chatted and he jested
With the uncanny brood of monsters,
He would feel their claws and horns or
Pull their tails. But shrewdly all the
While he would observe their faces,
Coarse and vicious, wild, uproarious
Phizzes, and within his silence
He meanwhile was jeering at them,
At the demons, and his silent
Laughter rang.

-- 21 --

Goya had forbidden anyone to visit him in the *ermita* save in the most urgent need. Only one person was allowed to come at any time, Cayetana.

She never inquired about his work. But one day she remarked, "You're almost never to be found anywhere but here. What exactly are you up to?"

"I'm putting down a few ideas that occurred to me," he answered, "whims, trifles. This new process with the aquatint is particularly well adapted to them. As I said, they're nothing of importance, chimeras, *caprichos*." He was angry with himself for making light of his work. He was hoping she would not ask him to show them to her, and waiting for her to do so.

She did not ask. And against his own will he said, "If you like I'll show you one or two of them."

He showed her the pages just as they came, leaving aside the ones that referred to her or could be so interpreted. She looked at the pictures quickly and in silence, as was her way. When she came to the one of the very ugly old woman looking at herself in the mirror and titivating, she said with satisfaction, "You'd better not let your María Luisa see that one." About the other drawings she said nothing.

He was disappointed. He handed her the sheets on which she herself appeared. She examined them with the same benevolent, impersonal interest. When she saw the one of the amorously conversing couple which were herself and him, with the two amorous little dogs at their feet, she said, "Your friends Manuel and Pepa won't be pleased with this one." For a split second he was surprised. But hadn't he seen it so often: no one recognizes himself?

She looked at the ghost pictures for longer than she was wont to look at pictures. "You've hit Brígida off very well," she said. But most of the pictures left her cool and obviously unaffected. "Strange," she said finally. "Trifles, you yourself called them. Frankly, I would have expected your trifles to be a little more amusing. '*Nous ne sommes pas amusées*,' " she quoted with an unkind little smile. Then she seized his notebook and wrote down for him: "Frankly, I find much of it brutal, barbaric." "And a good deal of it tasteless," she added, speaking the last words very clearly and articulately.

He stood dumbfounded. He had expected her to turn away from the drawings with a shudder; he would not have been surprised if she had been shocked. But to call them "barbaric, tasteless!" There she had before her all he had learned, the fruits of these last five years of bliss and despair, his America which he had discovered after a journey fraught with danger. And all she could find to say was "tasteless." The judgment of a grandee. It was all right for *her* to dance the *desmayo*, all right for *her* to kill her husband when he was a little in the way. But when he conjured up the demons who wanted to destroy him and triumphed over them, that was tasteless.

In a matter of seconds he had swallowed his anger. He ought to have foreseen her lack of understanding, ought never to have shown the sheets to her. The phrase "*Idioma universal*" came into his head. "Young Quintana was mistaken," he thought, and smiled. "What are you smiling at?" she asked. "At those things there that I've done," he answered, shuffled the *Caprichos* together, and put them back in the chest.

Next day he made another drawing. He drew a man and a woman, bound to each other and to the trunk of a tree, desperately trying to get free from each other. But over their heads was a monstrous night owl in spectacles, its wings spread, one claw clutching at the trunk of the tree, the other at the woman's hair. Jovellanos and Quintana would doubtless take the huge night owl with the glasses for the Church and her laws, guarding the holy indissolubility of the marriage bond. And Manuel would see the owl as the fatality which bound Miguel to Lucía, while Miguel would think the owl represented Manuel's bondage to Pepa; but he knew that the drawing was all of those things and also the indissoluble bond between himself and Cayetana.

A few days later Doctor Peral unexpectedly announced himself at the Quinta del Sordo. Goya, suspicious by nature, and more so since his deafness, told himself at once that Peral had come at Cayetana's behest. So this was the effect of his new art! For a very short space he felt the black flood sweeping down on him. Then he decided to make light of Cayetana's attitude. After all, she had made no secret of what she thought of the pictures, and if she could take herself for Pepa why shouldn't she take him for a fool?

"Come on, admit it, Doctor," he said with forced joviality. "Doña Cayetana sent you, to have a look how I'm getting on." With equal good humour Peral replied, "Yes and no, Don Francisco. My visit was certainly prompted by Doña Cayetana, but it is the painter Goya I have come to see, not my former patient. The Duchess told me you have done a great deal of work lately, drawings and etchings. You know how much I admire you. I would be proud and happy if you would let me see some of your new work."

"Be honest, Don Joaquín," Francisco replied. "Cayetana has told you I've been shutting myself up and doing crazy stuff. She has told you," he went on, now suddenly angry, "that I'm off my head again, melancholic, crazy, unhinged." He spoke more and more furiously. "Insane, demented, mad, maniacal, lunatic, bereft of reason," he was shouting now. "You have plenty of scientific terms, classifications for it, headings and categories." To himself he thought, "I really must take hold of myself or he'll be right in saying I'm mad."

Very quietly Doctor Peral replied, "Doña Cayetana found your drawings strange. But during our Italian journey, and even before, I discovered that Her Grace's artistic judgment is capricious." "Yes," said Francisco, "witches have their own theories of art." Peral went on as if he had not heard. "And you know yourself how many prejudices a master must fight when he produces something new. I am reluctant to press you, but please don't take it for idle curiosity or professional interest if I am eager to see what you have done."

After Cayetana's foolish talk and behaviour it was a temptation to Goya to hear the verdict of this judicious man with his expert knowledge of art. "Come to my studio in the city tomorrow afternoon," he said. "You know, in the Calle San Bernardino. No, not tomorrow," he corrected himself, "tomorrow is Tuesday, the unlucky day. Come Wednesday afternoon. But I can't absolutely promise I'll be there."

Peral came on Wednesday. Goya was there.

He showed the doctor some of the drawings of the *Satires* and watched Don Joaquín eagerly examining the sheets with expert eyes; he showed him more, among them some of the *Caprichos*. He felt the gusto with which Peral inhaled the incense and sulphur that arose from them, and he showed him Cayetana flying above the men's heads to the witches' Sabbath. And he rejoiced at the wicked gleam of triumph which came into Peral's eye.

And he asked him, "Am I crazy,
Doctor? Is that madness that I've
Drawn there?" But the other, with the
Utmost of respect, responded,
"If there are things here I do not
Altogether comprehend, the
Reason is that so much less I
Know than you do. You have shown us
Hell as though yourself had been there,
So that when I look at what you've
Drawn I'm dizzy." But Francisco
Said, "Indeed I've been there, Doctor,
Been in Hell, as you should know if
Anybody should. It made me
Giddy too. So now if others
In their turn are giddy, that is
Just precisely what I wanted.
Quite right, Doctor!" and with boyish
Glee he thumped him on the shoulder.

-- 22 --

He had been neglecting his portrait work; his clients were growing impatient. Agustín reminded him that the picture of the Conde Miranda should have been delivered three weeks ago; that the Duque de Montillano had also sent a reminder. He, Agustín, had done all that was in his power to advance the work on the two portraits; now it was up to Francisco to finish them off.

"Finish them off yourself," replied Francisco, casually indifferent. "Do you really mean it?" Agustín asked eagerly. "But of course," Goya answered. Since Cayetana had looked at the *Caprichos* he cared less for the opinions of his noble sitters.

Agustín worked with all his might and after ten days the pictures were completed. The Conde Miranda was most satisfied, the Duque de Montillano no less so.

After this Goya more and more often left his Agustín to finish pictures of which he himself had painted scarcely more than the initial outlines. Nobody noticed. Francisco was amused by the beholders' lack of comprehension.

He said to Agustín, "Doña Cayetana wants a new portrait of herself. When I paint her I put too much of myself into the picture, I know. You know exactly how I'd like it to be, so get to work. Sketches and studies are there in plenty, more than you'll need. Then I'll put in a few brush strokes and the signature, and decorum is preserved." Agustín looked at him, surprised and suspicious. Francisco said challengingly, "Well, do you think you're not up to it?" Agustín was thinking to himself that it was a dangerous game and that if it turned out badly he himself would be the one to suffer for it. "You must know," he said uncertainly, "how much the Duchess knows about art." "She knows just as much as the rest of them," said Francisco.

Agustín painted the picture. It was a success. The lady of the painting was the Duchess of Alba; hers was the clear, pure, flawlessly beautiful oval face with the enormous eyes, the arrogant brows, the exciting black hair. But no ghostly Brígida inhabited that brow; one would never have suspected this woman of hastening her husband's death or that she imposed hellish tortures on those she loved by her moods, her pride, her devilries. Francisco gave the picture a thorough examination. Then he added a few strokes of the brush and signed it. Gave it a last look. It was for all that a picture by Agustín Esteve. "Excellent," he pronounced. "You'll see, Cayetana will be pleased with it."

So it was, for Cayetana
Liked the pure, proud, tranquil features
Looking at her from the canvas.
"That you've painted better pictures
Of me may well be, Francisco,
Yet I must say this one pleases
Me the best. Don Joaquín, am I
Right?" The doctor in confusion
Stood there, for he guessed that Goya
Had been playing some grim kind of
Joke. At length he answered, saying,
"Yes, this portrait is a worthy
Complement to your collection."
Goya saw and heard and did not
Crack a smile. With Cayetana
He was quits.

-- 23 --

On that evening when his friends had been with Jovellanos for the last time, Agustín had predicted with gloomy decisiveness that Don Manuel would revoke Urquijo's daring edict on the independence of the Spanish Church. Don Gaspar's fanatical repudiation, "They wouldn't dare!" had impressed and encouraged him, then. But now Don Manuel had actually by royal decree restored the old, bitter, costly, dependence of the Spanish Church on Rome, and this event, though not unexpected, struck Agustín with the force of a new calamity.

He longed to pour his heart out to Francisco. When the latter had allowed him to collaborate so extensively on pictures which he himself signed, Agustín had taken it to be the promise of a closer bond between them. But his happiness had not lasted long. For weeks Goya had given him no opportunity for intimate talk, and now he wasn't there, just when he most needed him. Slowly his mounting anger fixed itself on Francisco.

He was aware that nothing provoked the latter more than to be disturbed in the *ermita*. He rushed to the *ermita*.

When Agustín entered, Goya angrily pushed aside the plate on which he was at work, so that Agustín could not see it. "Am I disturbing you?" Agustín asked. "What did you say?" Goya asked crossly and handed him the writing pad. "Am I disturbing you?" wrote Agustín, with rising resentment. "Yes!" thundered Francisco, and added, "What do you want?" "Manuel has revoked the edict," Agustín announced very clearly, in outraged tones. "What edict?" Goya asked. Agustín could control himself no longer. "You know perfectly well," he shouted, "and you have your fair share of blame in the matter." "You fool, you idiot, you quadruple ass!" said Francisco with dangerous calm. Then he too began to shout. "And you dare to disturb me with that!" he yelled. "Couldn't I perfectly well have been told this evening? What do you think I'm going to do about it? Do you imagine I'm going to rush straight off to Don Manuel and stab him, or what?" "Don't shout so!" said Agustín angrily. "All this stupid dangerous stuff you're talking, and screaming it at the top of your lungs at that." And he wrote down, "This house has thin walls. You don't want to provoke any more denunciations." Then he lowered his voice and went on with bitter clarity, "Here you sit, following your own affairs, and when a friend comes to you because his heart is overflowing, you shout at him to go away and leave you in peace! What have you been doing all this time while they have been pushing Spain down into the stinking darkness? You've been painting Don Manuel, the leader of these criminals, as Cæsar and Alexander and Frederick rolled into one. That was all you had to contribute. Francisco! Have you been utterly debauched and corrupted?"

"Don't shout like that," replied Goya indifferently. "Haven't you yourself just pointed out what thin walls the house has?" He had become completely calm. He was almost amused by Agustín's contortions. Was there another man who in the last bitter months had seen the peril of the country with more sinister clarity than he, Francisco Goya? Was there another man who had shown it up more clearly? And there stood the doughty Agustín, within reach of the *Caprichos*, and drivelled at him about his blindness, his laziness, his thick skin.

"Even now," Agustín rumbled and grumbled on, "it goes to my heart when I think of Jovellanos and the way he spoke to you: 'Spain! Spain! Work for Spain! Paint for Spain!' You had no right to close your eyes, if only for the sake of your work. But you think only of yourself. Mister First Painter has to be careful. His Excellency mustn't risk anything that might annoy the well-dressed mob. What servitude! What a thralldom! *Qué vergüenza!*"

Francisco remained calm, he even smiled. That provoked Agustín still more. "Of course that woman's to blame for it all," he said. "You're rotting away at her side. You shrug your shoulders with a smile at what a Jovellanos has to say to you, and you play with trifles while Spain goes to the dogs."

In Agustín's accusations Goya could hear all the latter's helpless anger over Dona Lucía. "You pathetic fool," he said, almost with pity. "You eternal student! You have got a glimmer of understanding of art, but you don't begin to know anything about the world and men and me. You really believe I've been sitting here all these months, brooding conceitedly over my romantic temperament. No, you wiseacre, you connoisseur of souls, I've been doing something else." And he unlocked the chest and took out a pile of drawings and a pile of etchings and stacked them up in front of Agustín.

Agustín was seething inwardly at Goya's scornful words. But his desire to lay eyes on what Francisco had been doing all this time was more passionate than his sense of injury.

So he sat and gazed. And suddenly, fiercely, the world of the *Caprichos* overwhelmed him, this cornucopia of incredible experiences more real than reality. He scrutinized each single drawing over and over again, unable to tear himself away, then laid it aside, too eager to see the others. He forgot himself, forgot Don Manuel's edict. Burrowed his way inside the new world. Gazed, smacked his lips, his face twitched. Goya let him take his time.

He watched him as he looked, and that in itself was a powerful satisfaction.

At last, shaken, overcome, so that he could barely speak, and Goya could hardly read the words from his lips, Agustín said, "And you let us talk, you let us go prosing on! What blind fools you must have thought us all!" Then, seeing that Francisco didn't fully understand, he began to use sign language, gesticulating vehemently, but it was too slow for him and he relapsed into his gabbling and smacking. "You had all this in you, perhaps some of it even already on paper, and you let us go on talking." Still holding up the sheets again and again, unable to part with them, exulting and admiring, he scolded, "A low dog, that's what you are. You sit here in secret and do this. You underhanded sneak! Yes, this time you've got them all up against the wall, all of them, past and present!" He laughed foolishly, happily, and put his arm round Goya's shoulders. He was like a child, and Goya was delighted. "At last you've noticed what a wonderful fellow your friend Goya is! All you can do is to scold. You've no faith in me at all. You can't wait, you have to break in on me at the *ermita*. Well, *am* I degenerate? *Am* I debauched and corrupted?" Again and again he asked, "Tell me, aren't they fun, my drawings? Have I made good use of your technique?"

Agustín, his eye on a particularly weird drawing, said almost humbly, "I don't understand this one properly, not yet. But I understand them all as a whole. Everyone must understand their horror and enchantment. They *must* understand. *Idioma universal*" —he smiled.

Goya listened and felt strangely cast down. He had of course occasionally wondered how the sketches would affect other people, and even whether he ought to show them to other people at all, but he had immediately, almost fearfully, thrust such considerations aside. Since Cayetana had confronted the drawings with such galling lack of comprehension he had actually resolved that no other eye should behold them. The absurd and terrible struggle with the demons remained his own highly personal affair. To show the *Caprichos* to all and sundry would have been like running naked through the streets of Madrid.

Agustín read his friend's embarrassment in his face and came back to earth. He suddenly realized what Goya naturally also must have realized, namely that these sheets were dangerous, deadly dangerous. Any man who showed such drawings to others might just as well go and give himself up at once to the Inquisition as an arch heretic. Such were Agustín's reflections, and he realized his friend Francisco's isolation in all its chill reality. All alone this man had wrung these dreadful grotesqueries from himself, had had the courage all alone to commit them to paper, without the hope that others could ever share the burden of his horrible, magnificent apparitions.

As if Agustín had spoken his thoughts aloud, Francisco said, "I ought to have been more sensible. It might have been better if even your eyes had not beheld these drawings." And he shuffled the pages together. Agustín stood by, not daring to help.

But when Goya crossly threw the drawings back into the chest, Agustín pulled himself out of his daze. It was unthinkable that the drawings should stay there in the chest, unseen, perhaps, forever. "You must at least show them to your friends," he begged, "to Quintana and Miguel. Don't be so proud and withdrawn, Francho! You positively force one to think you're unfeeling."

Goya made an ungracious face, grumbled, raised objections. But in his heart of hearts he longed to show his friends his work.

He invited Miguel and Quintana to the *ermita*. His son Javier he also asked to come.

It was the first time that more than one person had been at the *ermita* at the same time. To Goya it seemed almost like a profanation. The friends sat about in embarrassment, all of them except Javier seemed awkward and oddly in suspense. Goya had ordered wine, sandwiches, cheese; he told them to help themselves. He was gruff and taciturn.

Finally, circumstantially and with marked awkwardness, he fetched the sheets out of the chest.

They passed them from hand to hand. And suddenly the *ermita* was filled by this throng of supernatural creatures and monsters, these half-animals, half-devils. The friends looked, and they perceived that in spite of their masks, behind their masks, these figures had more naked faces than creatures of flesh and blood. They were creatures whom they knew, yet cruelly stripped of this appearance and equipped with another one, much more malignant. And the horrible and ridiculous demons of these drawings were the monstrous yet intangible chimeras by which they themselves were threatened, which lurked within themselves, wretched, ignorant yet full of dubious knowledge, mean, treacherous, modest and immodest, gay, innocent, utterly vicious.

No one spoke. Finally Goya said, "Drink, drink! Eat and drink. Fill up the glasses, Javier!" And as they still kept silent he said, "I call these sheets *Caprichos*, whims, ideas, fantasies." Still there was silence. Only young Javier said, "I understand."

At last Quintana pulled himself together. "*Caprichos!*" he cried. "You put the world on paper and call it *Caprichos!*" Goya thrust out his underlip, the corners of his mouth lifted into a slight smile. But Quintana could no longer suppress his enthusiasm. "You have utterly bowled me over, Goya!" he cried. "What a feeble bungler you make me seem with my pathetic verses. In the face of these drawings I'm like a little boy going to school for the first time whose head swims with all the letters on the blackboard."

Miguel said, "It's not easy for an art historian when something new comes and upsets all his theories. I shall have to revise my ideas, Francisco. All the same, I congratulate you." He cleared his throat. "I hope," he went on, "you won't take it amiss if I detect the influence of older masters in some of the drawings, the influence, for example, of certain pictures by Bosch in the Escorial, of certain pew carvings in the cathedrals of Avila and Toledo, and of course the influence of the carvings of the Pilar in Saragossa." Javier observed, "Even the greatest artist stands on the shoulders of another." His impudence embarrassed the friends, but Goya looked indulgently at his wiseacre son with a smile of agreement.

Miguel went on ruminatively, "The sense of most of the pictures is clear enough, but some of them, forgive me, Francisco, are quite beyond me." "I'm sorry to hear that," Goya answered. "I don't understand all of them myself as a matter of fact, and I had hoped you might be able to explain them to me." "That's how it struck me too," Javier officially agreed. "One understands nothing and everything at the same time."

At this point Agustín upset his glass of wine. The wine ran over the table and spotted two of the drawings. The others looked as if Agustín had committed a sacrilege.

Quintana turned rather irritably to Miguel. "Even if the sense of the one or the other drawings eludes you," he said, "you must admit that the sense of the whole is within the grasp of everybody. *Idioma universal!* You wait and see, Don Miguel, the people will understand these pictures." "You are mistaken," answered Miguel. "The people will certainly *not* understand these pictures. Few educated people will be able to understand them either. It's a pity your opinion can't be put to the proof." "And why can't it?" asked Quintana belligerently. "Do you really recommend that these marvellous works should remain shut up in the *ermita* on the Calle San Bernardino?" "What else?" Miguel asked. "Do you want to bring Francisco to the stake?" "If people got to see these pictures," Augustín put in dourly, "the Inquisition would light such a fire as would make any earlier auto-da-fé look like a miserable tallow candle, you know that yourself." "You'd make cowards of us all with your damned caution," Quintana cried bitterly. Agustín pointed to some of the drawings. "Do you think that ought to be published, or this?" "Some of them would have to be kept back," Quintana admitted, "but most of it could be made public." "Most of it could *not* be made public," Miguel returned sharply. "You couldn't leave enough of it out to prevent the Inquisition from intervening and the Crown courts as well." As the others sat in helpless dejection he consoled them politely, "You must wait for the right moment." "When your 'right moment' comes," said Quintana, "these pictures will no longer be necessary. They'll just be pictures, and superfluous." "Well, after all, that's the fate of artists," said Javier reflectively. But Quintana stuck to his guns. "Art is pointless unless it is effective. Don Francisco has made visible the fear, the deep secret fear, which lies over the whole country. One needs only to show it up and it vanishes at once. You have only to strip the clothes off Coco, Black Peter, and he ceases to be dangerous. Is Goya to have created these masterpieces for us five and no one else?"

They exchanged question and answer as if Goya were not present. He listened in silence, looking from one mouth to the other, and although he did not understand everything he was familiar enough with the individuals involved to form a pretty good impression of the arguments they used.

At last they had exhausted the subject and looked at him expectantly. He declared cannily, in a thoughtful voice, "Very persuasive, what you have said, Don Miguel, and your point of view, Don José, has a lot to be said for it also. But as the two opinions are unfortunately diametrically opposed, I shall have to think it all over very carefully. And I must also take into consideration," he went on with a grin, "that I can't afford to have done all this work for nothing. I need money."

With which he stacked the drawings and engravings together and shut them up in the chest.

And they all looked on, dejected,
As the new, wild world of magic
Sank from sight. Among the daily
Noises of the house, within the
Dull, unsightly chest they lay there,
All unseen, the very greatest
Since Velázquez by a Spanish
Hand was ever made. So caught and
Tamed, within the chest they lay there,
Lay the grisly Spanish demons.

Yet, had they been tamed, when no one
Dared to show them? Did they not even
Show their power precisely therein?
Lying in the chest they proved their
Power was magic, was not canny.

And the friends as they departed
From the *ermita*, in amazement,
Quite transported, and yet even
So depressed, were followed at their
Heels by the uncanny, wild and
Beastly shadows of the spectres
And the even more uncanny
Ones of men.

-- 24 --

Goya liked to hear the impression his work made on others. Since his friends, well disposed and well informed though they were, had failed to understand many of the *Caprichos*, he set to work to weed out what was too obscure, too personal among them, and to arrange the others in an intelligible order.

After he had arranged them, he began to give the individual sheets titles, for after all a good drawing must have its name just as much as a good Christian. If he thought the title of an engraving too dull he furnished it with a short explanation. Finally every sheet had not only its name but its own commentary. Sometimes the title was simple and proper and the commentary the more biting, sometimes the title was sly and subtle, the interpretation all the more naïvely edifying.

"Tantalus," he wrote underneath the drawings of the despairing lover with his dead beloved peeping up at him, and made fun of himself in adding the comment, "If he were more chivalrous and less boring she would come to life again." "No one recognizes himself," he wrote under the masked ball, and beneath the old lady in front of the mirror expensively and laboriously being decked out for her seventy-fifth birthday he wrote, "Until death." To the drawing of the *maja* being dressed up while Brígida, the procuress, says the Rosary, he commented, "She is praying for her, and isn't she right to do so? That God may send her good fortune and deliver her from evil and from leeches, doctors, and bailiffs, and make her dexterous, lively, and ready to help everybody like her dear departed mother." But under the picture of the poor prostitute sitting before the Secretary of the Holy Tribunal, listening to her sentence, he wrote, "To treat a good, brave woman like that who has served the world so willingly and industriously for her bread and butter, shame! shame!" And to the engraving of the witch sitting on the satyr's shoulders and pronouncing the blasphemous oath before the superior ghosts he wrote, "Do you swear to honour and obey your pastors and masters? To sweep attics? To ring bells? To howl, to screech? To fly, to anoint, to suck, to blow, to roast? Always to do anything no matter what or when you're told?—I swear— Good, my daughter, now you are a witch. Hearty congratulations."

He deliberated a long time over which sheet to put at the beginning. He decided to give first place to the drawing in which he himself appeared, stretched out over the table, hiding his eyes from the ghosts. And he called the sheet "*Idioma Universal.*" But then the title struck him as too presumptuous, so he called the drawing "The Sleep of Reason." And elucidated, "As long as reason sleeps imagination will produce dreams of monsters. But allied to reason, imagination becomes the mother of art and all its miracles."

To conclude the *Caprichos* he did an entirely new drawing.

One sees coming towards one a huge, incredibly ugly monk, running in a panic; behind him a second monk, and right in front with his mouth wide open stands one of those brainless, spectral grandees, one of the sloths, the chinchillas, and yet another spookish figure is there, a monkish one, screaming. And at the bottom of the sheet Goya wrote the screamed words that were issuing from the four horrible, monstrously gaping jaws:

"*Ya es hora!*" It was here, the
Hour, the time had now run out. And
Everyone must see that it *was*
There, the hour. It was all up with
All the spectres, they must go, they
Must be off: the dummy grandees,
And their fellows, monks and prelates.
"*Ya es hora!*" That was right. It
Was the proper one to finish
Off the drawings, the *Caprichos*.
"*Ya es hora!*"

— 25 —

Since Goya had shown the *Caprichos* to his friends he took less trouble to preserve the tacit inviolability of his *ermita*. Friends came more often and without formality.

One day when all three had come together, Agustín, Miguel, and Quintana, Miguel smilingly indicated the young poet and wrote down for Goya, "He has brought something for you." And while Goya looked questioningly at the blushing Quintana, Miguel went on, "He has written an ode which concerns you." Hesitantly Quintana extracted the manuscript from his portfolio and made as if to hand it to Goya. But Agustín urged, "Read the verses aloud to us, please." And Goya chimed in, "Yes, please read them aloud, Don José! I like to watch you when you are reading. I can understand most of it."

Quintana began to read. They were sonorous verses.

"Ah, fallen is the Empire, the world dominion
Evanished. Only the fire that in Velázquez,
That in Murillo burned, still goes on glowing,
It glows now in our Goya.
Before his magic phantasmagorias
Reality pales, empoverished sinks from sight.
A day will come, it will soon come, when we,
When the whole sphere, Goya, will bow before
Thy name, as now today it bows before Raphael's.
And from all nations on earth they will to Spain
Make pilgrimage; they will enraptured stand
Before thy art,
Francisco Goya, glory of Spain!"

The others, much moved, looked at Goya with smiles on their faces, and he smiled himself, rather sheepishly, but he was affected too.

"*Si, vendrá un día,*
Vendrá también, O Goya, en que a tu nombre
El extranjero extático se incline,"

he repeated Quintana's lines, and everyone was astonished at how well he had understood them. Quintana's blushes deepened. "A trifle extravagant, don't you think so yourself?" Goya asked with a smile. "If you had said I was better than my colleague Jacques-Louis David, even that would have been quite a claim, but actually better than Raphael, well, isn't that something of an exaggeration?"

But Quintana answered impetuously, "The highest word of praise is not enough for the man who created these drawings!"

Goya was aware of Quintana's childlike naïveté, of the childlike naïveté of his verses; nor did he need to be told that he was Spain's greatest painter since Velázquez. What did that amount to anyhow? Nonetheless he had felt a surge of happiness. These were noble hymnic verses which the young man had written to his "brutal, barbaric, tasteless" drawings. And written, what was more, before they had been arranged, while they were still hard to understand.

Goya said as casually as he could, "By the way, I've put the *Caprichos* in the right order now and have given them titles. And I've added commentaries," he went on slyly, "for the stupids who need explanations."

He put the engravings on the table. Yes, the order in which Goya had arranged the sheets brought out their true meaning for the first time. Even the temperate Miguel said, almost with reverence, "This thing that you've done is your best, your greatest portrait. Now you have done the face of the whole of Spain."

Young Quintana said, "Of course I'm a free-thinker, but from now on I'll see demons and witches in every corner." And Agustín, grimly satirical, remarked, "And there are still people who think Jacques-Louis David is an artist."

They had come to the last sheet, to the engraving of the fleeing, screaming, monkish monsters. "*Ya es hora!*" cried Quintana. "*Cierra, España!*" he uttered the old battlecry, glowing with enthusiasm.

Miguel said thoughtfully, "The titles are extraordinary, many of them excellent. If I understand aright, they are intended to take the sting out of the pictures themselves. But they often serve rather to accentuate it." "Do they really?" Goya asked with a mischievous air of surprise. "Of course I know only too well," he went on, "that my clumsy Spanish is inadequate to express what is in my mind. After all, I *am* rough."

Miguel was uneasy. Why had Francisco, who was unhandy with words, gone to the trouble of devising all these titles and commentaries? Was he really playing with the idea of publishing the *Caprichos?*

The longer Miguel thought about it, the more worried he became. Doubtless Goya, inspired simpleton that he was, had been infected by Quintana's crazy fanaticism. Miguel pondered and pondered how to go about restraining his friend from such a fatal indiscretion.

There was only one person who could help: Lucía.

Miguel's relations with Lucía were as equivocal as ever. When he told her he had tendered his resignation as he could no longer approve of Don Manuel's ruinous policies, Lucía had consoled him understandingly, civilly, and without warmth. Probably she had already heard it all from Pepa, perhaps even from Manuel himself.

Lucía genuinely regretted Miguel's quarrel with Manuel, for which she was to blame. She schemed to reconcile them. But only in the future. For the next few months Manuel would have an experienced, patriotic, and reliable adviser, Don Diego.

Yes, the Grand Inquisitor had been true to his pact with the First Minister and the Abbé had been released from the cloister. Not that the Holy Office had annulled the verdict, but the agents of the Inquisition turned a blind eye to him, the green messengers of the Santa passed him by, and though he would not have dared show himself in the neighbourhood of the royal residences, Manuel had assured him that he could return secretly to the capital as long as the Court was not there.

Miguel naturally knew all about it. He suffered deeply under the knowledge that Lucía and Manuel had eliminated him and put the Abbé in his place.

Now, in his anxiety over Goya, he had a pretext for a confidential talk with Lucía. Having first knowledgeably extolled the novelty and stirring grandeur of the *Caprichos*, he told her of Goya's insane intention to make the sheets public and complained eloquently of the folly of mankind in general and of clever men in particular. Lucía heartily agreed. Finally, at his request, she promised to try and dissuade Goya from his folly.

She went to him. "I hear," she said, "that you have made a series of very remarkable engravings. It's unkind of you to keep them from an old friend." Goya was outraged at Miguel's weakness and lack of discretion. But had he not himself, against his own better judgment, shown the engravings to Cayetana?

Lucía asked him straight out when she could see the *Caprichos*. Incidentally, she would not come alone, she would be bringing a mutual friend. "Whom?" Goya asked suspiciously. He thought it would be Pepa and he did not wish to show her the *Caprichos*. But Lucía answered, "I would like to inspect your new engravings with Don Diego." Stupid with surprise, Goya asked, "Is the Abbé here? Then is it—?" "No, it is not allowed," answered Lucía. "But he is here."

Goya was upset. If he were to allow a condemned heretic, whose auto-da-fé he himself had attended, to cross his threshold, would it not be a most insolent challenge to the Holy Office? Lucía perceived his confusion. Her narrow, slanting eyes looked him full in the face, a small, subtle, mocking smile played about her wide mouth. "Do you think I'm a spy of the Inquisition?" she asked.

Goya had in very truth for a moment entertained the suspicion that she wished to deliver him into the hands of the Inquisition. Had she not, for some accursed whim, hounded Jovellanos into exile? But of course that was nonsense. And his reluctance to see the Abbé, that too was nonsense. If the latter could show himself in Madrid without being arrested, they could scarcely object if Francisco did not bar the door to him.

Furthermore he was quite eager to show Lucía the *Caprichos*. She had always obscurely attracted him for all his hostile wariness. There was something in common between them. She had, and therein lay her strength, brought the deeps with her onto the heights, just as he had. He was sure she would understand the *Caprichos* much more profoundly than any other woman whom he knew. Yes, he had a feeling of revenging himself on Cayetana in showing Lucía the *Caprichos*.

"If you please, Doña Lucía," he said dryly, "my greetings to Don Diego, and give me the honour of visiting me with him on Thursday afternoon at three o'clock in my studio on the Calle San Bernardino."

The Abbé came, and seemed little changed. He wore a simple, highly elegant suit in the latest French fashion and strove to appear airy, superior, witty, slightly cynical, as had been his custom. But Goya perceived the effort which this cost him and felt rather ill at ease. He hastened to cut short the preliminary conversation and to fetch the engravings from the chest.

Doña Lucía and the Abbé inspected the *Caprichos*. It was just as Goya had foreseen. Lucía's face lost its masklike quality, a kind of fanatical affirmation spread over it. With all her untamed nature she absorbed the vehement life which emanated from the pages and reflected it back again.

With the first group of engravings, the "realistic" ones, the Abbé showed himself as the expert art lover which he was and made clever observations on technical points. But as the pages became bolder and more fantastic he fell silent and slowly his face also assumed that fervent absorption visible on Lucía's features.

Now they were both bent over the engraving of the couple chained to each other, at whose heads the owl of fate is clawing.

"Will no one set us free?" Goya had entitled the picture, and Francisco observed with profound satisfaction the avidity with which Lucía and the Abbé were gazing at the sheet and their own destiny. And from that moment onwards, while they looked at the rest of the *Caprichos*, there existed a sympathy between the three which went beyond words.

At last, hiding his pleasure under *brusquerie*, Goya said, "There, that's enough," and made as if to gather the drawings together. But the Abbé cried out, "No! No!" with childish lack of restraint, and Lucía showed no intention of relinquishing the sheet she held in her hand. "I thought I'd seen through the titled canaille," she said, "but you've let us really see for the first time how horrifyingly they combine vice and stupidity." She gave herself a shake. "*Mierda!*" she said, and it was strange to hear the ugly oath issuing from the lady's wide, aristocratically curling lips.

Indicating the pagination, the Abbé said, "So there are supposed to be seventy-six drawings here? But here are thousands. Here is the whole world! The whole of Spanish greatness, the whole of Spanish misery!"

But now Francisco really did put the engravings away; they disappeared into the chest.

The Abbé stared at the chest, a wild, lost look on his face. Goya realized what he was feeling. For he had seen him kneeling before the tribunal in Tarragona. These *Caprichos* were the vengeance of all the oppressed, the Abbé's vengeance also; in the *Caprichos* he too screamed his hatred and contempt into the face of insolent power.

The Abbé actually spoke out now, quietly, slowly, with emphasis. "It is inconceivable that this should be in the world, and yet not in the world."

Goya was immediately infected by the Abbé's passionate desire that all the world might see the naked countenance of the evil ones who were ruling Spain today as he had mirrored them in the pages shut up here in the chest. Stronger than ever became the temptation to launch the *Caprichos* on the world. "I will send them into the world," he declared hoarsely.

At this, however, the Abbé wrenched himself from his absorption back into the reality of the studio and the city of Madrid. In a light conversational tone he said, "Of course you are joking, Don Francisco."

Goya looked at him closely and behind the elegant mask he saw the real face, the face of death. Yes, this man was dead. He was going about secretly, unsanctioned, suspected, in the same Madrid where once he had been wont to shine in all the salons and to have a finger in every pie, living by the favour and compassion of the woman for whose sake he had taken this annihilation upon himself. A dead man sat before him, trying to make light, witty conversation. Goya saw a *Capricho:* a putrefying corpse, leaning elegantly against a piano, smoking a cigar.

He felt something like awe before this creature who went about like a living being and yet was dead. "I didn't understand," he said rather stupidly.

Lucía looked him in the face, indignantly, without mockery. "The Abbé means that you ought to be more intelligent," she said very clearly.

Suddenly he realized the significance of it all. Realized that Lucía had brought the Abbé to him so that he might see with his own eyes the fate of martyrs. Lucía's reproof was timely. He had been like a child. "Spain's Glory." Quintana's verses had gone to his head, vanity had swamped his powers of reason. He had wanted to lay hands on his "glory." He deserved Lucía's severe looks, her reprimand. She had done well to bring Don Diego to him, so that the sight of him might recall him to reason, unteachable fool that he was.

And he said quite simply, "You are
Right, Doña Lucía," and to
Don Diego too he said, "You
Are quite right."

But then Lucía,
At their parting, pointing to the
Chest where lay his truest claim to
Fame, and shaping clear and loud each
Syllable, said, "I thank you, Goya,
Now I know these sheets exist, I
Need no longer feel ashamed to
Be a Spaniard." Then in front of
Don Diego, unashamed and
Warmly, kissed him, kissed Francisco
On the mouth.

— 26 —

Doctor Peral visited Goya in the *ermita*. Francisco perceived at once that he had come on important business.

"I have something to tell you," Peral said after a few introductory civilities. "I have hesitated whether to speak to you, and perhaps it is quite wrong of me to do so. But you allowed me to see Doña Cayetana with your eyes in the *Caprichos*, and you allowed me to be a witness when you put Doña Cayetana's judgment to the test in the matter of that portrait. I think I can assume that both you and I are close friends of the Duquesita."

Goya was silent, his massive face inexpressive, biding his time. Hesitating, then making a dash for it, Peral went on. Had Goya noticed very recently a slight change in Cayetana? he asked. "Aha," Francisco said to himself, "she's discovered the trick with Agustín and he's come to warn me." "Yes," he said, "Doña Cayetana has seemed a little changed in the last few days." With feigned casualness Peral replied, "She *has* changed. She is pregnant."

Goya asked himself if he had heard aright, but he knew he had. "*Está preñada,*" Peral had said. *Palabra preñada,* a word pregnant with meaning, Goya thought idiotically. There was a tumult within him which he strove to suppress. Peral should not have spoken. Francisco wished to know nothing of these things, had no wish to be mixed up in the unpleasant intimacies of Cayetana's life. But Peral was proceeding with his unwelcome confidences; he was even writing them down. "Before, in such cases," he wrote, "Doña Cayetana took care to rid herself of the condition in time. But this time for the first few weeks she was clearly minded to bring the child into the world, and changed her mind only later. Dangerously late. For if she sticks to her decision it might not be without risk."

Goya read what he had written. "Why are you telling *me* all this?" he asked angrily. Peral did not answer, he only looked at him, and Goya knew what he had really grasped from the first, namely that it was his own child that was in question. It was his child whom Cayetana had wished to bring to birth, and now no longer wished to.

Peral wrote, "It would be well, Don Francisco, if you could persuade Doña Cayetana against any attempt at interference."

Hoarsely, and very loudly, Goya said, "It is not for me to intervene in the Duchess's affairs. I never have, and I never will." He thought wildly, "*Preñada. Palabra preñada.* She killed her husband, she killed my Elena, now she means to kill this child of mine too." He said very loudly, "I am not going to talk to her, not one word will I speak to her about it." Peral had grown slightly paler. He wrote down, "Please understand, Don Francisco, an attempted interruption is not without danger." Goya read. Shrugged his shoulders. "I cannot talk to her, Doctor," he said in a tortured voice; it sounded like an apology. "I cannot." Doctor Peral neither said nor wrote anything further. He jerked the sheet off the pad and tore it into tiny pieces.

Goya said, "Forgive my vehemence, Don Joaquín."

He fetched the *Caprichos* out of the chest, selected two pages, the one showing Cayetana being carried in her infamy to heaven or hell on the cloud of three men's heads, the other of the two-faced Cayetana, the possessed lover, the brood of demons all about and the enchanted castle in the air. "Would you care to have these two sheets, Doctor?" he asked. Peral flushed deeply. "Thank you, Don Francisco," he said.

A few days later a message came from Peral that Goya should come at once to Moncloa. He drove thither, saw Peral's face, and knew there was no hope.

Perfume had been sprayed about the darkened room in which Cayetana lay, but it was not able to overpower the faint, sweetish, evil smell from the alcove. The curtains of the alcove were lowered. Peral made Goya a sign to draw them aside, then he withdrew. Francisco opened the curtain. At the side of the bed, withered, rigid, turned to stone, sat the dueña. Francisco stepped to the other side of the bed.

Cayetana lay there, her face waxen-yellow, the sunken eyes closed. Francisco had often thought of her high brows as being like great vaults, but what lay behind them he had never been able to discover. Now he felt a burning desire to have her open those closed waxen lids. He knew her eyes which hinted at bewildering richness and gave not the slightest promise of security. But this one last time, when she opened her eyes, he would perceive the truth.

Very clearly within him, as clearly as if they were bodily presences in the room, he could hear the last words which he had taken with him into his deafness from the speaking world, her words: "I've never loved anyone but you, Francho, no one but you, you silly, ugly old man. Only you, you impudent artist. Only you." And all the time she had known that this love for him would destroy her, the dead Brígida had told her so, and the living Eufemia. She had gone with her eyes open into love and into deadly peril. And he, often though she had begged him to do so, had not even painted her. He had been unable to paint her. But perhaps he had not painted her only because he did not wish to endanger her. And yet here she was, and dying in spite of it.

He gazed at her, his mind filled with a confusion of thoughts. It was simply unthinkable for her to die, one simply could not imagine that this warm, proud, wilful heart could cease to beat. He ordered her to move, to open her eyes, to recognize him, speak to him. He waited with volcanic impatience. He swore at her to himself for being so wayward yet again. But she did not open her eyes, nor did she speak, being wholly occupied with her weakness, her passing, her dying.

A vast feeling of isolation, of remoteness, assailed him. They had been bound to each other, he and she, as closely as two people can be bound, yet what strangers they were! How little she knew of his reality, his art! And how little he knew of her! His "Tantalus" was a lie, she was not peeping at him, she was dying.

Doña Eufemia came over to him, hard and hostile. She wrote out for him, "You must go now. The Marquesa of Villabranca is coming." He understood the dueña. He had dishonoured the Duchess of Alba all through the years and now the least he could do was to let her die with dignity. He almost smiled. It would have become this last of the Albas to die with a daring, insolent word of mockery on her lips. But there she lay, weak and ill smelling, and it wouldn't make her end any the more dignified if it took place in the presence of the Villabrancas rather than his own.

The dueña escorted him to the door. "You have killed her, Señor First Painter," she said, fathomless hatred in her eyes.

Peral was in the antechamber. The two men bowed to each other deeply, without words.

In dignified haste the priest strode through the hall with the viaticum. Goya knelt with the others. Cayetana would be as little aware of this visit as of his and the Villabrancas'.

The people of Madrid, always ready with a rumour, said that this also was a case of poisoning, that this time it was that foreigner, the Italian woman, the Queen, who had had her rival poisoned. They who had looked askance at the Duchess since the Duke's death were now filled with sympathy, love, and veneration. Touching anecdotes went the rounds: how unaffectedly she had spoken with everyone, without pride, as if they were her equals; how she had played at bullfights, with the children in the streets, how eagerly and generously she had given to anyone in need who had asked of her.

All Madrid was present at her burial; all the funeral pomp which her lofty rank dictated was displayed. The Villabrancas spared no expense, but they did not try to appear grieved. Good-natured Doña María Tomasa alone regretted Cayetana's passing, who had been so lovely, whose death had been so untimely and so dreadful. The old Marquesa looked down with contempt at the crowd's genuine sorrow. Cayetana had loved the masses, and the masses loved her. Doña María Antonia's face was hard and proud. The very same hand by which this deranged, depraved woman had contrived the death of her dear son had now done away with herself. The old Marquesa barely moved her lips during the prayers for the soul of the departed, and what she uttered were no pious wishes.

In her will the Duchess of Alba had settled large sums on the dueña Eufemia, the maid Fruela, the innumerable servants on her numerous estates; nor had she forgotten the jester Padilla. It was a capricious testament. People whom she had known only fleetingly were remembered with sums of money, sometimes considerable ones, students who had once crossed her path, a half-mad mendicant friar to whom she had given shelter on one of her estates, a foundling child who had been discovered in one of her castles, several actors and *toreros*. To the First Painter to the King, Francisco de Goya y Lucientes, Doña Cayetana left a plain ring, nothing else; to his son Javier a small income. Her physician Doctor Joaquín Peral, on the other hand, received half a million reals as well as one of the Andalusian estates and a string of choice paintings.

Doña María Luisa was vexed that jewellery the possession of which she had always envied the Duchess of Alba should now fall into the hands of servants and other rabble instead of her own; for, contrary to prevailing custom, Cayetana had left none of her possessions to the Catholic monarchs. Don Manuel was also disappointed. He had hoped to procure paintings from the galleries of the Albas by profitable exchange with the chief heir, the Marqués de Villabranca. Now these pictures were to pass into the possession of that disagreeable Doctor Peral, who was notorious for his stubbornness.

So both the Queen and the First Minister welcomed it when Don Luis María, Marqués de Villabranca, now fourteenth Duke of Alba, contested the will. Doña Cayetana had been credulous and lacking in business sense. The suspicion was obvious that some of the legacies, particularly the unreasonably large one to the doctor, and those to the dueña and the maid Fruela, had been extorted from the testatrix in some dubious way. The Duchess's sudden death was suspicious in itself. The obvious supposition was that the doctor, greedy and fanatical art lover that he was, had first made sure of his position in the will and then hastened his acquisition of the legacy by doing away with the Duchess.

The Queen assumed that proceedings against the doctor would quickly silence those rumours which connected her sacred person with Cayetana's death. She charged Don Manuel personally with the responsibility of seeing that a thorough investigation was made into the death of her first lady-in-waiting and her last will and testament.

Charges were made against Doctor Peral, the dueña, and the maid Fruela, in the first instance of *captación de herencia*, legacy-hunting. The accused were confined to prison, the inheritance sequestered. It was quickly proved that the testatrix had acted under undue influence. The will was declared invalid. The case against the three prisoners proceeded.

The legacies which had been found to be invalid were added to the main body of the inheritance, falling to the new Duke of Alba. He invited Don Manuel to select one or two paintings from the dead woman's collection and to accept them as a friendly return for his efforts in regulating the affair of the inheritance; several of the paintings, however, by which the Infante set store, had inexplicably disappeared. Doña María Luisa, who had been so disinterestedly anxious to clear up Doña Cayetana's mysterious death, was respectfully invited by the new Duke of Alba to choose certain pieces of jewellery from the personal estate of the dear departed and to accept them as a memento.

And so, soon, of Cayetana's
Famous pictures, some were hanging
In the gallery of the Infante.
While upon the neck and arms and
Fingers of the Queen there glittered
Rich adornments, rings and brooches,
From the world-renowned collection
Of the late Duquesa de Alba.

-- 27 --

Goya's friends could not induce him to talk to them about Cayetana's death. They were even afraid he might relapse into his black madness. But this he was spared.

Grim and taciturn, he sat about in the bare rooms of the *quinta*. He tried to recall Cayetana to his mind, but without success. He seemed to have retained nothing but the image of a waxen, dying woman, shut up inside herself, and her evil smell. With a final stroke of malice she had refused to open her eyes to him. His anger over the tortuousness of her character had diminished in the months before her sudden death; now that she was no longer there, it overcame him with new vehemence.

He went walking in his spacious garden, a dignified figure with his *bolívar* planted firmly on his head and his fine Malacca cane, carrying himself with Aragonese uprightness, brooding darkly. Cayetana was no longer there, quite simply no longer there, he knew it. He did not believe in the Heaven and Hell of the priestlings, his Hell and his Heaven were of this world. As Cayetana was no longer in this world, she no longer existed.

Nothing of her remained, and that was his fault. His portraits were poor, pathetic shadows which told nothing of how glorious she had been; even Agustín's bungling picture had more of her in it. His own art had failed. The side of her which he had caught in the *Caprichos* was all that he had succeeded in bringing out clearly. But that was the witch in her; nowhere, either in his drawings or his painting, was there anything of her magic, her brilliance.

"The dead open the eyes of the living," people said. The dead Cayetana had not opened his eyes. He did not understand her, did not understand her now, had never understood her. No other woman had remained as impervious to his art as she. "Tasteless and barbaric." Perhaps it had been the *Caprichos* which had changed her purpose, had caused her instead to kill his child before it saw the light of day.

He tried to be just to her. Of course, she had hated him from the first moment, but from the moment he had caught sight of her on the estrade he had hated her too. He had never got the better of her, nor would he ever do so. Always, even in their most burning moments, his passion had been mixed with hate. Cayetana had spoken words of love to him when she thought he was asleep; he could not even tell the dead woman he had loved her.

He wept. The unashamed, undignified tears rolled down, for himself and for her. But they washed nothing away, nothing of his hate or love.

It was base of him to curse the dead woman, the defenseless one. He crossed himself in front of the wooden image of the Virgin of Atocha, the very one which Cayetana had shrouded with her mantilla on that first night, so that the most blessed One should not be witness to their doings. He prayed. "Forgive her her trespasses as we forgive those who trespass against us." Even his prayers were base, since he did not forgive her.

He was as bare within as the *quinta*. Hitherto his life had been filled by the unremitting assault of his interests and his passions. Now for the first time he experienced boredom. Nothing tempted him, no pleasure of any kind, neither women, nor eating and drinking, neither ambition nor success. He was finished with everything, with his art as much as with Cayetana. He had said what he had had to say. The *Caprichos* lay in their chest, finished, exhausted.

He was not finished with Cayetana. He chafed at the wrong which the Queen and Don Manuel were doing to the dead woman. At the thought of the doctor and the dueña sitting in prison, of

Cayetana's memory soiled with ugly rumours, rage seized him. *He* might wrong the dead woman, but no one else might.

He was not finished with the *Caprichos* either. "Art is pointless unless it is effective," Quintana had said. There was something in it. If one hid one's work away from the eye of the beholder it was as though a woman strangled her child before birth.

He amused himself by imagining what would happen if he published the *Caprichos*. Sometimes if a man committed a really monstrous act of daring it had the effect of paralysing those in authority. In his early days, his young days, Goya had been fascinated by the idea of the really great gamble. If he now made plain to all the world what he thought of Cayetana's detractors, would it not be an expiation for the wrongs he had done her himself?

Admittedly to publish the *Caprichos* went against all reason; the others had proved it to him conclusively, he had proved it to himself. But had he grown so old and bloodless that he could act only according to reason? Had he turned into a leathery, dried-up Miguel? It was unworthy of him to hide the *Caprichos* away in the *ermita* like a cowardly old woman.

He interrupted Agustín at work. "I've had the horses put to," he said, "and you're to come with me. We're going to fetch the *Caprichos* to the *quinta*." Agustín, greatly surprised, looked at his grim, determined face and dared ask no questions.

They drove in silence to the Calle San Bernardino, walked up the stairs to the *ermita*, and laboriously, under the astonished gaze of the other inmates, carried the plates, the drawings, the engravings, the chest, and finally the heavy press down to the street and into the carriage. They had to go up and down the steep stairs several times before everything was stowed into the *carroza*. The servant Andreo wanted to lend a hand, but Goya waved him curtly away. And on the drive home he sat in grim silence, not taking his eyes off the chest. Then with Agustín's help he brought everything up to the studio in the *quinta*. He placed the chest against the wall, where no one could help noticing it.

Visitors came, the Duchess of Osuna, the Marqués de San Adrián, and others who had reason to consider themselves on close terms with Goya. He titillated their curiosity. "I daresay you would like to know what's in that chest," he taunted them. "Perhaps I will show you one of these days. It will be worth the trouble."

A visitor arrived from Cádiz, the ship-builder Sebastián Martínez. Briskly he wrote down for Francisco, "We have both lost much, Your Excellency. Her Grace the Duchess, a great lady, a glorious lady, the last flower of the old Spain," and he looked at Goya sympathetically. "A crying shame," he wrote further, "the manner in which the property of this great lady is being lost and dispersed. A whole series of pictures are simply not there. That mysterious naked Venus, from your hand, Excellency, that, too, unfortunately lost without trace. A suggestion: would it not be possible for a trustworthy, admiring connoisseur who pays a good price to acquire at least a copy?" Goya read, his face clouded over. Señor Martínez said hastily, "Nothing, nothing, don't trouble to say anything," and he took the paper and tore it up.

With interest and curiosity he peered about the bare studio, again and again his eyes went to the chest. Finally he inquired if he might be allowed to ask what the Señor First Painter had been doing in the past months. Goya, after considering for a moment, smiled and said graciously, "I am honoured by the interest of an art lover who knows his subject so well and pays so good a price." He fetched a few sheets out of the chest, first the donkey series, then several of the sheets with the *maja* episodes. And when he saw with what knowledge, amusement, and appreciation Señor Martínez examined the drawings, he made up his mind and showed him Cayetana's "Ascension."

Señor Martínez snorted, tittered, blushed. Said, "This one I must have. I must have everything that's in the chest! I must have the chest and all its contents!" He stumbled over his words, stammered, wrote in flying haste, but that was too slow for him, he relapsed into speech. "You've seen my collection, Don Francisco," he both said and wrote. "You must admit that these miracle works of yours belong in the Casa Martínez. Sell me the chest, Excellency! You will find no more deserving, no more admiring, client and connoisseur." "I call these engravings *Caprichos*," said Francisco. "An excellent title," said Señor Martínez with ready enthusiasm. " 'The fantastic inspirations of the Señor First Painter'—marvellous. Bosch and Brueghel and Callot rolled into one, and at the same time Spanish and therefore wilder and greater." "But what exactly do you want to buy, Señor?" Goya asked politely. "You have seen only a few pages out of the collection. There are five or six times as many in the chest. Ten times as many." "I will buy everything," declared Señor Martínez. "All the plates and prints and the chest thrown in. That is a firm offer. Name your price, Excellency!

"Make it high, I will not grumble
If it is a work of yours that
Is in question. No one save these
Two poor eyes of mine may ever
Look at these, your wonder-works!" "If
Ever I should print and publish
The *Caprichos*," Goya said, "I'll
Send you one of the first sets." "The
Very first!" implored him Señor
Martínez. "The first three," begged he,
"And the plates as well! The plates!" Poor
Goya had his work cut out to
Get the excited man to leave the
Quinta.

-- 28 --

That spring there came bad news of the fate of Don Gaspar Jovellanos. The Infante Manuel had not long withheld from the Inquisition the permission to proceed against Jovellanos, and one night the old man had been roused from his sleep and arrested on his estate near Gijón. They had taken the heretic the long journey to Barcelona, exposing him in chains to the public eye, and brought him to the island of Mallorca where they locked him up in a monastery, in a windowless cell. The use of books, paper, any contact with the outside world, were forbidden him.

"*Ya es hora*, the time has come," Goya said to Agustín. "I shall put the *Caprichos* in their final form. You must buy the paper for me and we shall print them together. I think three hundred prints will be enough for a start."

For weeks Agustín had noticed with concern how Goya went out of his way to draw his visitors' attention to the chest and its mysterious contents. "You really mean to—?" he stammered in confusion. "Does it surprise you?" asked Francisco with a sneer. "Didn't someone once come running to me in the *ermita*, screaming something about debauchery and corruption? At that time your Don Gaspar was only banished; now he's sitting chained up in a dungeon, without light or air." "You're out of your mind, Francho!" Agustín burst out. "You can't do this to us. You really can't mean to do the Inquisition such a favour." "We'll print three hundred copies!" Goya commanded. "There are others among my friends who would think this was just the thing, the only thing possible. A certain Quintana, for example." "I knew it," Agustín said bitterly. "Quintana's flattery has gone to your head. That stupid ode of his about your immortality." "I don't give a damn for immortality," Goya said calmly. "That's a damned lie!" Agustín answered angrily. "Don't swear," Goya told him, still conspicuously calm. "First you lose no opportunity to tell me I must use my art for political ends. And then, when they're persecuting Don Gaspar to death, you bid me be silent. That's just like you politicians and *Proyectistas*. 'Clever people talk, brave ones act.' " "It would be sheer madness," fumed Agustín, "to let the *Caprichos* out of their chest at this moment. We're at war, the Santa can do what it pleases. Be reasonable, Francisco! A man can kill his father and perhaps get away with it; but anyone who publishes such engravings today is simply committing suicide." "That's enough of that!" cried Goya. "I'm a Spaniard. A Spaniard does not commit suicide." "It *is* suicide," Agustín persisted, "and you know it. And you're not doing it from motives of decency, or of politics either. Since that woman died everything seems empty to you, so you want to make things a bit more colourful for yourself by some daredevilry. That's what it is. That woman's to blame for it all. She's going to involve you in disaster even now she's dead!"

Now Francisco also shouted
In a rage. "Now you just hold your
Jaw," he yelled, "and if you will not
Help me, then I'll find someone who
Will." "Go look, you'll find nobody,"
Jeered and taunted Agustín. "I
Am the only man so crazy
As to stick it out with you!" He

Left the room, he left the *quinta,*
And though Goya could not hear it
Slammed the outer door with all his
Might.

— 29 —

Overcoming his self-consciousness, Agustín hastened to Lucía. She was the only one who had succeeded before in talking Francisco out of the mad idea of publishing the *Caprichos.*

He complained to her that Señor de Goya, no doubt because of his recent bereavement, had made up his mind to print and publish the *Caprichos.* "Please help us, Doña Lucía," he besought her. "Please, Señora, don't let him run headlong into calamity! The greatest man in Spain!"

While he was talking in such helpless agitation Lucía was looking him attentively in the face. She saw what he was feeling. He loved her, but in his heart he accused her of having destroyed his friends, the Abbé, Miguel, and above all Jovellanos. She was sure it galled him to have to come to her for help. "You're a loyal friend, Don Agustín," she said. "I'll do what I can."

Lucía thought she could understand what was impelling Francisco to publish the *Caprichos* after all. To pull him out of the paralysis and emptiness of his grief, he needed to take risks, to gamble for high stakes. On the other hand, a peasant from Aragón was used to tempering daring with prudence; even if he were about to plunge into an adventure of his own seeking he would not scorn to be well armed.

She thought she saw a possibility of protecting him from the Inquisition. But her plan called for preparation. It all depended on preventing Francisco from being precipitate.

She went to him. "You know of course," she said to him, "the danger of what you mean to do?" "Yes, I know it," answered Goya. "There are ways in which we might reduce the danger," she declared. "I'm no longer a boy. I'd rather pick up a live coal with the tongs than with my naked hands," he told her, "but the tongs must be there." "The peace negotiations in Amiens are not going quite according to the personal wishes of Don Manuel," Lucía proceeded to elucidate. "What he really needs is a reliable agent. If Don Miguel could at this point declare his willingness to work with Don Manuel again, he might at the same time be able to do something for the cause of progress and for a man who is dear to him." Goya looked attentively at her lips. Doña Lucía went on, "I'm going to give a *tertulia* very soon, only for my most intimate friends. The Infante Manuel will be there, and Pepa, and I hope Don Miguel. May I count on you too, and on Don Agustín?" "Of course I will come," Goya told her, and went on warmly, "You're taking great trouble, Doña Lucía, to protect me from the consequences of my folly. You even want to smuggle one or two clauses into the peace treaty." He smiled broadly. "Now you're being more fox than lion," she said, smiling in her turn.

Political deals were child's play to Lucía, and the omens were favourable. At the Amiens conference, where England, France, and Spain were negotiating the peace of Europe, there were a whole string of questions to be settled in which, Lucía knew, the Infante Manuel's interest was personally engaged. He wished to obtain advantages for the Pope, from whom he was hoping to receive a very high honour. He had reason to wish to prove his indispensability to the Queen, and hoped therefore to obtain favourable terms for those Italian kingdoms whose princes were related to her. And, above all, he must be wanting to extend the territory of the Kingdom of Naples and drive out of the country the troops of General Bonaparte, the *gabachos*. For if he were successful in this, the last obstacle in the way of the proposed marriage between the heir to the throne of Naples and Doña María Luisa's youngest daughter would have been removed; and the latter, the Infanta Isabel—Don Manuel made no bones about it either to Pepa or to Lucía—was his child, and he had no doubt set his heart on getting a royal crown for his daughter. Thus Don Manuel's interests did not at every point coincide with the interests of Spain, and since Ambassador Azara, who was representing Spain at Amiens, was not precisely his friend, what the Infante needed at the conference was an agent who would show understanding of Don Manuel's interests. Lucía was convinced of this: Miguel could demand a high price for his readiness to go to Amiens as the Infante's representative.

Doña Lucía invited Manuel to her *tertulia* and observed with satisfaction how his face lit up when she told him that she expected Miguel to be there. Miguel himself was inclined to be coy, but he too was obviously glad of the opportunity to meet the Infante.

There gathered at Doña Lucía's the same small circle as on that evening when she had just brought her friend Pepa and Don Manuel together, except that the Abbé was missing.

The walls were hung with pictures from top to bottom, more densely than ever, with Miguel's collection. Among them Goya's portrait of Doña Lucía. Only recently had Miguel painfully acknowledged the whole magic truth of this picture. Francisco had divined Lucía's true nature and her future destiny with uncanny precision; now the bodily Lucía had become wholly the woman on the canvas.

On this evening on which he was to meet Don Manuel again under such favourable circumstances, Miguel's face maintained its accustomed serenity and friendly composure; but within he was all confusion. He told himself he was a lucky man. As a consequence of his enforced idleness during the past months, his great life work, his lexicon of artists, had prospered as much as he could have wished, it was almost completed. And here, in the midst of the art treasures which he loved, sat the woman he loved; the trouble between them was a thing of the past. And though he might have lost his beloved office of guiding Spain's destinies from the shadow, yet it had come to the point where the culprit who was responsible for his loss was compelled to entreat him to take it up again. Nevertheless his happy anticipation was mixed with uneasiness. The ground beneath his feet had trembled, his lovely security was gone. No doubt he could still tell himself and others with the old certainty, "This is good, and that is bad," but only his voice was still authoritative.

On the other hand, a sense of security, of satisfaction such as he had not felt for a long time, this evening filled the heart of Agustín Esteve. He knew nothing of the details of Lucía's plan, but it was obvious to him that she had arranged this *tertulia* in order to help Francisco. That Miguel and Manuel could meet again on good terms was in itself significant. Agustín patted himself on the back for having overcome his awe of Doña Lucía and been instrumental towards saving Francisco from the consequences of his folly. His own future seemed brighter to him since he had succeeded in this. Perhaps he could still become a Painter of the First Rank. He was slow and clumsy, but sometimes those who were the slowest to develop were the ones to achieve the most. Even if he were never to reach this goal he would not complain. It was fulfilment enough that it had been vouchsafed him to be a success as Francisco's assistant.

Lucía herself was enjoying her *tertulia*. Her guests had been through many vicissitudes since they had first assembled at her house, she had had her part in these vicissitudes, and was on the point of shaping destinies again, the destinies of her country and of those about her. It was a pity that Don Diego could not be there. He would relish to the full the sight of Manuel playing his part in preserving for the world in the *Caprichos* a lasting record of his own baseness.

Manuel had come with the firm purpose of getting Miguel back again. The Príncipe de la Paz was about to vindicate once more his principle, "One ounce of peace is better than a ton of victory." The gold and silver fleets from America would once again make port unmolested, Spain would be full of riches and rejoicing, and he would get the credit for it. Under such circumstances he would not find it difficult to be magnanimous to Miguel; and then, if Miguel were to shake the tree at Amiens, even more glorious fruits might drop from it.

So, barely giving himself time to kiss Doña Lucía's hand, he rushed up to Miguel, who was standing there very erect, clapped him on the shoulder, tried to embrace him. "How glad I am," he cried, "to see your face again. Last time we met I rather think you told me a few home truths, positively abused me, in fact, and I daresay I didn't express myself very diplomatically either. But I've forgotten all that nonsense. Just you forget it too, Miguelito! You know yourself what a tight place I was in at the time," he went on persuasively. "But things have changed. Once there is peace you'll be surprised at how quickly we shall drive back the priestlings, the *frailucos*. Don't make such a sour face, Miguel! I need you in Amiens! You simply can't refuse to do me and Spain this service."

"I don't doubt, Don Manuel," Miguel replied, "that today you are determined to be liberal in your politics. But no matter what the peace terms may look like, I'm afraid that in the end the only people to benefit from them will be the Pope, the Grand Inquisitor, and a few wolfish grandees."

Don Manuel swallowed his chagrin at Miguel's mistrust and resistance. He spoke of the magnificently progressive undertaking which he had in mind. He would put through the long-planned regulation of rivers, would set up model agricultural institutes and big laboratories. He was even considering the foundation of three more universities. It went without saying that he would relax the censorship, perhaps even abolish it altogether. "Bring me back a good peace treaty," he cried, "and you will see how Spain will blossom forth in the sun of enlightenment." His rich tenor rang out. Everyone was listening.

"Wonderful plans," said Miguel; he spoke dryly, unemotionally, the irony was barely perceptible. "I fear, Don Manuel," he went on, "that you underestimate the forces which are aligned against you. You probably have no very clear idea of how bold the Holy Office has become in recent months. Today a Francisco Goya has to think seriously whether he dare publish certain wonderful drawings."

Taken by surprise, Manuel turned to Goya. "Is that so, Francisco?" he asked. "What sort of drawings are they?" Pepa put in. "Why didn't you come to me, you secretive fellow?" Manuel scolded him playfully, and he took Goya by the shoulder and steered him to a table. "I want to hear more about these drawings," he said. Pepa insisted on sitting down with them.

Goya had perceived the skill with which Miguel had laid the trap for Manuel and he was delighted at the tremendous joke in which the dangerous adventure seemed to be going to end.

But his pleasure was short-lived. For, digging him confidentially in the ribs and winking at Pepa, Manuel said, "Here we are, my dear boy, and now confess, have you painted another naked Venus?" And he grinned all over his face.

Goya recalled Señor Martínez' allusions to the fate of the two pictures which he had painted at San Lúcar. Here was the solution to the mystery. From the loose expression on Manuel's face and the casual, mocking one on Pepa's, the fate of the pictures was plainly to be read. Obviously they had been found while the inventory of the estate was being made, the Nude Cayetana had been discovered behind the Clothed one, and probably the picture was now in Manuel's hands; the latter apparently interpreted Miguel's words to mean that he, Francisco, had recently done a similar painting and was for that reason in fear of the Inquisition.

He pictured to himself Manuel and Pepa standing together in front of the picture, feeling Cayetana's naked body up and down with their shameless eyes, stoking their own lust by the sight. He was filled with rage from the top of his head to the soles of his feet. It cost him an effort not to shout aloud.

With delicious apprehension Pepa watched his face grow dark. But Manuel misinterpreted his displeasure. "Yes, Don Francisco," he teased, clumsily roguish, "we've found you out. You're more cunning than you look. A Frenchman couldn't have done it better. But you need have no fear. The pictures have fallen into the hands of someone who is well able to protect you from the Inquisition. Both ladies, the one before, and the one after, are now in my gallery, arranged just as they were in the Casa de Haro."

With an effort Francisco controlled his rage; yes, he almost smiled. He reflected that it was to fall to the lot of this obscene fool to set himself up as the protector of the *Caprichos*, to build with his own hands the stage on which his own vileness was to be displayed. He, Francisco, would hold his peace, would do nothing to spoil his sweet, secret revenge.

Pepa sat there, lovely, white, indifferent, wholly the Countess Castillofiel. She had been silent till now. But her gratification that Francisco depended upon her favour sought outlet. "What sort of drawings are they, Don Francisco?" she inquired. "I'm sure the Infante will protect you if you publish them." "Are they drawings in the manner of the Venus?" Don Manuel asked greedily. "No, Your Highness," Francisco answered dryly, "there are very few sheets of an erotic nature in the whole collection." Genuinely surprised and slightly disappointed, Manuel asked, "But then why are you frightened?" "My friends," Goya explained, "have advised me against making them public because some of the engravings represent ghosts wearing cowls and soutanes. I think that as a whole the collection is most amusing. I call them *Caprichos*." "You've always had such outlandish ideas, Don Francisco," Pepa observed. Goya went on as if she had not spoken, "Grand Inquisitor Reynoso is no friend to my art." "Reynoso doesn't like me either," said Manuel noisily. "I've had to postpone some of ***my*** projects on his account too. But we won't have to pay attention to him much longer." He stood up, supporting himself with both hands on the table. He had become quite excited. "Our friend Goya won't have to wait long to show his cowl-wearing ghosts to the world," he announced. "All you have to do is to bring me the treaty of Amiens, Miguel, and the time will have come. Did you understand what I said, Francisco?" he bellowed at the deaf man. Francisco had been watching his lips closely. "I understood: the time has come, *ya es hora*," he said. "*Si, Señor*," Manuel answered with a ringing laugh, "*ya es hora.*" Delighted, Agustín rumbled, "*Ya es hora.*"

"But now we want to have a look at these dangerous ghosts of yours, Don Francisco," Pepa demanded. "Yes, now I'm *really* curious," Manuel chimed in. He clapped Francisco on the shoulder, declaring noisily, "I just want you to know: your ghosts and *Caprichos* shall be published, even if they do pluck at the Grand Inquisitor and his red robe. I'll place myself in front of you and then we'll see who dares come on. You must wait just a little longer, a few months, perhaps only weeks, till peace has been signed. This fellow here can speed things up if he only wants to," he said and pointed to Miguel.

He got up, and pulling Goya
Up to Miguel he took both men
By the shoulders. "This is a great
Day," he shouted. "We must all drink
To the Peace. You, Miguel, go to
Amiens, while you, Francisco,
Shall exhibit your *Caprichos*
To the world in flat defiance
Of all priesties and all ghosties
To the greater glory of our
Spanish art. And I will hold my
Hands protectingly above your
Head."

— 30 —

When Pepa heard the news of the Duchess of Alba's death and the strange circumstances which had attended it she had at first felt triumphant and pained at once and had wished to pay Goya a visit of condolence. But Lucía had been to the *ermita* more than once while he had not once invited her, Pepa, to come; the Countess Castillofiel was not one to force herself upon people.

Then later Manuel had led her in front of those shameless pictures and shown her the Duchess in her impudent *torero*-costume, and behind it the naked Duchess. These obscenities on the part of the Duchess and the godless Francho had revolted her, yet again and again she felt compelled to visit the picture, and she inspected the body of her rival often, at length, and with an expert eye. No, she had no cause to fear a comparison, no one would be able to understand that Francho could have preferred this shameless, lascivious, affected woman to herself.

At Lucía's *tertulia* she had unfortunately had no opportunity for a frank talk with Francho, but now that he had invoked her own and Manuel's assistance in the matter of the publication of his engravings, and since his concern over the negotiations at Amiens left Manuel without a minute to spare, she took over the task of inspecting these dangerous *Caprichos*.

She drove out to the *quinta* unannounced, excited, not wholly without embarrassment. She declared the purpose of her visit while Francisco listened politely.

It was fortunate that Don Agustín was not there. She and Francho were thus together once more, as in the old days, and since he did not seem displeased that she had come without Manuel, she felt it a favourable moment for a little friendly plain-speaking.

"You don't look as well as I should like to see you, Francho," she began. "This affair has taken it out of you badly. I was very sorry when I heard about your misfortune. But I'd always known she'd never do you any good, your Duchess." He said nothing. The portrait of the Duchess, the only painting in the barren room, provoked her to further speech. "You couldn't paint her either," she went on. "The way she's standing there is quite unnatural. And the way she's stretching out her index finger is almost ridiculous. But you were always like that: if something was wrong between you and your model you couldn't make a proper job of the portrait either."

Goya thrust out his underlip. Once again in his mind's eye he saw this impudent ninny standing before the Nude Cayetana with that blockhead, her fancyman. He had a violent impulse to seize her and throw her downstairs, but there was good reason for him to restrain himself. "If I understood rightly, Countess," he said, "you came at the Infante's behest to inspect my engravings." He spoke very politely. The Countess Castillofiel felt herself reprimanded.

He brought the *Caprichos*. She looked at them, and he saw at once—she understood. She had come to the series of the aristocratic donkeys. A haughty expression appeared on her face. Goya sensed danger. She had a great hold over Manuel; it lay within her power to turn Manuel against him, to ruin him, to bury the *Caprichos* forever in the chest. But all she said was, "You really have a colossal nerve, Francho." The haughty expression had gone from her face, she shook her lovely head gently from one side to the other, almost smiling.

His instinct had been good after all when he had taken up with her in the old days.

She enormously enjoyed the picture "*Hasta la muerte*—Unto death," in which the old crone appeared titivating in front of the mirror; she obviously recognized the Queen. If she recognized herself in any of the pathetic or opulently flaunting *majas* she did not show it. But she did show that she had recognized the Duchess. "You're cruel too, Francisco," she said. "I knew it. These engravings are extremely cruel. You treat women badly. I daresay you gave her a bad time too." She looked full at him with her languid, green, shameless eyes, and he saw—though he might treat women badly, she would not be unwilling to try it again with him herself.

She attracted him too, as she sat there in the splendour of her flesh. And it was decent of her to side with him against Manuel.

He felt something of the lazy, comfortably lukewarm desire

of their old irresponsible relationship. It wouldn't be at all unpleasant to have this smooth, white, plump, sensible, romantic Pepa in bed with him again. But he had a dislike of warmed-up dishes. "What's finished is finished," he said vaguely; she might take his words to apply to what she had said about his cruelty to Cayetana.

With apparent irrelevance and friendly malice she said to him, "What are you going to do, Francho? Are you going into a monastery?" "If you'll let me," he replied, "I'd like to visit you soon and take a look at the small boy of yours."

She turned back to the *Caprichos*. Dreamily she contemplated all the girls and women. The Duchess of Alba was there, she was there herself, and Lucía, and scores of others whom Francho obviously knew very well, or thought he knew well. And he loved and hated them all. And he had shown the Devil lurking within and around them all. He was a great artist, Francho, but he understood absolutely nothing about the world and people, and in particular about women. It was amazing, all the things he failed to see, and it was amazing how many things he saw that simply weren't there. He was poor, obsessed Francho, and one must be kind to him and encourage him.

"*Elles sont très intéressantes, vos 'Caprices,'*" she approved. "They'll fill an important place in your *œuvre*. I must say they're excellent, *remarquables*. I've only one criticism—they're exaggerated, altogether too gloomy and pessimistic. I've had my hard times too, but the world isn't *quite* so bad as all that, you can take it from me, Francho. You didn't see it yourself in such gloomy colours before. And at that time you weren't even First Painter." "Exaggerated," he thought, "pessimistic, barbaric, tasteless. My drawings aren't having an easy time with the dead or the living." She was thinking, "He was quite happy as long as he was with me. One can see what a miserable time he had with that other woman."

Aloud she said, "She was romantic, one must grant her that. But one can be romantic without breeding mischief all around one." As he remained silent she went on, "She brought bad luck to everybody. Even the money she left to the doctor only brought him bad luck. And she could never tell who was her friend and who her enemy. If she had, she would never have left it to him."

Goya listened without understanding all of what she said, and kept his temper. From her point of view she was right. She had often irritated him with her foolish talk but she had never brought him bad luck, and when she could help him she had done so.

"The things people are saying about Doctor Peral are not true," he told her. "Reality is often different from what your pretty romantic head imagines." She was rather put out that he still treated her as if she were some foolish little thing. Yet she was flattered that he should discuss with her affairs that were so near to his heart. There was still something of their old intimacy.

"What actually was the truth about that doctor?" she asked. "Did he kill her or didn't he?" With conviction and some heat he answered, "Peral is as much and as little to blame as I am. And you'll be doing a good deed if you bring that home to certain people." She was proud and glad that Francisco—for the first time—was openly asking a favour of her. "Would I be doing you a service, Francho?" she asked, looking straight at him. He answered rather dryly, "The thought of saving an innocent man ought to warm your heart as much as it does mine." She sighed. "You'll never admit," she complained, "that you care for me at all." "I do care for you," he returned, rather mockingly but not without tenderness.

Pepa, when they parted, told him,
"And on horseback you have still not
Painted me." "Of course I'll do it,
If you want me to," he said. "But
I advise against it." She said,
"Even the Queen looks well on horseback."
"Yes," Francisco answered dryly,
"*She* looks well." But Pepa grumbled,
"Why are you so damned straightforward
Always, Francho?" "Is not that the
Best part of our friendship, Pepa,
That we always tell each other
The plain truth?"

31

Señor Miguel Bermúdez came to say good-bye to Francisco. "Don Manuel's and the Queen's purely personal objectives," he declared to his friend, "can no doubt be attained at Amiens. But I can't bring back a good peace. The best I can do for Spain is to get some agreeable formula so that at least our prestige is preserved. I'm most reluctant to take part in these ungrateful negotiations; I'm only doing it because I want to strengthen my position with the Infante Manuel. The obscurantists must be sent back to their lairs and"—his face brightened—"one person at least shall benefit from the peace of Amiens—Francisco Goya." "I don't always agree with your ideas about art, Miguel," said Francisco, "but you're a true friend." He put on his tall hat and doffed it again to Miguel.

"How long do you think the conference will last?" he asked after a while. "Certainly not longer than two months," answered Miguel. "That will give me time and to spare," said Goya after a moment's calculation. "Three days after peace is signed I shall give notice of publication, and a week later everyone in Madrid will be able to see the *Caprichos*. And buy them, if they have the money," he ended with relish.

Rather hesitantly Miguel said, "I would have liked to see the *Caprichos* in their final form, before you launch them into the world. Could you wait till I am back from Amiens?" "No," said Goya flatly. Miguel pleaded with him, "You ought at least to take a second look at the pictures of Manuel and the Queen." "I've looked at them two thousand times," returned Goya. "When I was painting 'The Family of Carlos' I seem to remember someone croaking out dire prophecies. Incidentally," he went on slyly, "I'm going to make it quite clear in a detailed prospectus that the *Caprichos* are not directed at individual cases or at particular persons." "At least I would take out the donkey series," Miguel urged. Francisco refused. "Anyone looking at the *Caprichos* without malice," he said with satisfaction, "will take them at their face value. The malicious will always be able to read a malicious interpretation into the most innocent engravings." "Don't be too rash, Francisco," Miguel begged once more, "don't go too far." "I'm grateful to you, Miguel," Goya answered lightly, "and don't fear for me. Keep your mind free to deal with France. See to it that you do your job well, and I won't do my job too badly either."

In the days that followed Goya considered for the last time which of the *Caprichos* he should retain and which reject. But he did not consider what might offend Manuel or Doña María Luisa, he did not care for the Court, or for politics either.

It disturbed him, however, that the series was introduced by a Goya sprawled across the table, surrounded by ghosts. The Goya of this engraving was an idealization, he was much too slim and much too young. But, above all, it was unworthy, it was positively improper for the Goya of the first page to be hiding his head. The creator of so militant a work as the *Caprichos* must *show* his face. Must plant himself in front of his work, recognizable to all.

He had painted a number of self-portraits, the last one a bearded, desperate Goya, possessed by all the evil demons. Now the time had come to do the Goya of today, the Goya who had trod the hard way to wisdom and had learned to adjust himself to the ways of the world without acknowledging those ways to be the right ones.

He carefully combed his hair over his ears and considered for a long time the question of what he should wear. The *Caprichos* must have an impressive Goya, a dignified Goya, no acrobat or buffoon, but the First Painter to the King. He put on a neck-cloth which came right up to his chin, he slipped into his heavy grey frock coat and set his proud top hat, the broad-brimmed *bolívar*, upon his big round head.

Thus he drew himself, in profile, curious to see what would emerge.

When he finished, with amazement
He beheld his work. This grim old
Gentleman, was he that? Was that
Really he? Out of one corner
Sharp, ill-natured, peered his eyes at
The observer, while his lower
Lip protruded, sulky, drooping.

From the nose the hard folds ran down
To the thin and twisted upper
Lip. The head, austere, unfriendly,
Round and leonine and mighty,
Looked still more so seen beneath the
Mighty *bolívar.*

With mingled
Feelings Goya saw his drawing.
Did he really look so old and
So morose as that? Or had he
Drawn his lonely future and his
Misanthropic future self?

So
Lifting up his eyes he grimly
Stared ahead, then straightway signed his
Name to it: Francisco Goya
Y Lucientes, painter, saying,
"Look at him, how solemn and pompous!
But just take his hat off, open
Up his cranium, and you will
Look and marvel at what all is
Underneath."

— 32 —

All the bells in Madrid were ringing. The plenipotentiaries of the Catholic King and His Britannic Majesty had signed the treaty in Amiens: peace had come. There was rejoicing. The bad times were past. The ships from the territories across the seas would make harbour again. The treasures of both the Indies, a fructifying rain, would pour down upon the aridity of Spain. Life would be all one magnificence.

Goya had not looked for so speedy a result of the negotiations. But he was ready; the three hundred copies of the *Caprichos* had been printed, the prospectus which was to go with them was written.

One week after the proclamation of the peace treaty the *Caprichos* were advertised in the *Diario de Madrid.* Señor de Goya, the advertisement ran, had made a number of engravings whose theme was "*asuntos caprichosos*"—fantastic themes. From the many extravagances and inconsistencies of society, from among the countless prejudices and deceptions hallowed by custom, ignorance, and the profit motive, the artist had selected those which seemed to afford the best material for a production at once instructive and fantastic. Señor de Goya had by no means the intention of attacking or deriding definite persons or events; on the contrary, his object was to pillory typical characteristics, sins and perversions of all kinds. These *Caprichos* could be viewed and purchased in the shop of Señor Frágola, Calle de Desengaño 37. The portfolio contained seventy-six engravings. The price was one ounce of gold, the equivalent of two hundred and eighty-eight reals.

The Calle de Desengaño was quiet and elegant. Señor Frágola's small, intimate shop was pretty and expensively fitted up. In it were for sale choice perfumes, rare French liqueurs, lace from Valenciennes, rarities and antiques of all kinds. Agustín and Quintana had counselled against exhibiting the engravings in this abode of luxury and exclusiveness. But Goya insisted that the *Caprichos* must be on show there, of all places, a valuable among other valuables; from the very beginning they were to be regarded not as the means of political propaganda but as works of art. Then, too, he had been attracted by the street's significant name. For the word *desengaño* has two connotations: it can mean disappointment, disenchantment, disillusion, and it can also mean enlightenment, instruction, knowledge. The Calle de Desengaño was the right road for the *Caprichos.* He had gone this road himself, now let others take it too.

But these others, the people who came to look at the *Caprichos*, derived no knowledge from them, and if they were disappointed it was by the engravings themselves. They turned over the pages of the portfolio and it left them cold. Even the notices in the press displayed little warmth or understanding. Only the critic Antonio Ponz praised the novelty and depth of the work and wrote: " 'Four eyes at once,' runs the old saying, 'have never yet succeeded in seeing a ghost.' Goya gives this saying the lie."

Quintana, who had expected the *Caprichos* to turn the whole city upside down, was embittered. Not so Goya. He knew—a work like that took time to fall into the right hands.

After a short time, in fact, interest in the work increased, more and more people found their way to the Calle de Desengaño.

Some, indeed, found in the sketches,
This despite Goya's disclaimer,
Caricatures of actual persons
Of the highest rank and witty
Mockery of the Church's customs.
Whispers went around and snickering
Wanton comment. And the gentlemen
Of the Holy Office called quite
Often at the shop of Señor
Frágola.

33

Suddenly, stealthily, one of the green messengers appeared before Goya, and scuttled away. With uncertain fingers Goya opened the letter. He was bidden to appear next day before the Holy Office.

Deep within him he had always known this would happen, ever since he had had to witness Olavide's auto-da-fé. He had been warned many times, and forcibly. Nevertheless the summons came to him as a shattering blow.

He called on reason to aid him. He had the assurances of his friends, and now that the war was over Don Manuel could parry the attacks of the Holy Office without effort.

In spite of these calculations, wave after black wave of fear rolled over Francisco. He crouched in his chair, his face and whole body slack, and nobody would have recognized in this fear-ridden creature the dignified Goya who went about in a grey frock coat and *bolívar*.

Not one of his friends was in Madrid. Miguel and Lucía were still in France, Manuel and Pepa at Court in the Escorial, Quintana at the Council of the Indies in Seville. He ought at least to speak of the matter to Agustín, or to Javier. But fear of the sinister punishment which threatened those who transgressed the rule of secrecy was too much in his bones; he could actually feel the shuddering that had run over the boy each year when the Edict of Faith was pronounced.

He brought trouble upon everybody. His poor son Javier! Now he too would be ostracized and ruined.

Next day, inconspicuously dressed as the occasion demanded, he presented himself at the Santa Casa. He was shown into a small, ordinary room. A judge appeared, a quiet man in priestly garb, bespectacled, and followed by a secretary. Suddenly there were documents on the table, and a portfolio containing the *Caprichos*.

There was a soundlessness in the small room, more profound and oppressive than any the deaf man had ever known. No one moved his lips. The judge wrote down the questions he was to ask, handed what he had written to the secretary to be copied, and then passed it to Goya.

The judge had among his papers Goya's explanatory comments on the *Caprichos*. He showed it to Goya. It was the first copy. Agustín had set it up and he had corrected it himself. The judge asked, "Are your drawings intended to express only what is in this commentary, or other things beyond that?" Francisco looked at him stupidly; he was unable to collect his thoughts. In order to pull himself together he observed minutely the judge's face and hands. The face was calm, rather long, of a brownish pallor, eyes almond-shaped and expressionless behind the glasses; thin, well-formed hands. At last he regained command of himself; he said cautiously, "I am a simple man and not clever at putting things into words."

The judge waited till the secretary had written this answer into the record. Then he took one of the *Caprichos* out of the portfolio and showed it to Goya. It was *Capricho* number twenty-three, which showed the whore in the penitential shift on whom the Secretary of the Holy Tribunal pronounces sentence, while the devout crowd, shoulder to shoulder, stares and listens with eager curiosity. Goya looked at the page which the thin hand held out to him. It was a good drawing. The way in which the huge penitential cap stuck up into space and the woman's figure conveying nothing but dust, dirt, and ruin was masterly; and the professionally stolid, zealously reading secretary, looking just like the one then writing, his records in front of him, and this sea of heads, avidly curious and at the same time of a doltish piety, all this was excellent, he had no reason to be ashamed of this drawing. The judge, with measured gesture, laid it back on the table and held out the commentary to him. In it Goya had written, for this *Capricho* 23: "To treat a good, brave woman like this, who for her bread and butter has served the whole world so willingly and industriously—shame! shame!" The judge asked, "What did you mean to convey by this? Who is treating this woman badly? The Holy Tribunal? And if not, who?" The question lay before Goya, materialized in the clear, delicate characters, enormously dangerous. He would have to have a care with his answer or he was lost. And not only he but his son, and his son's sons into the farthest future.

"Who is treating this woman badly?" the question still lay before him, clutched at him. "Fate," he said. The smooth, elongated face gave no sign. The thin hand wrote, "What do you understand by fate? Divine Providence?"

His answer had been no answer at all. The question was still before him, though in a fresh guise, courteous, mocking, threatening. He must find an answer, a good, plausible answer. He sought desperately, but no answer came. They had him in the trap. The glasses before the judge's calm eyes winked and glittered. Francisco thought and racked his brains and racked his brains and thought. Neither the judge nor the secretary stirred, and the winking glasses never shifted from him. "Most blessed Virgin of Atocha," Goya prayed inwardly, "let me find an answer! Send me a good answer! If you have no pity for me, have pity on my son!"

With a very slight movement of his pen the judge indicated what he had written. "What do you understand by fate? Divine Providence?" demanded the hand, the pen, the paper. "The demons," he said, and was conscious that his voice sounded hoarse. The secretary wrote it into the record.

Another question, and another and ten more, and each one was torture and each pause between question and answer an eternity.

After eternities and more eternities the hearing was at an end. The secretary addressed himself to preparing the record for signature. Goya sat there and watched the hand as it wrote. It was a deft hand, but a fleshy, vulgar one. The room was an ordinary, everyday room; in it there was an ordinary, everyday table with documents on it, at which sat a well-dressed gentleman in priestly dress with a calm, polite, bespectacled face, while an ordinary, everyday hand wrote with quiet regularity. But to Goya it seemed that the room grew more and more sinister, more tomblike, as if the walls pressed closer and closer upon him, forcing him out, as if he were falling through time and out of the world altogether.

The secretary wrote with intolerable slowness. Goya waited for the report to be finished, at the same time wishing the secretary would write more slowly, need not finish, need never finish. For when he had finished they would present the report for his signature; he would have to sign, and as soon as he had signed the green ones would come and drag him away and he would disappear forever in the dungeons. The others would ask where he was, they would sit together and use big words. But they would not do anything, and he would rot in his dungeon.

He crouched there, waiting, feeling the weight of every limb. It was a great effort to hold himself up in his chair; in the next moment he would faint and slide down sideways. Now he knew what Hell was like.

The scribe was ready. The judge read the report through slowly, meticulously. Handed the document to Goya. Must he sign now? He looked fearfully at the judge. "Read it," the latter commanded, and since he need not yet sign, Goya breathed more freely.

He read, and the reading of it was a form of torture. There were the judge's questions, the cruelly crafty ones, each one a trap, and there were his foolish, ineffectual answers. Nonetheless he read slowly, for every second was so much time gained. He read the second page, the third, the fourth. The fifth page was only half-written on. And now he had read to the end. The secretary passed him a pen and pointed to the place where he must sign. The calm eyes dwelt on him, the glasses winked. He signed, with stiff, heavy fingers; then he had an inspiration. With a foolishly arch smile he looked across at the winking spectacles. "The *rúbrica* too?" he asked. The judge nodded. More time gained. Slowly, carefully, Goya inscribed the *rúbrica.* And now he had signed.

Nothing happened. He might take his
Leave and go. So step by step he
Went downstairs. He got into the
Air, it did him good and yet it
Hurt him, every movement on the
Way was pain and effort, like a
Man's who after serious illness
Has got up too soon from bed.

He
Was worn out, when he at last had
Reached there. Summoning Andreo
He demanded food. But when the
Servant brought it, he found Goya
Fast asleep.

-- 34 --

Young Señor Javier de Goya observed with surprise that his friends from among the *jeunesse dorée* no longer invited him and declined his invitations on various pretexts; no doubt this or that prelate or grandee had taken offence at the *Caprichos.*

Javier would gladly have spoken to his father about it. But in the past few days the latter had been so silent and morose that in spite of his boyish heedlessness Javier hesitated to burden him with his affairs. But he needed gaiety about him, friendship, recognition. He no longer felt at ease in Madrid, and as his father had, after all, promised to send him on an educational trip abroad, he reminded him about it in his most ingratiating tone. "You've reminded me at just the right time," Goya answered with unexpected kindliness. "Let us get everything ready at once."

Agustín Esteve too had observed with mounting uneasiness the void which surrounded Goya. Aristocrats who before had sought assiduously to have their portraits done now withdrew their commissions on threadbare pretexts. All at once Señor Frágola found himself unable to dispose of any further copies of the *Caprichos*. One only had to mention Goya's name and there was an awkwardness. Rumours flew about that the Holy Office was planning to proceed against him; the rumours seemed to have originated in the Santa Casa itself.

Agustín breathed a sigh of relief when he heard that the two Bermúdez would be coming back in the next few days.

Yes, Don Miguel had happily accomplished his mission in Amiens and was on his way back to Madrid.

He was aware that the peace he had brought about held no advantages for the Kingdom of Spain. But at least the successes he had achieved for Don Manuel and the Queen surpassed expectations. The possessions of the Italian states had been extended, the Duchy of Parma restored, France had promised shortly to withdraw her armies of occupation from papal territories, as well as from the Kingdoms of Naples and Etruria. Moreover, to Don Manuel's extreme satisfaction, Miguel had brought it about that the Spanish representative was in a position to sign the peace treaty with England several days before the plenipotentiaries of the French Republic. So much was certain: Miguel was entitled to the Infante's gratitude and he intended to call in the debt to the benefit of progress, civilization, and freedom.

It was in a contented frame of mind, then, that he travelled back to Madrid. But he had scarcely arrived before Agustín Esteve appeared in a state of agitation and reported to him the alarming events in connection with Francisco.

Don Miguel betook himself at once to Señor de Linares, the Chief of Police, to find out for himself how far Agustín's panic was well founded.

Señor de Linares, who had his spies in the Santa Casa, proved himself to be well informed, and what he revealed to Miguel aroused the latter's deepest misgivings.

Don Ramón de Reynoso y Arce, Archbishop of Burgos and

Saragossa, Patriarch of the two Indies, forty-fourth Grand Inquisitor, had declared that the temptation communicated by Francisco Goya's hellish works of art was more dangerous than all the books and speeches of Jovellanos. On another occasion he had declared that from the *Caprichos* arose the sulphurous stench of Hell. The Grand Inquisitor had made several such utterances, even to members of the laity, presumably with the intention that his words should go further. Unquestionably Reynoso was determined to proceed against the *Caprichos* and their creator. It was even said that the First Painter had already been interrogated.

Don Miguel thanked the Chief of Police and took counsel with Lucía. The Grand Inquisitor, a shrewd politician, who must long ago have realized how much his power was menaced by the conclusion of peace, was clearly seeking an immediate trial of strength, for which the *Caprichos* afforded a favourable opportunity. The danger was great, speedy action enjoined.

Lengthy discussions of the matter with Francisco would be purposeless. Miguel and Lucía devised a plan to nip the attacks of the Inquisitor in the bud. Miguel travelled the same day to the Escorial.

There he found Manuel in a state of noisy self-congratulation. Once more he had proved himself to be fortune's favourite. In the first place, he had been able to add to his existing titles and dignities a wonderful new one. In grateful recognition for what had been achieved at Amiens, the Pope had named him Principe di Bassano; moreover, it was his brother-in-law, who had had to hand him the title deed, the Infante Don Luis María, Primate of Spain, the same Don Luis María who had once looked through him as if he had been air. Further, he had once more proved to Doña María Luisa that Don Manuel the statesman could guide the destinies of her house past all hazards to ever loftier triumphs. Thirdly, he had contrived to make a queen of the Infanta Isabel, his own and her favourite daughter, queen of an independent Naples liberated from the *gabachos*. But apart from all this—and possibly this was Don Manuel's proudest triumph—his representatives had been the first to sign the treaty. Yes, it was a new feather in his cap: he, not the arrogant General Bonaparte, had restored peace to Europe. From now on the name of the Príncipe de la Paz would be glorified throughout the Kingdoms of Spain as reverently as that of the most blessed Virgin.

He was genuinely pleased to see Miguel again; he had not overlooked the fact that he had had a hand in the successes of Amiens, in fact, he had a surprise ready for him, a letter of thanks in His Catholic Majesty's own hand, new dignities and titles, and a considerable sum of money.

Unfortunately Miguel marred the pleasure of their first meeting. He introduced the subject of Goya's distressing position.

A small shadow clouded Don Manuel's face. His time had been fully occupied with the display of his new glory, he had had little leisure to worry about Goya. Certainly he had heard that Reynoso had knit his brows over the *Caprichos*. But was that not to have been foreseen? And it was a long way from a frown to an auto-da-fé. No, Miguel was taking too gloomy a view, the Grand Inquisitor would make a few peevish utterances and let it go at that. And the Infante sought to brush Don Miguel's anxieties aside with a man-of-the-world gesture.

But Miguel was not satisfied. He declared that the Grand Inquisitor intended to make a second Jovellanos case out of it, that was certain. If he wasn't stopped immediately, Francisco might soon find himself, within a few days even, in one of the dungeons of the Holy Tribunal. It would be considerably more difficult to rescue him from there than to take clear, effective measures today.

The Infante was reluctant to be involved in a conflict with the Santa Casa in the midst of the general rejoicing, but he agreed that he would have to do something. "You're right," he said, "we must take up the cudgels for our dear friend Francisco at once. And we shall do so. The double wedding in the royal family is to be celebrated with hitherto unknown magnificence. The city of Barcelona will be one great festival. And do you know whom I am going to suggest as director of festivities? Francisco Goya. Did not Philip the Great on a similar occasion distinguish Velázquez with a similar commission?" His animation grew. "You must admit, I've hit on just the thing. In this way we shall show the whole kingdom how high Francisco stands in the favour of Their Catholic Majesties. I shall speak to Doña María Luisa about it tomorrow. And then we shall see if Reynoso dares to molest our friend Goya further."

Miguel was voluble in his praise of the Infante's happy inspiration. But he was afraid even the highest honour would not suffice to turn aside the Grand Inquisitor's fanatical hatred. Measures would have to be taken with a direct bearing on the *Caprichos*. They must, so to speak, build an unscalable wall around the *Caprichos*. And though Manuel made a sour face, Miguel did not weaken. "How would it be," he suggested, "if our friend Francisco were to make Their Majesties a present on the auspicious occasion of the double wedding? And if he were to select for presentation the plates of the *Caprichos?* So that in future the *Caprichos* would be produced and published by the Royal Printing Establishment?"

The astonished Manuel was momentarily at a loss for a reply. He had given no more than a fleeting glance to the presentation copy of the *Caprichos* which Francisco had sent him. A faint suspicious had crossed his mind that here or there Goya's impudence might be directed against him, but before this impression had had time to crystallize the sense of his own success and importance had swept it away. The Infante had smiled at the caricature of Doña María Luisa and thought no more about it. The work as a whole had struck him as being an artistic prank, bold enough but fundamentally harmless.

But now that Miguel had made his daring proposal he was once more aware of that faint suspicion; he feared too that María Luisa might turn nasty if the *Caprichos* were brought so directly to her attention. But from motives which he did not wholly understand he kept this objection to himself. Instead he asked after a short pause, "How do you picture the thing? The *Caprichos* have, after all, already been published, they have been, so to speak, deflowered. Can one offer the King such a thing as a present? Are the plates worth anything at all once the drawings are on the market? Doña María Luisa is a shrewd calculator. Won't she think such a present insultingly shabby?"

Don Miguel was prepared for this objection. "For fear of the Inquisition, Señor Frágola stopped selling after only a few days," he answered. "As far as my information goes, there are less than two hundred copies in circulation. The plates are capable of producing from five to six thousand copies, the interest in them is immense, one copy can fetch an ounce of gold. You can see, Don Manuel, that the present Señor de Goya would be offering to the Catholic Kings is entirely worthy of the occasion."

Don Manuel made calculations in his head. The result was a million five hundred thousand reals. He whistled through his teeth.

"It's much more likely," Miguel went on with a smile, "that the Queen will wonder why Goya is making her such an expensive present, and will guess that he is seeking protection from the Holy Office. But that will only increase the value of the present in her eyes; she's certainly not averse to playing a trick on the Grand Inquisitor."

"Your arguments are most persuasive," observed the Infante. "But"—and here he was compelled to come out with his real thoughts—"if I remember rightly, there are certain pictures which Doña María Luisa can scarcely be expected to like. The Queen is sometimes very sensitive."

Prepared for this objection also, Don Miguel answered without hesitation, "It will surely occur to the Queen that no one would dare to offer the work to her if certain of its pages were directed against her. And if the Queen then publishes the work herself, then surely it will never enter anyone's head that some of the drawings point to her."

This made sense to Manuel. The way for a clever statesman to render a lampoon harmless is for him to circulate it himself. Hadn't General Bonaparte given orders for an abusive placard to be hung lower? Or had that been Frederick of Prussia? Whoever it was, Don Manuel and Doña María Luisa could follow his example. The idea of having the *Caprichos* published by the Royal Printing Establishment recommended itself to him more and more. "I shall speak to Doña María Luisa about the plan and Goya's present," he promised. "Thank you, Infante," answered Don Miguel.

He reported the success of his interview to Lucía. She went to see Goya.

She found him bitterly resentful that Miguel, after so long an absence, had travelled on to the Escorial without stopping to see him. That's what his friends were like, the worthless wretches. Now that he had fallen on evil days they were shamming dead.

But when he saw Lucía he brightened.

"They tell me the Inquisition isn't very happy about the *Caprichos*," she began. "Have you heard anything about it?" He fought the temptation to talk, to pour out all his despair to her, and said dryly, "Yes." "You are a strange creature, Don Francisco," she said. "Why didn't you come to us? We had made promises to you." "Promises!" was all Goya said, with an expressive shrug of the shoulders.

Lucía went on, "They have decided to celebrate the double wedding in Barcelona. You, Don Francisco, will be summoned to the Escorial. In a formal audience you will be entrusted with the task of designing and directing the course of the festivities. Like Velázquez in his day." Goya thought for a moment. "Will that be enough?" he asked practically. "Incidentally, I enjoy arranging celebrations of that kind about as much as I enjoy painting saints." Lucía said, "You will be expected to give the royal family a present on the occasion of the double wedding. Your friends feel the plates of the *Caprichos* would not be unsuitable for the purpose."

Goya thought he had misunderstood. "You'll have to write that down for me, Doña Lucía," he said. She did so, and as she sat there busily writing with her tongue in the corner of her mouth she was suddenly the almond-seller of the Prado again. Goya read what she had written. "Won't they throw me down the steps of the Escorial?" he asked. "They're very steep." Doña Lucía answered, "Your friends have calculated that if the Royal Printing Establishment produces them, the *Caprichos* are capable of making one and a half million reals. Your friends are doing their best to make this clear at Court."

Goya thought again, with growing satisfaction. "Did the plan originate with you, Doña Lucía?" he asked. She made no reply. Instead she said, "If I were in your shoes, there's one picture I *would* leave out if I were going to present the *Caprichos* to Their Majesties: the picture "*Hasta la muerte*—Unto death." "The old lady prinking herself?" asked Goya. "Yes," answered Lucia. "Ageing ladies are sometimes rather sensitive." But Goya declared with noisy joviality, "I shall leave nothing out. The old lady stays in. Unto death." Lucía seemed amused. "You're taking a big risk," she observed, "but I suppose you must know yourself how much the fun is worth to you."

Purposely misunderstanding her, Goya answered, "You're right. A simple painter shouldn't try to give the Catholic King such an expensive present." He considered briefly, then, brightening, spoke his thoughts aloud. "You're so clever, Doña Lucía, and Miguel is a diplomat. I've been meaning for a long time to send my son Javier on an educational journey through France and Italy. Couldn't we wangle it that at least the King would pay for that?"

Goya saw Lucía laughing,
Something that not often happened.
"Your idea is not so bad," she
Said. "For if the Court is slow to
Take your costly gift, one might hint
It would well become the King to
Put at the disposal of your
Gifted son a proper stipend
For his journey. Why should not Don
Carlos manifest his love of
Art, as in the father likewise
In the son?" And then—the gamine
Of the Prado and the peasant
Lad from Aragón—they sagely
Looked each other in the eye and
Laughed.

— 35 —

Don Carlos and Doña María Luisa were sitting on elevated chairs like thrones. Behind them stood the Infante Manuel, the Countess Castillofiel, other ladies and gentlemen. The First Painter to the King, Francisco de Goya, down on one knee at the steps of the throne, was offering his present, a portfolio containing the *Caprichos.*

As he knelt he tasted to the full the grim jest which was being enacted. It was surely the maddest gamble of his life, a life which had not been lacking in the maddest gambles, a *capricho* which in sombre humour surpassed any of the *caprichos* in the portfolio. Here was the Escorial, soaring, solemnly magnificent, here was the jovial, blockheaded monarch and his proud, lascivious queen, and here he was himself with his insolent engravings, his dignified donkeys, his apish whores, his ravaged crones, his spectres. And Their Catholic Majesties would graciously thank him for these creations of his most impertinent fancy, would assure him of their protection against attack from the Holy Office, would promise to show his caricatures to all the world. And all this over the very graves of the conquerors of old, the founders and champions of the Inquisition. Before Goya's eyes floated a new *capricho* in which these dead rulers struggled to raise the heavy lids of their silver sarcophagi with their skeleton hands, to put a stop to this blasphemous game.

Their Majesties examined the *Caprichos.*

They turned the pages, passing each other the engravings; their scrutiny lasted a long time and gradually Goya's grimly pleasurable sense of superiority dissolved. Uneasiness crept over him. Perhaps in defiance of all their calculations the Queen would lose her dignity at the sight of "*Hasta la muerte,*" would hurl his gift at his feet and abandon him to the Inquisition.

Manuel and Pepa were also observing the Queen with fascinated curiosity. She was undoubtedly intelligent enough to understand the sheets in question. Would she also have the intelligence to overlook them?

For the time being only Don Carlos spoke. He had enjoyed the *Caprichos.* The donkey series afforded him particular pleasure. "I can see a number of my grandees in this one," he said with satisfaction. "I feel I want to say *cubríos* to some of them. And you've achieved your effect by such simple means, my dear Don Francisco. Actually it's quite easy to do caricature, one makes a long nose longer, lean legs leaner, and calls it art. The next thing you know I shall be trying my hand at it myself."

For Doña María Luisa the past weeks had been a time of happy excitement. Once more her wishes had achieved glorious fulfilment. She had held her own against the vulgar, predatory French General; she had restored her children to their thrones; the Kingdoms of Portugal, Naples, and Etruria, the Duchy of Parma, were once more firmly in the hands of the dynasty; and once more her ships could sail the seven seas unmolested, to lay their treasures at her feet from all quarters of the globe.

It was in such a mood that she examined the *Caprichos.* He certainly had a glorious, impious eye, her painter Goya. With what incorruptible clarity did he portray humanity! He had penetrated to their turbulent, yet at the same time so empty, depths. And how well he knew women, how he loved and hated them, despised them and admired them, a proper masculine man. It was just such a struggle as Francisco depicted, when one was a woman. One had to adorn oneself, to take care that the comb was properly placed in one's hair, that one's stockings were pulled tight on one's legs, one had to calculate how far one could pluck the men and at the same time be on the watch against being too much plucked oneself, one had to be on one's guard against a hypocritical Grand Inquisitor preaching against one and thrusting one off the throne.

Surely this woman riding to Heaven, or possibly to Hell, was the Duchess of Alba? Of course it was. Her presence haunted several of the pages, proud and beautiful, but a witch. She had obviously sore beset her lover Francisco; she did not appear on these pages in a sympathetic light, for all her beauty. At all events she was now lying in her mausoleum in San Isidro, putrefying, already forgotten, the *Caprichos* could give her neither pain nor pleasure. She had been forced to abdicate with scandal and disgrace, this proud, insolent, beautiful rival of hers. But she herself, María Luisa, was still in full bloom, she still had an excellent appetite for life, and would make many more journeys on earth before her final journey to Heaven or Hell.

Goya gazed at Doña María Luisa's hands as they shuffled through his engravings, the fleshy, eager hands he had so often painted. He saw the many rings on these hands, among them the ring Cayetana had loved best to wear. He had so often seen this strange old ring, a connoisseur's piece, felt it, painted it, been irritated by it and sometimes very fond of it. He tasted bitterness to see it now on this finger. He had done well to perpetuate this Queen's debauched, lascivious ugliness in the *Caprichos;* if only for her meanness towards Cayetana she richly deserved it.

The Queen's face, as she looked in silence, was hard, attentive, controlled. And suddenly, much more powerfully than before, fear overcame Goya. With piercing clarity he perceived the monstrous impudence of his "present." He had been a fool to leave the picture "*Hasta la muerte*" in the collection against Lucía's advice. The Queen was sure to recognize herself. She was sure to recognize Cayetana. And sure to realize that in these pages he was coming to the feud on behalf of her hated rival.

Now she had come to it. Now the ageing, bedizened María Luisa was examining the ravaged, age-old crone bedizening herself.

She herself was by no means wizened, rather plump in fact, and at most half as old as this old crone. She did not wish to know, yet knew at once, that the pathetic old gargoyle in the picture was she. She caught her breath at the insult of it, the vilest she had ever received in a life that had been rich in insults. She stared vacantly at the number on the page: 55. "*Cincuenta cinco*," she thought mechanically. "*Cinquante-cinq*," again and again. And there stood this plebeian creature, this heap of dung, this nobody whom she had raised up and made First Painter, there he stood in the presence of her consort the Catholic King and of her friends and foes, and thrust this malignant picture under her nose. And they were all enjoying the spectacle, Manuel and his Pepa and all the rest of them. Was the proudest Queen on earth powerless, because she was over forty and not good to look upon?

Mechanically, in order to retain her composure, she reread and repeated to herself, "*Hasta la muerte, cincuenta cinco, cinquante-cinq*." She recalled the many pictures this Goya had painted of her. Even in them he had painted her uncomeliness, but also her power and dignity. She *was* a bird of prey, and an ugly one, but one with sharp eyes and good claws, one who could fly high, who was quick to sight the prey, quick and certain to clutch it. In this sheet 55 the man had spirited all her good points away, had rendered only the ugliness without the pride, without the power.

For a split second she felt nothing but a raging desire to destroy this fellow. She did not have to lift a finger herself. She had merely to decline the "present" on some pretext—and the Inquisition would look after the rest. But she was aware that everyone around her was watching expectantly to see what she would do. Unless she wished to be a laughing stock for some time to come, she knew she must counter this vulgar insult with mocking superiority.

She continued to look in silence. Manuel and Pepa waited with mounting apprehension. Had they gone too far after all? Over Goya himself there washed a new overpowering wave of fear that robbed him of breath.

At last María Luisa opened her mouth. Equably, with a gracious smile, so that her diamond teeth gleamed, she playfully admonished him, "This hideous old woman in front of her mirror, haven't you been just a little *too* unkind to our good friend Osuna's mother?" All three, Goya, Manuel, and Pepa, were immediately certain that the woman knew "*Hasta la muerte*" was aimed at herself. But she was standing her ground without flinching, it was impossible to get the better of her.

María Luisa shuffled once more rapidly through the *Caprichos.* Restored them to their portfolio. "They are good drawings," she declared, "mad, impudent, good. It's possible a few of our grandees may grumble. But in Parma we have a saying, 'Only a fool is angry with the mirror that reproduces his likeness.' " She remounted the steps and sat down again on her elevated chair. "This Spain of ours is old," she said without emotion, but not without dignity, "but in spite of certain of her neighbours there's plenty of life in her still. She can bear to be told a few truths about herself, particularly if they're told with spice and humour. All the same, perhaps you would do well to be careful in the future, Don Francisco; reason isn't always in the ascendant, and the day might come, Señor, when you were dependent upon fools."

With the finger which wore Cayetana's ring she indicated the *Caprichos,* a proprietary gesture. "We accept your gift, Don Francisco," she said. "It shall be our concern to see that your drawings are disseminated both inside our domains and beyond."

Don Carlos descended from the throne in his turn, gave Francisco a mighty clap on the back and said to the deaf man very loudly, and as if he were speaking to a child, "Excellent they are, your caricatures. They've given us great pleasure. *Muchas gracias.*"

But María Luisa had something more to say. "We have furthermore decided to make a three-year grant to your son for an extended educational tour. I wanted personally to inform you of this. Is he a handsome lad, your young son, Goya? Or does he take after you? Send him to see me before he goes abroad. And make a good job of things in Barcelona. These are great days of celebration for our children and our kingdom, and we rejoice in them."

Their Majesties withdrew. Goya, Manuel, and Pepa were overjoyed that it had all gone according to plan. Yet they had the feeling it was not they who had played a trick on the Queen but she on them.

María Luisa betook herself to her dressing room; she gave orders for the portfolio with the *Caprichos* to be brought after her. Her ladies applied themselves to changing the Queen's costume. But they had no more than removed her ceremonial robes before she let it be known that she wished to be alone.

Her toilet table had once been the property of Marie Antoinette, it was decorative, costly, recherché. On it stood a number of choice objects large and small, boxes and caskets, jars and bottles, combs, pomades, powder and make-up of all kinds, *frangipane*, *sans-pareille*, essence of amber and roses and other rare toilet waters, distilled by doctors and experts in the cosmetic art. With an impatient hand María Luisa brushed the whole collection aside and took up the *Caprichos*.

There lay the acid, insolent, seditious drawings amid the costly, frivolous trumpery on the costly table of a queen who had been executed on the scaffold. And Doña María Luisa set to work to examine the pages undisturbed, alone.

She examined the last page, the spectral monks and grandees fleeing in panic. "*Ya es hora*—the time has come," it said underneath. In a burning flash she realized the daring, seditious intention of the drawing. "*Ya es hora.*" Did he really think so? That's where he was wrong, this fellow from the dregs, this Mister First Painter. The hour was ***not*** come. Nor was it soon going to strike. She, María Luisa, had no intention of clearing out. Not till death.

Now she had come to the drawing "*Hasta la muerte*" again. It was a vile, despicable drawing. And what a stale joke it was, one that had been made millions of times already, to poke fun at an ageing coquette. A painter of his rank ought not to stoop to such cheapness.

But if the idea of the drawing was cheap, it was still a good drawing. The way the old thing was sitting eagerly looking into the mirror was not mere moralizing, nor yet just a shoddy joke, it was the tragic, naked, objective truth.

One whose gaze can penetrate so
Deep as that is dangerous, she
Thinks, and yet she does not fear him.
Dogs may bark, but the procession
Marches on. María Luisa
Feels indeed quite glad to have the
Painter in the world. For she, when
Someone looks into her deepest
Depths, can stand it; and, besides, she
Is acquainted with the demons
Too; and they belong together.

She and he, the queen and the painter,
Make a pair, two of a kind, the
Bold and resolute.

She puts the
Drawings down and in the mirror
She observes herself. She is not
Old, no, no! In no way is she
Like that ancient crone of Goya's.
She is fortunate. All that human
Heart could compass, she herself has
Now achieved.

And suddenly she
Starts to weep, the helpless, bitter,
Angry tears come falling ever
More and stormier, till her body
Is convulsed and shakes all over
With her sobbing.

With a start she
Pulls herself together, wipes her
Eyes and blows her nose and puts some
Powder on the tip with weeping
Red. She seats herself erect and
Rings her bell. Her waiting-women
Enter to a Queen that is a
Queen.

— 36 —

When Goya came back from Barcelona, tired, and loaded with new honours, he found that his affairs in Madrid had also been prospering. The Royal Printing Establishment, under Agustín's direction, had published a large edition of the *Caprichos* and a second was in preparation. The collection could be bought in all the larger cities of the kingdom. In the capital it was for sale in seven book and art shops.

Goya paid an occasional visit to Durán's bookshop to hear what people were saying about the *Caprichos*. The comely proprietress, Señora Felipa Durán, was always pleased to see him, and was willing and eager to keep him informed. A host of people came, particularly strangers, people from abroad, to see the *Caprichos*, and in spite of its high price the collection was selling well. Goya observed that Doña Felipa was privately somewhat surprised; for she didn't make much of the *Caprichos* herself. "What hideous dreams you must have, Don Francisco," she would say with a coquettish shake of the head. He laughed good-naturedly and returned her look; she attracted him.

The *Caprichos* probably left most people cold. In Goya's opinion the public's taste had been ruined by the classicism of his colleague David. If, nevertheless, many people came and put down their two hundred and eighty-eight reals for his *Caprichos*, it was because of all the gossip and sensation he and his work had provoked. People tried to identify every figure in the *Caprichos* with a living model, and probably something had also leaked out of his subterranean struggle with the Inquisition.

Of course a few, above all among younger people, saw the *Caprichos* as something more than a collection of piquant and sensational caricatures; they understood and admired them as a new, daring, independent form of art. From France and Italy too came letters of appreciation and admiration. Quintana declared triumphantly that his verses had already become the truth, that Goya's fame had travelled all over Europe.

There was a stream of visitors to the *quinta*, admirers and the merely curious. Goya received only a few.

One day to his surprise Doctor Joaquín Peral appeared.

Yes, he had been released. But he had been ordered to leave inside of two weeks and to show his face no more in the domains of Their Catholic Majesties. He had come to Goya to say good-bye and to thank him; for he was sure Don Francisco had played a part in procuring his release.

Goya was pleased that Pepa had "done him the favour." "It was not difficult to do something for you," he said. "Once the booty was redistributed there was no further object in detaining you."

Peral said, "I would have liked to give you one or two pictures from my collection as a memento, but unfortunately my entire property has been confiscated." Then suddenly, to Goya's astonishment, Peral's face changed, looked much younger, and he went on. "Perhaps I may be able to send you a token of my gratitude from the other side of the frontier," he observed. "Since I had had one or two bad experiences even before this last affair, I was already prepared for reverses. I am going to Saint Petersburg, and unless all my plans have gone astray, I shall find some of my favourite pieces from my collection awaiting me. All my Goyas, Don Francisco, including one of the *Caprichos* which has not appeared in the final collection." Although they were quite alone he went right up to him and whispered very articulately, "I'm hoping to find a painting by Velázquez there too, a wonderful, though very little known one, a Venus with a looking glass." "You're a resourceful man, Don Joaquín," said Francisco appreciatively. "You can certainly live without a care on the proceeds of that Velázquez." "I don't think I shall have to sell the Velázquez," answered Peral. "I don't think I shall fare badly at the Court of the Czar; my friends are dependable and hold out tempting prospects. All the same I shall miss Spain. And you, Don Francisco."

Peral's visit had affected Goya. With him had re-emerged from the depths memories of very happy years, and very wretched ones. It was with a dull feeling of emptiness that he now watched this man go, his friend-enemy who had known and understood more of his bitter-sweet relationship with Cayetana than anyone else.

Soon after this the final preparations were made for Javier's journey. The plan was for a long sojourn in Italy, and a long one in France; it was to be a journey of intensive study. Goya's son—it was his father's wish—travelled like a great gentleman, with a servant and quantities of luggage.

Francisco stood by the carriage with Javier while the last trunks were loaded on. "I'm very confident," said Javier. "Your son will come back to you as an artist of whom you can be proud. Yes, I have a faint hope that one day I shall be able to paint like you, father. Of course," he acknowledged, "no one but you could do the *Caprichos*."

And he drew his mantle round him,
Wide and modishly unwieldy,

Fastened with a silver clasp, a
Present from the Duchess of Alba,
At the throat, and sprang light-footed
Up the carriage step. Within, he
Stood with laughing face and waved his
Hat. The coachman raised his whip, the
Horses started up, the wheels went
Round. So Javier too departed.

There remained of him the picture
Of a young and charming lad, a
Laughing face untroubled by a
Thought, a hat that waved, a
Flapping mantle fastened at the
Neck by Cayetana's silver
Clasp.

-- 37 --

Goya went on living in the Quinta del Sordo, alone with Agustín and his pictures, those he had painted and those he had not.

In years alone he was not yet old, but in wisdom and vision he felt his years. He had forced the demons to serve him, but they were still unruly. He had realized it only recently, before the judge of the Inquisition, when the horrible fear had seized and throttled him. But however the demons might sport with him, they could no longer deprive him of his pleasure in life; the fact that he had been so afraid of the judge was proof of how much he still clung to life.

His thoughts went to Doña Felipa, the handsome book-dealer. She liked to see him, though he might be deaf and no longer young. If she did her best to make the *Caprichos* attractive to possible purchasers, she did it not for the sake of the engravings themselves but to please him. "What hideous dreams you have, Don Francisco!"

She haunted his dreams rather frequently herself. Soon he would paint her; and then one would see what happened next.

He took up his tall hat and cane. Went outdoors. Slowly he climbed the small rise behind the house. At the top he had had them set a wooden bench without a back. He sat down; he sat very upright as became a man from Aragón.

The countryside lay spread out before him, silvery in the late morning light. Beyond the faintly shimmering heath rose the mountains of the Guadarramas with their snow-capped peaks. Usually the sight gladdened his heart; today he was not even aware of it.

Mechanically he drew with his stick in the sand circles which became a jumble of objects, figures, and faces. He examined it with faint surprise and saw that once more he had drawn something that looked like his friend, Martín Big-nose.

He was often visited by the dead. He had more dead friends than living ones. "The dead open the eyes of the living." His eyes certainly ought to be wide open by now.

He had acquired a certain amount of wisdom. For example, he knew that however much he might curse at it, life was still worth the effort of living. In spite of everything. And would go on being worth the effort.

He would not be able to cry "*Ya es hora*" yet. But even if the hour should never strike, he would go on waiting for it and believing in it till his last breath.

He stared unseeingly at the heath and the mountains behind. He had reached a lofty ridge himself. But from it he was uneasily aware of how high the next ridge was, and how inconceivably high the summit. *Plus ultra* was easy enough to say. But the hard way was becoming steeper and stonier, and the rarefied cold air took one's breath away.

He began to draw in the sand again, playfully this time. An image which had often come to him of late, the outlines of a giant who sat there resting, foolishly dreaming, and above him a thin, miserable moon.

With an abrupt movement he stopped drawing, his expression grew tense, concentrated. He had sighted something new. To force this new something onto canvas or paper would cost him a tremendous effort. He would have to scale a wild, bitter-cold height. He would have to create colour values which had never been seen before, to make this new thing visible, a blackish sort of white and brown, a dirty grey-green, something livid and sombrely exciting. And then people would ask, "Do you call that painting?" It would be painting, *his* painting; yes, this was the only form of painting possible for *painting* the *Caprichos*, and next to the painted *Caprichos* the engravings would look like a harmless, childish joke.

"What hideous dreams you have, Don Francisco!" The dignified gentleman smiled a broad, malicious smile under his dignified *bolívar*. He went back to the house.

He went into his bedroom. Took off his grey frock coat, made himself comfortable. Put on his working smock which he had not worn in a long time: he smiled again—Josefa would have been glad to see him.

Wearing his working smock, he went down to the dining room and sat down between the bare walls.

No canvas was adequate for this new thing of which he had caught a glimpse. It was not something to be stretched onto a frame and carried about. It was part of his world and must stay there. It did not belong on a canvas, it must be firmly rooted to his walls.

He stared at the bare surface of the wall, closed his eyes, opened them, stared again, with a penetrating yet unseeing look. New strength flowed through his veins, strange and delectable.

This new giant of his was just the thing for the wall. He was something quite different from the giant he had seen so often hitherto, had smiled at and scribbled onto the sand. This new giant would be a doltish giant too, but a dangerous, greedy one, perhaps the one that ate Odysseus' companions, or the one called Saturn or something like that, the demon of Time, who devours his own children.

Yes, it was just such a man-eating giant who belonged here on the wall of his dining room. In the past he had sometimes encountered the noonday ghost *El Yantar* and had been afraid of and avoided it, though it was a comfortable, mildly grinning demon; now he had reached the point where he was not even afraid of *El Jayan*, the stupid, dangerous bully. On the contrary, he wanted to get used to him, to have him always before his eyes, the *ogro*, the *coloso*, the *gigante*, the gobbling, gulping, chewing, crushing giant who would end by devouring Goya himself. Everything that lives eats or is eaten, which is only right; and he wanted to keep it before his eyes as long as it was vouchsafed him to go on eating.

And the few friends whom he admitted to his table would also have to look at it. Anyone looking at his giant ought to feel bitten by doubly vivid pleasure that he was still alive. The *ogro* would eat them all, Miguel, Lucía, Agustín, and the fair bookseller, Doña Felipa. But for the time being one ate and was alive oneself. Vigour courses through one's body. One feels oneself a thousand times superior to the doltish giant on the wall. One sees through him in his omnipotence and impotence, in his dangerous malevolence and his pitiful absurdity. One can make fun of his doltishness and gluttony and spite, can mock and tease him as long as one is sitting at table oneself and eating. And even after one's own death one can go on laughing at the stupid *ogro* in the picture on the wall.

It is still a shadow picture,
His colossus, his *gigante*,
Greenish-brown and palish-black, and
Somehow shimmering, with the tiny
Little human figure in its
Horrid mouth. Someday the shadow
Will have body, it will live, for
Out of darkness will Francisco
Goya draw his giant to the
Day, which no day must be, only
Fallow light. He simply must be
On the wall, his giant!

Goya
Rose then, speaking to himself, and
Said, "The dead into the grave, the
Living to the table." So he
Went and sat down. All his teeth were
Still in place, his appetite was
Of the best.

When Agustín came
In, he was surprised to see his
Friend in working smock. And Goya,
Vastly pleased, and smiling smugly,

Said, "Yes, once again I'm painting,
And it's something new I'm painting.
These bare walls, I cannot stick them
Any more, I mean to paint me
Something on them, spicy, that will
Whet the appetite. Tomorrow
I'll begin to paint."